YOUN

THE FAIRWEATHERS

THE INHERITANCE

BY

ANNIE S. SWAN

SUNDAY MAIL EDITION

1933

YOUNG BLOOD

YOUNG BLOOD

BY

ANNIE S. SWAN

SUNDAY MAIL EDITION
1933

CONTENTS

CHAPTER I

THE INTRUDER

It was a typical and pleasant picture about half-past five, on a midsummer afternoon, in the garden at Balcraig, a large family house in the west end of Glasgow, where the Annans and their friends had gathered for tennis and tea out of doors.

It was one of the few fine Saturdays in a rather rainy June, and, though the courts were a little soft, some excellent play was in progress.

As Mrs. Annan, having dispensed tea to the last of the players, rearranged herself with her knitting in her comfortable basket-chair, on the terrace, she remarked to her husband, with an indulgent smile:

" It's nice to see them all enjoying themselves. Isn't it, Robert ? "

She was a comely, happy-faced, motherly woman of the old-fashioned sort, devoted to her husband and family, whom she thought the best and the finest in the world. There never had been any problem or vexation in her life since she had plighted her troth to Robert Russell Annan, then a junior partner, but now the head of the firm of Annan & Co., of Glasgow and Calcutta.

He was a handsome man, undoubtedly, now on the shady side of fifty, but well set-up, without a wrinkle on his smooth, clean-cut face, and breathing that air of assurance which is the reward of a diligent and successful business career.

He wore a light-grey flannel suit, a white waistcoat, and a Panama hat, and he played a quite strenuous set with three of the young ones before tea, just to show them that they could not have it all their own way. But he was quite ready to rest now, and to enjoy his fine cigar by the side of the wife, who was always his most admiring audience.

" Yes, it's very pleasant, Mary ; and the money laid out on the lawn was a good investment. Lisbeth plays a good game."

" She and John Marchbanks are well matched," she said, on the spur of the moment, and he seemed to knit his brows.

" I say, Mary ; I've been wondering once or twice, lately, whether we've been wise—encouraging young Marchbanks so much about the house. He's a taking chap, I grant you, but we don't want him to be casting his eyes at Lisbeth—do we ? "

Mrs. Annan gave a slight start at this, and sat forward in her chair, peering rather eagerly towards the tennis court, where the white-robed figures flitted to and fro. She quickly discerned that Lisbeth and young Marchbanks were not playing, but sitting out, as they might have done at a dance, on a cosy garden-seat, under the shade of a chestnut tree, and apparently very well pleased with themselves.

" Oh, I don't think he would, Robert," she said, but her voice had not a very confident ring. " He knows quite well that there is a difference; but he and Roger are such chums it isn't easy to keep them separate."

" That would be unnecessary ; but I'd slacken off a bit, if I were you, Mary. You needn't ask him to stop on to supper to-night, for instance ? "

"Oh, but he has always stopped on Saturday nights, and probably Lisbeth has already asked him," said Mrs. Annan, rather distressed. "It would look rather pointed. If he is to be discouraged it will need to be done very gently. It would make Lisbeth so angry! You've no idea how set she is in her ways, father, though she's only twenty-two! She always knows her own mind, and does exactly what she wants."

Robert Annan's jaw set a trifle less genially. He was both fond and proud of his daughter, but he had old-fashioned ideas about the discipline in which a family should be reared. He himself had been kept in strict bondage to it in his youth, and was fond of saying that he was a better man for it; in fact, he owed much, if not all his success, to his father's stern upbringing.

Yet, in his own family, he had not been able to enforce these ideas with the same strictness as the old moralists had been able to do. It seemed as if there was some element in the modern air antagonistic to it. The call for freedom was in the young blood, and all the efforts of the old could not still it.

So far, however, there had been no active trouble in the Annan household, chiefly because a loving mother was always ready to throw herself into the breach. She put out her hand now, and kindly patted her husband's knee, as she watched to see whether the ruffles would smooth from his brow.

He was a quick-tempered man, and, in his tempers, apt to be impulsive to the verge of injustice.

His wife had oiled the domestic wheels so that the household at Balcraig was a very happy one.

"That's all very well, Mary, but, after all, a girl's father and mother are the final judges of what is best for her. We haven't spent close on a thousand pounds on Lisbeth's education to give her to a bank clerk!"

All the middle-class pride and exclusiveness vibrated in his voice as he uttered these, which he intended to be irrevocable words. They provoked a little sigh from his wife's lips.

"I don't think there's anything of that kind in Lisbeth's head, father; but I'll try and get a word with her, in a roundabout, quiet kind of way, and find out how the land lies."

Mr. Annan, who had been sufficiently disturbed to leave off his smoke, now resumed it; but his face was still clouded.

"Of course, it doesn't do to interfere too much with a lad's choice of companions," he began, "but it would please me better to see Roger taking up with folk of his own class. Marchbanks has no folk—and we've all heard who his mother was."

"But that is no disgrace to him, Robert!" said his wife quickly. "And you would be the last man to visit the sins of the fathers on the children."

"That's good so far as it goes, Mary; but I put it to you now—'Would it please you to welcome the illegitimate son of a bit servant lass as a son-in-law?'"

Thus confronted with the naked truth, Mrs. Annan undoubtedly winced.

"I would rather it was somebody else," she confessed.

"And, besides, he's only a bank clerk. What are his prospects? When he's my age, probably he'll be a manager in some remote country town, with three hundred a year, and a house above the bank. That's all the prospect banking offers to the mediocre youth; and, so far as I've seen, there's nothing extra about Marchbanks, though, I admit, he has a taking way; and that's why I think he should be made less free of the house. Now, I'll not say any more. I'll just stroll across and split up that little *tête-à-tête* under the trees."

" Stop a minute, Robert. As we're talking about Lisbeth, we may as well thresh it out a bit. It might help me with her."

" Well, what is it, mother ? " he asked, as he knocked the ash from his cigar on the edge of the stone jar laden with gaily-coloured geraniums which, here and there, made such pleasant patches of colour along the edge of the terrace.

" What about Archie Dunsyre ? He comes here a lot, too. Would that please you, father ? "

Annan did not immediately answer, but watched the players for a moment. Archie Dunsyre was playing with one of his sisters, Roger Annan, and a pretty girl from a neighbouring house.

" It would be better than Marchbanks, Mary, but not quite good enough," he slowly delivered himself at last. " The ' Knockout ' would be a bit hard to swallow ! "

" Then, what would please you, Robert ? " asked his wife whimsically.

" Fine you know ! The kind of folk we met at Marienbad last year—these are Lisbeth's real circle."

Mrs. Annan rather doubtfully shook her head.

At the fashionable Austrian Spa they had met all sorts and conditions of men and women, many of them far below Mrs. Annan's own personal standard of life and conduct. But her husband, keen, shrewd man of business though he was, had been flattered and cajoled by some of the needy aristocrats they had got to know there, and had dreamed dreams of seeing his girl with a handle to her name.

He had never descended to plain assertion on the point, but had encouraged several advances in quarters neither Lisbeth nor her mother much favoured ; and had given invitations galore to some of their new-made friends to come to Scotland to visit them, either in Glasgow, or in their coast house on the Gareloch, where one of the prettiest and fastest yachts on the Clyde rode at anchor from May to October.

So far, none of these invitations had been accepted, though next month they were expecting to receive some of their travelling acquaintances at Kilcrean.

" Archie Dunsyre would be better than any of them, Robert. At least, we know all about him, where he has been brought up, and what kind of folk he has. It's better, in matrimony, to err on the safe side."

" Tuts, woman ! Nothing venture, nothing win. And, if I were a woman, I'd grip the sporting chance."

" Forgetting you had to live with a man, my dear ! " she put it drily. And they both laughed as he strolled away.

He walked quite deliberately round the end of the court, crossed the smooth turf to the seat under the chestnut tree, and sat down beside his daughter and young Marchbanks. His practised eye, alert at the moment, for signs, did not fail to observe Lisbeth's heightened colour and the sparkle in her eyes, as well as the earnest and openly adoring expression in the young man's. But he suffered no hint of his irritation to show itself, as he sat down, remarking affably :

" There's been a bit of good play this afternoon, and the court's improving. Isn't it, Lisbeth ? "

" It's all right, dad," answered Lisbeth, and, conscious of a little embarrassment, springing from she knew not where, she rose and said she would go and see how they were getting on at the other side.

A little group of those who were not playing were making merry at the summer-house door. Both men watched the lithe, slim figure, and the neatly-poised, small, dark head, as the girl moved away.

White suited Elizabeth, for, though she had little colour, her skin was clear and unblemished. She had magnificent dark eyes, a crown of abundant glossy brown hair, and an air of distinction which was undoubtedly her father's pride.

He exaggerated it, perhaps, and built too many castles in the air on it. What he would really have wished was to see Elizabeth married to a member of some county family, who would take up politics as a profession. Mr. Annan had cherished his own secret ambitions in that direction for several years, but the claims of business had prevented him from prosecuting them in earnest.

Elizabeth had a very pretty mouth, and few who admired its upward curve calculated the strength of character displayed in that daintily chiselled chin. It was her father's chin in a modified form, and once or twice just lately, since Elizabeth had come home for good from her fashionable boarding-school, he had come up against a wilfulness which amounted to a kind of dour determination. Elizabeth would listen to strictures and suggestions sometimes without protest, and then she was more dangerous. For she invariably proceeded thereafter to walk in the way which seemed good in her sight.

"There was less play when I was your age, Marchbanks," observed Mr. Annan, with a small preliminary cough. "No Saturday afternoons then! But banks have notoriously short hours, and I doubt very much whether it's a good thing for young men to have so much leisure."

"We have an occasional spurt of work, sir," said Marchbanks, his rather wide mouth curving into a little smile, which extraordinarily softened the rugged outline of his face.

Beside the smooth and handsome countenance of Mr. Annan, Marchbanks appeared, for the moment, plain. He had a rather thick-set figure, and did not wear his flannels with the lithe grace of his friend, Roger Annan. His face was sallow, too, and set in a strong mould, his eyes redeeming the face, however, giving it at times the necessary softness, just as his smile made his mouth more mobile. He had a fine square head, and a broad brow—what somebody has called the bull-dog breed, and he needed it all! He had been fighting for four-and-twenty years against the accident of his birth, regarding which he was sensitive to a degree, though he had behaved towards his mother with all the chivalry of his nature, putting her first in all things.

When Roger Annan had asked him first to come out to Balcraig, he had refused to come, until he had told of the stain of his birth, and awaited the decision of Roger's parents. They had been so touched and struck by the unusual proceeding, that they had made their welcome all the warmer on that account. But that was three years ago, before Elizabeth had come home from her final year at Neuilly.

"Spurts of work!" repeated Mr. Annan, with a fine touch of scorn. "A spurt is no use. It's dogged as does it! Do you know what I was saying to my wife a minute or two back? I was just wondering that you were content to hang on so long behind a bank counter! With Roger it's different. He's merely getting ready for Calcutta. But if I were in your shoes I'd cut my stick, and get abroad. Everything's possible to the man who makes himself a citizen of the world," he added, with one of his grandiloquent touches. "Here everything runs in grooves, necessarily so. Have you never thought of getting out of Glasgow?"

"I have, sir. I'm biding my time," he answered, quite modestly. "There can be as much time lost by over-restlessness as by waiting on."

Mr. Annan was struck by the remark.

" That may be true, too, provided that one doesn't wait too long. I've seen more promising careers killed by stagnation than by overpush."

Just then, Marchbanks was summoned to make up another set, and presently, Mr. Annan had an opportunity for a word with Elizabeth.

He did not think the waiting game would do, so far as Elizabeth was concerned, and surmised that the sooner they arrived at some idea of her attitude towards young Marchbanks the better it would be. As it happened, however, he blundered. As he strolled round by the path which skirted the lawn, he met her, and she stopped with a smile.

" We've had some splendid tennis this afternoon. Haven't we, father? The best this season ! "

" You think so, eh ? And who is the best player ? "

" Oh, John Marchbanks. Nobody can touch him ; but then, he does most things well."

She spoke with a spontaneous frankness which might have reassured him. But it did not.

" Oh, come ; don't glorify that mediocre youth. Any of them are as good. Look at Archie Dunsyre just now ! He'd be hard to beat ! "

" He isn't steady," said Elizabeth quietly. " As a partner, he's unsatisfactory. You never know what he'll do next."

Those few words were sufficient indication of the girl's attitude of mind towards the young man who, in her father's eyes, was a far more eligible suitor for her hand than the obscure bank clerk.

" It's nothing against him if he can't match Marchbanks on the tennis court," he said drily. " He gives his brains to something else. His father was telling me only the other day what splendid business qualities he is developing."

" At the Knockout," said Elizabeth, with a little rippling smile which indicated a mild scorn.

" Don't be sarcastic, my dear. It isn't a becoming weapon in a woman's hands. And don't think you are a judge of a man's qualities just because you can clip at them with your tongue."

Elizabeth looked startled, wounded ; and her face flushed with genuine vexation. She could not understand her father's mood, and thought his rebuke both untimely and undeserved. She was not able to banish it entirely from her mind, but only hid it in one of the inner chambers thereof, for future cogitation.

About seven, the bulk of the tennis party dispersed, the only ones remaining for supper being Archie Dunsyre and young Marchbanks.

Supper at Balcraig, on tennis evenings, was an informal meal, mostly cold, to suit the vagaries of the players.

The atmosphere round the table, and afterwards in the drawing-room, was a little less happy than usual. Elizabeth was conscious of some hostile quality in her father which was as unusual as it was disagreeable. To Marchbanks he was as short as the usages of politeness would permit. Mrs. Annan strove to make up for it by her motherly kindness, but she was glad when Marchbanks said he would leave earlier than usual. Archie Dunsyre and his sister rose too, and the evening came to an end before ten o'clock.

Elizabeth walked out through the garden with the visitors to let them out by the lane, and, though there was nothing unusual in that, Mr. Annan was annoyed. He did not, however, follow them, though he observed, from the library window, that Elizabeth and Marchbanks walked a little way behind.

Now, though this had happened at least fifty times before without occasioning the smallest remark, it annoyed Mr. Annan out of all proportion to its importance. Perhaps, at the back of his mind there lurked the fear that he was only trying to lock the door now the steed was stolen!

He would have been convinced of it had he heard what passed between the young pair in these few hurried moments they had to themselves, as they followed in the rear of the Dunsyres and Roger.

"I've offended your father, Betty," said young Marchbanks with a rueful air.

The very liberty he took in using a name proprietary only in very intimate circles would have filled Mr. Annan with unspeakable indignation.

"Oh, no," said Elizabeth, trying to speak quite naturally. "Probably it's his liver. Every now and again he gets like that, over nothing, then we know he's paying for the Calcutta years. We have to pay, too; but we must just pay cheerfully."

"He put a few leading questions to me to-night, on the seat over there, after you had gone. He wanted to know when I was going to clear out from Glasgow. A good and broad enough hint, wasn't it? I think I'll have to stop coming here, though I'll miss it, Betty. Heavens, won't I, just!"

"Oh, but," said Elizabeth a trifle unsteadily, "that would be foolish. Probably you'll find that next time you see father he'll be quite all right. I'll try and find out what upset him presently."

"I think I can guess. He's beginning to suspect that I have too warm an interest in certain quarters, and, very naturally, thinks it's too presumptuous."

To this Elizabeth made no demur, because the subject was delicate and the moment inopportune.

The gay laughter of the others was wafted back to them on warm night air, and a few steps more would bring them to the gate in the lane, and so end their brief *tête-à-tête*.

"I'm sure you'll find I'm right, and that it's only Indian liver, John," she said quickly.

"I hope so, but it's doubtful. I feel rather a worm that I haven't spoken up yet. When will you give me leave, Betty?"

"I don't know," she said hurriedly. "There isn't any hurry, really. Why can't everything go on as it has been doing?"

"Well, because I love you, and I want to do the square thing. I'll have to see your father soon, Betty. I can't go on like this."

"Well then, if you must, your blood will be on your own head! Supposing we have a talk over it to-morrow? I'll be coming out of the Girls' Club at half-past eight."

"Right. I'll be there," he answered. "Good-bye just now."

She slipped her hand in his, under cover of the friendly dark, and, risking the danger of being seen, he raised it to his lips. And, presently, they were drawn in by the trio at the gate, and for a few minutes there was the usual happy banter which passes between young creatures who have not yet plumbed the depths of care.

It was beginning to stalk them now, however, in more directions than one.

John Marchbanks had not the only uneasy heart in the little company.

Roger closed and locked the gate, and turned to recross the garden by his sister's side.

"What was the matter with the pater to-night, old girl? He wasn't very decent to John—seemed to have his knife in him."

"I don't know, I'm sure," said Elizabeth, very low.

"I felt it awfully, for, of course, I brought him to the house. And I asked leave before I did it, too. I'm going to have it out with the pater about it."

"Perhaps it would be better to let sleeping dogs lie," suggested Elizabeth, rather gravely.

But Roger Annan was nothing if not impetuous. About half an hour later, after his mother and sister had gone upstairs, he asked his father point-blank, in the library, what John Marchbanks had done to offend him.

"You were very short with him, sir, and he felt it—anybody could see that."

Mr. Annan winced slightly, for no man likes to be accused of lack of courtesy in his own house.

"Nonsense, Roger," he said rather sharply. "You exaggerate what was really nothing. But, since you've mentioned the subject, I may as well tell you that your mother and I have come to the conclusion that Marchbanks must not be made so free of the house."

"But why? It's too late now," said Roger blankly. "The time to show him the cold shoulder was at the beginning. You could have refused to let me bring him. I was fair and square, anyhow, though I argued with Jack till I was nearly blue in the face that the mere accident of his birth couldn't affect him, and that it was quite unnecessary to tell you. It was he himself who insisted that you should be told, and I don't think you ought to go back on it at all now."

"You are quite mistaken, my lad," said Mr. Annan drily. "Both your mother and I were glad to show a little kindness to a deserving young fellow under a cloud through no fault of his own. But your sister wasn't at home then. I suppose that even you would hardly declare him to be a suitable husband for Lisbeth?"

"Oh, but hang it all, there isn't anything of that kind! They're far too friendly for that. I think you're imagining things."

"It's better to err on the safe side, is it not? And I hope that after this hint you'll co-operate. It isn't necessary to give him the cold shoulder. Only, he needn't be made quite so free, you understand? We can go down to the Gareloch a week or two earlier than usual, and that will nip it in the bud. When you go out to the East the thing will, perhaps, drop of its own accord."

"Oh, but I say," began Roger, and his handsome face reddened, "that would be a simply rotten way to treat old John! He's been a most awfully decent pal to me, sir."

"We understand that and appreciate it; and we have no intention of cutting him altogether. The thing will die a natural death."

"No—a sudden death!" said Roger savagely. "If there's any more cold douche like he got to-night! John's a proud beggar, sir, and sensitive about most things. Directly he gets the impression he isn't wanted he'll be off like a shot, and there won't be anything more heard of him."

Mr. Annan smiled a superior smile, as he knocked the cigar ash from the sleeve of his velvet coat.

"You're a good champion, and I like to see it in you, but older people can see a bit further than you, Roger. It was a mistake to let young Marchbanks get on such a footing in the house. Your mother and I both see it now, and it is necessary to draw in before there is any serious harm done."

But Roger seemed uneasy.

"I owe a lot to Jack, father," he said moodily. "And I think it will be rotten to shunt him like that, when he has not done a single thing to deserve it."

CHAPTER II

DIPLOMATIC INTERFERENCE

UPSTAIRS, at the moment when Roger and his father had crossed swords, as it were, concerning young Marchbanks, Mrs. Annan made an attempt to discover Elizabeth's attitude of mind towards the young man. She did it rather clumsily, being a very simple, direct kind of person, who had never, in her own life, had anything to hide. She began, however, as she imagined, quite diplomatically.

"Lisbeth, your father is talking of going down to Kilcrean earlier than usual this year; in fact, I believe he wants to go next week or the week after."

"What for?" inquired Elizabeth, in her calm judicial voice.

"He didn't exactly say. But he seems to think it would be better for us to spend the most of the summer there this year."

"You and me, that means; for, you know, he finds two months quite long enough to travel up and down; so I suppose he means to stop here, while we go down. Why are we being banished? What have you been doing, mother—eh?"

She put the question lightly, and Mrs. Annan laughed a trifle embarrassedly.

"Oh, it isn't me he wants to get out of the way, Lisbeth. Put the question nearer home, lassie."

"What am I supposed to have been doing, then?" asked Lisbeth, and her tone perceptibly hardened.

"Nothing particular. I rather think he wants to be kind, in his own way, to John Marchbanks," said poor Mrs. Annan, blurting out the truth without further parley.

Elizabeth's face immediately assumed an expression of singular density, though her mother was quick enough to observe that her colour slightly rose.

"What has John Marchbanks got to do with our going to Kilcrean?" was all she said.

"My dear, you needn't pretend you don't understand. You are quick enough to see through most stone walls! It just means that father thinks that poor John may be thinking more about you than he ought. It was, perhaps, a mistake to encourage him so much here, but then, we did it for the best, and because he had been such a good friend to Roger."

"He's quite a good friend to Roger yet, mother, and he'll just come as much to Kilcrean as he does here. Last September—don't you remember?—he came with Roger nearly every Saturday."

Mrs. Annan remembered quite well. She had thought of it when her husband suggested Kilcrean as a possible safe retreat for Elizabeth, but had refrained from saying anything.

"I rather think, my dear, that your father intends that these visits to Kilcrean won't be encouraged in future."

Elizabeth was silent a moment, busying herself with a fragment of needlework she had begun to roll up, preparatory to getting ready for her bed. They were talking in her room, to which her mother did not often come after they had parted for the night, and which had been sufficient in itself to disquiet Elizabeth a little.

"What's father's idea about this?" she asked presently, in the same even, cold tones, and without looking at her mother.

"Can't you guess? He does not think—and I agree with him—that John Marchbanks would be a suitable husband for you. Of course, I told father there was nothing in it, but he thinks we'd better err on the safe side."

"And if it should be too late?" asked Elizabeth, quite quietly, after a brief pause.

Mrs. Annan gave a visible start, and took hold of the corner of the silver-laden dressing-table with a hand which, in spite of her, trembled a little.

"Lisbeth! You don't mean to tell me that there is anything between you and John Marchbanks?" she asked faintly.

Elizabeth shrugged her shoulders, and did not, for the moment, answer.

"Because your father will never give his consent," her mother added.

"But I'm of age, mother," said Elizabeth quietly. "And in these days fathers don't just issue orders for daughters to obey. Everything's changed."

Mrs. Annan was a gentle-hearted woman, but these coolly delivered words roused in her a quick and sudden anger.

"That's not a way to speak to me, Lisbeth—nor of your father! We've been very good to you, and we expect some consideration from you. I like John Marchbanks very well. I have always liked him. But, in the circumstances, he would be a most unsuitable husband for you, or anybody brought up like you. Why, he has only the pay of a bank clerk, and he has his mother to keep!"

"Oh, no, she is quite self-supporting!" said Elizabeth hotly. "And he is very proud of her though she only keeps a little shop in the Garscube Road."

Mrs. Annan's face wore an odd expression, which Elizabeth understood to mean that, regarded from a social point of view, Mrs. Marchbanks was impossible.

"He has never made any secret of her position, and you knew it, I am sure, all along, mother. It was a shame to let him come at the beginning, if you mean to treat him badly now, for he is just the same man as he was then."

"That has nothing to do with it, Lisbeth. You will have to let your father decide what is best for you here, my dear; and I hope you will show both obedience and common sense, and we don't want any dispeace in the family where we have all been so happy."

"Oh, mother!" said Elizabeth, as she jumped up, "you are talking like the tutor in 'Sandford and Merton.' Let's say good night What is to be, will be; and if John Marchbanks is my fate, why then, all the king's horses and all the king's men won't drag me back from it! Good night; and don't worry. I'll work out my own salvation. You leave father to me, and don't wrinkle your dear face over it."

She kissed and dismissed her mother as if the latter had been some petulant and unreasonable child.

Aware that nothing could be gained by further discussion at the moment, Mrs. Annan did not seek to prolong the conversation, but took the kiss, and went back to her own room.

She was in bed, but sitting wide awake, with her wrap about her shoulders, and her open "Daily Light" in front of her, when her husband came up. Then she cried out impulsively, because it had been her habit all her life to roll her worries on to his strong and capable shoulders:

"Oh, Robert, I do believe you were right after all. I've spoken to Lisbeth, and she doesn't take it at all well. I should not be surprised if there is something between them, after all!"

Robert Annan, his face a little grim, unfastened his substantial gold chain and began to wind his watch for the night.

"Tell me what she said?" he asked drily.

Mrs. Annan tried to give him a detailed and accurate account of what had passed.

"So she suggested that it might be too late?" he said significantly. "That's far enough—isn't it? Well—we needn't say any more about it to-night, my dear. I've just been threshing the same business out with Roger, and he was most impudent. It seems to me, Mary, that we've been mistaken in Marchbanks all along, and that he has wormed himself in with them both. For Roger, it doesn't matter a dump, but Lisbeth is a serious business. But it isn't going to come off, if I can help it! You leave it to me. I'll find a way."

Mrs. Annan sighed, and dropped a rather anxious tear on her pretty wrap, as she threw it off preparatory for sleep. For the first time, real friction was threatening to undermine the peaceful family relations, so necessary to her happiness. Peace at any price was practically the litany of her life.

Next morning a kind of strain was clearly felt in the family atmosphere, at breakfast. Mr. Annan was annoyed because Roger did not come down for breakfast, and his mother said nothing, fearful lest he should discover that Roger had come in rather late, and had only returned after midnight. She, lying awake in her bed, pondering on the sudden rift that had appeared in the lute of their harmonious family life, had heard him slip out, and the click of his latch-key on his return.

She was not less anxious about Roger than about Lisbeth. She was consumed with a gnawing anxiety on this score. Of late the vagaries of her second son's behaviour, and his frequent, and not easily explained, absences from home, had worried her very much. She had not spoken to her husband about it, because knowing that the two men possessed the same hot temper, she feared the inevitable explosion.

Mr. Annan was an office-bearer in one of the West End churches, and most regular in his attendance. He performed all his religious duties, as he did everything else, most thoroughly.

The young people, however, were less punctilious. In the last year, Elizabeth had taken to wandering on Sunday, and when her father had remonstrated had said quietly, looking at him straightly from her large, calm eyes—"I must go where I can get food for my soul."

It was rather a startling remark, to which no answer could be found.

Elizabeth was a serious person, taking herself and all her concerns with the utmost gravity, which is the characteristic of the youth of our time. It is only the old and the experienced who have leisure, apparently, for lightness of heart.

Elizabeth did not go out at all that Sunday morning, and after lunch her father suggested that they should go for a walk. She did not demur; nay, she agreed with the utmost readiness, though aware that her father had some ulterior motive, and that probably he intended to speak to her about John Marchbanks.

She was not mistaken. They had hardly turned their faces westward when he began, with an abruptness which left her in no doubt as to his seriousness.

"I say, Lisbeth, I want to speak to you about a rather difficult matter, and I won't beat about the bush. What is there between you and young Marchbanks?"

The question thus put nonplussed Elizabeth for the moment. She had prepared herself for a more delicate and devious approach, and an attack which she was going to parry, with all her skill and finesse; but, in front of this bald question, her colour angrily rose.

"I don't understand you," she said stonily.

"Oh, yes, you do," her father assured her. "You put on a good many airs, my dear, but the good, old-fashioned instincts are there, all the same. I'll put it differently, if you like—Are you in love with young Marchbanks, or he with you?"

"Don't be vulgar, father. We are quite good friends, and I won't discuss our friendship with you."

"Won't you, though?" asked Mr. Annan, with admirable good-humour, though the tone, no less than the words, nettled him. "Then you don't admit that either your mother or I have the smallest right, or even interest, in your future?"

"I don't say that; but, after all, I'm of age, father, and surely every human soul has a right to freedom."

"Within limits, yes, lass. But who is to set the limit?"

"There's the rub!" murmured Elizabeth, on the spur of the moment.

"We've done our best for you, Elizabeth—given you everything the heart of a girl could desire. And now, when you ought to be a little comfort to us, you're beginning to cause us a great deal of anxiety."

"I thought I was a very serious, well-intentioned person," said Elizabeth demurely.

"Too serious by half. If you took a leaf from Kitty Dunsyre's book, your mother and I would be better pleased. She's a real sunbeam at Ashendene!"

Elizabeth's lips merely tightened in an aggravating little smile. She had no great opinion of Kitty Dunsyre, whom she regarded as a soulless butterfly, wholly given up to frivolity and clothes.

"Is Kitty the man's ideal?" she asked coolly; and, once more, the veiled suggestion of superiority annoyed Mr. Annan, unaccustomed as he was to having his cherished opinions and judgment set aside.

He had in his nature a certain arrogance, as well as the somewhat over-bearing manner of the man accustomed to exact at least outward obedience and deference from those under him.

"Your tongue has the usual nip. But, let me tell you, my dear, that what you scornfully term 'the man's ideal' has served as an inspiration to the world for centuries before you were ever heard of, and will continue," he added firmly, "until long after you have passed away."

"Doubtful," commented Elizabeth. "Everything is changing, and there is going to be complete evolution by and by, when all the old shibboleths are shed. I hope I shall live to see it."

"Doubtful indeed!" repeated Mr. Annan briefly. "But meanwhile, what concerns us is what is happening at the moment. You haven't answered my question. Perhaps you don't mean to answer it, so I'll just drop a word of warning. If young Marchbanks has presumed on the liberty and the welcome we have given him at Balcraig, why, then, the time has come for him to be informed of the fact. If he has aspired to marry you, and you have encouraged him, understand that it is forbidden, that your mother and I will never give our consent to it."

"Why?" asked Elizabeth calmly. "I haven't said that such a contingency might happen, but, if it should, why not?"

"Why, because he is not the kind of person we wish as a member of our family. Personally, I have no objections to him. He is an inoffensive, mediocre youth, to whom we have gone out of the way to show a little kindness. Socially, he's impossible."

"But why? He occupies precisely the same position as Roger."

"The cases are entirely different. Roger is merely getting a knowledge of banking business, which is going to help him presently in the East, when he goes out to release George."

Elizabeth stalked on rather defiantly, hitting the ground with her short ebony stick, her head in the air, her eyes dangerously bright.

"What have you to say, Lisbeth?" he asked presently. "We don't want to resort to any drastic measures or to be needlessly unkind to young Marchbanks, so your mother is arranging to go down to Kilcrean a few weeks earlier than usual—about the end of this week, probably, or beginning of next."

"I won't go," said Elizabeth calmly. "I've got all sorts of ties here; it is inconvenient to break them before another month at least. So many people are away already, it is hardly possible to run my Club. For instance, I was single-handed last Sunday night, and probably will be the same to-night."

"It can be closed, then. Anyhow, it will be better for the girls to be out in the fresh air then mewed up in a stuffy club-room."

"We don't think that; and I can't close it. I'm only one member of Council, and I promised to hang on till the middle of July. One can't throw over one's responsibilities like that, father. Men don't do it, and women, happily, are learning something about *noblesse oblige*."

"*Noblesse oblige*," repeated Mr. Annan slowly. "And is there anything in it about honouring the father and mother, so that your days may be long in the land?" he asked, with a keen side-glance of his daughter's beautiful but rather hardly-set profile.

He was not getting on. He was dismally conscious that he had taken the wrong turning, that he was farther off than ever from understanding his own child.

"Honouring parents? Why, of course, all decent people honour their parents; but that needn't prevent them from insisting on the personal freedom which is the right of every soul."

"In other words—everybody is right in demanding his and her own way, in spite of other folk! It's a poor foundation to build your life on, my dear; and that you'll maybe find as you get a little farther on."

"I'm not afraid. And if there's any price to pay, I can pay it," she answered calmly. "Where are we going? Straight on, or over the hill?"

"I'm not minding. There's not the pleasure I used to have when I took you and your brothers for a scamper of a Sunday afternoon when you were all wee," answered Mr. Annan with a touch of pathos which impressed Elizabeth far more than his laying down of the law.

"Poor old father! It's a pity we all had to grow up. But never mind—you will get used to the new order by degrees."

"Meanwhile, the point I'm driving at, and which you have got to grasp, Lisbeth, is, that we don't accept John Marchbanks as a son-in-law, now, or at any future time."

"What's your objection to him—his poverty?"

"That's one bar, certainly. Do you imagine yourself fitted to be a poor man's wife, Lisbeth?"

" I haven't thought about it."

" Then, he has been brought up differently from you——"

" Of course. His mother is a widow, and has had to work very hard; but that is no disgrace to him."

Mr. Annan drew himself up rather stiffly. The thing he had to say was difficult, for he had all the old-fashioned ideas about gilding pills for feminine consumption; holding that certain facts of life were better ignored, or glossed over for them.

But Elizabeth, surely, was an exception. She was one of those terrible, clear-eyed, sharp-tongued young women who had no fear of shrinking from facts. Well then, she should hear them!

" So he has told you that his mother is a widow, has he? "

Elizabeth looked round in rather a startled way.

" Not in so many words. But, of course, she is a widow. She lives quite alone, and I know that she has a little shop, for he has told me so."

" When he was at it, he might have told the whole truth," said Mr. Annan grimly. " Has nobody ever told you, then, that John Marchbanks is an illegitimate son, and that his mother was a servant lass in Edinburgh, and came here to hide her shame? I hate telling you this, Lisbeth, but, apparently, it is the only way. Now do you understand that the barrier between you and him is insuperable? "

Lisbeth's face blanched. She could not help it. True to the traditions of her family, she visibly shrank from what was horrible and crude. The bar sinister seemed to strike her like a blow.

" It isn't true," she said in a low voice. " I don't believe it for a moment! Somebody has spoken this wicked calumny out of sheer spite."

" He told it himself, to me, in the library at Balcraig, my dear, the first time he came to the house. And I honoured and respected him for it then, because he was far too proud to come to the house under false pretences. I told him we did not belong to the Pharisees, who visit the sins of the fathers on the children."

" And why have you changed? " asked Elizabeth in a sudden flash.

" Why, because it is one thing offering a man under a cloud a friendly hand, and another to offer him the privilege of entering your family as a member. Have common sense, Lisbeth! Probably, had you not been in France then, we shouldn't have let him come too freely. But I accepted him at his own valuation. I believed him to be an honourable man, and, if he has overstepped the bounds of friendship where you are concerned, then he has behaved badly, and I will tell him so."

For the moment, Elizabeth had no answer ready. After a time, however, she got out some words:

" I don't think it is fair, the way things are kept from women," she said at last, in great bitterness. " I wasn't a baby or a fool, and I would have known how to behave in the circumstances."

" We acted for the best, my dear," said Mr. Annan mildly. " There are many things in life a man has to rub up against, which he would wish to keep from his women-folk. But now that you know about the bar sinister, the rest will be easy. We don't want to hurt the poor chap's feelings. We shall continue to show him as much kindness as we can; but he must be gently discouraged. You see that, Lisbeth? "

" It is too late, father," answered Elizabeth, without a tremor of the eyelids. " And I mean to marry him some day, in spite of the bar sinister, as you call it."

Mr. Annan's face grew a little white, and, wheeling about, he suggested that they should turn back.

Neither felt capable of continuing the discussion—the father finding nothing in his mood to correspond to the calm of the Sunday afternoon; and feeling the need of solitude to face this unexpected development.

Elizabeth walked along, silent, by his side, but her step and her mien conveyed protest and determination quite equal to her father's.

CHAPTER III

FATHER AND DAUGHTER

ELIZABETH did not go to her Club that evening, but sent a hasty note round to the house of the only substitute she could think of, asking her to take her place, as she had had a bad headache, and did not feel equal to the stuffy room and the effort of talking to the girls. At the same time she threw out the suggestion that it might be advisable, in the interests of everybody, to close the Club for at least a month. If necessary, she would herself come up from Kilcrean, in Fair Week, to look after such girls as could not afford to go to the coast with the great general exodus.

Elizabeth, while she was writing the note, and after it had been despatched, was fully conscious that, for the first time, she was not only shirking her duty, but evading the real issue !

Truth to tell, she had got an undoubted shock, and she did not feel herself able, as yet, to see John Marchbanks again, immediately, though she had trysted him to meet her after her Sunday evening mission was over.

She had to think things over, get her mind adjusted to an entirely new aspect of a question which might affect her whole life ; and she must have both time and solitude for the purpose.

She did not, however, send a message to John. She had none of the loving woman's solicitude or desire to save him inconvenience or pain.

The new womanhood does not shirk, in the same way as the old, either from the bearing of, or from the infliction of pain. They are all for facing facts, and dealing with them boldly and hardly ; and it is beginning to tell in the ordinary relations of life. Whether it will have any ultimate or lasting effect on human nature or life in the next generation still lies on the knees of the gods.

Poor John, journeying by tram from Shawlands, and then walking to the end of the obscure little street in the great western district, where Elizabeth had her club-room, had his journey and his wait for nothing ! He was very patient, and not at all angry, for it was so very unlike Elizabeth to do anything discourteous that he never thought of blaming her.

He watched the girls disperse, some of them showing a levity in the street which would undoubtedly have disturbed and disappointed those who laboured so hard for their improvement, and, finally, a small, demure, old-maidish person came out of the close-mouth, dangling a key over her finger. He then understood that Elizabeth had not turned up.

Chagrined, and slightly concerned, he walked idly out into the great western road, and was there arrested by the singular and enchanting beauty of the evening sky. It had been a very fine sunset, and great masses of purple clouds with fiery edges were making a wonderful background for the graceful outlines of the University Buildings.

John Marchbanks had a fine mind, and an eye acutely sensible to natural beauty, and the pictured scene caught hold of his imagination and fired it, to the exclusion of his more disquieting thoughts. It wooed his spirit even from the image of the woman he loved ; while, at the same time, as if from no will of his own, he felt himself being drawn, as by a magnet, in the direction of her home. There was no earthly reason why he should not call at Balcraig and make a personal inquiry regarding her non-appearance. He did not suppose that it would cause the smallest comment.

So he climbed the steep ascent towards the University, still revelling in the lovely panorama of the sky, and sought his road by devious ways to the stately avenue where Balcraig, with its square tower and large enclosing space, easily made a landmark.

As it happened, Mr. Annan, after the cold supper, which was the only part of the Sunday he actively disliked, but to which domestic arrangements demanded that he should conform as amiably as possible, was taking a cigar in the grounds. He had not seen Elizabeth since their return from their walk. She had not come down, either to tea or supper ; and when her mother had gone up to inquire after her she had found the door locked, and had been assured, from the other side, that Lisbeth was all right and wanted nothing.

This was in itself sufficient to upset the mother, because Elizabeth was a perfectly healthy and normal young woman where food was concerned, and enjoyed all her good meals. Rushing to her husband, he had informed her of what had passed that afternoon, and had sternly ordained that, in the meantime, the refractory and rebellious daughter was to be left severely alone.

Roger was not in to supper. None knew where he was ; but they supposed it probable that he was round in the next avenue, at the Dunsyres' house.

Mr. Annan, though feeling slightly soothed by the fragrance of his fine cigar, was by no means his usual complacent self as he paced the narrow path near the door in the lane, which was always kept locked on Sundays. He was not very far off it when he heard some one try the handle, and, hastening his steps, he threw it open to behold John Marchbanks.

John had been for several years now such a privileged person at Balcraig that it had even been suggested he might have a key, in common with all the members of the family. Mr. Annan's face, however, wore a distinct frown instead of the usual smile of welcome, as he recognised him.

" Good evening, Mr. Annan," said John, in his usual genial voice. " I tried the door on chance."

" We keep it locked on Sunday ; and, anyway, it doesn't do to let everybody make free with a private entrance," said Mr. Annan coldly.

John looked a trifle askance at this remarkably cool reception. His face flushed a little, and, had he obeyed his immediate impulse, he would have turned on his heel and walked off.

Mr. Annan, who had, at the very moment of interruption, been concocting a note which he intended to write and post that night, making an appointment with the young man next day, reflected that the matter could now be settled by a very few words, without further delay. That it was Sunday, and, therefore, the Day of Rest, need not count—the better the day the better the deed ! It would not be a very pleasant task, but, then, the strong man—and Mr. Annan prided himself on being that—does not shrink from the duty that is obvious, merely because it happens to be unpleasant.

" Come in," he said, a trifle ungraciously, but at the same time beckoning his entrance. " I rather want to see you anyway. It'll save writing."

Marchbanks stepped in, not so blithely as usual, for there was a kind of cold hostility about the man who had so often been his genial host. For the moment he did not associate his changed demeanour with Elizabeth, but presently he was left in no doubt.

Mr. Annan could not, by any stretch of the imagination, be described as a tactful man. He walked on a few steps away from the door by the young man's side; and, presently, as they neared the very trees where he had interrupted the *tête-à-tête* the previous afternoon, he stood still on the path and looked squarely into Marchbanks' astonished face.

"Would you mind stepping into the summer-house a minute, John? I have something I wish to say to you."

Marchbanks coloured violently, and lost at once his usual quiet manner.

"Of course, sir—anything you like," he murmured confusedly. "But why not outside here, just where we are?"

"Very well—we can walk up and down. It's very pleasant in the open certainly. I don't like what I have to say, Marchbanks, and I'm sorry that it should be necessary. Perhaps you can guess—indeed, it's very likely—it is about my daughter I wish to speak."

Marchbanks paled as rapidly as he had flushed, but made no remark.

"When you began to come to Balcraig first," began Mr. Annan, with great deliberation, "we were very pleased to welcome you, chiefly because you were a friend of Roger's, though afterwards," he added handsomely, "you were very welcome on your own account. You remember that night when you asked to see me in the library, and told me frankly of the great disability of your birth?"

"I remember perfectly, of course."

"I admired your courage and frankness that night, and both Mrs. Annan and I were agreed that your action, which must have cost you something, did you credit."

He paused there, but when Marchbanks made no response he hastened on. "But, at that time, Miss Annan was not at home. It was not so very long after she returned from abroad that her mother began to be a little uneasy, and confided her uneasiness to me. I made light of it, thinking it was only a woman spying ferlies where a love affair was concerned—you are following, John?—and I'm sure you would not make it more awkward or difficult for me?"

"I'm following you, of course," said Marchbanks a little harshly. "And I understand quite well that you are giving me my *congé* from Balcraig. Very well, Mr. Annan; I promise you I won't come back."

The tone was so quiet as to mislead Mr. Annan, who had expected some sort of indignant outburst. He turned, and looked rather anxiously into the young man's face, but the light was failing, and he was not able to read the fine shades of expression.

"I wish I could make it easier for you, lad," he said, with a touch of real kindness; for though somewhat pompous and condescending, he was far too kindly to enjoy what he was doing. "But you see it—don't you? She's our only daughter. We have quite proper ambitions for her—other views, in fact. In all probability she will marry out of Scotland altogether."

Still no answer. Then, getting slightly uncomfortable—even nettled, Mr. Annan stood still in the path and looked squarely and keenly into the young man's face.

"My advice to you—repeated from yesterday—is to leave Glasgow. You have certain abilities, I know; according to Roger, who is your devoted champion, they are of an exceptional kind. Get out into a wider area where the unfortunate accident of your birth won't militate against you. If you care for the East, I'll do what I can. I have no room in our Calcutta House just now; but I know some of the big jute folk there, and, if you like——"

"Thank you kindly, Mr. Annan; but I'll not be troubling you. And I'll say good night now," interrupted John's even, quiet voice.

"Don't go like that! You must see the reasonableness of what I've been saying?"

"I see it quite well; and I'm not complaining," said Marchbanks, and his tone was as dense and inscrutable as his face.

Grasping the fact that the young man was not going to make the slightest trouble, the kindlier side of Mr. Annan struggled for supremacy. It was a horrid thing he had had to do—to stab a sensitive nature in its most vulnerable part, and, while not departing an inch from his inflexible purpose, he would have made amends if he could. But Marchbanks, apparently, wanted none of his amends. He was already beginning to move in the direction of the door in the lane.

"I'm very sorry, my lad," said the great merchant almost humbly. "As we go through life, we have to give and take some hard knocks. You'll find that out, soon enough. But I'm nearly certain that the day will come when you'll thank me for this."

"When that day comes, Mr. Annan, I promise you that you'll hear from me."

It was not a threat, but, nevertheless, there seemed to sound something ominous in the unnaturally quiet voice.

Mr. Annan looked at him keenly once more, as he turned with him down the path.

"I hope I need not ask you to respect the confidence I have place in you?"

"The confidence?" repeated Marchbanks in a dazed kind of way.

"It is a mark of confidence, surely, when a man trusts another with his most intimate desires and intentions concerning his own!" retorted Mr. Annan in a slightly nettled voice. "But, if you want it put more plainly—Will you promise not to try to see Elizabeth or to write to her?"

"I make no promise, sir—none at all," answered Marchbanks, and a sudden fury swept his face. "But you'll be sorry for this, Mr. Annan—by God, you will! I'll take care that you are!"

And with that he hastened his steps, so that it would have been undignified for Mr. Annan to follow him.

A moment later the bang of the garden door as it answered to its chubb latch finally ended one of the most uncomfortable interviews Mr. Annan had ever taken part in. His handsome face was flushed, and he threw away the half-smoked cigar—sure sign of mental disturbance beyond the common.

He had been shaken by the experience, but Marchbanks' last words had removed the slight sting of remorse he had felt, and confirmed him in his own opinion and attitude.

But, if the parting words meant anything, the affair was by no means over. Marchbanks had declined to be bound—then, there was Elizabeth!

Once more, as he returned slowly to the house, Mr. Annan heaved a sigh over the vanished and purest joys of parenthood, when little arms had met about his neck, and every childish woe could be assuaged with chocolates, or the newest toy.

Presently, the next phase in the campaign was introduced by Elizabeth, who, having sighted the pair from her bedroom window, and watched Marchbanks' hurried exit, had rushed down to discover what had happened.

When her father saw her coming, his spirit frankly quailed!

Even the strongest and most domineering man is small match for a charming and determined daughter! Since the day had passed when he can shut her up, on bread and water, until her will is broken, his weapons are no match for hers. She is ready with her tongue; and even when she is silent, her woman's wit is like a polished shaft against his.

Elizabeth did not, on this occasion, beat about the bush. Looking directly into her father's face, she asked, in a voice almost as quiet as John's had been :

" What have you been saying to John Marchbanks ? And why has he gone away like that ? "

" I just told him, lass, that it would be better for us all, and, more particularly, for himself, that he should not come about the house as much as he has been doing."

" And what did he say to that ? "

" Very little ; but I think he agreed. He's a reasonable chap, if he's let alone, Lisbeth, and I should be glad to help him to get out of Glasgow, and to make a career for himself elsewhere."

" But why should he be hounded out of Glasgow just because you happen to have got a particular idea into your head ? " asked Elizabeth, in her most cutting voice.

" Oh, come, Lisbeth ! That's not a way for you to speak to me, and I won't have it—understand ! This affair is done with. I'm in earnest about it. So is your mother. I'm going in now to discuss arrangements for the summer with her. What would you say to the London trip now, that had to be put off because your mother was so poorly at Easter ? "

" I want to hear what John said ? " persisted Elizabeth. " And if you don't tell me, I'll go and see him to-morrow, at his mother's house."

Mr. Annan looked properly shocked at this unmaidenly speech.

" You're not in your right mind, or you'd never so far forget yourself, Lisbeth ! You know—or perhaps you don't know—what men say and think about women who hunt after them like that ! My daughter would not be capable of that, I know ! "

" Wouldn't she ? "

Elizabeth's tone was distinctly mocking.

" You're so old-fashioned—you and mother !—and you don't see that the new age has come—the age where men and women have met, or are going to meet, immediately, on equal terms ! Why shouldn't I go and see John at his mother's house ? How do you know I haven't been there already ? I'm tired of all this make-believe, father, of being treated like a child, when I'm a grown-up woman. Have you forgotten that I'm nearly twenty-three ? You can't whip me and put me to bed any longer ! "

" It's what I'd like to do when you behave like that, lass," retorted Mr. Annan sternly. " I was in hopes, after this afternoon, that you had looked the situation squarely in the face, and seen for yourself how impossible further association with John Marchbanks has become. I blame myself for not having foreseen and guarded against this contingency. One has to pay for good as well as for bad deeds, in this world ! But understand once for all, Lisbeth, that neither your mother nor myself will ever sanction an engagement or a marriage between you and John Marchbanks. I have already explained why ; and there are wheels within wheels in a case like this, which I would have spared you if I could. But the headstrong can be spared nothing ! You that read so much, and pose as a thinker and a reformer, should know that inherited tendencies are the most difficult of all to overcome. Supposing for a moment that we were so far left to ourselves as to let you marry young Marchbanks, how long would it be, do you think, before you rued the day ? Not long, my dear—not long ! He has acquired a certain veneer—not much, I admit, but enough to get along with—but what can the grain be, but coarse ? And it might even be something worse ! A bairn, born out of wedlock, hasn't a chance, Lisbeth. He or she is handicapped from the start, by the lawless strain. The bar sinister is deeper and more serious than is seen on the surface. It's that we would save you from, my dear. Try and picture what it would be like, tied to a man for life, in such close relationship as I have lived with your dear mother all these years. It is a test, Lisbeth, the supreme test. He would wound all your susceptibilities, you would become his critic and his judge ; and then, what but disaster would ensue ? For you have neither patience nor forbearance for the smallest worries of life, and where would you get them for the big things ? We've spoiled you, my dear ; and now we are trying to make what sorry amends we can by saving you from yourself."

Never had Mr. Annan presented a case more succinctly and more convincingly. The personal feeling under which he was labouring gave the necessary touch of poignancy to his appeal.

Elizabeth was impressed by it, even shaken. In the high-handed way of youth, she had already appraised and settled the mental calibre of the parent about whom she really knew very little. A successful business man—she had decided him to be—and nothing more ! And his exposition of the laws of heredity, and his lucid grasp of the possibilities of tragedy lurking in certain marriage unions, came to her as a complete surprise. She was shaken by it, and, for the moment, at a loss how to refute it.

Mr. Annan regarded her rebellious face wistfully.

" I'd like you to try and take this sensibly, Lisbeth ; and more especially, not to trouble your mother with it more than is necessary. She's not so strong as she was a year or two back. I have to shield her, my dear. Shall we make a little pact ? I promise you I'll do my best for John Marchbanks, and that he shall not suffer through what has happened. It may very easily be the making of him."

" I'd like to hear what he has to say about it," she answered, with the note of dull defiance in her voice—the voice of three-and-twenty.

" I can't prevent you seeing him, of course, as I can't shut you up," said Mr. Annan, the softness fading out of his voice as Elizabeth's hardened. " I can only trust, now, to your own common sense and your good, womanly feeling. Maybe I'll find them a broken reed ! "

" That's very likely," answered Elizabeth, and sped back to the house, her father watching her with troubled eyes until she disappeared.

He was not sure but that she had the best of it. Further, she had not even given him the smallest assurance that she would respect his wishes. It was a difficult family impasse in which he was quite helpless.

That he had done his duty he was completely assured. In all the circles of his wide acquaintance in the city of his birth he would not, he felt sure, find one solitary father to disagree with him on that point. He went over some of them in his mind, and, naturally, the Dunsyres came first. Supposing, for a moment, that Kitty, whom they had, mentally, assigned to Roger, should contemplate such a disastrous shipwreck of her future as, apparently, Lisbeth had faced—what would be the verdict of Joe Dunsyre —"Old Knockout," as he was popularly and affectionately called by his intimates, and the public at large ? Joe was one of the warm-hearted, choleric sort, subject to gusts of passion, yet quick and generous to make amends when he came to himself. He would have small quarter for a rebellious daughter like Elizabeth ! Yet, if she had looked at him out of those big, calm, confident eyes of hers, where would he be ?

" It's easy to judge and condemn when you're not in the dock," he muttered to himself. " But I wish I knew what to do with her."

He went in to see his wife, and found her in her boudoir already preparing for bed. Life flowed very placidly at Balcraig on Sundays—always kept as a day of complete rest.

" You've surely been a long time over your smoke, Bob ? " she said, looking round with the wifely smile that had never failed him once in over thirty years.

" I'm not easy in my mind, Mary. I've had it out with John Marchbanks, and, in a less degree, with Lisbeth."

Mrs. Annan paused in her task of brushing out her still luxuriant hair, and looked at her husband in consternation.

" You mean you've told him he isn't to come back ? Oh, Bob, I hope you put it nicely ! I couldn't have done it ! "

Mr. Annan could have laughed outright at this characteristic, womanly speech, which embodied the entire philosophy of his wife's life. She could hurt the feelings of no human being, even her servants, who were often trying, and unappreciative of the best mistress in Glasgow.

" I did the best I could. But it had to be done, and the methods can't always be chosen. You've to take it as it comes."

" And how did he take it ? "

" Quietly enough. He would give no promise not to see Lisbeth, or write ; but I left him in no doubt as to our intentions and resolves—I advised him to get out of Glasgow, and suggested the East. I'll make a point of seeing William Kinnaird to-morrow, when I go into the city, and get him to make a berth for the lad. When he gets away to new scenes he'll forget."

" And Lisbeth, father ? " was the next anxious question.

Mr. Annan shrugged his shoulders.

" That'll have to be your job, my dear, for I've no understanding of the creature. Find out whether she cares, and what will be the best thing to do. I've done my job—it's your turn now."

Mrs. Annan smiled ruefully as she answered :

" I'm not sure but that you have left me the hardest row to hoe, Bob ! "

CHAPTER IV

TROUBLED WATERS

Ellen Marchbanks, sitting alone by the window of her sitting-room above the shop in the Shawlands Road, was interested, though rather less keenly than usual, in the Sunday strollers, who had found the quickest and easiest way of getting a glimpse of the green country, for which human nature seems to long more on Sundays than other days.

About nine o'clock, in the golden dusk, happy but tired family parties, the children hanging on to father's hand, or to mother's skirts, the biggest ones bearing triumphal branches of the white hawthorn which can still be discovered by the discerning, in hedges quite near Glasgow, toiled by on their way to the car which would bear them inwards to the city.

It was rather a quaint, old-world little house wherein Ellen Marchbanks had pitched her camp—one of the few remaining bits of old Glasgow which are still to be found here and there on the outskirts, though they are rapidly being swept away.

After the tragedy of her young life, Ellen Marchbanks had been so fortunate as to find a real Christian friend in her mistress, who occupied one of the fine old mansion houses in Shawlands. A maiden lady, given up to good work, and with a discerning heart beyond the common, Miss Galbraith had heard the young woman's pitiful story before she engaged her, and determined to give her a chance. She did so, and never rued it, for Ellen remained her faithful and devoted servant to the day of her death.

She left two hundred pounds to Ellen, and certain articles of furniture and plenishing sufficient to equip a small house. Great was Ellen's joy, and she immediately pounced on the little shop and house in the Shawlands Road, near the car terminus, and there proceeded to make a home for herself and her fatherless boy.

Instead of merely spending his Sunday afternoons in Miss Galbraith's house and garden, the boy was brought in altogether from the house of his foster-mother, an old neighbour of Ellen's, in Miss Galbraith's service, married to a ship's carpenter, at Whiteinch, and having no children of her own; to a real home with his mother.

It was a great day when little Jake, as he was familiarly called, had that home-coming! It was a Saturday afternoon, and Mrs. Houston had brought him, with all his clothes in a carpet-bag, making a great mystery out of it all. His mother had received him with tears, which had mystified and discomfited Jake, he being unversed in the strange contradictions of a woman's heart. His childish imagination could not, in any way, connect tears with an occasion to joyful. For Jake loved Shawlands as much as he loathed the ugly crowded street near the river, where he had lived with the Houstons.

When he discovered that the joys of his new home were further enhanced by the possession of a shop where you could weigh sugar and things out of real scales, his satisfaction knew no bounds!

Ellen's little venture had been a complete success. Thrifty, capable, and with a sunshiny smile for everybody, even the humblest customer who had merely a farthing to expend, her little emporium became quickly known, trusted, and beloved. And when, as the years went by, and other flourishing establishments with enormous sheets of plate-glass for the display of attractive goods, arrived for Shawlands, Ellen's popularity did not wane. She made an excellent living for herself, and laid by every penny she could for her boy's future. She was one of the still, silent kind, who voiced her ambitions and her secret hopes to none. To Jake, now and again, she would confide her hope that he would work hard at school and learn everything he could, so as to become a useful and successful man. In her secret soul she yearned to send him to the University; but, at the time when the necessary decision had to be made, Jake had decided against it, and had taken a place in a bank, beside one of his chums

On reflection, Ellen, who was necessarily elemental in certain parts of her intelligence, decided that a bank was very good, and that a young man of ability, like Jake, would have as fair a chance there as anywhere else. He was a good lad, and had never caused her any anxiety.

As he grew older, she encouraged him to find friends and associates beyond their very narrow circle, and was specially pleased over his friendship with the Annans. She had heard of them through her old mistress, who had been distantly connected, in some way, with Mrs. Annan.

Ellen imagined that she had prepared herself for the day when her son would finally drift away from her, into what she called his proper sphere, among people who were his equals, according to some crude laws of heredity, which she had worked out for herself. But, though she imagined herself ready for that supreme sacrifice when, if need be, she should stand aside and efface herself completely in order not to be a bar in his way, she none the less dreaded its approach.

As she sat there, idle, her book lying open on the little table in front, she was conscious of a most unusual depression of spirits. The passing show in the street below hardly interested her at all—nay, she saw the moving figures as in a dream.

When she suddenly saw her son swing himself off the car, newly arrived at the terminus, her face flushed with pleasure. So often he went out to supper on a Sunday night, leaving her alone; but she had never grumbled, nay, she had gloried in it.

A little apprehension followed hard upon her joy as she watched him striding across the road. Love-sharpened eyes are quick to read and mark every expression on the face beloved, and John's expression was unusually gloomy. All his features were grimly set. It was as if a cloud suddenly obscured the sky of summer for the mother, the sole light of whose life he was.

She rose quickly, her housewifely mind turning for a swift moment towards creature comforts. It was seldom she had him to supper on Sunday evenings, but the remains of their midday dinner, with a little skill and embroidery, would furnish forth no mean meal.

But quickly, very quickly, Ellen's mind was diverted from material things, for, when her son came into her presence, she knew that more than a passing gloom held him in thrall.

She received him at the door, where the light was dim; and, when he entered the sitting-room, the first thing he did was to pull the cord of the incandescent burner and flood the room with light. It shone, rather pitilessly, on both. On Ellen, in her neat black frock, with the little glimpse of white at the throat, which relieved the sombre hue and gave to her face a kind of wistful, girlish sweetness.

Time had dealt very gently with Ellen Marchbanks, and at forty-five she had an enviable air of youth. Her hair was particularly beautiful, though too demurely plaited to show to the best advantage. Her figure was slim, her eyes clear, and, though she had very little colour, having spent the greater portion of her life indoors, it was not an unhealthy, sallow pallor.

" You're home early, Jake," she said, striving to smile with her usual readiness, and to speak naturally, as was her wont.

" Am I ? It's after nine," he answered dully, and she had no idea—poor soul !—that his soul revolted, at the moment, from her, blaming her for the suffering and humiliation he had that night undergone, and might yet have to undergo !

" But there's plenty to eat in the house. What would you like, Jake—a slice of cold meat or a bit of yesterday's pie ? " she asked hesitatingly. Her voice was nicely modulated, though her accent was a little laboured.

For her son's sake she had abandoned, even in private life, the use of the broad Scots, which was her natural channel of expression. He did not like it ; he never used it himself ; and was often railing at the Glasgow accent, which he professed to think the ugliest on earth ! He took immense pains to keep it in check in his own speech, and had succeeded in a quite remarkable degree. For there is nothing so clinging as accent—the ivy has not a chance beside it !

" I don't want anything to eat. It would choke me, at the minute ! " he said with unnecessary harshness. " Come and sit down here ; I want to ask you something."

" Yes, Jake," she said, a trifle faintly, for something seemed to sweep over her heart—the first wave of an unnamable fear.

She sat down nervously on the edge of the chair by the table, while he, striding to the window, pulled down the blind with a jerk.

" I've been kicked out of Balcraig, mother," he said, with an undertone of savageness.

" Kicked out of Balcraig ! But what for ? " she asked blankly.

He shrugged his shoulders.

" Ask me another——" he said gruffly.

" Ah, but, Jake ; there's no use answering me like that. As you've told me so much, tell me the rest. What happened ? "

" Can't you guess ? " he asked roughly.

" I might guess wrong. And, anyway, it's your business to tell me," she answered, with a certain amount of that dignity which, just now and again, flashed out from the recesses of her grey humble life, and lifted it up.

" I might have known what would happen ! And I had a very good mind to tell Mr. Annan to his face, that it would have been a kinder, and more Christian act, if he had showed me the door three years ago, instead of to-night——"

" What reason did he give ? "

" Oh, you know. I presumed to lift my eyes to his daughter. But she cares, mother, I'm sure ! And, if she cares enough, I'll have her in spite of all the fathers in the world ! "

" Have you asked her, then ? " inquired Ellen Marchbanks in a low voice, in which pain predominated—the pain of the mother when she learns for the first time that another woman has a claim upon her son. It was poignant enough, even to dull that other pain which had long slept, but was now about to leap into newness of life.

" Not exactly asked her. We've drifted into it, you know how——" he said, with an odd simplicity. " And they must have been blind bats if they didn't see it. Roger has a guess, I'm sure ; but Mr. Annan told me to-night, quite straightly, that it was no use. In other words—he forbade me the house."

"And did he give his reasons ?" asked Ellen in a hollow voice which bore little resemblance to her own.

"Reasons ! Why, of course. You can guess. I'll tell you now, what I didn't mention at the time, for fear of hurting you. When I began to go about Balcraig first, I made up my mind I would not go under false pretences, and I told him—you know what——"

"But I want to know who told you first, Jake, since the subject had never been mentioned between us ?"

"Well—it was Mrs. Houston—far back, when I was at the school, and wanted to have a father, like other chaps. I couldn't ask you ; and I wanted desperately to find out——"

"And what did Mrs. Houston tell you ?" asked Ellen, in a sort of cold, passionless voice, which gave no index to the seething cauldron within.

"She just told me the truth—that I was an illegitimate bairn," said John ruthlessly. "And now I know what a curse that is to a man ! I wish you had done something to me when I was born——"

It must be supposed that John Marchbanks, smarting under his own acute personal suffering, had no real conception of what he was saying. It was an enormity he was perpetrating—hurling such words at the mother who bore him ! But when does youth make pause to consider whether its winged words will hurt, or slay ?

Ellen sat very still ; but the pallor of her face seemed to deaden until it became grey and full of woe.

"And now, I think the time has come when you should tell me who my father was, mother ?"

"And why ?" she asked, in her low, quiet voice. "Of what earthly use would that be ?"

"It might help. I asked Mrs. Houston, but she either didn't know, or wouldn't tell me—which was it ?"

"She didn't know. And you will never know either, my man. For, while I live, his name shall never pass my lips."

"Then there is no more to be said," said John, in a hard level voice. "And we'd better change the subject."

"That we can do to advantage," she replied. "But this I will say to you, Jake, before my lips close over the subject I can't discuss with you : you are right to blame me—nobody but me. I've been trying to get ready for this day, which has brought me my punishment—punishment that no sinner escapes. But I didn't think it would be so hard——"

Her voice, in spite of her effort to steady it, trailed away into a little cadence of pain. But, apparently, her son heard it unmoved.

"If you would tell me his name," he said between his teeth, "I would seek him out and get even with him, if I have to go to the ends of the earth to find him !"

She looked at him with eyes that were calm and wondering.

She was, in some respects, an elemental creature, whom suffering had made wise. And she discerned that, for the moment, the powers of evil had got hold of her boy and were trying to work their will with him. She, who would have given the last drop of her blood for him, had brought a heart, naturally kind, to this point of fury when naught but the desire for revenge was uppermost.

She stretched out her hands with a little impassioned gesture, but either he did not see it, or hardened himself against it.

"I'll leave Glasgow," he said harshly. "And show Mr. Annan that it is possible for a man to rise in spite of the bar sinister—which was the grand name he gave it. Then, maybe, I'll get a chance, another day, to fling back their stinking pride in their faces, and stand up to them, man for man——"

"You'll rise, Jake. There's nothing surer—and you'll get over this, too!" she murmured feverishly. "What can I say to you, laddie? Me, that has a broken heart."

But he passed on, in the unheeding way of youth, stumbling blindly, with eyes shut and ears deaf to the poignant appeal in his mother's voice.

"And, if I liked, I could put a spoke in their wheel now! Roger's a very good chap; but I know things about him! I've shielded him too; and hauled him out of a lot of scrapes which, if they were known, would bring down his father's pride."

"Wheesht, laddie, that's not worthy of you!" cried Ellen, with a real anguish in her voice. "If I were you I'd take a vow not to be revenged; for revenge never gave anybody a scrap of satisfaction yet. But to rise by your own efforts to a high place in the world! You can do it, Jake—you've a terrible determination when you like!"

John smiled grimly as he answered, with a merciless simplicity:

"It's very easy for you to speak. You've never been out in the world. You don't know how people like the Annans view things. And they don't stand by themselves—they're a type. No!—I'll have to get out of this rotten country, and try my luck where the moral laws don't hang together by such mighty fine hairbreadths. I'll give in my resignation at the bank to-morrow; and if they can let me off without working the usual month's notice, the better I'll be pleased."

She rose at that with a little quick, nervous gesture, and said she would be seeing after some supper.

John permitted her to go without further word. Obsessed by his own humiliation and pain, he had no thought to spare for her, not even a wave of grateful recognition for her self-denying labours on his behalf. Had the question been driven home to him at the moment, he would most probably have replied that the initial injustice, the accident of his birth, wiped out all the rest.

Ellen felt that it did. As she shut herself up in the little kitchen she put her hand sharply to her heart, and her breath came in a short, shuddering moan.

At the back of her mind she had always known that this day would come; but the suffering far transcended her anticipation. She did not rebel altogether, taking it as her just punishment; but, away back in the dimmest recesses of her being, there was a faint rebellion against the inevitable law which ordains that the woman should pay, not only first and last, but all through.

The Almighty has thus ordained it, no doubt, in order that the stability and the purity of home life may be maintained.

There was but little eaten at that humble supper-table that night, and Ellen said good night early. But retiral to her room did not mean sleep. Nay! Long after he was in his own bed, where he tossed, restless and gloomy, John could hear her moving in the adjoining room.

She seemed to be opening and shutting drawers a good deal. There was an old-fashioned bureau in one corner of her bedroom, one of the many useful articles left to her by Miss Galbraith's will. From one of its inmost and secret recesses she took some letters, tied with a string, two photographs, and some memoranda in a note-book, which she studied for some minutes.

The letters she read over one by one, methodically and with an effort, for it was like opening a grave. Love-letters they were, breathing a passion which might and ought to have been strong enough to conquer fate; instead of lying there, in a secret drawer, years after, of no use except to torture a woman's heart!

Yet, so strangely constituted was that heart, that it took a sad but exquisite pleasure in words that had ceased to live save in memory alone!

The handwriting was educated, and of a bold decisive type; and the words were gallant as well as sweet—the outpourings of a heart stirred to the depths. They had been both true and deep when they were penned; and they were strong still, to move the heart of a desolate woman after more than twenty years.

Through all these years, no other image had ousted that of the writer from her faithful heart. Where he was now she knew not, nor even whether he was alive or dead, and, in spite of the bitter words her son had spoken, there was no bitterness against the man who had left her to bear the brunt alone. Nay—her eyes grew tender, and a smile of indescribable sweetness crept about her sad mouth as she looked once more on the pictured face, recalling, rather than imagining, the winning smile that had lurked in the depths of those bright eyes.

It was near midnight before she could tear herself away from that strange tryst with memory; it might be, with death. None knew of it, nor, perhaps, would ever know. Who that knew the small, friendly, obliging shopkeeper near Shawlands Cross would have pictured her the heroine of a romance which had a side so tragic!

Strange as it may seem, that little dip into the archives of the past both soothed and strengthened her, and even after a time she was able to sleep a dreamless and refreshing sleep, which contrasted sharply with John's somewhat bitter and dream-haunted rest.

Of late years, in deference to John's strongly expressed wishes, Ellen had requisitioned the services of a woman in the early hours of the day to light fires and clean the shop and do the roughest work. This enabled her to attend to some of the little refinements of life, by which her boy, since he had reached man's estate, had begun to set store. This worthy's name was Katrine Polson, and she was a queer little, hump-backed, dwarf-like creature, with a shrewd, peaked little face, and a pair of uncanny black eyes.

Her physical strength was prodigious, and she was simply devoted to Mrs. Marchbanks, who had been kind to her in a great variety of ways.

In addition to her unusual physical strength, Katrine had certain odd qualities of mind and heart out of the common. For instance, she claimed the gift of second sight, and augmented her slender earnings by the surreptitious reading of fortunes among those foolish enough to cross her palm with silver for the purpose.

The moment the door was opened for her on that Monday morning, she gathered from the expression of Mrs. Marchbanks' face that all was not well with her mistress. The voice that wished her "good morning" had lost its blithesome ring.

"Ay, it's a guid enough mornin'; naething the matter wi' it, in fact, as far as I can see. But you hinna sleepit."

"Oh, yes, I have!" Ellen hastened to assure her. "Not so long, maybe, as usual. I was late in getting in my bed. The kettle's boiling on the gas-ring—come and get your cup of tea."

This early morning cup they always shared together; and nobody but the little hunchback herself knew how much she appreciated this kindly start to the day. At the same time, nobody knew better than she exactly how much it meant; for Ellen had a quiet dignity of her own, which would have been quick enough to resent the smallest undue familiarity.

" Mrs. Marchbanks is a rale leddy," Katrine was fond of saying. " An' she kens her place. She hasna aye stood ahint a coonter."

One Shawlands worthy, to whom Katrine had ventured this remark, had derisively pointed out that, after all, Mrs. Marchbanks had only been servant to Miss Galbraith.

" Servant or nae servant, she's a rale leddy," Katrine stoutly maintained. " There's mair ahint yon face than the common e'e can see."

The faithful soul, as she took the pin out of her tartan shawl, was disturbed by something she saw in her kind friend's face that morning ; and when they had concluded their early meal, Ellen found her, a few minutes later, intently studying the tea-leaves at the bottom of the cup she had used.

" It's rather early in the morning for fortune-telling ! Isn't it, Katrine ? Yours and mine are long told, anyhow ! "

" I'm no' so sure," retorted Katrine. " This is your cup, an' there's a fell heap o' things in it for a Monday mornin' ! "

" What kind of things ? " asked Ellen, with a slight smile of interest on her face, as she prepared to go into the shop to uncover the counters.

" A' kinds o' things—great, big, muckle cheenges ! Ech me ! Fair earthquakes ! I see a voyage to furrin pairts for somebody—Maister Jake, likely ; an' a lot o' queer things on the ither side, forby folk. An' a big, tall, buirdly man wi' a pair o' dancin' e'en that ye hinna seen for lang enough. You'll see them again, though, when your ship comes in—but there's a heap o' water to row under the brig afore that time. But you're to keep your hert up, my dear. The best bit o' your life's to come."

" Havers, Katrine ! Away and get your sweep's brush, and be sure you put it as far up the lum as you can reach, for there was some soot falling yesterday. I'm not needing to get the sweep afore the Fair."

Katrine went chuckling to her work, as if she had had some very good news which she was in no particular hurry to pass on, confident that its proof and distribution was in other hands than hers.

CHAPTER V

RAGGED EDGES

THERE was, naturally, very little said by John Marchbanks or his mother at the breakfast table that morning.

On Ellen's part it was a mere pretence of a meal. She came in and sat down at the table and poured out tea for her son; but when he took the lid off the bacon-dish, she shook her head.

" No, thank you, Jake. I'm not much of a breakfast woman, as you know. And I took an extra big slice of bread with Katrine this morning, so I'm needing nothing but a mouthful of tea."

" But that's bad, mother," said John; and his eyes roamed, with a furtive anxiety, to his mother's face.

The morning had so far restored and healed that he could regret part, at least, of what he had said the night before.

That it was all true took nothing away from its cruelty.

There are moments when it is necessary, if we are to preserve the decencies of life, that truth shall be graciously veiled, just as there are moments when it is necessary for her to appear in all her nakedness, if justice is to be done.

John Marchbanks loved his mother, and admired her, too—which is a different thing. Away from the perspective set by the Annans, he was even proud of her. In the silent night-watches he had cursed the beginning of his friendship with Roger, of which he had once been so proud.

If he had only been wise and prudent enough to be content with the more modest limits of his own set, how much better for them both! Then this anguish and strain would have been spared them! But the milk being spilt, why cry? He sought to apply the homely maxim by trying to assume a cheerfulness he did not feel.

" I won't have that way of going on, mother! You'll be getting ill! Eat your breakfast, and don't let us have any more nonsense."

It was a very good imitation of the old playful masterfulness, and it brought a little wavering smile to Ellen's grave lips.

" I'll eat a morsel to please you, my dear; but I'm not needing it." Then, after a moment, she asked hesitatingly: " Did you sleep? "

" Off and on. It was warm in the night. I sometimes wish you could get out of Glasgow, mother. Wouldn't it run to a little house at the coast, which you would let for a while in the summer, if you should happen to want a change? "

It was a delicate way of intimating his growing disgust with the shop.

He had evolved this scheme in the night, fortified by the reflection that quite nice people let their country houses on occasion, when they wanted a change themselves. He even recalled the memorable year when the Annans had let Balcraig and gone abroad. But that was before Elizabeth came home.

Ellen shook her head.

" It would be too quiet for me, at the coast—especially in the winter."

" But at Rothesay there's a kind of winter season; and people who know say the coast is delightful in the winter after the crowds have dispersed."

" Ay, maybe. But I'll not give up my business, Jake. It's meat and drink to me ; and all the folks that come about are my friends, in a kind of way you would maybe find it difficult to understand. I know that you are ashamed of it ; but, if you really mean what you said last night and are going to leave Glasgow, what's the odds, where I am concerned ? "

Without being studied, the words conveyed a certain reproach. Ellen, in the colder light of day, was disposed to resent the fact that her son was ready to kick away the ladder by which he had risen, even to his present modest height. She might so easily have done less for, or by him ! She could, for instance, have remained in service and apprenticed him to the shipyard, or to any other respectable trade which would have kept him on the Houston's level. Perhaps that might even have been a wiser plan, and made him happier ?

John's lips tightened, for, though he wanted and, indeed, intended to be kind, his feelings were raw yet, and would not bear much handling.

He ate the rest of his breakfast in silence, and left the house without giving his mother any further satisfaction regarding his plans or intentions.

In the pleasant stir of Monday morning business, which was even brisker than usual, Ellen somewhat lost the edge of her inward care. She had a very busy forenoon ; for, after the rush of housewives for their Monday's stores slackened, she had various visits from travellers, representing the firms she dealt with. She was a great favourite, and each and all went out of their way to show her some kindness whenever they had a chance.

About half-past two in the afternoon, always a slack time, came one called Drummond, from Edinburgh, representing a firm of biscuit-makers. He was a fine-looking, well-set-up man, about forty-five, and a favourite of Ellen's, who had known him since ever she started her little business venture.

Because she liked him, she gave him more orders than perhaps, strictly speaking, she ought to have done, if it is the right thing to encourage home industries. She could not plead the excuse that there were not goods as fine in the Glasgow market.

I am afraid that Ellen, woman-like, gave very little thought to that. She was loyal to her friends, and Drummond had shown her a good deal of kindness, earlier in her business career, and had, once at least, helped her out of a rather tight place by his timely and practical advice.

She had always a smile for him ; and often invited him into the back shop for a chat and a cup of tea, while the errand boy, whom she was trying, at intervals, to train for the counter, donned his white apron and took her place.

Drummond called that Monday afternoon, and she received him with her usual cordiality, but he had not talked with her long when he discovered that something was troubling her.

" You don't seem yourself to-day, Mrs. Marchbanks," he said kindly. " Got anything vexing you ? "

" Yes," she admitted. " It's a very private affair, but there is no reason why I shouldn't tell you. It's my son—he is tired of Glasgow, and is going away abroad. I believe he's resigning his place in the bank to-day. Of course, it'll make a great difference to me."

" That's to be expected. But I am not surprised that he is not content with the slow rise possible in a bank. But I can see that it would leave you very lonely."

The tone, so kind and sympathetic, brought a sudden quiver to Ellen's face, and her hands, lying with unusual idleness on her lap, involuntarily clenched.

These signs of distress in a woman in whom he had long been interested put Drummond so far off his guard, that the secret he had intended to keep forever was wrested from him. His face flushed, and, getting up from his chair, he stood before her humbly yet eagerly, and began to plead his cause.

"Look here, Mrs. Marchbanks, I don't know if you've guessed—maybe not—because I've tried honestly to get the better of it, thinking myself an old fool, and a cut-and-dried bachelor as well. But, if you're going to be left as you say, perhaps you might do worse?—I'm lonely too—there's only my sister, and she has her own income, and wants to travel about, and see a bit of the world. I've money saved; and a nice little house at Granton, looking out over the Forth. If you'll marry me I'll do my best to make you happy; for you're the pluckiest and the best little woman I've ever met, and I never thought it was in me to care so much for anybody."

The greatness of her surprise prevented Ellen from interrupting him, so that he was allowed to deliver his soul to the end. She rose then, too; flushing deeply, and looking shy and troubled as any girl.

"Oh, Mr. Drummond, I'm so sorry! I hadn't any idea, of course. But it is not possible I could think of it. I would be a most unsuitable wife for you, or for any man."

"I don't see it!" he said eagerly. "You haven't taken any sort of vow not to marry again, have you?"

"I haven't," answered Ellen faintly. "But, all the same, I won't turn another page of that kind of life. I've had enough of it."

Drummond naturally inferred, from these words, that she had had an unfortunate matrimonial experience.

"But all men are not the same," he said blunderingly. "I'm no great shakes, maybe; but you'd find me very easy to live with. My sister would tell you that. Won't you take a day or two to think it over, before you say no, finally?"

Once more, but very firmly, Ellen shook her head.

"No, I couldn't do that, Mr. Drummond. I've nothing left to marry on—if you understand. I gave all, once, and there's nothing left. But, all the same, I'll never forget this. It—it has done me good—more good than you'll ever know, or than I can explain."

There was something final about her words, and, though he saw her struggling with her tears, Drummond understood that he had no chance.

"If you ever change your mind, you can let me know," he said, with a somewhat rueful smile. "And, in the meantime, I hope this won't make any difference to our friendship. I promise not to offend again, so I hope you won't shut the door to me in future."

"How could I do that? I hope you'll come, just the same," she answered, and they shook hands upon it.

He did not stay longer then, because a certain awkwardness arose out of the situation, which could not be bridged all in a moment. He was not due for another call for a month, so that there would be time for the old friendly relationship to settle down again. He left the house a disappointed man, and he had not the faintest idea of the strange tumult his offer had created in Ellen's mind.

She cared nothing for him, save as one cares for a casual friend, yet, left alone, a mighty temptation swept over her.

It was her first real offer of marriage, for she had, in all the years offered such a stony front to men that not one, even when he was attracted, as had been the case more than once, ever presumed.

She had now got the chance by one step to climb to the height of married respectability, and could, vulgarly speaking, snap her fingers at John and his fine friends!

As Mrs. Drummond, of Forth House, Granton, she would be above all reproach, and could hold up her head with the best of them.

For one mad moment she even contemplated writing to Drummond, and telling him that, on reflection, she had changed her mind. But, very soon, better thoughts came to her, and she put it all behind her. But the incident had done her good, and restored in large measure her self-respect.

Meanwhile, John, true to his resolve, asked to see his manager directly he arrived. The bank where he was employed was situated in Renfield Street, and the manager was both a capable and a popular man.

Young Marchbanks was a favourite of his, and he often cited him as a concrete example of what a young man ought to be who desires to succeed in the world.

He had, therefore, a pleasant smile for him when he came through the door of his private room, after having obtained permission to leave his desk for a few minutes.

" Morning, Marchbanks. And what is it I can do for you ? "

" Nothing much, Mr. Craighead ; it's only that I want to resign."

The manager sat back in astonishment, this being the very first hint he had received that Marchbanks was other than contented.

" You surprise me ! What has happened ? Somebody enticed you away —eh ? "

" Oh no, sir. It's only that I want to leave Glasgow altogether. Probably I am going abroad."

" To something definite, I suppose ? Has Mr. Annan offered something in Calcutta ? He was speaking about you the other day."

The mention of Mr. Annan's name was sufficient to bring the dull red flush to the young man's face.

" Oh no ! He's got nothing to do with it," he said, with more haste than accuracy. " I'm tired of Glasgow, and I want to get off as quickly as possible. If you could fill my place, sir, so as to let me away soon, I would be grateful."

Mr. Craighead sat back in his chair and, putting his hands together, looked rather keenly into the young man's face. The request was not only unusual, but, coming from this particular youth, quite unexpected. It might mean one of two things—that he had got into some personal scrape, or that the circumstances of his home life were pushing him to an extreme decision.

The first he dismissed as unlikely, having proved Marchbanks to be a youth of blameless character ; the second he did not feel himself justified in probing into, no information being volunteered. But the situation both interested and piqued him.

" I'm very sorry, of course, and, as it is our slack time, there won't be any great difficulty in filling your place. But I'm sorry to hear what you tell me, and I would like to be sure that you're acting in your own best interests."

" I think I am, sir, and, anyway, it's nobody's business but my own."

Some hint of the bitterness he was feeling vibrated in his voice, and the kindly interest deepened in the manger's eyes.

" Do your home people approve of this ? " he asked.

" I have no home people—only my mother," answered Marchbanks simply ; then, after a second's hesitation, he added, rather stumblingly, " And she knows I've got to go."

" I see. But you haven't an idea where your next berth is going to be ? "

" No, sir. At the present moment I haven't."

" It sounds a bit rash, and I thought you had more foresight, Marchbanks. But, as you say, it's your own concern. Very well, I suppose I must accept your resignation. You'd better send it in in writing. If I can be of any use to you, let me know. Only, before I can be so you'll have to give me some idea of what part of the world you propose to go to."

"Thank you, sir," said Marchbanks, and passed out. He was relieved that the initial step had been taken.

As he went back to his desk he had to pass Roger Annan, who gave his arm a tug.

"Morning, Jack. You look glum. Been getting what for—eh?"

He spoke with his accustomed lightness, not having been made aware of what had passed at Balcraig on the previous evening. But John merely grunted and passed by, and he did not so much as turn his eyes once in Roger's direction in the next two hours.

Mr. Craighead thought so much about young Marchbanks in the course of the morning, that, departing from his usual no-lunch rule, he walked over to a popular dining-room at one o'clock, knowing that, most likely, he would find Mr. Annan there.

They were old friends and schoolfellows. Mr. Annan was much pleased to see him, and made room at a little table where he sat alone.

"Morning, Willie. Have you fallen away from grace? I thought you had joined the no-lunch brigade?"

"So I have, but I daresay they'll let me sit here while I drink my glass of milk. How are you? And I hope Mrs. Annan is well?"

"Not so very. I'm sending them down to Kilcrean a bit earlier. They'll probably be gone by the end of the week."

"Very good plan. It's been hot, these last few days. What I really popped in for, was to ask you a question about young Marchbanks. I know that he and your Roger are very thick. He's chucked his billet, this morning, for no reason under heaven that I can discover, and he hasn't another in view. I thought you might know something about it, as he goes about your house?"

Mr. Annan picked his cutlet bone very clean before he answered.

"I do happen to know something about it. He's been going rather too much to the house—Lisbeth, you know—won't do at all."

"I see. Who does he belong to? He's been in Renfield Street just over seven years, and I don't even know where he lives! Very remiss on my part, but he's a reticent chap that doesn't invite questions."

"Lives out Shawlands way," said Mr. Annan, then dropped his voice and added something which startled his listener.

"You don't mean it? You surprise me very much! Well—he's a credit to his mother, and she must be a woman out of the common. But I quite see your point, of course. A handsome, marriageable daughter undoubtedly complicates life."

Mr. Craighead was the father of four sons, and the lack of a daughter was one of the minor disappointments of his life.

"And that's true, too! But I tell you what, Willie—girls give a lot of trouble nowadays, and are not so easily managed as they were in our young days."

"But surely, Miss Annan would look a bit higher than a bank clerk! Has it gone far enough to be a difficult job?"

"That's just what I don't know, Willie. She told me, no later than yesterday afternoon, that she would marry him in spite of me. Then I had to tell her what I've just told you. It gave her a shock, I could see, but the barometer is a bit stormy at our house, and that's why I'm in a hurry to get them down to Kilcrean."

"He doesn't mean to make trouble, evidently," said Mr. Craighead, and there was a kindly, regretful note in his voice. "I'm sorry for the lad, and it is the best thing he can do, undoubtedly, to leave the city. I must try and get some more talk with him, and see whether I can't give him a push on."

Mr. Annan made no demur to this ; in fact, he was secretly glad to hear it, for, though he had found it necessary to take drastic measures to nip this love affair in the bud, he wished young Marchbanks no active ill.

When Mr. Craighead went through to his own room, just after two o'clock, he tapped Marchbanks on the shoulder.

" Come through before you go, Marchbanks. I'd like a word with you."

" Yes, sir," said John, readily enough, but the invitation did not elate him in the least.

He had begun to expect nothing from life but rebuff and disappointment. Frankly, he had expected to have had a line or a sign from Elizabeth, but none had come, and he was tormented by the doubt that her love, of which he had been almost, if not quite assured, had after all, been but a very light thing, unable to stand the slightest test.

Roger Annan, quite well aware that something was amiss with his friend, had not had an opportunity of questioning him further, for they did not go out to lunch together. When he saw him disappear into the manager's room soon after four o'clock, he did not connect it in any way with the undoubted gloom that had been on his face all day. There had to be frequent consultations in the manager's room with the junior members of the staff, relating to bank business.

" Shut the door, John," said Mr. Craighead kindly, when John presented himself. " I've been thinking about what you told me this morning, and I would like to hear whether you have any definite ideas about your future ? "

" In the meantime I've none, sir ; except that I want to get out of Glasgow, as I said in the morning."

" But he's a foolish man that burns his boats ! " observed the manager, as he bent his shrewd brows on the young man's face. " Wouldn't it be better to make sure of the next step before you take this rather serious one ? "

" Oh, I'll find something," answered John. " My wants are few. And I've got a few pounds saved which will serve me till I get another berth."

" But there's nothing easier in the world than to begin drifting, lad. If you could give me any indication of what bent you would like to follow I might be able to lend a hand. What particular bit of the Colonies are you thinking of ? If it's Canada, we have corresponding houses in all the principal towns, as you know, and I'll be pleased to do what I can."

Into John's dull face crept a quickening ray.

" I don't think I have thought seriously of it, sir—at least, not to settle anything. But Canada doesn't attract me. From all I can hear it's a pretty tough fight out there, with the climate—and other things. I'd rather try the Argentine, I think. I saw a man from Buenos Ayres last summer "—he did not add that it was at the Annans' house he had met him—" and he advised me to go out there. He says there are plenty of chances for a chap, and that it's the coming country. There's a lot of money in it now, and more to be made ; so I think I'll make tracks for South America."

" Well, and you might do worse. Though there's always something to be said for the British flag, boy. I'll think over the Argentine, and see what letters of introduction I can furbish up. But don't do anything in a hurry that you may be sorry for—even if you have very few people to consider."

It was the nearest approach he dared make to John's private affairs, though, if he had not talked with Mr. Annan, he would probably have asked him about his people, and put a more direct question.

It gave John an opening, if he wished to offer any confidences, concerning the tragedy of his life, but apparently he could not bring himself to it. All he said was :

" I won't be rash, sir ; but I'm twenty-four, and, if I am to make a fresh start, the sooner the better."

When he left the private room his expression was certainly brighter, and he looked a little less like a man at war with fate.

Roger glanced at him furtively, and smiled significantly when their eyes met. To his relief, John smiled back.

Between five and six they left the bank together.

" What's up, old chap ? You look most frightfully down on your luck ! " said Roger, as he tucked his arm in his, his handsome face quite solicitous.

" Nothing much," answered Marchbanks, with a note of strain in his voice. " At least, nothing I can talk about to you."

" Going home, now ? Come up to the Club, and have a peg ? "

John shook his head.

" Not to-day. I'm going out home."

" Will you be along at Balcraig to-night ? I'm asking, because I won't be in."

" No," answered John, with a quick hardening of his voice. " I won't be there, Roger." Then, after a moment, he added, with a whole world of concentrated bitterness in his voice—" Never again ! "

CHAPTER VI

IRONS IN THE FIRE

On his way to his Club, in Gordon Street, Roger Annan suddenly saw, on the other side of the street, a very attractive figure in white, with a pink parasol that matched the rose-trimmed hat sitting so jauntily on Kitty Dunsyre's fair hair. A few strides through the traffic took him to her side.

" Now, this is a bit of jolly good luck ! Had tea ? I hope not, for I'm hungering and thirsting for mine ! "

Tea was not his usual objective at the Club at the close of his day's work, but it served the purpose at the moment.

" I've had some. Mother and I have been at Mrs. Murdoch-Thompson's ' At Home ' ; and now she's gone to fetch father with the carriage. I've been keeping a dressmakers' appointment—I shouldn't at all mind another cup."

" Come then."

He was immensely pleased and proud to be cavalier to such an alluring vision, and Kitty herself seemed not averse.

She was a small, dainty creature, with a pretty rose-leaf face, and big innocent blue eyes, and nobody would have given her credit for being a person of strong will and decisive character.

A very short walk, during which they discoursed on things in general, brought them to a tea-room, a little out of the beaten track, noted for the daintiness and the exclusiveness both of its viands and its service. It was a café which the rich and exclusive preferred to the more popular places of refreshment.

It was very well known to Kitty Dunsyre. Several, already seated at the tables, smiled and exchanged glances at sight of this attractive, well-matched pair, representatives of two very well-known West End families. It gave colour to some of the rumours that had been lately afloat about them.

Roger skilfully guided his companion to a retired corner, gave his order, and then regarded her admiringly.

Poor Roger had been blessed—or cursed—with a quick, appreciative eye for a petticoat, and had seldom, since his boyhood, been free of a love affair. In fact, he had had so many that his susceptibility had passed into a proverb. He had been desperately in love with Kitty, off and on, but she had treated him very cavalierly, and nobody guessed that her heart was really set on him. She had sufficient strength of character to judge that a man who was such a general lover was not at all likely to make a very satisfactory husband.

She was quite well aware that her father and mother would have welcomed the alliance ; and that either Tom or Roger would have been acceptable as a son-in-law. Tom was older and graver, and though he, too, had admired Kitty greatly, and paid her a good deal of attention the last winter he was at home on furlough from Calcutta, she had not responded. Like many another woman, she loved the n'er do weel, and hoped that one day he would settle down.

In the meantime, she was happy enough at home, and had a great many interests in her life, and was by no means given up wholly to pleasure, as were so many of her companions. She had quite as grave a side to her character as her great friend Elizabeth Annan, and was naturally a far more lovable creature.

" Say, Kitty, I've got some news for you, I do believe ! " began Roger confidentially, as he leaned his elbow on the table and looked across at her.

He was looking very handsome in his well-cut, light suit of summer tweed, and his curls, closely cropped about his shapely head, made him resemble an old Greek statue. Kitty, while inwardly admiring him immensely, and rather thrilled by this unexpected *tête-à-tête*, preserved an air of provoking coolness.

" Your news is never worth very much, my dear," she answered, beginning to draw off her long white gloves. " But what is it ? "

" Oh, if you're going to be saucy," he began, and she laughed so prettily that Roger's susceptible heart began to get warm immediately.

" I don't want your news, and I hope they won't be too long with tea, because I forgot I promised Elizabeth to go and hear Barnard sing to-night."

" When did you see Lisbeth ? " asked Roger interestedly.

" This morning."

" And was she all right ? "

" Well, no ; I don't think she was. She seemed in a bit of a temper ; and very short about everything in general."

" Something's happened, at our place, about Jack Marchbanks," said Roger.

A look of deepest interest immediately sprang into Kitty's face.

" Oh, I say ! You don't mean it ? What kind of a thing ? Do you suppose that he has proposed ? "

" As to that, I don't know, but the Guvnor is afraid that he means to, and has nipped it in the bud."

" Told Elizabeth—you mean—that he won't do ? " asked Kitty breathlessly.

" I don't know about Elizabeth, I rather think he has told Jack himself."

Kitty dropped her eyes on her plate, at the moment, as the waitress brought their tea. She had been for some time aware of the fact concerning John Marchbanks' birth, which Elizabeth had only learned the day before, but it was, of course, not one she could discuss with Roger.

" I rather wonder—we all have—that Mr. Annan hasn't spotted it before," said Kitty, as she stirred the tea in the pot—a little gesture which showed her pretty hands to perfection. " If he doesn't think Jack good enough now, I don't really think you all ought to have encouraged him about the house as much as you have done. Didn't you see it, and couldn't you have done something ? "

" I never thought ! " Roger confessed. " You see, a chap doesn't, when it's his own sister. Though where another girl is concerned, he's quick enough."

" I don't see where the difference lies. But how thrilling ! And is there going to be trouble ? Lisbeth is a dear, but she's very determined, Roger, and has been talking a great deal lately about living her own life."

" There's going to be trouble, but not serious, I hope, for Jack has made up his mind to leave Glasgow."

" Rather hard on him, don't you think, Roger ? "

" Hard ! I think it's perfectly abominable. But, of course, well—he isn't exactly a match for Lisbeth—is he ? "

"I suppose not. I wonder what will be the end of it? And does he know where he is going?"

"He doesn't, and, what's more, he doesn't care. I'm sorry for poor old Jack. He hasn't deserved this, Kitty."

Kitty's blue eyes were full of sympathy, and her expression dangerously sweet.

"I say—you're looking positively ripping to-day! And I can't help it if you're angry. I've simply got to tell you."

"Don't be silly. And how many girls have you told that to to-day?"

"Honour bright, I haven't spoken to one since I saw you last!"

"That was only last night," she reminded him. "Do you mean to say, not a girl has been in the bank to-day?"

"Heaps of them. But I simply didn't see them! Don't be so unkind, Kitty. Tell me what I've done to offend you, and I'll promise to be a better boy in future."

Kitty smiled, a rather abstracted smile, and drank her last mouthful of tea.

"I'd give a good deal to know just how Lisbeth feels about this, and whether she'll stick to him. I like him. Don't you, Roger? And I believe he'll get on, wherever he goes. He's one of the quiet sort who get there, while others are talking about it."

"Is that a dig at me?" inquired Roger ruefully—"And you haven't made half a tea!"

"I've had as much as is good for me two hours before dinner, and thank you very much, Roger. You needn't put the cap on unless it fits, you know," she added, with a demure yet adorable glance, which further confirmed the young man's belief that she was the only girl in the world.

Yet, not half an hour later, he was talking, if not with the same passion, yet with considerably more impressiveness than Kitty would have approved or sanctioned, to another girl! Young blood will have its riot in the lap of spring, whatever be the suffering or the cost!

As they left the café together, the carriage, which was the pride of Mrs. Dunsyre's heart, came rolling smoothly up the street, and was hailed, with great satisfaction, by Kitty. Roger, however, declined the offer of a seat beside her, opposite the comfortable pair who seemed to breathe success at every pore.

Dan Dunsyre had been an errand boy at "The Knockout," when it was a modest, two-storied building, with one window on either side of the door. A concrete example of the self-made man, he had many of the faults as well as most of the virtues of his type.

Steady industry, which spared neither himself nor any associated with him, a sharp eye to the main chance always, small profits and quick returns, a swift, unerring grip of every opportunity, even the most slender—these were Dan Dunstyre's simple recipes for success. His salvage stocks were always the largest and cheapest, and his name was held in due reverence by thrifty Glasgow housewives, whose limited pocket money went so much farther at "The Knockout" than anywhere else.

In appearance he was large, fat, and comfortable, with a rather cherubic face which had stood him in good stead through many a hard bargain. Anything more unlike one's preconceived ideas of a sharp man of business could not well be imagined than that big, comfortable, smiling man, whose blue eyes—so like Kitty's—had such an innocent, childlike expression.

He was good-natured up to a point, and his personal kindnesses were legion. He was adored by his entire staff, and their devotion to him had lined his pockets. He had long taken as his axiom, that an unwilling army is poor in fighting qualities, therefore he had adopted a system of profit-sharing which had bound the whole of "The Knockout" employees in one corporate body, with but one aim—the general good.

Neither of his sons could hold a candle to him, and further, they both despised the business, though they did their best to hide it from their father, in whose eyes that was the unpardonable sin.

Mrs. Dunsyre was a less lovable person than her spouse, and her social ambition, which her own personality could not do much to further, kept her in a state of perpetual warfare and unrest. She had all the jealousy, discontent and irritability sometimes seen in those not sure of their position.

Instead of being content with such friends as she could procure easily, and trying to make the best of a really enviable lot, she was constantly striving after the things that were out of her reach.

For there are things which money is powerless to buy, even in an age corrupted by it, and Mrs. Dunsyre was not wise and discriminating enough to leave it at that.

She had tried, and was still trying, most of the avenues open to the climber, of which organised philanthropy is, perhaps, the chief. Of every big bazaar, Mrs. Dunsyre was one of the heads, and nothing pleased her better than to see her name flourishing as a patroness on prospectuses and announcements, beside those of titled folks. She had done her best to shove Dan into public life, but he had good-naturedly, but quite resolutely, declined to be brought forward.

"Leave it to the lads, Joan," he was fond of saying, "and leave me to mind my own business. Mak' Dan or Airchie a Councillor and Lord Provost if ye like, or Member of Parliament, I'll pay up to a point, but leave me alane."

Dan, the elder boy, however, had disappointed every hope, and after causing them untold misery and anxiety, had disappeared, no one knew whither.

Archie promised better, and, sobered by the example of wastage set by his brother, was apparently working contentedly at "The Knockout." But he loathed the place and everything connected with it, and longed to be free.

Such, then, was the state of affairs at Whinstone House, Dowanhill, the home of the Dunsyres, at the moment when Kitty, leaving the café door, took the carriage seat opposite to her mother.

No objection was taken to her escort, even by her mother. She respected the Annans, though she professed not to understand Mr. Annan, who preferred to live the quiet domestic life, and made not the smallest effort to soar.

Roger, having declined the offer of a seat, lifted his straw hat and strode off. Then Mr. Dunsyre bent teasing brows on Kitty's sweet face.

His younger girl was the apple of his eye. The elder one—Marion—had married the principal buyer at "The Knockout," who had then been given a small partnership. They lived in the country, and occupied, on the whole, a satisfactory position.

But it was Kitty all her mother's hopes were fixed on.

"Now, then, Puss, that's what ye are after! I thought your mother said dressmaking? Was ye tryin' it on, in front of Roger?"

Such broad sallies were Dan Dunsyre's idea of the native wit, on which he rather prided himself.

Kitty merely smiled back. She was very fond of her father, to whom she gave much more of her sweet confidence than to the mother, who was always correcting, and putting her in her place.

Mrs. Dunsyre did not smile now. Her face, under her much-beflowered toque, looked rather sour and vinegary, and her eyes had the hawk-like expression of those who seek but never find.

"Don't glare at me like that, mother," said Kitty unperturbably. "I just met Roger by accident, in the street. He was going to the Club for his tea, and took me into Hartley's instead."

"You'll be getting yourself talked about," said Mrs. Dunsyre primly. "And that is bad for any girl's chances."

"What kind of chances, mother?" asked Kitty, as her laughing eyes met her father's in an understanding flash. "If it's matrimonial—I'm not on! As long as I've got my old dad, I don't want another sweetheart."

These words rather accurately describe the relations between Dan Dunsyre and his youngest girl. He reached over and patted her hand, and his expression was very soft and kindly.

"That's richt, lass; stick to your old dad, and defy them a'!"

"You're nothing but a pair of silly creatures," said Mrs. Dunsyre severely. "And don't be pawing at one another in that ridiculous manner in the street!"

"We're in the carriage, mother," put in Kitty swiftly.

"Don't nip me up like that!" retorted her mother sharply, and, after that little skirmish, conversation languished, until Dan created a diversion by drawing attention to the arrangement of certain windows in Sauchiehall Street, where he had rather a formidable rival in business, whose methods he was always calling in question.

It was half-past six when they got home, and Kitty followed her father into his den to tell him about John Marchbanks.

Whinstone House was a large, imposing enough house, but had no ground about it, and, standing sheer at the juncture of three streets, had rather a forbidding look. But it was roomy and comfortable inside, with that solid comfort which takes big cheques to pay for. Axminster and Turkey carpets in which the feet sank deliciously, and highly polished, if rather ornate furniture, and plenty of mirrors everywhere, as well as pictures, conspicuous for their great size and the massiveness of their gilt frames, rather than for any special artistic merit, all combined to give an air of comfort and solidity to the successful merchant's home. His own little den was a pleasant little smoky, stuffy place, hung in old-gold plush, and smelling of much tobacco and the very strong cigars which he permitted himself in his off time.

"You shouldn't rag your mother like that, Kate; she dislikes it," began Dan, when they were alone.

"Oh, she doesn't mind. Mother and I don't quarrel, dad, really. I just let her speak," answered Kitty flippantly. "I want to tell you something frightfully exciting. It's a real love story—good enough for a book! You know John Marchbanks? Well—he's in love with Lisbeth Annan, and, I believe, she's in love with him, and the Annans are in an awful rage about it, and Mr. Annan has showed him to the door!"

"I'm not surprised, for they're very ambitious for that lang-leggit lassie o' theirs. But what do they think she's going to get?"

"That I don't know; but what interests me more than anything is to see what Lisbeth is going to do! But that isn't all, father! Have you ever heard who John Marchbanks really is?"

"A bank clerk, beside Roger, isn't he? And I mind, when he came here once or twice, your mother was very feared about you."

Kitty hardly smiled.

"He's not my style at all. He's far too solemn and quiet. But, dad, I must tell you the real reason—his mother was never married, so, of course, the Annans would not think him good enough for Lisbeth. What I'm waiting to see is, whether Lisbeth will be strong-minded enough to brave it out, and take him in spite of that. You have no idea what opinions Lisbeth holds, and what queer, rather terrible things, she says on social subjects ! "

" Well, I suppose we'll see, if we wait long enough," said Mr. Dunsyre, and his face was thoughtful, as if he were pondering something at the back of his mind. " If what you say is true, I'm sorry for the lad, and he hasn't been well treated. It would have been far kinder had they never invited him to the house."

" That's what I say. But perhaps they didn't know ? " suggested Kitty.

" Who told you, lass ? "

Kitty's cheeks reddened a little.

" A girl I know," she answered evasively.

" Well, it's not a subject you should be discussing freely with your girl friends, my dear," said Dan, with a fatherly touch. " I'm sorry for that lad. He has a stiff fight in front of him. If he wants to get on, I'll try to do something for him, I think."

" I was sure you would, daddy. That's why I told you. But don't say anything to mother about what he is—I mean, it would make her so angry ; and, of course, she would forbid me to speak to him again."

Dan eyed the child's sweet face with a new solicitude.

" You're sure you have no truck with him, Kitty ? "

" Oh, sure, daddy—quite. You may keep your mind easy on that point," answered Kitty, and her candid eyes met his unflinchingly. " I just thought you'd be interested."

" I am interested. Do you happen to know his private address ? "

" No ; but I daresay Roger does. I could get it from him. You're going to write to him—aren't you ? "

" Maybe aye, and maybe no. Is Roger coming round to-night ? "

" He didn't say. But I'll ring him up about dinner-time and get the address anyway."

So another iron was put in the fire on John Marchbanks' account, and, as he rode home, rather gloomily, to Shawlands, in the clear golden evening he had no idea how many unexpected people were giving kindly consideration to his case.

It was about seven when he got home ; for, though he had left the bank before six, he had paid a call at more than one of the emigration and steamship offices for the purpose of making some preliminary inquiries regarding both his possible destination and the cost of getting there.

He did not go through the shop, as usual, that night, but entered the house by the door at the side of the business premises, and his mother, in the little back-shop, heard his step in the sitting-room above, and knew that he had come home.

She did not, however, hasten up. She too had had a somewhat exciting day, both within and without. She had hardly yet recovered from the upheaval made by the very unexpected offer of marriage from Hector Drummond.

Eight o'clock was the usual closing hour, but sometimes, when business was very slack, she would put the shutters up earlier.

She sent the boy off about a quarter to eight, after he had put the shutters up but eight was pealing from the city bells before she closed and bolted the door.

In the days before their close and kindly relationship had been so sadly disturbed, it had been John's frequent custom to come down to the back-shop, about closing time, and help her with her ledger. Then they would go upstairs to supper together.

But something told her he would not come down that night, and she had no heart for her ledger; so the moment the lad disappeared she went upstairs. She had, earlier in the evening, laid the table for their high tea, and something savoury had been cooking a long time in the oven, its delicious odour filling the whole house.

"You're there, John," she said, striving to speak cheerfully. "Supper's just ready."

When he gave no answer, she retired to the kitchen, swallowing something in her throat. The terrible change in him indicated how badly he was hit, and, incidentally (which perhaps wounded the mother as much as anything), how keen was his disappointment over the untimely check to his love affair.

Presently, to her astonishment, she heard him cross the little passage, and, as she was about to lift the tray on which she had placed the food they were going to share, as she imagined, very uncomfortably together, he took it from her hands, set it on the dresser, and standing in front of her, looked her straight in the face.

"I'm sorry, mother. I said more than I meant to. Please forgive me. I've resigned at the bank, and, like as not, will be off to Buenos Ayres next week. It'll be for the best in the end, I don't doubt; and I'm sorry I vexed you."

She who had been so brave when harsh and unforgettable words had been spoken thereupon burst into tears.

Such emotional passages were very rare between that mother and son; in fact, this was the first that had occurred.

John did not know how to act. Finally, he did what was probably the best thing in the circumstances—lifted the tray and carried it to its place on the sitting-room table. Then he came back to the passage, and called to her as cheerfully as he could:

"I'm not worth greeting about, mother. Come to your supper, and let's try and forget what's passed."

CHAPTER VII

SHINE AND SHADE

When, about half an hour later, Kitty Dunsyre rang up Balcraig her call was answered by Elizabeth, which was very awkward, the question she wished to ask having relation to John Marchbanks, presumably now a forbidden name in the Annans' house. But Kitty had very nimble wits, and merely inquired, innocently, whether Roger was in the house, as her father wished to speak to him.

"No, he isn't in," came Elizabeth's clear, cool answer across the wires. "And he has 'phoned to say he won't be home to dinner. Mother has just told me."

"Oh, it doesn't matter—another time will do," said Kitty. "Well, what about the concert? Where are we to meet?"

Elizabeth seemed to ponder a moment.

"If you don't mind, Kitty, I'd rather not go to-night, after all. I am not feeling up to it. I suppose it's the heat. Can you use the ticket?"

"I daresay I could get Maisy Carstairs to go with me. But I'm not very keen myself—summer concerts, except in the open air, are an abomination."

"All right, then. When can I see you?"

"I'm not sure. I'm sorry your brother isn't in. I must just tell daddy he'll have to wait."

"You don't happen to know what he wanted—do you? Perhaps one of us can fill the gap?" suggested Elizabeth.

"I daresay you could," chirped Kitty blithely. "It's only John Marchbanks' private address—something daddy wanted to write to him about—he didn't say."

Again there was a second pause.

"I can give you that," said Elizabeth, then—"Of course, we all know it here, through Roger—18 Methven Street, Shawlands."

"Right-o! I'll just write it down, for I never can remember anything beyond a minute. Thanks awfully. I've got it—18 Methven Street, Shawlands."

"That's right. And you don't know what Mr. Dunsyre wanted it for?"

"Oh, no. Something to do with business, possibly the bank," answered Kitty on the spur of the moment. It sufficed to lull, for the moment, Elizabeth's active curiosity, and the conversation came to an end.

But later, her judgment assured her that it was very unlikely that Mr. Dunsyre would have to write privately to John Marchbanks concerning bank business, more especially as she knew he did not deal with that particular bank. She had the odd sense of things happening, or about to happen—a consciousness, which was not dispelled by her father's manner at dinner.

It was almost elaborately natural, so to speak, and he cracked a great many jokes, at which his wife laughed dutifully, though Elizabeth remained stolid and unresponsive.

It had been a very uncomfortable day at Balcraig, and Mrs. Annan had welcomed her husband's return with joy. She had, indeed, delivered herself, just before dinner, of a piece of philosophy which nobody could have guessed was in her repertoire :

" There is something to be said, after all, for the childless state, Bob. What peace or comfort have we with Elizabeth ? She hasn't spoken a word to me all day ! "

" Oh, she'll get over that, lass," Mr. Annan had answered, but his expression was not quite so assured as his words.

His wife shook her head.

" I hope she will. I don't understand her, dear. Really, to-day, one would think her father and mother, who have been so good to her, are nothing but her natural enemies ! I must tell Susan, next time she bemoans her childless state, that she has her compensation."

Susan was Mr. Annan's sister, the wife of a rich lawyer, for whom all else in life was as ashes in the mouth because she had no children.

" Don't take it so seriously, my dear," said Mr. Annan, with a kindly pat on the shoulder. " Lisbeth will come to herself by and by, and discover who are her best friends. Meantime, what do you think is in her mind ? Has she given you any inkling ? "

" Not she. She has not spoken a word, I tell you, since you went out of the house. She was down town all the morning, and took her lunch in the city. I was wondering whether she had seen John. It is quite possible that they may have had an appointment."

" Well, we can't help that. It'll soon come to an end ; but we must be firm, my dear, very firm, if we are to steer clear of this catastrophe."

Kitty Dunsyre conveyed the desired information to her father at the dinner table, and, later in the evening, he wrote a brief note to John Marchbanks, asking him to call, if convenient, at " The Knockout," next day, at the luncheon hour. This note, which was addressed in the big, sprawling handwriting of the uneducated man, John found by his plate when he came in to breakfast next morning.

He put it in his pocket without saying anything about it, though his mother, watching him keenly, saw the expression of surprise which flitted across his face while he was reading it.

Things were better between the mother and son, but the old delightful confidence was broken, perhaps never to be restored, at least on the old lines. Both were passing through strange alterations of feeling, all of them poignant. John alternated between indignation, shame, and pity for his mother, and, when one is in the throes of such passions, it is not easy for the outward manner to be quite normal.

John had a very slight acquaintance with Mr. Dunsyre, for, though very intimate at Balcraig, he had been seldom invited to Whinstone House. This was partly owing, no doubt, to the fact that Archie and he did not get on well together. In his better moments, Archie had serious thoughts of Elizabeth Annan, and concluded that, very probably, he would settle down with her later on. He thought Marchbanks' aspirations in that direction confounded impudence !

It may be asked how he knew that John had such aspirations ; but there is nobody quicker to sense a love affair than the man who has one of his own ; and it is a natural and very human weakness for him to imagine that the eyes of all men are turned towards the object of his special adoration. That Elizabeth had so very little to say to him Archie blamed entirely on Marchbanks, whom he hated accordingly, describing him as a bounder and an outsider, and other choice epithets, which the modern young blood has ready for those who fall under the ban of his displeasure.

What he was too ignorant to see was that Elizabeth's soul, naturally pure and lofty, shrank from him as from something unclean. Many stories of young Dunsyre's private life were abroad in the West End of Glasgow; but, though few of them reached Elizabeth's ears, she knew, and shrank from him accordingly.

As Archie Dunsyre left the front door of "The Knockout" to seek his luncheon—which he could have obtained very comfortably in the establishment itself, only it did not suit his tastes—he was astonished to meet Marchbanks in the vestibule. He was so astonished, indeed, that he stood stock-still and said "Hulloa!"

"I'm going to see Mr. Dunsyre," said John, on the spur of the moment, and immediately wished he had not satisfied his evident curiosity.

"Oh, all right. You'll find him inside, I don't doubt," answered Archie coolly, as he turned away.

Marchbanks, who had never been inside "The Knockout" in his life, was bewildered both by its size and, what his orderly mind would have described as, its confusion. It was an enormous place, very low in the ceiling, being, indeed, part of old Glasgow, and the great interior was rather dark; even in the middle of a summer day it had to be lighted by immense arc lamps, which spread an uncanny brilliance very trying to the complexion.

But the principal patrons of "The Knockout" had very little time or thought to bestow on their complexions, and they adored the brightness and cosiness of "The Knockout," which was their cheeriest rendezvous in summer-time and their escape from the dullness of the foggy winter days.

The long counters, piled high with their merchandise, in what looked to John inextricable confusion, had all a method, however, and had even been thus carelessly arranged to give the impression of opulent plenty. A woman will stop and look at piles of things on a counter, handle and buy them, when she would not make pause for an assistant to show her something out of a box. The ethics of selling are intricately woven in with the ethics of buying, and the shopkeeper who studies his customers knows exactly what they want, and what induces them to buy in the profusion which spells his success.

"Bargains" is the word to conjure with in that particular branch of the trade in which Dan Dunsyre had made his fortune.

The average young man, like John Marchbanks, is helpless in such an emporium; nay, it fills him with a kind of terror! He even, if his imagination is brilliant, can picture himself being hauled ruthlessly up to counters and made to pay for piles of stuff for which he has not the slightest use!

John was rescued, however, almost at his very entrance, by a sleek shop-walker, who looked doubtful when he asked for Mr. Dunsyre.

"He's at his lunch, and, I don't know——" he began doubtfully. But John held out the card Mr. Dunsyre had enclosed, with the hour written on it, which immediately altered the expression of the shop-walker's face.

John found himself being ushered, with all due respect, up long stairs and through endless passages, to what appeared to be a kind of annex at the back, given over to counting-houses and offices. And there, in a small room, he found Mr. Dunsyre, taking his modest luncheon, which consisted of a glass of milk and two slices from a brown loaf, spread thick with country butter. He took the last mouthful of milk as he rose to bid the young man a friendly good day.

"Sit down. I suppose you've had your lunch?"

John admitted that he had.

"Well, so have I, so now we can talk in peace. I daresay you wonder what made me ask you to come here to-day?"

"Naturally, Mr. Dunsyre."

"Well—there's no use beating about the bush. My daughter told me last night what has happened at the Annans, and that you're wanting to leave Glasgow. If you have nothing else in your mind, I think I can help you to get away."

John's face flushed. This was the second man of standing in the city who had offered to help, and it was comforting to realise that after all the hand of every man was not against him.

"It's very kind of you, Mr. Dunsyre, and I'm sure I don't know why you should be willing to do me such a kindness."

"As it happens, the story interests me—and it's not the first time I've come up against the hardships of it. There's nothing surer than that we pay for the sins of our youth; some have to go on paying to the end of their lives, and the innocent have to suffer with them—that's the worst of it. You're quite right to get away from Glasgow. You'd never have a chance to rise here. It would aye be comin' up against ye. Now tell me what plan you have made for your future."

John was obliged to say that, so far, he had made none.

"I've been thinking of the Argentine. I hear it's a good place for getting on in. I've got a turn for languages, and last winter I took up Spanish. They speak Spanish in the interior of the country, and that's where the money is to be made."

Mr. Dunsyre looked deeply interested.

"Now, that's queer, for I've often had a wish to see South America—more especially Buenos Ayres. There's a big fortune there for the folk that can raise the capital to open a big drapery store. The prices are terrible out there, and money is so plentiful that they pay whatever is asked, and they'll ha'e the things at ony price. But drapery is hardly in your line o' things?"

"Hardly," answered John, with a faint smile.

"But your mother micht ha'e done worse than apprentice ye to the drapery. Whatever made ye choose a bank? There's nae future there, unless just for one or two. The rank and file havena a ghost of a chance."

"It was my fault. My mother wanted me to go to the university."

"Did she, though? That was very game of her!" said Dan admiringly. "I've nae personal interest in Buenos Ayres, but I daresay I could get ye an introduction or two. If ye would try Canada now, that would be a different story."

John shook his head.

"Canada's no use unless you have capital. I have only what will pay my fare and leave me a little to live on till I get a fresh billet. But I'm not afraid to try my luck in South America. I can speak French and German fluently, and I've a smattering of Spanish and Italian and even a little Hindustani. Surely that'll help me out there—and Mr. Craighead said he would give me a letter to some friends of his."

"Did he? Well, that would be of more value than mine. But I'll tell you what, Marchbanks—I'll advance a bit of money to you, any time you want it. Go out, and if you see a chance of turning over a bit, you can write to me and I'll send you a letter of credit. If I'm satisfied that there's a prospect of success for you I won't be stingy."

John Marchbanks' face was a study.

"Mr. Dunsyre, you overwhelm me! Why should you do this for me? I am almost a stranger to you."

" I micht ha'e a private reason. Sufficient for you that I'm interested. And from all I can hear, you're an industrious, sober-minded chap, that sticks to his work, and disna squander what he earns. They're no' so common that we can afford to despise them. Take my advice, and dinna ask ower mony questions, but tak' what comes along, and mak' the best of it."

This homely advice, and the extreme kindliness of Dan Dunsyre's look and tone, warmed John Marchbanks and put fresh courage and a certain kind of ambition into him. His eye began to glow, and his whole personality seemed to be quickened by the encouragement thus given.

Dan Dunsyre noted these symptoms with approval and a secret compassion, not unmingled with envy. Neither of his two sons, he felt sure, would have exhibited such a spirit in the like circumstances. Everything had been made too easy for them. He was fully aware of that, but had not been able to apply the brake in time.

" Are ye thinkin' on goin' soon ? " he asked.

" As soon as ever I can get away."

Dunsyre nodded.

" Very well. You come to me when all your arrangements are made, and we'll ha'e another talk. What I want ye to understand is, that you've a friend in the world, and I think none the less of ye because of what ye are. Whatever your mother may be like, you're a credit to her, and ye can tell her Dan Dunsyre said it—and he's no' sic' a bad judge of human nature efter a' ! "

John, thus dismissed, rose blithely to his feet.

This was one of the great surprises of his life, undoubtedly. But before he could give expression of his gratitude Dan Dunsyre spoke again :

" And as for the thing that's at the bottom of a' this dinna let it tak' ower big a grip o' ye. I admire Miss Annan—at a distance—very much, but what you've got to remember, lad, is, that there are as guid fish in the sea. Wait till ye get oot to South America, and see the Spanish gipsies ! You'll forget a' aboot the Scotch lasses. And wha kens ! Speaking a' thae languages, ye micht come back wi' a Princess to astonish Glesca ! '

He gave a huge guffaw at his own joke, and accompanied his visitor to the top of the grand staircase, where he dismissed him with a cordial shake of the hand.

John trod the ground very lightly as he passed through the swing-doors of " The Knockout " into the sunny street. He had not been more than a quarter of an hour inside them, but it sufficed to make a great change in his outlook. He was no longer a mere adventurer who might or might not be a fortunate voyager on unknown seas, but felt himself to be a properly accredited person with solid backing.

For the first time in the last forty-eight hours he felt himself a man again, instead of a shrinking creature against whom the hand of every man was directed.

After all, the Annans represented a very small portion of the world. Dan Dunsyre's big-hearted, generous kindness might be typical of a far wider and finer section of humanity.

He was going forth into a big, wide world, where he would be judged entirely on his own merits, where he would get clean away from all the trammels of conventionality, as they existed in the West End of Glasgow.

The idea began to fire his imagination and his blood, and he walked back to his post with a step as light as air.

Before he reached Renfield Street, however, he was disquieted by meeting Elizabeth full in the face, at an angle where it was impossible to avoid recognition. Smarting under the knowledge that she had made no sign during these days of suspense and suffering, he shrank from meeting her face to face.

She coloured violently, and even looked wildly round as if seeking some means of escape. But none offered, and they walked towards one another, both feeling, perhaps, that the sooner the ordeal was over the better it would be for both. Elizabeth was looking charming, and she thought that John had never carried himself so well. He had not the look of a man convicted of disgrace or ineligibility, never had he carried his well-built figure more stiffly nor held his head higher.

He took off his hat when they met, but she did not offer her hand.

" How are you down in this direction ? " she asked. " I promised to meet Kitty at her father's shop at two o'clock."

" It will soon be two. I have been there——" he answered lamely. Then they both stood silent for a moment, looking the picture of discomfort. But John had the undoubted advantage, for Elizabeth knew that she had not behaved well.

" Perhaps I'd better tell you now, in case we don't meet again," he said abruptly, " I'm leaving Glasgow next week."

" You are ? " she said faintly. " And where are you going ? "

" It isn't definitely settled, but, probably, South America."

" But why South America ? Do you know anybody there ? "

" Not yet."

" Is it a good place to go to ? " she asked stupidly ; for, somehow, the world grew dark to her, and her heart began to ache intolerably.

" As good as any other," he answered shortly. " I've been advised to it, anyway, by more than one. It's thought to be the coming country."

" I suppose you'll take your mother with you ? " said Elizabeth then, goaded to mention her name, though, as she spoke, the red dyed her cheek.

" No," answered John quietly. " I have no intention of taking my mother."

" Oh but how hard that will be for her ! She's so devoted to you. She won't like it at all."

" I can't help that. She is comfortable where she is. I'm going out on pure spec, and nobody knows what the upshot of the venture may be. My mother is a reasonable person," he added, quite slowly and distinctly, " and that is the very last thing she will expect."

" And I suppose you'll be away for years ? "

" That is quite possible," he said rather curtly, for the whole trend of Elizabeth's speech and manner was intolerable. He could not believe they were part of the same woman who had spoken such sweet, heartening words to him in the garden at Balcraig on Saturday night. What had changed her ? What could have changed her, except the one damning fact which had changed everything ?

Standing there, on the edge of the sunlit street, with the tide of life—the luncheon-hour life of one of the busiest cities in the world—surging by them, John dealt mercilessly with the situation, determined to discover, once for all, where he stood. But even as he put the question he had no doubt. The stony set of Elizabeth's features when they met had left him in no doubt.

" I suppose they've told you, Betty, and it's all up with me ? "

" They've told me, of course ; and I ought to have known before. It was a shame I did not," she said, with her eyes stormily fixed on the opposite side of the street.

" I was hardly to blame, my dear ; your father knew. I told him when he asked me to the house first. But it was not a subject I could discuss with you."

"Why not?" she asked rebelliously. "See what suffering comes of wrapping women like me up in cotton-wool! If I had known at the beginning it would have made a great difference."

"What difference would it have made?" asked John rather sternly.

"Well, things would never have got so far," she admitted. "It wasn't right, or fair. I don't know, or care, who has been to blame, but it ought not to have happened. I should have been told."

To this passionate protest John made no answer.

"It's a futile business discussing it here, Betty. The only thing that concerns me is whether there is anything to carry away with me—anything in the nature of hope, I mean? I'm going to do big things out there. If, as I believe, I can conquer fate, is there any use in my coming back?"

She brought her eyes back, wonderingly, to his face.

"Whatever you do out there—would it alter the one, great, big fact?" she asked, not aware, evidently, of the brutality of the words.

John whitened a little; set his jaw like iron; lifted his hat, and walked away.

CHAPTER VIII

A SIDE TRACK

The last hope quenched, John Marchbanks might now set his face towards the next great epoch-making turn of his life, and seek the undiscovered country which experience has lying in wait for every human soul.

There are moments when indignation or a righteous wrath can take the edge off the keenest personal suffering life has to offer. John tasted that bitterness of disappointed hope, which in the life of the heart has a varying effect on a man's character, sending him sometimes to the underworld, and sometimes to the heights of achievement.

On that sunny summer day, in the city of his birth, as he climbed the steep slope of Renfield Street, John saw nothing of the sunshine which makes glad the heart of man. It was his hour for walking on the shady side of the street; he squared his shoulders to it, and lifted his head, and swore that it should not conquer him. But he had gotten a blow.

Yet as he bent gloomily over his desk, where the work happened to be of a sheer routine which permitted his thoughts to stray elsewhere, he reflected on the strange social fabric in which the souls of men and women are caught, as it were, in a net.

Elizabeth Annan loved him; she had admitted it both in words and in those indefinable sweet ways which send a man's pulses bounding; yet she had not had the courage or strength to fling conventions to the wind, and stick to him, in the face of the opposition of her set.

That being the case, she was surely not worth consideration or regret —his, or any man's. So common sense whispered, but the ache at his heart remained. But he would forget her, tear her from his heart, while, at the same time, he remembered what she had done!

Her indifference, her coldness, her absolute failure when the supreme test came, would merely act as a spur. One day, he told himself, he would come back to Glasgow, and show her what she had lost. If there was anything worth the winning out in the great new world towards which his eyes were set, why then, he would win it, not for her sake, but merely to prove that she and her set had no power to keep him back, nor to retard for a moment his triumphal progress.

There is nothing to hinder a bank clerk from trailing his dreams of glory across the pages of his ledger, and John Marchbanks did trail them that afternoon, and forgot, for two mortal hours, where he was, even while he mechanically, and without the smallest slip or error, performed the task for which he was paid.

The end of that day beheld him a different man, who had risen to meet its responsibilities and opportunities; he felt it in the very marrow of his bones. A harder, less kindly, charitable man, but a stronger one—that was how the day of decision left him.

Roger, watching him furtively, from an angle which permitted a full view of his profile, saw that he was brooding, and that he had shut him out of his life for the time being.

But Roger, who loved John, and owed much to him in the years of their friendship, determined that he would not be shut out.

"Look here, Jack," he said, nudging his elbow, when the moment came for their labours to relax, "I want you to dine with me to-night at the Club."

"Thanks," answered John quietly and steadily; "but I'm not coming."

"Why?"

"I'm busy," he answered evasively. "I'm leaving next week, and there are a lot of things to see to."

"But nobody sees to things in the late evening! If you won't come, I'll rout you out at Shawlands, Jack. I've often threatened to do it."

John's face flushed a dull red.

"You won't do that, I think, Roger. Just leave it. We've been good enough pals, but it's over, that's all."

"It's not over where I'm concerned. I don't exactly know what's happened, old man, but I'm not in it—you may take that from me," said Roger passionately.

"You'll give offence to your people," said John; and the remark was unworthy of him in the face of Roger's quite genuine protest.

"Haven't I just said I'm not in it?" asked Roger quickly. "Don't be a pig-headed ass, Jack. You and I can't split like this! After all that's been between us, we can't, I tell you, and we're not going to, so there!"

In spite of himself John's face relaxed.

"I won't come to-night, old chap," he said in a more natural voice; "but I'll promise we'll have a night together before I go."

"We must get up a supper or something to give you a good send-off."

But at this suggestion John's face quickly darkened again.

"No, you won't. I shan't come, if you do. I don't want any fuss made. I'm simply going to get out and get under," he added with a grim touch.

"I've a jolly good mind to chuck it and go with you!" said Roger eagerly.

"Oh, that would be stupid. Especially as you're booked for Calcutta in October. Things would have come to a natural conclusion between us any way in the autumn."

"Is that all you amount to as a chum?" asked Roger. "Now we know where we are!"

Some one interrupted them at the moment, and, while Roger was engaged talking elsewhere, John took the opportunity to slip out of the bank. He was in that hurt, sore frame of mind which makes a man aggressive, even to his dearest friends.

Five was ringing from all the church clocks as he emerged into the streets once more, to find them crowded with shoppers.

All the world seemed to be abroad that afternoon, and John found that he had to lift his hat every few minutes to some fashionably attired lady whom he had met at Balcraig or elsewhere, and whose gracious recognition seemed to accentuate the outer darkness into which he had been thrust. For, if they knew, one and all of them would, probably, cut him dead.

The thought brought rather a grim smile to his lips, and he was in an exceedingly bitter mood when he suddenly met an acquaintance who was neither fashionable nor richly dressed, but a sweet, quiet, lady-like girl, who appeared moved to an extraordinary pleasure at sight of him.

He was quick enough to recognise her as the orphan niece of the Houstons at Whiteinch, who was now their adopted daughter, and made their house her home while engaged at one of the fashionable dressmakers' emporiums in the west end.

She was very far removed from the smart set who frequented Balcraig and houses of the same standing, but her look was so sweetly kind that John stopped readily for a word with her.

They had known one another as boy and girl in the days when he had lived with the Houstons, and her parents still survived—the far-back days which he had almost forgotten, though Annie Houston cherished them in fondest memory.

"Hullo, Annie! It's a long time since we met. What has become of you all these months?"

"Nothing particular. I might say, what has become of you? Aunt Lizzie was saying only the other day you hadn't been at Whiteinch for over a year!"

"You don't say so! I must pop over one of these days. But why don't you ever come to Shawlands now?"

"I'm often there; only I don't see you, Jack. I was there last Sunday night."

"I'm not often at home on Sundays," he admitted. "Have you seen the mater this week?"

"I saw her on Sunday; it isn't forty-eight hours yet!"

"Neither it is. But so many things have happened I've lost count of time, I suppose. I'm leaving Glasgow, Annie."

"Leaving Glasgow!" she repeated, and her voice seemed to falter. "Whatever for?"

"Fed up with it. I'm going abroad—to South America, probably; and I don't care if I never see the bally place again. I've had my fill of it."

The girl had no answer ready, and had John Marchbanks been a vain man, he could easily have read, in the face that had perceptibly paled, much that was flattering to himself.

But he was not a vain man, and he had not an idea that the playmate of his youth, who was no more than the casual acquaintance of his later years, loved him hopelessly, but with a devotion that would have shrunk from no sacrifice to prove itself.

She had no great dignity, perhaps, but for the moment she could not hide her pain. When she did not speak, John bent his eyes more searchingly on the modest, sweet face, on which the evidences of distress were plainly written. Somehow the sight had thrilled him, and, drawing her a little apart, into a doorway, he said, in a low voice:

"It's very good of you to mind, Annie. I'm not worth it. I'm afraid I'm going to be a waster—leaving my country for my country's good!"

"No, no!" she said, and now she was struggling vainly with her tears. "Don't call yourself names, Jack; and, won't this kill your mother? She hadn't any idea of it when I saw her on Sunday night. Whatever made you take it into your head all of a sudden?"

"I can't tell you here; but I'd like to tell you, Annie," said Marchbanks, the longing for sympathy—a woman's sympathy, dangerous to a man in his mood—sweeping irresistibly over him. "I suppose you're not off duty yet?"

"Not till seven."

"Well, I'll come down and meet you, and we'll go out a bit on the top of a car, and I'll tell you the whole story. You've been as good as a sister to me; and, anyway, I'd like the opinion of another woman."

"There's your mother——?"

"She's the last person I can talk things over with," he answered.

"Must you go now? Good-bye, then; seven sharp, at Charing Cross. I'll be there. I'll just have time to go home and see my mother first."

Annie, whose face was now radiant, because no such thrilling excitement had come into her quiet and lonely life for many months, eagerly promised that she would be there ; and they parted.

It was a foolish tryst which John Marchbanks had made that night ; one that was destined to complicate his immediate future. There was no one to warn him against it, for he did not mention to his mother that he had seen Annie, and certainly never would he have told her about his tryst.

Like many another, in his moment of disillusionment, John Marchbanks found himself thrown back upon humbler friends whose worth he had hardly appreciated. Very gradually he had drifted completely away from the Houstons ; and, though Mrs. Houston still kept a warm place in her heart for the boy she had mothered, George himself was furious at the way John had given them the cold shoulder after he began to get on. Had he ventured to Whiteinch lately he would have found there was a very warm reception waiting him from the ship's carpenter who had no hesitation about calling a spade a spade !

Annie found it very difficult to give her mind to her work during the last hour she bent over it in Madame Valerie's establishment, where she was now the first hand. She was a very clever fitter and designer, and had largely increased her employer's rich clientele, among whom were the Annans and the Dunsyres.

The Dunsyres did not get their clothes made at "The Knockout," though the latest Paris fashions were ceaselessly advertised as to be procured there, at undreamed-of—in fact, at "knock-out" prices.

Annie Houston, though simply dressed, did not wear cheap clothes, and she was a very attractive figure as she stepped forward to meet John, a few minutes after seven, having given him time to be at the trysting-place first.

"There you are, Annie, and we'll have a fine blow out west. But don't you want something to eat first ?"

"Oh, no, thank you. I've had my tea. I was going back from it, that time you met me, at five o'clock. Madame Valerie thought I looked pale, and I had a headache ; so she thought the walk would do me good. Besides, I had to match up something in Buchanan Street."

"I see. Well, we can have a snack somewhere when we get back to town again. I told mother not to wait supper for me."

He helped her to the top of one of the waiting cars, and, as there was nobody either behind or in front of them, it was possible to talk unrestrainedly.

John was surprised at his feeling of comfort and security in the company of his old playmate, with whom it was not necessary to be on guard in the smallest degree. For one thing they knew one another with that real intimacy born of childish friendship ; then their positions were somewhat different now, and naturally Annie looked up to him, and had respect and full appreciation for him, which a girl in Elizabeth Annan's position could not be expected to feel or to exhibit. In a word, Annie's obvious deference and eager joy in his presence was gratifying and comforting, and helped largely to soothe his wounded pride. But, on the other hand, it threw him off his guard.

"It's a long story, but I'm to go through with it, Annie," he said, and his arm stole along the back of the seat, and he bent his manly head so that he need not raise his voice, all unconscious how his proximity sent the blood bounding in the girl's pulses, and her heart beating almost to pain.

But presently she forgot her own merely personal feelings in indignation over the treatment he had received.

He did not mention what Mr. Annan had called the bar sinister, but merely suffered Annie to infer that it was because he had aspired to the daughter of the house that he had been offered the cold shoulder at Balcraig.

" She has a good deal of impudence. They all have ! " cried Annie indignantly. " To do that to you, Jack, of all folk ! But I'm not surprised. She isn't a nice woman—Miss Annan. I've never met anybody yet who really likes her ! "

" Do you know her ? " asked John, in surprise.

" She comes to Madame Valerie's for her frocks, and she's very ill to please. Sometimes she comes with Miss Dunsyre—but she's a dear, so kind and friendly ! Miss Annan is so stuck up—I can't think what you find to admire in her ! " she added, with a little outburst of womanly indignation such as was secretly flattering to John's wounded feelings.

Of course, it was all very small of him, to be thus impressed by the simple adoration of a girl of no importance, and of whose acquaintance, in some of his more exalted moments, he would certainly not have boasted. But the best and the strongest of us have our weak moments, and, just then, John was in a very lonely, hurt, and dangerous mood, and therefore fair game for any designing woman. Not that Annie was designing. Indeed, anything further from the type could not well be imagined, but her very ingenuousness, her frank and simple worship, made her specially dangerous at the moment.

" She's not like that, when you know her," he said, and heaved a prodigious sigh.

" Well, anyway, she has no right to be so horrid to you," said Annie, with considerable spirit. " And, if I were you, I wouldn't leave Glasgow —not me ! I'd stop here, and show her I didn't care a scrap for her and her pride, or for any of them ! "

" But I want to get away, to make a big thing of my life ! And there are precious few chances for a chap here—even if——"

He paused there, and broke off, remembering that the subject nearest to his heart, the *raison d'être* for all this upheaval, must be taboo between him and the girl by his side.

" There are chances everywhere, if only you look for them," said Annie shrewdly. " Do stop, Jack. I'm sure your mother will break her heart if you go away. Hasn't she said that ? On Sunday night she didn't seem to be herself. She thinks of nothing but you, Jack, and it doesn't seem fair, hardly, to go away and leave her now, just when you are such a comfort to her ! "

" She should have thought of that——" began John hardly, and then drew himself up again. " Fact is, Annie, there are wheels within wheels, and I can't explain everything. If you like, you can ask my mother, after I'm away, and, if she likes, she can tell you that I simply haven't any choice, and she knows it. Besides, I've got a queer sort of a feeling inside, that it's Kismet—don't you know ? "

" What's Kismet ? "

" Fate—ordained from the beginning. I've got to take the turning."

" And what if it should be the wrong turning ? "

" It won't be, in the long run, though I may take one or two side-slips, before I get there. But that I will get there, is certain ! I've taken a vow, and the stars in their courses are fighting in my favour."

" You talk like old Katrine Polson when she's reading the teacups ! " said Annie flippantly. " And after you've done all the big things you've settled in your own mind to do, what happens ? Do you come back in a coach and four, and marry Miss Annan ? "

Her voice, as she uttered the name, sounded very dry and slightly bitter.

" No, and that I won't lassie ! No woman will get the chance to wipe her feet on me twice ! Come back I most certainly will ; and show them what a Glasgow lad, without a friend or any help from them and their set, can do——"

" How long will that be ? " asked Annie, in a voice of curious quiet.

" How can I tell—' it may be for years, and it may be for ever,' " he quoted lightly. " What are you crying for, Annie ? "

The sight of her wet eyes oddly moved him, and, almost unconsciously, his arm tightened along the back of the seat, till it encircled her shoulder. " Is it me you're crying for, Annie ? I'm not worth it——"

" I can't help it, Jack ! I hate your going away. Glasgow won't be the same place. Even if I don't see you often, I always know you are there——"

" But I haven't done anything to deserve that you shall think so kindly of me."

" No—you haven't," she admitted, and a wan little smile crept through the mist of her tears. " But, you see, I'm that kind. Whatever the folk I like do, I never go back on them."

" By God, that's the kind of woman for me ! " said John a trifle hoarsely. And on the spur of the moment, and there being nobody particular to see them, he bent his head lower and kissed her cheek.

" Oh, Jack ! " cried the girl, and the flame flew to her face and her eyes shone like stars.

" It's all right, Annie," he whispered, rather foolishly. " I made a mistake, trying to get out of my own line. I see that now, but, fortunately, it isn't too late."

" And you really like me, after all ? " she asked, her smile shining through her tears like the sun through the rain. " Oh, I never, never thought this would come, or that I should be so happy ! But you won't go away now, Jack ? Now, you know, I don't care what you are, or whether you earn a big salary or a little one. Simple things would do for me. And, oh, I will be the happiest woman in the world ! "

A sort of grey pallor spread instantaneously over John Marchbanks' face, as he realised, in that stupendous, enlightening moment, the magnitude of his own foolishness.

He had not an idea of his danger, he thought that with Annie he was perfectly safe, that she was nearly, if not quite, his sister, to whom he could speak with the utmost freedom. Oh, the ghastly, irretrievable mistake ! It sank, like a knell, into his soul, even as the smiling, tear-stained face was raised to his !

" Let's get down here," he said abruptly, " and take a walk across the fields."

She agreed with alacrity, for it was going to be a lovers' walk, and she had entered into a new world. So overwhelming and passionate was her own love that she was content with the lees and dregs he had to offer her. Besides, he had not laid stress on his feelings for Elizabeth Annan, but had, rather, dwelt on the assumption of the Annans that he had aspired to her hand.

He had only given a half-confidence, just enough to awaken sympathy. And lo, he had awakened something more !

He walked stupidly by the girl's side across the road and entered the field path leading to one of the new roads, laid out by the builder exploiting that particular suburb. She clung to his arm, her sweet face aglow with the first joy of possession.

"Do you think your mother will be pleased, Jack?" she asked, a trifle wistfully. "Do you think she likes me?"

"Oh, she likes you, all right," he answered recklessly. "She's always singing your praises."

"And will you tell her when you get home to-night?"

"Tell her what?"

"That we're engaged."

"Are we engaged?" he asked, with a conscious laugh. "It's been all very rapid, and it's very precarious, too, Annie, for it's my fortune I'm going to seek, and I may be long enough away."

"But won't you stop at home, now, instead of going?" she asked pleadingly. "We could be so happy."

"I couldn't. I've got to show them——"

"But, perhaps now, you won't care to stop away so long?" she said, with something of the pride of the woman who believes herself beloved.

"Maybe not," he answered stolidly. "But it's as well to face the risks, and I've no right to bind you or anybody——" he added earnestly. "For I might never come back alive."

"You're only saying that to frighten me, Jack, and you will come back! I'll see that you do. I'll ask you, every letter I write, and pray for your coming back, every night. And, after a while, you'll begin to feel the same as me, and that you can't stop away!"

But John, under his breath, even while his lips smiled a weak assent, said "God forbid!"

CHAPTER IX

A MAKESHIFT LOVER

If the true and secret history of marriage could be written, it would astound the world. But it would serve no good purpose, it would not be of the slightest value as an object-lesson or a sign-post, for the coming generation, like each individual, has to dree its own weird, and work out its own salvation.

But how many lives have been sacrificed, how many hopes destroyed, how many ambitions quenched by weakness in a supreme moment, is one of the phases of our mortal life which must make the angels weep !

John Marchbanks had not a particle of love, in the lovers' sense, for Annie Houston, in his heart. His thought of her, had it been put into words, might have described her as a good little thing, far below him in mental gifts, in gifts of all kinds. Her sweet face and her kindly manner did her credit, but they were not the things a man will fight and die for.

She was too colourless, she was of no more account in his life than the fly upon the pane. And yet he found himself annexed, bound,—hateful word,—engaged, before he returned that night to his mother's house.

He took Annie dutifully home to Whiteinch, but, when he stopped at the end of the horrid, little grey street, on whose pavement his boyhood's playtime had been largely passed, she looked with shy pride into his face. She had babbled, more or less, all the way home, as if love had unloosed a tongue naturally shy. It had transformed her, while it had petrified her lover. But she was too happy and too blind to mark or digest the true case.

" Won't you come in, Jack, and tell Aunt Lizzie ? My, she will be pleased ! It will shut their mouths, anyway, for they think you've grown too proud and big to know them, now."

" They must go on thinking it, for one more night, Annie," he answered stolidly. " For I can't go in to-night. It is time, and more than time, I went home. Ten, just ringing—your aunt will think you're lost."

" She'll be all right when she knows who I've been with." answered Annie bravely. " Will I see you to-morrow, Jack ? "

" Oh, yes—maybe—I don't know. Anyway, I'll write," he answered, and his tone was heavy. For, if he lived, he must write and make clear the ghastly mistake into which the girl had fallen, and his soul, naturally kindly, quailed at the prospect.

Weak where he ought to have been strong, he had let her babble on about their future, she, all unconscious of anything wrong, and that the babbling ought, by every right of precedent, to have been on his side. He had hardly listened, indeed, but had walked grimly by her side, spellbound by the tragic comedy of the whole situation.

" Well, dear, I must really go," he said, as he took her hand, and longed for people to come along in droves so that theirs could be no lovers' parting !

But none came—only a solitary policeman, whose rubber soles gave forth no sound. When he had passed, and the face was lifted to his, what could he do but kiss it ? And he did, though, when he felt the clinging of her arm about his neck, he knew himself a coward and a braggart, and his heart was as lead in his breast, as he managed to break away.

But she went, singing, up the little street, and, before she lifted the latch of the door, raised her brimming eyes to heaven in a mute glance of gratitude unspeakable.

John's steps rang hard upon the pavement, as he strode away, cursing his folly, and, in a lesser degree, cursing even her who had wrought it. How was he to get out? There was only one way—he must not delay. Every hour spent, now, in Glasgow, would forge the shackles more strongly on him. She might even marry him before he could get away! These small, clinging women, have a terrible persistence and staying power, a way of getting all they want without striking a blow, or even raising their voices to obtain it!

As he rode back to his home, on various tramcars, with the soft, cool air of the beautiful night playing about him, smoking desperately, he tried to get some clear perspective of what had happened. But nothing was very clear. True, he had put his arms about her, and kissed her, on the impulse of a kindly moment, when he had felt grateful for her sympathy, but surely, never did kiss accomplish so much!

Even in this clumsy adventure the fates had been against him! He had never been a philanderer, but had kept his respectful distance from women, chiefly because he was very shy, and had a reverence for womanhood, in the inmost recesses of his being. He had heard both Roger Annan and Archie Dunsyre make light of love adventures, such as had made him stand aghast. How many kisses, for instance, will a man like Archie Dunsyre bandy in the course of a year? Hundreds! For they were the small change of his life. Yet there was nobody, apparently, more free from entanglements than he.

Arrived home, near eleven o'clock, John was thankful to find that his mother had gone to her room. There was still a light in her window, but presumably, she was in bed, for she did not come out to speak to him, or even to tell him to lock up. She had left his supper on the end of the table, but he looked at it with loathing.

She heard his every movement, and was consumed with anxiety as to where he had spent the evening, since Balcraig, his usual haunt, was barred. She had no very clear idea how his love affair was progressing, or what attitude Elizabeth Annan had actually taken up. With all a mother's natural pride in the son whom she thought a match for the best woman that ever breathed, she thought it probable that they had met, that evening, to discuss things. Perhaps, even, they might have contemplated and arranged something desperate, to counteract the decision of their elders. Supposing Jack took the law into his own hands, and ran off with the hope of the Annans, what could they do? Why, nothing, but make the best of it! She was quite unaware of the half-hearted pause Elizabeth had made at this crisis in her life, and could not have conceived a woman who loved could act so.

Poor Ellen's only experience of the passion had been overwhelming, nothing but a flood tide, on which she had been borne to her own undoing. Her view, like her experience, was limited, and her thoughts ran in one narrow groove. She had given all to the man she loved, and had known nothing of the calculations which enter into the love schemes of the modern woman, who is anxious to get the most out of life.

But does she get the most? Ah, who shall answer that stupendous question? I shall not even try.

Had Ellen known of the extraordinary move in the game which had taken place, that night, in a place so prosaic as the outside of a tramcar, how great would have been her consternation!

Annie Houston occupied a very small place in her regard. She was a person she never remembered, unless when she saw her, and that was not very often—just occasionally, on a Sunday, when she happened to drop in to tea, and for a chat. Annie was a simple, elemental sort of creature, who had given no thought to the deeper things of life, and Ellen had little use for her, except as a casual acquaintance. She was always kind to her, but, on that last Sunday evening, as she had listened to her perpetual babble of all the microscopic interests of her life, she had been rather bored, and filled with a kind of sadness to see that any human being could be so obsessed with the infinitely little! Ellen could not have expressed it in these words, but of what account was it to her that Madame Valerie had changed her style of hair-dressing, decided to cheapen her prices a little in the off-season, and to undertake "alterations" scorned in the full one, and what she said, and the others said, and all the conclusions of supreme moment to the little dressmaker—these had beat, like the sound of far-off surf, on Ellen's languid ear. The only girl that mattered, in her present outlook, was Elizabeth, whom she had never so much as seen! But she longed to see her, and had already considered various schemes whereby her desire might be compassed.

These were testing days for Ellen Marchbanks, when the mother-instinct was fighting hard for its rights—days on which she afterwards looked back with dislike, and some remorse.

Katrine Polson, watching fiercely over the woman she loved, with the faithful devotion of a creature somewhat shunned by most, and who was, therefore, grateful for the smallest kindness, saw, each morning, as she arrived to her task, that the cloud was deepening on Mrs. Marchbanks' brow.

"You're worryin' yourself to daith!" she said, next morning, as she received her morning tea from Ellen's hand. "An' it's no' worth it—naething is, in this world. Sons, or brithers, or ony o' the tribe, are no' worth ony o' the saut tears that are shed for them. I suppose they're needit, puir craters, to do some o' the wark o' the world, but the Almichty maun aften be geyan sorry He fashed to mak' them."

Ellen smiled faintly at this sally.

"He must get rather tired of the whole thing, Katrine, that's what I think. Folk make sic havoc and hash of everything! There's hardly a life run on straight lines—least, I've never come across one."

"Nor me. There's some fun in lookin' on, but the puir deevils that tak' the plunge!—Weel, they jist ha'e to dree their weird. Ay, ay, there's a heap o' dreein' in this warld! But is onything settled aboot Maister Jack? Is he really gaun awa'?"

"Oh yes, very soon. Next week, I believe, Katrine. He's doing everything in a hurry, and not saying very much to me about it."

"That's jist hoo they serve them that toil and strive for them," said Katrine resignedly. "Weel, we maun jist gang. As sure as daith, the day will come when he'll ken what you've been and dune for him! Meanwhile, if I was you, I wadna fash my thoomb. What wey no' mairry again, yersel'? A wise-like wummin like you could get your pick. Ye micht dae waur, I say. I ha'e nae great opeenion o' men, but there's a kind o' wummin that's happier when she has wan to trauchle efter."

Ellen's face reddened, as she gave a conscious laugh.

"Katrine, you're really an awful body! What will you say next? A woman of my age has something better to do than think on marrying. We'll leave that to the young ones. Well, I must away to the shop, and get things seen to."

She was still in the shop when the postman came, about a quarter-past eight, with the letters. Breakfast was at half-past eight, and already the savoury odour of bacon Katrine was sizzling in the pan was filling the whole atmosphere.

There were always letters, for Ellen had a considerable business correspondence, and quite a few came to John likewise. After she had passed the time of the day with the postman she sorted them out on the counter. Instantly, her eye was riveted by an envelope of rough hand-made paper, with a small, neat, black crest on the flap, addressed to her son in a pretty, rather precise woman's handwriting. It bore the south-western postmark, and she had no difficulty in deciding who and where it came from.

She pushed it aside, opened some of her own comparatively uninteresting letters, glancing over their contents without much comprehension, her eyes and attention coming back to the one addressed to John. There were others, but this was the only one that mattered!

An almost superhuman desire to open it and devour the contents swept over her, and once she even gripped it feverishly and held the little ivory knife ready. But she restrained herself with difficulty, and, standing there with her brows knit under her dark hair, tried to guess at the probable contents.

Did it contain a final pronouncement on the big question of her future—hers and John's? Or undying protestations of faithfulness, a vow to stick to him at any cost? She would have given much to know, and the temptation was certainly sharp.

As she stood there, a small, barefoot child came up to the counter for a pennyworth of tea, which she served her without weighing or measuring, and when the little shadow had passed out by the doorway again Ellen's decision was taken.

Something told her that it was a disquieting letter, and that it would be better John should not get it. A sudden fury of determination laid hold of her, and, retiring into the back-shop, she opened the business desk which stood there, and carefully hid the letter under a pile of cash books. Then she closed and locked the desk, gathered up the rest of the post, and, after making sure that the breakfast was nearly ready, mounted the stairs.

John was in the sitting-room glancing at the paper. He gave his mother the usual good morning, and beyond the fact that he looked a little paler than usual, and was somewhat heavy-eyed, there was nothing special to mark in his appearance. His tone was quite cordial as he inquired whether there were any letters.

She handed him three, which she had brought up with her own, and, walking to the table, busied herself with the coffee machine, which was nearly ready to bubble up.

There was nothing interesting evidently in John's letters, and he tossed them aside at the moment when Katrine, bearing the breakfast tray, entered the room. He gave her a nod, and drew in his chair as if in a hurry to get on with his meal.

For a few minutes not a word passed, then, quite suddenly John said abruptly: "It's on the cards I may go sooner than I intended, mother. I'll know this morning when I get down town. I'll wire or 'phone to you if I can get a message through."

"Have you heard something this morning?" she asked, and her hands trembled as they busied themselves about the making of the coffee.

"Imphm," he answered, and the monosyllable, while committing him to nothing, might mean anything.

"I can't understand the need for such terrible hurry unless it's an appointment that has to be taken up at a moment's notice," she said presently, with a slight ring of complaint in her voice. "And if that has happened I think you should tell me?"

"It has not happened, and you know all I know myself about my future," he answered shortly.

Another silence ensued, emphasised by the horrid sense of a steadily widening gulf.

As John ate diligently at his ham-and-eggs, he asked himself whether by any chance he could tell his mother the incredible thing that had happened to him last night on the tramcar.

No—he could not ! It would make him feel too contemptible. It was a thing he would never be able to explain away to her or to anybody else. It seemed even more appalling in the cold light of day than it had done before, and the worst of it was that it must go on getting worse and worse as the girl sought to establish and make good her claim upon him !

" Mother," he said suddenly, " it would be a good thing if there was a law passed to shut up some of us between the ages of, say, nineteen and twenty-five ! "

" Mercy me, laddie ! What for ? "

" It would save a lot of trouble to an astonishing number of folk," was all the satisfaction he gave her.

She had no doubt that he was referring to his love affair with Elizabeth Annan, though not sure as to whether these words indicated any change of front.

" Most of us are no more capable of managing our affairs than an unborn bairn," he went on. " That's why there is such a lot of misery in the world. We're not born strong enough or with enough of common sense."

" But we are put into the world to acquire both strength and common sense," she answered him. " That's what life is supposed to mean."

" Then it's a poor and rotten show, mother, for most folks die before they get enough," he said enigmatically. " Well, I'll be off. It's a fine morning, and there's nothing the matter with the outside world—it's only the folk in it ! "

After he had collected all his small belongings, and bidden her good morning, and gone down to the bottom of the stairs, he came up again.

" Look here, mother—I'm an awful fool ! Really, a far bigger one than you've any idea of. I'm not worth ten minutes of your worry or anxiety. I'm sorry ! I wish I was different, but you won't bear me any grudge—will you ? "

His tone was wistful and boyish, almost he seemed to have slipped back to the old sweet days when she had been the only star in his firmament, her smile or frown the sole arbiter of fate !

" Oh, Jack, what a chap you are, and what things you say ! Off you go ! You're just my ain laddie, and none o' them will ever take ye away from me a'thegither, I do believe ! " she cried, going back, in that moment of emotion, to the speech with which she had been familiar in her youth.

" I believe it, too, old lady ! So, here's a kiss to the better days that are coming ! " said John, rather shamefacedly, and went whistling down the stair.

His mother had a light-hearted morning, yet, before the day closed, she became aware of a singular return of her depression. It could not be the shadow of the parting which had been more affectionate than any she could recall.

But she was certainly more anxious than usual for his return, and watched the clock, after the usual hour had come and gone, and made frequent pilgrimages to the corner window, to keep an eye on the incoming cars.

Six—seven—eight o'clock, and still no sign ! But she did not know what to do. There was no one she could ask, or telegraph to, or even send a message to. She knew that he usually left the Bank about six o'clock ; sometimes coming straight home or sometimes spending an hour down town with a friend. Always, when he was to be late altogether, he would contrive to let her know.

But this day no message came. About twenty minutes past eight, while she was watching from the window, she suddenly saw Annie Houston alight from the car, and come across the street.

She was surprised, because Annie seldom paid her two visits so close together; but she was pleased, too, for she was a lonely creature, shut up in that house, and her anxiety, for some unexplained reason, was becoming acute. She had the door ready opened when Annie came up the wide stairs, and bade her good evening cordially.

"It's a hunger and a burst with you, lassie!" she said, striving to speak naturally. "You hadn't been near me for over two months, and now you come twice in a week! Maybe I said too much on Sunday; I didn't mean you to take me too literally or to put yourself about to come."

"It's all right. I wanted to come," answered the girl, smiling prettily.

After they had entered the sitting-room, where the light was beginning to fade a little, Mrs. Marchbanks was struck by something more than usually attractive about her—a certain glow and radiance, which were rather arresting.

"You are looking very well, my dear. And how is your Aunt Lizzie?"

"All right. I suppose you weren't expecting me—were you, Mrs. Marchbanks?" asked Annie, looking round the room a little wistfully, even disappointedly—Ellen thought.

"No, I was hardly expecting you, as this in only Wednesday."

"Didn't Jack say anything?"

"Jack? What about?"

"About me," said the girl, reddening shyly.

Ellen shook her head, completely mystified.

"Nothing. When did you see him?"

"Last night. He didn't say a word, then?"

"Not a word. Was he at Whiteinch late last night then, that he was so late in getting home?"

"Oh no—we met outside," said the girl. "But where is Jack? Doesn't he get home usually before this time?"

"Sometimes, and sometimes not. But I wish he would come, for he didn't say anything about being late, this morning. He's rather unsettled, and very busy. I suppose I may tell you he's thinking of leaving Glasgow immediately."

"I know," said Annie proudly. "He told me every single thing about it last night."

Ellen looked the surprise she felt. Some new element in the little dressmaker's personality began to disturb and repel her.

Truth to tell, she hardly believed her at first, for she knew that John had seldom had a thought to bestow on Annie Houston, and had, on more than one occasion, gone out, of a set purpose, when she was expected.

"You met him accidentally, I suppose, and he mentioned it," said Ellen, with a slight hesitation, her pride forbidding her to question the girl, yet her curiosity getting the better of her.

"No—I met him by tryst. We were more than two hours together last night, walking in the fields, far beyond the car line."

"Oh!" said Ellen, and her lips seemed to shut together. "Whatever for?"

"He hasn't told you, then? But there's no reason why I shouldn't do it, for it's not going to be a secret. He asked me to be his wife, Mrs. Marchbanks, and I'm to wait until he sends for me, or comes back."

CHAPTER X

FRENCH LEAVE

ELLEN looked at the girl in sheer amazement which had pity rather than resentment in it.

"Ye are dreaming, lassie," she faltered, at length. "The thing could never happen, it's clean impossible!"

"It has happened. We're engaged, anyway," Annie maintained stoutly. She had none of the more complex nature's shrinking from handling delicate facts, and this one was vital to her. Thinking over what had happened as she bent to her work at Madame Valerie's, she had frankly faced the possible opposition, or at least the coldness, of John's mother. She had listened too often to her ambitious forecasts for him, her frequent allusions to the coming day when he should be somewhere at the top, while she, his mother, remained with lesser lights at the bottom.

Annie, frankly, had never liked such talk. She was a very sanely balanced, common-sense little person, and, moreover was under no very great illusions regarding John Marchbanks.

That she loved him passionately did not prevent her from tabulating his faults. She thought he was altogether too lordly and superior, and his mother too meek—though she had never gone the lengths in blame of the situation as her Uncle George and her Aunt Lizzie. Nay, she had defended him at Whiteinch often when the atmosphere surrounding his name got a little warm.

Not at all abashed, therefore, she smiled, and nodded cheerfully into Ellen Marchbanks' blank face.

"Oh, but it's quite true! Jack'll tell you when he comes. I'll wait till he does come."

Perhaps there was a lack of delicacy in the suggestion, and Ellen, less than just, looked at her with a growing distrust. Who was she—with her little, piquant face, her dancing black eyes, and her common origin—to aspire to such a height? It was preposterous, and, though she was in ignorance of what ground she had for her assumption, she was prepared to combat it without remorse.

"Ye can wait if ye like, of course, Annie Houston. I can't prevent ye," she said, in her most hostile voice. "But I tell ye, the thing ye say is clean impossible. Jack's as good as engaged to Miss Annan of Balcraig. That's why he is leaving Glasgow to get on faster, for her sake."

It was quite a mother-like view of the case, though not strictly accurate. Annie received it with the maddening smile of superior knowledge.

"Jack told me all about it, last night—every single thing," she repeated. "There was something, of course, between him and that stuck-up affair. I know what she is, coming to our place for her clothes, and there's no pleasing her—and she can't put them on, when she gets them!" said Annie, woman-like, wiping out her rival in one fell sentence! "Of course she would like to get Jack, and tried her level best, for it's not everybody that would look at her, though she is Miss Annan of Balcraig! But Jack has seen through her in time. He told me that they had given him the cold shoulder, and that now he sees what a mistake he has made, forgetting his best friends—at Whiteinch, principally,"—she added, with a malicious little touch—" and it's all right between us, for he knows I never would treat him as they have, and, as I say, we're to get married as soon as he comes back—if he can wait as long. If not, he'll send for me."

The last sentence was pure assumption, as the wish is father to the thought. That wish had been born, in the course of the day's brooding, when she had tried to face calmly an indefinite separation, and now she believed it implicitly. Of course Jack felt like that, because she did. Perhaps, even, he might marry her and take her with him! He would—she felt sure—given time and opportunity. Poor Annie would have risen up, at his bidding, and followed him to the ends of the earth, not only without scrip or wallet, but without question or doubt.

Such was the gift of love she had to give, but, unfortunately, John was not in the mood to appreciate it.

At all this, Ellen grew angry, for, if it was true, she had been horribly misled, and, moreover, made to feel cheap in the presence of a creature, whom, if she did not despise, at least, she had hardly given a place in her regard. Her nerves, rasped already, were in no fit state to stand this strain, so she said sharply:

" It's a queer story, and I'm no' taking' it in till I've seen my son. But I'm not keen on your stoppin', now, Annie. It's nearly nine o'clock, and now, Jack will not be in to supper. He'll be with some of his friends that dine late, and, probably, won't be here before eleven o'clock."

Before Annie could reply, there was a loud double knock at the door, and Ellen, apprehensive of evil, ran to see what it might portend. It was too late for an ordinary telegram, but, in these days of strain, anything might happen.

It was a post office special messenger, bearing an express letter, which he removed from his wallet, got a signature for, and departed, saying there was no answer.

Ellen saw that it was John's handwriting, and, so sick was her soul with apprehension, that she was afraid to open it. She went into the kitchen for that purpose, not minded to have the prying eyes of Annie Houston upon her, and, after a few minutes which seemed quite interminable to the waiting girl, she came walking back to the parlour, holding out the missive.

" Ye can read that. It'll do for your castle in the air, lassie," she said, not kindly, but with a terrible intensity which smote cold on the girl's ear.

Annie grabbed the letter, without further invitation.

This was all it contained:

"G.P.O.

" *Wednesday night.*

" DEAR MOTHER,—By the time you get this, I'll be speeding south, in the London train. Circumstances I can't explain have arisen, which make it necessary, as well as expedient, for me to leave Glasgow at a moment's notice. I hadn't time to come out to Shawlands, and I didn't wire, because I thought an interview and a good-bye at the railway station would be an ordeal for us both.

" Some day you'll understand that what I've done to-day was more than it seems. And I'll never forget you, mother. One day I'll come back, and make up for all this. I fear I've not been all I should, as a son, but there—it is difficult for a man to be all he could wish in every relation of his life. The forces keeping him back are too many and too strong for him. I'll get on, I mean to get on, and you'll see me back in Glasgow, maybe sooner than you think, cured and whole.

" I'll be much obliged if you'll pack up all my stuff, in readiness for an address I'll send to you when I know it myself. Meanwhile, I'm nothing more or less than a bit of drift on the sea of life, and I don't know what port I may make. Any port in a storm, I suppose it will be ! If you can still pray, you can ask that I may be guided aright.

" JACK."

It was a poignant document, and every word seared itself on Annie's heart. Ellen, watching her relentlessly, less kind than her usual, real self, beheld the gradual whitening of her cheek, but was amazed when the sheet fell from her hands and she fluttered, like a leaf from the tree, to the floor.

It was a timely diversion, for Ellen's better thoughts and her natural kindness of heart prompted her to swift action. She bent over the stricken girl, pitying her weakness, even while she resented its cause, with that fierce, possessive resentment, peculiarly characteristic of the mothers of only sons, did the necessary ministry, and, raising the light figure, laid it on the sofa. Presently, she was rewarded by the girl's return to consciousness.

" Where am I ? " asked Annie confusedly. " What happened ? Oh yes— I remember. I'm sorry. I couldn't help it. Something came over me. I won't do it again—— "

She laughed rather helplessly, as she tried to struggle up to a sitting posture.

" Lie still," said Ellen warningly, " and I'll get ye something—a cup of tea, or a drop of brandy—— "

" I'm not needing anything," said the girl with a touch of spirit. " I'm sorry it happened. I'll be getting back to Whiteinch now."

" You can't go yet," said Ellen severely. " It wouldn't be safe."

As she spoke, she turned and picked up the fallen letter, folded it, thrust it into her pocket.

They looked at one another, then, but not a word was spoken regarding it.

Ellen went to the kitchen, put the already hot kettle on the gas ring, and began mechanically, to set a little tray. Her face was nearly as white as Annie's, and her lips were set in a long, thin, hard line. She had got all her thanks in one day, from an ungrateful son, who was a coward as well !

Bit by bit she pieced things together, and, though she could not, by any stretch of imagination, reconstruct the love scene between him and the girl in the parlour, she arrived at a conclusion which was not so very far from the truth.

In a moment of weakness, tempted to give confidence in a too sympathetic quarter, he had fallen before a woman's wiles, and, in the sober light of day, had quailed at the consequences of what he had done. So he had run away, had taken the time-honoured way of escape for the coward !

A dry smile of exceeding bitterness wreathed the lips of the mother who had made an idol of her son, and now found him made of clay. And very inferior clay at that ! It was no heroic figure he cut that night, whether in his own estimation or in the estimation of the two women sitting in judgment on him. Of the two, strangely enough, Annie was the more loyal.

When Ellen brought in the tray, and, pouring out a cup of strong tea, forced Annie to drink it as well as to eat a morsel of scone and butter, she remarked, in a voice that had an edge to it :

" He's a burning and a shining light—is my Jack, Annie Houston, and no great catch for any woman. My advice to you, my dear, is to forget him as quick as ye can. He's worth naebody's tears or fainting. I'm his mother, and I ken—— "

" Oh, but—— " said Annie, rather hotly, " it can be explained, I'm sure! He hasn't told you everything. Men never do. Uncle Joe keeps back the chief bit in everything. They're made like that, they can't help it. Some day everything will be made plain. And, anyway, no good will be done by you and me ca'in him names. Let ither folk do that."

Ellen's maternal instincts were still too clamorous to permit her graceful acknowledgment of Annie's assumed rights.

" I don't, of course, know what happened last night, Annie," she said grimly. " But he has run away. There's no gettin' away from that bonnie fact! And if ye had a spunk of common sense or pride, you would snap your fingers at him, and marry the first man that asked ye. That's the only way to serve them! Let them wipe their boots on ye, and ye can be the doormat from first to last. I thocht my son was different, but they're a' tarred wi' the' same stick! "

Never had Annie Houston heard such bitterness on the lips of Mrs. Marchbanks. Some idea of what the mother was suffering came to her, and made her forget for a moment the sharpness of her own pain.

" It's very queer, I don't understand it at all! " she said feverishly. " It's as if some demon had got inside of Jack. He is not like that, really. And if you had heard him last night—he spoke quite different! Perhaps "—she added, trying to introduce a cheerful note—" if we just wait for a while, we'll hear from him again, and everything will come right."

" And as for sending his clothes on after him," went on Ellen, precisely as if she had not heard—" I'll do a heap less! What for should I be put to such trouble? I'll no' send him a haet."

Annie forbore to make any comment on this statement.

" Well—I'll better be getting away home," she said ruefully. " And I can't imagine what Aunt Lizzie will say! I wish now I hadn't said a word to her last night! "

" The less said, where men are concerned, the sooner mended, lass. But are you sure you feel able to go all that long distance in the car? I could easily gi'e ye a bed."

" Oh, no. We should have Uncle George out here afore twelve o'clock, making trouble. He carries on dreadfully if I'm out after ten! What had I better say to them, then? "

Ellen seemed to ponder on these words—the first of Annie's utterances to which she had paid serious attention. Once more the inborn instinct to protect and shield her own crept up, and she said, rather gratefully:

" It's very good of you to think about that, because, if what ye told me was true—I—— "

" Why do you harp on that, Mrs. Marchbanks? " interrupted Annie. " Is it likely, now, I'd make up a story about me and Jack? Am I that kind? I don't think you are fair to me."

" Maybe I'm not, lassie—that may very well be. Well—since ye ask me—why not just say that Jack has had a sudden call away abroad, and that both you and me has to wait till we hear from him? Until we do, there's nothing to tell. It's a horrid position to be in, but there it is! "

Annie picked up her gloves, drew them on, and turned to go. She would have liked to utter a word of sympathy to the obviously stricken mother, but something in Ellen's face forbade it.

They parted at the door with a handshake, and Ellen did say, not ungraciously, that she would be pleased to see her again soon, as well as to have a postcard announcing that she had reached home safely.

When the door was shut and she was quite alone in the little house, Ellen sat down helplessly, on the edge of one of the parlour chairs, all unconscious that she had left the gas flaring on the ring in the kitchen, as well as turned full on above the fireplace. If she had known, perhaps she would not have minded. Small economies, all the routine of household affairs, had ceased to have a meaning, since the being who had inspired them had deliberately turned his back on it all! It was a cruel blow, and a blow—she told herself passionately—which she had not deserved. Her head began to ache with thinking, and, presently, her nostrils being assailed by the strong odour of the gas, she picked herself up, and walked into the kitchen to make things right.

Then, having lowered the lights, she stepped into her son's room. It was, of a set purpose, the best in the house, the largest, and airiest, and quietest, away from the front street where the traffic hardly slackened, even in the night.

He had had the best, always! The new carpet, a rich Axminster, had been his last birthday gift from her, and it gave a very cosy appearance to the large pleasant room. A brass single-bedstead, hung with pretty chintz, a well-made wardrobe and dressing-table for which she had given over thirty pounds, and many other little comforts, gave evidence of her care and forethought he had so ill repaid.

The room gave her a sharp pang, for it was as he had left it in the morning, his ivory-backed brushes, and other toilet accessories, lying on the snow-white mat, and his pyjamas folded neatly, where the bed had been turned back, earlier in the evening. She threw open the wardrobe door, to find it full of clothes, very neatly arranged, for she had trained her son to orderly habits, and he was somewhat of an old bachelor in his precise ways.

Almost in spite of herself she began to take out some of the garments and lay them out on the bed. And just then her eye was arrested afresh by the framed photographs, standing about in lavish profusion on the mantelpiece.

There were mostly photographs of men friends, but two were of girls—a head-and-shoulders of Kitty Dunsyre, which made a very pretty picture; and a half-length of Elizabeth Annan, in a riding costume and small felt hat, which suited her rather severe style almost better than frills and furbelows.

Ellen walked deliberately up to it, and looked at the highbred, impassive face, with the long, straight nose, and the firm, but rather beautiful mouth. It was a handsome face, but hardly a winning one. There was a hardness, and the eye seemed unnecessarily severe.

Such a passion shook Ellen Marchbanks at the pictured face of the woman who, as she decided, had been the author of all this misery, that she snatched it up and tore it across! Then, ashamed of her childish outburst, she sought to piece it together again. But it was no use, and, finally, to get rid of some imagined reproach in the deep eyes, she walked into the kitchen and put it in the fire, even standing by to watch it burn. Then she went back to the room, got out the suitcase and a kit-bag he took on holidays, and actually started packing up.

The mere mechanical exercise had a soothing effect, and she found her nervous tension gradually relaxing. It was after midnight before she made pause, and by that time the wardrobe and chest of drawers were pretty well emptied.

Feeling rather faint, for she had had nothing to eat since her tea, about four in the afternoon, she closed the door and went back into the kitchen to make more tea and get herself something from the larder.

The house was horribly empty and silent, and she felt an odd nervousness, quite new to her, for she had often slept in the house during John's frequent absences for week-ends and the like, though, just lately, she had been considering the advisability of inviting Katrine Polson to become a permanent servant in the house. Now it would be necessary, since it would not be possible, or wise, for her to remain entirely and always alone.

It was nearly one o'clock when she at last retired to her own room for the night, and then she could not settle.

There was something else she wanted to do—something to which she felt goaded, and from which she inwardly shrank. In the room below, still hidden under the account books in the bureau, was the letter from Miss Annan which she had purposely held back, and which might, perhaps, have made a difference had John been permitted to read it. She was very uneasy in her mind about that, and even, in a dim way, wondered whether what had happened to-night was, in some sort, a punishment for what she had done.

It needs no special code of honour to prove that tampering with a letter addressed to another person is, if not an unforgivable sin, at least a very serious one.

Ellen fully realised its seriousness, and she had even decided in the course of the day to give the letter to her son that night, saying nothing of how it had been delayed. But now the opportunity was gone; and in view of all that had happened, especially concerning Annie Houston, it would perhaps be better if John's eyes should never rest upon it.

It was useless trying to fight against the desire which possessed her, so at last she drew her dressing-gown about her, lit a candle, and descended the back stairs to the regions below.

Scotty, the little Aberdeen terrier whose business it was to guard the shop, came blinking from his box under the counter, much surprised, evidently, to see his mistress at such an untimely hour. She spoke a word of reassurance to him, and entered the back parlour, where she quickly got a brilliant light.

The letter was still there safe and sound, and she drew it out, looking at it lingeringly, aware that the thing she wished and intended to do was wrong, yet too weak to resist. Finally, stifling the still small voice, she put a knitting-needle lying handy into the flap and slit it open.

There were only a very few words written on the sheet, but they might have gladdened John's heart had his eyes been permitted to behold them.

"BALCRAIG,
"*Tuesday night*.

"DEAR JOHN,—I don't know what to do. I'm miserable. I must see you. I can make a special errand to the Club to-night, and if you could be about at half-past nine I'll be there.

"BETTY."

Somehow these few words which said so little and yet might mean so much smote Ellen with a kind of terror. If John had got them in the morning surely he would not now be speeding through the Cumberland Hills on the London train! What could she do? She did not know. She shivered a little as she arose to her feet, again hesitating a moment whether to destroy the letter or leave it intact. Finally she decided to keep it, and, undoing the secret flap of the bureau, put it beside some special papers which it was her business to keep safe from every prying eye.

When the spring had clicked securely into its place again she relit her candle, said good night to Scotty, and toiled wearily up the stairs. From the narrow window on the half-landing she saw the friendly policeman on the beat opposite turn his flashlight on her window, as if uncertain about the flickering candle she carried.

In ten minutes more she was in her bed. But dawn found her wide-eyed and unrested, thinking, thinking—something beating like a sledge-hammer in her brain.

Two other women were sleepless that night in Glasgow on John Marchbanks' account—Elizabeth Annan, in her luxurious bedroom at Balcraig; and Annie Houston, on her hard woollen mattress underneath the stars in the attic at Whiteinch. Both were awake—thinking of him.

But John himself slept the sleep of the just—or of the unjust—with his head against a station pillow and a railway rug about his knees.

CHAPTER XI

COUNTRY COUSIN

It was not John Marchbanks' first visit to London. He had spent two holidays in it, one with Roger, and one on his own account; so he was robbed of that vivid feeling of anticipation which invests the first journey to the greatest city in the world.

Although he had had what any experienced traveller would call a good night in the train, he felt tired and unrefreshed as he stepped out at Euston, in the grey, close haze of a summer morning, before the sun had broken through. His belongings, all brand new, purchased in the nearest outfitter's when he had decided to take the plunge, consisted of a small brief-bag containing a suit of pyjamas, a clean collar, and his toilet things. These he carried into the Euston Hotel, to get a bath and some breakfast.

He began to realise, then, the magnitude of the step he had taken, and his own helplessness at the moment. For, in spite of the fact that he had money in his purse, he was as veritably a waif on London streets as any of the loafers about the station gates. He had neither business, occupation, nor destination.

Also friends were very few. One or two casual acquaintances he certainly had, but, beyond expressing a certain polite astonishment at sight of him, they would be unlikely to do anything for him.

But John had no intention of asking them. He was out upon the great adventure, and would trust to what the day or the hour might bring forth. It did not dismay him, for he was filled with youth's unconquerable ardour, and inspired by the hope which nothing daunts.

Also he had a substantial backing in the hundred pounds lying snugly in his pocket-book; and, moreover, knew where to get more. Aided and abetted by his mother, John had been saving steadily for the last eight years, having started a bank book at the tender age of sixteen. In the last two years he had, for private reasons, opened another banking account in a different bank from the one where he was employed; and it was from that source he had drawn the notes and gold which filled his pocket-book. He had thus not betrayed himself in Renfield Street, out of which he had simply taken French leave.

He did not feel himself to be a very heroic figure, however. Can the man who runs away ever be that? It may be answered that it all depends on what he runs away from. Sometimes a man may scale heroic heights in trying to escape from his worst self.

But John had only run away from a girl, a little dressmaker's hand, whose guileful eyes and sweet tongue had betrayed him in a moment of sentimental weakness. When, in the waking intervals during the night, his contemptible conduct rose accusingly in front of him, he had mentally cursed the female sex which is at the bottom of all, or nearly all, the worst troubles of life. He was able to defend himself by many a line of specious argument; but all the same his mind was far from easy, and he welcomed the end of his journey with delight, sure that the lure of London would quickly sweep everything else from his mind.

When he entered the big, comfortable coffee-room of the hotel he was quite ready for his breakfast, and had the alert, well-groomed air of the man who has an assured position, and no doubt about the future. Obviously it was the only spirit in which to attack the great adventure.

He looked round the room with interest. About fifty men were devouring food, in most cases, with newspapers propped up in front of them ; and all were absorbed, either in themselves, or in the news of the day.

Mostly of the commercial type, they interested him not a little, since any one of them might very easily become a potential friend.

There was not a table vacant, and he was placed at one where two were seated—one of them getting through his breakfast with no idea, apparently, but to mark time. John gave them both " Good morning ! " The one behind the newspaper merely grunted, the other nodded curtly, then raised his voice to inquire of the waiter, in a voice of rasping quality, why it is impossible to get an egg boiled so that any Christian can eat it in any hotel under heaven !

The waiter, without protest or enlargement, simply carried away the offending fluid ; and, while the irate one waited for another to come, he repeated his question to John.

" The egg," he said sententiously, " one of the simplest and most wholesome of Nature's foods, is barbarously murdered, mutilated, and destroyed in every country under heaven, except in France."

" But they can't boil them there either," said John, waxing reminiscent. " I saw a man heave his one day at a waiter in a hotel in the Rue St. Honoré. It just missed him and bashed against the wall. He said he would do it if he got a third morning an egg that had only walked through luke-warm water—and he did."

The stranger, a large, fierce-looking, bearded man, laughed rather grimly, as if the story pleased him.

" If there was an egg-throwing brigade established among egg-eaters, perhaps a reform might be accomplished. Nothing is done without organisation. Try the porridge—they can make it here ; but a man's soul can't be sustained exclusively on mush."

John sampled the porridge, and found it good. Some more talk passed between them ; and presently the man reading the newspaper looked annoyed, as if his meditations on the affairs of the State were unduly disturbed. He rose up, pushed back his chair noisily, and walked away.

" English table manners," said the bearded one with scorn. " Yet people wonder why the British are the worst-hated race on the face of the earth ! "

" Are they, though ? " asked John. " Have you been all over the face of the earth ? "

The stranger laughed at this neat sally.

" Had me there ! But I've been pretty well all over it, and every time I come back to London I ask myself why any sane man wants to come. We never get away from the tie forged at birth. We may try, but we don't succeed."

John felt his face redden. It was odd that this stranger should let fall a remark so apropos, as well as significant.

" I don't agree with you. Many men, some of the most distinguished, have risen above the mere accident of their birth."

" To outward seeming, but their souls bear the mark to the day of their deaths. And why not ? There must be something immutable in a changing world ! It is necessary for the continuation of the race that something should stand."

The words sounded sententious, and did not impress John in the least.

He regarded their utterer with a closer interest, however, wondering what could be his standing, his occupation, or his nationality. He had a foreign look, and his face was bronzed as if he had lived under tropical suns.

"Are you English, then?" he asked bluntly.

"I was born at Battersea, in one of the little old houses that used to lie far down on the shore. It's gone; and there's an abomination, in the shape of a hide factory, belching forth horrible smells, in its stead. That's the curse when the traveller returns; everything is changed—he, most of all!"

"You've been out of England, then, some considerable time?"

"Seventeen years roving; but, latterly, in the Argentine. I've come from there now."

John started.

"The Argentine!" he repeated. "Queer you should say that! I'm going there."

He spoke positively, in order to fortify himself, and give him an immediate standing in the world, and in the estimation of men. Obviously, the world he wished to bring to his feet could offer no consideration to the loafer and to the invertebrate, who were without rudder or compass!

Instantly, the stranger's eyes narrowed, and he looked, with more keenness than he had yet done, into the young man's face.

"What part of the Argentine, may I ask?"

"Oh, Buenos Ayres in the first instance."

"Going to a post of some kind, I suppose? I know it, from end to end, and every name in it that counts. Where are you going to?"

The question obviously embarrassed John, but he answered truthfully enough.

"I'm going out on spec."

"Oh—on spec! It's all right, if you've got money at your back. As a country, it's a sink for money; but it's only big things that pay. What's your line of things?"

"I'm afraid it wouldn't interest you," said John modestly, yet with a certain quiet courage. "I'm only a Scotch bank clerk on the make; fed up with things in general, and Glasgow in particular, and having a fancy to see a bit of the world before I die."

"It's the right spirit," said the stranger heartily. "And I wish you good luck. You've a pretty steep proposition in front of you; but nothing beats an honest trial."

"I suppose there are a good many Scotch out there?"

"Thousands of them," said the stranger, with a queer, slow grin, meant to be facetious. "No offence; but when your countrymen are to be observed gathering in their hosts like that, it's time for the non-Scot to look out!"

John laughed good-humouredly, preferring to take the statement as a compliment rather than as a jibe.

"I suppose they know a good thing when they see it, and I don't blame them."

"That's right! Who's blaming them? I was only stating a fact for your encouragement. But, while there is no doubt you'll get there eventually, you must be prepared for certain hindrances which are liable to assail the stranger in any new country, when he arrives first. I don't want to pry—but, you have money, I suppose, to keep you for a little while after you get there? That is, supposing you don't fall into a rich billet at once."

"I've enough," answered John, still modestly and a little guardedly. "And I can get more."

"Ah, that's good; you're safe; and nothing but your own slackness and lack of perspicacity can prevent your rise. Well, I must be off. I've a couple of important appointments in the city to-day—one, due in an hour's time."

"Are you stopping here?" asked John, not eager to let this chance of first-hand information concerning his prospective country slip away from him without effort. "I'd like to have another talk with you about things out there. All my information up to date is second hand, so to speak—through emigration agents and the like."

The stranger made a wry face.

"Umph! They either tell you too much or too little. Well, as a matter of fact, I was leaving here to-day. It's not my style of place. When a man comes to my age he wants a little bit more comfort than is to be found in a jumping-off place like this."

Now John had thought it very comfortable, but, as assertion on that point might easily mark his inexperience to this seasoned traveller, he merely nodded, and said he understood.

"I might stop another night, though. It really doesn't matter, and I'd like to put you on the right lines; in fact, I wouldn't mind giving you a few introductions."

"Oh, thank you," said John, with real gratitude. "That would indeed make a mighty difference!"

"Well, I'm busy this morning up to twelve-thirty, at least. I've an important consultation with a big engineering syndicate in Queen Victoria Street. It's about some bridge work on a railway they happen to want to plant on my land. There's a hint for you now! Get land where there is likely to be development, and wait. Money's simply coining for you while you're doing nothing!"

John's eyes gleamed at the prospect of such an Eldorado. He had read of such things. Are not our emigration pamphlets full of them?

"If you're not otherwise booked up, and care to meet me in the city for lunch, we can have another talk, and go deeper into the business. I think I can help you. In fact, I know I can; and you seem one of those straight, honest chaps it would be a pity to see go off the line for lack of a friendly signpost."

John's face flushed with pleasure at this flattering summing up of the situation, and he immediately gave himself away.

"I've nothing on earth to do. Haven't I told you I'm out on the make, ready to grab every opportunity? I'll meet you anywhere, at any hour you like; for, ten to one, I'll never have such a chance offered to me again! Meanwhile, my time's yours. I've nothing else to do with it."

"All right. One o'clock at the Strand Palace, shall we say? Or Simpson's—which?"

John was obliged to admit that he was unfamiliar with either.

"We'd better say Simpson's—prime joints there—no frozen mutton. Not that frozen mutton, in its place, doesn't serve its purpose! Would you like the net shipment of frozen mutton from the Argentine in one season? Get into that, now, and your fortune's made. But the work's harder than the waiting game on land which the developer happens to want."

All this, as may be imagined, was more than fascinating to the unsophisticated mind of John Marchbanks, and he blessed his good luck which had thrown such an obliging and influential stranger in his way.

When he was alone and a slight doubt assailed him, he dismissed it with an angry rebuke to himself for his Scotch caution.

Carried to excess, that excellent quality undoubtedly stands in the way of a man's advancement, and closes likely doors which seldom open a second time.

The appointment was made, and the stranger took his leave, John accompanying him to the vestibule of the hotel, where the obsequious attentions of the porter convinced him that the stranger was a person of importance.

It was only after he had actually gone that John remembered that he had not asked his name. But that was a small matter. His personality was a little unusual, and would easily be discernible even in a crowded Strand restaurant at the luncheon hour.

Left alone, the first thing John did was to make a definite statement at the desk and book a room until further orders, at the same time explaining that his luggage was coming on.

Then he sent a wire to his mother, telling her to forward his belongings by first passenger train to the Euston Hotel. Thereafter he went to the writing-room to indite a letter to her.

His breakfast table experience made his task somewhat easier, for he was now able to give her some definite information regarding his future movements.

About the immediate cause of his hurried and undignified departure from Glasgow he prudently decided to say nothing at all. His one hope was that he might be able to get clean away from England before Annie Houston should go and expatiate on the tramcar episode to his mother.

Having indited a very diplomatic and, to himself, satisfactory epistle to his mother, he also wrote one to Annie. In this he acted upon the principle of clearing the ground from under his feet, and, so to speak, burning all his boats.

That letter, though short, took him a full hour to write. When finished it was a model of how much a man can say without saying anything at all. Its gist was regret over what had happened, and an attempt to show how precarious and uncertain his future was, and how little he had, or was ever likely to have to offer any woman. It was, in its way, a masterpiece, and when he read it over he told himself it ought to convince any woman.

If, at the back of his mind, there was a feeling of meanness and shame, he quenched it by the reflection that he had been, in a manner, trapped into a love affair of which his whole heart and intention were innocent.

These two necessary letters written and posted, he felt as light as air, and was able to give his whole mind to dreams and aspirations for the future.

The mere fact of his having, at the very outset, so to speak, met a man who had it in his power to guide him at this important turning point in his career, was proof—if any were needed—that heaven approved of him. He did not put it exactly in these words, but that was the essence of his inner consciousness.

Before the day closed, however, he was destined to be a little less assured of the favour of heaven.

About half-past eleven, having set his house in order, so to speak, he issued forth from the hotel smoking a cigarette, and looking both prosperous and well pleased with himself.

A new world was before him, and as yet he had not begun to regret the old one on which he had turned his back.

Such glorious half-hours are only possible to youth. Experience knows that they always have to be paid for, sometimes in coin with which it is hard to part.

John rode on the top of an omnibus to the Strand, enjoying himself immensely all the way. It was a beautiful summer day, and old London looked her best. The throng of the streets, the perpetual blockage in the roadway, the good-natured chaff of the 'bus drivers—his own and others—filled him with lively amusement.

He found it hard to realise that, only twenty-four hours before, he was glued to a stool in the Renfield Street Bank, seeing nothing but the blur of summer rain on the panes when he looked up. His last day in Glasgow had been very typical of the western city's moist climate—presumably she had been shedding tears over the departure of one more of her promising sons.

At Trafalgar Square he got down, for he had still forty minutes to wait for his luncheon appointment, and the memory of London sights was not vivid enough to dull his present interest in them. The fountains about the Nelson Column were in full play, the urchins dabbling delightedly in them just as they had been four years before ; the loafers lined the seats, and the flower-sellers bawled their wares. It all had the charm of novelty for him, and he enjoyed it to the full.

Arrived at the imposing entrance to Simpson's, he had to wait about seven minutes, and was at last rewarded by seeing his new acquaintance dashing up in a taxicab.

" Sorry to be late," he said, with the brusque air of a man endeavouring to crowd the business of two days into one. " It took double the time I expected to bring the Syndicate to terms, but I have managed it, and we'll drink success to the Soraca-beya Light Railway."

He paid and dismissed the cab, and they entered the restaurant, which was already filling up comfortably. A nod and a tip to the waiter, however, quickly secured the necessary quiet for John and his new friend, and they were soon discussing a prime cut from the joint.

The stranger's manner was that of a man who was flushed with the success which had attended his morning effort. His manner was a trifle jerky, and he was inclined to much speech. He ordered champagne, but John observed that he was very abstemious himself, while continuing to press it upon his guest.

" Drink it up, man ! At your age I was afraid of nothing ! After forty a man, especially if he has to live in the tropics even half the year, touches champagne at his peril. But it's the only stuff worth drinking—the wine of youth, in fact. Drink it up ! "

John drank it up, though at home he had been practically a teetotaller, and, before very long, he had reached the garrulous stage.

" I don't yet know the name of my new friend who is doing me so well," he said, as he leaned across the table. " Please enlighten me now."

" What's in a name ? " asked the stranger lightly. " But it's natural you should like to know mine. It's Shuttleworth, really ; that's my Battersea name ; but, on my own estates, part of which I inherited from my wife's family on condition that I took their name, at least for Argentine use, I'm Senhor Lope-de-Vègas."

John seemed to sense a familiar sound in the name, and attributed it to the standing of his new friend in the Argentine. Doubtless he had seen it on some share prospectuses which had to be laid out on the counters of the bank.

" I seem to have heard the name," he said quickly.

" Ah, no doubt," said the stranger modestly. " As I told you in the morning, it is well known out there, and appears in public print pretty often. Well, I daresay you are anxious to know what I have done on your behalf this morning ? I didn't forget you in the midst of my own pressing affairs, and, I think, at a word from me, the Syndicate will be willing to give you a small appointment in Buenos Ayres, where the principal offices are. If you will call at King William Street to-morrow morning, mentioning my name, you'll see the Managing Director, and can, I have no doubt, clinch the business. I would offer to go with you, but, unfortunately, I have to start this evening for Paris to meet another man, who has a big stake in this new venture. There are wheels within wheels, my dear sir, in these gigantic schemes which shake the entire financial world. To-morrow every London paper will devote considerable space to the business, discussed this morning, with my Syndicate in King William Street."

Much more of the same talk passed between them, and it was about half-past two before they rose from their table. By this time various pencilled directions had changed hands, and they parted at the restaurant door with many mutual expressions of regret. When John attempted to thank his new friend rather effusively for his kind interest, and more especially for the introductions with which he had been so lavish, Shuttleworth—or de Vègas, as he preferred to be called—reproved him airily.

"My dear boy, what I have done amounts to nothing, as you will find—probably to less than nothing. A man's success depends entirely on his own initiative, ability and that sang-froid without which no diplomat is complete. And there is more diplomacy in successful business than is visible to the ordinary eye. One day, when I am free from my multitudinous obligations, it is my intention to write a book embodying the best business maxims. I'll put you on the free list."

With a laugh at his own pleasantry he shook hands, and, hailing a taxi, jumped in and was immediately driven off.

John did not hear the address given ; indeed, he made no attempt to hear it. His new friend had given him already a considerable portion of his time, much good advice, and an excellent lunch. No reasonable man could expect more.

It was now three in the afternoon, and John decided to take the rest of the day as a holiday. Seeing a motor omnibus, labelled Hammersmith and Kew Bridge, he recalled a pleasant Sunday afternoon spent at Kew Gardens on the occasion of his last London visit. On the spur of the moment he climbed to the top of it, got a comfortable seat, and lit a cigarette. Then he took out his leather case to look, for the second time, at the various address cards he had obtained from de Vègas. These were three in number, and, for greater safety, he decided to transfer them to his pocket-book, which he carried in a special inner pocket.

Putting his hand against the spot where it ought to be, he was startled to find a curious flatness. His hand plunged in convulsively, and so sharply that a woman, on the opposite seat, regarded him with some apprehension.

Then he stood up, searched violently in every pocket, but found no sign of the fat little receptacle in which he had snugly hidden one hundred and five pounds, in notes !

It was all gone ; and, for the moment, the truth did not dawn upon him that he had added one more to the long list of Verdant Greens who have come to grief among the sharpers of London !

CHAPTER XII

THE GRIM REALITY

Poor John stood up, searching the floor of the omnibus, and looked round rather wildly, after the manner of the person who has had a serious loss, and then stopped the 'bus.

"You've lost something?" said the lady opposite, and the cheerful simplicity of the question so enraged John that he had some difficulty in answering civilly in the affirmative.

The conductor, aggrieved at being stopped at an inconvenient point, had only a scowl for him as he descended the stairs.

"Might a' waited till we made the Circus round the corner," he said grumblingly.

"I've lost my pocket-book!" said Marchbanks excitedly. "Over a hundred pounds in it. Perhaps you'd like me to go to the Circus—now!"

"Sorry, sir. Go back to the Yard, I would. Only wish I could find it!" said the man, much less sympathetic than he might have been, at the same time jerking the cord again, with the result that the car started forward, and the passenger was pitched, with more force than grace, into the street.

The conductor's tone had not only been indifferent—it had been incredulous—which was the last straw to the unhappy loser. John jumped on a 'bus going in the opposite direction, and was, ere long, deposited at the door of the restaurant he had left little more than half an hour before.

It was now slackening inside, and the luncheon room was nearly empty. But when he confided his loss to the head waiter he did not find him conspicuously sympathetic.

"Can't 'ave lost it 'ere, sir. It bein' as you describe, it would' ave bin seen. Can you look? Why, yes, of course, sir! What do you think? I carn't say as I remember you, sir. Whereabouts did you sit?"

John found the table, and every inch of the narrow floor space was eagerly scanned; but the result was nil.

"Been pinched outside, sir, I should say," observed the waiter. "See the manager? Oh, yes, if you like; though he carn't do nothing. Why, he wasn't even in the 'ouse for his own luncheon to-day. See 'im by all means, but I assure you the Yard's the only plice. If it's bin found by an honest person it'll be there by now. Did you 'ave it out while in the room, sir?"

John was obliged to admit that he had not, as having been a guest he had had to pay nothing.

"Then as like as not it's at 'ome, or at your 'otel, in another coat, or somewhere else. I'd advise you to go back an' see, sir. It's best to make sure in a case of this kind, on account of other people, sir."

John perceived the justice of this suggestion, and left the building without insisting on seeing the manager.

Not anxious to court a snub at Scotland Yard he made haste back to the Euston Hotel, cherishing the vain hope that, by some chance, he might find his pocket-book there. All the way back the waiter's suggestive word "pinched" rang in his ears. He had, of course, frequently heard tales of the countryman in London falling into the hands of its professional sharks, but that such a humiliating experience should have happened to him was not to be entertained. He refused to entertain it, anyhow, until every other avenue was closed.

Arrived back at the hotel, he went to the room he had selected in the morning, turned out the very modest little handbag, standing meekly on the luggage tray, examined the pockets of the overcoat he had left hanging on the peg behind the door; but, of course, without result.

Deciding to say nothing to the manager of the hotel until he had consulted expert opinion at Scotland Yard, he again left the house, and proceeded, by tortuous ways, to the Lost Property Office on the Embankment, where losses are made good in the most astounding way, which reflects the utmost credit on mankind in general.

But John's luck was against him. Having given the particulars, he was informed that it was too early yet to expect the pocket-book, supposing it had fallen into honest hands, to have been restored; he was asked to come back on the morrow, or in a couple of days, and dismissed. No comment was made, though particulars of his movements for the day were taken. The misery of the next forty-eight hours may be imagined, and the final extinction of the faint hopes of the recovery of his money which had upheld him.

While the hundred and five pounds did not represent his entire worldly possessions, it was on it he had depended to get over the first stages on the road to El Dorado. In the bank where he had been employed he had a very modest deposit account, amounting to about £28, too small to be of much practical value. And, moreover, to apply for that would give information at Renfield Street, which he at the moment wished to withhold. In the course of the second day his luggage arrived from Glasgow, but contained no line or message from his mother. She had done no more and no less than he had asked.

In spite of the bright sunshine and the cheerful aspect of London, in the heyday of summer, acute depression quickly made John its prey. During these interminable hours, many of which he passed plying between Euston and Charing Cross, the conviction was forced upon him that he had been "done," and that his friend with the specious tongue, instead of being Senhor Lope-de-Vègas, of Buenos Ayres, and the world at large, was probably nothing but an ordinary swindler who waxes fat on the green innocence of such as he.

It was not a very palatable thought to an independent spirit that rather fancied its own powers and aspirations; but none the less it was the particular kind of spur John needed at the moment.

It was when they assured him at Scotland Yard that he might now give up any hope of seeing his pocket-book again that he ventured to voice the impression that perhaps it had been stolen from him by a man with whom he had lunched at Simpson's. The officer proceeded to question him sharply, his interest quickening to an extraordinary degree, and when John proceeded to describe the individual he waxed indignant.

"Now, why, in the name of all that's wonderful, didn't you lodge all this information before, sir?" asked the man with real aggrievedness in his voice. "That's how we're treated here by the public! They come and tell half a story, and expect us to fill in all the gaps, they keeping back more than half the time the only bit that really matters. Depend upon it, that's where your notes have gone. I know the chap—he's one of the light-fingered crew that gets the better of chaps like you. And now you've gone and given him fifty-six hours' start, and expect the Yard to lay his fingers on him in a moment! I put it to you, now, is it fair?"

Marchbanks was obliged to confess that it was hardly fair.

"But you see it isn't easy to bring a charge of that kind against a man who may be perfectly innocent."

"The mistake, of course, was in your chumming up with him. I'm not blaming you, sir; but I put it to you, now—Is it likely the sort of help he offered is going begging in London or anywhere else? Why, it was written fraud, on the very face of it! We'll do what we can, of course; but I don't, myself, promise anything, or think there's a chance of your ever seeing your money again."

That finally disposed of, there was nothing for our unhappy voyager but to take immediate and exact stock of his position, means, and prospects.

In the purse he had kept apart for incidental expenses in London he had over seven pounds and a handful of loose silver, which would, roughly speaking, keep him idle in London, if he practised economy, for about three weeks. In the interval he could obtain his last resources from home. Even they were inadequate to take him out to the port he had in view. But somehow the glamour was off Buenos Ayres. The shameful way in which an alleged citizen of that great Republic had treated him had given him a distaste for its very name, which must forever be associated with that of the sharper who had betrayed him.

Then he could go back, of course, and take up his old position, or another, in the city of his birth; but he quickly, with reddening cheek and with hardening heart, put that idea behind him. Finally, it was open to him to seek a berth in London, and start to save afresh, always having in front the hope that something might turn up to further his ambitions and give him the chance he so eagerly sought.

After reflection he decided on the latter course, and began the dreary round of searching for employment, which more quickly reduces the fibre of manhood than any other quest on earth.

Before he set out on this pilgrimage he very prudently removed himself and his belongings from the Euston Hotel to a modest boarding-house in Guildford Street, where, for the sum of twenty-one shillings per week, he could obtain breakfast, dinner, and a room to sleep in. Making careful calculation, by this economy he could extend the period of his unproductive waiting for a week or two longer.

It was a very strange and searching experience for a young man, who had hitherto been nursed, if not exactly in the lap of luxury, at least in the bosom of a very comfortable home.

His search for work, the daily rebuffs, the gradual sinking of hope and consequent lowering of self-confidence, the descent from the heights of the ideal to the stern and grim reality of the mere fight for existence—all these have been described by abler pens than mine. When not unduly prolonged, such an experience is not without its value and influence on the human character.

Long before the end of the first week John Marchbanks had, willy-nilly, adjusted his values, as well as his attitude towards life. For one thing, the character, attainment, and real grit of his mother stood out, clear-cut, like a cameo. He began to realise, as he had not yet done, something of the nature of the struggle which she, unaided, had made, as well as the magnitude of the small success she had achieved. If he, well equipped for the world of business, with nothing to handicap him in the race, could achieve so little by his own unaided exertion, what must the fight have been for a woman who had few friends, and who, moreover, had to conduct the fight under a cloud?

Ellen never knew of the unwritten letters which might have reached her that week bearing the London postmark!

What a book could be compiled of the unwritten letters of the world! What thoughts that soar and words that burn could thereby be added to the records of imperishable fame!

But John Marchbanks' unwritten and fervent letters to his mother will never see the light. He did not even transcribe them on the tablets of a handy diary. When a line, or a postcard, would have reassured the heart which, mother-like, quickly forgot its brief indignation, he maintained the silence of death.

Happily for her she imagined him a voyager on happy and prosperous seas, speeding towards the haven where, doubtless, full recognition and success awaited him.

The divine and unquenchable hope of motherhood is one of the buttresses of the world.

John Marchbanks had disappeared, quite near home, as men have been known to disappear for various reasons, some of them unaccountable, since the beginning of all time. There are well-authenticated cases of family men escaping like shadows from the trammels of an obligation against which they had been chafing for years, and going no farther away than the next street! It is only in great cities that such things are possible, and John, in the greatest city in the world, had no difficulty in joining the endless ranks of the unknown and the unrecognised. In fact, the difficulty was to escape from them. His whole being, notably the pride of his manhood, revolted from becoming merely a guest in a cheap boarding-house, welcome only so long as he could pay his way, and a unit in crowded streets at whom none cast the glance of kindly recognition or offered the hand of friendship.

It is certain that John's rather sensitive nature could not long have stood the stupendous strain. He would have gone under quickly, and probably with great completeness, had there not been some timely intervention.

It was on the thirteenth day of his search for work that he found it, not in any dramatic or exciting way, but just merely and practically by the simple answer to an advertisement. By all the known laws that govern cause and effect he ought not to have obtained the situation, because he could give no satisfactory account of himself; that he got it shows that the overruling Providence had him in full view.

From the pages of a newspaper which he feverishly studied each morning at his breakfast table, proceeding from it generally to the nearest reading-room to implement his list from various other journals, he culled one which asked for the services of a temporary clerk, well up in languages, at a place of business in London Wall.

The soles of John's well-made Glasgow boots, for which, under Roger Annan's chaperonage, he had paid the high price of two guineas, were beginning to show signs of wear, and to tire his hot feet after a long day's tramp. That morning he decided not to test them further, but to get to London Wall by the fastest means of transit possible.

He was there on the stroke of 9.30, and looked askance at two other young men, entering the palatial building at the same moment, perhaps on the same errand.

He found the address to be one of those immense and gorgeous blocks of business buildings which in London are so rapidly superseding the old-fashioned types of business premises. This one rejoiced in the name of Havelock House, and, once inside, John discovered that the firm of Trent,

Bartlett & Hume, shippers, occupied two floors, while the others were let off.

The third name on the enormous, dazzling brass plate, shining like real gold in the sunlight, somewhat reassured John, while it also slightly chastened him. In his peregrinations and adventures through the business part of London during the last fortnight he had discovered that his own countrymen were the least inclined to take him at his own valuation. It had invariably been a Scotchman who had put the crucial question which he either could not or would not answer, and which had barred his chance.

When asked why he had left his last place, the simple answer " Private reasons " had never in any single instance satisfied a Scotch questioner. But John had stuck to it with an odd pertinacity, as determined he would not budge from the attitude he had taken up as they were determined to be at the bottom of it.

His heart somehow was a little lighter that morning, though, if questioned, he could certainly not have given the smallest justification for it. He was, indeed, getting very near the end of his tether now ; and had only sufficient to pay his week's board in advance, and leave a very few shillings to go on with. His next move, failing success to-day, must be to take a step lower, and seek some manual labour, which would give him daily bread.

In spite of the trying experiences through which he had passed he had not altogether lost the confident air characteristic of him in Glasgow, which was to stand him in good stead on this particular day of destiny.

He was put, along with the two other applicants, into a small and quite bare waiting-room, where the only thing to divert attention was a copy of a financial paper and some pictures of steamships sailing over beautiful bright blue seas hanging on the walls.

John was the last to be summoned to the hall of judgment, and then, as those in front of him did not return to the waiting-room, but had, presumably, been shown directly to the stairs, he had no opportunity of knowing whether either had been successful, leaving him to be seen merely as a matter of courtesy or formula.

When he entered the room, two men were in it—an elderly, grey-haired one, tall, thin, and spare, with a very keen eye and a somewhat severe face ; and a young man, about thirty, possibly his son, as he had the same fine looks combined with the charm of youth.

" Morning, Mr. Marchbanks," said the elder one. " You have come after the post we advertised. What business training have you had ? "

John briefly explained that he had been in a bank the whole of his working life. At this statement the elder gentleman looked disappointed, even slightly annoyed.

" It does not sound promising for our purpose—does it, Gilbert ? You read the advertisement, I suppose ? It is a knowledge of languages that is the first essential. The two candidates who have just gone out speak nothing but English. The waste of time—ours and their own—is obvious."

He played with the gold eyeglass, which he had taken from his nose at John's entrance, and continued to regard him rather severely, as if to rebuke him before being proven of the crime.

" It was the paragraph about the languages which encouraged me to come," answered John. " I speak French and German fluently, and I know enough Spanish to be able to write it correctly, though I have not had sufficient opportunity for speaking it to be able to do so fluently."

The elderly gentleman's face visibly brightened.

" This is better. It is probable that you will suit our purpose ; but, unfortunately, a word was omitted from the advertisement which ought to have appeared, and that word was ' temporary.' Our foreign correspondent has had a nervous breakdown, and is off on three months' leave. Possibly a man with your qualifications—and credentials "—he added, with a slight emphasis on the word, though he had not asked for any yet—" may not care to take a temporary post ? "

" At the present moment, sir, I shall be glad to get it," answered John, trying to restrain the note of eagerness in his voice. " And I may as well tell you that, although I could get references from Glasgow, and from my former employers, I would much prefer not to ask them. As the job is only temporary, perhaps you could dispense with them ? I promise I shall do my best to fulfil your requirements, and I think I can do so."

Sir Edward Trent, who had continued his study of John's face while he was uttering these words, wheeled round on his chair to look at his nephew and junior partner.

" The circumstances are a little unusual, Gilbert, but what do you think ? Shall we risk it ? "

" I think we might," answered the younger man, and it relieved John immensely to catch the Scots accent. " Anyhow, the matter is urgent, and perhaps Mr. Marchbanks might tide us over the worst."

" You say you prefer not to have your references taken up ? " continued Sir Edward. " You understand, of course, that this is an unusual attitude ? And one—if you'll excuse me—likely to mitigate against any advancement for yourself."

" I am quite aware of it, sir. I left Glasgow for purely family and private reasons, and my business life is unimpeachable. But for a bit of ill-luck, I should not be in London now, but in Buenos Ayres, which was my destination when I left Scotland," answered John, but did not mention the loss that had befallen him, reflecting that it was hardly a heroic story.

" I understand. Well, we don't want to pry into that ; and, as it happens, our business is urgent—more especially the Spanish part of it. So you may consider yourself engaged. Can you come in to-morrow morning."

" Yes, sir—to-day, if you like. I can stop now."

" Well, if you could, some part of the correspondence could be at once disposed of. We have had to requisition the services of an outside translator ; but that we don't care about. Can you stay now, then ? "

John said that he could.

" And about salary—three pounds a week, shall we say ? It's not, of course, what we have been paying the member, of our regular staff, whose work you will have to do ; but, meanwhile, it is all we are prepared to offer."

" I accept it," said John manfully, his pulses beginning to bound at the prospect of being once more enrolled among the wage-earners of the world.

" Perhaps, before you go to work, Mr. Marchbanks, you may like to know who we are ? I am Sir Edward Trent, and this is my nephew, Mr. Gilbert Hume. He will show you what you have to do. You can go now, Gilbert, for I think I had better not keep Gascon waiting longer."

So in a few minutes' time John had taken a new step on the ladder of progress, and, instructed by a very friendly Scotchman in the person of Gilbert Hume, proceeded to give a very good account of himself, so far as his mastery of languages was concerned.

He had an interesting and not very strenuous day, which had sufficed to make him realise, if not altogether grasp, the magnitude of the commercial operations associated with the name of Trent, Bartlett & Hume.

He registered a view that he would make such good use of the next three months that his services would be deemed indispensable.

He did not write to his mother. Nothing, perhaps, can explain or mitigate his strange cruelty in this direction.

He decided to disappear, at least until his three months of probation were up, and he knew what chances of promotion were likely to be his. He could not bring himself to the humiliating confession that all his fine effort and ambition had ended in such meagre achievement.

He decided, therefore, in the meantime, to add one more to the great army of those whom London's capacious, ravening maw has swallowed up.

CHAPTER XIII

THE GIRL HE LEFT BEHIND HIM

WHILE these adventures were befalling John Marchbanks in London, certain persons interested in him were not without concern in Glasgow.

On the morning of the third day of his non-attendance at his desk at Renfield Street, Mr. Craighead sent out the youngest clerk for Roger Annan.

"Know anything about Marchbanks, Roger? I suppose he's ill, but it's not like him to send no explanation of his absence."

"I don't know anything about him, sir. I haven't seen him since Tuesday."

"Queer, isn't it? I suppose you knew he had given notice, and was contemplating leaving Glasgow?"

"Oh, yes," answered Roger with a certain amount of restraint in his pleasant voice. "I knew all about that."

"Got his home address?"

"Yes—I know where he lives; but I've never been there."

"You haven't inquired, then?" Mr. Craighead said, and his voice undoubtedly expressed surprise. "Could you go out this afternoon?"

"I could go in the evening after dinner. I'm due at tennis at six o'clock, or as near it as I can get. It's only tennis at home, of course," he added hastily. "But I know they are counting on me to-day."

"All right. I daresay we'll hear to-morrow; but, if we'd happened to be busy I should have had something to say about this."

So uncomfortable did Roger feel, that, in about an hour's time, he indited a prepaid telegram to Marchbanks, and sent it out, asking for the reply to come direct to the bank.

In about an hour's time the reply, containing these disquieting words, was handed in: "John not here. Know nothing about him."

Now rather excited, Roger immediately took it through to the manager's room.

"I felt so uneasy after you spoke to me, sir, that I sent this wire—and look at the answer! Very queer, isn't it?"

Mr. Craighead sat in silence regarding the ominous words on the pink slip.

"It is certainly strange. He has a small account here, I believe; I wonder if it has been touched?"

Roger, who kept the ledgers, could assure him that it hadn't.

"I hope nothing has happened to him," said the manager, in rather a troubled voice. "I had a talk with him the day he informed me he was leaving, and I could see that he was not in a very good state of mind."

Roger's face flushed, his imagination leaping up without further incentive.

"You don't think John would do anything foolish, sir? Do away with himself, for instance? He wasn't that sort."

His voice thickened a little, for he was genuinely fond of his chum, and his grief over the rupture brought about by others was both deep and sincere.

"One never knows," answered the manager, who had had a dyspeptic morning, and was inclined to take gloomy views. "It's a very queer thing. I must write—or try to see the mother. Know anything about her, Roger?"

"I've never seen her. Fact is, Jack had a sort of reticence about her. More pride than anything, I always said. None of his friends, I know, have ever seen her."

"But I suppose she exists," said the manager grimly, "and this has got to be explained. I'll try and see her myself. At least, between now and Monday. It's a queer story, and I wish I could get to the bottom of it. He was the very last man I should have thought to do anything rash or foolish—if it had been you, now, Roger——"

A slow smile summed up most of the possibilities, but Roger was too concerned to respond to it. He was in a frightful hurry to get home; not for the tennis, altogether, but to throw the bomb into the peaceful family circle which he held responsible for the loss of his chum. Roger was very hurt and sore in these days, and his family had not found him easy to get on with; in fact, on two nights, he had taken more liquor than was good for him, to his mother's terrible grief.

A love of strong drink was Roger's besetting sin, and John's influence, though his people did not credit it, had pulled him up sharp, and kept him straight. This was the explanation of the younger son's long residence in Glasgow when, according to family tradition, he ought to have taken his turn in the East.

A fiery-faced grandfather, now deceased, who had lived hard, and distinguished himself in other fields than business, though he had made an immense fortune there, was held mainly responsible for Roger's unhappy tendency. They hoped, however, that he had mastered it, though his mother's anxiety seldom slept. It was the skeleton in the Annan cupboard, and the one they were most anxious to keep from the knowledge of the Dunsyres.

Old Dan Dunsyre had absolutely no quarter for any dereliction in that respect. A strict teetotaller himself, he had pulled the strings so tightly at home that both his boys had broken loose. No drink of any kind was to be seen on the Dunsyre's table; while at Balcraig, on the other hand, it appeared lavishly on every occasion; even the tennis tea-table was incomplete without claret-cup and whisky-and-soda.

When Roger got home the game was already started, though there was a scarcity of men. Archie Dunsyre was the only one visible, and Roger's return was hailed with delight. The sett being just over, when he came through the door in the lane they collected about him to hear his news, and to reprove him for being late.

"Couldn't help it. We're doing double-tides at present—short of our cashier. Say—what! Poor Jack Marchbanks has disappeared, nobody knows where; not even his mother!"

He uttered these words as they were walking towards the veranda, where some of those who had dropped into tea without wishing to play were grouped about the host and hostess.

Elizabeth, happily, was not in his immediate vicinity, but Roger took great delight in repeating his news when they got nearer so that everybody got the benefit of it.

"We've got a mild sensation at Renfield Street," he said, addressing his mother more particularly. "Jack Marchbanks hasn't been at business since Tuesday; and to-day old Craighead came through to ask did I know where he was as he hadn't sent the usual explanation and apology? I said

I didn't, of course, and old Craighead, I could see, thought it quite on the cards—that he may have shuffled off this mortal coil, I mean—for his mother knows nothing about him."

This bomb caused quite as much sensation as was expected. Somehow, most eyes turned towards Elizabeth, for Jack's infatuation for her was a matter of common talk in the little circle.

"Has his mother been seen?" asked Mrs. Annan, stepping mother-like into the breach at once. "Lisbeth, I wish you would go and bring me a handkerchief. I can't find one in my work-bag."

Elizabeth did not move, but, keeping her eyes on her brother's face, waited for his further remarks.

"His mother hasn't been seen, but she's been wired to. I've got the answer here. There it is! 'John not here. Know nothing about him.' Quite explicit, isn't it? The question is, where is John? Mr. Craighead, as I said, thinks he's shuffled off. It's significant that he hasn't touched the money he has at the bank."

Mr. Annan, with reddening face, cleared his throat. He was quite well aware that Roger's words were directed at him; and, while resenting them, he could not, in face of the gaping crowd, strung up to the highest pitch of excitement by this unusual occurrence, say just what he liked.

He was angry with Roger for several things at the moment.

The week had been a most trying and disappointing one, and this was the crowning act of offence. As he said later, "If you had an atom of horse sense, you would have kept dark about Marchbanks till all these grinning apes were cleared out."

When really angry Mr. Annan did not mince his words.

He attempted to pooh-pooh the whole situation.

"Possibly there is some quite simple explanation; Roger is aye spying ferlies! And, anyway, if young Marchbanks elects to take some foolish and unnecessary step to worry his own folk, and any that happen to know him, the heavens needn't fall! Your mother asked you to get her a handkerchief, Lisbeth. Did you hear her?"

"Did she ask me that? All right—I'll get it," said Elizabeth in a clear, low voice that had not a tremor in it.

Though admirably mistress of herself, her face had visibly whitened, and she was glad to get away.

Kitty, who obtained all the proof she needed that she had no feeling, was very indignant. She had watched the growth of the love affair with all a girl's intense interest, and had even had a small bet on its ultimate issue. And now, convinced that Betty had been merely playing herself, she was indignant. For John Marchbanks had always acted like a gentleman, even if the Annans withheld that title from him.

A short discussion failed to throw any light on the mystery, and presently the little crowd, whose interest was, palpably, of the evanescent order, hurried back to the court to continue their play.

Roger, declining his mother's offer of tea, said he would go and get into his flannels. On the stairs he met his sister, and both stopped involuntarily.

"I suppose you know nothing about this, Lisbeth?" he asked rather harshly. "I tried to gather from your face whether you did."

"I know nothing about it," Elizabeth answered in a low voice.

"But you're at the bottom of it, all the same," said Roger brutally. "Jack was the best chum in the world till you had him through your hands. You've spoiled and ruined his life! If you didn't care, you might have left him alone."

Elizabeth, strung to the highest pitch, laughed shrilly.

"How delicious! So you think I did all that, do you? Well, your welcome to your opinion. I don't care what you think. The truth will come out some day, maybe, then you'll know!"

She passed on quickly, with her head in the air; and Roger retired to his own room to fume in secret over what he did not fully understand. In his own mind, he was perfectly convinced that some underhand game had been going on, and it was because they had kept him in the dark that he was so furious.

He was certain from the expression of his mother's face that she even knew more than appeared on the surface, and the few words his father had uttered had had the ring of acute personal discomfort. But Roger swore to be at the bottom of it, and decided that he would make a point of seeing John's mother, when he left the bank, early on his free Saturday afternoon.

But he was forestalled in that desire by his father, who, meeting Elizabeth in the hall as she came down, put a straight question to her.

"You know knothing about this, Lisbeth? Marchbanks did not confide in you, or—or tell you what he meant to do?"

Elizabeth looked strangely at him.

"When a man wants to commit suicide," she answered clearly, "he doesn't usually take the whole world into his confidence."

Mr. Annan started back and threw up a deprecating hand. The words gave him an undoubted shock, though they merely crystallised a vague fear that had crept to the back of his mind.

"You don't think that, Lisbeth! It isn't possible—men don't do that sort of thing."

"Don't they? Well, perhaps not. But whatever ill happens to John Marchbanks, father, you are to blame—you, and the system that treats women like babies, or fools, who are not fit to hear the facts of life!"

So saying she passed on, not caring what kind of a wound she inflicted so long as she found vent to her own misery.

Now, Elizabeth did not believe for one moment that Marchbanks had taken his own life, and it was her pride that was suffering, undoubtedly, more than any of the deeper feelings of her heart. She had humbled herself to write to John, and he had ignored her appeal.

Mr. Annan stood about aimlessly for a few moments after she had passed out to the terrace, not caring to go back and hear platitudes from his wife about the affair, and entirely out of tune with the pretty picture of domestic happiness and social peace to be observed in the garden.

Suddenly a resolve came to him. He would himself go to Shawlands and interview the mother of the delinquent—the woman who, after all, was the prime factor in this unhappy business. Glad of a scapegoat—as the remorseful usually are—he mentally put her in the pillory all the way citywards.

It is a considerable ride from the extreme west end of Glasgow to the Shawlands side, and it was seven o'clock when Mr. Annan descended from the car at a familiar terminus which Ellen Marchbanks had so often watched from her window above the shop.

As he stood for a moment somewhat undecided, in the middle of the road, fumbling for the address which Roger had given him on the last Saturday night, his eye was suddenly arrested by the name, "E. Marchbanks, Groceries, Sundries," staring him in the face.

The old-fashioned word now so seldom seen, though it embodied Ellen's ideas of the merchandise she wished to sell, caused him to smile, and thrusting his letter-case back to his pocket, he made a line for the door of the shop.

Stepping right in, he was confronted by a very small boy in a very large white apron, behind the counter—Jimmy Duguid, the errand boy, playing the part of shopman to his own entire satisfaction. He was permitted to do this frequently during the slack hours of the day, and never surely was shop better served. Jimmy was never idle for a moment. He was weighing up pounds of sugar now with a nice exactitude. Strictly just, without being generous, he scarcely permitted the scale to turn a hair's-breadth in the customer's favour, though instructed by his mistress to remember that "the poke," as she called it, weighed something.

"Is Mrs. Marchbanks in, my man?" inquired Mr. Annan, as the small, grave face turned from his engrossing occupation to inquire his business.

"Up the stair," he answered shortly.

"And how do I get up the stair?" inquired Mr. Annan blandly.

"Round the corner—first door to the left. But I can cry her, if ye like?"

But Mr. Annan, reflecting that the crying process might deprive the interview of its preliminary dignity, said he would ascend by the orthodox way.

Jimmy nodded, and went on, imperturbably, with his sugar weighing, not even stopping to take a lick now, though it was the luscious brown stuff that he loved.

The door at the side was shut, and when Mr. Annan rang the bell he felt the jerk of the pull at the top of the stair which admitted him. A long clean passage and a whitened stone stair rather narrow and dark, took him to the first floor of the house, where Mrs. Marchbanks stood waiting, her face wearing rather a fretful look, for she was in no doubt that it was Annie Houston again, and she had had just about enough of the girl, though she was sorry for her.

When she saw the portly figure of Mr. Annan she stood at attention, as it were, even on the defensive, and waited for him to speak.

"Mrs. Marchbanks?" he said, making pause two steps from the top, and taking off his hat.

"That's my name," she said ungraciously.

"Mine is Annan. Can I come in, ma'am?"

"Yes, I suppose so," she said drily, and, stepping back into the passage, held the door open wide.

The passage was necessarily dark, as it had only borrowed light; but, after his eyes grew accustomed to the gloom, Mr. Annan found the lobby table, where he deposited his hat and stick, and proceeded towards the sitting-room door, where Mrs. Marchbanks waited, hesitatingly, for him to follow.

He was surprised to find himself immediately in a large and very pleasant room, with a rounden end, and three long windows commanding a noble prospect of the immediate neighbourhood. It was nicely furnished, too, with a sideboard and piano, and one or two quite good engravings, and some well-filled book-shelves against the wall-space not utilised by furniture.

Mr. Annan took this general view at a glance, as it were, but his main interest, of course, was Ellen herself.

She stood by the table, a tall, slight, rather sombre figure in black, with a neat collar fastened by a small gold brooch at the neck. She was very good-looking and quite lady-like, he decided, and John had borne very little resemblance to her.

She was in no hurry evidently, but stood there quite quietly, waiting for him to make his deliverance. Experienced man of the world though he was, Robert Annan felt himself rather nonplussed, and even wished he had not come.

" My name is Annan," he repeated, in a subdued tone of voice. " No doubt it is familiar to you ? "

" I have heard it," was all she said.

" I have come—I have come—well, in fact, to ask a question about your son. My boy, Roger, came home from the bank to-day much perturbed, because he has disappeared from Glasgow, it seems, and you wired, in reply to his inquiry, that you knew nothing about him. Is that absolutely true, Mrs. Marchbanks ? "

" It is quite true," she answered, in her quiet, even, steady voice, which had an aggravating quality. Evidently she had not the smallest intention of helping him out with his difficult task.

" Do you mean to say that he has left without saying a word to you, or having given you the smallest clue to his whereabouts or intentions ? " asked Mr. Annan incredulously.

Then Ellen began to speak, evidently without emotion and without raising her voice.

" On Wednesday my son went out to his office as usual, and he did not come home in the evening. I was waiting for him here, about nine o'clock, not very anxious, for he was often late, and had ways to go that were no concern of his mother's, when I got an express letter from the Post Office saying he was away in the London train. The next morning I got a telegram from him, asking me to send his clothes and things to the Euston Hotel in London. Both these messages are here—you can look at them. That is all I know."

She drew them from what appeared to be a capacious pocket and handed them over. Mr. Annan ran his eyes over both, and, while he was relieved, he did not feel one whit more comfortable.

" So he has cut his stick ! " he said, trying to speak naturally, and even jovially. " Well, perhaps it'll be the making of him. It shows initiative and pluck, and he was a very fine fellow, Mrs. Marchbanks. I had a great respect for him."

" Had you ? " she asked, and, had her face not been so impassive, he might have imagined that she spoke in scorn.

" I had. We all had ; and my boy Roger was devoted to him. We are very sorry this has happened, but, I repeat, it may be the best thing for him in the end."

" It may be," said Ellen, and her quiet unresponsiveness began to get on Mr. Annan's nerves.

Never had he tried to manage an interview more difficult, and all the specious sentences he had planned to speak to soothe and mollify an irate mother seemed impossible of utterance. Trying to describe the interview afterwards to his own docile and simple-minded wife, he remarked that " it was just like butting against a stone wall."

" You are not anxious about him now, presumably ? " he said, feeling that he ought to be moving doorwards, and yet lingering in the hope of getting some satisfaction out of the pale silent figure opposite to him. A slight curiosity also was his. He would like to pierce that strange cold reticence and reserve, and find the real woman. That she existed he had no manner of doubt. Her whole personality seemed to breathe depth, capability, even passion. She was no common woman, and Mr. Annan understood that he had made one of the few failures in judgment of his life.

" Oh, no ; I'm not anxious about him at all," she answered, as if the question surprised her.

Then Mr. Annan ventured farther—perhaps foolishly.

" We are all sorry to lose him at Balcraig. I suppose you know he came a good deal about our house ? "

A quiver then galvanised Ellen's features into life.

" I know that he went a good deal about Balcraig," she repeated.

" And nobody deplored more than myself and my wife the misunderstanding that arose," Mr. Annan blundered on.

" What misunderstanding ? " she asked ; then, before Mr. Annan could frame an answer to this difficult question, her passion rose. " You've come into a humble home, Mr. Annan, and destroyed its peace. You've taken her son away from a woman that never harmed you ; I don't know whose blame it is, first or last ; but the blow came from your house. Let it stop at that. And don't you, or any bearing your name, come now, trying to pry into the outs and ins of it. My son has left me—I don't know where he is, or what he means to do ; but, among you, you've stolen him from me ! That's all I know or care about. I don't want to hear any more you have to say. If I'd known who was at the bottom of the stair, I'd have locked and double-locked the door ! No, I won't listen ! All the talking in the world is not going to mend the thing you have done to me and mine. We're poor folk, but we have feelings ; and, maybe, we have pride too that can match your own, though, according to the lights of you and your kind, we are outside the pale ! "

The next moment Mr. Annan, propelled by some inward force which forbade him to seek to stem the flood, was outside the room and the house.

It was an experience that had shaken him. He even trembled a little as he walked away in haste from the corner, trying to calm his nerves before he got into a car to bear him back to his own side of the city.

CHAPTER XIV

THREE WOMEN—ONE MAN

Mr. Annan, even with the aid of a taxicab, was nearly half an hour late for dinner, which, in summer evenings, except Saturdays, was usually served at eight o'clock.

All the company had gone when he reached home, and his family were waiting for him with some impatience. Roger, who had an appointment elsewhere, was obviously chafing, but his mother refused to begin without the head of the house.

" It can't be anything so very important, and your father may come in any moment, Roger. We must just wait."

They heard the hoot and whir of the motor at the moment, and she ran out to welcome him back.

" Sorry to be late, my dear ; I'll tell you all about it later. Tell them to begin serving. I'll just pop up and wash my hands."

They were all at the table when he entered the dining-room, but he sat down without offering any explanation of his absence. It was so unusual for him to leave the house after he once returned to it, after business hours, that it had caused some speculation.

Elizabeth had changed into another white frock, in which she looked singularly colourless. Her face was paler than usual, and her eyes slightly shadowed. Her father did not think that she looked well.

" How is it," he asked irritably, as he took his seat, " that it seems so difficult to get away to Kilcrean ? Why, I thought that long ago everything we wanted had been collected there, mother ! I must insist on you and Lisbeth going down to-morrow. I'll take you myself, and come in again on Monday."

" We were really going on Monday, dear," his wife assured him in her gentle pacific voice. " I think we'd better leave it at that ; they'll be quite ready for us on Monday."

" Ought to be ready any moment ! Who are you going to leave here ? You needn't consider me—if I have Barbara Chisholm here, she'll do all that's necessary for me and Roger."

" We thought of taking her only, and leaving the rest to wind up the house by degrees," his wife suggested.

" You thought of it, you mean, mother. I don't see why we want to wind up the house five or six weeks earlier than usual. I get enough of Kilcrean, and I am not keen on going out of town, yet. Nobody is even thinking about it ! "

Elizabeth's voice was hard and metallic.

" You look as if you would be the better of it, lass," her father said with a kind of dry solicitude. " There's something the matter with that soup—it's got too much salt in it. Who wants very hot, salt soup on a midsummer's night ? "

Mr. Annan was not a grumbler at meal-time, and his wife showed an instant and becoming solicitude. Roger glumly pushed his aside, and the next course was hurried on in a kind of grim silence. A more uncomfortable meal, indeed, had seldom been eaten at Balcraig, and Elizabeth, without any apology, left the table while the last course was in progress. The moment the door was closed, her father spoke up.

" I've been out to see John Marchbank's mother," he said, addressing nobody in particular.

" And did you see her ? " asked Roger, in rather a tense voice.

" I did."

" A nice woman—eh, father ? " asked Mrs. Annan timidly.

" She might be ; but she was not so civil as she might have been to me. A regular madam, she is, in her way ! She keeps a little ' a'thing ' shop at Shawlands Cross, but she has the airs of a duchess. There's a pretty long and queer story behind that face, or I am much mistaken."

" What did she say about Jack ? " asked Roger hotly.

" Very little. She merely supplemented what you told us at tea-time. He's wired for his clothes to be sent to the Euston Hotel in London ; but, beyond that, apparently she knows nothing. At least, that is what she says. We needn't discuss the subject any further. I thought I'd tell you ; and, as long as we know no harm has come to him, he can be left alone. He has doubtless his own reasons for what he has done, but they are no concern of ours."

Roger grunted, finished his glass of port, and, excusing himself to his mother, left the room.

Then she leaned, somewhat agitatedly, across the table, and spoke in her quiet pleading voice :

" I'm glad you went, Robert. I am sure it was the right thing to do. And you were not very favourably impressed by her ? "

" I didn't like her, Mary ; but she's not the kind of woman either you or I had pictured. There isn't anything common about her, and she must have been very pretty in her youth. She has both brains and grit. It's been a most unfortunate affair all through ; but I'm thankful the lad is safe out of Glasgow, out of Lisbeth's way. I wish she was more like other lasses, my dear, so that we could get at the bottom of her. Don't you think Kilcrean is the place for her at the moment ? "

Fatherly anxiety vibrated in his voice, but his wife only sighed rather pensively as she answered :

" I don't really think places matter much to Lisbeth, Robert. She's just the same Lisbeth at Kilcrean as she is here, and not a bit easier to understand. I wonder, now, whether we did right to nip the thing in the bud ? I mean—after all it wasn't his fault, and he was a very good lad. I liked him. If you had been kind, Bob, and sent him out to George in Calcutta he might have done you great credit ; and Lisbeth could have gone out to him, and been married from Agnes Kinnear's house. I was thinking it all over yesterday."

Mr. Annan was angry as well as surprised, and showed it.

" I wonder to hear you, Mary ! It's a preposterous suggestion."

" Not so very, is it ? It might have made Lisbeth more human. She'll never be right till she has some little bairns of her own, father, and she'll need them soon. She minds me of a flower that begins to close up when the frosts come——"

" What are you talking about, Mary ? " asked Mr. Annan testily. " Has Lisbeth been confiding in you ? "

Tears started in the mother's eyes.

" If that had happened my heart would not be so sore, Bob ; but she tells me nothing. She treats me as if I were a big bairn, and I suppose I am.

You've sheltered me so carefully all our married life."

"Why, of course; that's every man's duty," said the elderly husband gallantly. "That's what the ordinance of marriage means, if it means anything at all. There can't be two heads to a body, my dear, and I'm sure Scripture is explicit enough on the relationship."

"Lisbeth doesn't like the Bible teaching on marriage, father—she say's it's blasphemous."

"She says that, does she? The blasphemy is nearer home!" said Mr. Annan wrathfully. "Now, understand, I don't want you to be fretting over this, Mary. It's over, and there'll be no more of it. I'll try and arrange to take you and Lisbeth over to Switzerland in about a month's time. And you might write to the Baroness in the interval, and ask whether the invitation to Hungary holds good. That would be a complete change now, and lift Lisbeth clean out of herself!"

Mrs. Annan made no promise. She was not very keen about paying visits to queer foreigners in Hungary, however charming they might have proved themselves at the health resort where they had all met.

Her heart was very anxious about two of her children, and often she longed for the return of George, her eldest son, and principal mainstay—her very own boy, as she sometimes whispered in her heart—who united in himself his father's business ability and the strict integrity which is so comforting to a mother's heart.

"I'm not very easy in my mind about Roger, Bob," she said to her husband, a little later in the evening. "And if you send him to Calcutta in October, and bring George home, I'm afraid you'll find it won't work."

"He's got to make a kirk or a mill of it, Mary," answered the father, with a sudden harshness. "And I wonder to hear you suggest that George should not come home! He's had a pretty fair spell of the East, and you know he likes Scotland best."

Mrs. Annan did not in the least resent this aspersion of her motherly affection. Secure in her own just perception of the state of affairs, she went on:

"There is no doubt that John Marchbanks was a good influence for Roger—we can say that much, at least, now he is away. And I'd like to tell his mother that——"

"Well, you can take a car out to Shawlands to-morrow, my dear, if that's your mind; but, I warn you you'll not like what you get there."

The suggestion caught Mrs. Annan's imagination, but she was not one to act very quickly on impulse, but generally considered well all her actions. That was why she had had so few to regret in her uneventful life.

Elizabeth, who so often acted without consideration, spent a sleepless night. Like many another, she was now beginning to prize to the full what she had lost.

For one thing, John must have cared tremendously, since he was unable to suffer existence in Glasgow deprived of the opportunity of seeing her and of hoping for a future she would share.

She was desperately anxious to discover whether the letter she had written had ever reached him, and, forgetful of her dignity and the pride of the Annans, she decided to go out to Shawlands next day, and pay a surreptitious call on John's mother.

The idea embodied a certain amount of adventure and daring which were quite sufficient to commend the step to her. She was just in the mood to do something foolish, and, perhaps, irretrievable. In fact, had John Marchbanks appeared suddenly on the scene at that juncture and asked her to take the irrevocable step and share his precarious fortunes, there is little doubt but that he would not have had to ask twice.

A certain lawlessness had crept into Elizabeth's blood. She had been in revolt for some time against the conventional trammels of her life, and was seeking for some outlet whereby she could express herself. That was a favourable expression of hers, and meant tremendous things to her.

So far the Suffrage Movement had not been much of a lure to her, though she was interested, and had even joined the non-militant party, though not as a very active member.

She rose betimes next morning, and appeared at the breakfast table apparently her usual calm collected self. Her mother did not come down, and, quite conscious of her father's pointed, if rather furtive scrutiny of her, she talked quite naturally about the usual affairs of the morning.

The weather was atrocious; the long spell of summer glow and beauty had been suddenly quenched, a cold east wind had sprung up from that sinister quarter, and the rain was lashing on the panes.

Roger, who had been very late on the previous evening, was grumpy, and ate no breakfast to speak of; only gulped down two cups of very strong coffee. He left the house before his father, as if he did not care to have his company down.

Mr. Annan, usually cheerful in the morning, seemed depressed by events.

"Roger's a fool, Lisbeth!" he said irritably as she helped him on with his big mackintosh in the hall. "He doesn't seem to know which side his bread is buttered on. He'll maybe get an awakening one of these days. I'll see that he does!"

"He has too little to do, father," was Elizabeth's unexpected contribution to the subject. "He ought to work like George and you. That's what is the matter with the most of us out here; we have too little to do. I'm thinking of hiring out as a typist."

These words provided food for reflection for Mr. Annan all the way into town.

Lisbeth spent half an hour over the newspapers, looked languidly at the uninteresting post, and about ten went up to her mother's room, to find her sitting propped up in bed getting ready her letter for the Indian mail.

"Give my love to George, mother. Will he get that letter before he leaves in October?"

"Oh, surely. But I'm not very sure whether your father won't change his mind about sending Roger out in his stead. I'm anxious about Roger, Lisbeth; and I've been wondering this morning whether there is anything between him and Kitty."

Elizabeth laughed rather disagreeably.

"Nothing. Roger's a general lover, and Kitty plays up to him, that's all. She doesn't care a fig for him. Besides, Mr. Dunsyre will only let Kitty marry a teetotaller, and Roger can hardly be said to be that! I'm going down town. Can I get anything for you?"

"It's an awful morning, my dear! Unless there's anything urgent, why go out in such a deluge?"

"I like it—I love the rain; it washes everything clean. It's a pity there can't be rain for the soul as well as the body! It would do a lot of good."

Elizabeth's energy was certainly prodigious. She walked all the way into the city, where she got her tramcar for Shawlands. It was all quite deliberately done, and, when she stepped off the car, opposite to Ellen Marchbanks' house, she looked about her interestedly, and with a certain verve which indicated that it was something of an adventure.

Like her father, she quickly caught sight of the signboard, and walked across the dripping street, towards the door of the modest emporium, where she very quietly lowered her umbrella, shook the rain from it, and left it outside.

Ellen was behind the counter, though at the farther end, making some entry in the ledger. There was no one else in the shop, Jimmy having been dispatched to ask for the day's orders at the few houses of the better sort, who had a weekly book, and were called on daily.

Ellen stepped forward, with her usual alacrity, smiling pleasantly.

Although all the world had changed, her motto was " business as usual," and now, in her secret heart, she had a fresh ambition, in which, for the first time since his birth, her son had no part.

" You don't know me, Mrs. Marchbanks," said Elizabeth in a rather difficult voice, for, like her father, she was a little surprised at Ellen's appearance, and realised that she was not the sort that could be patronised or put into any convenient corner.

" I don't," answered Ellen bluntly ; but her colour rose as she began to suspect the stranger's identity.

" I'm Miss Annan—from Balcraig. And I should like to speak to you for a minute, if I may."

" Oh, yes, certainly. Come upstairs—no, I'm sorry—it'll have to be the backshop only, for my message boy's out, and I can't go so far from the shop."

" Anywhere will do," said Elizabeth, with a touch of graciousness which did not impress Ellen as intended.

She opened the flap in the counter, and held it up for Miss Annan to pass through ; and, together, they entered the little snuggery at the back. A small clear fire burned there and somewhat relieved the general gloom ; but it was only a backshop after all, and was filled with evidences of the work which went on in the front.

Ellen stood by the table, and did not so much as offer a chair.

The moment of waiting was even more tense than that of the previous evening, when Mr. Annan and Ellen had faced one another upstairs. Had Elizabeth known of that interview possibly she would not have come.

" I'm Miss Annan," she repeated, and, though her voice was steady, her face betrayed the inward strain. " We have heard from my brother Roger that your son John has left Glasgow. We are all sorry about it, and I came to tell you that I hope he will come back soon."

It was a lame and unconvincing speech, delivered in a halting voice, with a pair of very hard, merciless eyes fixed on her face. Elizabeth already desperately regretted having come ; but, being there, she must get through with it somehow. Here was no transparent, elemental creature, whom she could hold in the hollow of her superior hands, but a woman of unusual mental vigour and very strong personality !

" Yes," said Ellen quietly, " and that's very kind of you I am sure."

She did not mean to mock, but the girl's sensitive colour rose.

" I hope that you have heard from him, since he went away ? "

" I have heard that he is in London. I have sent his luggage on," said Ellen quite quietly. " I told Mr. Annan all that last night," she added ; and the words seemed to imply that she might have been spared the repetition.

" I did not know my father had been here," put in Elizabeth hastily.

" He was here last night asking these very questions. It is very kind of you all to take so much interest in my son ; but the only person who could, perhaps, answer all your questions is the young lady he is engaged to," said Ellen ; and, afterwards calling herself to account, she could not explain what evil spirit entered into her at the moment. All she knew was that she wished desperately to make some of these people suffer who had robbed her of her son! She saw Elizabeth start, though she gave no other sign.

"I believe you may know something of her, though she is only a working woman, as I am. Her name is Houston—Miss Annie Houston. She's one of the first hands at Valerie's, where, I think, you get some of your frocks made. Maybe she has the latest news—you could take it on the way home."

Elizabeth drew herself up, ever so slightly, and, when she spoke, her voice was extraordinarily gentle.

"I don't think I shall trouble to do that," she said. "I am sorry your son has gone away as he has done—more especially for your sake. And my actual errand here to-day was to ask whether a letter I posted to him on Tuesday reached him before he left?"

"I don't know," answered Ellen, without flinching. "I have never heard him say."

"Then probably he did get it. Ah, well, nothing more can be done, and I need not take up your valuable time," said Elizabeth gallantly.

Ellen stood aside immediately for her to pass into the front shop.

On the customer's side of the counter Elizabeth paused, and looked round a little wistfully.

"It must be very pleasant to be independent, and to have some definite work to do, Mrs. Marchbanks."

"You think so?" asked Ellen with difficulty, and trying to harden the heart which something winning about Elizabeth Annan strove to soften.

John had never even tried to describe her to his mother, but, in her mind, she had had a very different vision.

There was nothing lordly or arrogant about the girl; nay, she seemed very simple, kindly, and sincere. Ellen desperately regretted some of her hard thoughts, and at least one of her deeds—the way that she had made away with the letter meant for John, and which she had had no right to tamper with.

"Yes; well, good-bye. Won't you shake hands, Mrs. Marchbanks? I'd like to tell you—but, no, I haven't the right. Good-bye, I hope your trouble and anxiety will soon be over."

"I have none," said Ellen bravely. "If it is my son you are speaking about, he is perfectly able to look after himself, and wherever he goes he will succeed. He has got that in him, and he has been feeling for a long time, that he has no scope in Glasgow. Good-bye, Miss Annan. It was very kind of you to come; but somebody what writes books has said that the East and West can never meet."

"It was Kipling who said it; but he did not refer to the East and West, but to the Far East," said Elizabeth, with a faint, melancholy smile.

The smile faded away immediately, however, as she walked away from the door, quite unaware that Ellen had even stepped there after her, and almost inaudibly called her back. But she did not hear, and the opportunity which might so easily have been fraught with rich consequences to both of them was lost.

Elizabeth's morning was not yet over. The one thought uppermost in her mind now was anger against John Marchbanks. If what his mother had said was true how dared he say what he had said to her not later than last Saturday night? Engaged to a dressmaker at Valerie's! She did not know her by name, but some magnet seemed to draw her to the place where it was the easiest thing in the world to create an errand.

When she entered the well-known atelier she was informed that Madame

Valerie had gone to Paris, but that Miss Houston would see her if it was anything urgent.

Elizabeth indicated that she would see Miss Houston, and sat down to look at some fashion-books until she was fetched.

She rose up when she saw the small, slight figure in a flowing black gown, only worn when she had to take her principal's place, come through the door at the other end of the spacious, cool, grey-and-white waiting-room.

" I can do something for you, perhaps ? " said Annie, in her cool, well-modulated voice. " Madame is away in Paris, but she'll be back on Monday with the newest things."

" Ah, well, perhaps I had better wait—unless you could show me some linen coats and skirts ? I'm going down to the coast on Monday, but they could be sent after me, if you haven't what I want now."

" I can show you some," said Annie ; and, beckoning to a younger assistant, proceeded with the business for which she was paid.

All the while a normal conversation was going on about the advantages of white over coloured linen for summer frocks both these young women were conscious of something psychological between them. Annie, not sufficiently versed in such matters, only knew that if she had had her way she would have been quite openly rude to Miss Annan. But she was a loyal little soul, and did her duty to her employer as faithfully as if she had been on the spot to watch her.

Elizabeth, on the other hand, made a study of the girl, grudgingly admitted her sweet looks, the charming dimple in her chin, the pretty way her hair waved about her delicate ears, the air of refinement which characterised her.

She would have liked to question her, to tear the truth from her ruthlessly; but not a word passed between them the whole world could not have heard.

To her surprise, Annie found Miss Annan gentler and much more considerate than usual, and wondered whether she, too, was mourning over John Marchbanks' disappearance.

When Elizabeth reached home she found her mother in the garden, anxiously scanning the roses, which she found it very difficult to coax into bloom, in the trim parterres.

" I was looking for you, Lisbeth. Kitty has been ringing up—wants you to go round to them for lunch."

" I'm not going, mother ; and, I think if you don't mind I'll run down to Kilcrean to-night and help them to get ready for next week."

Mrs. Annan's clear eyes, a little wistful, scanned her daughter's face.

" I never know where to have you, lassie ! Why, just last night, you were vowing no power on earth would take you to Kilcrean ! "

" I'm miserable, mother. Everything's out of joint in my life. Don't ask any questions, but just let me please myself, and, above everything, keep father from asking me questions ! "

So saying she dashed into the house. Her mother bent over a wilting rose tree, with the shadow deepening in her gentle, motherly eyes.

She understood, without further hint, that her child had entered upon one phase of the woman's lot—to suffer in silence, so that the world shall not know.

CHAPTER XV

PASTURES NEW

THE circumstances in which John Marchbanks now found himself, called up most of the reserves of his nature, and made special demands on certain Scottish characteristics which, from time immemorial, have contributed to the national success.

He was industrious by nature, and his mother had early dinned into his ears that no lasting or worthy success can be achieved without hard work, though other attributes, of course, might help. But, first and foremost, she, who had been a working woman all her life, had preached, both by precept and example, the doctrine of hard work to her only boy, in the full belief that she was thus rendering him the greatest in her power.

During the period of his apprenticeship, he had enjoyed very little of the amusement or diversion lads of his age usually seek for themselves. He had been sent to a night-school, where he had perfected his natural love of languages ; it was more than an aptitude with him, it amounted to a gift. Although not supposed to be musical in the ordinary sense, his ear seemed extraordinarily receptive to the sounds ; and his retentive memory made what was a task to most, mere pastime to him.

Once fairly established at his new post, and with daily demonstration of the utmost value a knowledge of foreign and strange tongues was, in such a business, he lost no time in finding the means to increase his store of equipment.

In London, there is nothing easier ; since facilities for the young man to increase his knowledge, both in the ways of good and evil, abound.

To John, London presented little temptation to lure him from the right path. His mother had grounded him well ; and, moreover, in his heart there glowed a deep and indomitable purpose which nothing would set aside. He had vowed to rise by his own effort, to the highest rung of the ladder, and to return to the city he had left under a partial cloud, to flaunt his success. This, in plain language, embodied the motive which made Marchbanks work like a galley-slave during his first months in London.

It is not surprising that such devotion to business, more rare in the young manhood of Britain than of yore, commanded the attention, respect and approbation of his employers. Sir Edward Trent, especially, watched him with an interest which, though for a few weeks it did not find any expression, continued to increase. Of Gilbert Hume, John did not see very much ; evidently, he was the more active partner, and the exigencies of his daily work took him far afield.

John learned that the interests of the firm were confined to no country or clime, but, practically, embraced all the markets of the world. There was much in the vast operations, with which his handling of foreign correspondence put him in touch, to fire the imagination of a young man. John's desire to go abroad grew until it became a perfect passion.

He was very quiet, unassuming, reticent rather than communicative ; and, after a few overtures, he was left pretty much alone by his fellow-workers. His work, being of a more intimate nature than the ordinary routine, necessitated many visits to the private rooms of the heads of the firm, where he quickly became a person much liked, and, what was more important, fully trusted.

One morning, after two hours' close application to foreign correspondence, under the supervision of Sir Edward Trent, the words for which John had been dreading and trying to prepare himself, fell on his ears like a knell.

It was now the seventeenth day of October, and he had been seventeen weeks in London—fifteen at his post in London Wall.

" Our Mr. Tiverton will be able to return next Monday, Mr. Marchbanks. I daresay Mr. Hume has mentioned it to you ? "

" He hasn't, Sir Edward," answered John, and his voice sounded dry and rasping, as his heart sank down to his boots.

" We are very pleased to have Tiverton back ; it has been touch and go with him," said the old gentleman, in his kindliest manner, which was the only one he had ever shown to Marchbanks.

There was another side, however ; a fiery side for evil-doers, which long residence in the East had helped to exaggerate. But there had been nothing about young Marchbanks to call for counsel or reproof. So John naturally regarded him as a very mild-mannered old gentleman, who left the more strenuous manipulation of their world-wide interests to the younger hands.

" Yes, of course, you must be," John said, trying to speak naturally. " Then, do I understand, that after Monday, my services will not be required ? "

" Not here. Though, between ourselves, you have suited us very well here, and we shall miss you. But we can make room for you elsewhere—if you would care to go abroad, that is. There will be, of course, no vacancy here, after Tiverton comes back."

If he cared ! The blood surged up to John's face, and his heart began to beat like a sledge-hammer. Had not the call of the East been in his ears, for years ; and, had it not of late begun to beat so insistently, that it gave him no rest, night or day ? One night, at a concert in the Scottish Club, near his own boarding-house, the rendering of Kipling's song—" The Road to Mandalay "—had made him almost want to cry, for which he had taken himself severely to task. He was sometimes at a loss to understand this longing, though, in his saner moments, he attributed it partly to his associations with the Annans, whose interests were so largely in India.

Sir Edward regarded him interestedly, wondering what that quick flush might portend.

" You wouldn't care about it—eh ? "

" Care about it, sir ! It's been the dream of my life ! " stammered poor John. " And I was beginning to fear I should never get a chance ! "

" Then you would be willing to go on short notice ? "

" On a day's notice, if you like ! " cried John eagerly.

" As it happens, it would be five days' notice. This is Monday—could you be ready to sail for Calcutta on the P. and O. boat, on Friday ? "

" I am quite ready, sir ! "

Sir Edward regarded him with deepening interest.

" You are able to decide quickly. Have you no people who might be inclined to throw cold water on such an expedition ? "

" Only my mother, sir ; and she would not throw any cold water on it," answered John, and the note in his voice struck a minor key.

" Where does she live ? "

" In Glasgow, sir."

" Would you wish to go there, to say good-bye to her ? There hardly seems to be time for that."

" It would not be necessary. I could write and explain. She knew that when I left home, I hoped to go abroad right away ; but things did not go well with me, at the start."

" Ah, I see. Well, I don't want to pry into your private affairs. I will see Mr. Gilbert when he comes in, and, very probably, the appointment will be confirmed ; then you can hear the details. It is a very delicate and important negotiation we wish you to put through, and we think you are the man for it. You know how to hold your tongue, and that is something—in addition to the fact that you can hold it in so many different languages ! " said Sir Edward, with a dry delightful smile.

John's face flushed with pleasure.

" I like languages, sir ; I learn them easily ; and, since I've been here, I've been studying hard at an Oriental class. My teacher says I've made astonishing progress—— "

" I could believe that. Well, it will give me pleasure if you will come and dine at my house, this evening, at a quarter to eight. I live in Lowndes Square. By the by, you may meet some fellow-passengers, who will be on the *Ortolan,* if you sail on Friday. Are you disengaged ? "

" Yes, sir ; thank you," said John, and, when left to himself, his thoughts were in a whirl.

Less than four months' continuous and conscientious labour and application to the first duty at hand had had more pleasing results than fall to the lot of the average plodder.

At one fell swoop, John's self-confidence, which had sustained several rude shocks during the first few days in London, leaped to the highest pitch. Perhaps the invitation to dine pleased him most of all. It raised him to the platform almost of equality with his employer, and certainly, during these months, John's social advantages had been very few. Such as were open to him he had availed himself of rather sparingly, though he was always a welcome visitor at the Scottish Club, which has done so much for the young men who cross the Border to seek their various fortunes.

On the way home, he could not refrain from calling there, to acquaint his kind old friend, the Secretary of the Club, with the good fortune that had befallen him. The words of congratulation and counsel warmed his heart, and his only other errand was to visit, at the last moment, a handy outfitter's shop, to purchase a white tie.

He had not donned his dress clothes since he left Glasgow, the last occasion on which he had worn them having been at a subscription dance he had attended with the Annans and their set.

He thought of that night, as he took his clothes from the drawer, anxiously inspecting them, lest, by any chance, they should not pass muster in the high latitudes in which he was to carry them that evening.

It was a well-made suit, however, bought under the supervision of Roger Annan, who was the chaperon in all matters pertaining to the social amenities.

When he got into his evening clothes and surveyed himself, he was not ill-pleased with what the cheap boarding-house mirror reflected back at him. His face, though thinner than it had been when he left home, had gained in manliness and seriousness of expression. He looked older, by at least five years ; but that pleased him, for it might help him in the strange untried fields where his lot was about to be cast.

He left the boarding-house at half-past seven, took a taxi from the nearest rank and drove, correctly and in proper style, to Lowndes Square.

He was admitted by a footman, who awed him slightly, for there had been no menservants at Balcraig, which had hitherto been his standard of high life. The house, however, was smaller than Balcraig, and less magnificent. The colouring was subdued, and there were a good many evidences of Eastern culture in it—old and priceless Indian and Persian rugs, for instance, whose value and beauty John's untrained eyes hardly gauged. To him they seemed bare and even poor, though he was conscious of the subtle atmosphere, which differed from that of any house he had been in before.

When he heard his name announced loudly and not quite correctly—it being a difficult one for the Southern tongue to compass—he felt his colour rise. As he advanced up the long room he suddenly became conscious that there was nobody in it but a lady, who, however, did not seem at all embarrassed.

"How do you do, Mr. Marchbanks? I'm sorry my uncle is not down yet. But it is not a party—only Major and Mrs. Eastcote, with whom I am travelling to India on Friday, and my brother Gilbert. I hear from Uncle Edward that you are going out in the same boat. How you will love it!—not the boat, nor, necessarily, the company!"—she added, with a demure, somewhat roguish glance which surprised John in a lady so stately and correct.

Long afterwards, trying to describe his first impression of Beatrice Hume, "stately" was the word John used. She was very tall, and though graceful the poise of her shoulders gave the impression of strength, capability, and resource both physical and mental.

She had pale brown hair which, in a bright light, would turn surreptitiously to gold, and very clear grey eyes, which had so candid and direct a glance that it was impossible to shift or prevaricate under their steady light.

She wore a gown of some soft, noiseless, yellow stuff like crepe, with a big damask rose fastened at the waist-band, and a string of pearls about her white neck. Gracious, serene, with that fine unconsciousness of self which is the prerogative of the well and truly bred, she put the shy young man from the North immediately and perceptibly at his ease.

He felt all his pulses quicken, his being awaken, as it were, as he put himself on his mettle. On the social impression he made that night in such company much of his future advancement might depend.

"I am sure I shall like the voyage; but I am afraid I shall not have the opportunity of travelling with you and your friends, Miss Hume. My passage was taken to-day; and, of course, being but a humble representative of the firm, it is a second-class one."

"Oh, but you can come over to dine, of an evening. They often do. A lot of our boys travel second-class, because most of them are hard-up, and none of them have money to throw about. I have never travelled second-cabin myself, but, if I were a man, I should sample everything. It adds so immensely to one's knowledge and experience."

She spoke kindly and sincerely, very favourably impressed by the young Scotsman's direct, sincere mode of speech, and his obvious desire not to sail under any false colours.

Her uncle had already told her all he deemed necessary about him, and she discovered that she had been too ready to dismiss him with the usual casual thought given to chance guests who often appeared without much notice at her uncle's table.

"You think knowledge is power, then?" suggested John with a smile so like his mother's, which so altered his face, as it did hers. Both had a habitual gravity of expression, which some mistook for dullness.

Beatrice Hume, herself a keen student of human nature, noted and responded to that smile, because she was herself a creature of moods and loved the sun.

"It's a very trite old saying, but full of wisdom, as the old things are. I wonder what your impression of India will be. To me, its principal characteristic is antiquity. That and mystery. They are so around one—breathing into one's inner consciousness from the very air that almost it seems for us an impertinence to foist on them our newer civilisation! It is like the pang one feels on seeing Brummagem goods in the native Bazaars."

"But our rule in India is good—isn't it?" asked John, with all the vivid interests he felt in this big new fascinating theme.

"I think so; but you will meet a man to-night—Major Eastcote, of the Diplomatic Service—who is an authority. I believe that he thinks that the British rule in India is in the last stages of the melting-pot, and that something is coming within the next five years to prove it to the uttermost. Either it will be proven practically flawless, or it will be overthrown.

"But what could happen, to bring things to a crisis? —another Mutiny, such as the sedition-mongers, here and in India, are always predicting and trying to fan into life?"

She nodded understandingly.

"Oh no; there will never be another Mutiny! I can't tell you why; but people who have been born in India, and really know and love it, know that it will be something quite outside British rule in India. I've heard them discuss it in military and diplomatic circles. I believe it is a European war they are always thinking of. But, how serious we are becoming! And how late everybody is! If my uncle happened to be down he would have been furious! To-night he will not be able to say a word about decadent London manners!"

"You were born in India then?" asked John Marchbanks.

"Yes—at Simla. My father has a house there on the hills. He is in Calcutta now, and I am going out to attend my sister's marriage in December. I shall stay until the spring, and then I must come back to my uncle—he is so very lonely."

"You keep house for him here?"

"Yes. He came out to us five years ago, after my aunt died, stayed a whole year, and refused to live without me! I have never been back since, though most of my people have been home. I shall love going back, but I should like to take Uncle Edward with me. He says he is too old, and will only send his blessing. Ah, here is Uncle Edward, bringing the Eastcotes—and Gilbert in the rear! I'm so glad to have had this little chat, Mr. Marchbanks; and I shall look forward later on to hearing your opinion—or rather your first impressions of India. I don't believe"—she added, with that straight, earnest glance of hers—"that you will belong to the Brigade who deliver themselves of a final judgment on British rule in India, and can write books about it after they have been three weeks in the country!"

She moved forward to receive her guests—a tall, greyhaired, moustached man, with a very small brown wife, who looked as if the Indian suns had worked their will with her. She was very badly dressed, and showed to little advantage beside Beatrice Hume's vivid and fascinating personality; but later, Marchbanks discovered that Mrs. Eastcote had a charm of her own, and that, further, she had kept the passionate devotion of her distinguished husband through a long life of trial and stress. He learned later, when he knew more of Indian life, that she had braved the terrors and perils of the climate and gone with him everywhere, on the most trying expeditions, making, by her personal devotion and attention, many things possible to him.

She had, early in their married life, made a study of Oriental languages, so that she might be of use; and, though she was now rather frail for the long and adventurous journeys to the very outposts of Empire, which had once been the wonder and despair of her friends, she was still Major Eastcote's right hand.

The atmosphere of that small and most perfectly appointed dinner-table was so quiet and friendly and delightful that more and more young Marchbanks felt himself at his ease.

He had often been less so at the Annans' table, when other guests had been present, and he had even sometimes obtained, in a subtle fashion, the impression that he was there by accident, and that he was expected to efface himself.

But in this new environment there was no such suggestion. Everybody was kind and friendly to him, and he heard much that interested him deeply about the country to which he was going.

Once his opinion on some trivial point was asked, and he replied frankly that he was not entitled to offer any. This so astonished Major Eastcote that he fixed his very keen, penetrating eyes for a long instant on his face.

"It's rather refreshing to hear that from a youngster; and if you carry it out to India you'll do well," he said—a remark which somewhat confused John, who desired nothing less than to attract attention to himself.

When the ladies left the table, Major Eastcote quite deliberately drew his chair towards John, and proceeded to engage him in further conversation, which, incidentally, turned upon the qualities which best fit a man for life in any of the great dependencies of the British Empire.

"Grit, push, and an open eye for the most useful accomplishments," he said emphatically. "And, incidentally, a command of languages. That we have succeeded so well in most parts of the globe, on our very meagre accomplishments in that line, proves that we've got most of the other qualities. I'm sorry I have no children, but if I'd had a round dozen, I'd have seen to it that at least the half of them became expert linguists!"

John ventured to explain modestly that the study of languages was the one he was most interested in.

"Well, stick to it, and you'll never regret it. A man I know away up in the northernest frontier, a man who has done unheard-of service for us in India, but who prefers to remain practically unrewarded, owes his success to his extraordinary command of the native tongue. Through it, he has acquired inside knowledge of the native mind, which is of more value than all the text-books on government, or on war, in the world. Mark, learn, and inwardly digest that, and you may have a chance in India. We tried to din it into the ears of various subalterns, but they don't heed——"

"Is the man you speak of a soldier?" asked John, deeply interested.

"No—a civilian; but he's done a sight more for India than many soldiers. I tell him he must come to his own one of these days. I haven't seen him for six years. He hasn't been out of Afghanistan since then."

"May I ask his name?"

"Oh, yes; why not? He's a countryman of yours—came from the Lowlands, I believe—belongs to a very good southern family—name of Jardine—Langham Jardine, to give him his full title and designation. He has the worst signature in Christendom; more difficult to decipher than Hindustani!"

At that moment some one else interrupted, and the talk became more general.

But the name lingered in John's mind ; and, after he was back in his boarding-house bedroom, he wrote it down in his diary against the date which had undoubtedly marked an epoch in his career.

The evening, so far as he was concerned, had been a complete success, and he left the house with the pleasant and comfortable assurance that he had created an impression at least not unfavourable.

Next morning this consciousness was confirmed by Sir Edward Trent, when they met at Haviland House.

" Morning, Marchbanks. I hope you enjoyed yourself last night ? You made a new friend ; and, I can tell you, that is an event in a man's life—especially when it happens to be a friend of such quality ! "

The ready flush sprang to John's face. He was often annoyed at what his new knowledge of the world inclined him to regard as a foolish habit, not aware that it made part of the personality which won him friends in unexpected quarters.

" Major Eastcote had a great many questions to put to me about you after you left ; and, if you take my advice, you'll make the most of your opportunities on board. He is in a position to help any young fellow along in the East, though I told him he must not poach on our preserves ! "

" It is very kind of Major Eastcote, and it was a tremendous privilege for me to meet him. I am very grateful to you, sir, for giving me the chance."

" That's all right. And I was saying to Gilbert this morning that, as you know the Eastcotes and my niece now, it might be better if you travelled in the same class. We don't usually allow more than second-class fare to our people, except under special circumstances, but I think this occasion will warrant it. You'll have to see about your kit this morning. Mr. Gilbert will be at liberty at eleven, and will go out with you. There isn't anything pertaining to Indian outfit he hasn't at his finger-ends."

This sudden change and uplift in his position and prospects was calculated to send John's thoughts in a whirl. The next two days passed as in the twinkling of an eye, and even had he been more than anxious, he could not have spared the time to go to Scotland and bid his mother goodbye.

Yet, strange to say, he thought more of her during these strenuous days, and with a deeper tenderness and yearning, than at any period since he left her.

It was on the last night of his London life in his boarding-house room, with his travelling gear and the debris of his packing all about him, that he sat down to write to her for the first time since he left Glasgow. He found words difficult, nay, almost impossible to come ; and, though it was a kind, regretful letter, breathing part of the remorse which undoubtedly lurked at the bottom of his heart, it failed to express a tithe of his feelings.

Another great opportunity was lost. Another milestone passed ! And, before the letter reached its destination, John Marchbanks was tossing in the Bay of Biscay.

Much, very much was to happen of tremendous import to him before he, once more, set foot in his native land !

CHAPTER XVI

JOHN'S MOTHER

MR. ANNAN held somewhat patriarchal ideas about family life.

One of a large family himself, he had been reared with the utmost strictness on the old Calvinistic lines. A considerable residence in the East had somewhat broadened these lines, but to some of the old tenets of parenthood he still adhered, and so he was full of wrath against the continuous and insistent cry for liberty on the part of the rising generation.

One of his favourite axioms was that the young had no need, nor indeed any right to money until it was earned by themselves.

In the twentieth century in a luxurious Glasgow home it is a little difficult to enforce these old-fashioned ideas. His conscientious endeavour to do so had been the cause of much of the family friction.

Elizabeth, for instance, had never had a dress allowance, nor any money she could legitimately regard and use as her own. Her father—still in pursuit of the patriarchal idea—had frequently informed her that so long as women got all they wanted in the way of clothes, and an occasional half-sovereign for pocket-money, they surely needed nothing more.

In vain Elizabeth had tried to point out the false logic of this, disclaiming passionately against the treatment of her sex as a mere chattel, and had even gone the length of threatening to go out and earn her own living.

Her father had never taken this threat seriously, and had added insult to injury on the occasion when it was made by presenting her with a five pound note which was, figuratively speaking, a soothing pat on the back. Now, Elizabeth ought to have refused this bounty with suitable indignation, but a five pound note is a five pound note, and she, a very woman, had never been able to refuse it.

She was a queer mass of contradictions, and what her nature needed, undoubtedly, was discipline.

With the boys the hard-and-fast rule regarding money had been less successful. George, who had always been a solid, steady boy, had resented it deeply, but escaped from it sooner by being sent out to Calcutta to the care of James Wilson, the Manager of the Calcutta branch, when a disordered liver demanded his father's release from India. It had also been rather disastrous for Roger. Obviously, when a young man or maiden is reared without being taught the spending value of money, mistakes and disasters are bound to ensue. Just occasionally some of them may prove to be irreparable.

Roger Annan was a young man of expensive tastes, and his bank salary was insufficient to meet them.

Mr. Annan made the mistake of charging him nothing for his board, and considered, perhaps justly, that two pounds per week was quite sufficient money to throw about on trifles. Roger never had enough, and was constantly floundering in a sea of unpaid bills. What the lad needed was a little honest and kindly guiding which, oddly enough, he received from neither of his parents though they were such good and conscientious people.

John Marchbanks had been his salvation time and again, and the Annans owed far more than they had the slightest idea of to that ineligible young man, whom they had, with the instinct of self-preservation, hounded from their house.

Marchbanks, reared in a harder school, and knowing to the uttermost the spending value of every penny, had no inclination to waste money, and had acted as a very considerable and useful brake on Roger. But remove the brake from any machine standing on an incline and what happens? It begins, slowly but surely to slide down towards the bottom.

On the Monday following John Marchbanks' departure from Glasgow the Annans, as a family, went to their house on the Gareloch. Roger, however, elected to remain at Balcraig, where the gardener and his wife—an old family servant—were left as caretakers.

This arrangement had worked excellently for several years now, and there was no objection made to it on this occasion, although Mrs. Annan had some secret fears concerning Roger.

Some of these she voiced to him on the Sunday night, when she came into his room to say good night.

"I've been thinking, Roger, that it would be much happier and cheerier for us all if you just travelled up and down with father instead of stopping here."

Roger, who was winding his watch at the dressing-table, turned round with his smile which was always ready, even in his black hours.

"Mater, I don't think! You know how I hate getting up so early on beastly wet mornings and sailing at unholy hours. What's put this into your dear little noddle?"

Roger had a caressing way with women, and he was undoubtedly fond of his mother.

"I would feel happier. But you will be a good boy—won't you?—and not vex father. He has enough of worries; and the last letter from George doesn't give a very good account of things in Calcutta. Father was actually saying it was possible he might have to go out."

"The pater looks on the dark side," answered Roger lightly. "And we mustn't encourage him. Of course I'll be a good boy, though I'm feeling it pretty rotten in Glasgow, now Jack has gone away."

Mrs. Annan winced, for her conscience was not quite clear about John Marchbanks.

"You must try and get over that. After all, he wasn't your only friend, Roger."

"No—only the best one," he answered gloomily; and these words were sufficient to keep his mother awake half the night.

Roger had his way, and remained in town after his family had departed to Kilcrean, to which he wended his way usually on Saturday afternoons for the week-end.

The Dunsyres had a palatial place at Hunter's Quay, with a yacht, and all the other luxuries the rich man can collect for his family; but oddly enough, not one of the young people whom fortune had favoured was really happy, but all were straining after something beyond reach.

Had Roger been really in love with Kitty, all might have been well; she was more than favourably inclined towards him, but he was a very slack wooer; and when he did not look near Hunter's Quay for a whole month after they settled there for the summer, her pride came to her assistance.

Truth to tell, Roger was not playing the game in Glasgow; but it is unnecessary to enter into particulars regarding these wasted weeks.

When a young man turns his eyes and his feet towards the broad road, there are plenty to encourage him down the steep incline. One secret sin his father had only a very little inkling of, and that was his passion for gambling in any form, but more particularly at cards; and he was the fastest and most reckless member of a little gang that had its head-quarters in one of the most fashionable west-end clubs.

Now, it being one of the unwritten laws that gambling debts must be paid on the spot, Roger Annan was often in a tight hole for the lack of ready money. He borrowed where he could, but there came a day, in the late autumn, when he was at his wits' end, and when a clean breast must be made of things to his father and mother if he were to get clear of the horrible entanglement in which he found himself.

From just such a hole John Marchbanks had pulled him about a year before, and a critical and perilous moment seemed to accentuate his loss to an unendurable degree.

This was the simple explanation of a visit Ellen Marchbanks had, one beautiful autumn night, from a wild-eyed and rather dissipated-looking young man, who dropped off the car between six and seven o'clock, at the moment when he ought, according to arrangement and expectations, to have been getting ready for his father's dinner-table.

Ellen was still prosecuting her calling at Shawlands, and had now taken Katrine Polson as a permanent inmate of her house. It was an excellent arrangement for both parties, for Katrine was not only a demon for work, but she was a most cheerful, philosophical, and original-minded companion.

Her gratitude and astonishment at having been offered a permanent home was so great that no amount of service rendered could ever repay the debt she imagined she owed to Mrs. Marchbanks.

The only way her elemental soul could repay that debt was by the prodigious and unceasing labour of her hands, and a personal devotion such as is bestowed on very few. Ellen found herself so mothered and cared for, and looked after, that she soon wondered how she had managed to exist before. The house was a marvel of cleanliness and daintiness, and Katrine, promoted to black frock cap, and apron, was very proud of herself.

The great ambition of her life was to be allowed occasional service in the shop, and she took surreptitious lessons from Jimmy in the art of careful and just weighing and certain other mysteries known only to the successful shop-keeper.

Katrine opened the door to the gentleman asking for her mistress, but when he mentioned his name, she regarded him askance. Somehow, Katrine associated all her mistress's darker moods with the name of Annan, and had, therefore, no love for the sound thereof. So her affirmative answer to his civil inquiry for Mrs. Marchbanks was very dry, even suspicious in tone.

"She's in," she admitted. "Bide there, an' I'll ask whether she'll see ye."

So Roger was left to kick his heels on the stone landing till the ungracious vassal came back and indicated, by a jerk of her thumb and a queer little nod, that he might enter.

He left his hat and stick on the lobby table, and passed through the open door in to the sitting-room where Ellen was sitting quietly at her sewing.

She rose to welcome him with a polite good evening, but did not offer her hand. She seemed to stiffen a little, though there was something about the forlorn appearance of the young man which appealed to her motherly heart. And John had been very fond of him, and had said more than once during what Ellen now, in her mind, called "the black week," which had stolen him from her, that Roger was not to blame for what happened.

"I've often heard of you, Mrs. Marchbanks," said Roger, quite humbly.

"I suppose Jack must have mentioned my name to you once or twice?"

"He often spoke of you, Mr. Annan."

"My name's Roger," said the young man, "and I've come to ask whether you've heard anything about Jack?"

Ellen's face was very serene, and in her eyes there was a deep content. The hunger of her heart had been stilled by the letter written on the last night John had spent in London, telling her of his plans and bidding her good-bye. It had not been a long letter, but its tone had entirely satisfied her; and it was lying now inside the bodice of her gown, near her heart, where it had lain since its arrival.

"I had a letter from him on Friday night," she answered, and there was a thrill of pride in her voice.

"No," said Roger with a start. "And where is he? I've wanted to come ever so often, Mrs. Marchbanks, but, somehow, I felt I hadn't the right."

"John never blamed you for what happened, Mr. Roger; and, anyway, it wasn't a bad thing in the end. It has been the making of him. He sailed on Friday to take up a splendid appointment in Calcutta."

"In Calcutta!" repeated Roger in amazement. "Why, I expected to go there this month, but my governor's changed his mind, and says he'll need to go himself. Calcutta! Fancy old Jack in Calcutta! Who is he with?"

"A very large and splendid firm," said the mother with her air of quiet pride. "They have branches all over the world."

"Wonder he didn't go to the Argentine then. That was the country he was always talking about. India's played out. I wouldn't have gone there if I had been in his shoes."

"Ah, but you see, the firm he has been with since ever he went to London——"

"Hasn't he been any further than London all this time?" interrupted Roger in a puzzled voice. "If I'd known, I'd have run up for a week-end to see him."

"He has been in the London office."

"What's the name of the firm? I might just happen to know it."

"Messrs. Trent, Bartlett & Hume, Haviland House, London Wall," answered Ellen, who had learned all the salient points in her son's letter by heart.

"I'll ask my pater, like as not he knows them. Most of the big firms have a sort of corresponding connection, don't you know. So old Jack only sailed yesterday! And how is he!"

"He is very well, and writes in the best of spirits. He was dining with a number of distinguished people at Sir Edward Trent's house on the night he wrote my letter. He was very sorry he could not take a run home, but it was all arranged in a hurry, and he was the only man who could do the work required. It has something to do with languages. My son was always fond of languages."

"And swotted no end at them!" added Roger. "I'm jolly sorry I didn't know that he was in London all this time. Glasgow hasn't been the same since he left it, Mrs. Marchbanks. I'll never have a pal like him again!"

To this Ellen made no reply, but her mouth hardened a little as she took up her sewing again and put a fresh thread in her needle.

All the time she was wondering what had brought Roger Annan to see her at this late day, and though her indignation against the family had cooled, she had no desire to encourage any of them about the house.

"What's the name of the boat he sailed on? If I'd known I'd have been on it, too!" he cried with a sudden passion. "For I'm mortally sick of Glasgow and all it contains."

"Oh, but you shouldn't talk like that, my man—you that has everything Glasgow can give you," said Ellen with an odd mixture of sadness and reproof.

"Everything Glasgow can give me!" he cried in a burst of passion which surprised her. "I haven't as much in my pocket now as would tinkle on a tombstone! And I'm in such a hole that I don't know what to do with myself! If I'd had Jack, I never would have been in this hole. No, nor anywhere near it! I tell you they had no business to rob me of my best pal and leave me on my beam-ends."

At this poignant cry Ellen's face softened wonderfully. Born to trouble herself, companioned by it all through life, she had kinship with the suffering and the tried, so many of whom she had helped to take the right turning.

"I suppose it's because he was always so jolly, so ready to help, so understanding; and because he never sat in judgment, that I want Jack so badly to-night, that I came here. I'll be going now, Mrs. Marchbanks, for, of course, I had no right to come, and I apologise for it now."

"Sit down, my dear. As Jack isn't here, perhaps Jack's mother might help," she said, and the change that came over her was marvellous. "I've seen a lot of trouble—I've supped with it, and risen with it in the morning, and I'll help you if I can for my own son's sake."

"Would you, though? But I don't know if you can, but I'd like to tell you if you'd listen, for I am in a black pit of trouble, and I don't know how I am to get out of it!"

"Tell me," she said gently, "and don't hurry yourself. I've nothing else to do but listen, and it'll be a queer thing if I can't help. There are few troubles in this life I don't know something about."

"Ah, but this I've brought on myself!" said Roger hotly. "Perhaps you won't understand—though Jack did, because he came about Balcraig, and knew how we lived there. It's a big house, and my father reigns in it like a sort of autocrat, and what he forgets is that we are all grown up, and need a different sort of handling than what we got when we were children."

"That's a fault common to parents," said Ellen with a slight smile. "But it sorts itself out in the end."

"That may be, but sometimes the end comes rather late to be of much use. One thing he doesn't understand and never will understand till the day of doom—that a young man needs money and can't live without it!"

"But don't you have enough to live on?" asked Ellen in amazement. "Johnnie used to say that you had all your salary to do what you liked with, and that it was a mistake."

"I know he thought that. But Jack had no expensive tastes," groaned Roger. "You brought him up with common sense. My salary!—What is it? A beggarly two pounds a week! My tailor's bill swallows more than the half of it, and I never have the clothes I want! Then there are other expenses a man incurs about town when he belongs to an expensive club, and hob-nobs with chaps who have unlimited cash. I got myself into a pretty tight hole once, about eighteen months ago, incurring a debt that couldn't wait, and I hadn't the money, and Jack found it—did he tell you?"

Ellen shook her head.

"That's the last thing he would have told me, my dear," she said with a quiet glow of pride in her kind eyes.

"I owed sixty-eight pounds, by Gad! And Jack paid every penny of it, and I've never paid him back—that's the beastly thing that's rankling in my mind, and so, now, you know how bad I felt about the way they treated him at home. I hoped to get away to Calcutta this month. I might even have been sailing in Jack's boat if my governor hadn't put a fresh spoke in my wheel! It's this being treated like a baby which undermines a chap and makes him don't care what he does next."

"But your father, whom I saw once, struck me as being a very shrewd man of business. Probably he has good and sufficient reasons for his change of plans."

"Oh, I dare say they seem that to him, but they've dished me, and he knows it—but he'll maybe know it better soon, unless I can get out of this hole I'm in."

"What is the hole?" asked Ellen. "Maybe I can help you as Jack did."

Roger shook his head.

"It isn't likely. But I will tell you, for I have been in hell for the last week, and now my people have come up from the coast I live in a sort of terror. I owed money—not so much as before, but forty-seven pounds odd, and I—I helped myself from the bank, don't you know? And if I don't make it good before the end of the week, why, I suppose I'll maybe see the inside of Duke Street, then my father will maybe know what he has brought on me and himself."

Ellen listened, not in the least horrified; for many sordid stories had she listened to in the last twenty years—stories of human weakness, crime, and misery, and she had become a sort of expert in dealing with them.

There is no more unerring judge of human nature than the soul in jeopardy; it has a sort of homing instinct for the one who is able and willing to help.

She put down her needlework and sat forward a little, looking at the pale, distraught face of Roger Annan with a mingling of sadness and compassion which gave much sweetness to her own. It was the face of the mother whose heart is big enough for the woes of all childhood; indeed, to her Roger Annan seemed nothing more than a big, inconsequent, reckless child who, hunting about for a scapegoat, had no blame for himself.

"Was this what happened before?" she said.

"Yes, just the same. And Jack, though he paid the money, was awfully hard on me. You should have heard him, Mrs. Marchbanks! And I really kept straight, and didn't touch a card or a drop of anything stronger than claret and water for over six months! Then, somehow, I got a bit slack. It was beginning just before he left Glasgow, and, of course, after they actually hounded him away it was all up with me."

Into Ellen's heart as she listened crept a quiet, unutterable thankfulness. For she—the poor woman, the despised by her west-end neighbours—had been spared such suffering, and could still be proud of, and thank God for, her son!

"I've got the money, my dear," she said gently, but with a kind of quiet firmness. "And though every penny of it has been earned, I could give it to you without missing it. But I'm not sure whether I ought, for your sake. Will you take a little advice from Jack's mother?"

"Advice? Of course! I'm gasping for it! It's because Jack wasn't about with his that I'm in this hole," he said disconsolately.

"Well, if you were my son, I would pray God to touch your heart so that you'd go and make a clean breast of it to your father and mother."

"To my mother I might, but my father would put me out of the house!" he said gloomily. "And my mother hasn't got any money except what he gives her. We live in the regular old patriarchal style—all dependent on his bounty. George is the only one that has escaped, and even he has to give strict account from Calcutta. What my father never seems to think is that when he's done with it all he'll have to leave us without a notion how to use it ! Spend it we could, of course, and pretty soon make ducks and drakes of it ! "

The truth underlying these bitter words smote hard on Ellen Marchbank's heart.

" Go home and sleep on it, my dear. But before you sleep, make a big effort and lay bare your heart to your father. Talk to him as you've talked to me. It may be that he doesn't know how things are with you because nobody has pointed it out to him. And he must have a father's heart ; try and get to it ; and, if everything fails, come back to me here to-morrow night and I'll lend you the money, to be paid back in instalments at a fixed rate of interest, for I'm not a millionaire like Jack, and I don't intend to lose it."

She smiled as she spoke, and Roger's gloomy face suddenly became illumined as he sprang to his feet.

" Mrs. Marchbanks if you do this for me I'll—I'll turn over a new leaf for your sake ! "

" Not for my sake, but for your own mother's sake. But I haven't your promise that you will try and make a clean breast of it to your father ? Believe me, laddie, that will be your best course. If I know anything about men, it'll be the right way with Mr. Annan. He came here once, and I think he would not be ill to deal with if you took him the right way."

Roger somewhat hopelessly shook his head.

" I'll try, since you put it like that, but I don't believe for a minute it'll be of the slightest use."

" It's worth trying. I've been through seas and oceans of trouble, my dear, and have proved that the only path is the straight path. It's a wee bit harder to keep at the moment, but it pays—pays in the end. Get into it, and bide in it ; and the first step is to take your own father into your confidence. It's because you've left him on the outside this big wall has grown up between you. Fathers and mothers don't like the outside edge, my dear. Maybe some day when you've little bairns of your own you'll mind these words and know how true they are."

He wrung her hand and promised again at the door that he would take her advice, every bit of it ; and, further, that she might expect to see him next night about the same time.

After he had gone Katrine Polson, deeply interested, came creeping back to the parlour ostensibly for the purpose of laying the supper cloth.

" That's a likely young fellow," she said experimentally. " But he has trouble in his e'e. He'll ha'e trouble frae a big broad-shouldered man wi' white hair an' a reddish face."

" Katrine, stop your nonsense ! " said her mistress with unwonted sharpness. " I wish you wouldn't turn everything into your teacup haivers ! "

" They're as guid a sign-post as ony," observed Katrine stolidly. " I've never kent them wrang. Did I no' tell ye aboot the letter ye got on Friday ? It was at the bottom o' my cup for mair nor a week afore postie brocht it."

But Ellen did not answer, her thoughts being far away.

" I've jist been lookin' in my cup for him while he was in here, an' there's the shadow o' the jile ower him—that wad bring doon the high Annan pride ! "

" Hold your tongue, you uncanny creature ! " cried Ellen sharply. " I believe you've been listening at the door."

" Me an' my kind disna need to listen at doors," observed Katrine with her slow, dry smile. " I wadna wonder, noo, but that you've gien him money in spite o' a' they've dune to ye ! What they did to Maister Jack didna maitter —they were but the instruments o' destiny. But dinna you haud oot hard-earned siller to ony Annan among them ! Faur better gie it to me to tak' care o'."

" Go and bring my supper in and talk less, my woman," said Ellen, but her tone had regained its ordinary level.

She was struck by Katrine's forecast, and however much she might deride her prognostications, some of them had come perilously near what had actually happened.

This particular one was fully verified, for, when Roger Annan entered the Balcraig smoking-room that night for the purpose of trying the barometer as it were, such black thunder was on his father's brow that he knew his confession had been forestalled.

It was an awful moment when he rose to face him.

And then the storm burst—such a storm as had never before been heard in the house of Balcraig !

CHAPTER XVII

REAL TROUBLE

THERE was some excuse for Mr. Annan's wrath.

He had prided himself through a long and successful career on the blamelessness of his methods, his impregnable integrity, his business and family honour. That it should be threatened by any bearing his name had never come within the farthest limits of possibility.

But it had come, and his brows were dark as they bent on the son who had brought shame upon the name he bore.

" Shut that door ! " he said thickly. " Shut it close, for there may be that between me and you that it won't do for the rest of the house to hear."

Roger shut the door and set his back against it. He did not lack courage, and now that the worst had come, he would meet it as best he could. Nay, with it, there was a certain amount of relief which was welcome.

" Craighead has been here," his father began in a harsh, high voice, which bore little resemblance to his usual well-modulated pleasant tones.

" Oh, he has—has he ? " answered Roger fatuously. " And what did old Craighead say ? "

Roger's flippancy, though merely assumed to hide genuine consternation, so enraged his father that his hand involuntarily clenched by his side.

" Don't stand there like a grinning ape when you know your guilt ! That you, my son, bearing my name, should descend to the level of the common thief ! "

" Hold hard—I'm not that ! " said Roger, wincing. " I helped myself, I own, but I can pay it back. I've got the money—at least, I shall have it to-morrow. Where is old Craighead ? I can settle his little account."

" It is settled," said Mr. Annan, and the veins were standing out on his temples as he made the admission which cost him dear. " He came here quietly like the friend he is to tell me privately what had happened, and to offer to let you off. If it weren't for your mother and for other things there would be no letting off, my man ! What's to hinder me from telephoning now to the police station and having you arrested as you deserve ?"

" Nothing in the world," Roger admitted with a queer, jaunty little crack in his voice. " Why not do it now ? "

A look of anguish that was almost malignant passed over the elder man's face. He had no inward discernment, and could not grasp the fact that the boy was actually writhing under the lash of his tongue and was not responsible for any words that might fall from his lips.

" It seems useless to try to bring you to any realisation of the depths you've sunk to, Roger. I shall not even try. But can you tell me how or why you became capable of this infamy—you, who have had everything all your life which a lad's heart could desire ? "

"Everything but one thing," said Roger sullenly. "Proper guiding and direction about money. We've never been treated like men. Even George has told me how it has handicapped him out in Calcutta! You can't make bricks without straw, and the chap who is treated like a child behaves like one to the end of the chapter, that's all. You've tried to drive us like a little flock of sheep in front of you, and one of us has strayed out of bounds—that's all the explanation there is. Well—if you're going to speak on the telephone, get it over. I'm ready, and I don't care a hang anyway!"

Mr. Annan took a faltering step across the floor, pushing his hand through his thinning grey hair which this might easily turn white.

"I won't telephone, because Craighead, like the good friend he is, has given you a chance. No—you don't go back to the bank—there are limits to man's mercy just as there are limits to divine mercy."

"What do you know about that anyway?" asked Roger rather mockingly. "You've never had to take it. It's only the like of me that needs it; and I'm not afraid of its quality! It isn't so hard as the mercy of human beings."

This tremendous truth did not strike Mr. Annan at the moment, though afterwards it came back on him like an avalanche.

"Look here, Roger," he said sternly. "Such speech is unbecoming in the circumstances, even criminal. What you don't appear to understand is that through the amazing kindness and consideration of Mr. Craighead, you are going to escape the felon's cell."

"Shouldn't care a hang if I were in it now!" said Roger again. "At least, it would save me posing as anything else."

"The money has been paid, and you will sail by the earliest possible boat for Calcutta. I will cable to George in the morning to wait my instructions. Wilson and George may be able to do what I apparently have been unable to do. I haven't deserved your reproaches, Roger, and the day will perhaps come when they will recoil on your own head. You've had a good home, the best of everything, and you've never appreciated any of it. Now you will taste some of the hards. Wilson will be told the truth—likewise George."

"Not George, father?" said Roger, and for the moment the old, wistful look crept back to the lad's face, the pleading look one sees in the eyes of a child.

It made a curious appeal to his father, but he hardened his heart.

"George shall be told," he said firmly. "It is due to him. He has never cost me a moment's anxiety, and he must know why he is condemned to another year out there when his time is up, and he had been promised a long furlough."

"I can go about yet without a leading string!" said Roger quickly. "And I refuse to go to India on these terms."

Mr. Annan, who had paused by the desk, made as if to lift the receiver from the telephone.

Roger did not wince.

"I don't care. Do it if you like, it would save a lot of bother and shift the responsibility from you. And, while we're threshing out all this, I may as well tell you that you did me a very ill turn when you hounded John Marchbanks out of Glasgow. He was my best friend—the only one who kept me straight. He took me out of the same kind of hole eighteen months ago—never hesitated a moment—paid sixty-eight pounds down on the nail for me, and he's never had a penny of it back. He didn't think anything of that, because Jack, though you chose to despise him, had a prince's heart, and money was just like the dirt under his feet. He didn't set it up and worship it like a god as they do out here. It has its uses, and one of them was to help the lame dogs like me over stiles. If he'd been here yet this would never have happened, for I kept straight for his sake and nobody else's for over a year; I'd have been straight now if you hadn't hounded him away.

Mr. Annan winced at this long indictment.

"It only shows what a low estimate of friendship and honour you have," he said in the same stern voice. "To take money from a man in Marchbanks' position! You ought to have had more respect for yourself and the name you bear! I can see that this talk is going from bad to worse, Roger, and we'd better end it. Your mother knows nothing about this, and it is my desire that you should not tell her. She is not very strong, and there is no knowing what disastrous consequences it might have for her. Can you be relied on to hold your tongue?"

"I don't know. My mother would understand at least. She ought to have been the father, and there would never have been any trouble of this kind! One can explain things to her. You never would have understood explanations—even if they had been offered! What you expect is that everybody should be melted and poured into the Annan mould! I tell you it can't be done. You may consider it the best in the world, but there's nothing human about it."

These home-truths delivered for the first time certainly left nothing to the imagination! Poor Mr. Annan seemed to shrivel under the weight of them even while his indignation and wrath knew no bounds.

While he was trying to frame some further and more convincing remonstrance, Roger very quietly opened the door and walked out.

The interview so eminently unsatisfactory on both sides ended miserably, leaving the father in the throes of distress. He desired, if possible, to keep the truth from his wife, yet never had he needed her counsel and sympathy more.

While he was standing helplessly by the table pondering on the downfall of his family hopes stricken by the first breath of disgrace, for, though Craighead had generously promised absolute secrecy, the knowledge that he knew was bitter to Robert Annan's taste; while he was thus pondering, half distraught, the door opened softly and his wife came in.

Never had she looked more like an angel in the house. Her sweet face so delicately coloured seemed accentuated by the soft lilac of the pretty evening frock she wore. Mrs. Annan had lost none of the daintiness of her youth, and bestowed more pains on her toilet than Elizabeth approved. Her answer would be that it was a woman's duty to make herself as attractive as possible; more especially for those in the house with her.

Elizabeth had not yet reached this high standard, and affected to regard it as a sign of the subjection of women.

"Something gone wrong, dear?" she said, hastening to her husband's side. "That was Roger who went out and banged the door. And why was Mr. Craighead here? Why did he go in a hurry, too? What kind of bad things are happening, or going to happen?"

Then he blurted it all out. She was not in the least surprised. Neither did she collapse, nor even exhibit the signs of distress which he fully expected, not without anxiety as to their effects.

It is in the sorrows of life that women prove themselves often stronger, more patient, and more resourceful than men, more especially those sorrows of the heart which so continually remind us that here we have no abiding city.

Men quail and stagger under them, their fighting powers being reserved for the strife of the market-place. So, while her cheeks whitened and her lips grew wan, Mrs. Annan maintained her calmness of manner, and was even able to throw a little light on the dark cloud.

"No—I'm not surprised as you would think, Robert; for, of course, I've known for a long time that Roger has not been behaving himself."

"You've known it for a long time!" he repeated irritably. "Then why in heaven's name didn't you mention it? Something might have been done to prevent things coming to this horrible position."

"You have very little patience with the bairns, my dear, unless they are walking in a straight line behind you," she said rather sadly, repeating, word for word almost Roger's charge against him, though in a different spirit. "And I was always hoping something would happen—that Kitty would pull him up sharply, maybe, and make a man of him by marrying him."

"Catch a Dunsyre marrying an undesirable! You may trust old Dan for that, Mary! Depend upon it, he knows all about our Roger—he must do so, because Archie is so often in the same boat; but he wouldn't let any girl of his marry where there is no money or, as in this case, no character——"

Mrs. Annan permitted this bitter reflection to pass unchallenged.

"And what are you going to do then, Bob? You've paid the money to Mr. Craighead, you say, and he won't take proceedings; but, of course, he can't be expected to let Roger come back to the bank."

"No, no! That door is shut for ever, as every other door would be, if the truth were known. I've told Roger he'll go to Calcutta next week, and I'll wire to Wilson in the morning and tell him to prepare and wait for my letter. And George can't come home till the spring—maybe not till next autumn. This has knocked every plan on the head, and we've all got to suffer for it."

Mrs. Annan felt the injustice and also the futility of such a programme. It embodied the whole weakness of her husband's character—that secret of inner weakness which is known only to the wife of a man's bosom.

So mightily afraid was he of any smirch on the name of Annan, so determined that Roger should be cleared out before anything should leak out, that he did not care who might suffer in the process.

George had been seven years in Calcutta without a break, and he was very home-sick. The very boat for his return had been fixed in his last letter, and only his mother knew, from private bits he had enclosed in his home letters, how his heart and soul were set upon it. But, so well did she know her husband's cast of mind, that she did not press the point at the moment. Instead, she asked abruptly:

"Where has Roger gone? And were you very hard on him, Robert?"

"Hard on him! Hard on him! Woman, I wonder to hear you! I told him the truth, man to man. It's not a moment for soft sawder! You don't appear to realise what he's done, Mary."

"I realise it very well; but I know what the laddie is—what a mixture of weakness and good qualities. He has never been in his right place, my dear, not had enough of responsibility——"

"Good heavens! Haven't I told you all along I've been waiting for him to show himself worthy of it?"

"Responsibility makes men," she answered him with spirit. "What state was he in when he left the house? You don't think," she added with a furtive anxiety, "that he would do any harm to himself?"

"Tch!" cried Mr. Annan in extreme scorn. "More likely he's gone for a blow-out with some of his cronies. He took it as light as air here, and is farther off from comprehending what he has done, or that he has any responsibility towards me, than he ever was! Where he's got that black strain in him I don't know! It makes one hark back to his grandfather Dempster——"

Grandfather Dempster being Mrs. Annan's own father, the affront was very personal; but her charity was large enough to bury it decently. She knew that her husband was not himself, that his pride had gotten a serious blow and that it would require all her wifely tact and skill to tide over this terrible crisis in the family history.

She sat down suddenly on the edge of a chair, but said nothing about the faintness which threatened her heart. It had been coming oftener of late, and she would often have to pause, breathless, at the top of the shallowest stair and feel for the faint fluttering of a rebellious and halting heart.

"Lisbeth has been saying a good deal lately about India, Robert," she began in a very low quiet voice. "How would it do to send her out with Roger to spend the winter with Mrs. Wilson? She needs a change, and that would be the best she could get."

"Send her as jailer to her brother! A bonnie pair they'd make! Why, she might end up the voyage by eloping with the purser!"

Mrs. Annan's lips tightened.

"She's not that kind, and I still think you were very hard on her about John Marchbanks. And Roger has missed him terribly. I wish I were easy in my mind about it. I can't help thinking that all this may be a judgment on us for what we did to that lad."

This was the last straw for Mr. Annan, and resulted in an exhibition towards his wife of which he was seldom guilty. She retired in the midst of it with some dignity, telling him she would come back and talk to him when he knew how to behave himself and how to control himself, though her tears fell as she began to mount the stairs.

Altogether there never had been a sharper, more painful interlude between that husband and wife, and both were perfectly convinced that only the other was to blame. Mr. Annan was, if anything, the more uncomfortable, however, as he had listened to a great many startling and very plain spoken statements, some of which, his inner consciousness assured him, were perfectly true.

The truth in family matters is bound to be unpalatable to some one, truth's function being the tearing of scales from blinded eyes.

Meanwhile, the cause of this black cloud that had descended upon a peaceable home, having flung himself out of the house, had no idea where to go for a crumb of comfort. At the cross-ways just opposite the closed gates of Balcraig he hesitated as to whether he would go to the Dunsyres and tell Kitty all about it. But the uncertainty of finding her alone and the difficulty of concocting a very coherent or plausible story out of what had happened deterred him. He accordingly walked to the nearest point where a tram could be obtained and took the first one going citywards.

Arrived there, he hesitated betwixt two—wondering whether he would go and have a regular burst at the club and paint the town red, or whether he would go out to Shawlands once more and acquaint John's mother with the miserable attempt to follow her advice to make a clean breast of it to his father. He had gone home with the best intentions, but some strange spark of rebellion, which at the moment had almost amounted to hate, had thrust back all his softer impulses and forced to his lips words that had only fanned the flame.

To seek John's mother, won ; and he got out to Shawlands between half-past eight and nine. He ran up the stone stairs and rang the bell and expected the cross-eyed weird-looking servant to admit him. But instead, a girl opened the door—a very sweet-faced, winning girl, in a blue serge skirt, a white lingerie blouse as pure as drifted snow, and a coquettish little hat pushed back on her head so that the gold of her hair was visible. An extraordinarily pretty girl ! And Roger's heart was always soft to any of that ilk !

" I'm sorry to trouble you, but I want to see Mrs. Marchbanks," he said very courteously.

" Oh, come in. She won't be long. She's gone with her servant to see a woman across the street who fell down in a fit. They're always sending for her like that—she's the nearest doctor ! "

She smiled as she spoke these words and held the door invitingly open.

Roger walked in.

" Well—if you think she won't be long ? "

" She would be sorry if you went away without seeing her, Mr. —— "

" My name is Annan," said Roger ; and fortunately at the moment, Annie Houston had turned towards the sitting-room door so that he did not notice the little start she gave.

A meal was spread on one end of the table—rather a dainty meal—and when Roger saw the tempting-looking dish of tongue and salad, and the fresh pats of butter and the new white scones, he remembered that he had had no dinner.

" You don't live here, do you ? You are not by any chance a Miss Marchbanks, are you ? "

" No, no. My name is Houston. I'm a sort of relation of Mrs. Marchbanks—that is to say, her son and I were brought up in the same house for a few years. It seems rather muddly, but that's how it is."

" You mean that you lived here with him in this house ? " hazarded Roger, wondering that Jack had never spoken of this charming inmate of his mother's house.

" Oh, no, not here. It was at Whiteinch," said Annie, and then changed the subject as if she felt it was one she ought not to pursue.

Roger was mystified.

John Marchbanks being extraordinarily sensitive concerning his inner home life had certainly never mentioned even to his best friend the years he had spent in the shipcarpenter's house at Whiteinch, not altogether out of pride, but simply because it was a very delicate situation which he did not feel called upon to explain even to Roger.

Annie, whose perceptions were quick enough, knew exactly what had happened, and she had no intention of satisfying any casual curiosity of a young man bearing the name of Annan. At the same time she was much interested in the situation, and at the moment, likewise, in the young man.

Annie was a very ordinary, healthy-minded young woman, and every young man interested her in some degree. She was the stuff of which good wives and mothers are made, the homely, warm-hearted sort easy to know, and not at all stand-offish. And she had no quarrel with him, so she was quite prepared to be very pleasant with him while she kept him waiting Mrs. Marchbanks' return.

" I've heard Jack speak about you," she said.

" Well, he might have told me about you ! " said Roger in his best manner, for the face was very sweet, and he admired the way she sat on the chair with her pretty hands folded demurely on her knee.

Annie showed her even white teeth in a merry smile.

" Oh, he wouldn't do that ! I suppose you know that he has written to his mother this last week, and that he has gone to India ? "

" Yes, I know. This is my second visit to Mrs. Marchbanks, though I was never in this house in my life until this evening."

This announcement both interested and surprised Annie Houston, but before she could make any comment they were disturbed by the opening of the outer door.

Ellen came directly to the sitting-room and visibly started in the doorway at sight of Roger Annan sitting calmly talking to Annie.

Roger at once sprang to his feet.

" I must apologise, Mrs. Marchbanks, but I thought I would like to tell you the result of my interview this evening."

" Oh, yes. Well—after supper perhaps. Will you take a cup of tea or coffee with us ? You know we don't dine late. I suppose you two have introduced yourselves. This is Miss Annie Houston, an old friend from Whiteinch. You can go and make the tea, Annie, if you like, for I think Katrine has to get something ready for the woman down the street."

Annie obediently withdrew, then Ellen looked inquiringly into the young man's face.

" When I got home, Mrs. Marchbanks, I found that Mr. Craighead had been before me."

" Oh ! And what is going to happen now ? " said Ellen breathlessly.

" My father has paid the money, but there has been the most awful row between him and me. Honestly, Mrs. Marchbanks, I tried to remember what you said and to appeal—I think that was the word you used. But you've no idea how difficult it is with a man like my father ! You see, he has been so steady all his life—nothing has ever been a temptation to him, and he hasn't the smallest mercy on poor wretches like me. The upshot is that I'm to be shipped off like a bad egg to India by the very first available boat."

" Oh, then, Mr. Craighead isn't going to make any fuss ? "

" No. He has been very decent about it, very ! If old Craighead was my father now, I would be different."

" Then you won't want the money after all ? " said Ellen, and before Roger could reply Annie Houston entered carrying a little tray whereon stood the teapot and the hot water jug.

They drew their chairs in to the table and had quite a pleasant little meal together. He did not hurry away, and somehow it fell out in the end that Annie and he left the house together just before ten o'clock.

And while poor Mrs. Annan was working herself up into a state of frantic anxiety as to what her prodigal was about and anticipating some foolish, perhaps irretrievable, step he might have taken in desperation after his quarrel with his father, he was only adding one more to the romantic and agreeable episodes of his career—seeing home one of the prettiest girls he had met for a long time.

That little car ride out to Whiteinch, however, was destined to have much further-reaching effects on Roger Annan's career than any of the characters in this little drama dreamed.

CHAPTER XVIII

ACROSS THE SEAS

THE change from the grey skies of England to the gorgeous pageant of the East is a dazzling one.

Seen for the first time by the possessor of a vivid and impressionable imagination it quickens all the pulses of life, opens the doors to a thousand fascinating possibilities, and for the time being gilds the whole horizon with mystery and romance. Even the unimaginative it fills with a dull vague wonder.

Undoubtedly that voyage in the *Ortolan* was a turning-point in John Marchbanks' career. Being taken under the protection as it were of the Eastcotes and their party gave him a certain cachet which he might have taken years to acquire.

The nameless waif whom Glasgow had not thought good enough for her more exclusive privileges was, at one strange move in the game, transferred to a position which would have compelled their respect.

The Eastcotes, though without pretention or display, were distinguished people quite well known to those *au fait* with Indian governmental life. Their position, so fully assured, required no bolstering, and they could afford to do as they pleased concerning their social affairs.

Sir Edward Trent, asked a few questions concerning the modest youth who had created a favourable impression at his dinner-table, had replied that he knew nothing of him beyond his business capabilities, which were of a high order.

The Eastcotes had evidently decided to take him at that valuation; they asked no awkward questions, and bestowed on John a good deal of unobtrusive kindness during the first days of the voyage before he had made any acquaintances. John was not the man to abuse such kindness. Day by day he endeared himself more to the Eastcotes and Mrs. Eastcote was quite warm in her commendation.

"I should like to know something more about that young man, Arthur. I like him so much. And he reminds me of someone, I can't think who."

"'Someone' is rather vague, Lucy! I always seem to remember Jardine when I'm listening to him. It's the Scotch tongue, I suppose. Yes, I like him, and we can show him a little kindness in Calcutta. I foresee you mothering yet another of Britain's exiled sons!"

He smiled as he chaffed her mildly, but his eyes were seriously tender. Perhaps even he did not know how many mothers' sons her mothering had saved, and kept immune from the fiery temptations of the East.

For the first week Beatrice Hume, a wretched sailor, was not seen at all. About the eighth day she came up looking almost as white as the frock she had donned for the tropical heat, and Marchbanks, who caught sight of her the moment she appeared at the head of the companion-way, was shocked and concerned, and hastened forward to see whether he could be of any use.

"I'm looking for Mrs. Eastcote," she said, smiling reassuringly. "Yes, thank you, I'm quite all right now. I forgot to tell you I'm always a week in durance vile on every sea no matter how kind it is. You are all right I can see, and enjoying the voyage."

"It surpasses anything I've ever imagined, and I should like it to last for ever!" he said on the impulse of the moment.

"Hardly! It becomes deadly monotonous after the first week. But I can't remember ever having such a thrill as you are experiencing, for, you see, I began traversing this particular ocean when I was three, and I've been doing it at stated intervals ever since. The things which thrill a child are generally outside adult experience or understanding, don't you think?"

Such unexpected questions opening up whole vistas of thought and experience made one of the chief charms of Beatrice Hume's conversation and personality. There was nothing conventional, or even quite ordinary about her, and most certainly nothing trivial, though she could still take a child's joy in simple things. She was indeed in some respects curiously young in outlook and character, and there was nothing blasé or woman-of-the-world about her.

Then her complete unconsciousness of self, her most perfect naturalness stood out, giving to her a singular charm. Purity, lofty purpose, sincerity all shone in the clear candid depths of her starry eyes. But it was only the sincere and good who felt drawn to her. There seemed to be a sort of aura about her which repelled those who had base thoughts of womanhood and did not do it full honour.

She was much admired on the ship because her looks were regal and winning, but she was hardly popular.

Much speculation was rife as to the relations between her and the dark-eyed, capable-looking young man by whose side she was content to sit or to walk, and to whom she talked with so much animation. He was quite unconscious of the greatness of his own triumph. For Beatrice, towards the average man, was as cold as ice.

"My dear," said Mrs. Eastcote to her one day, "be careful what you are doing. Don't spoil my new protégé. It is very good for him to be smiled on by the inaccessible star, but it will be very bad for him if he draws too near and, like the moth, scorches his wings. We don't want him nipped in the bud, so to speak."

Beatrice laughed merrily. She had a lovely laugh, pure and sweet as the spring which rushes between the stones, or like the trill of a bird on the wing.

"Aunt Lucy," she said, lingering affectionately on the courtesy-title permitted, "you are always on the look out for danger signals which are seldom hoisted. I like John Marchbanks very much; he is very refreshing, as naïve as a child, and he has seen nothing. It is only the elementary stages of his education I am attending to so that he may make a proper début in Calcutta."

"But he is only a clerk, and apparently he has no people—at least, none that can be talked about. It is my duty as your chaperon to protest," said Mrs. Eastcote, but her eyes were smiling even while her mouth voiced prudence and wisdom. "Your mother won't hold me guiltless," she added quietly.

"My darling mother knows that I am capable of looking after myself. Dear Aunt Lucy, when have I ever made a false step? I'm not going to now. But this young man interests me. He is refreshing, he is so simple and modest, and, moreover, he is clever. If he is a clerk now—how I hate the word—he will not long remain one. He has success written on his marble brow!"

Her quizzical speech somewhat reassured Mrs. Eastcote. " I agree with you ; and Arthur is enthusiastic about him. I shall not be surprised if a little later he wiles him away from your firm. He says he is the stuff the Intelligence Department wants—so discreet ! A man who can be silent in half a dozen languages is increasingly difficult to find."

" It would be a big jump from a Glasgow bank stool to the Government Intelligence Department," said Beatrice musingly.

" Is that where he sprang from ? " asked Mrs. Eastcote interestedly.

" Yes. I have discovered that, and also that he has a mother whom in some secret fastness of his soul he adores and reverences. It has taken me thirteen days to discover that, so it is true that he can be silent in at least one language. Most men are over-anxious to deluge you with all the pros and cons of their uninteresting careers ; Marchbanks will go on making his while others talk about it."

When she was alone Mrs. Eastcote pondered on this high and unusual commendation from Beatrice Hume, and it made her a little uneasy.

As they were dressing in their state-room that night she voiced part of that uneasiness to her husband.

" Arthur, do you think that Beatrice and young Marchbanks are too much together ? "

" If they are it can't be prevented now, Lucy, and Beatrice is a strong-minded young woman capable of looking after herself."

" Would you call her that, Arthur ? She is such a dear, and one always knows exactly where one is with her, she's so sincere. But she likes young Marchbanks—I shall be glad when we get to Calcutta."

" You don't think——? "

" No—I don't think anything. But she speaks warmly of him, and you know she is like her mother, not guided or bound by any known laws of social convention."

" I hope they won't blame us then, Lucy. I wondered when they sent him out on the same deck with us. It was, to say the least of it, unusual. But I like the young man, and further, I'm of opinion that he'll go far. He has ambition of the right sort that doesn't scorn the drudgery that is going to realise it. But the Humes will want something very much more assured for Beatrice than this young Scotsman on the make. Besides——"

" Besides what ? " asked Mrs. Eastcote, wrinkling her brow with anxiety.

" He has given me a certain confidence which I am not at liberty to divulge. I've taken to him, Lucy, and I won't lose sight of him, but there must be no complication with Beatrice Hume or any other girl in her position, and he knows it——"

" But why ? Such things have happened before and the heavens did not fall ! "

" In Marchbanks' case there is an insuperable obstacle—the bar sinister, in fact, Lucy. Don't ask any more questions."

Mrs. Eastcote was profoundly surprised, likewise a little shocked, but she was not the woman to turn against a young man for a fault not his own.

" If you have known that all along, Arthur——"

" My dear, I haven't. He only told me yesterday, and there are only three more days to go. It is up to you to take care that no die is cast in the interval."

Mrs. Eastcote smiled rather inscrutably and said no more. But she certainly surprised Beatrice by her close watch during the last days of the voyage, a watch which effectively prevented much private talk with John Marchbanks.

On the last evening, however, when Mrs. Eastcote, travelling without a maid, was busy with her packing, John had the chance of a last stroll round the deck with Beatrice. By this time Glasgow and the old life had faded into insignificance, and the memory of Elizabeth Annan had become very dim.

There was no one to blame but herself. She had had her chance and she had failed at the moment when his heart was aching for some crumbs of comfort and hope.

John was only human and, besides, the new star in the firmament was a very brilliant one. While realising fully that it was far beyond his reach, there was no harm in worshipping from afar. He had learned much from Beatrice Hume in these precious and enriching weeks, far more, he told himself passionately, than he could ever acknowledge or repay. She had given him much friendly counsel, listened to some of his dreams and visions of the future, and never discouraged him once. She was too innately womanly to fling the sharp stings of criticism against him as Elizabeth had so often done.

John was less humble now than he had once been, and would not perhaps have stood so much. But Beatrice never tried him, and as they sauntered together round and round the moonlit deck with the glamour of the East already enveloping them in its languorous folds, he tried to thank her.

" Oh, I have done very, very little ! " she said lightly, " listened chiefly. And you have never bored me ! Do you know that the capacity of boring people is very pronounced in the average young man ? He talks everlastingly about himself and has no doubt as to it being the one theme of interest to a waiting world ! "

" If I have done that——"

" Haven't I explicitly declared that you have not ? " she said quaintly. " And now, after to-morrow, I suppose Calcutta and all the whirl of new business interests will swallow you, and perhaps we shan't meet again ! "

" I hope we shall," said John wistfully. " But I suppose it is hardly likely. I don't exactly know what my duties are going to be. I'm travelling in a sense under sealed orders, that is, I'm to get my instructions when I land."

" My father will give you them, I don't doubt," said Beatrice with a little laugh. " I wonder how you will like him ! He is not at all like Uncle Edward, yet both are splendid business men. But my father takes much interest in public affairs. He is one of the best-known men in Calcutta."

John already knew this from Major Eastcote, and somehow his spirits seemed to sink to zero. The prospect of seeing the new star again seemed to fade away into the dimmest region of possiblity.

" I shall hear from my father how you are getting on, and where you are to be sent. It is somewhere in the interior, I know, for I heard Uncle Edward talking to the Eastcotes about it the night you dined in Lowndes Square. But I have an idea——"

" What sort of idea ? " asked John eagerly.

" That Major Eastcote means to annex you. The Service he is engaged in is fascinating—far more interesting than business, because there is no end to the things one can learn and discover. I am sure that is going to be your career."

The confidence with which she spoke absolutely thrilled John.

" Whatever I may do in the future I shall never forget this voyage and your kindness. You don't know what you have done for me, Miss Hume ! "

" What have I done ? Just put it into words," she said suddenly.

" I can't," he answered simply, it won't go ! "

5*

At this she laughed, but the beam in her eyes was very kindly.

"Oh, come! You mustn't begin your life in the East on the hills of imagination! I can assure you you will need to take a firm grip of yourself to keep within the bounds of common sense, and practical politics!—Yes, Aunt Lucy, I am here," she added, and a little whimsical smile crept to her lips as she saw Mrs. Eastcote come forward with her queer little glide-walk to find her.

"You are a very naughty girl to be out so late, Beatrice!" she said. "As it is the last night I suppose we mustn't say more, but I insist that you come downstairs now.—Good night, Mr. Marchbanks. Everything must have an end—even the finest voyage in the world! And this has been a very fine one."

"The finest in the world!" repeated John fervently, not quite, perhaps, master of himself.

Mrs. Eastcote hurried her charge down the companionway, but said nothing serious till they had entered Beatrice's state-room.

"You've done the mischief after all! My dear, what did I say at the beginning? It is a shame, for he is a very respectable young man and deserved a better fate!"

"To what fate have I consigned him, Aunt Lucy?" asked Beatrice demurely.

"You've finished him off quite. He was looking at you to-night with a dumb and hopeless adoration in his eyes, and it won't do, my dear. Even you must admit that he would hardly pass the bar of your father's judgment!"

"He won't be asked, I'm sure, nor will he seek it himself," Beatrice answered; but her face was turned away so that Mrs. Eastcote could not read its expression. "He will presently be swallowed up by the big wheels of Messrs. Trent, Bartlett & Hume, and we shall see him no more. I think I'm very glad to come back, Aunt Lucy. Aren't you? After all, India is a home to the like of us—isn't it?"

The conversation she adroitly turned could hardly be pursued, and Mrs. Eastcote said no more.

When the great ship reached the dock and all the stir and bustle of greetings and arrival sent the thoughts of the passengers whirling in a thousand new directions, John Marchbanks was made to feel acutely that he was a lonely unit of the British Empire, of whom, at the moment, nobody had any particular need. His modest luggage, quickly accounted for, claimed very little of his attention. He was therefore at liberty to watch the proceedings with the detached air and singular discernment of the looker-on.

Quite a large little crowd had assembled to meet the Eastcotes and Miss Hume. As John watched her, the centre of affection and admiring welcome, he realised both the privilege that had been his and the futility of any future hopes. He had assured himself gallantly that he had cherished none, and that he had spoken truly when he had thanked her in halting but sincere terms for her friendly kindness to one whom she need not have so much as noticed.

But all the same his heart ached and he made haste on to the landing-stage to hide himself from every eye and make what arrangements he could for his own comfort and habitation.

He realised as he hurried off the deck that, amid much friendly talk and counsel, there had been a strange and complete omission of practical details. He had not even the smallest idea where to turn to obtain a bed for the night!

The pride that forbade him hanging on the outskirts of the brilliant throng surrounding his fellow-travellers could not help him to a choice; also, it assured him rather gloomily that he was a person of no importance, merely a new servant in a great Company, whose sole duty in the immediate future was to get himself housed somewhere and report himself to his employers in due course.

The scene on any landing-stage when a big liner arrives is an animated one, where many of the outstanding traits of human nature get fullest play; but when the scene is transferred to some Eastern port, with its striking contrasts of gorgeousness and squalor, and mystery, the painful impression of the solitary and unknown voyager becomes rather acute.

Having removed himself from the immediate vicinity of the only persons with whom he could claim any acquaintance, John stood a moment irresolutely by his baggage at a loss which way to turn.

Of vehicles there were hundreds, and the howling mob of native porters threatened to engulf him. He had even to lay strenuous hands on his baggage to prevent it being whisked away from his sight and ken.

Presently the sight of the welcome word "Cook" on the hatband of a man in the familiar livery of the world-wide agents filled him with joy and relief.

The man spotted him at the moment and came forward willingly.

"Where can I direct you to?"

John pondered a moment, thinking it would be indiscreet and undignified to be absolutely vague about the destination.

"There's a Y.M.C.A. here, isn't there?" he asked on the spur of the moment, the memory of the great friendly, invaluable organisation, of which he had been a member in his younger manhood, rising before him like an oasis in the desert.

"Yes, sure. Here, you!" cried the agent, signing to a coolie, who instantly came forward all eager for service.

A few words spoken in Hindustani, which John already partly understood, resulted in the baggage being transferred to a cab, and in a few minutes he was driven off through the strange, bewildering vista of Calcutta streets.

In common with many young men who have made use of the Y.M.C.A. at various periods of their lives, there was a lurking reluctance at the back of John's mind to have his fine friends know of his indebtedness to it. He had the idea—a quite mistaken one—that he might have fallen in Major Eastcote's estimation if he had mentioned the Y.M.C.A. as his only port in Calcutta.

He realised his mistake one day a little later when he heard Major Eastcote speak in the hall of the Institution, paying a striking tribute to the work it carried on.

The friendly welcome of the Secretary put him at his ease at once, and he was very thankful indeed to find himself under a friendly roof where he could obtain all the information necessary regarding lodgings and other amenities so important to a young man arriving alone and friendless in an unfamiliar city.

He realised for the first time the vastness of the Empire, and also the insularity and genuine ignorance of the average Britisher. He had read much about India, and incidentally, through the Annans, heard a good deal of talk about life in the East; but it was a stupendous revelation to him, and, for the time being, drove every other consideration and regret from his mind.

It did not occur to him that he would be missed by his fellow-travellers or that they would display the concern they did about his disappearance.

After all the excitement and the babel of the greetings were over, Mr. Michael Hume asked what they had done with young Marchbanks, regarding whom he had had advices from the London house.

" He was here just before we docked, father," answered Beatrice. " Major Eastcote, have you seen Mr. Marchbanks ? He seems to have disappeared ! "

Nobody had ; and Mr. Hume—a large, somewhat pompous-looking man, whose fiery temper was balanced by the genuine kindness of heart and his vast knowledge of most affairs pertaining to India—looked distinctly annoyed.

" Now, that is most awkward, because we can't begin searching for him here like a needle in a haystack ! Had he anybody to meet him, do you know ? "

" Nobody," answered Beatrice promptly. " He did not know a living soul in Calcutta ; though he knows George Annan's people in Glasgow he has never met him. Now I wonder where he has got to ? "

" Don't trouble about him," said Major Eastcote easily. His head is very firmly screwed on and he won't get into any hole. He'll turn up to-morrow morning for business, I don't doubt, Mr. Hume, on the stroke of the hour."

" That may be so, but I'd like to have seen him," fumed John's new master. " He was a fool to disappear like that! He must have known I would be here."

But nothing could be done. As he remarked, it was like looking for a needle in a haystack to seek for a solitary unit in such an indescribable and motley throng, so they began to take their separate ways.

The delinquent who had thus caused a momentary anxiety and irritation in a quarter where he would have wished to avoid it spent a most delightful and profitable evening, wandering about Calcutta in company of a clerk from one of the great Banks whom he met in the Institute.

The business day was over when he arrived, and the long delicious evening, the warm sunshine, the wonderful feast of movement and colour as the ever-varying pageant of Eastern life unrolled itself before his vision, made a picture which never afterwards faded from John's memory.

Much depends on first impressions of a new place or country, and John's impression of Calcutta was as a pageant of moving and gorgeous colouring which seemed to accentuate in his memory the greyness of the tight little Island he had left behind. And yet the day was to come, as it comes to every exile, when he would have bartered all the gold of the East for one little glimpse of the low grey skies of home ; and when his eyes, grown sick and weary of the burnished gold and copper of the heavens, longed for the patter of the rain on the panes and the comfortable, enveloping greyness of mist rolling in from the sea !

Next morning he was up betimes and, as early as he deemed advisable, went to report himself at the gorgeous premises of the firm of which he had the honour to be a properly accredited servant.

He was shown at once to the principal's room. He found him to be an elderly man of full figure, with a somewhat rubicund face and rather fierce black eyes glowering out from under bushy white brows ; a white moustache somewhat softened the harsher outlines of his mouth. He gave the impression of power, of a driving force which nothing could resist. His son Gilbert was a little like him, but the younger type was more gracious and a little less aggressive.

" Marchbanks—ah, there you are ! stand forward and let me get a look at you. Where did you get to yesterday, and where were you last night—

eh? I spent at least five minutes of good time worrying about you at the landing-stage."

"I'm sorry, sir; but I thought my business was to find quarters at once and get ready to report myself this morning."

"And where did you find quarters—eh?"

John informed him where he had spent the night.

"You belong to that crowd, do you? Well, it's a very good crowd, within limits, but the limits have to be adhered to. You might do worse than stop there meanwhile, for you won't be stationary in Calcutta. Sir Edward and my son tell me you have some knowledge of Hindustani?"

"Only a little, sir. But I was glad to be able to understand when Cook's man spoke to the coolies at the landing-stage."

"Oh, you'll soon master it. You've got the gift. If you haven't, you may hammer for years at it and come out a dead failure in the end. Well, I've nothing to say to you specially to-day. You can take a look round and pick up impressions, and remember that the language and the study of the native mind is to be your business."

"It's a large one," answered John on the spur of the moment.

"The native mind is, I grant it," said Mr. Hume, more pleased than he cared to show by the answer.

He had experience of all sorts and conditions of men in India, and knew the type which despises the native, and dismisses him in one contemptuous sentence. This man was different, and he concluded that those at home had made no mistake and had not over-praised Marchbanks.

All unconscious of the immensely favourable impression he was making, John continued:

"I'll do my best, sir. I've no prejudices. I don't know anything about India. I'm here to learn, and when I've learned, to serve the firm to the best of my ability."

"I don't need anything else," said Hume briefly as he held out his hand. "It's a good working creed; stick to it and you'll go as far as there is any need for. I'll see you tomorrow. Meanwhile, go through the place, and if you come across Andrew Rintoul, glue yourself to him. There are five Scotchmen here, but he is the one that counts."

John took his dismissal with the pleasant assurance that his career had certainly begun, and under auspices which might be distinctly labelled as favourable.

CHAPTER XIX

GETTING EVEN

George Annan, in a comfortable bamboo chair, on the deep verandah of his club, in the cool of the afternoon, studied the list of the passengers who had arrived by the *Ortolan*.

Two names therein gave him to think—those of Beatrice Hume and John Marchbanks. That they should appear together, under those of the Eastcotes, was significant, and appeared to indicate that they were of one party.

Now, George Annan had not met Beatrice Hume for six long years, but he had never forgotten her. She had been a beautiful young girl the first year he had spent in Calcutta, and he had met her often, both at her father's house and at the houses of mutual friends.

The Humes—a considerable family—were all married now, except the eldest daughter and the youngest, for whose wedding invitations had already gone out. George Annan had received and accepted one, for it was to be one of the most brilliant social events in the Calcutta season, the bridegroom being a member of the Government staff.

George Annan knit his brows over John Marchbanks' name, with which he was perfectly familiar through his home letters.

His mother wrote the copious, womanly letters from which the exile learns everything. Such letters, full of minute detail, crammed to overflowing with a record of trivial happenings, though derided by some critics, are never derided by their lucky recipients abroad. It is a question if those at home fully realise how insatiable is the hunger for news of home in the exile's heart, and how he inwardly blesses the pens which supply him. They are mostly womanly pens; for the mind of the average man is incapable of hoarding minute details or of passing them on. He can never tell you the cut of the new skirt, nor has he the latest items of social intelligence neatly tabulated and dovetailed into the mosaic of social affairs. It is a woman's job; and it is a far more potent factor in existence than anybody dreams. True, it is sometimes abused, and "the long bow" shamelessly drawn, but, in the main, we should be the poorer if the labours of such conscientious scribes were withdrawn or curtailed.

It was Mrs. Annan's custom to begin her next Indian letter the day after she had despatched the previous one, and to add to it day by day such items as were of interest in the family life. She was often teased about this amazing industry, on which Elizabeth was specially hard. Elizabeth could write brilliantly when she liked, but her efforts were spasmodic, and she had an aggravating habit of leaving out precisely what George most wanted to hear.

He had an orderly mind, with an immense capacity for detail, and his mother's letters were, in very truth, an oasis in the desert of his life in the East. He had the home instincts strongly developed, and would never be able to settle down like other Anglo-Indians. He was always holding himself on the eve of departure, as it were, and his mother's letter, announcing the arrival, by an early boat, of both Roger and Elizabeth, had seriously incommoded and upset him.

All his plans for leaving India had been made, and James Wilson, the faithful manager, who had been lately promoted to a small partnership, had agreed willingly to go on single-handed for two or three months until Roger should come out.

Mrs. Annan had laid the entire story before her elder son as far as she knew it. George, therefore, was aware of the rupture with John Marchbanks, with whom he was perfectly familiar in spirit, though he had never met him in the flesh. Everything, down to the bar sinister, had been passed on to him, so that he had a comprehensive view of the whole situation.

And it was, therefore, quite natural when he saw John Marchbanks' name on the passenger list of the *Ortolan* that he should suspect collusion between him and Elizabeth, and jump to the conclusion that the scene of the incipient and undesirable love affair had merely been shifted! This thought so disquieted him that involuntarily he rose to his feet, with the feeling that he must do something to nip this obviously premeditated plan in the bud.

George, the faithful plodder, the tortoise of the Annan family, had a good deal of pride hidden under his quiet, unassuming exterior. He was a very careful man about his own intimates, and was incapable of understanding Roger's heroic and enthusiastic attachments to people quite outside the usual pale. Roger had been like that all his days: at the Academy he had never failed to take up with boys nobody else cared to know, and he was always championing what he imagined to be the cause of the distressed or unfairly treated.

That this was a fine and a lovable trait in his queer, loosely-hung character none of the Annans believed. They did not like it, any of them; they were so eminently respectable and conventional that they wanted everybody to walk in the appointed path. George, however, was the only one who had, persistently and obediently, walked in it all the days of his life. He was the pillar in the family life, but not a very interesting person beyond it. Outsiders found him dull, and his reputation in Calcutta was that of a decent plodder. Just past his thirtieth birthday now, he was fast approaching the set bachelor habit of life, from which it is so difficult to break away.

That a young man of John Marchbanks' position and antecedents should have presumed to make up to his sister annoyed George Annan very much, and he foresaw, in imagination, a most difficult and tiresome time in front of him. He was a little like his father in determination, and could be very hard on occasion.

As he stood up and pulled down his white waistcoat, and decided that something must be done before the boat bearing his brother and sister arrived in Calcutta, he conceived the idea of getting hold of Marchbanks first, and having a friendly, but quite decisive talk with him. He would tell him quite frankly that he was not playing the game, that it wouldn't do, and all the other polite platitudes with which the undesirable can be crushed.

But first he had, in the language of the proverb, to catch his hare.

It was not yet beyond calling hours. He would, therefore, present himself at the Humes' house, obviously with the purpose of welcoming Miss Hume back to the city that had been a city of night without her, but in reality to find out what he could about John Marchbanks, but more especially where he could see and talk with him.

As he drove towards the spacious mansion of the Humes he reflected that the printing of their names together on the *Ortolan's* list was, in all probability, a mere coincidence, it being hardly within the limits of possibility that there could be any acquaintance between a being so obscure as John Marchbanks and people like the Eastcotes and Beatrice Hume.

George Annan, while he was not a conceited man, had a full and unassailable belief in himself. His looks, of the average kind, were carefully husbanded; he was immaculate in his dress; but while his lean brown face was pleasant enough to look upon, he had none of Roger's unexpected charm. He was good, and solid, and hardly likely to fire the imagination of a woman like Beatrice Hume. He felt oddly comforted by the reflection that she was still single, and, though not given to flights of imagination, it did occur to him that, perhaps, fate had had a hand in the postponement of his departure from India. Perhaps the stars in their courses had decreed that Beatrice and he should meet again!

He had the good fortune to find Miss Hume at home alone, her mother and the prospective bride having gone forth to fulfil some social engagement which did not appeal to Beatrice.

He was startled by the change in Beatrice, who had now reached the zenith of beautiful womanhood. The elusive charm of the girl had certainly gone, but something far more alluring and attractive to George had come in its place. Indeed, he felt all his pulses leap at sight of her, and decided on the spot that she was the woman.

Her greeting was friendly, cordial, and sincere.

"Now, how very kind of you to come so quickly to renew an old friendship, Mr. Annan!" she said, as she offered a frank, gracious hand. "Do you know you are the very first of the old friends I have seen? I was too tired to go with them to the Government House—and why are you not there?"

It was on the tip of his tongue to say he had not received an invitation, but he prudently refrained, not wishing to belittle himself in any degree before her eyes.

"I have been very busy lately. I expected to have gone home this month, and I was most awfully disappointed over it, but now I'm not. This compensates for everything!"

Beatrice listened in some surprise, for such speeches had not been usual on George Annan's serious lips.

"I perceive," she said demurely, "that though you have changed very little outwardly the inner man has—shall we say?—deteriorated. I don't remember the George Annan of seven years ago paying such outrageous compliments, and as I haven't been used to them in the interval (for London is a serious place), shall we rule them out of court?"

George smiled delightedly, imagining that the words so sweetly spoken opened the door to more friendly intimacy.

"It's not a compliment at all, I assure you!" he said eagerly. "It's nothing but the truth. Seven years is it? Perish the thought! You don't look a day older."

"But the years have left their mark for all that," she said quietly. "Sit down, and tell me how it is with you. I somehow did not expect to find you in Calcutta. Of course, I heard from them here that you were going home this autumn. What happened to prevent it?"

George settled himself comfortably and joyfully for what he imagined would be a long and intimate talk.

"I heard from home that I was to wait here until my brother and sister arrived."

"Your sister is coming out!" said Beatrice interestedly, though she seemed surprised. "Only for a trip, I suppose."

" She will spend the winter, and look after my young brother, who," he added frankly, " seems to have been getting himself into some kind of a scrape."

" Then he will retrieve it here, beside you," said Beatrice quite sincerely. " When do you expect them ? "

" By the next boat. It was a wonder they did not sail on the *Ortolan*."

" That would have been interesting. I must ask my mother to send them both a card for the wedding. It would be a good chance for your sister to meet everybody."

" Thank you. Yes, it would," admitted George.

Then there fell a slight silence.

" I was looking over the *Ortolan's* list to-day, and I saw your name, and that of a man I've heard about, from home—John Marchbanks."

" Yes," said Beatrice, and, was it imagination, or did her colour faintly rise ?

George decided that it was pure imagination.

" He was on board," said she. " A very nice man. He came from Haviland House."

" Do you mean that he is in employment there ? "

" He is ; though it was Uncle Edward and my brother Gilbert who discovered and engaged him. They think he is a real find. He has a gift for languages, and they have got something very particular for him to do in the interior, I believe—something to do with rugs and carpets, if we must descend to sordid details ! "

" Oh ! " said George meditatively. " But, of course, you wouldn't see much of him on board, as he would be travelling second class ? "

" No, he wasn't. He was on our deck, and sat at our table ; and I walked round the deck with him at least six times every day of the voyage."

" But—but," stammered George, for this did not coincide at all with the account of Marchbanks he had heard from Glasgow, " I don't understand how he came to be there, don't you know ? I've heard of this chap from my people at home. They seem to think him an outsider."

" Then they were wrong," said Beatrice, quite quietly and sincerely. " He is a gentleman. And when I tell you that Major Eastcote has his eye on him, you can conclude that he has some ability a little out of the common."

" Where has he gone for quarters, do you know ? Perhaps he is staying here ? " suggested George rather sourly.

" Oh, no he isn't. I think I heard my father say at tiffin that he had got quarters for the time being at the Y.M.C.A."

" That would just about suit him, I should say," observed George with a kind of quiet scorn which nettled Beatrice.

" It won't matter where he finds quarters, the right quarter will find him," she said rather scathingly. " And it isn't like you, George Annan, to be so uncharitable and dog-in-the-mangerish about a fellow-creature. I want to know what it means ? "

" Well, as it happens, I can't exactly tell you. All I can say is that he used to go about my people in Glasgow, and that they had to give him a hint to stop it. Something happened. But I must leave it at that."

" But you can't," said Beatrice candidly and straightly. " Don't you see, if you go about Calcutta making remarks of that kind he won't have a chance ? Either you must speak out plainly, or hold your peace for evermore."

" I could tell a man, but I can't tell you," said George desperately.

" If you are trying to tell me he has been guilty of some moral offence, then I shall tell you that I don't believe it. Nothing on this earth would ever make me believe it!"

"He is fortunate in his champion," said George rather drily, "and has evidently made the best of his opportunities."

"That may be, but we have sufficient lying and blackening of reputations here in Calcutta, goodness knows, and I never expected George Annan to join the scandal-mongering brigade! I'm going to ask you not to, in fact, but to do your best for John Marchbanks. You ought to, as he's a countryman of yours, and comes from the same city."

George pondered a moment, acutely conscious of her clear, disapproving eyes upon him, and altogether disconcerted by the turn affairs had taken. He did not know how to extricate himself from his dilemma since the head and front of John's offence had been to lift his eyes to Elizabeth. Supposing he told Beatrice that, she would probably instantly ask why that should condemn him.

"It has nothing to do with him personally, I believe," he said at last. "But concerns his people."

"He hasn't any people except a mother whom he worships," said Beatrice quietly. "And apparently she has suffered a great deal, and he hopes to live to make up for it all to her."

George rose to his feet, feeling that the conversation must come to an end. The interview had disappointed him deeply, and he felt that he had not made at all the impression he had hoped and desired. He decided mentally that he must see John without delay, and point out to him, if need be, the enormity of the offence he had committed in trying to worm himself into the good graces of people whose social position was such as he could not share. Obviously something would have to be done before the arrival of the next boat with Roger and Elizabeth on board should complicate the situation.

Beatrice suffered him to go without protest or without expressing the hope that they should meet again. He did not interest her in the least, and she considered his prim ways and narrow, conventional outlook as very typical of the man. She quickly dismissed him from her thoughts, however, though she could not dismiss so quickly her wonder as to the real story behind John Marchbanks' life.

George made his way by easy stages, for he encountered many acquaintances on the way to the Institute, where he was fortunate enough to find John Marchbanks reading the evening papers, before dressing to go out to dinner at the Humes'.

Beatrice had not mentioned that he was expected, because she had not heard that he had been invited.

"My name's Annan," said George, when they met. "I dare say you've heard it before."

John sprang up with slightly flushing face and a pleased smile. But something in George Annan's manner chilled him, and he withdrew the hand he had rather eagerly thrust forward.

"Oh, yes, of course, you are George Annan. I've heard your brother Roger speak about you often. But how kind of you to look me up so quickly. Why, I only arrived last night! How did you hear I was here?"

"I saw your name among the list of arrivals on the *Ortolan*, but, as a matter of fact, it was Miss Hume who told me you were living here."

He watched narrowly, and was rewarded by the sudden consciousness which sprang into John Marchbanks' face. Studying the face keenly, with the eye of a rival, in fact, George was somewhat cheered by the fact that Marchbanks had no very distinguished looks, but was very ordinary. He was to discover, as others did, that the quiet charm of the man grew, and that very soon he imparted a subtle sense of power which is as difficult to put into words as it is impossible to acquire. It is native born.

" Oh, yes—Miss Hume. I'm dining there to-night."

" You're dining there to-night ! They're going to do you well apparently. What capacity have you come out in ? "

" I don't just know yet. It is going to be some kind of a confidential agency, I think, and I don't expect I'm to stop long in Calcutta."

" You're very lucky to have got such a post—especially after what happened in Glasgow."

" What did happen in Glasgow ? " asked John, on the defensive at once. He felt the subtle, inward hostility of George Annan, whose personality, so different from Roger's, was a grievous disappointment. He had always heard of the Annans' eldest hope spoken of as the salt of the earth, who had never been known to harbour a wrong thought or do an ignoble deed.

As he spoke his colour had heightened, and his eyes grew dangerously bright. He was less shrinking than he had been in Glasgow, and now stood in no awe of any bearing the name of Annan. In the last months he had found that there are kind hearts and discerning eyes even out in the big world, where the fight for existence goes on day by day.

George Annan faced with the question realised that he had made a ghastly mistake, besides perpetrating a breach of good feeling, and even good manners, which it would be difficult to explain away.

" I suppose they've been writing to you," said John, with a kind of steady heat. " All they could do would be to bring a charge against my mother, but, what I can tell you is, that she is a better woman than many who would not think her good enough to speak to ! You can do me harm here if you care to try, I don't doubt—that is, among people whose opinion is not worth caring about. I can look after the other sort myself."

It was a tremendous outburst for a person of John Marchbanks' peaceable disposition, but the feeling that the Annans were pursuing him relentlessly caused him for a moment to lose his sense of proportion.

His outburst, however, impressed George Annan, who made a clumsy attempt to apologise.

" I didn't mean anything," he began, but John, as if freshly enraged by the words, interrupted.

" If you didn't mean anything you'd better choose your words more carefully next time ! After what happened in Glasgow was what you said. That might mean anything. I'm waiting to hear exactly what you meant to imply ? There's nothing against my character. If they say there is it's a lie ! I left Glasgow without making any talk about it because, as things were, it was difficult to keep on. It was your people who made them difficult, and if they try to put spokes in my wheel out here, I'll fight them—by God I will, with every weapon in my power ! "

He was raised to a white heat of fury by the reflection that the sinister Annan influence might operate in certain quarters where it was of paramount importance that his character should be well esteemed.

In the last few months, or rather weeks, John had learned much and had got beyond the alphabet of social life. The voyage had taught him the importance of the trifles he had been apt to despise. He had learned that there is a code a man has to observe strictly if he would pass into the charmed circles where that code is honoured and observed. It was a different code from the Annan code, something finer, more subtle, and more enduring. Money was the Annans' standard, and they had no desire to have friends where money did not exist.

John longed to throw this discovery in the smug face of George Annan, and only refrained because his own knowledge was yet new and crude.

"Oh, come!" said Annan. "There is no use getting into such a rage. What did I say after all? Perhaps I've got the facts wrong, but I certainly got the impression that you found it wise to leave Glasgow."

"Then you'll revise your impression before you pass it on!" said John savagely. "You'd better write to your brother Roger for the facts. He was a good sort when they let him alone. If he tells you the truth you'll understand maybe that he was the one who ought to have been hounded out of Glasgow. But I won't say any more. I'll bid you good afternoon, Mr. Annan. I've come to Calcutta to get my living, and I'm going to get it, and, maybe, something more in spite of all the efforts of the west-end of Glasgow to keep me back!"

So saying he walked quite deliberately past George Annan, and left him standing in the cool vestibule feeling a little cheap. But there is no doubt that the outburst, though almost immediately regretted by the person who had been guilty of it, had the wholesome effect of making George Annan respect him.

George could have kicked himself for coming at all to look up the newcomer, and also for not having kept a better guard on his tongue. He would have it out with Roger next week. It was rather a difficult and delicate situation, and the fact that Marchbanks had been taken up by the Humes and the Eastcotes, whose position in the Anglo-Indian colony was assured, complicated it rather hopelessly.

John retired to his upstairs bedroom heartily ashamed of himself. His outbursts of anger were very few, and he could not remember having given way before, and he had a healthy mind's contempt for lack of self-control. There is no doubt that the knowledge that Annan had it in his power to damage him with Beatrice Hume was at the back of it.

But the mischief being done and, presumably, George Annan made an enemy of, he must stand by the consequences. In the course of the brief and stormy interview, Annan had not had the chance to inform John of the impending arrival of Roger and Elizabeth. John, therefore, inwardly concocted an indignant letter to his old friend, pointing out to him that he had better put a muzzle on his brother, unless he wanted trouble.

That letter was never written, however. The evening spent at the Humes' soothed his ruffled feathers, and gave him a fresh opportunity of consolidating his position. He saw very little of Beatrice, for their was a considerable party present. The Eastcotes were not there, but he was sent down to dinner with a charming girl who was very kind to him, and with whom he got on well.

Next day the absorbing interests of his business claimed him, and gradually his indignation against the name of Annan faded into the background.

But only for a little. About three weeks later he was invited to dine for the second time at the Humes' house, when he entered the drawing-room, he was aghast to behold in the distance talking to his hostess Elizabeth Annan!

CHAPTER XX

A NEW SETTING

It was certainly an awkward moment. Mrs. Hume, catching sight of John, turned to him smilingly.

"Ah, there is Mr. Marchbanks—a countryman of yours. I believe he is to take you in to dinner."

Elizabeth wheeled round so suddenly that her pince-nez fell from her nose. Stooping to pick them up perhaps accounted for the sudden rush of fiery colour to her face.

John's face was rather pale, and his lips were set. His rage against fate was profound, and as he took these few ghastly steps up the room he felt the hidden tragedy of the moment. He remembered in a sudden flash all the foolish lovemaking in the garden at Balcraig, the tender passages which had been so heavenly and so pregnant for him in his callow youth, but which he now knew to have been mere bubbles on the surface.

Love does not come like that, creeping gradually and cautiously on; nay, he had proved that the love that lives and uplifts a man to the highest heights has something in it akin to the tempestuous floods!

Here, in one room, surely were gathered once more some of the elements of tragedy inseparable from the eternal triangle—two women and one man, or two men and one woman!

In John's case here were the woman he had imagined himself in love with and the one who was already fixed in his firmament as its most desirable, if somewhat inaccessible star!

Elizabeth was the first to recover herself, and, smiling a trifle confusedly, she extended her hand.

"Mr. Marchbanks and I have met before in Glasgow. How do you do, John? Strange, isn't it, that we should meet here?"

"It is indeed," he said drily, his voice seeming to crack in his throat.

He took her hand limply in his own and tried to smile amiably even while he wished that the floor would open and engulf him.

"You seem most frightfully surprised! Why should you be so? I thought George had seen you and told you we were coming?"

He shook his head.

"He did not mention any names or that he expected Glasgow folk. Who are 'we'?" he asked stupidly.

"I see I may leave you two to renew old acquaintance," said their kind hostess beaming as she sped away, so that they were left quite alone in a wide corner of the spacious drawing-room under the spreading palms.

"Didn't George tell you that Roger and I were coming out?" asked Elizabeth quickly.

"Roger! Is he here?" asked John looking vaguely round.

"No. He and George had another dinner engagement. Miss Hume only asked me this afternoon when she came to call, when I happened to mention that I would be alone in the evening."

"But I don't understand what you are doing here!" said John in the same stupid, wondering voice.

"I might say the same! What are you doing here?" asked Elizabeth with a kind of gentle banter. "Of all places in the world to meet you here and in this house!"

"Queer, isn't it?" said John with a slow smile. "I am surprised myself! But there! One never knows what odd surprises life has in store. I suppose Roger has come out to release your other brother."

In spite of himself his tone hardened so that he could not speak the name.

"He has, but George isn't going home yet. We've had trouble at home, John—horrid trouble! In fact, nothing has gone right since you went away."

She spoke with the same kindly feelings as of yore, and the eyes behind the pince-nez were distinctly wistful.

"Sorry," he murmured, but his tone was listless, and his manner had entirely lost the slightly deferential air which had been characteristic of him in the old Glasgow days. "But I hope your father and mother are well in spite of it?"

"Oh, yes; they are all right. Roger was the trouble. They only discovered after you had gone away how good your friendship was for him, and they are very grateful and understand things better," she added bravely.

She said all these things because they were what she believed, and also she had some idea of atonement. All the time, uppermost in her mind, was the memory of the little appealing letter she had written in that memorable week, the letter which, had it reached its destination, might have materially altered everything. She grasped the fact that it was going to be difficult to bring her lover back to the old footing, and while she liked his pride, she wished that he had more discernment. Elizabeth's own pride was very high, and already she had risked it considerably. Believing that this indifference was assumed, however, she went on bravely.

"We must meet and I'll tell you all about Roger. Perhaps even there might be a chance to-night. I should like to tell you before you see him."

"Perhaps Roger might object," said John casually, and his eyes were roving towards the door, where at the moment some members of the family were entering with some other guests.

Had Elizabeth been watching keenly at the moment, or had she been a little less assured that her own image was still paramount in John Marchbanks' heart, she might have guessed there and then what had happened.

"It's so wonderful to meet you here!" she babbled on. "Quite like a piece out of a story-book, don't you think?"

"Oh, quite," he assented, and at that moment Beatrice came sailing up.

She had on a wonderful gown of robin's-egg blue, so delicate, so filmy, so beautiful against the clear pallor of her skin that somehow she made every woman look common and ordinary. The damask roses she loved were not lacking, but nestled in a vivid cluster at her waistband, the rich perfume wafting to them as she came swiftly towards them.

"Here we are again, Miss Annan! You and Mr. Marchbanks are quite old friends, I suppose. That is one of the charms of Calcutta—one never knows whom one may meet round the next corner! Well, I hear from father that you are going up-country on Monday on a very important mission."

John replied, and for a few moments they discussed the impending journey, of which Beatrice seemed to have considerable knowledge.

"But the Eastcotes know every inch of it, and they are coming to-night," said she.

"They have asked me to tiffin on Sunday," said John modestly.

"How nice of them, they are dear people! Ah, there they are! Excuse me, I must go on."

She glided off again, and something in the man's eyes as they followed the perfect grace of her movements sent a strange and sudden chill to Elizabeth's heart.

" How long have you known her, John ? " she asked rather sharply. " It is so strange to meet you here in this house ! "

" I met her in London. I'm in the employment of her father's firm. I suppose you knew that ? "

" George just mentioned it, but he didn't say anything about meeting you here."

" I've never met him here," said John hastily and aggressively.

" Oh, haven't you ? I quite thought you had. It is going to be a big party evidently. I do hope they'll send us down together ! It would be quite like old times at Balcraig ! They seem far away now, don't they ? "

" Just as if they had never happened at all," he answered, and the too-ready assent wounded her.

But she had no opportunity for making any more experimental remarks at the moment, for their host came up and told John he was to take her down to dinner.

John would infinitely have preferred the most colourless and uninteresting stranger ; the last thing on earth he desired now was a *tête-à-tête* or intimate conversation with Elizabeth Annan ! He even wondered as she laid her hand on his arm that he had ever been thrilled by her touch. " Calf love ! " he said to himself with the nip of scorn in the words.

And he devoutly hoped that she so regarded that past episode, and would cease being reminiscent.

But it was a vain hope ! No sooner were they seated at table with plenty of elbow-space between them and the next guests—for Mrs. Hume's table was never crowded—than Elizabeth began to go back on the days that were not and never would be again.

" I want to tell you about Roger, John," she said as she drew off her gloves. " You haven't seen him, I know——"

" I haven't. I suppose I must thank your other brother for that, Miss Annan. He highly disapproves of me. He has been trying to put several spokes in my wheel ever since I came out to Calcutta, but I didn't think Roger would have gone back on me like that."

" I don't believe he has. But you see, George has very strict orders as to how he is to behave to Roger, who is in disgrace. He did a quite dreadful thing, and, if you weren't such an old friend of the family, I would rather die than mention it. He took some money from the bank. Mr. Craighead was very good about it. When he discovered it he came straight to father, and, of course, it was all comfortably hushed up. I blame Archie Dunsyre myself—that was a horrid set he introduced Roger to—and after you left Glasgow he didn't seem to care somehow, and began to have the late nights which worry mother so dreadfully. Altogether, we've had a most wretched autumn."

John Marchbanks was interested, naturally, because it was his best chum she was talking of, but his interest was painfully divided, because he was trying to hear part of the conversation going on on the opposite side of the table between Beatrice Hume and an uncommonly handsome young man whom he knew to be a member of the Governmental Staff.

" I'm sorry. Yes—it was a bad set, and Roger will be better out of Glasgow," he said casually.

" Didn't Miss Hume say something about your leaving Calcutta next week ? " asked Elizabeth then.

" Yes. I'm going up-country on Monday."

" Won't you try and see Roger first ? Couldn't you come to our house—— ? "

" I couldn't do that after what passed between your brother George and me."

" What did pass ? " she asked quickly. " He only told me he had seen you, and I could gather from his manner that the interview hadn't been very satisfactory."

" He was very insulting to me," said John quietly. " And, while I don't bear him any special ill-will, I don't propose to meet him again of my own free will until he chooses to apologise."

" Oh, I can't believe it is you actually speaking, John ! You are not the same man you were in Glasgow."

" I hope I'm not. I was too much of a worm there," he answered rather bitterly. " And I'm going to have an up-hill fight for it yet out here if your brother George can secure it for me."

" Oh, don't say that, John ! And, anyhow, you know I am just the same. I'll speak to George—— "

" Pray don't. It wouldn't do any good. Besides, candidly, I'm not keen on his friendship. I don't need it. Thank goodness I can forge ahead without it ! "

" I am sure you can. Now tell me about your mother. Have you heard from her since you came out ? "

" Yes, I had a letter yesterday."

Elizabeth waited a moment hoping that she would hear more, but she waited in vain. In the silence that ensued the man on her other side ventured a remark, and John eagerly seized the opportunity of speaking to the lady on his left, and after that the conversation became more general.

He took care that there should be no renewal of private or intimate talk, and when she crossed the room to bid him good night she asked a question which embarrassed him considerably. It cost her something to ask it, but she was determined that she would not lose the opportunity.

" Good night, John. I hope we'll meet again before you go on Monday. Is it a long journey, and will it take you out of Calcutta for long ? "

" They tell me I might be away six months."

" Six months ! " her face fell. " Oh, that is a long time ! Well, good night. It's been disappointing, our meeting ; everything seems changed—we most of all."

" It is inevitable in a world where nothing stands still, he answered rather sententiously.

" Good night and good-bye then, John. There is just one thing more—Did you ever get a letter I wrote to you the day after we met that afternoon in Renfield Street ? Do you remember ? "

" We met a lot of times in Renfield Street," he answered, not meeting her gaze. " And I never got any letter before I left Glasgow."

Her face brightened at this.

" You got no letter ! I wish I knew where it went ! But, of course, that explains several things I've been blaming you in my thoughts for. Now I wonder what became of it ? "

John shook his head and asked no questions as to what the letter had contained. There was not an atom of lover's eagerness about him, and again the chill descended on Elizabeth's heart.

In spite of her father's Spartan ideas regarding the upbringing of children she had in reality been denied nothing in all her twenty-four years of life. A pliable mother fills up many gaps in the man-ridden household. The Annan children had discovered that quite early in their respective careers.

But there are things which even a pliable mother is powerless to obtain for the children of her love.

Elizabeth, as she stood face to face with this grave-faced young man whose polite but slightly bored manner indicated that he might have been meeting her for the first time, and was not even casually interested, realised that she was now confronted with Life.

" Nothing is the same ! " she repeated petulantly. " I can't imagine what has happened to change you so."

" I'll tell you "—and there was a rising note of passion in his voice—" The change was made that day we met in Renfield Street, and you went back on me ! A man can't go on laying himself open to such blows. Good night."

He turned from her abruptly, leaving her, in a manner, stunned.

The John Marchbanks she had known could never have been capable of such incredible harshness ! What did it mean ? How dared he speak to her like that ? Where could she look for the explanation ?

She found it without searching at that very moment, when her eyes fell on his leave-taking with Beatrice Hume at the other end of the room.

There was no lassitude, no stiffness or aloofness in his bearing now. Nay, his face was eager and impassioned, his expression that of a man who hangs on a woman's words.

Instantly the most bitter feelings that can ravage the human heart entered into Elizabeth Annan and took possession. A raging jealousy gnawed at her heart ; but, in the midst of her most bitter pain, there lurked the still more bitter feeling of hopeless futility. In Glasgow she had been a person of some importance—flattered, sought after, deferred to an account of her position ; but here she was a mere nobody, only one of a crowd !

Then her inner consciousness, with avenging truthfulness, assured her that against Beatrice Hume she had no chance. Brilliant, beautiful, winning, moving with the grace of an assured position, and a beloved personality in the most exclusive Calcutta society, Beatrice had the ball at her feet.

Of course John Marchbanks was dazzled by her gracious and condescending kindness, but to dream that he had made the smallest impression on her was unthinkable. But Elizabeth, woman-like, was feverishly determined to find out.

For that purpose she did not hasten her own departure, but lingered, seeking an opportunity for a little private talk with Miss Hume. It came quickly enough, for, observing her alone, Beatrice came swiftly towards her.

" You enjoyed meeting your old friend, Miss Annan, I am sure ? " she said, plunging into the crucial subject at once, simply because she knew of no reason why she should avoid it.

" Yes—and yet I don't know. He doesn't seem the same, somehow."

" But improved, I am sure ? " suggested Beatrice amiably. " Vastly improved ! He is the kind of man who not only grasps every opportunity but creates opportunities for himself."

" You think so ? He was only considered a very mediocre person at home, and people are spoiling him here. There is no doubt about it."

Beatrice eyed her rather narrowly, quite aware of the petulant edge to her voice, and wondering just what it meant.

" He is certainly very much liked," said Beatrice quietly. " Major and Mrs. Eastcote have taken a great fancy to him, and their opinion is worth a good deal out here."

" I never was more surprised in my life than when I met him here," said Elizabeth, and the venom deepened into her tongue. Then she hesitated just a moment. She knew the eyes of the other woman to be gravely rebuking, and she decided to put a permanent spoke in John Marchbanks' wheel.

It was an impulse born of the devil, and immediately regretted; but she gave way to the brief and base temptation.

"I was much surprised, and nobody knows better than he that he has no right here. If all were known about him, fewer doors would be opened to him."

"What is there to be known about him?" asked Beatrice, and her eyes were dangerously bright, glowing like twin-lamps or danger signals; only Elizabeth, undiscerning, blundered on.

"Well—socially, he is impossible," she said nervously.

"But that has to be explained?" answered Beatrice mercilessly. "This is the second time I've heard something of the same sort. It was your brother who said it last time, and I say to you what I said to him—that it isn't fair to throw out innuendoes against a man's character unless they can be substantiated. It is worse than stabbing him in the dark."

"Oh, there was nothing against his character!" said Elizabeth weakly, and her colour rose high in her cheeks.

"Well, then, what was it? Don't you think you ought to tell me, Miss Annan? In fact, I think I must insist on it. We have received Mr. Marchbanks here as an equal and a friend."

"Oh, but it's impossible he can be either, and nobody knows that better than he does! He had to leave Glasgow because his social connections were so impossible. His—his mother has never been married."

It was out, and for a moment there was a strained silence.

But the steady light in Beatrice Hume's eyes suffered no quenching; in fact, the glow deepened there, the righteous glow of anger against cruelty and injustice, the desire to champion the weak and wronged.

"He can't help that, Miss Annan," she said in a lowered voice, but quite clearly. "And in the twentieth century we don't visit the sins of the fathers, or of the mothers, either on the children—at least, some of us don't. Good night."

She turned away without so much as offering her hand, and Elizabeth, crushed by something fine, even majestic, in her rival, had to slip quietly up the long room, bid good night to her hostess, and, even while she listened to her cordial repetitions of welcome and farewell, to realise that she had closed one of the most exclusive doors in Calcutta against herself.

Beatrice Hume might not even mention what had passed between them, but none the less surely and swiftly she would act.

Elizabeth had never suffered so acutely in her life and could have cursed the day of her arrival in Calcutta, even although it had brought her again face to face with her lover.

Her lover? But he was no longer that, and Beatrice Hume had supplanted her!

There is no more discerning judge of the fluctuations in the love-life of a man than the woman who has shared them. Elizabeth was amazed, humiliated, rebellious at the extraordinary wave of rage and wounded pride that had swept over her, transforming her from a rather reserved, standoffish young woman into something which her finer consciousness assured her was both common and unclean.

There rose uppermost in her mind, as she was quickly borne in her rickshaw to her brother's house, some foolish but deeply significant words of Rudyard Kipling's, penned under these very skies of the East which now smiled upon her:

"The Colonel's lady and Julia O'Grady
Are sisters, under their skin."

And this was the second humiliation John Marchbanks had meted out to her! She had not forgotten Annie Houston.

An exceeding bitter smile curved her lips as she thought of Beatrice Hume's face, should she ever hear of that episode! Even had it been only the figment of a girl's imagination, the mere fact that she had sufficient acquaintance with him to create it, would not be very pleasant hearing for the proud Miss Hume!

What could be easier than to acquaint her with that too? Elizabeth's own imagination ran riot that night, and she arrived at home a flaming creature, quite ready to speak bitter words in the hearing of her brothers if she found them there.

She found only George, smoking tranquilly on the verandah.

"Well, had a good time, old girl? Roger's gone upstairs. He's had too many whisky pegs. He'll have to learn that a man can't play fast and loose with himself out here the way he can do at home. But it strikes me that I'll have a pretty tough job with him. Well, sit down and tell me who was there?"

He looked at her rather critically as she dropped her pink satin wrap on the nearest chair. Her face looked tired, and even a little drawn. He concluded privately that his sister had gone off in looks or, rather, had not fulfilled the promise of her girlhood.

"The worst set of uninteresting fossils it has ever been my lot to meet!" she snapped. "I was bored to tears."

"I am surprised. And I rather wish the Humes could hear you! They rather fancy themselves—don't you know?—on their exclusiveness."

"That may be, but they didn't show it to-night," she answered, and after a moment added, "John Marchbanks was there, George."

"That outsider! And I suppose he came prancing up to you with all the assurance in life?—claiming that he had known you for a thousand years!"

"He didn't do anything of the kind. He has no use for us now—he thinks he has climbed a step higher."

"But he didn't cut you?" said George threateningly.

"He couldn't very well, being told off to take me in to dinner, but he showed me pretty plainly that he is off, so far as Balcraig, Glasgow, Scotland, is concerned."

"The bounder! But of course one can understand it. He's afraid they get to know things. The question is how far we are justified in holding our tongues. The Humes, and that lot are most exclusive; and, if it was known who he was, there would be no more invitations to dinner! He would be kept very properly and completely in his place."

"Well, they know now," said Elizabeth with a touch of sullenness. "Miss Hume aggravated me to the extent, after he had gone away, that I just told her."

George Annan took his cigar from his mouth.

"You don't mean it! Well, what did she say?" he asked eagerly.

Elizabeth shrugged her shoulders.

"She said that the twentieth century didn't visit the sins of the fathers on the children."

"It's just what she would say. But we'll see how it works out in practice. I could almost bet my bottom dollar there'll be no more invitations to the Maidan for John Marchbanks!"

The reflection, however, did not appear to afford either of them any very lively satisfaction.

"I'll go to bed," said Elizabeth wearily as she rose to her feet. "I simply hate and loathe India, and I'll never stop here through the winter, whatever happens to Roger ! I don't see why I should be sacrificed for him, anyway."

"Oh, this episode will soon blow over, and Marchbanks will receive the extinguisher. You just wait and see !" said George consolingly, as he bade her good night.

Elizabeth went to bed, indeed, but not to sleep. Kipling's words rang in her ears, between the snatches, till morning :

"The Colonel's lady and Julia O'Grady
Are sisters, under their skin."

CHAPTER XXI

HIS CHANCE

BEATRICE HUME'S father and Major Eastcote were friends of long standing, between whom ceremony was not much observed. No other person would the head of the big Calcutta firm have admitted on unauthorised business at his office between nine and ten in the morning when the letters for the day had to be sorted out.

This happened on the Saturday following the little informal dinner at his house on the Maidan, at which certain persons we are interested in had been present.

" Major Eastcote !—Major Eastcote, at nine o'clock on a Saturday morning ! " he said when the name was brought to him.

" Well, show him in. He must have something to say or he wouldn't bother us—eh, Jamie ? "

He addressed his query to his manager, James Kinnear, a native of Dundee, who had now been one of the buttresses of the Calcutta House for over fifteen years.

He was a typical Scot—short, rather broadset, keen, shrewd and kindly. A man of few words but tremendous deeds—everything he took in hand arrived ultimately, even though it might be slowly, at the pinnacle of success. Had he been an ambitious man, he might have launched out on his own account with reasonable prospects of success, but being childless there was no particular reason why he should push personal ambition to the utmost limits.

He was, therefore, quite happy and contented, and his position in Trent, Bartlett & Humes, and the small partnership lately offered had completely satisfied him as well as consolidated his standing in the City. His wife, a small, plump-cheeked little woman from the Carse of Gowrie, whose face the suns of India had failed to rob of its fresh north-country colour, had no fault to find with India, being one of the apostles of cheerfulness of whom there are too few in a weary world.

She was a woman absolutely without pretentions, who had never sought to get beyond her birth and upbringing, who took things as they came, and had an enormous capacity for friendship. She was as talkative and merry as her husband was silent and uncommunicative ; nevertheless, between her and " oor Jimse," as she called him, there was a complete understanding, and he was happier than most men.

They were discussing the details of John Marchbanks' journey into the interior, but he himself was not present.

" I think he'll do ; though it's not to be expected but that there'll be some mistakes made," observed Kinnear, as he gathered up a map and some papers they had been studying together. " But there's this to be said about him—he'll never give up. My wife had a long pow-wow with him last night, and she says that about him. He'll be a terrible stayer, and reverses won't daunt him. Yes—he'll do."

" I'm glad you think that, Jamie. I hope the Major hasn't come about him. He's been casting sheep's eyes at him ever since he came ; though, as I told him on Wednesday, there is no reason why the Government, that takes most things from us, should cast felonious eyes on all our likely young men ! "

Kinnear smiled as he made himself scarce through one of the doors at the moment when Major Eastcote entered by another.

" Morning, Hume. I see by your face that I've chosen the wrong minute!"

" Since you're so sure of it, Major, we won't contest the point. But sit down, and tell me what I can do for you."

" Well, you can do a considerable deal if you have the mind and disposition," said the Major, a dry smile illumining his lean brown face. " I may as well out with it. I want your young man."

" Marchbanks ? Then, by gad, you won't get him ! " exclaimed Mr. Hume, bringing a choleric fist down on the table. " I've just this minute sworn it to Jamie Kinnear."

" O, but the curse causeless shall not come," observed the Major, casually. " I've had my marching orders last night. There's going to be trouble on the old Border, and I'm going to leave my wife behind this time, and, with your permission, take Marchbanks."

Hume sat back in his chair and looked attentively at the Major's face. He knew him of yore, his quiet persistence, his terrible unmatched capacity for obtaining that on which he set his heart.

" We've been seeking for this youth all our lives, Major," he growled.

" So have I ! " was the answer. " And it's your duty to hand him over to a grateful country without delay."

" But why ? "

" Because his quality is what we need."

" It's what I need, too, Major, and mean to keep——"

" You won't ! Any man can appraise merchandise."

" Can he ! That only shows your ignorance, Major—an ignorance greater than the civilian's ignorance of military caste and precedent."

" But it takes a certain cast of mind to put through the ticklish jobs threatening us on the Frontier. I want to get through to Jardine. Do you know that nothing has been heard of him for thirteen months ? He's got to be found, Hume. His own silence is not so disquieting as the fact that nothing has been heard of him. He can be felt here when he isn't seen. Either they've finished him off at last or he's in a tight place. Anyhow, I've got to go and see. I want someone to help me, and I'm going to take your young man."

Inwardly pleased, Hume outwardly continued to fume.

" You have all the special characteristics of your class abnormally developed, Major."

" Yes. What are they ? " asked the Major languidly, as he sat down on the corner of the desk, and proceeded to make himself a cigarette. " I've heard 'em all before, but it'll compose your mind to marshal the catalogue of the crimes, committed in my name ! Forge ahead."

" The principal, and most objectionable, is your disposition to commandeer whatever you cast eyes on and covet."

" It's the first law of warfare, and we have the best authority for holding that all life is a warfare," said the Major, who always enjoyed these little discussions with his old friend more particularly when he could work up Hume's fiery temper to a certain pitch of heat. But, though sometimes hot words passed between them there had not been a single break in their friendship for over twenty years.

" If only you had been forty-eight hours later, he'd have been gone."

" If I had been forty-eight hours later I should deserve to be chucked.

Nobody has the right to be forty-eight hours late any more than forty-eight hours too early. The one can be as disastrous as the other. The time is the psychological moment. Mine is now. Can I see Marchbanks here? Is he in the house?"

"He is in the house, and he leaves on the business for which he is paid and for which he was sent out from London, the day after to-morrow," said Mr. Hume firmly.

"He will cover part of the same ground, and, if there is any time to spare from my particular wallet of instructions, he can do his business for you. That's a handsome compromise, old friend. Bring him in."

"He's young and inexperienced," suggested Mr. Hume, in a warning voice, as his hand began to wander towards the bell-push.

"The man who knows is the abomination of desolation, for none of us know anything. It is only the one who is willing to learn, who gets there in the true sense; and, when he has learned one page of his art, he only knows that the next one is a thousand times more difficult. Get him in, my boy, for time is passing."

"Perhaps he'll refuse. Indeed, he may very well do that; if he has a proper sense of what is due. We paid his first-class fare out."

"That was the initial mistake. It gave me my chance. If you had glued him to the second cabin, I would not have probed him as I did. So, you see, the stars in their courses have decreed it. I need him, Tom; and, remember, it is not lost what a friend gets."

"It's a bit of luck for him," said Mr. Hume. "Only, I'm not so sure. You and Mrs. Eastcote lead a charmed life. Perhaps he may be less fortunate."

"A man dies but once, Tom," said the Major, a trifle impatiently. "Get him in!"

Marchbanks was accordingly summoned; and, as he entered the room, he was obviously surprised to find Eastcote closeted with his chief.

"Let me speak, Tom!" said the Major with a wave of his hand. "Morning, Marchbanks. I've come here to ask whether your firm will lend you to me for an indefinite period. I'm going up-country immediately; destination unknown; business vague and possibly unsatisfactory; date of return uncertain. Will you take it on?"

Naturally, John turned towards his chief for confirmation of this extraordinary statement. Mr. Hume nodded gravely.

"The facts are as stated, Marchbanks. And we've got to fall in, at least, I have, though at great inconvenience. But the final decision, of course, rests with yourself."

Marchbanks at this strange pronouncement looked somewhat bewildered.

"It is right that you should look the thing squarely in the face," his chief went on; "we've brought you out here under certain conditions, and to do certain work, in the hope that you would do it very successfully, and, in plain words, become a valuable asset to the firm. But, on the other hand, should you have disappointed us, you would still have had a comfortable berth and some prospect. That's so, isn't it, Major? I believe we have the reputation of being a generous as well as an enterprising concern."

"You have," answered the Major, "and you are quite right to point it out to our young friend. It is my duty to point out to him that, in making the exchange, he may very easily find a less considerate employer. The British Government has a curious system of rewards and punishments which do not always reach the recipients in fair sequence. But, on the other hand——" He made pause there, and his eye rested with extreme kindliness on Marchbanks' flushed face. "While I can't give a definite pledge as to what my Government may or may not do, I can promise you plenty of work of the most interesting kind in the world, and what personal consideration I have to give. As to the pay—that is on the knees of the gods, for, in the first instance, your connection with me will be unofficial. It's one of my privileges and prerogatives, and they leave me pretty well alone. But, if you could get speech with some of the Government servants, in fairly high places in India, they would probably tell you that the man who trusts me doesn't often regret it."

"No thought of doubt was in my mind, sir!" said John, with the same modest earnestness which gave such an odd charm to his diffident manner. "I am only concerned as to whether I should be doing my duty to leave my firm who have done so much for me. In London they took me without credentials, and when I was absolutely unable to answer any questions they might have chosen to ask. But they did not ask any, and I feel that it may be my first duty to stick to my post, more especially as I have to set out on a journey for them so soon."

"But, if you were absolutely free—your choice?" suggested the Major questioningly.

"Oh, sir," cried John, "there could only be one! The mere idea of travelling through India with you fires my blood!"

"It won't be travelling through India exactly," corrected the Major with a smile of exceeding dryness. "But merely a small and very uninteresting section of it where the hardships may very easily be considerable."

"Then you accept?" broke in Mr. Hume abruptly.

"Yes sir, if you do not hold me."

"I can't, in view of what the Major has said."

"And when do I leave?"

"To-morrow morning, at six o'clock. I'll see you later in the day. If you can come to my quarters, at half-past five, this evening, I'll give you your instructions and tell you what it will be necessary for you to take."

John, thus dismissed, but with his brain in a whirl, bowed and left the room.

"There's something about that young man which makes an appeal, Tom," observed the Major as the door closed. "He's singularly unspoiled. Whatever his upbringing may have been, it has been conducted with wisdom and discernment. He has had some sort of special example."

"Couldn't say, I'm sure," commented Hume. "What's bothering me now is the excuse or explanation I'll have to fake up for London. Marchbanks was Sir Edward's find—or Gilbert's, and they'll be furious over your annexation."

"Shall I write to Sir Edward?" asked the Major as mildly as a dove, now he had achieved that on which he had set his heart.

"Oh, no; I'll muddle through somehow. We can't control these things. I know that's your opinion. You hold a great many queer ideas on the subject of destiny and what not; and no doubt, 'it is written,' as they say here."

About five o'clock that afternoon, John Marchbanks, in a state of mind that could hardly be analysed or described, left the business premises in which he had begun to take a mild proprietary interest to seek the quarters of the Eastcotes.

A little way down the street he met Roger Annan, and, though smarting still under the weight of the Annans' baleful influence on his life and affairs, he could not pass Roger by. There was a moment's awkwardness, however, at the meeting.

"Hulloa, old chappie!" said Roger, and then stopped short.

He was not looking well. The worry of the past weeks, and the means he had taken to still the accusing voice of conscience, had given to him a somewhat worn and dissipated appearance. He had hardly recovered from his over-indulgence of the previous evening at a club dinner, which had been the occasion of some very sharp words between George and himself.

John did not refuse nor ignore the hand, but the clasp was less cordial and warm than of old. He suddenly felt that already there was an immense distance between him and the Annans, once the galaxy of fixed stars in his firmament! He even was conscious of a new and mild contempt for Roger's weakness and feeble achievements. India had nothing to offer such as he. Now that he had seen with his own eyes the kind of life in Calcutta, its amazing network of special temptations for human weaknesses, he marvelled that Mr. Annan had been so blind as to entrust Roger to its tender mercies. It was uncommonly like getting rid of the prodigal son and pushing the shadow as far as possible from the immediate family hearth.

But there was no hardness in John's heart. Wider vision was teaching him tolerance, and his own prospects were so amazingly bright that he could afford to be lenient and kind to all the world. Never had life seemed so rich and fine a thing.

On the other hand, it was to Roger a well-nigh intolerable burden. Smarting under the sense of harsh personal injustice meted out to him by his father; stung by his self-righteous brother's tongue, and by Elizabeth's cold criticism and disapproval; and already loathing India, he was in the mood either to be easily cheered or easily disheartened.

Now, Roger had heard much talk of John Marchbanks from his sister since his arrival in Calcutta, and his brain was a little muddled as to the clearness of the issue. He did not know actually what had happened to John, or how he had gone out to Calcutta. George's suggestion being that it was the outcome of colossal cheek, and some sort of underhand doing it was hardly permissible to define. For this reason he had kept away, but his heart now warmed to his old chum, and he wanted desperately to carry him away to some quiet corner so that they might, in a sense, have it out.

"Seems queer meeting you here, in a Calcutta street, old Jack!" he said with an odd little fatuous laugh. "Doesn't it, now?"

"A bit queer, perhaps," said John absently.

"I suppose you've wondered why I haven't looked you up?"

"I have, rather, when I had time to think about it; but I don't seem to have had much of that commodity since I arrived."

"I suppose you are in great request—dining with all the big bugs, etcetera," said Roger drily. "Well, where can we meet? Can you come now to the club and have a peg and a pow-wow?"

John shook his head.

"I can't, unfortunately. I have a very important appointment in a quarter of an hour's time, and I'm leaving Calcutta to-morrow morning."

"So soon as that! I heard from George that they were moving you on somewhere. But can't we meet to-night yet, after you have kept the appointment? I have oceans of things to tell you. I've had a particularly lively and rotten time since you chucked me, Jack!"

John permitted the accusation to pass.

"I'm sorry. Well, I don't know how long I shall be engaged—no, I can't dine; but, if you like to come to my rooms at nine——"

"Where are they?" asked Roger eagerly; but when he heard, he gave his shoulders a little shrug. "Gone in with the pijaw crowd! Find it pays—eh? Well, I suppose it does, at a certain stage in a chap's life. All right—nine o'clock. I saw your mother, Jack, the week before I sailed, but neither of us had an idea I should be seeing you here."

" I'll hear about it later," said John as he darted off, fully aware that he must on no account be late for the appointment on which so much might hinge.

He was kept till half-past eight with the Major, dined with him at his club, and left in full possession of the first details of the momentous journey they were to take on the morrow.

When he reached his own quarters at the Y.M.C.A. he found Roger impatiently striding to and fro on the pavement in front.

" Ah, there you are, Johnnie! I hadn't the cheek to enter," called out Roger cheerfully, having fortified himself with a good dinner before he arrived. " Though I'm the particular brand they'd love to pluck from the burning, and elevate, as an object-lesson—eh, what ? "

" Shut up, you ass ! " said John. " You don't know what you're talking about."

" Perhaps not, and being a chastened observer I don't argue any more," said Roger meekly. " Do they permit a friendly cigar—or is that banned also ? "

John vouchsafed no answer until they had reached the wide, pleasant bed-sitting-room where he had made himself very comfortable since his arrival in Calcutta, then he produced some excellent cigarettes, and presently it almost seemed as if the old days of comradeship had come back.

" Queer, that we should be smoking over a Calcutta back garden ! " commented Roger, feeling himself soothed and comforted, already the old charm of John's personal friendship asserting itself. " But it isn't a patch on old Glasgow with her smoke and her rainy skies ! Has my sweet brother told you anything about the circumstances which led up to my being kicked out over the paternal doorstep ? "

John shook his head.

" I have had only one conversation with your brother, Roger, and I'll take care not to have another. Not that I bear him any ill-will, but he and I are on opposite sides of the pavement, and will continue to remain so. What happened in Glasgow ? "

After a minute's hesitation Roger confided the story of his second temptation and fall to his old friend. John listened with much gravity.

" Why don't you chuck it, old man ? That sort of thing doesn't pay. It's the very deuce all round ! What do you get out of it anyway at the best ? The game isn't worth the candle. And what will Archie Dunsyre or any of that lot do for you ? Why, nothing but snap their fingers at you after you get into the hole where they've helped to put you ! "

" Right-o ! You have the distressing faculty of being right every time. But it is the least pleasing trait in your otherwise fine character," observed Roger banteringly. " I do it because it's in my blood, and I've got to go on, don't you know, until the poison's all worked out."

" A rotten theory, Roger. Besides, it won't hold water. A man can and ought to be master of his own fate."

" Doubtful. Most of us start handicapped. In my case the offender to be blamed was my grandfather. Heredity counts for a lot more than people imagine ; and it serves some poor beggars as a decent cloak."

" They've no right to it," said John emphatically. " Do try and pull yourself together, old chap. It's worth while. What's in front if you don't ? You'll wear out the patience of your own folk."

" Oh, that's all worn out long since ! " answered Roger lightly. " Not that there was ever any very big reserve, except perhaps in my mother. Now tell me about yourself. Your mother gave me an outline that night I saw her. She was most awfully good to me, Jack ! She'd have given me the money, only, old Craighead went to my pater and got it. Just as well! I'd have hated taking it from your mother, especially as I haven't paid back what I borrowed from you. But I will pay it some day, Jack. 'Pon my honour, I will. Now, tell me just what you are going to do next? Where are they sending you, and what for?"

"I can't give you particulars because I don't know much myself as yet. Major Eastcote will tell me as we go along."

"What has he got to do with it?"

"I'm going with him."

"With him! But he's in the Government service. He hasn't anything to do with Trent, Bartlett & Hume's people!"

"I've been transferred then to Government Service," said John with an air of quiet pride. "At least, I'm travelling to-morrow with Major Eastcote, and Trent, Bartletts have released me from my engagement to them."

"Well, that's confoundedly queer!" said Roger staring hard. "And I'd like uncommonly to know how you've done it!"

They sat talking for a considerable time, and when Roger got back to his brother's house he took uncommon pleasure in passing on the bit of news he had learned.

"See here, you're all wrong about John Marchbanks, George. You've made a mistake, old boy, and snubbed the wrong person! What do you think? He's a Government servant now—attached to Major Eastcote's staff, and is starting for the interior to-morrow. Something very mysterious and important it is, and much secrecy is being observed. And it shows what Eastcote thinks of Marchbanks that he has got the Trent, Bartletts to release him! Now, what do you think?"

Elizabeth, who had made pause in the delicate bit of embroidery she was busy with near the shaded lamp on the centre table, began to work again, with a very curious expression on her face.

"It's nothing but cheek, confounded cheek, I call it! Excuse me, Elizabeth, but I haven't patience discussing that upstart! It won't be long before he's found out! I don't want to hear any more about your precious chum from the Glasgow slums. He has done quite sufficient damage to the family as it is leaving his mark on you——"

At this Elizabeth laughed so quickly and spontaneously, yet with such a harsh, mirthless note in her voice, that Roger felt a cold chill creep over him.

"It's all very funny," she said in explanation. "And it was quite worth while coming out to India to see!"

CHAPTER XXII

THE INTERIOR

THREE days and four nights did John Marchbanks spend in an Indian train, which crawled through a sun-baked land as if it were in no hurry to reach its destination.

For the first part of the journey he found his chief disappointing, and apparently disinclined for talk. It was as if some shadow brooded over his heart, some presentiment that the journey they had undertaken was destined to be a fateful one for him. But whatever his inward thoughts, he made no attempt to voice them, nor did he take any pains to give his subordinate information regarding the country through which they were passing with all the deliberation which characterises the Indian railway system.

Once or twice Marchbanks, disliking the solitude, ventured to put certain questions, and was rather sharply snubbed.

"Don't ask questions, boy. First-hand information is best. Use your eyes and ears, then you've less chance of becoming a nuisance."

After being thus thrust into the background Marchbanks remained there, and it was the third day when they had left the plains behind and were approaching a highly mountainous country that the Major suddenly roused up and began to be more lively.

The first thing he said threw light on the immediate object of their journey.

"We're going to find Jardine. Headquarters are anxious about him, and even fear that he is dead. It will be our business to make sure. Our destination is his station at the mouth of the Narkander Pass."

John, deeply interested, ventured a timid question.

"What is he doing there? Is he in charge of a garrison?"

The Major drily smiled.

"He's a civilian, not a soldier. He's doing the work of the Indian Survey. But he began quite early in his career to strike out for himself, and now his work is ten times more valuable than any survey, because it strikes deeper—goes to the root of things. That's what makes him such an interesting man. But he's elusive as such lonely, detached souls are. Nobody has ever really come up with him so to speak."

"Does he live alone then, without staff or assistance?" asked Marchbanks, his eyes travelling in the direction of the range of desolate-looking hills towards which the train was crawling.

"Quite alone, except for his native servants. One he took with him from the plains in whom he puts implicit confidence. His name is Ram Shicka Dass. I don't care for the fellow myself, but Jardine only smiled his queer slow smile when I told him so, and said he was beyond price. I had, and still have, my doubts, for I've never known a man of his caste who had not his price. The tribesmen are different. They are without bowels, and they kill a man as fast as look at him, but they have a quite clearly defined sense of honour. I've heard Jardine waxing eloquent over it. According to him the West has everything to learn in that direction from the East, but once more, I have my doubts."

The picture the Major drew was fascinating, and Marchbanks felt it sinking into his soul.

" But what I can't understand is how a man can stand the loneliness and isolation. Hasn't he any people, sir ? "

" Ah, there you ask me a question I can't answer ! He belongs to good people, but apparently has no near home-ties. Yet he has looks, and a queer odd winning way with him ! "

" I don't just grasp it. What does he get out of it ? "

" Ah, there you have me again. He's one of the few who don't stop to think what they are going to get out of it. He likes the free, roving life, the spirit of adventure, the insecurity, the risks. He can sleep with an eye and an ear open because I've seen him at it."

" But he must have had a past. Something to hide perhaps. Men don't wipe themselves out like that for nothing."

" He isn't wiped out by any means ! He has done work for us which can never be adequately acknowledged or repaid. You never can tell what induces a certain type of man to disappear like that. It happens oftener than you think—even in London I know of two who disappeared and were never more heard of, though I haven't the smallest doubt but that they are in London still."

" It reminds me of stories I have heard of the French Foreign Legion, though the most of them, I understand, are criminals."

" Don't you believe that," said the Major with a quick note of warning in his voice. " That's the popular idea fostered by novelists who have found the theme fruitful. There are plenty of gallant and priceless souls in the Foreign Legion. You never can tell," he repeated gravely. " There comes a certain break in a man's life and everything is changed. Then, perhaps, he takes some tremendous plunge which effectually wipes out his former life. In a small way you did it yourself."

" I did. But I had no temptation to cut myself off from my kind, and to come out to a God-forsaken place like this. I can't imagine where the lure or the fascination lies."

" Jardine, if we are so lucky as to find him, will tell us. But we shall have to coax him to the mood when we get off this infernal train. Shut that window now, for I've got a shiver in the small of my back which may mean anything, and the night dews in these high altitudes are dangerous and not to be trifled with. What I want to say is, that we've a thirteen mile ride after we get off this train."

Marchbanks sprang up to close the window, at the same time looking at his companion with a quick solicitude.

It was the first time he had ever heard him make a personal remark or shown himself to be susceptible to the physical conditions which affect other men.

" I'm all right. I get a touch of ague now and again, but I can't afford to have it at this juncture, when I'm going to see what has become of Jardine. He hasn't been seen or heard of for twelve months."

" He may have been ill."

" That is within the bounds of possibility. But it is more likely that some mishap has befallen him. Just beyond the Narkander Pass at the mouth of which Jardine keeps his lonely outpost there is a particularly difficult and hostile set of tribesmen. Jardine professes to have them in the hollow of his hand, and certainly he has kept them in check successfully for the last five years. But they are treacherous, and would take advantage of the smallest sign of weakness. That's what makes me so anxious about him."

Here he drew out his watch and timed the train.

" Seven hours late ! And we shall be tumbled out in an hour's time on the stroke of midnight at a station where there is hardly a decent dak bungalow. If we can get horses we might, with luck, reach Jardine's station by three of the morning. Charming prospect, but it's all in the day's work."

It fell out precisely as the Major said, and on the stroke of midnight in beautiful, clear, cool moonlight they were deposited on the little side-track of the station nearest to their destination.

Across a stretch of level country Marchbanks could see the sharp frowning outline of the hills, which seemed to thrust themselves upon them with a certain menace. Beyond these hills in the fastnesses of the tribal regions was hidden part of the mystery and the peril of the East.

His impressionable mind was full of the lonely man whom they had come perhaps to succour, but he forbore to express the wonder he felt that they should be so few in number, so inadequate for any emergency which might easily arise. Like many of the uninitiated, he was inclined to attach too much importance to the outward evidences of power and prestige, forgetful of the other forces which in the hands of the competent and the understanding are far more powerful and successful in dealing with racial difficulties.

The whole situation was intensely interesting to Marchbanks, and as he stood there, in the odorous and mysterious darkness of the Indian night, he could hardly believe himself to be the same man who, less than a year ago, was tied to the routine of a stool in a Glasgow bank.

Two native officials met the train, and to them Eastcote spoke rapidly in Hindustani, of which Marchbanks had already sufficient knowledge to be able to follow the conversation perfectly. This pleased him much, for the station-master had a strange accent, which bore no resemblance to that of the Eastern scholar who had given Marchbanks his first lesson in the language.

From the salaaming and obsequious official they learned that no horses were nearer than seven miles, but that they could be fetched at dawn. Meanwhile they would have to wait in the rude little shelter which did duty as a station house.

In a long bamboo chair Eastcote curled himself without delay, and wrapping his rugs about him was soon asleep, his fine face looking so attenuated, so sharply defined in the strange half-light that Marchbanks was conscious of a sudden pang. Supposing that by any chance his chief should become seriously ill, or die, out in that wilderness, how awful would be the problem for one, single-handed and ignorant, as he was !

The thought was so terrifying and insupportable that he stole out of the station house and walking up and down the platform to the evident disquietude of the official watched for the dawn.

It came tenderly and sweetly with a roseate flush on the far horizon, which presently enveloped the hills in a mysterious halo, robbing them of their towering menace. It grew warmer as the sun drew near to bless the waiting earth, and Marchbanks, with a soul full of poetry for which he had no vehicle of expression, watched the incomparable mystery grow until it became a glorious reality at daybreak.

Meanwhile through the window he could see that Eastcote slept with his chin on his breast, and his face, still ethereal and disquieting, turned towards the dawn.

Promptly at daybreak the second man who had received them returned with the horses, and when Marchbanks realised that he was expected to mount and ride one of the fiery-eyed beasts, he was in the utmost consternation.

" I've never been on a horse's back in my life ! " he said ruefully to the

Major, conscious of how sadly his education for this vivid and crowded life had been neglected.

" A fault soon mended. This will be your steed, she's past her first youth, and we can go slowly. It's only a matter of thirteen miles or so. The chap must bring up the baggage on the mule. Thirteen miles—and this is the thirteenth day of the month ! " he added as an afterthought.

" I think I'd be safer on the mule," said Marchbanks with an odd smile.

But the Major shook his head.

" It takes a master-hand to guide an Indian mule," he said oracularly. " Get up, sit tight, and hold on for all you're worth. We'll get there I don't doubt."

They got there through course of time, but it was a laborious, even painful experience for poor Marchbanks—one which he never forgot. His physical anxiety and discomfort prevented him from taking in the full beauty of the scenery by which they were surrounded, and which comprised one of the most fascinating parts of Northern India.

The mountains, now sharply outlined against the heavenly blue of the sky, showed themselves to be peaks of no mean height ; in fact, some of the farthest and highest had snow on their caps. The region did not seem to be well populated ; they did not even in the thirteen miles of their ride pass a single village, though occasionally, they would see native workers in the sparse fields and a little hut in a sheltered spot.

The track was little more than a bridle path, and led them straight towards a narrow defile between the mountains which, Marchbanks learned, was the Narkander Pass, famous in history, and the scene of a good many bloody fights.

It smiled fair and entirely peaceful upon them as they rode upward in the sweet freshness of the new day before the burning heat overtook them. Suddenly Eastcote, who naturally rode in front, and seemed little concerned by his young companion's frantic efforts to appear at home on the back of a horse, stopped and pointed to a little spur of a wooded hill where the long low outline of a bungalow could be plainly seen.

" Jardine's quarters ! God send we may find him there, but I must say I haven't too strong a hope. There's an air of desertion about it, but we'll soon see and hear for ourselves."

As they rode towards the wide compound where there was a blaze of tropical flowers, a figure appeared on the verandah swathed in white, though they were too far off to distinguish the wearer.

" I don't think it is Jardine," commented the Major. " More likely it is that rascal Ram Shicka Dass. But, any how, it's life, and we'll soon tear the truth out of him."

John, as yet unused to the native, stood aside wonderingly, while the conversation went on between Jardine's servant and Major Eastcote. A free translation of it ran somewhat as follows :

" Where is Sahib Jardine ? Do we find him in the house ? "

" Alas, no, Excellency. Ten fatal moons have arisen and set since the Sahib went away."

" But where has he gone ? Ram Shicka Dass, answer me that truly at your peril ? "

" Most noble one, ten moon rises ago the Sahib, my master, grew very sick. Sick to death I saw that he was, and I begged him to let me go to Dosoor to fetch the Doctor Sahib. I go, but the Doctor Sahib himself sick, and not able to come, but promised to send another doctor Sahib, summoning him by the little wires which do not lie. Then I come back, and lo, my master is gone, and none can tell me where he is."

The expression of the Major's face as he listened to the native's story was such as might have terrified the bravest.

"Ram Shicka Dass, are these words you speak in my ear true words?"

"Most noble one, the words are true words," said the man; and he wore an injured air, which indicated that he resented the imputation cast on his veracity.

"But you have remained for ten moons you have said, and made no effort to find him. How do you explain that, Ram Shicka Dass?"

"Excellency, I waited for the Doctor Sahib, and for some private information. That I have not obtained; and, before another moon, I go to seek my master."

"Ay—where?" asked the Major curtly.

Ram Shicka Dass made a weird evolution of his arms in the direction of the Pass.

"You think the tribesmen have carried him off?"

"No, Excellency; but, on the day he was taken ill, a message had come to my master from beyond the Pass. What was in the message I know not, for it was not permitted my humble eyes to see. It was brought by a beggar who asked me for alms, and whom I was driving away, when Sahib Jardeen stayed my hand. You know his heart, Excellency. It is as wide as the heavens and as tender as a suckling dove. And afterwards, when the man was rested and fed, he gave his message; and my master announced to me next day we must go through the Pass, and right to the place of the hillmen where that barbarian Bukha Saizan lives."

"Well, and when the next day came he was too ill?—or what happened?"

"The Sahib has said it. The fire was in his veins, and his limbs were as the limbs of a woman or a young child, and there was no strength left in him. He said to me, Sahib, that perhaps the great gods of his ancestors had need of him. Then my heart died within me, and, when he slept, I set out to find the Doctor Sahib."

"And when you returned you found him gone—eh? Well, you failed in your duty, Ram Shicka Dass, for you ought not to have left him when he was incapable of taking care of himself."

"It pleases the Sahib to blame; but when a man is alone, and his master is no longer able to guide him by the hand or the tongue, what can happen but disaster?" said the native with a humility which was, to John, inexpressibly touching.

The impression he got was that he had done his best, and that he was distraught over the strange thing that had happened to his master. But it pleased Eastcote to mistrust and doubt every word and act of Jardine's servant, and, presumably, he knew sufficient of the native mind to justify his harshness.

"We'd better get inside and unload, and get something to eat. This requires some thinking over," said Eastcote shortly as he turned away.

Marchbanks stepped forward at once to wait upon him, as a young subordinate would. The Major's manner was absent, and it was not until they were right inside the bungalow, and he was glancing round the sitting-room, that he spoke an enlightening word.

Then, all he said was:

"That rascal, Ram Shicka Dass, lied to us, Marchbanks. I saw it in his wicked eye. He knows what has become of Jardine, and is a party to it. And there is going to be trouble in the Narkander Pass."

These words filled Marchbanks with the utmost surprise.

"He struck me as being sincere enough, and he was evidently distressed," he ventured to say.

" He protested too much. My theory is that Ram planned to leave, on pretext of bringing the doctor, and that, in his absence, the hillmen came down and carried Jardine off. He is in their way, you see—holding the mouth of the Pass, as it were, and reporting every movement in and beyond it."

" And do you suppose they have killed him ? "

The Major shrugged his shoulders.

" That depends. He had an odd power over the native mind, and they may content themselves with keeping him shut up, out of the way, until their nefarious little scheme has time to ripen."

" What form would the scheme take ? "

" Oh, there is always trouble on the frontiers. India is full of little wars of which the home people hear but little. They've grown scarcer of late years ; either the new generation has at last digested the essence of British policy or they have lost a bit of the old fire. But up here, in the Narkander Pass, there has always been a cauldron seething and bubbling over. That it has never been drastically dealt with is one of the mysterious lapses you get occasionally in the best administration in the world."

" It is a very comfortable little billet, here," said John, looking round with uncommon interest.

It was an ordinary and very typical Indian bungalow sitting-room, furnished in bamboo and basket work, with one or two gaily-coloured rugs, and a bookcase with more books than are usually found in a place so remote. There were no photographs or other pictures, however, which rather deepened the impression that it had been the home of a very solitary man who had successfully cut himself off from the ordinary channels of life.

" It's all right, and, presently, that rascal Ram Shicka will set before us a very perfect little meal. I remember, last time I ate in this little bungalow, I complimented Jardine on his cook. But I shan't eat much of it. I'm not feeling very fit, Marchbanks—in fact, there's a bout of fever brewing. When we get our kits unslung I'll dose myself, and, after I've tried to eat, I'll go to bed. By to-morrow I'll have decided what it will be best to do."

It all fell out as the Major said. A meal of surpassing excellence was set before them, after an interval so short as to occasion surprise, even to the Major. And after they had refreshed themselves he said he would go and lie down.

Marchbanks followed him into the bedroom and carefully covered him up, as he complained of shivering though it was hot enough outside. After taking a dose of quinine he settled himself to sleep on Jardine's camp bed, and Marchbanks was left to his own devices.

In surroundings so new and strange he was not likely to find time hang heavily on his hands.

He sauntered out to the verandah, lit a comfortable pipe, and then began to take a fresh inventory of the contents of the room behind. He felt an extraordinary quick and personal interest in it, and there was something weird and pathetic in the way they had come to take possession of an empty house, as one might open an inviting casket, only to find the jewel gone.

There were very few personal belongings about ; indeed, the orderly neatness of the place seemed to point to the somewhat finicky habits of the confirmed bachelor. Some English magazines, however, though not of recent date, struck a homely note ; and Marchbanks felt a distinct thrill, as he came across a year-old copy of a well-known Scottish newspaper.

The sight of the flabby, well-thumbed sheets seemed to establish at once a strange link between this remote Indian station and the land of his birth, and even, in some strange subtle way, to draw him nearer to the man whose pictured face even he had not seen.

He roamed about, looking for some hint or token of the man's actual bodily presence ; and soon on a little, cheap, hanging bracket he saw an old-fashioned daguerreotype case leaning against a bit of some queer Indian carving. Without thought of prying he took down the little case and touched the spring.

Then he stood stock still, and the blood receded from his face, and something throbbed and hammered in his brain.

For the face—smiling and young and girlish, as sweet a picture as the eyes of man had ever rested on—was undoubtedly the face of his own mother.

There were the level brows, the straight, calm eyes, the tender, rather appealing mouth. His mother !

Such a terror took hold of John Marchbanks that he staggered against the wall, shaking, as if struck by a sudden ague.

CHAPTER XXIII

THE BACK OF BEYOND

JOHN MARCHBANKS did not consider himself, nor was he considered by others, a very imaginative or flighty person. Nay, most of his actions had been characterised by a deliberation and sound common sense not too frequently found in a man of his age. But, as he started back from the corner where he had found that amazing thing, a portrait of his mother, he began to wonder whether the lure of the East had been too much for his mental balance.

He still clutched the daguerreotype case in his hand and, on the verandah, where the light was certainly clearer and steadier than in the well-shaded room beyond, he proceeded to make a closer study of the picture.

His common sense assured him that probably the likeness was merely accidental—one of these odd coincidences which often confront us in life, sometimes to our perplexity, occasionally to our alarm; but, as he stood there on the extreme edge of the verandah, with nothing between him and the vivid light of the smiling heavens, something told him there was no mistake. If not a portrait of his mother in her youth, then there must be another woman her exact prototype somewhere in the world whom this represented!

He removed the little gilt-edged picture from its faded velvet bed and looked on the back. A small square label was pasted there and, though the printing was very indistinct, it was possible to read it: "J. Geikie, Photo Artist, Portobello."

The name, somehow, suggested a travelling photographer in summer. He tried to imagine the scene—his mother on Portobello sands, strolling by the side of some unknown admirer, the man, perhaps, whom her son had come out to the wilds of India to seek! It gave him an odd, unspeakable thrill, and, hard upon it, followed an absurd memory of certain words Katrine Polson had spoken concerning him one day when he was still in his teens, when he had chanced to find her in one of her excitable prophetic moods.

"Ay, laddie," she had said. "It's easy to see you're no' to be a bide-at-hame! I see heaps o' trouble for you, and what looks like a coffin, but is only a ship. Ay, ay, ye'll traivel far and hae mony ups and doons. But syne, at the lang last, a big, fair man will bring ye happiness and peace. But ye'll hae to seek the world wide for him. It's no gaun to be a' the comforts o' the Saut Market for you, lad. But we've a' got to dree oor weird."

It was extraordinary the vividness with which these long-forgotten words smote back upon his memory; almost he saw the queer old face of the woman before him, and heard her shrill but not unpleasant voice crooning over the teacups.

But presently, pulling himself together sharply, he was about to turn and replace the portrait case, when he suddenly became uncomfortably conscious that he was being watched by the exceedingly sharp eyes of Ram Shicka

Dass, who stood at the bottom of the verandah steps salaaming violently.

"Well, what is it, my man?" he asked in rather sharp accents.

"Could the son of the base-born speak one word in the Sahib's ear?" inquired the native in his smooth, winning voice.

"Yes, of course. What is it?" asked Marchbanks still abruptly, feeling for the first time a rather keen sense of personal aversion to the brown skin and the cringing manner of lower India.

"Will the Sahib, then, deign to come forward a little way into the shade so that none may hear?" he asked.

"In a moment," said Marchbanks, and walking over to the corner of the room he restored the portrait case to its place, Ram Dass's eyes watching him through their narrow slits with something more than passing interest.

"Does the Sahib know, that in all the house which holds his treasures, that is the greatest treasure of my master? And never before has his servant known him to depart to any destination and leave it behind, which shows beyond doubt, Sahib, that he was treacherously dealt with and removed against his will."

Marchbanks, feeling that he might be on the eve of momentous revelations, preceded the man down the verandah steps into the shade of the thicket, which protected one side of the compound from the sun.

"The Sahib is perhaps of the same blood as my revered master and knows the mem-sahib whose picture it is?" pursued the Oriental in his smooth suggestive voice.

"No, no; I have never seen your master. I am only here as the colleague and helper of the Sahib Major. And I do not know the lady—though she is like someone I do know. Who is she? The wife of the Sahib Jardine?"

"It is not permitted the base-born to know, for why? My master would not stoop to discuss the affairs of his heart with his servant. He is far too great and high for such a descent. It is the picture of one cherished by His Excellency, my master, beyond all others. Have I not seen him with his eyes studying it by the light of sun and moon, with that yearning in his eyes which is born of the heart's desire? The Sahib knows not whence she comes or whither she has gone?"

Marchbanks shook his head. He could not really make any positive assertion; for now, removed from his startling presentation of the face that had been the star of his boyhood, if it had waned a little in his manhood, the old common-sense suggestion of a chance likeness came uppermost.

At this gesture, Ram Shicka Dass seemed disappointed, and a certain wistfulness like that of a child who is cheated of something on which he has set his heart crossed his face.

Suddenly, however, his manner changed and he began to talk with amazing volubility which Marchbanks, whose knowledge of Hindustani was of very recent date, had to check more than once before he could get the gist of his observations.

"Listen, oh, Sahib, to the words of Ram Shicka Dass, for they be words of truth and wise council! The Sahib Jardine has been spirited away by that evil beast, Bukta Saizan, and nothing but the high power of the white sahibs will bring him back. I know where he is—at least I know sufficient to guide me. But what would it avail for the son of the base-born to go himself on such a pilgrimage? Why, nothing at all! Probably poor Ram Dass would pay with his head—though that he would sell dearly! But Bukta, though he shouts so loud, and brandishes the sword of his ancestors, is nothing but a babe and a braggart who mightily fears the might of the white sahibs. For that reason he skulks in his fastnesses and flies before the approach."

" Well, and what has all that got to do with me ? " inquired Marchbanks rather impatiently.

" Excellency, it has everything to do. To-morrow the Sahib Major will be even more sick than he is to-day, and for several days he will know nothing. I have seen that fever before, and nursed the Sahib Jardine through it. Ram Shicka Dass, therefore, knows that of which he talks."

" But I still don't know what it has got to do with me, unless you are going to suggest that I get the doctor from somewhere ? "

" Excellency, the Doctor Sahib will be here to-day at sunset, for he has given his word ; and even now I see the dust of his coming on the road."

" Then what in Heaven's name do you want me to do ? "

" To-morrow, before the sun is up, we shall go forth, Excellency, trusting himself to the son of the base-born Ram Shicka Dass, who has never had lying words upon his lips, to find the Sahib Jardine."

Marchbanks stared at the small, thin, eager face, and the flashing, mysterious, almond-shaped eyes devouring his face. It was uncanny, and involuntarily he took a step backward, saying inwardly, " I don't think ! " Aloud he said—" And leave my chief, the Sahib Major ! It is quite impossible, Ram Shicka Dass, and you are a fool and knave to suggest it."

" Excellency, there is nothing you can do for the Sahib Major, whom the gods will cure in their own good time, if they will—and if not——" Here he shrugged his shoulders and implied the rest. " And, moreover, the Doctor Sahib will be here. Behold, as I said, the dust of his coming on the road. And they two can very well be left while we go to find my master."

" But who will do for them ?—cook, make their meals, look after them ? " asked Marchbanks descending in spite of himself to details, for the idea, somehow, fired his blood.

In the heart of every man, even the most commonplace, there lurks the spirit of adventure, the desire to go forth to seek and conquer the unknown. Marchbanks was no exception, though, even while the lure began to work, his common sense warned him that it was a thing queer and risky, beyond telling, that he proposed to do.

" That, Ram Shicka Dass will see to ; in the night watches he will bring his substitute, if only Excellency gives his promise for the morrow."

" But it is a long ride, Ram. I'd be done for in the first half-day, for I am not at home on the back of a horse."

" Excellency, there is a little one in the stable, whose back is made for the uneasy," he said, never at a loss for a picturesque phrase. " She shall be saddled at dawn if only the word is given, and none has ever ridden her but the Sahib Jardine, whom Allah preserve ! "

Marchbanks remained silent, looking intently into the Oriental's face. It sounded like a wild-goose chase, and a mad adventure to trust himself to a man he now saw for the first time, and to go in search of another whom he had never seen at all.

" And what do you suppose would be the issue, Ram Shicka Dass ? Probably I shall lose my head."

" The quicker to Paradise, Excellency ! " came the answer glibly. " But I will pledge my own that no harm shall come to you."

" It would not particularly please me to behold your head on a charger, fool, if my own were to follow suit," said Marchbanks on the spur of the moment.

At this pleasantry Ram clapped his hands, and his eyes rolled in their sockets in uncontrollable ecstasy.

"Just so was my master, the Sahib Jardine, wont to speak to the base-born! Lo, it is written! Allah has decreed!"

"What is written? And what has Allah decreed, since you seem to have such an intimate knowledge of affairs celestial?"

"It is written that you, the unspoiled and unsullied son of the morning, should come to bring back the Sahib Jardine. I knew it this morning when my unworthy eyes rested on your face. Did Excellency not observe how, while the ears of his servant listened respectfully to the words and commands of the Sahib Major, his whole heart and mind were elsewhere?"

"I observed nothing of that kind. Well, and here is the doctor coming up to the house. Say nothing, Ram Shicka Dass, but let this be between us till the morning, when we will talk further of it."

So saying he moved forward to receive the doctor, who was on horseback, with a servant riding behind.

Thrown into a situation where he had to take the initiative on every point, Marchbanks was quite equal to it, but when he heard the doctor's hearty voice with the unmistakable North Country accent, he was filled with a lively joy.

"Scotch, by Jove!" he cried joyfully. "What's your name?"

"Pringle—Andrew Hepburn Pringle, at your service. Commonly called Andy for short. What's the matter here—eh? Our brown-faced friend was a trifle vague about symptoms yesterday, though picturesquely violent as to the haste necessary. Is Jardine ill, and have you come up to look after him?"

"Jardine isn't here. I arrived last night with Major Eastcote and it is he who is ill."

The Scotsman's cherubic face took on a more serious expression.

"The great, the inimitable Major Eastcote of the Intelligence Department?"

Marchbanks nodded.

"We came up to make inquiries about Jardine, but it seems he has been mysteriously spirited away."

"It was certainly Jardine I was invited by Ram Shicka Dass to come and prescribe for. Who has spirited him away?"

Marchbanks shrugged his shoulders.

"It seems to be an unholy mystery, but come and see the Major, and we can talk it out afterwards. I'm very anxious about him. He hasn't really been well all the way up."

"That so? I heard he was on furlough in England."

"So he has been. He hasn't been over a month back," said Marchbanks as he led the way into the house.

Sickness in tropical countries moves by rapid stages and a few hours can bring about acute symptoms which take much longer to develop at home. These few hours had so increased the fever in the Major's veins that his face was highly flushed, his temperature up, and his consciousness partly clouded.

He did not recognise the doctor as a stranger even, but kept addressing him alternately as "Billy" and "Jardine," which helped to indicate the direction in which his thoughts were running.

"By Jove, he's bad! But I've got everything needful, and that chap with the heathenish name should prove a faithful attendant, I should imagine. We must press him into the service at once."

"He's talking of setting out on a wild-goose chase after his own master to-morrow," said Marchbanks, as they left the sick-room together.

He had reason to express surprise almost immediately at the variety of completeness of the stores carried on the spare horse. Nothing had been forgotten, there was even a small refrigerator packed with ice.

"You see, I've never been up to Jardine's quarters, and from what I'd heard, I thought it unlikely he would have much comfort. I brought all I could carry between us, and I'm glad of it, for I'll have to stop a few days if he is to be pulled through."

"Is it so serious as that?"

Pringle nodded as he carefully sorted out his medical stores on the coolest corner of the verandah.

"I've heard a good deal about Jardine since I came up to Dosoor—God-forsaken station it is, too! And it seems he's been in the habit of doctoring himself. What's Ram Shicka Dass's theory about his disappearance?"

Marchbanks briefly explained it. The doctor listened interestedly as he puffed away at a particularly fragrant cigar.

"And he wants you to go off with him on a search expedition? A bit risky, don't you think?"

"That's what I'm inclined to think, but, on the other hand, I don't deny that the idea is rather fascinating."

"It would doubtless be a bit of an adventure. But has the engaging native informed you that this ruffian, Bukta, is the terror of his own district and all the others within his reach?"

"He has called him a few names certainly."

"And, his idea being that Bukta has abducted Jardine, does he think that there is a chance of his being alive still?"

"He seems to think so."

"To fervently believe it, do you mean?" asked Pringle, making pause.

"Yes—certainly he fervently believes it; also he asserts that if he can take a white man with him he'll be able to bring Jardine back, and to put the fear of death on the marauder somehow."

"So!" said the Scotsman, drawing a long breath. "Well, if Ram says that, depend upon it, there may be a grain of truth in it. They are queer beggars, the natives, and when they speak the truth they speak it hard. It may be swallowed whole. But I suppose you've sampled them in plenty, and I needn't air my scanty knowledge."

At this pronouncement Marchbanks naturally laughed.

"I haven't been six weeks in India yet!"

"Bless my heart and soul! And yet you are cheerfully contemplating a raid into an alien and hostile territory! It's the sublime dash of ignorance surely. Of course, you can't speak the language?"

"I understand Ram, and can make him understand me," said Marchbanks modestly.

"Well, you're a rum 'un. It's a chance of seeing a bit of the mysterious East, I grant you, but I'd advise you to make your will before you set out. But you aren't really contemplating it, are you?"

"I was, but if you think so seriously of the Major's condition——"

"Oh, I can attend to that. I'll stop here and see him through whatever the upshot. And you wouldn't be of any use. My servant can do the chores, though he may be less capable than Ram, whose prowess as a cook has penetrated to Dosoor. They have tales of Jardine's bachelor dinners here which raise the envy of our station ladies beyond words!"

"Then you would advise me to go—would you?"

Pringle shrugged his broad shoulders.

" I advise no man. The man who is prodigal to advice in this country usually has none worth offering. For look, old chap, nothing can be tabulated, or arranged, or concluded here ! There are no foregone conclusions in India ; it is the unexpected that invariably happens. And, where the native is concerned, that holds most infernally true. But, on the other hand, a little common sense might assure you that Ram Dass could gain nothing by making an end of you, because at this stage of your career you are of no importance. No offence meant, but it's the truth—isn't it ? "

Marchbanks grinned a slow grin as he readily admitted it.

" Well, these being the facts I should try the little adventure. If it comes off and you rescue Jardine, who is one of the most valuable government servants, you score, and perhaps your modest fortune may be made. As it is you don't seem to have much to lose——"

" Perhaps there is more to gain anyway," said Marchbanks with a kind of steady resolution. " And, things being as you say, and as you are going to stop here to look after my chief, I'll go. It may be the best service I can render him—he's most frightfully anxious about this man Jardine, and he's been awfully good to me, so I want to do something to show my gratitude."

Pringle, though a " hard nut," was rather touched by the simple earnestness with which Marchbanks spoke. He was delighted with him altogether, and blessed the bit of luck which had led to his discovery, in a place where he had expected to keep a lonely vigil.

Everything his skill and devotion could suggest was done for the poor Major that night, and Pringle was rewarded when he succeeded in producing a sleep, which, if not altogether natural, would at least do something towards restoring the shaken balance of a strong constitution, that had been much tried, through a long life of strenuous service, such as few men could show.

The two Scotsmen ate a very good dinner together, and talked on the verandah afterwards, looking out over a wonderful world bathed in moonlight such as only India can show. And next morning, when Marchbanks was ready to depart, their parting was that of friends.

At the last Marchbanks was permitted to go into the Major's room, but the sick man did not recognise him. He was shocked at the change these few hours of suffering had wrought, and though his mind, in a sense, was easy, because he was leaving him in such good care, he felt a strange lingering doubt as to whether he would return to find Eastcote alive.

" You'll take jolly good care of him, dear old chap ! " he said with a catch in his voice, as he bundled out of the room with more haste than he had entered it, because of his rising emotion.

" Right-o. I'll leave nothing undone," returned Pringle. " He isn't any worse this morning anyhow, and that's a crumb of comfort to carry away with you. The thing has got to run its course, and the more virulent it is the sooner it's over. He has a lean, hard body, and immense endurance. I believe he'll pull through. It's the dysentery I'm most afraid of. A man can't stand it long. But I think it's arrested. Well, good-bye, old chap, and good luck. I'll look forward to seeing a triumphal procession, headed by you and old Jardine, and a following of repentant and obsequious ruffians from the fastnesses of the Narkander Pass."

Marchbanks listened to these heartening words with a somewhat detached expression on his face, indicating that his thoughts had travelled beyond the immediate moment.

" And when he asks for me, Pringle," he said, a little unsteadily ; " if he seems to wonder at what I've done—give him this."

He took an envelope from his pocket and passed it over, and Pringle promised to deliver it faithfully.

Then they shook hands warmly, but no further speech passed between them. A few hours before they had not known of one another's existence, but already bonds were forged which would stand the test of time and circumstance.

It is so, in the lone places of the earth, where human nature is stripped of the trappings which hamper it in the busier haunts of men. Too often these trappings cloak the real man, and create misunderstandings which are never cleared up this side the grave.

As Pringle watched the little cavalcade of two ride forth into the unknown, he muttered to himself:

"Oh, Scottie, great is thy faith!"

For forty-eight hours longer he devoted himself to the lone struggle against disease and death, and towards the dawn of the third morning knew that he had conquered.

When the Major came to himself and saw the friendly face, with its odd, upstanding fringe of red hair, and the clear, honest, blue eyes, regarding him kindly and quizzically, he appeared bewildered.

"Where am I?" he asked, trying to raise himself and make a survey of his surroundings.

"In Jardine's bungalow, at the mouth of the Narkander Pass, popularly designated the mouth of hell," answered Pringle softly. "I'm one Pringle—doing locum duty for Harwood Mayne at Dosoor. You've had a pretty lively fight for it, but it's over."

"I'm as weak as a kitten. But I remember now. Where's Marchbanks?"

"He'll be here presently, but you must sleep first," said the doctor, advancing with some of his nostrum in a glass.

"Anything been heard of Jardine?"

"Not yet; but there's going to be something heard pretty soon. Drink this, and sleep. We'll talk it out to-morrow."

On the morrow, the restoration of all save strength was so complete that Pringle saw nothing would be gained by keeping back the truth about Marchbanks.

"A headstrong and adventurous youth, Major, has gone into the jaws of hell to bring out Jardine."

The Major started.

"Through the pass, you mean—on his own?"

"Through the pass, most certainly; but not altogether on his own. He is accompanied by that son of light—or darkness—which, has yet to be proven, Ram Shicka; and together they will retrieve Jardine, unless he has passed beyond the reach of human retrieval, which Allah forbid!"

"Drop that stupid talk, man, and tell me exactly what has happened!" cried the Major, in a state of feverish excitement, immensely pleased, though astonished by what he heard.

For answer, Pringle placed Marchbanks' sealed envelope in his hand.

"I expect he'll set forth his own tale a little more concisely, Major. I'm sorry my flowery language gave offence. It's this place! And it's nothing, I hear, to the lingo Jardine could spin by the hour."

The Major was not listening. His eyes were devouring the contents of Marchbanks' brief note. Suddenly he looked up, with an odd expression on his face.

"Go back to the sitting-room, doctor, and see whether you can find a small photograph case, in leather, standing in a corner somewhere. Bring it here."

The case was immediately found, and Pringle watched while the Major made a study of the woman's face within. But what a portrait, presumably belonging to Jardine, and found in his quarters, could have to do with these strangers, Pringle could not succeed in divining.

It was several minutes before the Major spoke, and then, it was merely to give voice to a reflection as old as the hills.

" There are more things in heaven and earth, Horatio, than are dreamed of in our philosophy."

CHAPTER XXIV

EAST IS EAST

SUBLIME ignorance of the task he had undertaken was undoubtedly John Marchbank's best shield and buckler, as he rode, at sunrise, into the narrow defile of the Narkander Pass.

It is not too much to say that many a seasoned Indian veteran would have hesitated before trusting himself so guilelessly to the tender mercies and the good faith of Ram Shicka Dass.

The Oriental rode for a few paces behind his superior, and, save when addressed, offered neither remark nor comment. As they rode on, very slowly, owing partly to Marchbanks' poor and unskilled horsemanship, and partly to the rude nature of the bridle path, a panorama of amazing beauty and magnificence began to be unrolled before them.

Travellers who content themselves with the cities of India, and make no opportunity of penetrating into its rich and wonderful interior, have no idea of what they have missed.

In a few hours' ride that heavenly morning John Marchbanks beheld scenery unmatched in the most mountainous regions of Scotland, quite equal to the finest bits of Switzerland. It was very wild, richly and thickly wooded, and a river of quite respectable size washed the base of the hills. Visible sign of life there was none, and the stillness was only broken now and again by some strange cry from the thicket, indicating that there was both bird and animal life hidden in these fastnesses.

After a time, the silence, so profound, became rather eerie, and Marchbanks, drawing rein on a spur of the still ascending bridle path, signed to Ram Shicka Dass to come forward. He had felt once or twice an odd little shiver in the small of his back at the thought that, on that narrow path, and amid such desolate surroundings, he was wholly at the mercy of the native, and could not combat treachery were it shown.

His one comforting reflection was that he was such very small game as to be worthy of no man's attack.

Ram came forward with an encouraging smile on his shining face. Having secured that on which he had set his mind, and in no doubt but that he was marching to the triumphant recovery of the master he adored, he was ready to study the slightest wish or whim of the principal instrument in the quest.

" What wills, Excellency? To rest and refresh? Lo, tiffin is behind, in the saddle-bags, and can be spread in a moment."

" Ripping idea ! " said John. " At least, a drink would be acceptable. Perhaps we'd better get forward a few steps ; there seems to be a kind of plateau ahead."

" Excellency has said it, and from the further point we can see the far-off ridges where the hosts of Bukta Saizan are crouching in their lairs."

They pressed forward, and presently John, feeling stiff and sore, after a couple of hours' jogging in an unaccustomed seat, slid thankfully to the ground, at the same time somewhat ruefully rubbing his thighs.

Ram Dass, with a sympathetic grin, recommended some patent anodyne, which he pledged himself to produce when they paused for the night.

The horses were tethered, and John spread himself under the friendly shelter of the nearest tree, and permitted the native to wait on him with all the air of the first in command. It was a very novel situation, but Marchbanks accepted it as merely a part of the day's work. The adventure still interested him mightily, and he permitted no doubt of his companions to mar his present employment.

He was young, and to youth the unknown and the untried has an ever-beckoning finger. Then at the back of his mind was the passionate hope that here, in this remote and apparently untrodden part of the Indian Empire, he might find or make his chance. It struck him as virgin country, every span and root of it, though it was all safely tabulated in the records of the Indian Survey, the very bridle path from which they had just turned aside being marked in good indelible ink on the Ordnance Map!

From his pack Ram Shicka Dass produced a luncheon which Marchbanks thought fit for the gods. He himself had given no orders concerning it, and was surprised at the neatness, perfection and daintiness of the meal served out to him, unaware that Dass—a very perfect servant—had been fully trained by Jardine himself. Many a time they had travelled together over the same bridle path, and slept in the open, and shared all the incidents, perils, and pleasures of the surveyor's life.

Marchbanks, enjoying his luncheon tremendously, was ready with his praise, and after he lit his cheroot he lay back in the shade at peace with God and man.

"Now, perhaps you will be good enough to give me a little more information, Ram Shicka Dass, as to where we are going, how we are to get there, and what we expect we shall find at the end of the journey?"

"Excellency, if all goes well with us, we reach the farthest ridge by the third sundown. See, yonder—where the sun touches the horizon—that is our destination."

"Faith, it looks like the edge of beyond!" said Marchbanks. "In actual fact, what is it?"

"The stronghold of Bukta Saizan."

"A stronghold! Do you mean a fortress, a castle, or something of that kind?"

Dass shrugged his shoulders, uncomprehending, but immediately began to expatiate with his usual voluble picturesqueness.

"Excellency, once upon a time there were walled cities on these ridges, and beyond the walls no stranger might pass without danger—nay, without certainty of being put to the sword. All the life there was hidden from those without. But the Government of the Heaven-born has changed all that, and now the walled cities of Narkander are but a remnant of half-empty houses huddled upon the mountain-sides. In the old tribal wars the walls have been broken down, both from within and without. But to Narkander Bukta Saizan, ingrate and fool, tries to cling, though he must know that the stars in their courses have decreed that he shall not longer rule in the place of his ancestors."

"It is like a page out of the *Arabian Nights*, Dass. Please go on," said Marchbanks, enjoying himself immensely.

Dass had never heard of the *Arabian Nights*, but perceiving that, beyond doubt, the Sahib was pleased with him, he proceeded with his tale—a curious mixture of fact and fiction.

He told of the old tribal life in the walled cities and of the fierce fights which took place between hostile tribesmen, fired by racial jealousies and all desirous of supremacy.

Marchbanks marvelled at the whole recital, but more especially that so much forgotten lore should dwell under the stolid exterior of Ram Shicka Dass. But before the long recital finished sleep overcame him, and the heat of the day was passed in peaceful slumber which undoubtedly refreshed him for the evening ride.

Dass withdrew to a respectful distance, and his wonder and devotion grew at the confidence this stranger was reposing in him who might so easily betray it most foully.

Later, Marchbanks found that the ridges, which seemed to meet, and even to cleave to the far horizon, were much more remote from each other than he had imagined.

When they came to make camp for the night they seemed more inaccessible than ever.

Dass had forgotten nothing necessary for the striking of a comfortable camp. There were no dak bungalows in the Narkander Pass, but the swift unrolling of a folded tent provided the necessary shelter for the white sahib, while the Dass squatted on the dry short grass without.

Marchbanks slept like a boy tired with adventure and the novel experiences of the day. Also, an odd reverence and awe descended upon his spirit, which comes to the unspoiled soul alone with nature in her noblest moods, when she spreads for him some pictures fresh, as it were, from the hand of God.

As he arranged his head on the air pillow which was one of the portable comforts Ram Dass had brought from the station, he thought with pity, of the thousands of British-born toiling in the streets of the dusty capitals of India, spending their lives there, and returning home without having rested and refreshed their vision with the inward beauty and the wonder of the country of their exile.

Three days and three nights did they thus travel, rest and encamp, for the Pass seemed interminable. And with each lap on the way it became wilder and grander, more solitary, more cut off from the ordinary world of men. There were beasts of prey near them on their last camp, and in the intervals of his sleep Marchbanks heard strange sounds and wild cries, but was perfectly satisfied because Ram Dass had betrayed no fear and said he had means to keep them at bay.

On the evening of the third day he saw quite distinctly, in the near distance, the low outline of the wall which shut in what remained of the city of Meeristan. When he would have questioned Ram Dass, with some eagerness, he found that a strange reserve and silence had fallen upon the native. As he looked at his impassive face, in which the almond-shaped eyes seemed to have sunk until they were mere slits, the first sensation of apprehension—though it could hardly be called fear—descended on Marchbanks' mind.

It was an immense adventure he had essayed, and might easily—how very easily he now realised—have death for its issue. For here in the fastnesses of the mountains, with but a single arm between him and unimagined evil, and that arm untrained to fight or kill, his chance might be of the slenderest.

" Answer, you son of a thousand apes ! How soon do we reach the gates ? And how do we pass through them ? And what will befall us, supposing we ever do get through ? "

Ram Dass shook an impassive head.

" We will encamp here to-night, Excellency, and while you sleep I will make reconnoitre further."

"Ram Dass, you do no such thing on your own! You won't leave me here to the jackals and any other stray and choice specimens of the jungle fraternity!"

Ram Dass permitted himself a faint smile.

"Excellency, there is no jungle here, no anything to hurt or harm. A few prowling jackals there may be, but they fear the face of man, for they were hunted without cessation. If Excellency wills and prefers it, I can wait for the dawn."

Marchbanks did will and prefer it, but for the first time since they started out on their so strange pilgrimage the native disobeyed.

Marchbanks slept, though he had not expected it, his nerves being now in slightly frayed condition, but he awoke with a start and sat up on his elbow to listen, and something within him told him he was alone on the far side of the mountain facing the walls of mystery and of menace beyond!

He rose, drew on his boots, and cautiously pulled back the flap of his tent door. He was in no way surprised to find Ram Dass absent from his accustomed place. Both the horses were tethered near, however, so that if he had gone it must have been on foot.

Now thoroughly awakened, and in a sense alarmed, he looked at his watch only to find that it had stopped, which chagrined him oddly, for a time-keeping watch is a friendly and live thing which gives a man a sense of companionship.

A curious sensation of finality overcame Marchbanks for a moment, and he experienced what he supposed might be some of the feelings of a man under sentence of death. For if Ram Shicka Dass, for some underhand or treacherous reason of his own, had deserted him within sight of the walls of Meeristan, what more likely than that he was in collusion with the scoundrel he had so vigorously denounced?

But presently his common sense came to the rescue, and he asked himself scornfully what object Ram could possibly have in betraying him—a person of no importance either to him or to the Indian Government with which his connection was purely personal and unofficial.

He plunged down on the short dry grass and proceeded to make the best of the extraordinary situation in which he found himself, and also to watch the holy mystery of the dawn from a vantage point withheld from most men.

The presence of the animals near by gave him a feeling of companionship and comfort. The pretty creature he had been riding for three days had grown accustomed to his awkward handling, and had responded to his undoubted kindness, while he had become familiar with her gait and manners, and so had found himself a more comfortable seat. These had been days of great awakening for Marchbanks, and he had had the strange feeling of being handled and driven by fate, which had ordained certain things to come to pass.

This somewhat fatalistic doctrine, so prevalent in India that it detaches a certain value from both human life and effort, steadied his nerve and purpose, and he vowed that, whatever befell him, whether Ram Dass should return or not, he would himself take the risks of penetrating beyond the walls of Meeristan. He would not come so near only to be baulked of the crown of his great adventure.

The sun rose, leaping from peak to peak in glorious splendour, and flushing softly with rose and gold the low white walls of the mysterious city. Marchbanks, whose eyes were good, strained them in vain towards these walls, hoping to be rewarded by the sight of a white speck he could translate into the returning native.

But his quest was vain. He felt himself totally at a loss. Judging the distance to the best of his ability, he concluded that he was a couple of hours' ride from the gates, which, however, he had yet to discover. Apparently the wall offered an unbroken line, and nothing showed beyond it—not one of the minarets or shining roofs common to Indian towns and cities, and which, often raised to great height, and flashing in the sun, serve as landmarks to the traveller at immense distances.

Either the city was buried in the hollow beyond, or presented its front to the further horizon. It added to the mystery and also to the menace, but Marchbanks determined that at all costs he would go forward.

The bridle path, quite clearly defined, was very steep and rocky. He had first to descend into the valley, then climb, on the other side, to the city walls, and prospect for the gates, or, at least, some smaller entrance which would let him through.

As he followed this procedure certain stories of the horrors, mysteries and atrocities of the mutiny marshalled themselves before an imagination which had never been clearer nor more vivid. Also, he had read stories of tortured Englishmen in Thibet, and though he was, geographically, far from Thibet, the conditions seemed disconcertingly similar. " A man dies but once," he muttered, recalling the Major's words ; " only, he wants to die quickly. Bah ! These days of incredible cruelty must be past ! "

Mingling with his natural fears, however, was a strain of assurance that he was being guided for some definite object.

In his own mind there was no doubt but that he would find this man Jardine, and, having found him, that the stranger would have a profound influence on his life. While not permitting himself to believe that it was actually his own father he was seeking, something stirred in his veins—that mysterious call of the blood which has pursued men from shore to shore, and altered the current of lives innumerable.

John Marchbanks, in the midst of these strange, heart-searching experiences, became older, wiser, and more manly, one from whom the smaller trappings of life fell away, like some useless garment. And when a man achieves that in the days of his youth, either there is a limit set to his earthly life or it is destined that he shall travel far on the highways of human effort and achievement.

He surveyed the horses, munching peaceably at the scanty herbage, somewhat at a loss whether to take them or to leave them, in the hope that Ram Shicka Dass might return quickly, and take charge of the little camp.

He had not sufficient skill in the handling of horses to enable him to establish that unity of purpose which so often exists between man and beast ; but again, supposing any mischance befell them, the means of transit were cut off, and the only way of getting back to the station at the mouth of the Pass would be by going on foot.

It is difficult to gauge distances, travelling as they had done, but Marchbanks had the idea that they must have come, at least, sixty or seventy miles. He imagined now that he was only a couple of miles or so from the fortress city. The actual distance, however, was much further.

Distances, in these high and clear altitudes, are as elusive and misleading as at sea.

Finally, he decided to leave the horses and foot it.

He gave them some provender to content them, patted their noses, and turned his face down the steep and winding path which led to the valley.

A mind less detached would have found it a most enchanting walk, full of beauty and possibility. As he descended, the wild luxuriance of the vegetation increased, and, after a very short time, he became aware that he had somehow missed the path. This was easy enough to do, as the tangles hid it effectually. But that seemed a matter of small consequence, as he had still the walls on the opposite height to guide him.

Seen from the lower slopes, the city appeared as far off and as inaccessible almost as the snowy peaks on the far horizon. But he held bravely on, making pause now and again to try and find his bearings in the thicket, and hoping presently to make the bridle path again or to descend into the good road usually found at the bottom of every valley.

But he seemed only to wander more hopelessly, and very soon found that he was not moving in a straight line, but in a slanting, uneven direction, which was causing his road to recede still farther from him. That goal, indeed, seemed as elusive and disappointing as some mirage in the desert; very soon it might be lost in the sun mists, and become a mere figment of the imagination or simply a dream.

Suddenly, he came to a little clearing in the thicket, before the face of an overhanging rock, covered with the trails of some brilliant creeper, growing in fantastic and luxuriant loveliness. As Marchbanks approached to inspect it, and to touch, with interested, curious fingers, the weird, orchid-like blooms which starred it here and there, he suddenly became aware that there was an aperture behind, which, undoubtedly, the creeper had been carefully trained to hide.

A thicket, a concealed entrance, a mysterious cave! Could the heart of a boy desire more? And Marchbanks was still a boy at heart, though a man in years. Of fear he had none—even of snakes, or noxious beasts, which a more experienced traveller might have warned him were likely to be part of the hidden dangers of such a place.

But through the curious adventure, which was destined to be one of the freshest and most extraordinary of Marchbanks' career in the East, he never parted with that strange buoyant hopefulness of outlook and absolute immunity from fear.

It was not till long afterwards, when he heard others talk of it, that he realised what the actual peril of that adventure had been.

To brush the creeper trails aside was the work of a moment, then, very cautiously, he pushed himself through the aperture, and was in no way surprised by the instant feeling of spacious coolness which surrounded him. In his pocket he had one of the electric torches, then newly on the market, which are found so useful a part of the soldier's or the civilian's travelling outfit.

The sudden flash revealed a narrow passage, apparently hewn out of the solid rock, from which the cool moist air from beyond rushed as through a funnel.

Moving cautiously, and with the eerie feeling that he might presently find himself in strange company, or, at least, in the presence of life of some sort, he found himself in a spacious inner chamber so vast and mysterious that it could never have been prepared by man, but must have been hollowed out by some great cataclysm in the days when nature was at war.

His interest and awe and apprehension deepened every moment, because man, more especially when solitary, is strangely susceptible to natural influences and easily awed by forces he does not understand and therefore cannot easily combat.

But presently he forgot all his natural fears as the flashlight revealed something lying, inert across the floor of the cavern, prone on its face—a figure attired in native dress.

It lay so still that a small shiver passed over Marchbanks, lest he should be in the presence of a dead man. And, if one dead man, why not many? And what mysteries and horrors might he not yet discover provided he had courage to go on?

He turned involuntarily to look back towards the narrow path, which the gracious and friendly daylight illumined in part, but was again impelled forward by some force he was powerless to combat.

And presently he was kneeling on the dry floor of the cave, with his torch turned full on the prostrate figure, from which he could feel a certain heat emanate indicating that life was still in the veins. The little green lizards, clinging to the wall, made pause in their play to watch him, and close by was a writhing black thing, wriggling in the dust, one of the most dangerous of the whip-snake breed which might have dealt immediate death.

But, apparently, his life was charmed for nothing touched him, and, fixing his flashlight by a little ingenious hold on the button, he, rather gingerly it must be confessed, proceeded to turn the prostrate figure over.

It was a tall, lean figure, not heavy, though the voluminous folds of the native dress completely disguised the outlines. The folds of the turban, however, had come unswathed, and Marchbanks instantly noticed that the hair, though dark, was very closely cropped, and bore little resemblance to any native head he had ever seen. The face was brown, however, with the clear brown of the native skin.

As he eased the figure over and laid it on its back the eyes opened suddenly—eyes that bore no resemblance whatever to such eyes as Ram Shicka Dass's, and a very weak, but quite clear astonished voice, said wonderingly:

" And who is this ? "

CHAPTER XXV

THE FINGER OF GOD

"I'M a Scotsman from Calcutta," answered John. "What might happen to be your name?"

Although the accent was all right it behoved him to be careful, with a man wearing a disguise, and he decided to give nothing away.

"I'm Scotch, too," answered the prostrate man feebly.

"Are you, by any chance, Mr. Jardine?" asked John, then, rather eagerly.

The man, however, vouchsafed no immediate answer.

"How did you get here?" he asked. "And what are you doing in this cave in the Narkander Pass? Are you with an expedition or what?"

"I'm with an expedition—yes; but, until you tell me your name, you've no right to mine, nor yet to any other information."

"My name is Jardine. I suppose the expedition came after me. Ram Shicka Dass always prophesied I would have to be rescued, some day, from Bukta Saizan's clutches by a British Expeditionary Force!"

Marchbanks gave a queer little cackle of mingled enjoyment and embarrassment.

Deep in his heart there was a livelier feeling even than satisfaction at having realised the main object of his quest, something near and intimate and real, which he did not at the moment seek to understand.

It is just possible that Jardine was conscious of it too, for his feverish eyes grew wistful as they fixed themselves on the young man's face.

"Where's the rest of the expedition then? And why are you in mufti?"

"I'm not a soldier. I'm only a clerk—at least, I was. I don't rightly know what I am now. Major Eastcote could probably tell you."

"Eastcote! Is Eastcote here? But he can't be! I heard he had gone home."

"He's ill at your station at the mouth of the Pass."

"Then who are you, and what's your part in the expedition? Where has it gone?"

"The expedition is very small and entirely voluntary," said Marchbanks drily. "It consists of your servant, Ram Shicka Dass, who may at this moment, for all I know, be interviewing the interesting bandit you call Bukta Saizan. I may as well tell you as quickly as possible, because the sooner we get out of here the better I shall be pleased. Major Eastcote came out to Doosoor for the purpose of making inquiry after you, but immediately we reached the bungalow he was suddenly taken ill with fever. It was an unofficial journey altogether, and he invited me to accompany him—also unofficially. He was taken ill, as I say. We left him in charge of the doctor from Doosoor, and, being urged by Ram Shicka Dass, I came off with a couple of horses, and here I am."

Jardine, listening intently, comprehended every word, but remained partly puzzled.

"Ram Dass has gone to interview Bukta, you say? Then very probably by this time he is dead—as I would have been, and was fully expected to be, only I had the good luck to escape."

"Well, that's interesting. But I hope for his own sake that old Ram Dass won't get hung up first thing, for he struck me as a very decent chap, though I have been assailed by a few doubts since he left me. But we had better not go on talking any more. I must get you out of here. I've got two horses—one of them your own mare, and her back is like an easy-chair, as I can testify, never having been on horseback before. They're up at the top of the ridge, a good half-mile away. Question is, how are we to get you there."

"I can't walk," said Jardine slowly. "Though it is possible that if I were raised up I might try to hobble."

"We must try everything. For, if it is as you say, and they fall foul of Ram Dass, what more certain than that they'll come out to hunt down the remnant of the Expeditionary Force?"

Without further ado Marchbanks put one of his strong arms about the prostrate figure and essayed to get the man partially to his feet.

Jardine groaned once or twice, for he was not only weak but was suffering from some wounds which, through neglect, had grown septic, and occasioned such intolerable suffering that he had actually crept into the cave expecting and hoping to die.

By slow degrees Marchbanks at last got him out into the sunshine, and then began surely the strangest little pilgrimage that had ever been undertaken even in India.

He quickly perceived that the movement of the limbs even strongly supported as he was occasioned Jardine excruciating suffering, and that in all probability his feeble reserve of strength would be completely exhausted long before they reached the little camp in the shade of the plateau.

"Look here," he said, after they had gone about a hundred yards, "this won't do. We'll never get there. This is the path right enough, I left some landmarks as I came down so that I wouldn't get wandered."

"Wouldn't get wandered!" smiled Jardine feebly. "That was never heard south of the Tweed!"

But John felt too serious to smile. He felt nervous at the idea of Bukta Saizan and his warriors riding out of the walled city after having obtained by hook or by crook some information from Ram Shicka Dass. To such a catastrophe there could be but one end.

Now, life is never fairer than at the moment when it is threatened, either by disease or danger, and John decided that he would take no risks.

"I'm going to carry you, Mr. Jardine. The question is what is going to be the most comfortable position for you, and how I am going to get you up? Once at the camp do you think you could sit astride a horse?"

"I could ride my own Nameena," said Jardine with positive assurance. "But I don't see you carrying me! You're a slim chap, and I'm a six-footer, and though I haven't much flesh on my bones these same bones are a pretty solid weight."

"It's got to be done. Let's try," said Marchbanks readily; and after considerable manœuvring he managed to get the long lank figure hoisted to his shoulders.

It was a toilsome, difficult ascent, and there were not many words spoken while it was in progress. Never, surely, had half-mile been so interminably long, and poor Marchbanks had to make pause frequently, especially towards the end of the journey. The sweat was simply pouring off him, and his own legs trembled when at last he deposited his burden on the plateau.

He was thankful to find the camp had not suffered any disturbance in his absence.

"We'll have a drink now," he said, and made for the little store which Ram Shicka Dass with rare forethought had got ready for almost any emergency.

Accustomed to the white man's love for the peg of whisky, he had not forgotten the little flask, and though John did not touch it himself, he was pleased to see that it had an immediate effect on his exhausted companion.

When they had refreshed themselves with food and drink, Marchbanks began anxiously to urge the continuance of their journey.

"I don't mind telling you I want to put a wider span between me and these mysterious walls," he said, shading his eyes as they swept the further ridges across the valley. "If you think you're able, let us get on."

"I am quite able, if you can get me on Nameena's back. How long have you been coming up ?"

"About three days, I believe ; but one loses count out here. What about Ram Dass ? Do we leave him to his fate ?"

"We can't do anything to help him, and the native has a wonderful way of slithering out of tight places. He's been as good as dead a score of times since I got him !"

"Well, I hope he'll turn up this time, too ; for, though he's a rum chap, he's done me a good turn in more ways than one."

Marchbanks had occasion to long most poignantly for Ram Shicka Dass's quick panther-like movement and nimble intelligence during the next few ghastly days.

After the superhuman effort of getting Jardine on Nameena's back, it was found impossible for him to sustain the riding position. He essayed it bravely, then casting one piteous look into the anxious face of his young companion, he fainted clean away.

This necessitated considerable delay, while Marchbanks dragged him as tenderly as possible to the ground again and applied such remedies as he had to his hand. He had practically no knowledge of medical aid—what healthy young man has ?—but his level common sense, which forbade panic, guided him to do the right thing.

It was admittedly a situation in which a moderate amount of panic might have been justified. Two Englishmen—one of them *hors de combat*, in a hostile country, where any moment a band of marauders might strike out for them, with the menace of a mysterious city behind, and a three days' journey in front ! How the journey was to be made now Marchbanks had not the least idea, and he almost regretted the superhuman effort which had got Jardine away from his hiding-place, and out upon the open track before there was adequate means provided for his complete rescue.

He tried to comfort himself while he waited for Jardine to regain consciousness with the reflection that it was unlikely the cave would be unknown to Bukta Saizan and his followers, and that the discovery of the fugitive in his hiding-place could not have been a matter of many days. Then there was the action and the fate of Ram Shicka Dass to be reckoned with. Supposing he reached the city in safety and betrayed them, how long would it take for the myrmidons of Bukta Saizan to track them down ? On the other hand, if he proved faithful, what could be the object of his journey, or its issue, now that Jardine was without the city walls ?

It was a hopeless problem, and he wisely decided that he had better leave the native servant out of his calculations altogether, and trust to his own resources.

All these thoughts passed in rapid and quite orderly review through his brain as he knelt by Jardine's side, once more conscious of the sense of nearness, of some mysterious call of the blood which, doubtless, had but one meaning.

Further than the actual stupendous fact of which his heart rather than his head assured him, Marchbanks did not care to go. Like the walled city of mystery both the past and the intervening years must meanwhile remain to him a sealed book. Perhaps it might even be sealed for ever here, on the desolate highway in the Indian mountains, by the angel of death himself. That, indeed, would be the very irony of fate, and Marchbanks' sense of justice forbade it.

Presently the breath came fluttering to the lips of the prostrate man, and after an interval his lashes feebly stirred and his eyes opened. A faint flicker of a smile accompanied his whispered words.

"No good, old chappie. Better leave me to be carrion, and 'mak' siccar for yourself."

"No, by Heavens, I won't do that. And only fifty miles perhaps from the station! I'll get you there somehow."

The prostrate man slowly moved his head in dissent.

"It's what I've gone through in that abominable city where savagery is still rampant. My poor body is a mass of raw sores yet, and you can understand how the effort to keep an upright position caused red-hot pains to overcome me. It won't be that way, friend, but——"

"Then there's another," said Marchbanks firmly. "But can't anything be done to ease the wound before we try anything else?"

Jardine appeared to reflect a moment.

"In this district," he began presently, "there are leaves of healing all around us—but they have to be known," he said in his feeble halting voice.

"Describe them to me and tell me the likely places and I'll find them," said Marchbanks, jumping up.

Jardine did his best to describe the wonderful medicinal plants which has long residence in India, and his intimate knowledge of the ways and habits and resources of its people had revealed to him.

For one interminable half-hour Marchbanks conducted a plant hunt, and after many failures brought back a handful of the precious leaves. He was then instructed how to apply them to the wounds on Jardine's body which looked as if they had been caused by some instrument of torture, and which had begun to fester, causing intolerable pain.

First, instructed by Jardine's feeble voice, he washed them clean, then applied the cool leaves and bound them up with some strips of his own handkerchief. It was a strange, rather pathetic scene, a comment on the wild life of India, and the difficulties and dangers not yet permanently removed from British rule; a scene, which formed a tie between these two men, which nothing afterwards could break.

Jardine winced once or twice while undergoing treatment at the somewhat clumsy, but very willing and kind hands of his rescuer, and when all was over he closed his eyes again and lay so still that Marchbanks feared he had fainted once more, or that the breath had finally left his body. But presently he was reassured, and when the voice spoke again it was distinctly stronger.

"Already I feel better. How can I thank you? Now we may perhaps get along. You will have to ride Nameena and lay me across the saddle in front of you."

It was a stiff proposition for a man with so little skill or knowledge of horses, and Marchbanks looked for the moment dismayed. Realising quickly enough that it was a stern necessity and assured by Jardine that the docile Nameena was quite equal to the double burden though she looked such a fragile, dainty creature, after considerable manœuvring and many breakdowns a start was made.

It was impossible for Marchbanks to attempt to lead or guide the other horse, but Jardine assured him she would follow of her own accord. His voice seemed to have a wonderful effect on the animals; it was a familiar and a beloved voice, and its frequent use undoubtedly was the only thing which made the venture possible.

Soon then and very, very slowly they began the long and toilsome descent. It was not possible to take long spans at first, because the torture to Jardine was still acute, and Marchbanks had to watch lest his feeble strength should ebb utterly away. The first span they made was only a mile or two, and the whole journey, which was destined to be written in fiery letters on their book of remembrance, occupied them four whole days.

It is unnecessary to go into the details of these days, each one being a practical repetition of the other.

They made the utmost use of the coolest hours, and rested while the sun was at its meridian, and in a most astonishing way Jardine's strength was not only maintained, but increased, probably as much by relief and hope as by actual betterment.

There was very little talk between them, and though Marchbanks longed to hear the full story of Jardine's experiences in the walled city, the present business was sufficient to engross their whole attention.

One odd omission may be chronicled. In their intercourse Jardine did not appear curious regarding the name of his deliverer, and addressed him in various affectionate terms such as a man might use to one of his own blood. John had not noticed the omission, he had plenty much more engrossing matters to engage his attention.

On the evening of the fourth day in the cool sundown they sighted the open mouth of the Narkander Pass and the sweep of the great plain beyond.

Jardine was very tired, but his eyes lit up with satisfaction as he realised that he was actually within sight and reach of his own station where peace and safety reigned. During that long-drawn and difficult journey they had not been molested by man or beast. Of the former they had not seen even one—a mystery explained by Jardine by the fact that certain very strict religious observances were taking place in Meeristan, which had practically tied Bukta Saizan and his people to their walled city. Otherwise they could not have escaped in such complete safety.

Major Eastcote had recovered sufficiently from his sharp attack of illness to be fretting at his own inactivity. He had sent full particulars of what had transpired to Calcutta, and was waiting results, but there is no haste in India except when there is acute trouble in the air, and the fate of one lost Englishman is not sufficient to set all the wires in vibrant motion.

Eastcote, however, was sorry that his urgent messages had brought so little response, and employed his leisure in writing diatribes against the slowness and pigheadedness of the Indian Intelligence Department. It was a favourite occupation of his though his effusions did not always see the light.

Being relieved from his locum-tenency at Doosoor, and in no particular request elsewhere, Pringle, the Scotch doctor, partly because he was deeply interested in the story, and partly because he did not think it wise from a professional point of view to leave Eastcote alone in Jardine's bungalow, had taken up his quarters there.

They were sitting together on the verandah of the bungalow talking Indian politics and waiting a summons to dinner when the Major's sharp and wandering eye beheld some strange objects on the bridle path emerging from the Pass.

" Something comes, Pringle ! Get the glasses, and make sure, for there hasn't been a sign of life at hell's mouth since I was able to sit again on the verandah."

Pringle brought the glasses from the inner room, and after a brief survey passed them over to Eastcote.

" It's the horses that left here, and as far as I can make out, Marchbanks is on one, and he has something queer in front of him that might be a native's body. He might have left Ram Shicka Dass in the tombs of his ancestors if he has kicked the bucket. Don't get excited, Major ! "

The Major had sprung up and hobbled to the extreme edge of the verandah, and his hands were trembling as he sought to focus the glasses.

His eyes, more practised than Pringle's, confirmed him, however, in every detail.

" It is Marchbanks, and it is Ram Shicka Dass's body undoubtedly, but surely it is a live body, for Marchbanks is no fool ! Half an hour will bring them, and the story we shall hear, Doctor, will be worth while listening to."

The pace of the little cavalcade was very slow, as if it was reduced to the last stage of weariness. Pringle presently emerged from the verandah shade, and went forward some paces to meet them, and he saw then that Marchbanks' face was drawn and set, and that he looked like a man who had been through some terrific bodily or mental strain.

" Hulloa, old chappie ! " he called out cheerily. " Welcome home ! What ho, and what luck ? "

But Marchbanks answered not, only shook a melancholy head.

Pringle stepped forward then and eyeing the huddled figure in front of the rider gave vent to an exclamation of surprise.

" It's Mr. Jardine ! " said Marchbanks quickly. " And he's just about played out. Help me to get him down and into the house. I'm very nearly pegging out myself."

By the time they crossed the compound to the verandah steps the Major had hobbled down, and his surprise and consternation were very great. Seeing the urgency of the case he forbore to ask a single question, but lent what aid he could to get his poor friend into the house.

Jardine spoke not at all, nor seemed to take the smallest interest in his surroundings or, indeed, to be aware that he had been brought home. His eyes were dim, and he had the dazed look of a man suffering either from severe pain or from extreme weakness.

The native servants flocked round to help, and in a very short space of time they had undressed him and laid him in his own bed.

Marchbanks, thankful to roll his responsibility on to the capable shoulders of Pringle, left the bedroom at once and walked back somewhat unsteadily to the verandah to report himself to his chief.

That extraordinary week had left its marks on Marchbanks. He had grown thin and worn, and his face had the wrung expression of a man who has been held at high tension for a long spell.

" Well," said Eastcote with a curious thrill in his voice. " You've done a big thing, my man—something that won't be forgotten by the powers that be ! I'll see to that. Are you able to give me a few particulars now ? If not, I can wait."

" I can give you an outline," said Marchbanks rather faintly, as he sank into one of the chairs. " We were three days getting within hail of the walled city. Then Ram Dass said he would go on alone and asked me to keep the camp until he returned either with Mr. Jardine or with some report of him. He did not come back, and I set out on my own to follow him when I came across a cave or rather a series of caves in the mountain-side, and in one I found Mr. Jardine. I thought he was a dead native at first until he spoke to me in English.

" I got him up—carried him, in fact, to the camp, and after we had rested and refreshed we began the return journey. It's been a tough business, and I never thought we should get here alive. No—we haven't been molested. In fact, we haven't seen any human life since we started. Mr. Jardine told me when he was able to speak that they are celebrating some great religious festival which keeps them strictly to their mosques.

" He seemed to improve the first day or two, but yesterday he got worse. He has got a lot of horrible wounds, sir. He hasn't been able to give me his story, but I gathered that he had been tortured somewhere. I did my best for him. I hope Pringle will be able to save his life, but it hardly seems like it. It's disappointing, very, because——"

Here his voice trailed away into a rather feeble cadence, and to the Major's alarm he slid from the chair and fainted clean away.

Pringle, hastily summoned, ordered him to bed and assured the Major that it was only the reaction after the superhuman strain of the last few days.

He was also very reassuring about Jardine, and later in the evening the Major was permitted to see him. By this time he was attired in his own pyjamas, and the brown stain being washed from his face he looked more like the Jardine of old, though woefully thin and pallid, and with great dark circles under his eyes.

" Well, old pal," said the Major, with a little catch in his voice. " A couple of nice old crocks we are ! And what, may I ask, do you think of yourself and your latest escapade ? "

" It was worth while—you'll know that, when I'm able to tell the yarn, Arthur ! " said Jardine, with a slight but very satisfied smile. " I own I'm uncommonly glad to be in my own bed again, and that chap of yours has saved my life. What he's done for me can never be acknowledged or repaid ! Tell me about him ? I don't even know his name ! I seem to remember asking it once or twice, and then not hearing the answer. But I may have dreamed that with the rest. Where does he come from ? "

" Scotland."

" I know that, my boy. But what part ? And where did you get a hold of him ? "

" I met him first at Sir Edward Bartlett's house in London, and he came out to Calcutta in the same boat. He is, or rather was, in Trent, Bartlett's employment, but I annexed him when I wanted to come up here. Lucy isn't able any more for these adventures, Jardine, but she sent you her love."

Jardine's lips parted in a smile.

" And you took this young man from Trent, Bartlett's ! But that doesn't tell me all I want to know about him. Where was he reared ? Who are his people ? And what's his name ? "

" I believe he belongs to Glasgow, and he was born under a cloud. His name is Marchbanks—Good God, what's happened now ! "

For Jardine had fallen back upon his pillow, and the pallor of death seemed to overspread his face.

" It is the finger of God," he muttered under his breath. But would say no more.

CHAPTER XXVI

MY SON!

A NIGHT'S sound sleep restored Marchbanks fully, and he awoke next morning with a lively sense that the world was a beautiful place, full of heavenly possibilities.

The words of his chief recurred to his mind as he lay there in the quiet room, and his own inner consciousness assured him that the adventure and achievement of the last ten days were likely to have vast and far-reaching effect on his future life.

Eastcote was a man chary both of praise and blame. Marchbanks had heard him say that many a promising career had been nipped in the bud by an undue need of both. But his eyes had been full of a lively satisfaction even effection as he had gripped Marchbanks' hand and thanked him for what he had done.

There are golden moments in the life of a man, the influence of which never afterwards wholly leaves him, and do its part when subsequent frosts of fate may overtake him. But youth is not prone to contemplate frosts of fate, and Marchbanks, though he had the very haziest idea what the next part of his official or unofficial programme might be, had certainly no anticipation of a set-back.

He admitted to himself that the rosiest vision glorifying his accomplished task was the thought of Beatrice Hume's face when she should hear the record of these gallant and difficult days. Thoughts of his mother also strangely mingled with the rest, but something whispered that other hands than his would build up the broken fabric of her life.

Presently so bewildering and overwhelming were all the vistas opening with the new day that he sprang from his bed and went to seek his bath eager for, and yet hanging back from the next milestones of the way.

In an Indian bungalow there are few of these homely household sounds to which we are accustomed. The native servants move with a stealthy quiet, and when well trained do not permit themselves to chatter about their work.

The sound of voices from the far end of the verandah assured Marchbanks that some other members of the household were astir. His watch had been stopped for over three days, and he had no means of knowing the time, though his fresh eyelids had convinced him that he had had the full modicum of sleep. He made haste with his toilet and when he emerged clad in a fresh linen suit on the verandah he found the Major and Pringle at their breakfast.

The Major rose to wish him good morning—a little ceremony significant in itself. Marchbanks at once felt that he had been lifted high in the estimation of his chief, and there are few things which can fire a young man's ambition more quickly and ardently. His face flushed as he received the salute, then the warm handshake and congratulation on his rested appearance.

" Yes, I've slept like a top, thank you, sir. But how is Mr. Jardine this morning ? "

He nodded and smiled to Pringle as he put the question.

"He's been more or less restless all night, and I've been up with him part of it. There's some fever from the wounds, though they've been treated as well as could be expected in the circumstances. In fact, better than we had the right to look for."

"He gave me my orders about the medicine plant, and passed each leaf before it was applied," said Marchbanks. "But he was rather far gone at the time, and I was in a mortal funk in case there should be anything poisonous, and that the remedy would be worse than the disease. I had several ghastly moments about it, more especially in the last twenty-four hours, when I saw him plainly going down the hill, as it were."

"You've done marvels, Marchbanks. Sit down and have some breakfast," said the Major briefly.

"Yes, sir; thank you. But you think he'll get better, Doctor, don't you?" asked Marchbanks wistfully. "It would be very disappointing—if——"

"It won't happen," said Pringle reassuringly. "He has a very tough constitution, but he's come through something that'll have to be explained and—wiped out—eh, Major?"

The Major merely bent his head and flicked his eyelids with an odd, little nervous gesture, Marchbanks had often noticed when he was speaking with strong feeling. But he did not trust his voice.

As they sat there they plied Marchbanks with questions, all of which he answered to the best of his ability, glossing over and concealing nothing, though trying to make light of what he had done.

Once or twice the Major eyed him curiously, thinking of the little episode in Jardine's room the night before, and after Pringle had left them, to attend once more to his patient, the Major sat forward and fixed his deep, searching eyes on Marchbanks' pleasant face.

It looked very young and boyish in the clear morning light, and it had lost the strain, the anguish of the past few days, and become once more a face of peace. It was very serious, however, as if thoughts too deep for words lay somewhere at the back.

"Life's a strange thing, my boy," said the older man, as he passed the cigar-case, and absently began to trim his own cigar. "And, somehow, in India one gets nearer the bedrock of things. There is less superficiality, and there is something in the contention that the East is the home of the occult. Certainly we get closer to the things we can't explain out here; but, when one has the courage to probe deep enough, it is generally found that everything is attributable to the inexorable working of natural law."

"Yes," said Marchbanks, and, though his monosyllable was brief, his tone was tense.

"Now, take your own case. Our meeting was purely accidental, looked at from the ordinary common-sense standpoint, everything happened quite naturally, and without effect or strain. I happened to want some one like you who would be pliable enough to fall in with my methods, and not for ever be thrusting his own ideas and opinions under my nose, which is the principal failing of what we may call the technically trained youth. But all the time I had the feeling that there were other forces at work, with which I, personally, had very little to do, but was merely the instrument for the furtherance of their operations. I should uncommonly like to hear more fully what you have felt about it, though I gathered from the note you left for me that you have shared, in some degree, this rather uncommon feeling."

It was a moment before Marchbanks spoke.

"I have had the feeling all along that I was being pushed by destiny, sir," he said then, quite quietly, and, rising, disappeared into the room beyond, the Major following him with rather wondering, staring eyes.

In a moment he returned bearing in his hand the little daguerreotype case, which he had examined and restored to its place on Jardine's bracket.

He clicked the little spring open, and held the pictured face out for the Major's inspection.

"This bears out what you say, sir. Do you remember the story I told you on board the *Ortolan?* That is a portrait of my mother."

The Major, whose face most certainly wore an expression of profound astonishment, studied the sweet face for several moments in silence. Once only he glanced towards Marchbanks, where he leaned against the verandah rail, as if seeking to find and establish the necessary resemblance.

"Where and how did you find this?"

"It was the day after we arrived, sir. I was mooning about, feeling very anxious about you, and not knowing what to do with myself. I looked at that out of idle curiosity, as one looks at objects in a room, to fill up time, and I was very curious about the master of this house. I have had a strange deep interest in his personality ever since you first mentioned his name in Sir Edward Trent's house in London."

"Did I speak of him there? Then what inference do you draw?"

"I have been afraid to draw any, but the natural one would be that—that he is my father."

The words came out with a little jerk, indicating the emotion which the mere supposition called forth.

"I think you are right, my boy," said the Major, and his hard-bitten face assumed a strange softness of expression. "Last night, in the midst of his pain, he was thinking and speaking entirely of you. He asked me where you had come from, and what people you had—and finally your name."

"Didn't he know that?" asked Marchbanks in surprise. "I seem to remember that he asked it."

"He seemed to remember that too; but apparently you had not answered him. When I mentioned it he got into a strange state of excitement, and said, 'It is the finger of God.' It all points to one issue, John," said the Major, using his Christian name for the first time; "and we shall have to leave to the same Finger the final unravelling."

Marchbanks' face twitched, and he was for some minutes unable to speak. And then it was to go back on the past—on his boyhood, which, though not unhappy, had always been shadowed by the lack of what is so precious and necessary in the life of a boy—his father's guidance and love.

From these detached and sometimes rather broken sentences the Major obtained a very clear, cameo-like portrait of the mother; and, when the day came on which he met her face to face there was no surprise for him. For Ellen had left her mark on her boy, and had established her own image in faithful portraiture in his heart.

John did not seek to smooth or gloss over the somewhat ungrateful part he had played towards her in the last year, but the Major, the most understanding of men, thought none the less of him for his frank admission.

"I shall have to be getting back to Calcutta," he said presently. "And, anyhow, it will be better that you and he should be here alone at first."

But at this suggestion Marchbanks drew back with a strange shyness.

"Oh, sir, don't leave us yet! You see, there is nothing established, and—and perhaps the story may have a more painful unfolding than we think. Twenty-five years is a lifetime in which many things may happen. How am

I to know that he will care to acknowledge the tie between us, even if it is proven? Men don't always care to perpetuate, or even to acknowledge, the faults of their youth."

"That is true enough; but in this case I do not anticipate any such refusal on Jardine's part. To begin with, he is not that kind of man. So far as I can gather, his life has been completely solitary, and he has had no womenkind mixed up in it. India is the grave of many a man's reputation, but there has never been even one hint of scandal concerning his. Yet, he was one who might easily have scored that kind of success had he cared for it. My wife was always rubbing that fact into me, and wondering about his past.

"Well, nothing can be done till Jardine is out of danger, and we must just leave him in Pringle's very capable hands. Meanwhile, you and I will ride into Doosoor to-day, and see the Commissioner there. It will interest him to see the new hero of the Narkander Pass, and from Doosoor I can telegraph to Calcutta that we have found Jardine."

They carried out that part of the programme, and, in a typical Indian administrative station, Marchbanks found himself treated like a man who has done something. In fact, the attention lavished on him somewhat embarrassed him.

"Look here, sir," he said, as they rode back in the cool evening. "Don't let them go on like that. What did I do, after all, more or less than any other man would have done? And there must be hundreds and thousands of Englishmen and Scotsmen doing their bit as conscientiously, and nobody ever hears a word about them!"

"And that's true, too, my young friend. The graves of India are full of them, and their monument is the growing power and prestige of the British rule, which, when it is put to the supreme test, will not be found wanting, any more than the loyalty of the land that has been redeemed from heathen darkness by its policy."

They found that Jardine had had a quiet day, and was distinctly better. The Major was permitted to see him, but he did not ask for Marchbanks, nor even mention him again, to his old friend.

Jardine's account of himself disposed of Ram Shicka Dass's emphatically expressed conviction that he had actually been kidnapped by Bukta Saizan. He had deliberately risen, with the fever upon him, and, dressing himself in native garb, set out for the mountains, with the quite definite purpose of reaching Meeristan, and, there mingling with the native life, make his own observations.

He had succeeded, even beyond his own expectations, and was just about to effect his escape back to the plains when he was betrayed by a native whom he had trusted, and who had suspected, and finally discovered his secret. Regarding his experiences after he was actually laid hold of by Bukta Saizan he evidently preferred to say little.

"He's a heathen, Arthur; and he behaved like one. Let us leave it at that. I don't want to make capital out of my sufferings, though they were genuine enough. I learned a good deal; and for all knowledge there is a price to pay. I've paid it, and now I can pass that knowledge on. Bukta has got to be crushed, Arthur, and your business is to see that there is nothing mealy-mouthed about the crushing. It must be done thoroughly, once and for all. So the Expeditionary Force must be adequate. Do you hear?"

Eastcote heard, and entirely and wholeheartedly agreed.

He was delighted with the vivid clearness of Jardine's mind and his firm grip of affairs. Jardine's voice, though weak was steady, and the expression of pain had disappeared from his face, leaving it serene and stamped with a certain nobility which suffering bestows.

"I think you shouldn't lose any time, Arthur," he went on a trifle restlessly. "Get back to Calcutta without delay and set them by the ears."

"Not until you are able to travel with us," said the Major firmly. "Bukta might very easily make a raid on this lonely station."

"He won't," said Jardine confidently. "He's a coward at heart, and knows very well by this time that he'll have to pay for what he did to me. I wish you'd start out for Calcutta to-morrow. You can wire for some troops to lie at Doosoor, if you like, as a concession to possibilities. And there is one other thing I want you to do before you go——"

"It's done, Billie, before you ask it!"

"Is it, old chap? I'm not so sure about that! I want you to leave your young man, my rescuer, behind, for a few days at least. He and I have still a little score to settle."

"Very well; that will please him, I'm sure," said the Major, and something in his voice, a subtle cadence, caused Jardine to look at him with singular intentness.

"You see nothing out of the way in that request, then, Arthur?"

"Nothing. He has rendered you the biggest service, I suppose, that one man can render to another—he has saved your life, and it might very easily have been at the expense of his own."

"Easily! But the odd thing was that that didn't seem to enter into his calculations. It's an older score than the trek through the Narkander Pass I have to settle with him, Arthur, but I can't say more now." After a moment's silence he added abruptly: "A queer old book, the Bible! And we don't, any of us, get away from it, however hard we try. Some men's sins go before, to judgment, and some follow after. Was there ever a deeper truth than that penned since the world began?"

Eastcote assented and waited, but no further confidence was given, and he felt glad of it.

He informed Marchbanks that night that he intended to return to Calcutta next day, and that it was Jardine's express desire that he should remain behind. Fancying a slight hesitation, even a mild dismay, in the young man's expression, he said kindly:

"If the mystery of your parentage and the whole tragedy of Jardine's life are ever to be cleared, it will be here and now, John, and you will be best alone. Cheer up, I foresee a happy future for you, a future which your mother is going to share in a way undreamed of, either by her or you. We cannot get away from the march of destiny."

Marchbanks could not demur, for the wisdom of the words was indisputable. Nevertheless, next morning when the Major was mounted for the ride back to Doosoor, and Pringle was ready to accompany him, he was conscious of a singular feeling of forlornness. He preserved an outward cheerfulness, however, and after impressing on Pringle the necessity for coming up not later than next day to see his patient, he walked back to the edge of the verandah.

And there, to his unspeakable amazement, who should bob up, smiling remotely, and engagingly, but Ram Shicka Dass!

The sight of that friendly face was quite sufficient to banish his momentary dismay at being left stranded in Jardine's bungalow.

"You rascal!" he stammered, quite unable to keep the joy out of his voice. "Where have you sprung from?"

"Excellency, I have been making my way on foot, night and day, without slumber or halt, through the jungle from Meeristan."

" The jungle ! What jungle ? I didn't see any—unless you mean the cave where I found your master, the Sahib Jardine."

Here Ram Shicka Dass bestrayed signs of the liveliest distress.

" Woe is me, Excellency, that Ram Shicka Dass, after all his bombast, should have proved himself of so little use, while the son of the heaven-born, without so much as lifting his little finger, did the great deed ! "

" There you are wrong, Ram Dass, for I lifted not only my little finger, but my whole body, and it is aching yet. Say, have you ever climbed the slopes of the Narkander Pass carrying a six-foot man unable to help himself ? "

" Excellency, I have done many things, but not just that—— "

" Then don't presume to sit in judgment. I'll hear your adventures later. I suppose you have seen your master ? "

" I have, O Excellency ; and once more the sun is high in the heavens for Ram Shicka Dass, and life, an offering to the gods ! "

" Well, anyhow, we accomplished it between us, and half the credit is yours," said Marchbanks generously as he sauntered into the house.

Then, across the sitting-room, he heard a voice calling him, and with step that halted slightly, he made his way through the open doors into Jardine's bedroom.

He was now sitting up in bed, looking thin and worn still, but otherwise well ; and he had a quick smile of welcome for Marchbanks as he bade him come in.

" So your companion-at-arms has escaped from Meeristan, too, and Bukta hasn't even one scalp to his girdle ! Have they all gone ? "

" Just ridden away, sir ; and I have the feeling that I ought to have been by the Major's side."

" You'll follow on presently. Meanwhile, you and I have a little score to settle—not perhaps a little one, but a very long one. I want you to sit down here, by my bed, and tell me from the beginning the whole story of your life."

" It is easily told," said Marchbanks, but his voice had an odd thrill and vibration in it. " Until I came to India it was quite uneventful."

" I particularly wish to hear about your mother—all about her—her name, her looks, her occupation, her mode of life, her smile, her voice, her outlook on life ; and understand that I ask these questions not out of idle curiosity, but because it is a matter of life and death to me."

Marchbanks, sitting on the extreme edge of a bamboo chair, leaning slightly forward, began the simple, bald recital.

He laid some stress on the loneliness and isolation of his boyhood during the years when his mother had been earning her livelihood in the house of another.

Engrossed by his own recital, and obsessed by the memories which rose so thick and fast upon him, he hardly noticed the growing excitement in his listener. Once, when he halted, at a loss for some phrase to carry him on, Jardine leaned forward eagerly.

" Go on ! Don't wait—go on ! Tell me how she looked when last you saw her ? I think I understand the rest."

Marchbanks, then labouring under an almost incontrollable emotion, rose, pushed back his chair, and strode into the other room. When he returned he held in his hand the open daguerreotype.

" This is my mother," he said simply. " You have seen her face as well as I."

Then a cry broke from William Jardine's lips, and he stretched out both his hands.

"My son!" he said. "Oh, my son!"

Marchbanks, without a question or a doubt, completely overwhelmed by that one supreme fact of existence, fell on his knees by the bedside, and Jardine's hands were laid almost in patriarchal blessing on his head.

Strangest of all was the fact that, though he had once sworn vengeance against the man who had wrecked his mother's life, and placed the bar sinister in his path, all that bitterness had died out of his heart. All he felt was that he had found a father, and that, from these lips, which some inner instinct told him could never lie, he would hear, at the fitting moment, some full and adequate explanation of the tragedy of his life.

CHAPTER XXVII

ROGER'S WIFE

JOHN MARCHBANKS, a free man and a happy one, to whom all the world seemed fair, walking in the principal street of Calcutta, on his way to call on the Humes within prescribed hours, suddenly beheld in front of a shop window under the deep awning, a sight which froze his blood.

I use the words deliberately, for, in the cheerful sunshine, among the moving pageant unsurpassed in any capital in the world, John suddenly felt as if he were walking on a grave!

Not a closed grave, but one ready to open and engulf him—the yawning mouth of a youthful and innocent folly rising up to confront and dismay him in what he had thought to be his hour of triumph.

And yet, there was nothing surely in the spectacle of a slim girlish figure in white from top to toe, even to the tips of her dainty shoes, with a young, gentle, serious face under the brim of a drooping hat, to disquiet a man so utterly.

And yet, before such vision, a man has been known to quail who never quailed before, even in front of the enemy's hosts.

John Marchbanks' step undoubtedly faltered, his cheek reddened, then paled; and the light of happiness left his eyes as he recognised the face and the figure of Annie Houston—the girl whom he had called cousin in the old, friendly, far-off days, and who had of her own accord desired a dearer tie.

In his utmost confusion, and having no doubt whatever but that she was a fresh Nemesis on his path, he tried to recall, before he should speak (since speak, he must, his courage urging him to face the evil and grip it with both hands), what had actually passed between them, on that fateful night, on the Whiteinch car, and to decide what position he had actually occupied towards her when he fled away from Glasgow and from her.

But before his thoughts would march to his order, she turned her pretty head and saw him. It was a strange moment, and, while he held himself breathless for the scene he considered to be inevitable, she suddenly advanced, smiling demurely, with even a touch of coquetry in her face.

"Well, Jack," she said blithely. "So here we are! I was wondering how long it would be before we ran across each other here in this funny place among all the dark folk."

Now, though her tone was of the friendliest, there was absolutely nothing proprietary in it, and her whole manner was quite casual and detached, and with an odd hint of mischief in it which completely puzzled him.

He, however, reached forth and took her frankly offered hand, stammering a little in his speech, which seemed to add much to the sum of her enjoyment.

"Annie Houston!" he cried. "Here, in Calcutta! Are wonders never to cease, then, in this most wonderful country in the world?"

"It's very hot to wonder about anything, and if you'll take me somewhere to get a cool drink, some iced tea, maybe, it would be a very good way to treat an old friend!"

John, realising that there could be no escape from this, and burning, besides, to hear the explanation of this miraculous vision, instantly acquiesced.

Though not very familiar as yet with the accredited afternoon resorts of Calcutta, he managed to pilot her to a suitable place, and there, in a quiet corner of a large and spacious tea-room, prepared to hear the worst.

He was apprehensive, yet not unduly alarmed, for there was neither reproach nor anger in the girl's manner, but rather an odd detachment, which seemed to assure him that he had no place in her present scheme of things.

He gave an order hurriedly to the waiter, and then looked fully at her while she began to draw off and to smooth her long white gloves with the utmost care, taking particular pains with the left-hand one.

"I'm waiting to hear how you got here, Annie, and the sooner you tell me the better I'll be pleased. I'm not a good one at waiting."

"Are you not? But you'll have to do your share of it maybe, before ye dree your full weird—as Katrine used to say. She had a fell job with what she called coffin-ships in her teacups this back-end; but, you see, we've all got here safe and sound, in spite of her!"

"When did you come out—and why?" he asked, realising that she meant to keep him on the tenter-hooks for some time, and tell him just what she thought proper in her own time.

And he, having neither the right nor the desire to complain, must wait that time with as much patience as he could command.

It was a new rôle for John to adopt towards the little playmate of his boyhood, and, coming to him in what was an undoubted flush of triumph, acted as a kind of wholesome discipline.

For this small, slender woman of no importance, so shortly since a paid hand in a fashionable dressmaker's shop, and the inmate of an artisan's home, had it in her power to do him some harm in Calcutta. She could at least delay and confuse, if she did not actually destroy, his dearest hopes.

But there was no vindictiveness in her looks, but rather a demure and most aggravating playfulness, which certainly became her, and imparted an air of mystery, tantalising, though charming.

"I came out ten days ago on the *Star of the East*," she answered. "And I heard that you were away upcountry somewhere; so, of course, it was a surprise to meet you to-day."

"Nothing to my surprise at meeting you, Annie," he blurted out. "And I shall be very much obliged if you'll tell me what brought you to Calcutta?"

At last the crucial, momentous question was bluntly put; but even that did not bring the ready answer.

"I daresay you would like to know that, Jack; there's a few more would like to get at the bottom of it; and all you need know is that it has nothing to do with you."

"Well, I'm glad to hear that, any way," he said, plunging deeper into the mire.

At this, her laughter pealed through the cool recesses, a laugh so spontaneous and so merry that it provoked a smile on more than one face in the café.

"Poor dear Jackie! Will I tell him just what he was thinking? That a certain poor little Scotch lass, that shall be nameless, had crossed the seas to hunt after him! My dear, it will be very good for you and your kind to remember that you are not the only pebbles on the beach."

With that she brought up the hitherto shy left hand, which, always shapely and small, had grown very white after six weeks of enforced idleness, and spread it out on the bamboo table in front of him.

On the third finger there glittered the shining band of a brand-new wedding-ring.

As he gazed stupidly at it John could have kissed it; he very nearly did so in his ecstasy of relief, while the girl-wife's merry, slightly mocking eyes transfixed the confusion on his face.

"You're never married, Annie!"

"And why not? Am I so very plain, then? What just do you mean by that, Jack? And you've got to be very respectful to me now! No more Annies, if you please, but Mrs. Roger Annan, at your service!"

"Mrs. Roger Annan? It can't be true! You! Married to Roger! But how—where in the name of all that's wonderful did it take place?"

"It took place in a Registry Office in Glasgow before he sailed, and I came on after; and it was his mother who gave me the money to come. She's an angel, Jack, if ever there was one, and I'll say my prayers to her for the rest of my life!"

Here the girl's voice broke and trembled, and diamond drops sprang to her pretty eyes.

"I was to wait till he sent for me, but when she found out—he wrote a letter to her from the ship and asked her to go to my Aunt Lizzie's house and see me—she came that very day and took me back with her to Balcraig and made me like her daughter, and my passage was paid, and I came out like a lady and Roger met me at the ship-side—and here I am!"

To this vivid and slightly emotional recital John Marchbanks listened like a man in a dream.

"It's a beautiful story, Annie, but what I don't understand is how and where you met Roger?"

"I met him where I met you—in your mother's house! She's another of the angels; and it's you men that are the poor crowd and that will never get near heaven's gates at all unless there's a lot of us round to push you through when there is nobody looking."

A little silence fell upon them then which Marchbanks found it difficult to break. He longed intensely to say something about the little episode which had resulted in a few hours' engagement between them. But he did not dare.

In matters of the heart it is the woman who can take the initiative, and Annie presently referred to the affair as if it had been quite a little joke.

"You did me a good turn, Jack, when it might easily have been a bad one," she said, turning her ring round on her finger, with a delicious little matronly air. "I had what they call the calf-love very badly. Just think how awful it would have been if we had really got married! We would never have been able to stand one another for any length of time."

"I'm glad you can take that view of it, Annie," said John quite humbly. "For, I can tell you, I had a good many bad hours over that same."

She laughed lightly.

"You needn't have had. It was my stupid fault. I might have known you didn't mean it. Lassies are often silly, Jack—though they seldom get to the heights of silliness men achieve! So, now we've got that cleared up tell me something about yourself, for what the Annans tell me I can't take in altogether. I'm very happy with my man, Jack, but I do not like his brother George, nor am I very sure about his sister. She has not been so very kind to me, and she is sailing back to bonnie Scotland next week."

"Is she?"

"She's another of the disappointed ones; and they've all got their knife in you, Jack, so I suppose you must be getting on. When folk are poor and humble—as I was, in Uncle George's house at Whiteinch—nobody meddles with them or bothers to tell lies about them."

"What lies have they been telling you about me?"

She shrugged her shoulders.

"Heaps of them! George said that the firm that brought you out to India had dismissed you in a week or two because you didn't come up to the mark."

"They very kindly released me because I was wanted by a more important man," said Marchbanks quickly. "And you can tell them that I'm to be taken on to the permanent staff of the Intelligence Department, through the influence of somebody I don't suppose they ever heard of, though he is very well known in Government circles."

"That's very exciting; and I hope it'll be a good thing for you, Jack, and bring you in good pay. I hope you are writing to your mother, for she deserves that you should keep mind of her, now that you are getting in with big folk. Mind, it was she that made you, to begin with."

Marchbanks hesitated a moment, and another look at the kind, rather wistful, little face decided him.

"Annie, you're such an old friend, both to me and to my mother, and you've been so decent to me when you might easily have been different, and nobody could have blamed you, I must tell you—what do you think would be the most astounding thing that could happen to me in India?"

"If you had married a black wife—one of these princesses they carry about in the queer little chairs!" she said, on the spur of the moment.

But John's very serious face reproved her.

"Well, I've found my father," he said then, quite baldly and simply.

"Found your father?" repeated Annie in a puzzled voice. "I never knew you had one—I mean," she added rather confusedly, "everybody thought that he didn't count; that he'd never even been heard of."

"I've found him all the same. We're living together in Calcutta. But he is sailing for home, just as soon as he is able, to see my mother."

"But how grand and terrible!" said Annie wonderingly. "And what kind of a man is he, Jack—a father worth having?"

At this John pushed back his chair rather noisily.

"He's a splendid father, Annie—the kind of father a son would die for! I very nearly did die for him up there in these infernal mountains, where we were lost together for days! It's of my mother I'm thinking. You are a woman, Annie; you know something of a woman's heart—what she feels about these things. What do you think my mother will do when she sees him? It is keeping me awake at nights."

Annie sat forward, her bonnie eyes glowing.

"Everything depends on whether—on whether—she has forgotten him. I've never heard her speak of him nor has anybody—even Aunt Lizzie that neighboured her at Miss Galbraith's, not so very long after it all happened. Has he explained it to you? How he happened to leave her, as she was then? We can speak quite freely now, Jack, as I'm a married woman, and you are like my own brother."

"He has explained to me. But what I am not sure about is whether the explanation will be enough for her. She's a terrible deep-thinking, far-seeing woman, my mother, Annie, and you can never know her through and through. Do you think there is anything I could do to help? Could I write?"

"You could, but you will not, Jack; for, after all, it is no business of yours, except from the outside like. When everything else fails you might write; but in the meantime I would let him go back and make his own explanation; and let them read it up together. It's not your story nor mine, Jack; and, as far as I can see, nobody can help them. As Katrine says, they must dree their weird. Tell me, has he fair hair, Jack? For Katrine has harped on about the fair-haired man that was to bring weal or woe to you, since ever you went away."

"Yes, he has fair hair. It has even, I believe, a tinge of red in it."

"Then everything will come right, I don't doubt. I must be going, for I don't suppose my very proper sister-in-law would approve of such goings-on! Can I tell her I've seen you, Jack?"

"As to that, you can please yourself."

His tone was cold and indifferent, and Annie eyed him keenly.

"You're not sweet in that quarter any longer then, Jack? Now, I wonder where you've cast that roving eye of yours this time."

He laughed embarrassedly, and said he had cast it nowhere.

"Tell that to the marines, lad, and not to me that has known you since you were a child!"

"I haven't got over my consternation yet, Annie—Mrs. Roger Annan, as I must call you! I hope you will be very happy."

"I am happy," she said tranquilly.

"And that you will make the very best of Roger. He's a good chap—a very good chap, Annie, but easily led."

"But it's me that's going to do the leading now, and I'll see that it's in the right road," she answered, with the same ready confidence.

"The Annans may yet bless the day you took Roger in hand. I believe they will, my dear," he said, on the spur of the moment.

She nodded, and her lips tightened a little as she fastened her gloves.

"The only opinion among them I care a button for is his mother's. And what I promised her I'll do; for she was an angel to me, and I've got a mother now, Johnnie, that had only an auntie before."

John, more moved than he cared to own, stood aside for his old friend in this new guise to pass before him. They parted in the sunny street with a warm handshake and a promise to meet again; and he hied him to the house of the Humes to seek an interview with Beatrice.

Hope beat high in his breast, higher even than it had done an hour ago, for the altogether unexpected and, in a way, unprecedented interview just ended had cleared every obstacle from his path.

He was able to anticipate the words Beatrice might speak of good comradeship and congratulation, for surely she would be glad that he had fared so well on the fateful journey, in regard to which she had already wished him well. Doubtless by now she had heard part of the story, at least, from the Eastcotes, though its most exciting chapter, concerning the relationship to Jardine might very possibly not yet have leaked out.

He was again fortunate in finding Miss Hume in the house and disengaged. He asked for her with a boldness he could scarcely have ventured upon, before he left Calcutta, a few weeks previously; but, when shown into her presence, the old diffidence returned.

A man honestly and sincerely in love is always humble and diffident, but that humility sat better on John than arrogance or assurance would have done.

Beatrice looked very regal and simple in a plain white frock, and she rose from her desk to receive him with a frank, friendly smile.

"Now, this is good! For I heard you had only returned yesterday. May I say how glad I am about everything?"

As their hands met Marchbanks longed to ask what " everything " might mean ; but his tongue seemed strangely to cleave to the roof of his mouth.

She, apparently not noticing his embarrassment, asked him to be seated, and sat down herself opposite to him, as if quite ready to hear his story.

" Of course, we've heard part of the wonderful story from the Eastcotes, but it will be so much more interesting first hand. How splendid it was of you to make that terrible journey, and bring poor Mr. Jardine back.

" It was the thing I was brought out to India to do," said John simply.

She seemed struck by the words.

" Why do you say that ? Mr. Jardine was a stranger to you. What could be the compulsion ? "

Her large luminous eyes fixed themselves on John's changing face intently, and he saw that Eastcote had not dropped any hint of the relationship which had been so strangely discovered at the mouth of the Narkander Pass.

" It is an extraordinary story, and one which I can't explain to you just yet. But—but Mr. Jardine is my father ! "

" Your father ? "

She repeated the words a little breathlessly, then sat forward and began to speak, rather quickly and warmly.

" Then I may tell you now what I have often longed to do, that I have sympathised with you in your difficult position. The Annans told us things about your family history."

" The one big, damaging fact, at least, I suppose ! " he said, rather stiffly. " You knew it before I left Calcutta then ? "

" Oh, yes, I knew it, even before that. Do you remember a dinner-party, at which Miss Annan was present ? "

" Of course, I remember it."

" She told me that night ; but I had already heard the story from her brother George. They wished, for some reason or another to damage you in our eyes, but they did not succeed, Mr. Marchbanks. I should like you to know that I have heard my father and the Eastcotes discuss it, so you were welcome here, on your own account, as you are welcome now."

" God bless you for these words," said John, quite simply. " I hope that one day the whole mystery and difficulty will be cleared up. My father is going home to Scotland as soon as he is able for the voyage."

" Home to Scotland—to see your mother ? "

" That is the object of his journey."

" How thrilling ! Has there ever been a romance like it ? How long have they been separated ? "

" Five-and-twenty years."

" Twenty-five years ! They will take some bridging, but love is a wonderful thing. I think it will all come right, don't you ? I will pray that it may. And you will remain here, in the interval, I suppose ? I hear from Major Eastcote that you have basely turned your back on Trent Bartlett's ! "

" No, no ! " said John deprecatingly. " They released me of their own accord."

" Aided by some slight pressure from without, shall we say ? " she asked, with a touch of coquetry. " Come and talk to my mother. She is as interested in it all as if you were her son."

John rose, for he had no valid reason for refusing, though these moments were very precious.

" Life has been so full and so extraordinary since I came to India that I hardly know myself."

"A common complaint," she answered brightly. "But others are always ready to assist us in the interesting process of self-education."

"I'm very ignorant," he began, but she held up a warning finger.

"Hush! No member of the Intelligence Department, even the most callow, admits ignorance."

He laughed.

"'Callow' is the word. But I'm going to work like a galley slave."

"I'm sure of it. You have the face of a worker, but don't become a slave to work. There are other things——"

"Yes, many of them! But it is through work they are attained," he said, rather quickly. "When a man sets his heart on some inaccessible height he has to climb for it first."

"What is your inaccessible height?" she asked, as if goaded to the question.

"I haven't the right to say," he made answer, and his voice was very full. "But, please God, the day will come."

She could not mistake his meaning. The colour leaped in a flame to her cheek, and she turned to the door rather hurriedly.

"Come and see mother," was all she said, but as her eyes met his they were full of an enchanting sweetness which did not forbid him to hope.

Meanwhile, in George Annan's house, where the quartette were still living, with only a moderate degree of comfort together, Roger's wife "got even" with her sister-in-law by giving her a very vivid description of her meeting with John Marchbanks.

Elizabeth listened without a word spoken, but her face looked tired and old in the half-light, and there were sad, even peevish, lines about her mouth.

She knew now, beyond all doubt, that the lover whom she had esteemed too lightly, had passed completely out of her life, and her one desire now was to put the breadth of the sea between herself and him.

CHAPTER XXVIII

THE SECOND SPRING

KATRINE POLSON, very busy with a surreptitious spring-cleaning, in the most unusual absence of her mistress, was singing at her work. It was about eleven of the morning, and she had the rest of the day in front, for her mistress would not return until late in the following day.

The only thing which disturbed the hard-working and conscientious serving-woman was the presence of strangers in the shop below.

Since her son's departure and consequent diminution of household expenses, Ellen had begun to save herself, in the way of labour, in a quite remarkable way. Also, she began to exhibit towards the close of the year, a very marked disgust with her surroundings, and a growing distaste for her work behind the counter. Finally, she announced to Katrine one day that she was going to retire from business, and go into private life.

Now, this decision would only have been a blow to Katrine had it involved her own dismissal, but, being assured that her mistress had no intention of parting with her, she was able to take a very lively interest in the new scheme of things.

It was a very simple one; merely the transfer of Ellen's home to a comfortable roomy villa at the coast, which she could let, in any season when she desired to augment her income, or have a little change for herself.

This big change necessitated many excursions to the coast; and it was some time before a decision was come to concerning the actual and final destination.

Ellen favoured Hunter's Quay, and in the end took a house there, standing back from the sea, on high ground, and commanding a view unsurpassed by any in Scotland. When she took the house she put a few things in it, furnishing a sitting-room and a bedroom simply, so that she would have a roof to cover her, until she could transfer her own substantial furniture from Shawlands Cross.

She would not part with any of her belongings there, for they had come from a good house, and were of a quality seldom met with in these more meretricious days, when people are loth to pay the price for quality alone, but are all for the outside veneer.

Ellen possessed a Georgian sideboard that had stood in Miss Galbraith's house, the value of which she did not actually know. The other things were in keeping, and had always imparted to the unpretentious house above the shop an air of solidarity and distinction which had surprised many.

A smart young shop assistant now took the bulk of the counter work off Ellen; and, though the customers frankly deplored the change, for they all loved her, the business in no way suffered. Her idea, in the meantime, was to give him an interest in the business, which would enable him to marry and live above the shop. She would thus be sure of an income herself, and at the same time be of some practical use to a couple of very deserving people who might otherwise have to postpone their marriage indefinitely.

This was the position of affairs in the early spring, nearly a year after John had gone away. Ellen's heart was now completely at rest about him, for he wrote regularly, and she was aware that he was doing very well. True, she was not very clear about his position in the Indian Intelligence Department, but, apparently, it was Government work, well paid, and offering considerable scope.

She had heard some account of how such a post came to him, and knew that he had made a perilous journey into the interior and rescued somebody whose personality was of value to the Government, but her knowledge and information stopped there.

Undoubtedly the principal cause of her restless desire for change was her loneliness. The main object of her striving and hope had been suddenly wrested from her. Her son was now standing on his own legs, fighting his own battle, and, though she had equipped him, he had no need of her now.

It was sometimes a bitter thought, and, now that Annie Houston also had been swallowed up by the mysterious East, she had very little to interest her beyond work and business.

What she hoped for from the drastic change from the city to the country she hardly knew ; but for the time being the idea pleased her, and took up her time and thoughts much as a new toy might please and occupy the mind of a child.

Singing at her work, then, having finished the parlour the day before, and now " thrang," as she expressed it, with her mistress's bedroom, with a duster tied above her neatly fitting cap and a huge blue-striped apron over her white one, Katrine Polson was disturbed about eleven of the morning by a very decided and rather imperative peal at the bell.

" Noo, wha can that be ? I've a very guid mind to let them ring ! She's awa', onyhoo, and it'll be somebody for her."

But Mrs. Marchbanks, who had been trained in very strict integrity regarding the answering of the door by Miss Galbraith, now deceased, had impressed on Katrine that it is wrong to lie or prevaricate to any caller, no matter what his or her business.

So, while the echoes of the bell died away, Katrine, with a sigh, took off her blue apron, untied her head-duster, rolled down her sleeves, and proceeded to the door.

When she opened it a very large, tall man, wearing a fur-trimmed coat, though it was a very sunny March day, and warm for the season, gave her a polite good morning, and inquired whether he could see Mrs. Marchbanks.

" No, sir, ye canna, for she is not at hame. She's doon the watter."

" Oh," he said, extreme disappointment in his voice. " But she lives here, doesn't she ? "

He had a very pleasant, well-modulated voice, and, though the light was insufficient for Katrine to obtain the clearest vision of his face, she thought she liked its outline. Also, frankly, her curiosity was great, for by this time she knew most of Mrs. Marchbanks' visitors, and this was a new one.

" She bides here when she is at hame, of course," she answered civilly. " And she is not coming back till the morn's nicht."

" I have come a long way to see her. I suppose she is too far away to permit of my following her ? "

Katrine hesitated a moment, for, undoubtedly this was a poser ! Finally she decided to parly judiciously with the visitor.

" Will ye no come in, sir, and I'll get ye the address ? It's a queer-soondin' name, but the mistress she wrote it doon for me afore she gaed awa' just in case onything micht happen."

The stranger thanked her, and with much alacrity followed her along the passage with the borrowed light and into the big, pleasant, and immaculately clean sitting-room, which certainly surprised him. Having ushered him in, Katrine folded her small, wrinkled hands above her apron and eyed him intently. " A big, fair man ! " she muttered voicelessly. " I do believe it's him, efter a' ! "

Aloud she said, quietly and respectfully :

" My mistress has a hoose doon the watter. She's goin' to live in it a'thegither in the month o' May. She's there—here's the address."

From the top of the black marble clock with the Corinthian pillars, which had been one of the glories of Miss Galbraith's dining-room, she took the envelope which bore, in Ellen's neat, rather precise, handwriting, the legend : " Ian Mohr, Hunter's Quay."

" And this is where Mrs. Marchbanks is ? " he asked, as his eyes, steadied by a pair of eyeglasses on a gold chain, which impressed Katrine immensely, fixed the written words.

" Yes, sir ; that's whaur she is. We're movin' doon there in May. She's tired o' the shop ; and it's no afore time, I may say, for she has been sair trauchled by that same."

Now, afterwards called to task for giving the whole story away at a moment's notice, Katrine was wholly unable to defend herself. All she said was " I just had to do it. It had naething to do wi' me, I jist had to."

The stranger listened intently, his kindly but very deep and rather searching eyes fixed on Katrine's face.

" Hunter's Quay ! I know the name very well of course, though I have never been there. It's on the Clyde, isn't it ? Very near Dunoon ? "

" It's no' faur frae Dunoon, certainly—there's Kirn first. Was ye thinkin' o' goin' doon, then ? "

" I will go down this afternoon if you assure me she is there. I have come a long way to see her, and my business is important."

" You'll get plenty o' trains an' boats. We've had fine weather this month, for a wonder, and they have put mair on," said Katrine. " Can I offer ye onything ? " she added, on the spur of the moment, feeling that to this stranger the whole hospitality of her mistress's house was somehow due.

This was the more extraordinary a concession on Katrine's part, for she was not naturally a hospitable, but rather a prickly aggressive person.

The stranger thanked her with an infinite courtesy.

" My name is Jardine," he said, and at the same time drew a visiting-card from his pocket and laid it on the table. " This is lest by some unlucky chance I should miss seeing Mrs. Marchbanks at Hunter's Quay, in which case I shall certainly come back here."

With this he took his departure, and Katrine viewed him from behind the window-curtain as he waited for the car to start, his eyes fixed on the white corner house which her mistress had inhabited so long.

What more natural than that Katrine should flee to her tea-cups—more especially as what she called her " eleeven 'oors," was considerable overdue ?

Jardine followed Katrine's directions faithfully, and, after various delays, reached Kirn Pier about half-past three of the afternoon.

It was an enchanting spring day, soft and balmy, the sky shining with a soft radiance, flecked here and there by fleecy white clouds sailing like little birds of passage across the blue. The sea was kindly, and the enchanting beauty of the scenery filled Jardine with amazement.

He could not recall that he had ever seen it before, and now understood Glasgow's pride in her queen of rivers.

On the purser's advice, he landed at Kirn Pier, and proceeded to walk by the shore-road toward's Hunter's Quay. But, as he neared his destination his interest in the scenery began to wane and was swallowed up in poignant anticipation of the interview, so charged with destiny that he almost feared its imminence.

On, on he went ; and presently, being directed, found himself on a somewhat broken, uneven hill road leading to a small cottage residence, picturesquely built on a fir-clad slope overlooking the Holy Loch, where already many yachts rode at anchor, making a picture both fair and suggestive.

Slightly heated by the walk, he had taken off his heavy overcoat and slung it over his arm, so that his slim, well-carried, rather soldierly figure in dark grey tweed was shown to advantage.

Ellen, who had had a busy morning measuring floors for carpets and walls for furniture, had made pause to get herself a cup of tea, which she had spread daintily with a white cloth on the end of the sitting-room table. She had just carried the teapot from the kitchen and put it under the cosy when, happening to glance over the white silk blinds which her busy fingers had fashioned for the front windows, she saw a strange man fumbling at the gate.

In no way apprehensive, for various people had already called—tradesmen asking for custom, and others—she settled the cosy more firmly over the teapot, gave the fire a little stir to make it cheerful, and went to the glass door which opened in a little porch gay with pots of daffodil and hyacinth.

When she opened the door, however, and her eyes saw before her a face which twenty-five years had not altered sufficiently to defy recognition, her own went deathly white, and, for a moment, she felt her senses slipping from her.

" Willie ! " she said at last, in a faint, almost inaudible whisper, " Willie Jardine, come back to life—and to me ! "

It was neither the welcome nor the repulse he had expected, but it was something which opened the door of possibility. So, with his strong right hand he just closed the door and went by her side, quite gently but firmly, into the room and closed that door, too, so that they were quite alone in the world where none could come between them.

She steadied herself by the table, her face still white as the bit of lace about her neck, her pale lips fluttering, her eyes, full of something that was not terror nor yet joy, but a mingling of both.

" Where have you come from, Willie Jardine ?—and why—why are you here ? "

" I've come from the other side of the world, Ellen, to find you that I thought was dead and buried long ago ! "

" What cause had you to think that ? " she asked ; and as strength came back to her after the first shock had expended itself her voice hardened. " I gave you none."

" You disappeared, and all my searching could not find you, my dear——"

" I was driven out from your father's house with harsh words, and you must have known it ! They told me they would leave nothing to chance, and that they would part us for ever. That I did not mind, for it was a natural thing for them to be angry because you should have had a love affair with one who was their servant. I bore them no ill will, but I have never forgiven you, Willie Jardine, and I never will—for your base desertion ! "

" You can't look me in the face steadily, Ellen, and say that again ! " he said in his strange, quiet, measured voice.

" Oh, but yes, I can ! " she said, but she did not look at him—for why ?—

the old love was creeping back to her heart! "Where did I go? Only to Glasgow! And you made no effort to seek me out. You did not even write to the address I sent you."

"Where did you send that address? I never got it, Ellen, as God is my witness!"

"I wrote to you after you had gone back to London and told you everything that had happened and some of the things—but not all—your mother said to me."

"I never got that letter, Ellen. Perhaps I was away to India before it arrived, but I swear to you that I tried everything in my power to discover you, even after my mother wrote that she had heard you had died in a Manchester hospital."

"A Manchester hospital!" repeated Ellen, in a strangely ironical voice. "How did I get to Manchester? She invented every word of that, and her one idea was to keep us apart. For me, I was not minding, for I was sick with the shame and the sin of the whole affair, and very nearly took my own life. I was not the first lassie to give up all for a man and get her thanks in one day! For myself, I would not have minded, but the bairn lived, Willie, and the sin of his father and the mother has been visited on him, for he has been driven from his home and his country by what they call the bar sinister. For myself, I have never complained, for they that sin deserve their punishment, and should take it humbly. But that the innocent should suffer is the bitterness of all sin, and my son will suffer through me to the end of his days."

She spoke with such passion that a streak of red illumined her white cheek and her eyes blazed with something of the fire of youth. And he, studying her face intently, marvelled that time had dealt so gently with her, even while he marvelled, too, at the passion which beat in his own veins.

"Ellen"—he said, and his voice took on a note of harshness through the very intensity of his feeling—"my mother is dead, and it is not well to speak ill of the dead. I was her only son, and, no doubt, my love for you disappointed her grievously. She assured me, not in one letter, but in twenty, that she had absolute proof of your death, and for that reason, and for that alone, I have never cared to come back to Scotland, nor to England, even. I have spent all these years in India."

"It can matter nothing to me where you have spent them," she said a little wildly. "And I don't know what for you seek to come here to disturb my peace. I have no need nor use for you now, Willie Jardine! We did wrong in our youth, and I, at least, have paid the full price. Let it be at that! I have repented and been forgiven by God, I do believe; but I am not needing to have all the black, bitter past raked up again, nor do I think that I have deserved this at your hands."

She looked him full in the face then with defiance in her own. His expression was very gentle and serious, and the tenderness in his eyes melted her inward heart so that she trembled visibly.

Ah, me! The heart of such a woman never forgets, but cherishes and remembers even the faithless to the bitter end!

Ellen rebelled with all her might against her growing weakness and cried out in her heart that she had not deserved this, the final blow!

"Listen, my dear; there have been forces at work in your life and mine which we are powerless to set aside. I have been living for years back on the outskirts of civilisation doing my bit where other men did not care about it, and not six months ago I had a most marvellous escape from certain death. I had undertaken on my own account a certain journey into the interior of India, into a hostile region where, I knew very well, I carried my life in my hand. But that was a small matter to me, and the man who does not greatly value his life usually finds it preserved for him in quite unexpected ways. It was Government work, and I wanted to find out something which was to be of the utmost value to them. And I did find it out, though at considerable cost. My disguise as a native was discovered, I was arrested and tortured, and escaped from a cruel death by the skin of my teeth. But I was too weak and spent to make the journey back to my station, and I had crawled into a cave to die at peace when I was rescued by a young Scotsman new to the work, to the country, to everything—yet he succeeded where twenty others might easily have failed! Can you guess, Ellen, who he was? Your son—and mine! That is how I am here this day."

"Your son and mine!" she repeated, in a voiceless whisper. "My Jack—out in India—rescued you and sent you here!"

"That is the whole matter in a nutshell, my woman."

"And—and—does he know?"

"He knows. He knew, or at least suspected, before he set out on his quest, and this was his guide and director. Do you remember the day we spent together on Portobello sands, and you had this taken for me?"

From his pocket he drew the faded little daguerreotype case, touched the spring, and showed her her own face.

Again silence fell upon them, and she, as if suddenly grown weak and spent, sat down, let her arms rest on the table so that her head fell on them and her face was hidden.

It was then that Jardine knelt at her feet.

In the gloaming, after a fiery sunset which gilded the incomparable scene with a radiant mystery, she walked with him to the little gate.

Much had passed between them in the interval, and some peace was made, but while he still urged, Ellen continued to shake her head.

"I would be afraid, Willie, for I know that the gulf between us was greater then than I understood. I was but an ignorant servant lass and your mother was a woman of the world, and knew what she was talking about. A hard world has taught me, and I don't blame her any more, because I understand. I've paid the price, and I'm willing to go on paying it. It's only peace I want now."

"But I would try to give you peace, Ellen," he said. "I'm not a fighting man, even my worst enemy could not call me that."

She continued to shake her head.

"It would not do, it would not do at all to marry now. What difference could it make to Johnnie, and he is the only one that matters."

"I don't agree that he is the only one that matters, Ellen, but it would make a great deal of difference to Johnnie, in fact, so much that I could never begin to put it into words."

"In what way?" she asked, and her look was a little startled and eager.

"In a thousand ways. I shall have to come back to-morrow and tell you. May I come back to-morrow and plead Johnnie's cause, since I've failed so miserably in my own."

"No, I don't think so; you'd better go back to Glasgow. I'll be going back myself to-morrow."

"I won't leave this place to-night. I'll stop down there at the Kirn Hotel and feast my eyes on the beauty of the sea and the heavens. Promise you'll let me see you to-morrow."

"What's the good? It can serve no end nor give any satisfaction, and it hurts us both. I've told you what I feel."

" But one thing you have not told me, Ellen."

" What's that ? " she asked, in the same startled voice which seemed to bring back her lost youth.

" That you hate me and will never forgive me. If you'll look me straight in the eyes here and now, and say you have grown completely indifferent I'll go away and never come back. There never has been any other woman in my life, Ellen. I remained true with all that was best in me, to what I believed to be your memory. I honoured that memory ; it was all I could do in the way of atonement for the wrong of youth."

She made no answer, but her eyes grown a little stormy and wistful looked out to sea.

" If you tell me you don't care any more I'll go away back to India and torment you no more, my dear," he said gently.

Then quite suddenly she laid her head down on the parapet of the gate and burst into tears.

" I can't tell a lie, Willie, I've loved you all my life."

That was practically the end of the story.

The first holiday inmates of the little house, called Ian Mohr, were a honeymoon couple past their first youth, whose extraordinary story was known in Scotland only to a faithful servant who would rather have died than declare it. But the latter part of their summer was spent in the south countryside of Scotland, in a great house which had cradled the branch of the Jardine family to which Ellen's husband belonged.

And when she saw it, and realised that it was Johnnie's heritage and would one day pass to him, the mystery and the awfulness of life made her afraid.

But most of all she was afraid of her own happiness, of the late blooming of love in her life which was something finer and sweeter and more steadfast than the passion of youth.

Finally, in the late autumn, they set sail for India, where the rest of the story had to be unravelled, and Johnnie's home-sickness appeased. If there had been something mysterious about the first honeymoon couple who visited Ian Mohr there was no hole-and-corner business about the affairs of the second, for they were young and gallant, described by Katrine Polson as a " sicht for sair een."

Thus did the announcement of their marriage run :

" At St. George's, Hanover Square, on the fifteenth of April, John Marchbanks Jardine, younger, of Knock Settle, Wigtownshire, to Beatrice Mary, eldest daughter of Gavin Hume, Esq., Calcutta and London and niece of Sir Edward Trent, Lowndes Square, S.W., and Alton Pagnell, Bucks."

That announcement appearing in the *Glasgow Herald* caused considerable astonishment and some heart-burning both in Glasgow and Calcutta, but very few knew that it hastened a marriage between Elizabeth Annan and an elderly widower, very rich, but with a ready-made family who were opposed to the marriage for private and selfish reasons. So Elizabeth, who had not had the courage to stand the test of adversity when love knocked first at the door of her heart, had to be content with the second-best in the end.

There is a rough and ready justice in life after all, and those who made study of it, see that the scales are pretty evenly balanced, and that most of us get our deserts in due course.

THE END

THE FAIRWEATHERS

THE FAIRWEATHERS

BY

ANNIE S. SWAN

SUNDAY MAIL EDITION

1933

CONTENTS

CHAPTER I

WHAT JANET THOUGHT

THE Fairweathers as a family were undistinguished. They had lived in the town of Balgarnie all their days, the inoffensive existence of Scottish gentlewomen of presumably independent means. They were the motherless daughters of a well-known practitioner, who for over forty years had attended to the physical well-being of the town and neighbourhood where he was both respected and beloved. Dr. Fairweather had much in common with the type of country doctor beloved of the fiction-writer, but he differed from him in one respect, that he did very little work for which he did not exact payment in some form.

He was of the firm opinion that charity makes paupers, and that nobody values that for which he does not pay.

He could be, and often was, content with a very small fee, but during the whole period of his working life he had required some recognition of his services, and had lost neither respect nor liking by adhering fast to this rule.

He had a somewhat abrupt manner, which repelled those who did not know him, and such a hatred of shams that one could not live in his presence. It was strange that one so upright and so conscientious in all his ways should have one failing, an inordinate desire to get rich, and to get rich quick. Now a north-country practitioner has seldom been known to die a rich man, unless he has had private means or some other way of adding to the income earned by his professional skill. But somehow it was generally supposed by the inhabitants of Balgarnie, with perhaps one exception, that Dr. Fairweather was a very rich man.

When he died suddenly in his gig one evening as he drove through Killairn Pass, after a hard day in the hills, it was never for a moment suspected that he could possibly have left his daughters in straits. There were four of them, quiet, unobtrusive women, well liked in the place, but wholly undistinguished.

They were so, simply because no circumstance had occurred to make any demand upon their reserve powers. They had simply vegetated in their father's lifetime, each contributing a little towards the comfort and the charm of the home he had well loved. When he died they began to live.

The shock of his sudden death kept them very quiet and subdued for a few days. They did not, until the day of the funeral, even speak to one another of the kind of life they would live henceforth.

As for money matters, they did not, apparently, give them a thought. They supposed that there would be enough, and that they could keep on living at The Croft, the big, roomy, old-fashioned house in the pretty garden which was the only home they had ever known.

It fell to the lot of Archibald Maclaine, the Balgarnie lawyer, to acquaint them with their changed circumstances, and he did so on the evening of the funeral day, when he paid a special visit to The Croft for the purpose. Maclaine did not enjoy his walk from his office in the High Street to the doctor's house, which stood on the outside of the town just overlooking the railway station. Fairweather's father had built it, and it had been added to once. Maclaine thought, as he approached its somewhat dignified entrance, that it was a pity there was such a heavy mortgage upon it. It was the month of January, when gardens, in the north especially, are apt to wear their most desolate and forbidding look.

There was, however, a great deal of ornamental shrubbery about The Croft, which gave it a green and pretty appearance even in winter. It was well kept, too, the avenue and the paths smoothly rolled, and not a weed to be seen in the trim borders. Away to the left of the house, sheltered all round by a high hedge of laurel, was a tennis lawn, the envy of a good many folks in Balgarnie. The Misses Fairweather did not play much tennis, which gave a sort of discontented edge to the general envy of their lawn.

The blinds were decorously drawn half-way down, and there was about the whole place that subdued air which follows hard upon the visitation of death. Maclaine, naturally a noisy and demonstrative man, instinctively stilled his hand on the bell pull, so that it gave only a gentle tinkle. It was answered immediately by the middle-aged, well-trained servant, who had been fifteen years at The Croft.

"Are the ladies in, Ellen?" Maclaine asked in the familiar way of the man who knows the house and its ways.

"Only Miss Janet, sir; the rest have gone to the kirkyard at Fintry, but Miss Janet had a cold, and they would not let her go out."

"I'll see Miss Janet, if you please," said Maclaine, and there was a note of distinct relief in his tone. He had been rather appalled at the idea of interviewing the Misses Fairweather collectively. He knew them well, and if he had been asked to choose which one he would go to in a difficulty or dilemma, he would undoubtedly have named Janet, who was the third. It is sometimes said that all the gifts of the family find their culmination in the third child. Certainly Janet Fairweather had a good deal of character, and her sisters had learned instinctively to appeal to her in any small matter requiring consideration or decision. Up till now no large or serious business had ever required their attention.

Maclaine was shown into the drawing-room, which was not used every day, but had a fire lit in it only for special occasions. A good many persons had come from a distance that day, however, to pay their respects to the memory of the doctor, but Maclaine did not expect to find any relatives staying in the house, for the simple reason that, so far as he was aware, the Fairweathers had none. The doctor had been an only son, and his one sister, married to an Indian civil servant, had died abroad.

The Croft drawing-room was a conventional place, in which there was a good deal of rather ugly needlework. The furniture was walnut, of a light and shining grain, kept in a high state of polish, and the carpet was a good stout Brussels of a faded tan colour, with large bunches of aggressive roses scattered over it. A grey goatskin rug lay before the fireplace, and a black timepiece and ornaments on the mantelpiece showed up in startling contrast to the white grain of the marble.

Portraits of the four sisters and their parents done in chalk, and framed in gilt, adorned the walls, and some studies of fruit in colour made an odd medley. But at the close of a sharp autumn day the crimson curtains across the windows and the glow from a bright fire composed of coal and peat gave an impression of comfort to the room. Janet Fairweather was sitting in a small *prie-Dieu* chair rather close to the fire, for she was feeling shivery in the first stages of a cold. She rose up when Maclaine entered, and looked a tall, angular figure against the white of the mantelpiece, her frock of dead black seeming to add to her height.

She was not a pretty woman, nor yet a graceful one, though she might have been both had she known how to dress herself, and how to arrange her plentiful and certainly beautiful hair. Her age was twenty-six, but she looked easily thirty, especially that day with darker rims than usual under her eyes, and a certain grim seriousness about her mouth.

She was not in the least disturbed by a visit from Maclaine, who was also a friend of the family. It was no unusual thing for a lawyer to call at a house where death had lately visited; in fact, it was part of all the dreary machinery of the occasion. She did not notice the extreme gloom of Maclaine's face as he bade her good evening,

"My sisters have gone to Fintry in the brougham from Balgarnie Arms, Mr. Maclaine. I would have gone, too, only for my cold. I caught it sitting in a draught at the open window last night. Sit down, won't you? I hope you don't feel this room too warm."

"It is very comfortable, thank you," said Maclaine, but he did not take the offered chair. When Janet had reseated herself, he simply stood against the mantelpiece and looked at her, wondering how she would take the piece of information he had to impart.

"I'm rather glad to find you alone, Miss Janet, and that's the truth," he said bluntly. "When a man has something to say he would rather not say, it is easier when he has only an audience of one."

"That, I should say, would entirely depend on the audience," she said shortly. "But I'm wondering what you can have to say to me that you would rather not say. Have any of us been getting into your black books?"

"That would be impossible. It's about your father's affairs, Miss Janet. There's very little left for you and your sisters; in fact, to be quite honest, there is practically nothing."

It was not a gracious speech. If the man had laid himself out to speed a thunderbolt of words, he could not have done it more successfully. But Janet Fairweather received it with apparent calm.

She leaned forward in her chair, and looked up at him keenly with a pair of the clearest grey eyes that could read a man's soul.

"Why is there nothing left? My father had a good practice, none of us have ever been extravagant, and we all thought he was saving money."

"He might have done; in fact, at odd times he did; but I have often wondered if any of you knew—but especially if you knew, Miss Janet—that Dr. Fairweather during the last ten years of his life was a victim to the mania for speculation."

"No, I didn't know, though I have sometimes wondered to see the rubbish about shares, and what not, that came through the post. And often he seemed worried. Pray, have you known of this all the time?"

"I have known of it for some time, and, of course, I remonstrated with him; but what was the good? This speculation is just like drink or any other vice, Miss Janet; it lays hold of a man, and there is hardly any power under Heaven strong enough to get the better of it. Of course, your father's desire was to make money, so that each of you might be left with a competency."

Janet Fairweather's face suddenly hardened, so that it looked like the nether millstone.

"He took the wrong way," she said with a touch of passion. "But I don't blame him, since it has been the way of men from the beginning of time. What he ought to have done was to teach us how to earn an honest livelihood for ourselves. Have you ever thought of the spectacle we are, Mr. Maclaine, four able-bodied and perfectly rational women, living like leeches off the hard labour of one man? I have rebelled against it all my life long, and sometimes I tried to set what was in my mind before our father. But he never would listen."

"He thought women should be sheltered, and so far I am with him."

"Faugh!" said Janet with something that looked like a snap of the fingers. "What he did was to create and maintain four parasites who preyed on him and on one another. We have had an idle, but we haven't had a happy, life. There was occupation here for only one woman. No house can be run successfully by four mistresses. For myself, I have often envied the outworker in the fields, but I've never had the courage to break the bonds."

Maclaine kept silence, much astonished at the hidden fires, the existence of which he had never suspected until now. The passion with which Janet Fairweather spoke drew and held him, and he admired her courage and her plain speech more than he could have expressed. He even at the moment admired her looks, for moments of strong feeling bring out in the human face all sorts of revealing traits, which must always be in the nature of a surprise.

"Do you mean to say that there is nothing left?" she asked suddenly in her normal voice.

"Nothing but the house, and that is mortgaged up to a thousand pounds."

"It is not worth more than fifteen hundred, is it?" she asked.

"Less; about twelve in the open market," he answered with his merciless candour. He knew his woman, and that plain speech now, though it might sound brutal, would save misunderstanding and confusion in the future.

"Of course, to anybody who happened to want it for business or professional purposes, it might be worth a hundred or two more," he said with a significance Janet did not fail to note. "Then there is the practice attached to it."

"My father disliked the idea of selling patients. He always said a doctor's business was a personal thing, and when the personal element was not in it, it was not worth having."

"That was one of Dr. Fairweather's ideals. His own personality was strong enough to uphold it. And his plain speech to his folk was liked because of the splendid qualities behind it."

"Is the practice worth anything, then, Mr. Maclaine? I'm not asking for myself, but for my sisters, especially Bella, who is not strong, and Nancy, who was my father's pet. Madge and I can fend for ourselves, I don't doubt."

"A death vacancy will not bring very much in the open market, Miss Janet," he answered slowly. "The only man to whom it would be worth anything is Dr. Ludlow."

Janet's colour slowly rose.

"My father did not like Dr. Ludlow; you know that, Mr. Maclaine," she said quickly. "I am sure the last thing he would have liked would be to think of him as his successor."

"But, Miss Janet, we can't afford to consider such things at the present moment. What we have to do—what I principally have to do—is to strain every effort in your behalf. I repeat that Dr. Ludlow is the only man to whom the interest in your father's business would be worth anything. He has already spoken to me about it."

Janet sat back in her chair with a very odd expression on her face.

"I am sure that I can speak for my sisters when I say that nothing on earth would induce us to sell the practice to Dr. Ludlow. I'm sure our father wouldn't sleep comfortably in the kirkyard of Fintry if he thought we had any traffic with him. He disliked and despised him. He did not think that he was either a good doctor or a gentleman."

Maclaine held his peace. That was no hardship for him. He was an adept at waiting till the storm blew past. And he intended to hold to his guns about Ludlow, against whom old Dr. Fairweather had cherished an unreasoning prejudice, which perhaps had its actual seat in professional jealousy.

But he could not hint at such a thing to his daughter.

"What has Ludlow said to you, Mr. Maclaine?" asked Janet with a sort of steel gleam in her quick eyes.

"He made a sort of proposition which, as your man of business, I shall be obliged to lay before you and your sisters."

"Tell it to me here and now," she said with her most peremptory air.

"He would pay a thousand pounds for the practice, and lease the house at a rental of forty pounds a year, provided he could get possession in a month."

"Like his impudence!" said Janet in high scorn. "Well, you can see him to-morrow, or to-night if you like, and tell him with our compliments that our answer is 'no'!"

"But, Miss Janet, are you empowered to speak so authoritatively for your sisters?"

"I know that they are of one mind with me about Dr. Ludlow; none of us can stand him. I would rather see the practice scattered, and the house let to strangers, than given to that man."

"But if you will only consider, Miss Janet, Dr. Ludlow is bound to get most of the patients except the few outlying ones who may prefer to send to Bridgton. I must point out to you that it is, well, rather foolish to talk like that. I think it would probably be better for me to say good night now, and call again to-morrow, when doubtless you will have talked it over with your sisters, and arrived at some definite conclusion. Miss Fairweather, for instance, may take a different view."

"Bella!" echoed Janet with just a touch of what in another would have seemed like scorn. "She does not bother her head about anything except keeping the house nice, but I'm very sure she will have nothing to do with an arrangement which includes Dr. Ludlow. And the others will do what I say."

"A 'majorful' man you are, Miss Janet," said Maclaine, with a slight smile.

"I hope I'm a sensible woman," she retorted. "Look here, Mr. Maclaine. Don't think we'll be beaten by this thing that has come upon us. We shan't. I wonder if you would believe me if I told you I'm glad it has happened? We've never known what it was to live up till now. We're going to begin now."

Maclaine listened with a kind of amazed interest. He had always respected Janet Fairweather, and had on more than one occasion remarked to his wife that she had most of the brains of the family. But he had never expected that she would meet the disastrous change in their circumstances with such splendid courage.

"What will you do, then?" he felt himself impelled to ask.

"I shall emigrate, probably to Canada. If any of them care to come, so much the better. If not, I'll go by myself. I ought to have been the man of the family, Mr. Maclaine, and if my father had given me what I wanted most in the world, it would have been a man's education. I could have taken his practice here after him if I had had the chance. But when I asked him to send me to Edinburgh or even to Dublin University, he just laughed in my face."

"It was a pity, Miss Janet, a desperate pity. Yes, that would have solved the difficulties of the situation. Well, then, and what am I to say to Ludlow to-night or to-morrow? He'll be at me at the earliest opportunity."

"I must talk it over with the rest first, of course, but I could give you their answer, I'm sure, without waiting for that," said Janet, with a high confidence which afterwards returned in memory to mock her. "None of them like Ludlow, and the thought of him in this house and carrying on our father's work would be as hateful to them as it is to me."

"But all the same, it is the easiest and the quickest way out of the difficulty, Miss Janet, believe me, and in a matter of this kind personal prejudices have to be sunk. You see, Ludlow is on the spot, and even if another man should come in here, he is bound to get the lion's share. Nothing can prevent that.

"Hadn't I better tell him you are considering his offer? If you'll let me advise you, Miss Janet—and, after all, that's what I'm here for, if I know my business at all—I should leave it at that. Do nothing in a hurry, and remember it is a terrible thing for four women to be cast on the world practically without resources. Every legitimate chance of improving the situation ought to be considered."

Janet smiled a superior smile as she walked with him to the door.

"Oh, we'll consider it all, but I can't see Dr. Ludlow here in our father's place, and I'm very sure that none of my sisters will care for the idea of it. Good night, and don't look so downcast about our affairs, Mr. Maclaine. We're not Scotch and Fairweathers for nothing. We'll win through."

"You have an astonishing pluck, anyhow," answered the lawyer, but as he went down the avenue between the naked branches of the limes he shook his head.

CHAPTER II

DAUGHTERS OF ONE RACE

JANET FAIRWEATHER returned to her seat by the fire after the lawyer had gone, and there remained until the roll of wheels in the quiet gloaming warned her of her sisters' return from the kirkyard of Fintry.

It had been Nancy's idea to go up with their own flowers after all the folk were away, and Janet felt pleased that it had fallen out thus, giving her the opportunity for private speech with Maclaine, and a certain amount of time to adjust her thoughts. She rose up to her feet when the drawing-room door opened, and was conscious of a quickened interest in her sisters. She looked at them, indeed, almost as if they were strangers, trying to picture them individually and collectively in circumstances that would undoubtedly try the mettle of their pasture.

Bella entered first and threw back her veil as she opened the door, saying the room seemed hot.

The eldest of the family, she was now thirty-two years of age, a woman of middle height, with a trim figure and a small, neat face a little inclined to shrewishness. Her colour, usually pink and white, was paler than usual, and even her lips, which were long and thin, seemed to have a bluish tinge. Her eyes were light blue and of a hardness like steel. But she seldom looked at you straight out of them ; she had a way of dropping her fair lashes quickly over them, as if afraid to reveal too much of her inner self. She had quantities of pale-coloured hair brushed primly back from her high forehead, and coiled up behind. It was a face that wanted softening, and, moreover, it was a mean face, which never won anybody at the first look.

" Sitting in the dark, are you, Janet ? " she said in her highly pitched treble voice. " It seemed to get dark all of a sudden, and it was cold up there."

" Was it ? " asked Janet mechanically, and stirred the fire so that it blazed upon Madge as she followed with her gloves in her hand, the white pillar of her throat showing against her black raiment in startling contrast. Madge was the beauty of the family, though that was a thing seldom spoken of. It was a strange, arresting kind of beauty, far removed from the ordinary standards, a weird beauty which Janet did not like, and which disquieted its own possessor. She had a milk-white skin and reddish hair and deep blue eyes, over which long curling auburn lashes swept, and a figure of lissom grace and soft, panther-like movements, half languorous, half restless. It was Madge who had hitherto created all the unrest that had ever been in the house ; she had fits of passion, when she seemed to lose control of herself, when she would say terrifying and unladylike things, and make her sisters regard her with mistrust and even a sort of dislike. It was chiefly between Bella and her the combat fell out. Bella was the embodiment of conventionality and prim propriety, while Madge might be said to represent elemental forces which had no legitimate outlet in their world.

She was now in her thirtieth year, and though she had gone decorously to the kirkyard and laid her offering on her father's grave, she had not mourned, but rejoiced, because death had removed the trammels from her life.

Already Madge Fairweather had laid her plans, and was prepared that very night to throw them like a bomb into the quiet of her sisters' lives.

Of Nancy, little need be said. She was a simple and quiet girl of sweet disposition and sweeter looks, young for her years, the sort of girl who would be moulded entirely by the husband of her choice, who would bear him children and fulfil all the requirements of her sex without an atom of protest. Of his four children, Nancy had been the only one the doctor understood.

" Is your cold any better, Jen ? " asked Nancy, slipping round to her sister's chair with that little air of concern which at the moment so oddly touched Janet Fairweather that she laid her hand with a caressing touch on her sister's arm. Demonstrations of affection were even more rare in that house than in most Scottish households. Life at The Croft was stripped of most of its embroideries. It was a gaunt and naked thing, which left each member of it hungry and cold. Doubtless the mother's influence had been missed ; the father had always been too much taken up with other folks' affairs to spare time or sympathy for his own household. They had been cheated, every one of them, and they were only beginning now to realise dimly that they had been cheated, and to rebel against it.

" Get off your things and come and sit down, all of you," said Janet with rather a peremptory air. " Archie Maclaine has been here talking business for one solid hour. Of course, he came to see all of us, but when there was only me, he talked just the same."

" What did he say ? " asked Bella, leaning against the edge of the table while Madge with a jerk pulled the catch of the incandescent gas burner so that a flood of light was immediately shed on the scene. She stood directly under its white, merciless glare, and stood the test well. Janet thought she had never seen her look more uncannily beautiful, and she felt glad of it with a kind of fierce gladness. Beyond a doubt Madge was the best equipped of them all for that which lay in front ; she possessed the gift which brings men to a woman's feet. The thought of it, while it filled Janet with a sort of slow concern, also brought bitterness to her mouth. Already Madge had had her love affairs, but they were not of a kind to boast about, but rather to forget. Once, indeed, the doctor had had to intervene in order to stop the talk of the town. Madge Fairweather possessed the power to attract men undoubtedly, but no man had yet asked her to be his wife.

" He has solved what we were talking about at breakfast this morning," said Janet quietly. " We were wondering how we could all go on living here without aim or object, getting narrower and narrower every day, until we shut up altogether. Well, we'll be spared that, because there isn't enough money left to keep us here or anywhere. We shall all have to turn out into the world and earn our own living."

For a moment the silence could be felt. On Bella's face sat a sort of grim dismay, Nancy looked wondering and interested, while in the eyes of Madge there burned a fierce flame, half exultation, half rage.

" Janet Fairweather, you must have misunderstood Archie Maclaine," said Bella shrilly. " If we were to be left like that, father would have prepared us."

" Would he, I wonder ? " asked Janet quietly. " He was never prepared himself for anything that happened. He was casual in every act of his life. But I question even if he knew. Archie Maclaine knows all about it, anyhow, and he has made it clear enough to me. We haven't even the house. It's mortgaged, and his one solution of the problem is to let Bobby Ludlow have it along with the practice."

Again there was silence, in the midst of which Madge came out from under the glare of the light and walked into the shadow.

" I have been thinking about the practice," said Bella quietly, " and, of course, we must admit that Dr. Ludlow is the only man it would be worth anything to. He's on the spot. Has he said anything to Archie ? " she asked eagerly. " Or is it only a supposition on his part that Dr. Ludlow would consider it."

" He has spoken to Maclaine already," said Janet. " But I told him none of us would entertain the idea of Bob Ludlow as a successor to our father."

A slight flush rose to Bella's face.

" Who gave you the right to say that—to speak for all of us ? "

" Well, then, and was I wrong ? Do you all want to see that unspeakable outsider in our father's place ? "

Both Madge and Nancy kept silence, the former watching with an odd sort of enjoyment the first signs of contest between Bella and Janet.

The air was full of electrical forces which, long suppressed, were about to burst the bonds. Only respect for their father and a sort of childish fear of him, which they had never outgrown, had kept these four women quiescent for so long.

" If what Mr. Maclaine said had any truth in it, then it isn't what we want, but what we can get, that would seem to be the thing," said Bella calmly.

" Please to speak out and tell us everything he said. It would have been fairer and more respectful if he had just gone away when he found you were in the house alone, and come back to-morrow when we were all here."

She spoke out of the fullness of her heart, because she felt that Janet had gained an undue advantage. Bella had been jealous all her life of Janet, and solely on her account had maintained her absolute supremacy as the eldest of the four and her father's housekeeper. She had never taken a holiday from it, nor suffered her hands to relax for a moment on the reigns of government.

Janet proceeded to lay before them the substance of the lawyer's visit, and by the time she had finished, her voice was a little husky.

" What do *you* think, Madge ? " asked Bella in the same thin shrill voice, into which a new note of trembling eagerness had crept. " It is the money we need, and what can it matter to us who gets the practice ? "

" I don't see that it matters much. To me it doesn't matter a hang," said Madge, using the unconventional word without a moment's hesitation. " I'm leaving Balgarnie, and if I ever come back to it, then I'll deserve all I'll get."

Nancy's face blanched a little at the concentrated bitterness with which her sister spoke, and at the sudden chasm which seemed to yawn before her. She had never given a thought to the problem of existence, nor had it occurred to her that their father's death could possibly make much difference. But as yet she did not feel at all afraid for herself. She was mainly conscious that something had happened to all her sisters, that they did not look like themselves, that there were unpleasant things in the air. " That is what I am going to do too, Madge," said Janet quietly. " I am going to emigrate to Canada. What I'll do when I get there I don't know, but that is where I'm going."

" Well, we can go together," suggested Madge. " To me it doesn't matter much. The main thing is to put the breadth of the sea between me and this God-forgotten hole before I begin to live."

" So it would seem to be you and Nancy who are undecided, Bella," said Janet, looking with a sudden tenderness at Nancy's sweet face. " Perhaps there will be enough saved from the cataclysm to keep you two together in a little cottage on Waffan's Brae. Madge and I will ask no more than our passage-money."

" Right you are," assented Madge, and it was at Bella they both looked, for her face was inscrutable.

" You are very kind, arranging a cottage for me on Waffan's Brae, thank you," she said, and never had her voice sounded more nippy. " But I think I'm capable of managing my own affairs. Nothing can be decided until we have seen Mr. Maclaine again, and if he does not see the propriety of calling here in a proper manner to see us all by ten o'clock to-morrow morning, I'll go down and give him a bit of straight talk."

She walked out of the room as she spoke, summoning all her dignity.

A silence followed upon her going, which was broken by the soft cooing of Nancy's sweet voice.

" I shouldn't like to go away from Balgarnie to any of these dreadful new colony places where everything is so rough. I'll ask Mrs. Dempster to let me teach the Manse bairns. I should love it, and I could do lots of odd jobs for her. She said to me only last week she wished I was her daughter. If she would let me go and live with her I should be quite happy."

In these few words did Nancy dispose of her destiny in an entirely fitting and satisfactory manner. Janet and Madge exchanged glances, admitting as much to one another.

" I daresay you could be happy there, my dear," said Janet softly, " though Mrs. Dempster and the minister, with his fiddling ways, would drive me crazy in a week."

Nancy smiled happily, and said that she would go and see her in the morning. The future had no terrors for Nancy Fairweather. The soul of sweet kindness herself, she had received naught else all her life. Even the occasional voice of her sister's strife was always stilled before her, who was the embodiment of peace.

" If we were all made like that bairn, Madge, it would be easier for us," observed Janet as the door also closed upon her.

Madge flung off her hat and stretched her arms above her head.

" You're right, Jen ; but, oh, to live ! I tell you frankly, if I had had to face another year of Balgarnie and—and Bella," she added viciously, " I should have committed some unheard-of crime. This is a merciful dispensation of Providence. How soon do you think we could decently go away ? "

" When things are wound up ; but, Madge," said Janet confidentially, " what do you suppose will become of Bella ? "

Madge was silent a moment. She beheld Bella's future stretch in front of her, unrolling like a scroll.

" Shall I tell you what was in her mind as she went out of the room, what is in her mind just now, upstairs, where I am nearly certain she's in front of the looking-glass counting her grey hairs and wondering what would take out those two tell-tale wrinkles between her eyes ? "

" Yes, if you like ; but your imagination runs away with you sometimes."

" It won't this time. She's going to get Bobbie Ludlow to take over the practice and come here to live. She'll stop on as his housekeeper, and in six months she'll be Mrs. Bobby ! "

" Oh, Madge Fairweather ! " cried Janet in a shocked voice. " She would never marry that man. How could she ? How could any woman ? "

" Bella will, you take my word for it. Just wait and see. She won't show her hand at once, but that's what she has in her mind. She'd marry anything, Janet, and so would I for the matter of that, bar Bobbie, if it would get me out of this place. But Bella will marry to keep her in it."

There was something uncanny in the bitterness with which Madge spoke, and Janet felt that her words were not wide of the mark.

" Who would have thought that three days could have made such a difference in us ? " she said musingly.

" We are not changed ; we're only wriggling out of our swaddling clothes. This has been coming on for a while, and it is certain that if this had not happened now I should have run away one of these days. Where to ? Ah, that I don't know, and I don't know that it would have mattered much. The thing was to get away. What do you propose to do in Canada ? "

" Anything ; I'm not particular. We'll find out, anyway, the truth in the report of the emigration agents. I suppose we can keep house, both of us. Anyway, we'll go out West and exploit such commodities as we have."

An odd smile curved for a moment Madge's red lips.

At the moment Ellen came to the door to say that the evening meal was on the table, and they scattered in haste to make ready for it.

Next morning, which was dull and wretched, immediately after she had given her orders in the kitchen, Bella slipped out by the back door, dressed in a short skirt and her mackintosh, and carrying her umbrella. This was not so unusual an occurrence that she required to do it in secret; she merely wished, for reasons of her own, not to be questioned by her sisters.

But Madge, who saw her come out from the end of the shrubbery walk, smiled to herself and then called Janet to witness that part of her prophecy was coming true.

Miss Fairweather walked with a purpose, and in seven minutes' time came to the office of Petersen and Maclaine in the High Street. She was immediately shown into Maclaine's room, and he rose to receive her with both respect and interest.

"Good morning, Mr. Maclaine. I was sorry we were out last night when you called. I had to come in the town this morning for my shopping, as usual, and thought I would look in. If you are not busy, will you give me a few minutes of your time?"

"Why, surely, I was thinking of coming up about eleven o'clock, Miss Fairweather."

"I thought probably you would, but first I wished to have a few words with you. Tell me, is it true that Dr. Ludlow has spoken to you already about my father's practice and the house?"

"Yes; he has done so," said Maclaine quickly, wondering what lay behind that small, neat, faintly smiling face.

"And Janet, I understand, told you we would not entertain it for a moment. Well, I have come to say that she spoke only for herself. It will not affect her one way or another, for it seems that she and Madge have already made up their minds to leave Balgarnie. I have called on my own behalf and that of Nancy, whom I shall have to look after, just to say that I should like to have an interview with Dr. Ludlow, and, if possible, to come to some arrangement with him."

Maclaine looked surprised, but, on the whole, gratified.

"I need hardly say that I am pleased to hear this, Miss Fairweather. It considerably lightens the difficulties of the situation. I don't know if Miss Janet made it clear to you that there will be very little left after all claims are settled."

"She said we were beggars or something to that effect," answered Bella, with a faint curl of her thin lips. "I allowed something for her exaggeration, but I understand that we shall be very poor. I don't want to leave Balgarnie, Mr. Maclaine, and if any arrangement can be come to with Dr. Ludlow, I shall be very glad. I suppose he would wish to live at The Croft. Indeed, he can't be very comfortable where he is now, and it is hardly dignified for a doctor to live in lodgings, however comfortable they may be. I don't see how his patients could like it or approve of it."

"Up to now the patients Dr. Ludlow has had don't mind it. But he is making his way, Miss Fairweather, and there can be no doubt this will open the door for him."

"I'm sure I hope it will. I have never joined in the outcry against him. I often thought my father both unjust and unfair to him. After all, he had the right to settle in the place if he thought he could get a living in it."

She spoke steadily and left the impression that she had come to say certain things with a definite object in view.

"I shall be glad either if you will see him on my behalf, or ask him to call at The Croft."

"There he is, Miss Fairweather, on his bicycle at the door," said Maclaine. "He has come to learn the result of my call at The Croft last night. He had a case up till midnight, so I could not see him sooner. What shall we do? Would you like to see him here?"

"Yes, I should," answered Miss Fairweather, and her colour rose slightly, and she unfastened her mackintosh and threw it back as if she suddenly felt some oppression in the atmosphere. Maclaine rose and passed into the outer office to bring the doctor to her presence.

CHAPTER III

BELLA LEGISLATES

Bobbie Ludlow, who had been such a thorn in the flesh of Dr. Fairweather, and whom his daughters spoke of so scoffingly, was certainly no great figure of a man. As he came with a somewhat shuffling gait into the lawyer's office he looked shabby, insignificant, undignified to the last degree. He was undersized, but did not carry himself with that perkiness often seen in small men. His diminutive body was crowned by a large head, and his features of no particular distinction had a somewhat vacuous expression, while his light blue eyes behind a pair of large spectacles, instead of being the mirrors of his soul, seemed to hide it—that is, such soul as he had. There were some in Balgarnie—and the Misses Fairweather had once been among them—who had denied him the possession of a soul. That he should come without invitation or encouragement into Balgarnie after he had "prospected," as he called it, and weighed up all the chances, was in itself a dire offence. He had been coldly received, and had suffered snubs which would have daunted most men, and in the first year of his professional existence in Balgarnie he made the handsome sum of fifteen pounds, three of which had never been paid to this day; but in spite of that dashing experience he had hung on. What he lived on was a mystery to all, since he had caused it to be known that he had no private means. But Robina Dick, in whose house in the High Street he lodged, had no fault to find with him, and said he owed her nothing. That he had some professional skill was proven by the fact that most of his patients recovered quickly, and thereafter became his partisans. It had been an acknowledged fight between the old methods and the new, between experience and that kind of blind confidence a man has before he has found out how little he knows.

Dr. Fairweather had been a dignified practitioner of the old school, very particular about dress and deportment, and his bedside manner was often spoken about admiringly. Bobby Ludlow owed nothing to these accessories of his craft. He wore a shabby tweed suit and an old cap of the same stuck far back on his head, and saved his washing bill by abstention from starched linen. Bella Fairweather, who worshipped the proprieties, looked at him with a cold disgust as he entered the lawyer's room, doffing his cap, and showing a head covered by scanty light-coloured hair inclined to baldness on the top. She made up her mind that Bobbie would not be a difficult man to subdue, and that in six months' time he would be walking in the way he should go. But that assurance only showed her ignorance of the world, especially the world of men.

Bobbie Ludlow knew Miss Fairweather perfectly well by sight, and did not in the least admire her. But at the moment his eye was desperately on the main chance which she represented. He must get the Fairweather suffrages on any pretext, and he was prepared to make himself as amiable as he knew how.

"Good morning, Maclaine," he said briefly, and waited for the introduction, which promptly came.

"I am pleased to meet you, of course, Miss Fairweather," he added courteously. "I have never been able to make out quite why we haven't met before. But that's one of the dark mysteries of provincial life."

As Archibald Maclaine said afterwards, this took the wind out of Bella's sails at the very beginning, and left her without a word to say.

"I promised myself the pleasure of calling on you one of these days, Miss Fairweather," he continued when she made no answer. "Have I your permission to do so?"

"Oh, yes, I think so," she answered vaguely. "I am sure my sisters will be pleased to see you, though everything at The Croft is so sadly altered now. But if there is a little business to talk over, hadn't we better do it now?—that is, if you have the time to spare."

"I must make the time," he answered, not quite so courteously, but rather in the manner of a man who does not care one way or another.

"You are busy, then?"

"I am, rather, and permit me to say," he added honestly, "that I very much regret the cause."

This remark served a double purpose—it expressed his sympathy, and informed Miss Fairweather that her father's practice was already coming in his direction. She looked at him steadily, and Archibald Maclaine, much amused inwardly, stood aside and watched all the little by-play of that preliminary interview.

In the presence of this perfect *sang-froid* Bella Fairweather found herself suddenly at a loss, and turned quickly to Mr. Maclaine.

"Perhaps you will kindly explain to Dr. Ludlow, Mr. Maclaine, that we might be willing to consider any proposition he has to make about my father's practice."

"Certainly, Miss Fairweather. There does not appear to me to be much difficulty in the way. Dr. Ludlow thinks he could keep the practice together, and you are willing that he should try for a consideration. The only thing that remains to be settled is the terms."

Ludlow nodded and concealed his surprise, for no later than the previous day Maclaine had assured him that he did not believe that the doctor's daughters would ever condescend to discuss terms with him, and that he had not the courage to suggest it. But things had marched quickly since then, and the whole complexion of the situation had altered. Janet had effectually lifted the veil from all their lives.

"Has Miss Fairweather any proposition?" inquired Dr. Ludlow as he tugged at his small, fair moustache, which somewhat concealed the strong upper lip.

"I might inquire whether Dr. Ludlow has any," retorted Miss Fairweather with a sort of formal coquetry which still further amused Archibald Maclaine.

"The whole question, of course, is the worth of the practice to me or to any man. Mr. Maclaine has doubtless told you that a death vacancy is not a very valuable asset in our profession. In Dr. Fairweather's case it is even of less value than usual. The circumstances of his death prevented him from making any arrangements for its being carried on, and at the present moment what is to hinder half a dozen men from squatting here and fighting for the crumbs?"

Bella winced at this very plain statement of facts.

"Mr. Maclaine seems to think, and I am inclined to agree with him, that the practice would be worth more to you than to any other man. Then there is the house. It has been a doctor's house for a great many years, and people are attached to it. We shall not, I regret to say, be able to live in it. Two of my sisters have intimated their intention of leaving Balgarnie immediately and going abroad. I don't wish to leave the town where I was born and where all my interests lie."

She paused here, not sure whether the atmosphere was sympathetic and encouraging.

"You would prefer to stay in the house, naturally. Well, if we could come to terms about the financial part of the business, would you be willing to take me as a boarder, Miss Fairweather?"

She winced again at the word, because the pride of the Fairweathers was very high, and they had never contemplated the idea of working for their living in any of the more sordid ways open to indigent females. Something genteel and ladylike, which would not compromise them in the eyes of society, was what Bella at least would have desired. The very course suggested by Dr. Ludlow had already matured in her mind, but she could have wished it called by another name. She regarded him doubtfully and with much dignity and reserve.

" You surprise me, Dr. Ludlow. It would mean a very great change for us all. I am not sure whether my sisters would agree to such a thing. It might be more dignified to leave the house altogether, and go into a smaller one, if it could be sold."

" But it would hurt the practice," he remarked eagerly. " If it is a concession to public opinion you are thinking of, I am sure most people would think our plan the best way out of a big difficulty. It would save you an immense lot of trouble, and it would give me the chance I want. It would help to establish me in the place."

Miss Fairweather still seemed to hesitate, though her heart was glowing at the prospect and at the ease with which her secret plan was being pushed forward.

" And though it does not seem very generous, I may remind you that any other man coming to the house and hoping to succeed to your father's, Dr. Fairweather's, practice would find it a pretty tough problem with me in the place. I've come to stay."

The vulgarity of the remark, its ruthless candour, Miss Fairweather passed by in dignified silence. She looked for the first time inquiringly at the lawyer's face.

" What does Mr. Maclaine think ? " she asked quickly.

" I think there is a good deal of truth in what Dr. Ludlow says," admitted Maclaine, " though perhaps," he added significantly, " he might have expressed it a little differently. But it is a hard world, Miss Fairweather, and I am sorry that you and your sisters have had to come up against it like this."

" Then you think I—that is, we—should accept Mr. Ludlow's offer ? "

" It is certainly worth your consideration, and I think you should go home and consult with your sisters."

Miss Fairweather looked out of the window, and her small, narrow face seemed to sharpen in the clear, still light.

" It concerns me chiefly—in fact, I may say entirely—as two of my sisters go abroad immediately, and I am disposed to accept your offer, Dr. Ludlow. The actual terms of the arrangement I must leave in your hands, Mr. Maclaine."

Dr. Ludlow looked immensely gratified.

" This is a very unexpected turn of events, Miss Fairweather, and I can only express my gratitude and appreciation. I promise you that my part of the bargain will be faithfully adhered to. As for my character," he added, with a curious laugh, " you are at perfect liberty to go for it to my landlady, Miss Robina Dick."

" I should not dream of such a thing. I hope that we are ladies, and that you are a gentleman, Dr. Ludlow," she answered with an air which once more secretly delighted Archibald Maclaine, and which he afterwards tried to reproduce with doubtful success for the benefit of his wife.

As she was about to go, feeling that the main object of the interview had been successfully accomplished, Bella looked at Ludlow with a smile.

" Then perhaps you would like to see through the house before you settle details with Mr. Maclaine. Will you come up to afternoon tea with me and my sisters to-day at four o'clock ? "

Ludlow, at most times a brave man, seemed to quail slightly at the prospect, but, immediately recovering himself, thanked her and accepted the invitation.

Miss Fairweather then, with much *empressement* of manner, bade them both good morning, and sailed out of the office, Archibald Maclaine accompanying her to the outer door.

" Please come up with Dr. Ludlow this afternoon, Mr. Maclaine, if you can spare the time. I shall have talked the matter over with my sisters before then, and it might be definitely settled. If the new arrangement is to be effected, it can't come into operation too soon, and there is no reason why Dr. Ludlow should not take up his abode at The Croft immediately. It would save all trouble of sending down messages to Robina Dick's lodgings."

"That is true, indeed, but you take my breath away, Miss Fairweather. When Ludlow spoke to me yesterday I warned him that even if there was a chance of making any arrangement between him and you, it would take weeks."

"Ah! that shows you don't know us, Mr. Maclaine," said Bella, and though she said "us" she meant "me." "In our dear father's lifetime, of course, it was not necessary for us to trouble about business matters in the smallest degree, but now I hope we shall make it clear to everybody that we are perfectly capable women, whom the exigencies of life do not daunt."

She bowed graciously and moved away from the door. Bobbie Ludlow, watching over the wire blind in the lawyer's room, saw her not ungraceful figure moving down the street with an odd interest. When Maclaine re-entered the room he burst into a small laugh.

"A clever woman, by Jove, Maclaine, a devilish clever woman, and no mistake. I begin now to understand a big part of Fairweather's success. It was his daughters who kept the thing together. That one is a born diplomatist, and now she's on my side I have the ball at my feet—eh, don't you think so?"

"She certainly knows her own mind, and, as you say, if she's on your side she'll stick up for you through thick and thin. Well, I'm glad it's fallen out like this. But, of course, though Miss Fairweather spoke so decidedly for her sisters, she hasn't consulted them yet. None of them are weak-minded, I assure you, so you are not out of the wood yet."

"If that woman and I have made up our minds—and we have, my good chap," said Ludlow cheerfully, "we'll knock the rest over like ninepins."

A little way down the street Miss Fairweather encountered Mr. Dempster, the parish minister, who from the other side of the roadway hastened to speak to her. He had seen her come out of the lawyer's office, and, with the insatiable curiosity which was natural to him, he desired to find out if possible what had been her business there. She was by no means indisposed to communicate it to him—in fact, it would be the simplest method of letting Balgarnie know what was going to happen.

Mr. Dempster was a tall, thin man with a somewhat nervous, fussy manner. He had been thirty years parish minister of Balgarnie, without winning the love and respect usually associated with his office. In some quarters he was even actively disliked, and it was only his wife's lovable personality which prevented the open grumbling of the parish. He had not good health, and his peevish, difficult ways, as well as his habit of poking into other people's business unasked, had made even the services of his church unacceptable to a large number of the parishioners, who had gone over in disconcerting numbers to the other denominations in the town. But Dr. Fairweather, conservative in all the relations of his life, had remained an elder in the parish church to the day of his death, and his daughters filled the wide pew set apart for The Croft every Sabbath day. But none of them like Mr. Dempster, though they sympathised heartily with his wife.

"Ah! good morning, Miss Fairweather," he said in his thin, raucous voice. "You are early abroad, surely. I am glad to think you are able to face the exigencies of life once more."

It was odd that he should make use of the word which a few moments before had been on Bella's lips, and she did not fail to note the coincidence.

"It is our duty, as Christian women, to put up a brave face to the weather, Mr. Dempster," she observed with a cheerfulness which was not all assumed. "I have just been having an important interview with Mr. Maclaine, and," she added impressively, "with Dr. Ludlow."

"Indeed!" said Mr. Dempster, and his small eyes positively shone with the keenness of his interest. " May I ask, without impertinence—you know the deep and abiding interest I take in your affairs on account of the long friendship between your late lamented father and myself——"

" You may ask, of course," she interrupted with a little touch of impatience not usual in her. " We have come to an arrangement with Dr. Ludlow. It will be ratified this afternoon. He will take over our father's practice."

" Indeed ! " said Mr. Dempster eagerly. " But he can hardly conduct such an important undertaking from Robina Dick's lodgings in the High Street."

" No, Mr. Dempster, he can't. He will take up his abode at The Croft," she said quietly. " Now I must hurry on. I hope Mrs. Dempster is very well. Will she be at home this afternoon immediately after our early dinner ? I rather think that Nancy is coming down to see her about the matter you have so often talked about—the teaching of your grandchildren."

" Of course she will be at home and delighted to see Nancy," answered the minister without a moment's hesitation. " But tell me more about Dr. Ludlow. I hope you have been well advised about this very momentous step."

" Oh, yes, we have ; it was the only way out, Mr. Dempster," she answered in a voice which closed the conversation, though he did not know it. " Now I must hurry on. My sisters are waiting to hear the result of my interview, and I must not keep them longer in suspense than is actually necessary."

She bowed quickly and hastened away, feeling herself to be a woman of affairs.

No thought of uttering an untruth was in her mind when she said her sisters were waiting for her ; this she honestly believed, and the cast of her mind was such that she regarded herself as the sole arbiter of their immediate destiny. She was, on the whole, well satisfied with her morning's work. She had in the space of one hour accomplished three things : made a definite offer to Dr. Ludlow, which had been accepted ; informed Mr. Dempster of the fact, which meant giving the news to Balgarnie as a whole ; and arranged an appointment for Nancy with Mrs. Dempster. After that, could anyone say with truth or propriety that she was incapable of managing her own affairs ?

Her step increased in buoyancy as she climbed the slightly rising ground towards The Croft. Most people would have pitied her because, after a life of ease and security, she was about to occupy an anomalous position. Not so, however, did Bella Fairweather regard the sudden change in their fortunes. Had she given an absolutely frank expression of her secret thoughts she would undoubtedly have answered that after the lean years she too now expected to begin to live.

She found Nancy in the garden busy with a hammer and nails repairing some damage that had been done to a climbing rose-tree by the wind in the night. She was standing on the smaller pair of kitchen steps, and the exertion of raising her arms to the drooping branch had brought the colour to her cheeks, and the wind had played among her hair, making a sweet disorder which became her rarely.

" Come down, Nancy, just half a moment," said Bella in her preceptor's voice. " I met Mr. Dempster in the town, and Mrs. Dempster would like to see you this afternoon between two and three about her grandchildren. You'll try and arrange it all, won't you, if I let you go alone, because it is important now that we should all get something to do."

Nancy turned round on the topmost step, looking a trifle bewildered at the haste with which her destiny seemed to be set.

" Already, Bella ? " she said breathlessly. " Have they talked about it, and are they willing to let me teach Mona and Charlie ? "

" I'm sure they're quite willing, but if Mrs. Dempster says anything about your salary——"

" My salary ! " echoed Nancy. " But I should like to do it because I love the children, and then, if I go there to live, I could not expect them to pay me as well."

" You can't do that, Nancy, because I shall need you here after Janet and Madge leave," answered Bella a trifle sharply.

" But I thought—at least Janet said—we can't afford to live here any longer."

" Things are going to be different from what we thought, and you and I will be quite able to live on here. Where are the girls, do you know ? "

" They are in the house, I think. When I came out about ten minutes ago Madge was in the dining-room with a map of Canada and British Columbia in front of her, and a lot of printed emigration books. I don't know where they came from. She seemed to get them all of a sudden. And she and Jen were talking for all they were worth about the place where they would like to go."

Bella turned quickly, sure that this was the psychological moment for the final announcement. But Nancy detained her with a wistful word.

" Don't you think it would be horribly dull here without Jen and Madge ? I wish they wouldn't go so very far away. We shall probably not see them again for years ; indeed, I don't see how we can, for Jen says it will take nearly fifty pounds each to get them there, unless they travel second class or steerage."

" Nobody thinks anything of going or coming to Canada in these days," said Bella lightly. " And we shall both be so busy, you with your teaching, and me with my housekeeping and other things that we shall hardly have time to miss them."

With which deliverance she passed into the house. She hung up her mackintosh in the little cloakroom off the hall, and put her umbrella in the stand, and then, hearing by the sound of voices from the dining-room that her sisters were still there, she marched boldly in. Both were seated at the table, with the map in front of them, at which Janet was peering through her pince-nez, which rather suited her style of face, giving an additional touch to its clever outline.

" You seem very busy," said Bella brightly. " Is it the All-red route you are mapping out ? "

" No, it's a resting-place for the sole of our feet we're seeking," answered Janet grimly. " Madge wants to go right to the Pacific coast and work our way back, if we don't find anything to suit us there. But I'm trying to point out to her that it would be the most economical way to stop half-way, about Winnipeg, for instance, and then, if we don't find anything to suit us, to travel west by degrees."

" I believe in plunging," said Madge, with her reckless, unfathomable smile.

" You look uncommonly well pleased with yourself, Bella. Have you succeeded in getting a penny or tuppence off the joint from old Adam Grant ? "

" No ; I've done a better stroke of work than that. I've sold the practice to Dr. Ludlow," she answered proudly.

The two younger sisters stared at one another, and Madge gave a small significant laugh.

" Have you been calling on Bobbie, then, at his lodgings ? " she asked with rather an odd look on her face.

" No, I merely called at Mr. Maclaine's by accident, and he happened to come in there, and somehow we got talking business, and it's all arranged, or at least nearly. But I needn't go into details here ; indeed, there aren't any to go into. He's coming this afternoon to tea at four o'clock to talk things over. But it's practically arranged that he comes here to live, and that I'll keep house for him."

" And we shall be gone to Canada, and Nancy planted out at the Manse ; you'll need to marry the man, Bella, to shut people's mouths," said Madge a trifle drily.

Bella tossed her head.

" You ought to be ashamed of yourself, Madge Fairweather, for taking such a low view of things. It's how you always look at everything ; but, thank God, other people have purer minds. Everybody in Balgarnie knows what I am, and there never has been, nor ever will be, any gossip of that kind about me. One in a family is quite enough."

Madge merely smiled a sort of meaning, aggravating smile, and walked out of the room.

The rain came down in the early afternoon, but, in spite of it, Madge, with her waterproof on, and an old cap above her glorious hair, stepped out into it soon after three, and so contrived her walk that she came up with Bobbie Ludlow as he approached the gate of The Croft.

She exchanged a cool greeting with him, and they passed through the gate together; then they stopped as if with one accord just where the high belt of the shrubbery hid them alike from view of the windows and possible scrutiny of the passers-by.

"Well?" said Madge, her white teeth parting in a mocking smile. "So you're going to become one of the family, Bobbie, eh?"

CHAPTER IV

THEIR SEPARATE WAYS

LUDLOW's colour rose at her mocking tone.

"That's as you like, Madge. I'm getting my foot in at least, and that's more than I've ever got yet. It's the worm's turn, don't you know."

"I'd dearly like to wait and watch the unfolding of the little comedy," she said as she picked a little bunch of elderberries from the tree and began to pull it to pieces.

"Well, stop, then. I want you to stop. Don't you see, Madge, this makes everything possible ? In a few months' time we might be able to marry and settle down."

"Have I ever said that I would marry you, Bobbie, under any circumstances ?" she asked deliberately.

"I don't remember the words, perhaps, but certainly I thought—that is, I hoped—that it was only the lack of money that stood between us," he said rather helplessly. He was desperately in love with her—had been since the first day he set eyes on her in the High Street of Balgarnie, and had noted her radiant, defiant beauty, and wondered who she was. Afterwards they had got to know one another, not in the usual conventional way, but simply by exchanging casual words on the lonely country road, after which they had met in secret a good many times.

Madge had never cared for him ; secretly and openly she had laughed at him ; but a string of some kind she must have to her bow, and since there were no eligibles in Balgarnie, why, then, she must amuse herself with ineligibles. The only time Madge had seen her father in a real fit of rage was one day when he had met her in Kinellan Woods with Dr. Ludlow in circumstances which made him think they had been love-making.

He had set an ultimatum before her then ; either she gave up Dr. Ludlow, or she must leave his house. Madge had quickly enough made her choice, but she had not altogether given up Dr. Ludlow—that is to say, though she made no further trysts with him, she continued to speak to him when they met casually, as they very often did on the road. But the idea of marrying him she had never entertained for one moment. A malicious desire to tell him so seized her now, when nothing mattered, when soon the breadth of the sea would lie between her and him.

She had not many kindly impulses ; she was one of those odd, heartless women who take their toll of men's hearts and give nothing in return.

It may be said that in the long run they suffer themselves, that they seldom achieve the happiness or the peace which simpler and better women enjoy. But again it may be answered that they receive only that which they deserve and can appreciate. Madge Fairweather had no womanly or housewifely gifts ; her only ambitions were in the direction of wealth and conquest, but especially conquest.

Bobbie Ludlow had only appealed to her imagination because he was absolutely forbidden fruit from every point of view. Her father hated and despised him to begin with, and he had not, and never probably would have, anything to offer a woman except himself. And that was no great gift. There are men for whom it is easily conceivable that a woman would make unheard-of sacrifices, but Bobbie Ludlow emphatically was not one of these. His looks were against him, and he had few noble or lovable qualities. He was frankly a tradesman in his profession, regarding it merely as a means of livelihood, and hating its ethical side with a mortal hatred. But he had been and was honestly enough in love with Madge Fairweather. Her coolness as well as her beauty nearly drove him to desperation.

" So you think the last obstacle is removed, do you, Bobbie ? Tell me, who arranged this afternoon call ? "

" Your sister at Maclaine's office this morning ; but she was merely your mouthpiece, yours and your other sisters'," he asserted, whereat Madge laughed again.

" That's all you know. Bella is engineering things for herself. Go right in now and propose to her for me, as the head of the family. Tell her you want to marry me, and then wait and see what happens. It'll astonish you."

" Why should it ? It might be a very good thing for the family as things have turned out. Of course, they could have a home with us."

At this Madge's mirth simply overflowed. It was not a noisy mirth, but rather a brimming of the eyes with incontrollable fun, a twitching of the lips, and broadening smile which spoke volumes.

" It's rich, very rich. The idea of you, Bobbie, in the house with four women ! Oh, it's very much married you'd be, poor old boy, and you'd not take long to sigh for the flesh-pots of Robina Dick."

" You turn everything into ridicule, Madge," he said sullenly. " But I don't believe, even if you go to Canada, that you'll stop there."

" I have never said I would. I've got the world in front of me at last ! " she said with a long, deep breath which was more eloquent than her words. " And with what joy I'll kick the dust of Balgarnie off my feet, Heaven alone knows ! Oh, yes, I'll come back, if not in a coach and four, then in a sixty-horse car. Nothing less will satisfy me."

" I suppose," he said, with a small sneer to which he was driven by her vivid picture of the future she hoped to achieve, " you'll set yourself out to marry a millionaire."

" Yes," she said, " that I will, and just as soon as ever it can be accomplished. My sister talks of helping to build up the great West. I'm going for the purpose of building my own fortune, for that, and nothing else."

" In the process it's just possible you may come a cropper," said the man bitterly, realising that he had been fooled for this woman's amusement, and that his honest affection had never been taken seriously by her for a moment.

" I suppose you hope I shall," she said, with a little mocking smile. " Thank you for your good wishes. I won't reciprocate them, because I know very well what your fate is going to be. You'd better go on to the house, Dr. Ludlow, and I'll follow presently."

As she turned away, a step sounded on the gravel of the outer road, and she stepped out from the shrubbery just in time to meet Archibald Maclaine.

" Good afternoon, Mr. Maclaine," she said demurely. " Dr. Ludlow is here. I've just met him. Will you take him up to the house, and I'll be back in a few minutes' time ? I don't suppose my presence is indispensable, anyway, to the family conclave."

" I should say it was, Miss Madge," answered Maclaine, and as he passed on there was a slightly puzzled expression in his eyes.

He felt sure that something more than an ordinary greeting had passed between Ludlow and Madge Fairweather. He was, of course, perfectly aware that there had been some talk about them in the place at one time. Ludlow had recovered himself, however, by the time Maclaine saw him, and they passed together into the house, while Madge, the amused mocking smile still lingering on her lips, walked down the road for a hundred yards or so, and when she had given them time to get inside the house, returned herself to it by the tradesmen's path to the kitchen door. Then she went up to her own room, and, having removed her outdoor things, went down to the drawing-room to see what was going on. She watched Bella with considerable interest and some surprise.

She had dressed herself with great care, paying conspicuous attention to her hair, which she had dressed in a new style. She wore the air of a person of importance without whom the business could not go on.

It is unnecessary to relate in detail what passed at the interview, which was practically a duologue between Bella and Dr. Ludlow, with occasional interjections from the others. Ludlow was not quite at his ease. The consciousness of the mockery at the back of Madge's flashing eyes disturbed him.

"I don't think it is necessary to talk about it much more, Miss Fairweather," he said pointedly at last. "In the long run it will have all to be embodied in one of Maclaine's wordy documents. I think we'd better leave the details to him, and, if necessary, meet at his office to discuss them a little later."

"There is not much time to spare," answered Bella with a convincing air, "because, you see, patients continue to come here. I have sent two messages down to Miss Dick's this morning already. Did you get them?"

"Yes, thank you very much."

"But surely you would like to see through the house. Will you come now?" she asked eagerly, and Ludlow consented. He did not really care anything about the house, which in his estimation was merely an adjunct to the practice. But he did not wish to offend Miss Fairweather, and he saw that she was making a point of it. He left the room with her; then Madge, who stood in no awe of Archibald Maclaine, burst out laughing.

"I can't help it, Mr. Maclaine, really. It's all so good a comedy. But poor Bella is over-anxious. It does not do to be like that with anything in this world, but more especially in dealings with your sex."

Maclaine laughingly agreed, and then changed the conversation by asking how soon they expected to sail for America.

"As soon as ever we can get the money for our passages," answered Madge promptly. "If Dr. Ludlow really decides to buy the practice, will he pay any money down?"

"I expect so, but if you require passage money, Miss Madge, you may draw on me to the extent of a hundred pounds."

"Do you hear that, Janet?" asked Madge, trying to draw Janet back into the conversation. During the later discussion of the business Janet had moved away from the tea-table group, and now stood at one of the windows looking out on the rain-dimmed landscape visible from the gable end of the house. Janet Fairweather was a sensible woman and a practical one, but there was something in the whole tone of the interview which she did not like, which jarred upon her, and filled her with distaste. She was not sure whether to blame it on Bella or Madge, or on Doctor Ludlow. She was going back just then on her father's life, on the views he entertained, and wondering how he would have felt could he have been an invisible listener to what had passed. The whole affair was so mercenary and so sordid that she was revolted by it. Though she had not been afraid to speak up to her sisters regarding what their father would have liked, she had been swept aside by the remark that they must now look after themselves. Her common sense assured her this was true enough, but at the same time something deep down in her heart was pained by the turn events had taken. They seemed to her to have marched with a haste that was almost indecent, and that the veil had been torn from them all with a ruthlessness which might have been modified.

"I hear, but I don't think it would be right for us to borrow money from Mr. Maclaine," she answered rather coldly. "There is no such desperate hurry."

"It would come out of the estate, stupid," said Madge a trifle impatiently "Would you propose to wait until everything is settled up, and till Bobbie—I mean Doctor Ludlow—comes here to live? For my part, I want to get away before that happy consummation, and I should like to take the earliest possible boat."

" It is not a good time for Canada," suggested Maclaine doubtfully. " All the emigration one ever hears of takes place in the spring. Would it not be wise to wait till then ? "

" No, some tragedy would happen before then," said Madge lightly. " And, besides, all seasons are alike for the Pacific coast. It's not within the Arctic zone. Here comes Nancy, looking well pleased with herself. Did you know she had gone down to try and get the post of governess to the Manse grandchildren, Mr. Maclaine ? "

" I didn't, but it's an excellent idea," said Maclaine, and turned with some relief to greet the young, sweet, girlish figure of the youngest daughter. He was a little tired of these three hard women, who had been discussing business so keenly, and he did not at all envy Ludlow what lay in front of him.

Nancy came in nodding brightly.

" How do you do, Mr. Maclaine ? Yes, it's all settled, and I'm to begin whenever I like. They would like me to go and live altogether at the Manse, but if it can't be arranged I'm to go immediately after breakfast every day. The children's father and mother are coming home from India in about a month, Mrs. Dempster says, and they'll stop in Balgarnie most of the winter, if Elsie is strong enough. Captain Frew has got six months' leave. They only had the letter this morning."

They were still talking over Nancy's prospects when Doctor Ludlow and Bella re-entered the room.

Bella looked much pleased with herself.

" Doctor Ludlow likes what he has seen of the house very much, especially the surgery arrangements," she said precisely. " And he thinks, if we are at all agreeable, he will come into residence with us next week."

Madge spoke up then.

" It might be better if Doctor Ludlow waited until Janet and I clear out. Probably that will be next week, if we can secure berths in the steamer which sails next Saturday."

At this Janet turned and walked out of the room. She was eager to go, but not in such haste. She felt that she must be alone for a little while to think things over, to realise the stupendous change that had come over the whole conditions of their lives. She climbed the stairs to the little back bedroom which she had made hers, because it commanded a view of Killairn Hill and Pass, where her father had been seized with his mortal illness. Many a long weary drive he had taken up that wild exposed road both by day and night, and now he slept in the old kirkyard of Fintry, which stood on one of the lower spurs of Killairn Hill.

She had often fretted against the dull order of their lives, against its narrow borders, but perhaps it had been better for them all. The freedom that had so sadly come to them seemed to be showing up in a cruel, garish light all the qualities that were least lovable in them. Nancy alone remained unspoiled. Janet Fairweather would have made a glorious wife and mother, she had all the qualities that go to their making, but she had never had a chance. Suitors were few in that dreary little country town. Mothers and fathers saw their daughters grow to womanhood, and pass on to grim middle age without having a chance to make homes of their own. The dull years were full of tragedy, and many a home in Balgarnie could have furnished sad instances of how nature, starved and cheated, at last revolts upon itself.

Such a tragedy had been very near the Fairweathers, if it had not actually begun. But would they wholly escape it, Janet wondered, now that no bar was put upon their flight into the world ? She wondered and doubted. They might get rid of one bondage, only to be encompassed by another. If she had told the whole truth, she would have confessed that she was a little afraid to set out on the new untried pilgrimage with Madge for a voyaging companion. There was a recklessness about Madge, a curious twist in her moral nature, which seemed to blind her to the finer sides of life. She was frankly selfish and material, and made no secret of the purpose for which she was going forth. To find a rich husband who would keep her in luxury and comfort was the one acknowledged object of her quest. Janet with a finer nature, took the larger view.

She wanted to see life, of course, but could carry with her some cherished ideals into the unknown. She would not go forth governed and moved by nothing but sordid aims. She would do her best, if opportunity offered, to help and uplift the life of the land to which she was going.

Presently Madge came to seek her with some little anxiety on her face. She could not afford to quarrel with Janet, or even to have her alienated in thought. It would pay them best to hang together.

" What was the matter, Jen ? " she asked, putting her face round the door and surveying Janet where she sat gloomily at the window. " Who put their foot in it ? Was it me, or Bella, or Bobby Ludlow, or all of us put together ? "

" I hate the whole business," said Janet, with a little passionate touch. " No, I can't put it into words, but there's something that isn't right. We're like fighters and grabbers, all of us. I was ashamed before those two men this afternoon. What must they think of us ? "

" I'm easy on that score," replied Madge carelessly. " You're a queer card, Jen, and nobody ever knows where you will break out next. But don't you think we'd better try and get away next week ? Bella will be glad if we do, I'm sure. Indeed, she has said so, because it's my room she proposes to fit up for Bobbie."

Madge came in, shut the door, and sat down opposite to her sister, and leaning her elbows on her knee, stared across at her anxiously.

" I simply can't bear the idea of his coming here. Father disliked him so much," said Janet with the same passionate touch.

" He is a little worm and no mistake, but harmless enough, and he's found favour in Bella's sight, and we must leave her to work out her own salvation and his."

Suddenly Janet looked across at Madge, and her eyes were full of searching appeal.

" Madge, I didn't like the way he looked at you this afternoon. Was there ever anything between you ? "

" Well, since you've put the question straight, there was, but it was all on his side. He asked me to marry him on two separate occasions, and again this afternoon in the shrubbery, when I went out for the express purpose of meeting him."

" Yet you would speak about his marrying Bella as if it could possibly happen," said Janet, in tones of disgust. " I'm sure she wouldn't have him here at all, if she knew."

" Oh yes, she would," said Madge cheerfully. " It's her last stand. But I wouldn't advise you to tell her. What would be the good ? It would only make her uncomfortable. I'm sure I don't care whether she marries him or not ; I shall be far enough away. Don't let us worry ourselves about that Jen, and do say you'll get ready to go next week. If I have many more weeks of this sort of thing I won't answer for the consequences, and I absolutely refuse to stop in this house till Bobbie comes. You can see for yourself it wouldn't do."

Janet did not speak for several minutes, then she looked very straightly across the intervening space into Madge's set, eager face.

" Madge, listen to me. I'm not sure of you. Remember that if we are to be travelling companions I shall expect you to behave yourself."

" Have you ever known me not to ? " asked Madge, with a small smile.

" Yes, I have. I won't have any ship-board flirtations or anything of that sort. I'm a quiet-living woman, with pride and self-respect. I won't be talked about,

Madge Fairweather, so I give you due warning. If anything of that sort happens, we split partnership."

" All right, old lady, don't worry yourself. I'll be as good as gold if only you'll let me write to the White Star or the Cunard people to-night about berths for next Saturday. We'll get the pick of them at this season of the year."

" But why Liverpool ? " asked Janet innocently, " when there are sailings from Glasgow every week for New York ? It would save a lot of money if we sailed from Glasgow."

" They're poor boats," answered Madge, but that was not her real reason for her wishing to sail from Liverpool. If she had declared it, Janet would have fought the issue with her. But in the end Madge had her way, and two berths were duly secured in the White Star steamer sailing for New York at the end of the following week.

CHAPTER V

"MAKING HAY"

"I HAVE never seen a more ugly or depressing place than Liverpool in the whole of my life," said Janet Fairweather discontentedly as she looked through the cab window upon the rain and grime of the streets.

"It's a wet day and there's a fog," said Madge in cheerful explanation. "Besides, you never see the best of a place between the railway station and the docks. I've heard that the chief streets of Liverpool are fine, and the outskirts by way of Prince's Park beautiful. Don't get too much down on your luck, Jen. Can't you be glad you've got clean away from Balgarnie at last?"

"No, I can't," answered Janet with a snap. "I've got some decent feeling left in me, and besides," she added enigmatically, "we haven't got clean away. Nobody ever does from the place where they have been born, even if they put the breadth of the seas between it and them."

"Oh, that's stuff and nonsense! I don't want to see it in a hurry again, and you can't deny that Bella was glad to see the last of us. It was written on her face and shining in her eyes, and even vibrating in her cheerful voice. It was the funniest and at the same time the most instructive thing I've ever seen."

"Madge, do be quiet! You always will take such a horrid view of things. I don't feel to-day as if I wanted to sail in that boat a bit, and here we are quite near the docks. I can see masts and funnels sticking up through the fog like ghosts."

Madge pushed her head out of the window, and observed in front several vehicles laden up with luggage, even as theirs was. During the last two weeks, after it became known what they had in contemplation, the Fairweathers had been in receipt of much advice concerning their voyage and the land whither they were bound. It was of a varied kind, one person assuring them that, to travel with the acme of comfort, one should have only hand baggage, and that everything suitable to a new country could always be obtained cheaply and conveniently on the spot, while others warned them that everything in America and in Canada had to be purchased at a king's ransom, and that they would be well advised to carry with them everything they could lay their hands on. They had listened to everything, and in the end, as commonly happens in such cases, each had followed the bent of her own inclination. Madge filled her boxes with her personal belongings, chiefly clothes of different sorts, most of which her own clever and undoubtedly artistic fingers had fashioned; while Janet, less vain about her appearance; discarded every superfluous article, and filled up her odd corners with household things. She had rather a vague idea of what she was going to do in Canada; she had even pictured herself taking up some land on her own account, and living in a shack upon it, after the fashion of a woman who had done it, and sent home the results of her experience to a magazine that had come into Janet's hands through the Magazine Club, which Mrs. Dempster ran, not very efficiently, for the benefit of the reading section of Balgarnie.

Janet had had to give in to Madge about travelling first-class on the boat, because Madge had flatly declared that she would travel thus or not at all.

"I don't care what happens on the other side," she said emphatically. "But I'm not going to herd with common folks in the boat. We'll need all the comfort we can get, especially if we have a bad passage."

But that was not Madge's true reason for what seemed to the others a bit of unwarranted extravagance. Janet was shrewd enough, but it was not until they had been three days out that Madge's true motive for taking the first-class passage began to dawn upon her.

When they got on board, and were shown to their state-room, a very small two-berth cabin at the lowest first-class rate, Janet sniffed and tossed her wraps in the bunk.

"And this is what we've paid nearly forty pounds for, and where we've got to live for the next week! It's to be hoped the weather will be fine so that we can get up on deck. It's rather close quarters for you and me, isn't it, Madge?"

"If you want to be seasick you can have it to yourself," answered Madge flippantly. "I shan't spend much time in it. It isn't for this we pay the money exactly, but for the big saloons, and the nice food, and the people we expect to meet. Just wait and see!"

Janet made no answer, but busied herself disposing of some of her more perishable belongings in the half of the microscopic hanging cupboard which was to do duty as a wardrobe. Madge had made herself a very pretty evening frock out of an old satin gown belonging to her mother, and a fine shawl of black silk Spanish lace that had belonged to her grandmother. She had made it quite low in the neck, and trimmed it with a good deal of jet, that sparkled under the electric lamp as she shook it out.

"You'll never wear that thing here, Madge Fairweather, and what will you do with it when you are seeking work on the other side?" inquired Janet scathingly.

"It'll serve its purpose," answered Madge equably. "I believe in being ready for any emergency. I haven't waited nearly thirty years for nothing."

Janet had contented herself with a frock of dull black silk made high at the neck, and only relieved by a small suggestion of white which gave her rather a widowed look, but, as it happened, it was several days before she was able to put it on. They had a stormy night to begin with, and poor Janet, a little run down with all the stress of the last weeks, and the final ordeal of saying good-bye to the two who were left, and all that remained of their old life, was not able to lift her head from her pillow for the better part of three days. Madge, perfectly well, and apparently enjoying the fresh roll of the Atlantic, was very attentive, running down at all sorts of odd times to inquire for her poor cabin companion, and offering to sit and read to her if she wished. But Janet's head was too stupid to be able to appreciate the attention, and she only begged to be left alone. But she had sufficient intelligence left to observe that Madge seemed to be having a good time on deck, that she looked well, even radiant, and that her steamer cap, with its filmy veil coquettishly arranged to drap her face, was most becoming. Madge had given her a few items of information regarding their fellow-passengers, and assured her she would enjoy the company of those who sat at the table as soon as she was able to join them.

On the third day the sea moderated, the sun came out, and Janet rose about eleven o'clock, feeling much better, but a little light in the head and uncertain on her feet. She had to ring for the stewardess, at last, to help her with her dressing, and by the time she had got on her big coat and her hat, she was quite ready for the light refreshment the stewardess pressed on her. Glancing into the mirror, she was rather dismayed to discover how much these three depressing days had taken out of her; all her colour was gone, and her cheeks had a sort of hollow look, as if she had fasted unduly.

"Oh, a day or so will mend that, miss. What a splendid sailor your sister is! She tramps round and round the deck even on stormy days, and never seems to be tired."

"Anybody with her?" asked Janet, struck by the fact that solitary perambulation of the deck must soon become monotonous.

The stewardess gave a little smile.

"Miss Fairweather, she don't walk much by herself, miss! They're all after 'er. It's as good as a play to see it. None of the ladies have a look in with her, an' I don't wonder, she's so pretty and so full of fun."

All this, though meant to be very complimentary, had a very disquieting effect on Janet, and, drawing on her warm, knit Shetland gloves, she made her way rather slowly towards the chief gangway, so that she might ascend to the deck. The fresh breeze meeting her on the upper landing felt delicious, and she stood still just a moment by the door to enjoy it. Then she peeped along the deck to see whether there was any sign of Madge.

Very few people were walking just then, the majority seemed to be lying out on steamer chairs, their legs wrapped up in plaid rugs, but there was another deck above, which was the favourite promenade. Janet ventured to take a few steps along the deck, and was astonished that she could walk quite steadily, for the ship was rolling a little yet, and the long green billows, like miniature mountains, undulated all round, making a fascinating picture. The gale had fallen, and though the breeze was still fresh, the air was mild and soft, and Janet inhaled it with the keen appreciation of one who had been cut off from it for some time.

Presently in her walk she came to the little ladder stairway which gave admittance to the upper deck, and now thoroughly interested in her surroundings she climbed up. A good many passengers were up there, walking to and fro, or sunning themselves in sheltered nooks. Presently, as she walked slowly round steadying herself by the rail, she caught sight of Madge. She was sitting on a steamer chair in a cosy corner, and another chair was in front of her, on which sat a man, at whom Janet immediately gazed with the most intense interest. He seemed to be tall, and he had a slim figure and a lean, brown face. He was not young; she could see the iron-grey of his hair under his cap, and his face had a good many lines on it. He was either talking or listening to Madge, with that air of absorption which indicates the deepest interest. In fact, neither of them seemed to be conscious of anything going on around them, though a good many of those passing cast amused and interested glances at them. During the few seconds Janet stood there she became acutely conscious that Madge was an object of singular interest to a good many people, and that evidently the passengers thought that a more than usually interesting steamer flirtation was in full swing. Janet did not know what to do. Certainly she wished to speak to Madge, but she was equally certain that she did not wish to intrude herself on them, but presently, turning her head, Madge observed her, and tried to struggle to her feet.

"It's my sister, Major!" Janet heard her say. "I didn't know she was getting up, or I should have been down."

The man rose, and they came together towards the spot where Janet stood.

"So you've managed to get on deck, Janet," said Madge gaily. "Why didn't you send somebody to tell me you wanted me?"

"But I didn't want you," said Janet drily. "The stewardess did all that was necessary."

"You see, I'm not the only one who exhibits Scotch independence, Major," said Madge, glancing at her companion with a saucy smile. "Janet, this is Major Haddon; my sister, Major. I've been telling him all along that when you came up I shouldn't have so much time to devote to him."

Madge spoke precisely as if she had known this stranger from her youth up. Janet, rather a shy person, blushed a trifle awkwardly as the Major raised his cap and in a pleasant, drawling voice, tinged by the true American accent, expressed his pleasure at meeting her.

"And yet I don't know, Miss Fairweather. If you're going to rob the ship of your sister's charming society, then I don't think that, properly speaking, we ought to welcome you at all."

"I'm not needing to rob the ship of anything," said Janet bluntly. "I can amuse myself."

Madge laughed, and gave her arm a little pat.

"We've just been discussing Scotch characteristics, Janet, and the Major refused to believe that most of us are prickly, like the thistle. I'm so glad you're proving it to him. Will you come and sit down here beside us? I assure you the Major is splendid at making you comfortable. As I tell him, he must be an old hand at it."

"Come, Miss Janet," said the Major affably, "I shall have the greatest pleasure in giving up my chair on condition that you allow me to have two turns round the deck with your sister before lunch."

The man had a pleasant way with him, and Janet decided that he was a gentleman. She suffered herself to be gently guided towards the steamer chairs, and in five minutes she was tucked cosily under the Major's rug, an illustrated magazine placed in her hand, and the two went off, Madge nodding gaily over her shoulder to her. Presently, while she was still pondering on the rapid strides this acquaintance seemed to have made, a small, insignificant-looking woman dressed in blue taffetas, with a flowing veil over her small, neat American hat, came up to her, smiling rather oddly.

"I ain't seen you before, surely," she said pleasantly. "Been sick up to now?"

"Yes," answered Janet, wondering whether it was usual for passengers to speak to one another immediately on board ship and ask intimate questions.

"First time over, perhaps?" said the small woman, showing some very dazzling white teeth, and, as she raised her hand at the moment to bring back a refractory end of her veil Janet caught the gleam of some very large diamonds on her fingers.

"Yes, the first time."

"Oh! never been to America before? Going to New York now, eh?"

"To New York first; afterwards I don't know."

"I saw you speaking to that Miss Fairweather who has hooked in Major Haddon. If you're a friend of hers, you might pass on a bit of advice to her from a woman who has known Ronk Haddon all his days."

"What's that?" asked Janet interestedly.

"Oh, well, he's only adding to his gallery of portraits, so to speak. He's a notorious flirt, and he's had two wives already, without making any of 'em happy. Is she a friend of yours?"

"She's my sister."

"Oh!" said the small woman with a gasp. "Never mind, I don't take back anything. She's mighty pretty, is your sister, and she thinks she's doing well. If she's only amusin' herself, it's all right; if she thinks it's the other thing, then it's all wrong. You do see some things on board ship, don't you? This is my eleventh time over. My, the things I've seen would fill a book!"

She sat down on the edge of the empty chair, and seemed quite ready for a gossiping talk.

"I bin trying to speak to your sister, but she ain't got much to say to women. I know her sort; not necessarily a bad sort, Miss Fairweather, only women don't interest her, see. You're different. Anyone can see it in your looks. What are you going to America for?"

"To earn our living," answered Janet. "I don't suppose there is much that women like us could get to do in New York, so probably we shall go on immediately through Canada to British Columbia."

"I don't think your sister is keen on that. I heard her and the Major discussing it right here yesterday. They weren't discussing it private either. I shouldn't wonder if she stopped in New York for a spell."

"Does Major Haddon live in New York?"

The little woman laughed.

" They'd be clever that could say where Ronk Haddon lives. I've never known him stop long in any one place. He was raised in Chicago, and the old Haddon homestead is on the outskirts of the city yet. They're in pork, the Haddons ; at least, the first generation was ; now it's wheat. Ronk has made a big pile, but he's a citizen of the world, and I mean it kindly, my dear, when I tell you to warn your sister to look out for herself."

At the moment the couple appeared in sight, arm in arm, and Janet's colour rose. She thought it not only strange, but not quite nice that Madge should in so short a time have made herself talked of on the ship.

" Now Ronk's looking at me," said the little woman. " He wonders what I'm saying. My name ? Oh, Field, Mrs. Alder K. Field, and I belong to Philadelphia. There's the luncheon gong. Hope we shall have another talk by and by."

CHAPTER VI

DREAMS

JANET made up her mind to keep her eyes and ears open and to say nothing to Madge just yet. They went in to lunch together, and Janet was surprised to find herself ready to enjoy the meal. They had a table for six in the alcove. Major Haddon sat next to Madge, and the other three were an elderly and rather deaf old gentleman, travelling with his niece and her fiancé, both so deeply in love that they had eyes and ears for nobody else. As the Major and Madge seemed engrossed with one another, Janet had to talk to the old gentleman, but as he did not hear well they did not make much progress. But the half-hour or forty minutes passed quite pleasantly, and on the whole Janet could find no fault with the Major's manner to Madge, though she certainly thought Madge rather free in her speech with a stranger. She ventured to say so when they found themselves alone together for a few minutes in the state-room after luncheon.

"Oh, you think so, because you've never seen anything, Janet," said Madge loftily. "On a big ship like this people don't stand on ceremony. Now, don't you think the Major a charming man?"

"I don't know enough about him. What's he a Major of, anyhow?"

"The United States Army, of course, and he's very proud of it. He has medals and things he got in the war, and he's immensely rich, but he doesn't seem to have a great many relations."

"There's something about his eyes I don't like," observed Janet guardedly. "They are set together too closely in his head."

"I call him a very handsome man. What has that horrid little Mrs. Field been saying to you? I heard from another American woman on the ship that she's been in love with the Major all her life, and, of course, she doesn't like him going about with me."

"I don't like it either. It seems to me that before a woman can get so friendly with a strange man in such a short time she must make herself rather cheap."

"Oh, Janet, try and take a bigger view of things, and if you can't enjoy yourself, don't prevent me from enjoying myself. I'm having the time of my life. I've promised to walk round the deck three times, that's a mile, with the Doctor, and I'm sure he's waiting for me now, and the Captain has asked me to tea in his cabin to-morrow. I must tell him you're coming too."

All the time Madge was busy coaxing her stray locks back under her veil, and dabbing a little powder or her red cheeks, which Janet observed with dismay. She had never seen such a thing in Balgarnie, and did not know that Madge had ever used it.

"I suppose you're going to lie down for an hour or so," said Madge, as she prepared to leave the state-room. "I'll come and fetch you at tea-time, and we'll have a little tea-party in the music-room. The Major and I have found a nice little corner, but we'll enlarge our borders to-day to admit you and the Doctor, so try and get a good sleep and come up cheery."

So saying Madge took herself off, and Janet lay down with an odd feeling of forlornness and isolation. She might just as well have been travelling alone so far as companionship went, for Madge was entirely engrossed with her new friends. But Janet could not help observing that very few women spoke to her, whereas when Janet herself appeared either in the drawing-room or on deck, the women were all quite kind and anxious to speak to her. The next twenty-four hours were full of new experiences for Janet Fairweather, and though she did not make Madge's rapid progress in friendships, she found a good deal to interest her and amuse her too. Madge and the Major spent most of their time together, and after dinner they would wander the deck in the dark, and often Madge was quite late in coming down to the cabin. Then she would say she was too tired and sleepy to talk. As the swift days went by and the end of the voyage approached Janet fancied that her sister began to look preoccupied and anxious. On the last afternoon, as she was sitting alone on deck, Madge being below gathering some of her scattered possessions together, the Major, coming out of the smoking-room, saw her and made for her side.

"Good afternoon, Miss Janet," he said in his languid, musical voice. "This is a bit of luck. It isn't often anybody gets the chance of speaking to you."

"I'm there most of the time," Janet made answer in her most ungracious voice.

There was something about the man she distrusted, and which put her on guard. She felt glad to think that after to-morrow probably they would not see him again, though that morning, while they were dressing, and she had tried to get Madge to agree to go on west without waiting even one night in New York, she had not found her very amiable.

The Major laughed as if he enjoyed her answer, and, leaning easily against the deck cabin door, asked whether he might smoke.

"It aids conversation, and I want to speak to you, Miss Janet, to ask you something."

"What is it?" asked Janet, and her eyes travelled seawards once more to the constant movement and mystery of the rolling billows, which had been scarcely stilled throughout the voyage.

"Your sister tells me you think of going to Canada; well, don't go. It's a one-horse country, and women there don't have a good time. It's nothing but work—sheer, hard work—and you and your sister ought to be, don't you know, like the lilies of the field," he added gallantly.

But his implied compliment did not even provoke a smile on Janet's grave lips.

"I am glad to hear there is work in Canada, because it is work we are looking for," she answered candidly.

"There are different kinds of work, and there isn't any use seeking for the hardest and the most sordid. Why not come out to our west? It's just as good, and you'd probably make better terms for yourselves, though I'm not very clear what it is you want to do. Your sister talks of housekeeping; well, there are heaps of jobs waiting in Chicago, where the domestic problems are as acute as in Canada. Also, there's more money."

But Janet's face was not encouraging. She remembered that Mrs. Field had told her the Major's real habitation was in Chicago, and it would mean a continuance of Madge's infatuation for him, which in the circumstances it was desirable should be stopped.

"It is very kind of you to be interested, Major Haddon, but it is always better to adhere to one's plans, unless some very strong reason arises for changing them. My sister and I will be more at home in Canada, because there are more Scotch folk there. I don't think," she added frankly, "that I should feel at home in America with American folk."

"Now that's unfair, seeing you've never even set foot in God's own country," said the Major in an aggrieved voice. "I don't think, between ourselves, that your sister is keen on Canada."

Janet made no answer, guessing that already Madge and this strange man had discussed the whole question, and that most probably Madge had arrived at some decision of her own.

" So you won't consider it ? I know what I'm talking about, mind," he said as he prepared himself another cigarette. " Besides, your sister wouldn't care for farm life. She likes movement and life and fun, and she's entitled to them. Every woman is, and she tells me you've been buried alive up to now."

" We had a happy home and many mercies," said Janet coldly, for though she had occasionally been in revolt against the narrowness of her life at Balgarnie, now it seemed a very haven of refuge ; and the idea of Madge belittling it to this stranger angered her.

Janet had the Scotch reserve in excess in her nature ; she could quite easily have spent the whole voyage in quiet observation without speaking to a soul. At that moment Madge appeared, and, seeing her sister and the Major together, joined them with unmistakable eagerness in her looks.

" Have you been speaking to Janet about Canada, Major ? "

" Yes, Miss Fairweather, but the good seed has dropped on stony ground," he answered flippantly, and his second scriptural allusion did nothing to improve Janet's opinion of him. Madge swooped her fine eyes keenly on her sister's face.

" Don't you think we should let ourselves be advised, Janet ? After all, though we are Scotch, we needn't be pig-headed. And Major Haddon knows what he is talking about."

" It is to Canada I'm going," answered Janet quietly, and, rising up, walked away. She knew that she was being ungracious, even a little rude, but something seemed to raise in her all her fighting qualities. She did not want to have anything further to do with Major Haddon ; she wished Madge's acquaintance with him to be cut here and now, and, above all, she wished to be left alone to carry out the programme they had drawn up. Never perhaps had Janet betrayed her provincialism to greater advantage ; she took up the position of the person who does not know, and who does not want to know. The Major and Madge exchanged glances as she turned her back on them.

" You see how I am badgered and hemmed in," said Madge, with a little glance of appeal, which made her look beautiful.

" There's only one thing to be done, then, split partnership," he said easily. " After all neither of you are kids. Surely it isn't necessary to hang together through thick and thin ? "

" It would be difficult to split," answered Madge, but did not explain that it was chiefly the financial difficulty which barred the way.

Janet had no further opportunity for private conversation with her sister until quite late that evening, after she had gone to bed. It was after eleven o'clock before Madge entered the cabin, and when Janet looked up from the book which she had been vainly trying to read, she saw that Madge's eyes were shining like stars.

" Not asleep yet, Jen ? " she said, with an odd note in her voice. " Just as well, as we must talk things over."

" I can't go to sleep till you come, Madge," answered Janet. " And I don't think it is right for you to be sitting up on deck with Major Haddon till this time of night. I am thankful that to-morrow will end it."

" But I don't know if it will," said Madge deliberately, as she sat down on the narrow sofa opposite the bunks and began to undo her veil.

" Are you absolutely dead-set on going on to Canada without trying your luck anywhere else ? "

" Absolutely."

" Well, then, I'd better tell you I'm not. I've made up my mind to go to Chicago instead. Major Haddon will help us all he can. He even says that his old home wants a housekeeper. Won't you come along, Jen, and let us try our luck together ? "

Janet sat up, raised herself on her elbow, and peered out with big, anxious eyes. " Madge, tell me just what this means. Has the Major said anything ? I mean, has he proposed to you ? "

" He can't, because he has a wife already, whom he is going to divorce. It's the only thing that has kept him from speaking. I know that, and don't you see, Jen, if I go to Canada with you and lose sight of him I'm letting slip the chance of a lifetime ? He's a millionaire, and just think what that would mean, not to me only, but to the whole of us. It would be the making of the family."

" I don't want to be made by Major Haddon," said Janet drily, and her face had a sort of wrung expression. She was younger than Madge, but in some respects her mind was older, and she felt an awful sense of responsibility towards her.

" You don't know enough about the man to take his word like that. He may only be an adventurer," she said desperately.

" You know he isn't that ; ask Mrs. Alder Field, if you don't believe me. She'd give her head to have the Major admire her and pay her the attention he does to me. See here, Jen, I don't care anything about the man ; I tell you quite frankly. But I do care for his money and his position, and if I can get them honestly, I mean to have them."

" Oh, Madge Fairweather, my blood runs cold to hear you ! " cried Janet in genuine pain.

" Why, we're out on the make, as they say on this side. You want to make a good thing out of it too. It's what we've come for, only you have a different idea of it. It's money I want, Jen, and the things money can buy, a big house, and a yacht, and Russian sables, and diamonds, and I don't care what they cost."

She spoke with feverish eagerness, and her white fingers worked nervously and unceasingly with her veil.

" It's far better to be candid, and you needn't look at me like that, Jen. I'm neither a fool nor a child. I can look after myself, and if you won't come with me, I'll promise to follow you, if I'm disappointed ; but in the meantime I am going to play my own game."

" Play my own game ! " The full significance of these words, as well as their vulgarity, chilled Janet Fairweather to the heart. She sank back on her pillow without saying another word ; then Madge came and knelt on the floor and pushed back the little curtain and looked into her face.

" I suppose you think I'm beyond redemption, Janet, but I'm not. I'm only a little more outspoken than the majority of women. Won't you come along to Chicago first and see the fun ? "

" I can't afford to do that, Madge, and you know it. We have only enough money to take us to the destination we had planned at first. If we fool it away, where are we ? Oh, I wish I had stood out firm about travelling second-class on the boat."

" And I'm thankful I stood out for first. Down below there would have been no Major Haddon, and I would not have got my chance. I knew that."

Jane turned her face to the wall, and all night long tossed sleeplessly on her narrow bed, asking herself what her duty was, and praying to be guided to do it. But Madge slept like a child, and her dreams were haunted by visions of a future so bright that it was going to make up for all the dreariness of the years that had gone before.

CHAPTER VII

PARTING OF THE WAYS

THERE are few places in the world where the stranger of moderate means can be made to feel so unwelcome as New York. It is pre-eminently a city for the rich. Toll begins to be taken from the traveller from the moment his foot touches its soil, and unless he has some wise, familiar friend to guide him, the day of his departure is better than the day of his arrival. As the great liner slowly approached her berth in the clear, still, autumnal light, the two Fairweathers stood together watching the animated scene on the quay with mingled feelings. The last twelve hours had been passed in discussion and in partial argument, but each remained firm in her own determination.

"Won't you stop at least a few days and see New York, Janet?" asked Madge in her insistent voice. "We never know; perhaps you'll never have a chance again."

"There isn't anything to see in the place," said Janet doggedly. "And besides, we can't afford it. Everybody knows that extremes meet here, and that there's no room in it for the middle sort, like ourselves."

"Oh, that's exaggeration, and Mrs. Field is to blame for it," snapped Madge. "And you really *are* going on into Canada this very afternoon?"

"The only thing that would make me stop, Madge, is the chance that I might persuade you to come along with me. You ought to, you know. It was never meant that we should split partnership so soon."

"I might say the same thing, and I'm the elder," said Madge shrewdly. "One person's word is as good as another's. After all, you've nothing but the emigration agent's reports to back you up. I have Major Haddon's word that there is plenty to do in Chicago, besides the offer of work from himself. Why not give that a chance first?"

"I don't like the idea of Chicago. I have heard what a big, wicked, terrible city it is, almost like Sodom and Gomorrah. I want to be in the open country among my own folk."

"Perhaps you won't like them so much when you get to them," said Madge. "A man on the boat told me that there isn't anything harder on earth than the Scottish-Canadian, and that he can draw money out of a stone."

"But, after all, they would be of our own kin, Madge, and we'd know how to deal with them," answered Janet courageously; then, after a moment, she added defiantly, "Besides, I don't like your Major Haddon."

"Why do you not like him? I'm sure he has been very kind and attentive to you all the way across."

"That's maybe just why I don't like him," said Janet in her most aggressive manner. "What for should he be so civil to us?"

"'Wha daur meddle wi' me?'" quoted Madge laughingly, and at the moment Major Haddon, dressed for landing in a becoming grey lounge suit, and a soft hat, sauntered up.

"I'm just trying to persuade my sister, Major," said Madge gaily, yet with that odd eagerness which was always infused into her manner in his presence. "I think I'll leave you to try what you can do. At present nothing will serve her, but that she'll make a rush for the Canadian train within the next five minutes."

"There are a good many preliminaries to be got over first with the custom-house gentry lined up for us in that shed just there," remarked the Major, showing his even white teeth in a smile. "Why are you so hostile to the American nation, Miss Janet? Has it done you any harm?"

"No; but when a person sets out to do a thing, why, then, they should do it," answered Janet, a form of logic which caused the Major to smile still more broadly. At the moment Madge, seeing someone else she wished to bid "Au revoir" to after her most fascinating and successful voyage, walked away and left them together. Then Janet looked up with her straight honest eyes into the Major's face.

"It is true, I suppose, that you have offered my sister a situation in Chicago, Major Haddon?"

The Major pulled his grizzled moustache thoughtfully.

"It seems impertinent to use the word in relation to your sister, but I did say to her that, failing anything better, she might keep house for me and my sister, Mrs. Ronderbusch, up at the old Haddon place."

"And would she be your servant or Mrs. Ronderbusch's?" pursued Janet mercilessly.

"As to that, I don't know. In one of her letters, Sallie merely mentioned that if I could find her a capable person in England I had better engage her. If your sister is inclined to go out west on that slender chance, well, I'll see that she doesn't lose by it."

"But then if Mrs. Ronderbusch has the engaging of her, she mightn't like her. Would she get something else quite easily?"

"A lady like Miss Fairweather would never be at a loss," said the Major gallantly, but it was a speech which annoyed Janet, and set her more strongly than ever against the Chicago prospect. She had not an ounce of imagination in her nature; most of her life she had been up against hard facts, and she wished to deal with them now.

The idea of Madge going forth to exploit herself, making use of her undoubted charms to smooth the difficult way, did not appeal at all to her, but merely filled her with a sort of disgust and dismay. She thought of their stern, pious old father, and remembered how grimly his face had set when he had to deal on two separate occasions with Madge's love affairs, and how, sore beset, he had even allowed that something was to be said for the Catholics, who could shut troublesome daughters up in nunneries.

Janet had no doubt but that Madge hoped to marry the American Major, but after what Mrs. Field had told her concerning his private affairs, she thought the contingency very remote. But, above all, she desired to have Madge under her own eye.

"I must go and see to my things, Major Haddon," she said stiffly. "So we had better say good-bye."

It was even in her mind as a last stratagem to tell him that as a housekeeper Madge was not likely to be worth much, since she had never exerted herself in that direction at home, but had left everything to their eldest sister, and occupied herself chiefly with her music and with the making and altering of such finery as she possessed. But, realising that such trivialities would not be likely to have power with the forces now operating in their lives, she refrained and walked away.

In spite of the fact that they landed about noon, it was late afternoon before they had got through all their affairs at the custom-house, and were free to go their separate ways. Janet had a quite clear and definite idea about her own journey now, and set out to go by the straightest and quickest route to Winnipeg. She parted from her sister without display of feeling. There was not a tear shed on either side.

"If you change your mind about coming to Canada after you have had a taste of Sodom and Gomorrah, Madge, you can let me know. Write, if you like, to the Immigration Offices at Winnipeg, or to Ellen Dunnet's address on Maxtone Avenue, and I'll let you know what I'm about."

"All right, my dear, then we'll see which one of us has chosen the better part," answered Madge lightly. They kissed one another as the train was about to move out, and as Janet saw the solitary figure left on the platform the tears, in spite of her, rose to her eyes. But Madge walked away with the lightest step, conscious of nothing but relief.

Full of high confidence and unutterable hope, she plunged into the unknown.

The weather was very beautiful for so late in the year.

"The fall," as Janet heard it repeatedly called, had all the soft radiance and glow of the Indian summer. During the three days and nights she had to spend in the train she had the opportunity of studying nature in many moods from the wide windows of the car, and more and more the land of immense distances brought home to her a sense of her own littleness and futility. As the train sped through vast tracts of wild and rocky scenery, intersected by innumerable lakes, seemingly without population or purpose, the wonder of it filled her soul.

She had heard and read many times that there is room and to spare for millions in the New World, but its realisation brought to her an odd sense of loneliness and pain. These desert places seemed so remote from all that was comfortable and warm and happy, that she wondered people could be found to inhabit them at all. When they would come suddenly upon some little wooden dwelling, standing sheer and lonely on its narrow patch of clearing, the stumps of the trees showing naked and gaunt among the hungry soil, she began even to doubt the report that had called it a land of plenty, flowing with milk and honey. But by and by they got beyond this vast, almost unsettled, wilderness, which can never be more than the lungs or the sporting ground of the country, and came to the level lands, where the wheat grows, and where smiling homesteads are everywhere to be seen, set at intervals with very exact precision, like so many watch-towers; her spirits rose. She was so deeply interested in what she saw, that she had no time to weary or even to worry about Madge. After all, she was of full age, and, as she herself had remarked, perfectly capable of looking after herself. She got very tired of the long journey, of the hot, weary days, and the stuffy nights, and when, at the end of the third day, the heavy train steamed into the big station at Winnipeg, just on the stroke of midnight, she stepped down with an odd sense of relief, not unmingled with apprehension. For it is not a pleasant thing for a lonely woman to be stranded in the middle of the night in a strange and great city, where she is without friends or place to lay her head.

She was standing a little irresolutely by her small baggage, looking round for a porter to whom she could speak regarding her big packages, and wondering to see so few men about for the arrival of such an important train, when a man came up, slightly touching his cap, and smiling at her from a pair of very honest, kind, grey eyes.

"Are you Miss Fairweather, if ye please?" he asked, and his tone had the pleasant Scotch twang which warms the heart of the exile when heard far from his native land.

"Yes," said Janet brightly. "And you?"

"Peter Rose, Ellen Dunnet's man. I've met the train twa nichts. She was that feared ye would arrive by yersel', the same as she did five year ago, and a fell state she was in, to be sure, though I was no mair than twa blocks away."

Now Ellen Dunnet had been a kitchen-woman at The Croft, and had only left to marry the sweetheart she had had since she was at the village school, a very decent, hard-working and skilled carpenter, who, lured by the promise of big wages at the other side of the sea, had emigrated to Canada, and then sent for Ellen to come to him. The gladness at Janet Fairweather's heart was reflected in her face as she held out a frank hand.

"Now this is more than kind, Mr. Rose, but how you knew I was coming this way beats me."

" Oh, Ellen's been hearing frae Balgarnie. Onywey, she wasna takin' ony chances. She kent the boat ye were to come by, and she hasna let me sleep twa nichts, or this train cam in," said Peter with his pawky smile, but his eyes never lost their kindly expression, which indicated that this little act of consideration had been as great a pleasure to himself as to his wife. " This is not a' ye hae, I suppose ? "

" Oh, no, there are big packages. Here are the checks."

" I'll see to them. They can be left in the station till the morn. You'll come hame with me, Miss Fairweather. Ellen's waiting and ready for ye, but she expected two Miss Fairweathers," he added in a puzzled voice.

" My sister went to Chicago. I'll explain to Ellen when I see her. And do you mean that Ellen can put me up ? "

" Prood to do it, miss, in oor little place. And there's the bairn forby. She's clean wild to show aff the bairn."

Janet suddenly felt that the desert had blossomed like the rose. With what thankfulness she relinquished the weird-looking iron tags which represented her baggage into Peter Rose's strong and capable hands, and with what joy she followed him a little later to the cab that was in waiting ! As they drove she recalled Ellen, as she had been in the days when she had charge of the kitchen at the Croft, when she had been wee Ellen, to distinguish her from the taller and more stately damsel that had waited on them upstairs. She remembered how fond her father had been of wee Ellen, how absolutely he had trusted her, and how he had deplored her departure to Canada, and had even selfishly done his best to keep her behind. And now all the kindness he had bestowed on the motherless girl from the moor of Rannoch was about to be amply repaid.

Peter Rose had not found the reports of the new country at all exaggerated. To a skilled and thrifty artisan like himself, it offered the warmest welcome. He had not had an idle day since his arrival, and now owned the house in which they lived, and was contemplating in the course of another year starting in the lumber business for himself.

All this he told to Miss Fairweather as they drove through the quiet streets to the outskirts, where his sonsy wife, in a tremendous state of excitement, had the table laid, and her best bedroom set out in the finest style for her old master's daughters.

When she heard the rumble of wheels far down the street, sure indication that Peter's second quest had been successful, she incontinently began to weep. She was laughing and crying in a breath, when the cab stopped at the door and Janet got out.

" Oh, Miss Janet, but I'm prood to see ye, but where's Miss Madge ? Not come at a', never mind ; I'm pleased to see ye. I hope ye did not mind comin' to our little hoose ? Peter said ye would laugh at it, and I jist clooted his lugs for it."

So much touched by this reception was Janet Fairweather that, as she gripped the good creature's hands, she bent towards her and kissed her, though kissing was not common in Balgarnie, except between sweethearts and such-like. Ellen flushed all over her bonnie face, and from that moment was her dear Miss Janet's bond slave.

Janet was pleased with everything. Indeed, after three or four days in the tourist portion of a west bound train, even a simple home is apt to present the acme of luxury. She praised everything, and when Ellen showed her the grass-bleached Balgarnie sheets on the bed, trimmed with her own fine hand-made crochet, she had no need to be disappointed with the appreciation of it all.

" Ye dinna look a day aulder, Miss Janet," said Ellen admiringly, as she looked keenly at her guest's face after her travelling hat had been laid off. " An' so the dear Doctor's awa'. I hope ye dinna mind, Miss Janet, that we ca'd the bairn Robert Fairweather efter him. Eh, he was kind to me, the doctor ; surely he was the very best man that ever lived."

Janet's mouth trembled. She was more than ready to agree with every word that Ellen spoke.

"That would have pleased my father, if he had lived to know it, Ellen, and when am I to see this wonderful bairn?"

"Oh, the morn; he's that gleg, if ye were to go in and look at him he wad open his een at wance, and syne there would be no more peace, till I gaed to my bed wi' him. And what do ye think of Canada as far as ye have seen it?"

"I'm not thinking much, except of its size, Ellen; the distances are terrible."

"An' you have come to seek your fortune?" said Ellen whimsically, as with her own hands she undid the buttons of Janet's enveloping travelling cloak. "Well, you'll no be long or ye get married here. I whiles tell Peter he had better be very ceevil to me, for I had three offers on the boat I cam oot on, besides fower more on the train, and that's as true as I stand here, and I'm no much to look at either."

Janet laughed heartily at this naïve speech, and patted Ellen's shoulder with a little shake of her head.

"You're a very bonnie woman, Ellen, and I have no doubt that Peter knows his good fortune. Do you like Canada?"

Ellen screwed her face.

"It's not that bad when ye count everything up. It's certainly better for workin' folk, especially if they hae a trade at their finger-ends, like my man. We're getting rich, an' syne we're gaun back to Scotland to bide half the year in Aberdeen an' the ither half on the Moor of Rannoch."

She sighed a little as if she saw before her the wind-swept moor with the purple of the heather on it, and for a moment the look these two women exchanged was rather pitiful.

"And what is it ye think of doing, Miss Janet? I don't suppose you'll stop here. It'll be further west you'll be going, where they have better winters, and where the big ranches are."

"I shall have to seek a housekeeper's place, Ellen; perhaps you will be able to help me to get one. Do you think I shall find it easily?"

"Oh, you'll get plenty work of a kind," said Ellen doubtfully. "But I do not think that there is any demand for lady housekeepers here. I fear ye will need to work wherever ye go, Miss Janet, and sorry am I to think ye should need."

"I hope I am not afraid of work. I can't help thinking what a splendid and lucky thing it is for me to have you here, right in Winnipeg, Ellen. Your advice will be worth so much."

"I don't know aboot that. The kind of places I know of wouldn't suit you, Miss Janet. Yes, Peter, we're coming. That's him whistlin' at the bottom o' the stairs. I daresay he's wantin' his supper. Will ye mind comin' doon, Miss Janet, jist as ye are. They're a' alike, men folk, they never can understand that a wummin would rather hae a good crack any day than a meal of meat."

With such deliverance on her kind Ellen led the way to the cosy little living-room, where the table was bountifully spread, and where Peter was waiting with more or less patience for the supper he had earned.

CHAPTER VIII

JANET FINDS A POST

NEXT day Janet Fairweather walked abroad in the wonderful new city of the plains, which is the gateway to the West.

It has achieved much since the day, not so far distant in the past, when it was but a handful of settler's huts dotted on the bank of the Red River, and known only as one of the Hudson Bay Company's stations.

Now it is a great city, with broad boulevards and amazing suburbs, lined with lordly dwelling places, each set like a gem in its little belt of garden ground, all open to the side walks, and guiltless of fence or sheltering wall. The keynote of freedom is struck here, and the cosmopolitan nature of its population is verified by a walk down the Main Street, where it is possible and indeed inevitable, to meet representatives of every nationality under heaven. Janet Fairweather walked slowly, keeping both eyes and ears open, and was very deeply interested in all she saw. There was a crudeness everywhere, an unfinished look, a strange and not too successful mingling of contrasting and sometimes hostile elements, both in the architecture and in the people. It was indeed a bit of a very new and a most amazing world. She felt her pulses stirred, however, for here was new life, young, strong, virile life, limitless possibility, potentialities scarcely yet realised.

Something of that young, strong, virile pulse seemed to beat in her veins. She, too, would become a part of this fresh young destiny, add her mite to the upbuilding of one of the greatest of the Empire's outposts. Old things, old traditions, old trammels dropped away from Janet Fairweather oddly that clear November morning, when the sun shone with the radiance of the late lingering summer, and there was scarcely a hint of the terrible grip of winter in the air.

Here all things seemed possible to her also ; it might be even hid in the womb of the future that she should achieve some high destiny in the land of her cheerful adoption ; there was an odd thrill and charm in the very dream. So strongly did it pursue her, that, being anxious to put her hand to the plough without a moment's delay, she asked to be directed to the Government Employment Bureau, which she had been told was established in Winnipeg for the use and benefit of those seeking work.

There was neither pride nor shame in Janet Fairweather's mind, nor in her looks, as she essayed her first journey into the unknown. She had come to the West for a definite purpose, and it was like her fine Scottish steadfastness and common sense that she should not seek to play about with the main issue. She had not said a word to Ellen Dunnet about her intention, for Ellen somehow had been discouraging about the kind of work her old master's daughter was seeking. Ellen had been five years in Winnipeg, and had no illusions concerning the life of the Far West, in so far as she knew it by experience and by repute.

Janet did not wish to put her kind entertainers to any trouble or anxiety on her behalf ; she also realised that it was neither possible nor desirable that she should stay long with the Roses, though they made her so welcome that she felt at once sad and glad.

Her suggestion that she should pay for her board had been received with such horror and pain by Ellen, and with such a queer hurt look by Peter, that she had hastily apologised. But soon she hoped to get a place, not perhaps to begin with very far from them, so that she could see them sometimes.

It is an amazing thing what the breadth of the sea can do in levelling down barriers, and weakening the class distinctions which buttress the life at home.

Janet had to wait with a few others in an outer room until the official within was at liberty to see her. She got a little shock to find him seated at his desk in his shirt sleeves, and smoking a cigar. The atmosphere of the room was stuffy, for though the weather was still mild for November the stove was on, and the close, dry heat quickly uses up the air space.

He looked round at Janet's entrance, and seeing a lady who from her looks seemed a little superior to the usual emigrants he had to interview, he took out his cigar and wheeled his chair round.

"Take a seat, ma'am. What can I do for you?"

He was a man about forty, with reddish hair and moustache, a sun-burned, almost parchment-like, face, and a pair of very piercing light-blue eyes, accustomed to take the measure of a person at a glance. But after staring a full second at the lady he felt himself at a loss.

"I have just come out from Scotland," said Janet clearly. "And I want something to do. I have to earn my own living. Can you find me a housekeeper's place?"

The official looked, as he felt, a trifle nonplussed.

He guessed that the kind of situation he could offer would not be quite within this lady's requirements.

"There are lots of places vacant of a kind, miss," he said civilly, "but they are of a kind, don't you know? Now I could almost bet my bottom dollar you haven't had to do much hard work in the old country."

"No," answered Janet frankly, "I haven't. But I know how to work, and I'm not afraid of it. Surely in this big country there must be some house where I could find something to do. Don't you know of any lady or gentleman needing someone to look after the house and the hired help, if there is one?"

"That's just the rub, ma'am, the hired help if there is one; but mostly there isn't. Now my sister-in-law hasn't had one inside of her house for seven weeks, and she's laid up now, and has nobody but an old Irishwoman who comes in for an hour or two every day. And there are some little children, too, want looking after badly, they do. I can tell you that."

"Do you think I would suit your sister-in-law?" inquired Janet without one moment's hesitation. "You see, I must buy my experience somewhere. I must get to know how Canadian houses are conducted before I can aim any higher. I'm not really worth much just now. Will you give me your sister-in-law's address, if you think I would suit?"

The official shifted uneasily in his chair, and on his face there was an odd mingling of admiration and hesitation.

"It's very seldom, Miss—Miss——"

"My name is Fairweather," supplemented Janet promptly.

"It's very seldom, Miss Fairweather, that the ladies who come out from the old country cheerfully expect so little. Mostly we get them critical and exacting. I have no doubt that you would suit my sister-in-law; she'd be mighty thankful to get anybody who knows how to run a house at all. And as for my brother himself, well, he ain't had a proper meal in his own house for a month. But, as I say, the question is whether she'd suit you——"

"Oh, that wouldn't enter," Janet assured him cheerfully. "Beggars can't be choosers. Will you give me your sister-in-law's address?"

"I'll just 'phone to Mrs. Nelson, if you don't mind," he said with some haste. "If I can't get on to her, I'll try Jack at the office."

He lifted the receiver, and called up the number, then waited in vain for the connection. After a long time a shrill, small voice answered him, and after speaking a few words in reply to it, he hung the receiver up.

" Just as I thought. Mrs. Nelson is in her bed and the kids running the show. That was little Cleveland, aged six, answering the 'phone. I'll just try if I can get on to my brother now."

" Would you like me to leave the room while you're speaking to him ? "

" Not necessary, thank you, Miss Fairweather. I'll only just mention that you're here. He'll know the state of his domestic barometer, so it won't take long."

Janet took up the newspaper, and ran her eye over the advertisement columns while the conversation was being conducted over the telephone. It did not last above a couple of minutes ; then Nelson spoke to her again.

" My brother will be very glad if you will go to his house, and see his wife. He'll telephone to her that you are coming, and if you would call at his office on the way down, he'd be glad to see you first. You pass it on the street car. Here's the address."

" Thank you very much, Mr. Nelson," said Janet warmly. " I'm sure you have been very kind to me, and if you treat all your emigrants like this I don't wonder you get so many of them."

" We don't get many of your kind, Miss Fairweather, believe me," said the agent with emphasis. " By the time they get this length their hearts are very often in their boots ; then our lot is not a happy one. Well, good day, and I wish you luck. If Mrs. Jack freezes on to you, we'll probably meet again."

Janet took the written card of address in her hand, bade him good day, and passed out, somewhat amused with the interview, and on the whole satisfied. It was an entirely novel experience for her to sue for anything, and she thought she had reason to congratulate herself on the treatment she had received. Nelson's manner, though a trifle free and easy, had been undoubtedly kind and friendly, and she felt that she was making progress. She found Mr. John P. Nelson's office without difficulty in a large block of new buildings on a street corner. The Dominion Land Company had long outgrown its first small quarters, and now needed a spacious floor and many clerks for its operations. John P. Nelson was its managing director, a tall, handsome man, of more imposing appearance than his brother at the Government Office. His manner had a certain brusqueness which Janet was beginning to understand was part of the foundation of Western manners. It was perhaps a trifle too aggressive for her taste, but she was not then in a mood to cavil at new experiences. However odd or even forbidding they might be, she approached her new life undoubtedly in the proper spirit, and had for the time being thrust all her critical faculties in the background.

" Good morning, Miss Fairweather," said Mr. John P. Nelson, when she was ushered into his room. " I have 'phoned my wife, and she will be pleased to see you at once. But supposing we have a little business talk here and now. There isn't anybody down at my home at the present moment capable of running it. Are you capable ? "

The straight question, accompanied by the glance of quick but not unkindly inquiry, was such as to appeal to Janet Fairweather's own practical side.

" I'll tell you just what I can do, Mr. Nelson. I am a doctor's daughter. I was one of four, and though I did not actually keep my father's house I think I may say there isn't a branch of housekeeping I don't know something about. I'm the domestic sort of woman, and though there are some things I haven't touched with my own hands, I wouldn't be afraid to undertake anything inside the four walls of a house."

" Good ! " said Mr. John P. Nelson, pleased with the answer. " You see, it's like this, Miss Fairweather. We get a lot of quite useless women, if you will excuse plain speech, out from England, who expect big things from us, and are not so particular about what they give in exchange. The kind that call themselves ladies, and are above soiling their little fingers in any honest work, Canada has no use for, and we've had our share of them."

"I understand, but I hope I shall not be as useless as that. I may say quite frankly, I hope, since frankness seems to be the order of the day, that I don't particularly want to black grates or scrub floors. If it is not absolutely necessary to do that, I would ask to be relieved of it. My theory is that I can do other things better, and that it would be what you men call an economic waste, to put me to it."

Janet was amazed at herself, but she smiled her broad, fine, and very winsome smile at this, and completed the subjugation of Mr. John P. Nelson where her capabilities were concerned.

"You won't need to do that. I quite agree with you, and I've often tried to point it out to my wife, but she don't see things just as I do—half the time. Somebody can be found to help. It's a boss my home wants at the present moment, Miss Fairweather, though I'm very sorry to say it."

"Mrs. Nelson has not good health," observed Janet sympathetically.

"She hasn't, but she might have, if she would make a little effort. See here, Miss Fairweather, when you are up against things, the best policy is to set your teeth and square your shoulders and go at them hard. I came here without a red cent, and now I'm a comfortable man. Addie—I mean my wife—don't see that. She's from the States, where women have the best time in the world. She thinks she has the worst, though I'm giving her the best I know how. That's the matter in a nutshell, and it's better to tell you straight before you see her. If she takes a fancy to you she'll be very sweet, and if my two kiddies don't win your heart, then I'll be astonished, that's all. Twenty-two Elinor Avenue, other side of the river, and good luck to you. I'll hope to come home to supper this evening and find you right there."

"Oh!" said Janet breathlessly. "Wouldn't to-morrow do? Isn't this what you call hustle?"

"The need is there, Miss Fairweather. If you're going to take pity on the Nelson block, don't lose any time. Good deeds don't improve by keeping. Mostly they're better done at once."

A little bewildered by the rapidity with which events were moving, Janet went out to the street cars once more, to seek her way to the Nelson house on the other side of the river. She found it one of the most beautiful of the suburban dwellings she had seen in Canada. It stood in the middle of fresh green lawns, as smooth as velvet, and the house itself was both roomy and architecturally beautiful. But it was not well kept. When Janet beheld soiled curtains and blinds awry she wondered how any woman who owned such a beautiful place could be so careless about its outward appearance. Presently, at the ringing of the bell, which chimed sonorously through the house, two small children in dirty holland overalls, bare legs, and sandalled feet, peered round one corner of the verandah. Their dirty faces were featured like the angels. Janet fell down and worshipped them on the spot, before they opened their mouths. She was engaged smiling at them and trying to entice them to come to her when an elderly help of dismal appearance opened the glass door which gave entrance from the verandah to the hall.

"I've come to see Mrs. Nelson," said Janet in her quiet, dignified way. "Please tell her Miss Fairweather is here. I think Mr. Nelson telephoned to her that I was coming."

The help grunted a little, and without inviting her to enter disappeared. Janet then renewed her attention to the children, and presently was rewarded by beholding them walking demurely along the verandah towards her hand in hand.

"Oh, you darlings; come and talk to me!" she said, kneeling on one knee. "Come and tell me your names."

"I am Cleveland Putnam Nelson," answered the little boy proudly. "This is Sadie."

" Well, and have you any kisses to spare, eh ? "

" Sadie has," volunteered Cleveland Putnam in his most lordly manner. " I'm a real large boy. I'll soon be six."

Janet caught the little girl to her, pushed back the tangle of gold from her eyes, and kissed her tenderly. Presently Cleveland Putnam, moved by some prehistoric jealousy, snuggled towards her, and put up his flower-like face. So Janet took them both to her heart, and they took her, and the fate of the Nelson block was sealed. It would have taken a very disagreeable mother now to have frightened Janet Fairweather away from that house. As a matter of fact, Addie Nelson was not disagreeable at all. She was merely languid and distrait. When the help came out presently she said ungraciously :

" Mrs. Nelson will see yer. It's there—— "

She jerked with her thumb across the pretty hall to a white panelled door, and left the stranger to find her.

Won't you take me to your mother, children ? " asked Janet, as she released them. Cleveland shook his wise head.

" We mayn't, cos we ain't bin told. You see, we make mammy's head ache most of the time."

" Well, I'll come back to you presently," she said, nodding brightly as she set out on her further voyage of discovery.

The interior of the house was well furnished, and full of lovely things, all bearing traces of neglect.

The dust was quite visible on the rich pile of the crimson carpet, and the white treads of the stairs looked as if they wanted attention, while the thick brass rods were dull and stained. Tapping lightly at the white door, Janet was bidden to enter by a sweet voice, and when she was inside the room she saw a small, elegant figure reclining on a big chintz-covered sofa, with a lot of pink silk cushions round her. The room looked like a boudoir ; it was really the smaller half of the drawing-room, which Mrs. Nelson used as her own sitting-room. It was furnished in perfect taste, had many beautiful objects of art, and fine pictures on the walls, also there were flowers everywhere, some of them needing much attention. It was the boudoir of a woman of ease and fashion, hardly the place where a Canadian housewife of moderate means should spend the whole of her days.

" You are Miss Fairweather," she said, leaning forward so that Janet got a good look at her pretty, peevish face, and noted the white fragility of her small hands flashing with diamonds. " Can it be possible that you are willing to come and housekeep here ? When my husband said so over the 'phone I asked him whether it was a fairy tale. Come in right here, and sit down, and let me look at you. You're a curiosity, don't you know ? I've been looking for a housekeeper that knew her business for months."

Janet closed the door and came forward to the couch.

" I am sorry you haven't good health, Mrs. Nelson," she said politely, not knowing anything else to say.

" I've never had any health since I came from the States to Canada," she answered with a strong American accent. " I keep telling Mr. Nelson I'll never be right till I have another winter in Washington or New York. You've seen New York, I suppose ? "

" I landed there on the White Star steamer, and drove to the railway station. That's all my acquaintance with New York."

" My ! and you didn't stop to get a real good look at it ! You don't know what you've missed ! You look like a lady. Whatever brought you to this horrid country ? "

" I suppose I came to seek my fortune, and because there are not many posts open to women like me in my own country," answered Janet frankly. " If you think I can manage your house capably I shall be glad to come."

" It's you that should know that, isn't it ? " said Mrs. Nelson with a little touch of shrewdness. " I'll be glad to have you come, even if you can't do much. For the kiddies, don't you know ! It ain't good for them to be round with that old Irishwoman most of the time, and I simply can't have them in here much. They make my head ache. If Mr. Nelson was pleased with you, and you're willing to come, why, then, come to-day, and I hope you'll be comfortable and stop for a bit. If you do, then I'll get away to New York, and have a month at Washington, with my mother. She's there for the season."

" You feel well enough to travel then ? " said Janet rather abruptly.

" Oh, yes ; it's the thing that would make me well. You see, I ain't been used to this sort of life, and I don't think it's right for a man to expect his wife to do it. All the Nelsons are like that ; they think their wives should slave at home all the time. They were Scotch right back, I believe, and I've heard that the Scotch are like that with their women-folk. Oh, but perhaps *you're* Scotch ? "

" Yes, I am."

" Oh, then you're bound to be a treasure," said Mrs. Nelson gleefully. " Do say you'll come. Did Mr. Nelson mention salary ? He didn't, well, we must leave it to him. You must just ask what you think fit. He'll pay. I don't mind. My ! this is a piece of luck for us, for me, especially now I see some chance of getting away myself. Where are you stopping ? I'm most frightened to let you out of the house in case you don't come back again."

" Oh, I'll come back right enough," said Janet, for every instinct in her was athirst to help in this helpless household, and, if possible, arouse in this selfish woman some sense of responsibility.

An hour later she walked into Ellen Dunnet's house, and electrified her with the announcement that she had obtained a housekeeper's place, and was entering on the spot.

CHAPTER IX

THE AMERICAN WIFE

THE household of Mr. John P. Nelson was a revelation to Janet Fairweather. Arriving with part of her belongings about four o'clock in the afternoon, she learned that she was expected both to order and to cook the evening meal.

Mrs. Flanagan, the casual day help, muddling around in the well-appointed but sadly neglected kitchen, was a little vague on the subject of meals.

" Shure, Miss, an' it's just annything whativer the children has. The masther, he don't come at all, at all. He goes to dinner at wan av the 'otels, which is the best thing a gintleman can do when his wife don't pay no attintion to his inside."

" But doesn't Mrs. Nelson herself have anything to eat ? "

Biddy Flanagan spread her massive hands on her hips and gave a disconcerting wink.

" She lives on chocolates, an' sthrong tea, an' bits av things. I nivver saw wan so bad nor, beggin' yer pardin, Miss, so useless ; an' yet the masther worships the ground she walks on. Shure, an' ain't it a lesson fur thim that thries to do their duty ? That's the God's thruth."

" Then they don't have late dinner," said Janet in tones of relief. " How would it do to order some cutlets and make a sort of high tea ? Mr. Nelson said he would come home to a meal this evening."

" Shure, an' annything at all will be better than they gets fur usual," answered Biddy. " The larder ? Oh, there ain't annything in there—nivver is. Ivrything comes up by that funny thing that rings the little bell. The misthress has it in her room. She tells it phwat she wants, loike, an' it's up inside av a jiffey."

Janet smiled at this summary of the wonders of the telephone, and proceeded to make herself at home as best she could in a house where there was no visible head.

Mrs. Nelson's headache being worse than usual, she had instructed Biddy to say that she was not to be disturbed till she rang her bell. In doubt as to what room she was to occupy, Janet caused her box to be set in the children's nursery.

Attired in an enveloping but not unbecoming overall, she proceeded to take an inventory of the house. It made her sad to see a house full of beautiful things so much neglected, such waste and destruction everywhere. She found Biddy putting fine damask table napkins to inglorious uses in the scullery, where the best china was to be seen cheek by jowl with pots and pans. It was less Biddy's fault than her misfortune that no previous experience had taught her to differentiate in the matter of the household gods. To her Limoges or Dresden or Derby conveyed no meaning—all were merely crockery to hold things, some of it " purtier " than the rest, though distressingly delicate to handle. The crested silver lay ignominiously beside its commoner kin in the dresser drawers—in short, the whole arrangement of the Nelson house was such as to fill Janet's orderly soul with pious wrath and indignation.

She was busy for two hours, and she saw further endless ones in front before she would be able to restore order from chaos, but she promised herself a good deal of pleasure in the process. Finding that Biddy knew nothing about the higher domestic grades, she set her first to scrub out all the saucepans, and then to pare potatoes for the evning meal, while she herself took the carpet sweeper to the dusty carpet in the dining-room, and afterwards got down on her knees to polish the ingrained surround.

She was thus engaged, breathless and merry, with the two children emulating her industriously in the hall, when Mr. John P. Nelson arrived. Just for a moment Janet's natural pride rebelled a little as she struggled to her feet. It was the first time she had engaged in actual menial work, and she did not like to be caught in the act by a mere man.

" I hoped to finish before you got home, Mr. Nelson," she said rather confusedly. " I hope you are not very hungry. I'll have something ready for you at seven. It is just twenty minutes past six now."

" That's all right," answered Nelson easily and with a very kindly look. " But surely this is not absolutely necessary. I don't want you to scrub floors—— "

" I wasn't scrubbing—only rubbing up—and it *was* necessary," Janet assured him softly. " I have only to dust round the furniture and lay the table. Then you shall have something to eat."

" Thank you," said Nelson, and with that brief reply he strode in the direction of his wife's door.

To his surprise he found her sitting in front of her escritoire, busy writing.

" Hulloa, Addie," he said cheerfully. " Are you fit to-day, little woman ? "

She turned to him with an unusually kind smile.

" I'm just writing to mommer. I could go east next week, couldn't I, Jack, now you have actually got the right person to come and keep house ? "

Nelson sat down on the edge of the table and looked a little askance. So far he had believed absolutely in his wife's profession of ill health.

" Are you able for the journey, Addie ? "

" I can get through it, I daresay, and it'll be all right when I get there. I do want so awfully to spend Christmas at home, Jack."

He winced at her use of the word *home*, but let it pass.

" Will you take Cleveland and Sadie ? "

She made a little gesture of dissent.

" I won't. How could I ? They'd be the death of me in the cars, and it would mean an expensive nurse at the other end—you must know that."

Nelson contracted his brows rather ominously.

Devoted to his children no less than to his wife, his chief grievance against her was that they were not properly cared for.

" Then you propose to leave them with Miss Fairweather ? "

" Why not ? Ain't she capable ? I'm sure she looks it, and I've heard her whisking about all the afternoon. It's what she's for, ain't it ? I suppose you're paying her ridiculous wages—how much, Jack ? "

" It hasn't been so much as mentioned between us. I found her on her knees in the dining-room polishing the floor. She's a lady, Addie, and you shouldn't treat her like that."

Mrs. Nelson shrugged her slender shoulders significantly.

" Oh, I'll go out, or have her in now, and go down on my knees to her this minute if it'll do any good or make you real happy, Jack. Only you must promise first to come to New York for Christmas."

" I shan't promise anything of the kind, Addie," he answered, and his voice had a warning note in it.

" You know you promised we shouldn't have to live in Winnipeg long, Jack. I never would have come if I'd thought it would be all these years. And I'm getting old, without ever having had a good time. Soon I shan't be pretty any more. Oh, what fools women are to give up everything for a man ! "

Nelson got up and took a turn across the floor.

" You really mean that, Addie ? " he said a trifle sadly.

" I mean it right enough—as far as it goes. If only you'd give me the winter in New York, Jack, I shouldn't mind spring and fall here, and summer at Muskoka," she said calmly. " Of course, the best thing would be if you'd go back to the New York office. I'm sure the company would let you if you asked——"

" But I don't want to ask, Addie. I'm doing a big thing here. I'll be a rich man in a few years' time."

" And in a few years' time we shall all be dead, or so old and ugly that we shan't care about anything. You know you've cheated me, Jack. You promised you'd stop here only long enough to build up the new business—five years at the outside. And this is the seventh. It's you who are in the wrong."

" I can't help myself, my dear, and it might be worse. If only you'd take an interest in things, you might easily be one of Winnipeg's leading women."

" But I don't want to be, thank you. I hate the city. It'a s poor, mean place, and the women in it are unspeakable. I'd like to tell them right here just what I think of them."

She was quite defiant now, with her hard little face turned to him, her big, child-like eyes meeting his without a tremor of the lids.

Nelson knew the mood. He had seen it on two previous occasions when she had broken into open rebellion. He sighed as he turned on his heel. But presently she called him back.

" If it'll make you any happier, Jack, I'll take the children. But, of course, I thought you wouldn't listen to it for a moment. I daresay my mother wouldn't mind, and we could get old Mammy up from Virginia to look after them. She'd just love to come."

There was a new eagerness in her voice, which might have warned Nelson that there was something else at the back of her mind. It is surprising how weak a hard-headed, clear-sighted man can become in the hands of a woman who understands him and who is unscrupulous in manipulating his weakness. John P. Nelson in the hands of his doll-faced wife was as clay to the potter.

" We can see about it later on," he said vaguely. " Won't you fix up and come into supper to-night, Addie ? It would only be civil to Miss Fairweather."

To his surprise his wife jumped up with alacrity.

" Why, yes, I don't mind if I do," she said sweetly. " I'd do anything to make you happy and comfortable if only I were strong. But there—even the John P. Nelsons of this world can't have everything."

She put her two hands on his shoulders and flashed an adorable glance at him, which said first of all that he had a great deal to be thankful for, and that he had to be reminded of the fact.

Meanwhile, very hot and a little tired with her unaccustomed exertions, Janet Fairweather had managed to create a very good semblance of comfort in the Nelson House. She had even taken time to pick some flaming maple leaves from the tree at the back of the house, and had scattered them with careless artistry on the snow of the damask, making a beautiful effect under the pink shade of the electrolier.

When Mrs. Nelson entered the room she made a very pretty gesture of surprise and pleasure.

" My ! That is real pretty—isn't it, Jack ?—and we are in luck and no mistake. Where are you, Miss Fairweather, so that I can thank you ? Only I don't think you should have set us on such a pinnacle the very first night. We are bound to have to come down again soon."

Janet Fairweather smiled, not being proof against the charm of Addie Nelson's manner. It was very soothing to her to be so sweetly treated, because she had not particularly enjoyed the rush of the afternoon, and had even wondered whether she would be able to continue it.

The next hour, when she sat at table with her employers and was treated by them as an honoured guest, served to mark as nothing else could have done the gulf fixed between the social conditions of the old world and the new. The woman who had cooked the meal was invited to partake of its choicest morsel, and was treated in every way as if she were a person of importance and distinction. It did not occur to Janet's honest mind that there could be any ulterior motive hidden beneath the flowers of Mrs. Nelson's flattering speeches. But a little later in the evening, when Nelson retired to answer some letters, Addie invited Miss Fairweather to come and have a confidential chat with her.

" See here, Miss Fairweather, you are the person I have been praying for for the last two years at least. It must be true, after all, that Providence hears us in the long run. You won't mind—will you ?—if I run away for a week or two, taking the kiddies with me ? You'll promise to stop till I come back at least and make my husband as comfortable as you have done to-night ? "

" I would do my best, of course, Mrs. Nelson, but it is rather a big thing—isn't it ?—to place so much trust in a stranger——"

" Oh, not at all, when it's you. Why, one has only to look at you to know that you are as steady as Gibraltar Rock. You see, it's like this, my dear. I'm an only child, and my parents didn't at all like my coming to Canada. They let us get married only on the understanding that we should stop here only a short time. And I've been married seven years. My people haven't seen the children for nearly two. Don't you think an only daughter owes something to her parents, and that I've been very good up to now ? I've never been very happy here. I'm an exile, and, though I have a very good husband, even the best of men never understand us—do they now ? "

" I don't know," answered Janet bluntly. " I have had very little experience of men, except my father, and he was always too busy to trouble much about us."

" Well, what I thought was that I'd go east to spend Christmas with my parents, and that Mr. Nelson would come for a few days then. And if you are here, looking after everything, just think how happy I should be about my home."

" I shall be very glad to do what I can," answered Janet simply. " I don't forget that I have to get my living, and I might have sought a long time before I got a place like this."

But afterwards she was not sure.

CHAPTER X

IN FULL POSSESSION

In the course of the following week Mrs. John P. Nelson departed in the east-bound train, taking the children with her. They started at eleven o'clock at night, but as they had the luxury of a drawing-room car for their own use the discomfort of the journey was considerably lessened.

Janet did not go to the station. After that long day's packing and running after Mrs. Nelson, she was so tired that when the carriage actually rolled away from the door she felt an odd inclination to drop into a chair and have a good cry. She did sit down just for a few minutes in one of the hall seats to reflect on the last twelve hours and all she had accomplished in them. She had cooked three meals, put the finishing touches to various rooms, packed the most of Mrs. Nelson's clothes, and made two journeys in the street cars to get things that lady wanted to take with her. In addition to all that, she had made the children entirely ready to accompany their mother, and incidentally given a little instruction to an incompetent nursemaid hired at the last minute to relieve Mrs. Nelson of the care of the children.

Hither and thither all day long had Janet flown, putting on a button here and a loop there, giving advice on this thing and that, receiving in return the sweetest of smiles and the most profuse of thanks. But the selfishness of the woman was amazing, colossal, overwhelming. Looking back on it, Janet felt a little hysterical. She pulled herself together with an effort, remembering that her work was not yet quite done. She had to straighten Mrs. Nelson's room before her husband could sleep in it. When she turned up the light on its pink-and-white draperies and saw the *débris* which is bound to be left behind such gigantic packing, she began to wonder what Mrs. Nelson wanted with so many things. She had taken practically all her belongings—her wardrobe and her drawers were empty except for useless or shabby trifles that no one could want.

" It looks as if she meant never to come back," said Janet to herself as she began mechanically to gather the paper and other rubbish into the waste-paper basket.

In ten minutes' time the room was straight. Then she began to be conscious that she was either very hungry or that she was in need of something to stimulate her failing energy. The evening meal had been necessarily hurried, and she herself had begged to be excused from sitting down. She went into the kitchen to see what she could find, and, at the risk of being kept awake half the night, she decided to warm some coffee left in a stone jug on the larder shelf. She was sitting at the end of the kitchen table, enjoying the fragrant stimulant, and eating with much relish one of her own buttered scones, when she heard the key turn in the door.

Nelson, observing the light shining from the kitchen passage, walked straight in.

" Not in bed yet, Miss Fairweather ? " he asked pleasantly. " I made sure you'd be asleep by now. Ain't you dead tired ? "

" I felt so hungry that I had to have something to eat. Surely you haven't been away long."

" No. The train was on time, for a wonder, and they did not stop in the station more than ten minutes. Phew ! but I'm tired, and I believe I am hungry too. Any coffee left in that pot ? "

" Yes—lots. And I can get you a slice of cold bacon if you like."

" Thank you. I'll eat it if you share it. Just on midnight this picnic, ain't it? Well, I guess we'll both sleep sound to-night."

" Won't I lay it in the dining-room ? " asked Janet, awaking to the incongruity of the situation.

" No, I'll have it right here or not at all. I wish I knew how to thank you, Miss Fairweather, but I don't. My wife is grateful, too. I hope she'll be all right, poor little woman. She never has travelled alone with the children before."

" I'm sure she'll be all right," answered Janet.

And for the life of her she could not prevent a dry note from creeping into her voice.

Nelson followed her into the larder and helped to carry out the viands, and they had an *al fresco* meal together, talking all through in friendly fashion, precisely as if they had been sister and brother.

Janet liked Nelson. He was the kind of man that a woman could be perfectly at home with, and she had not the slightest misgiving about remaining alone to keep house for him.

Ellen Dunnet, however, was considerably exercised regarding the whole matter.

" Eh, Miss Janet," she would say, " thae American wives is no feared. They tak' terrible liberties with their men. Whiles I say to Peter I'm gaun hame for six months. Then he says my job wad be filled by the time I cam' back. But with thae American kind naething seems to happen. The waur ye treat them the better they are. We must hae begun at the wrang end wi' our men-folk langsyne—I mean afore we were born. It was our grandmithers that made the mistake."

" But nobody can respect a man who makes himself a doormat for his wife," said Janet stoutly.

" Is that what Maister Nelson does ? But I hear Peter says he's a hard man aboot the toon wi' his business, an' that naebody ever gets the better of him."

" He's delightful in the house, certainly, and she does not treat him well. I had a good sample in the five days she was here with me."

" If I'd been her I'd hae been feared to leave ye wi' my man," said Ellen calmly. " For ye are very bonnie, Miss Janet, an' there's a something aboot ye that mak's folk baith respect an' love ye. Then, look at what ye can do ! If it were some men they wad be fa'in' in love wi' ye, wife or nae wife."

At this naïve deliverance Janet merely laughed. The possibility did not enter into her thoughts. Not only was Nelson devoted, body and soul, to his selfish wife, but Janet herself was absolutely above harbouring such a fancy even for a moment. She bore herself in a difficult situation with a courage and a high-souled delicacy which did her womanhood the greatest credit.

" It's getting very cold, isn't it ? " she asked, desirous of changing the subject. " Not in the house, of course. I've never seen such comfort as one gets indoors in this country."

" It's a' richt, but it's a close heat frae the furnace, an' at the end o' the winter you'll no hae sic fine red cheeks, Miss Janet. Ca' this cauld ? Stop or efter Christmas, when it gangs doon to forty or fifty below zero, an' ye get your nose and ears bitten ! This is naething."

Janet was not afraid of the winter, and she was both comfortable and happy at her post. In six weeks she had had three letters from Madge in Chicago—vague, unsatisfactory letters, which filled her with uneasiness. In none of them did the writer mention the names of Major Haddon or of Mrs. Ronderbusch, nor did she say how she was employed. The letters from home were cheering. Bobbie Ludlow was now in full possession at The Croft, filling Dr. Fairweather's place and apparently carrying all before him. Nancy was happy in her work of teaching the Manse grandchildren, spending her evenings at home with Bella.

Janet felt oddly out of it all, but in spite of sundry qualms of home-sickness she had not the smallest desire to go back. She had that comforting feeling, so dear to the true womanly heart, of being really useful and necessary in the place where her lot was cast, and she did an enormous lot of gratuitous work in the Nelson house, for which she would never get any thanks from the mistress. She overhauled it from top to bottom, and made an inventory of all the contents, besides darning and otherwise renovating whatever showed signs of wear and tear. She did not parade her efforts in front of her employer—she was far too Scotch and reserved for that. But he was fully conscious of the solid and abiding comfort of a well-ordered house and he showed his appreciation in many ways. True, he did not spend many hours in it. He had numerous friends in the city, and he was greatly in request at club dinners and the like, and he spent part of every Sunday at his brother's house.

Janet did not care for the other Nelsons. The wife was a bustling, active woman of the most aggressive Canadian type, always talking about her own achievements in the house—her baking and fruit-preserving and bacon-curing—and she had a supreme contempt for Mrs. John. She felt a little disappointed that the housekeeper, whose capabilities commanded her respect, declined altogether to discuss Mrs. John.

" She is my employer, and she was kind to me, Mrs. Nelson," she said at last in desperation, " and I don't want to talk about her, if you please."

After that there was a coolness between them.

At the beginning of Christmas week Nelson prepared for his journey east. He was rather concerned about leaving Janet alone.

" The house can be shut up quite well," he assured her. " Couldn't you go to your friends in Maxtone Avenue ? I'll be back inside of a week."

" I'll go to them for Christmas Day, but there isn't any need to worry about me, Mr. Nelson, now or ever. I am not the sort of person to be afraid of myself. I suppose it's my Scotch upbringing. We live a good part of our lives inside of ourselves. That has its good points as well as its bad, but at least it makes us independent."

" You are the most astonishing woman I've ever met," remarked Nelson candidly, " and if there were a few more like you—well, life would be shorn of its problems, and we'd never want to quit—see."

This quite sincere compliment warmed Janet's heart for days, and helped her through a decidedly lonesome Christmas week.

When Nelson returned on the second day of January, winter had descended with its terrible Arctic grip on the city of the plains. In spite of the underground furnace that heated the house, Janet found the water frozen solid in her bedroom, and she could not see through her window for the thick frost-pictures on the panes. Not much snow had fallen. It was one of those terrible, grim, black frosts which have little beauty to reconcile us to them. The people moved about the streets, enveloped up to the ears in what they called buffalo robes, though few of the skins had ever made acquaintance with the noble beast. Finding her outdoor clothing inadequate to the weather conditions, Janet stopped indoors, having plenty to occupy her, and being happy as only a well-balanced and contented mind can be anywhere. She was conscious, however, of a quite sincere feeling of gladness when the day came for her employer's return.

He arrived on a west-bound train about six o'clock in the evening, and came right home to a house that welcomed him to a dainty meal and to a friendly face that took the edge off his loneliness. His face brightened momentarily when Janet came forward in the hall to welcome him.

" Now, it's real good to see you, Miss Fairweather, and it makes a fellow feel not quite so lonely. How have you been ? Had a good time, eh ? "

" I've been quite happy, and not at all dull. How did you find Mrs. Nelson and the children ? I hope you had a happy Christmas."

" So so," he answered—and she saw the gloom descend on his face again.

She was far too wise and tactful to pursue the subject, but, just reminding him that supper would be ready in ten minutes, went to get it dished up.

Later in the evening he asked her to come and sit with him in his den while he smoked a comforting pipe.

"You've had six weeks of Winnipeg now, Miss Fairweather, and this is the worst time of the year. Do you think there is anything to prevent people from being happy in the place?"

"Nothing. But I've come to the conclusion that happiness has very little to do with places. It's inside of us," answered Janet.

"That's so, I suppose," he assented as he watched the blue smoke curling in wreaths from his pipe. "The place is good enough for me, but it seems I ain't to be allowed to stop in it. My father-in-law has offered me a job in Brooklyn, and I've got to take it."

"Have you? You don't speak as if it was going to be an improvement on this."

"Well, and it won't be. But, you see, my wife has made up her mind that she's going to stop down-east, and with me it's Hobson's choice."

Janet's colour rose. She felt angry, but reflected that it was not her place to criticise, or to pass an opinion on, any action of her employer's wife.

"Of course, there's a good deal to be said for the little woman," he said, precisely as if he divined Janet's unspoken thought. "She's an only child, and they simply worship her. It's a great thing for them to have her right there with the kiddies. Anyone can see that. A man shouldn't be unreasonable—should he, Miss Fairweather?"

"Nor a woman," Janet couldn't for the life of her help answering. "So you'll give up here and remove to Brooklyn?"

"To New York. I'll have to give three months' notice. I hope you'll be willing to stop on here with me till March, and then fix up the house when I quit."

"Do you mean that Mrs. Nelson is not coming back?"

"Well, why should she? She ain't strong enough for the work of moving. It would only be an extra worry and expense. The time'll pass slick enough, and if you'll stop I'll make it worth your while."

"I don't want any more than I've got. You pay me well," answered Janet quickly, "and I'll be very glad to stop."

She would have liked to say a great deal more, to cry out against the blind selfishness of the woman who was so sublimely indifferent to her responsibilities and her vows. But again she was silent.

"What I would like, and what my wife, I know, would like, would be for you to come east with us and settle down. We'll need you quite as badly there as we do here."

But Janet shook her head.

"I did not like what I saw of New York, Mr. Nelson. And, besides, I want to see a bit more of Canada. I really did not mean to stay in Winnipeg. When I leave you I'll go right out west."

"Well, I don't blame you. I'd like to go myself. It's the west, and not Kipling's east, that keeps a calling me. But I won't get there. Thank you for promising to stay till March. It won't be my fault if you don't have something good to go to when you quit here."

CHAPTER XI

NO CONTINUING CITY

THE next two months passed away quite uneventfully for Janet Fairweather. She was happy at her post, as, indeed, any woman might have been who was absolutely mistress of the house, with none to say yea or nay to her.

There were moments when John P. Nelson, fully appreciative of the unusual and ordered comfort of his home, thought how different his life might have been had fortune ordained him to wed a woman like Janet Fairweather. She was so sanely balanced, so cheerfully sensible, so full of resources, that she was a perpetual joy in the house. It was a new experience for him to be able to say over the telephone that he was bringing guests to dinner without fearing a storm of reproaches or hysterics. The only contribution Addie had ever been able to offer to an evening at home was her pretty face and well-dressed figure. The more substantial part, necessary to satisfy the inner man, was left to chance or the nearest cook-shop.

Sometimes he arrived with a guest without warning, but his housekeeper was never taken unawares. There was always something to eat. Simple it might be, but it never failed to be served appetisingly, with the sauce of a good-humoured and pleasant face to help it down. Small wonder that John P. Nelson began to spend many evenings at home, and even to do some of his work there, with the result that the club and the office after hours knew him no more.

He talked a good deal to Janet about his affairs, especially about the drastic step he felt obliged to take on his wife's account. He had established himself in Winnipeg, and the regret that was felt over his resignation was very widely expressed.

More than once Janet felt tempted to write to Mrs. Nelson, asking her if she realised and appreciated quite what it all meant to her husband. But she had not the right. She knew that, with all her sweetness, Adeline Nelson would not be slow to resent any interference from an unauthorised person. So she could only fume in secret, and do her utmost to make life easier for Nelson before he went. Evidences of Mrs. Nelson's appalling incompetency as a wife and a housekeeper she had found in plenty in the house, but she was very loyal to her employers, and she had never spoken of them except just on one or two occasions, when, unusually exasperated, she had vented her feelings in the hearing of Ellen Dunnet. But that discreet matron was far too wise and conscientious to turn over any words spoken to her by her dear Miss Janet.

The weeks flew by, and, at the end of February, acting on instructions given verbally by Mr. Nelson, and received by letter from his wife, Janet began to dismantle the pretty house and get ready for the removal. The city was still in the grip of winter, and all the great prairies were a vast, white, silent, and wonderful world. Janet had become quickly acclimatised, and she thoroughly enjoyed the clear, crystal atmosphere, only reminded of the lowness of the temperature when she rashly ventured forth to do her shopping on a very windy day. Her active life kept her healthy and well, her only worry being continued anxiety about Madge, who had intimated that she had gone to Los Angeles to take care of a hotel. There was something about it all that Janet did not like, and she had even contemplated devoting part of her savings to making a journey into California to see for herself what her sister was about. She was prevented from doing this, however, by the unfolding of her own future.

One evening early in March, about six o'clock, Nelson returned home for dinner, accompanied by a stranger. Janet was busy in the kitchen when she heard them come in, and, leaving a word of instruction with Biddy Flanagan—still the faithful, but much-improved, henchwoman of the Nelson house—she slipped out into the hall to greet them. Always mistress of a situation, and with a strong sense of the fitness of things, Janet dressed very soberly of an evening, even when guests were expected—invariably wearing a high black frock, which, however, her clear freshness of complexion enabled her to wear with great becomingness.

When she stepped forth into the pretty, well-lighted hall she saw that Nelson had with him a very tall, broad-shouldered man wearing an immense fur coat, which, of course, added to his dimensions.

" Good evening, Miss Fairweather," said Nelson pleasantly. " This is Mr. Yates Courtney from the north-west. He's stopping at the Malakoff House, but I brought him here specially to see you."

" Oh ! " said Janet rather confusedly, for this was a very direct and decidedly embarrassing speech. " That's unusual, isn't it ? "

The man called Courtney stepped forward and shook her cordially by the hand. " Mr. Nelson wants to do me a good turn, Miss Fairweather."

" Yes, indeed he does—to his own detriment and cost," said Nelson ruefully. " But we'll talk about it after. Come, Courtney, we'll go and wash."

Janet was conscious of a distinct thrill of curiosity and interest as she went back to superintend the final stages of the meal. She was conscious also of something else—an odd sense of reluctance and shrinking, the sort of feeling one very often has when meeting for the first time a person destined to exercise some strong influence over one's future.

She decided that she would not sit at table with them, and Nelson had learned that, when Biddy waited at table in a clean apron and with a shiny face, his housekeeper had her own reasons for not coming in. They were generally economic reasons, easily enough understood when he arrived with guests of whose coming he had given no notice. But he had taken the trouble to telephone that afternoon about four o'clock to say that he was bringing a man, and therefore he felt disappointed that she did not come to sit at the head of the table. He did not, however, send any message to her, feeling sure he would find her at the coffee tray by the hall fireplace, where they very often sat of an evening.

She was there when presently he rose from the table and looked through the half-open door. Nelson was a very abstemious man, and, as a rule, drank nothing but iced water or lager beer. When he and his guest came out, Janet thought the latter looked flushed, as if he had been partaking rather freely. Beside him Nelson looked a slim, almost boyish figure, a smaller man altogether both physically and mentally—more of the nervous, over-civilised, highly strung type to be found so largely in American cities. Courtney looked as if he had been bred of a race of sturdy yeomen. The type was pure Saxon. He had frank, fine blue eyes, a ruddy skin, and beautiful fair hair slightly waved above his broad forehead, reminding Janet of pictures she had seen of the Viking kings. He created an impression of strength and power, and when he spoke he had the pure English accent, entirely free from any Western taint.

" Mr. Courtney comes from Calgary way, Miss Fairweather, and his chief business in Winnipeg is to find somebody to go and keep house at his ranch. So now I'll leave you to settle it."

" Will Mr. Courtney take black coffee and sugar ? " asked Janet—and she was distinctly conscious of a tremor in her fingers as they closed over the handle of the coffee-pot.

" Black, and three lumps, if you please," said Courtney as he drew in a chair to the table and sat down. " It's soon said, Miss Fairweather. I've nobody at my place but a hired man, and I've a little chap of six, needing someone to look after him. He's boarded out while I'm down here. If there's anything in the forlorn spectacle of a widower's house that appeals to you, why, then, come. There's no more to be said."

It was all very rapid, but then, in the last two months, Janet had obtained a certain amount of knowledge regarding the unconventional and lightning methods prevailing in the New World. Nobody had time to consider all the pros and cons of things, even had they had the inclination. Opportunities simply flashed upon the horizon, and, if not immediately gripped with both hands, sailed by for ever.

" I would need some particulars, wouldn't I ? " she asked a trifle confusedly. " And so would you."

" I've had mine from Nelson," answered the new-comer promptly as he set down his coffee-cup after finding its contents good. " I don't know what else I can tell you. The life out west is pretty rough for women. It didn't suit my poor wife. But since her time I have made the house more comfortable, and there is generally somebody round to do the hard chores. When there isn't, I do them myself."

Janet had heard the word *chores* constantly used since her arrival in Winnipeg. It seemed to sum up every known species of domestic work. But in the Nelson house, where everything was so perfectly appointed, she had lacked for nothing, and house-work had been a pleasure rather than a drudgery.

" How long is it since Mrs. Courtney died ? " she asked sympathetically.

" Two years in the fall. Then a cousin of mine came out from England, but she got married eight months ago, and since then I've had nobody worth speaking of. So, as it was a slack time just before we get the Chinook, I thought I'd come east and see if they couldn't put me on to somebody at the Government Immigration Office. It was Mr. Nelson's brother there who told me about you."

" Mr. Courtney wants you at once, of course," said Nelson. " He hoped to take somebody back with him, but I've told him he must wait two weeks for you. You promised to see me through here, didn't you ? "

" Yes ; and I will, of course," answered Janet without a moment's hesitation. " But what if Mr. Courtney can't wait so long ? "

" Well, I've been without for eleven solid weeks, batching with the hired man, and the little chap at his Aunt Louie's. That's my only sister, married on a ranch nine miles away. If he could have stopped on at his aunt's I might have hung on till the month of June, when I had promised myself a little trip to the old country. But she has four kids of her own, and nobody to help. We're all in the same boat up west, and a paternal Government ought to do more for us in that direction than it does."

" How long have you been out in Canada ? " asked Janet with deepening interest.

This frank recital of his affairs appealed to her, and in fancy she saw herself home-making for a lonely man and a still lonelier little boy. Nelson saw how interested and touched she was, and felt a pang because he must let her go.

" I've never been home since I came out nine years ago. I did not even go home to be married—never could afford the time. My wife came out to me, but the life disappointed her. I suppose it looks different to a woman. I must prepare you for isolation and loneliness. We are fourteen miles from the railroad."

" But he has the fastest horses in Alberta, Miss Fairweather—bred on the ranch —and they annihilate distance, I assure you."

" I shan't mind the isolation. I am used to country life," answered Janet stoutly. " And I've been here for a good lot of weeks without much companionship. If you think I am suitable, Mr. Courtney, I shall be glad to come."

" Thank you. Now—the salary. It's a question for you entirely. I have had a lady at fifty pounds a year who would have been dear at fifty shillings. Shall we leave it till you get out there and size up the place and us ? "

"Oh, no," said Janet hastily. "Please say forty pounds to begin with. It can be adjusted after, if it is necessary."

"And you'll come up, honour bright, the moment Mr. Nelson can release you?" he said eagerly. "Nelson, you won't put any spoke in this particular wheel? After all, though Miss Fairweather's services are valuable to you, you have a wife, and, consequently, a home, waiting for you at New York. I'm the most needful beggar, I think, in the whole of Alberta."

Nelson promised, and when Janet, convinced that the two men had much to say to each other, quietly slipped away, she felt her head in a whirl.

"Life's like a kaleidoscope now, Biddy," she remarked to the help in the scullery.

But Biddy's intelligence did not soar to appreciation of the word.

"Wasn't the gintlemen's coffee roight, Miss?" she inquired anxiously.

"Oh, yes, quite right—at least they drank it all up. I am going out west when I leave here, Bridget—right out to Calgary at the foot of the Rockies."

"Wid the big gintleman?" inquired Biddy with the liveliest possible interest, sending the colour to Janet's face.

"Not exactly with him. We have to pack up this house first. But I expect I shall follow him when Mr. Nelson leaves Winnipeg."

Biddy gave a grunt and polished with renewed vigour at the saucepan lid.

"Shure, an' it moight be a good thing out there. I'm towld it isn't so cowld annyways. Would yez put up a good wurrd for the loikes av me, Miss? I'd loike oncommon to go there, only it takes a divil av a lot av money, I'm towld; but the wages is good because they can't get people to do the wurrk."

"I'll see, Biddy. Perhaps I might even find work for you at Mr. Courtney's place. I would very much like to have you myself."

"Glory be to God! An' that's jist what I'm afther," quoth Bridget joyfully. "I nivver served wid a rale leddy before, an' I loike it. Oh, Miss Janet, if yez do sind for me, I'll wurrk me fingers to the bone for yez."

"We'll see. I shall have to go first and prospect—as they say here. I've an odd feeling about it, Biddy. I want to go, and yet somehow I don't."

"Don't yez be feared, Miss. The Howly Virgin hersilf looks afther the loikes av you. For whereivver yez go a blissin follows; an' the big gintleman will foind out his blissid luck before ye've been a wake in his place."

Janet laughed at all this flattery and said Biddy was spoiling her completely.

Her dreams that night were a strange medley. She saw herself in a long, low house, painted green and white, standing lonely by the edge of a desert lake. The sun was shining on every corner of it save one, where a dark figure crouched as if in fear of being seen. When she drew near to discover the purport of this dark presence, she awoke with a little cry.

For the face, half-hidden by the drapery about the head, had a strange, alluring beauty of its own, and the eyes seemed to regard her with a mocking gleam. And, stranger than all, the features were familiar—the face was that of her sister Madge.

CHAPTER XII

THE BACK OF BEYOND

As the heavy train rolled along the prairie track, a hundred miles beyond Winnipeg, Janet's eyes grew tired of the monotony of the view. A wonderful west wind, in the middle of March, had swept the snow away to the back of beyond, and all the spring work was already started in the fields. Everywhere the immense heavy ploughs, some of them drawn by four and six horses, were busy upturning the soil, ready for the spring sowing. It was all very ugly and depressing, as seen from the train windows, and the absence of trees or hedges, of anything, indeed, to break the monotony, began to pall upon Janet's eyes, accustomed as they had long been to the rich variety of her native land. Perhaps she was just a little depressed at the somewhat abrupt termination of what had really been a very pleasant engagement. It was hardly to be expected that she would be so lucky again. She knew perfectly well that the comparative luxury of the Nelson house had not been a very good preparation for the privations she might be called upon to undergo further west. Ellen Dunnet had done her best to prepare her for them, drawing a dismal enough picture of what she had heard about western homesteads from those who had lived on them.

" I'm not easy in my mind about ye, Miss Janet, and baith Peter and me think it would hae been better for ye to go to New York with the Nelsons. Ye may hae everything to do at your new place, as like as not ye will. Hoo will ye like to wash and mend and bake for hired men ? maybe Doukhobors that are mair than half crazy, or thae terrible dirty Galicians that dinna ken what water is, for I'm feared aboot ye."

" If you had seen Mr. Courtney, Ellen, you wouldn't have another qualm, I'm sure. He is a splendid man."

Ellen sniffed unbelievingly.

" They're *a*' splendid when they're wantin' onything off ye. Even Peter leed aboot Winnipeg, an' I've never let it doon on him to this day. But mind, ye hae aye a hame here, Miss Janet, an' if things are not to your mind, jist you rise up an' come. You'll aye find an open door here."

Janet was thinking of these warm words as on the second day of her journey she began to anticipate its close. By six o'clock the following morning she expected to alight at the little station on the other side of Calgary, where Courtney had promised to meet her. But the Limited Imperial Express is a law to itself in the matter of arrival and departure, and it was eleven o'clock in the morning before it drew up heavily at the little wayside station of Fort Purbeck just lately planted down for the convenience of settlers who complained that Calgary was too far off. It was a raw, grey morning, but not very cold. Janet was conscious of a singular feeling of loneliness when, with the aid of the coloured porter, she stepped down from the high compartment on to the little wooden platform. She was absolutely the only passenger to alight, and in a few minutes her baggage was beside her, and the long train was moving off again, having discharged its particular duty towards her. She looked round askance, for apparently there was no one to greet her but a nondescript person in a very badly fitting overcoat who appeared to be the solitary official of Fort Purbeck.

She stepped up to him anxiously.

"I was to be met here by Mr. Courtney. Is he here, do you know?"

The stationmaster shook his head.

"No, Marm, he ain't, but thet ain't no reason why he shouldn't come by-'n-by."

"How far is his place?"

"A matter of fourteen or fifteen miles. No, there ain't no way of gittin' to it. The hotel? Oh, it's outside, across the side-walk, but they ain't got no team thet could take you. All the hosses are on the land at present. You'd better jes' come inside an' sit by the stove till Mr. Courtney gits 'ere. Sure theer's no mistake about the day? Of course, he's busy on the land jes' now—everybody is."

"There is no mistake about the day. If you'll look after my baggage, I'll just step out and have a look round, if you will be so kind as to point out the direction in which Mr. Courtney is likely to come."

"You won't git fur, Marm, for since the Chinook came, an' the snow melted all of a heap like, the roads ain't no great ketch. Like as not Mr. Courtney's rig may 'ave been swamped. Some of the slews over to his place'll be swollen no end. When the watter gits up to the axles, Marm, theer ain't no great speed possible even wi' cattle like Boss Courtney's."

He meant to be facetious, but Janet only partly understood him.

"Oh, nothin' won't happen to your baggage, Marm; there ain't no pinchers 'ere. So go an' 'ave a look round. My old woman could give you a cup of good coffee if ye needs it."

"Thank you, I've had breakfast on the train," answered Janet pleasantly, realising that the man meant to be really kind. She stepped through the dreary little booking-shed where the winter stove made the air too warm and close for comfort in the delicious spring morning, and from the open door beyond surveyed the world as it spread away from the railway track.

The abomination of desolation it looked in the still grey morning light, and one swift glance warned her that the stationmaster was right. It would not be possible for her to walk far. The wooden side-walks only extended from the station to the little hotel, about a hundred yards distant. A few small wooden shacks, and one miscellaneous store such as springs up in a night wherever there is a promise of settlement, comprised the township of Fort Purbeck. Away to westward, however, the line of the prairie was broken by a low range of hills which afforded much relief to eyes long tired of the plains, the foothills of the Rockies, Janet recognised them to be, having conscientiously studied her map and her time-tables during the interminable hours of her journey.

The roadway between the narrow side-walks was a sea of slush and mud, and when she had proceeded as far as the hotel, she stood still dismayed, realising that it would not be possible for her to go further without serious consequences to her boots.

Anything more dreary and discouraging than her first introduction to Fort Purbeck, Janet had never encountered in her life; she often recalled it afterwards, and always with a little shiver of disgust.

It looked like the limit of a world, with which no rational being would care to prosecute acquaintance. In this dejected mood she beheld in the distance, making a bold struggle through the heavy road, a team of horses hitched to what seemed to be a large waggon with a seat across it on which a tall figure was discernible. She surmised that it was Courtney even before he came near enough to be recognisable. Presently, observing and recognising her, he took off his cap and waved it. She picked her way across to the small verandah of the hotel, and there waited until the team came up.

"Good morning, Miss Fairweather," he called out cheerily, directly he was within earshot. "Sorry to be so late, but we've been held up half a dozen times. The roads are simply awful. How long have you been waiting?"

He drew up the panting horses with a sharp jerk in front of the hotel and sprang down at the moment that the proprietor came out to greet him. He did not look so smart and well groomed as when he had appeared at Nelson's house in Winnipeg, but Janet was unfeignedly glad to see him, as only a woman can be when stranded in an unfamiliar and not very home-like region, so far from civilisation and from home.

He represented the only link between her and absolute desolation. When he drew off his big glove and shook her hand heartily, smiling into her face with his frank, reassuring eyes, she smiled back.

"I haven't been here so very long, so don't look so disturbed. We were five hours late."

"I allowed for three," he answered, with his deep, sonorous laugh. "I started at four o'clock this morning, and now I'll have to take out the horses and let them get a rub down and a feed. I hope you don't mind. We can breakfast ourselves while they're at it. Where's the baggage?"

Janet pointed to the station, and just then the landlord's wife, a thin, brown-faced woman in a rusty black frock, her hair hanging in dreary wisps round her face, came out to welcome the stranger lady.

"Good morning, Mrs. Smithson," cried Courtney cheerily. "This is Miss Fairweather, who is going out to my place. Just make her comfortable, will you, till I get the horses out."

"Come inside, Miss, won't you?" said Mrs. Smithson in a lifeless voice, and Janet responded by following her into the house. She was met on the threshold by a warm, close air in which a variety of strange odours struggled for the mastery. There was no freshness, and the whole house had a slatternly, uncared-for look, which made Janet wonder that it got any patronage whatever. But when she reflected that there was no opposition, she understood, and sundry old tales of Bret Harte's she had read giving vivid word pictures of the stopping-places of the Californian stage coaches returned to her mind. She particularly remembered a woman of the name of Skaggs. Mrs. Smithson was a second edition of Mrs. Skaggs.

"Come out from the old country, I s'pose?" said Mrs. Smithson with an air of languid interest as she ushered Janet into the dining-room of the house, an apartment about fifteen feet square, barely furnished, and having a table in the middle of the floor covered with a white cloth of doubtful reputation. The floor, covered with a cheap oilcloth, had various spittoons standing about, and matches and other remains of smoking were plentifully in evidence. The odour there was of beer and stale tobacco mingled with that of some bacon of a particularly aggressive brand being cooked in the background.

"Any relation of Mr. Courtney's?" pursued Mrs. Smithson when she motioned her guest to the chair nearest the stove.

"No. I'm only going to be his housekeeper," Janet answered simply.

"Oh, his housekeeper. You don't look like that sort," answered Mrs. Smithson in a mild surprise. "Air you prepared fer the work up there? He ain't 'ad anybody but the hired man most of the winter, and you bet there'll be a lot to do. Don't you go, Miss. It ain't fer the like of you. It's plum hard for all wimmin-folk out here. It's jes' about finished me."

"I'm sorry," murmured Janet sympathetically as she regarded the drab, rather hopeless-looking figure. "But now I've come so far, I must give it fair trial."

"Men—they don't think—why should they?—what it means to wimmin to be cut off. You wouldn't think it, but when I come out 'ere to Joe Smithson I was as pretty an' peart a young gel as you could meet anywheere. Now the life's out of me, an' I've buried five. Thet takes it out of a woman, you bet."

Janet said she was sure it did, and her pity for the poor woman deepened.

"It's not so much the work, though thet's crooil 'ard, as the lonesomeness. It ain't so bad since Joe come here, when the station was opened. It was Mr. Courtney got the company to set this station down here. He has a powerful way with him, he has ; gits most he wants from everybody. It'll be a good thing fer the little boy, you goin' up, but don't you go fer to begin and make yourself a doormat to Boss Courtney. They takes it all as if it were their blessed right. If I 'ad me time to begin again, I wouldn't marry a Westerner, not me. Is thet them comin' back already ? Will you take tea or coffee ? There's fried potatoes with the bacon, and hot buckwheat cakes, if my fool gel ain't burned them. Smells kinder like as if she 'ad. I'll best go an' see."

She stepped across to a swing-door in the wall, pushed it back with her foot, and disappeared into the recesses of the cooking-place beyond. Janet leaned back in the dilapidated bent-wood chair, and looked about her with unmitigated disgust. Never had she been inside a more uninviting hostelry, never had she felt less inclined to sample its fare, but, curiously, when Courtney appeared in company with the unkempt-looking villain who was the landlord of the King Edward Hotel at Fort Purbeck, she found herself being completely dominated by him. She even sat down at the table with him and made a pretence of sharing his breakfast.

He took a prodigious meal, and seemed to be perfectly unconscious of the odour or flavour of the bacon, or the undrinkable nature of the coffee. He did not talk much while he ate, but after a while he began to ask her a lot of questions about her ourney and her final departure from Winnipeg.

"I didn't feel sure until I saw you, Miss Fairweather, that you would really come," he said frankly. "When I left Nelson that night, I didn't believe he'd ever let you go free. I hope you'll like Markyates, and stop a bit in it."

"Markyates," repeated Janet. "What a quaint, pretty name!"

"It's the name of the old place in England where I was born, but there's a mighty difference between the two."

Janet regarded him with an increased interest. She had not suspected him of any sentimental vein, and the idea of his calling his Western home after the place of his birth appealed to her. But presently their private conversation was interrupted by the reappearance of Mrs. Smithson, who hovered near them with friendly remarks, until Courtney pushed back his chair and said they must be thinking of going.

"Seen Mr. Courtney afore now, eh?" she inquired of Janet when he had left the dining-room after settling the bill.

"Yes, once, at Winnipeg," answered Janet, a little inclined to resent the woman's familiarity and openly avowed curiosity. She did not know that it was typically Western, and that Canadians will take no end of trouble to find out all about the stranger within their gates.

"Not a bad sort as men go, but he's got a temper. So had his wife. Then there were ructions. There were lots of stories going about Markyates."

"Excuse me, I don't want to hear them," said Janet hastily, beginning to move towards the door.

"I don't want to put you off your new boss," observed Mrs. Smithson, with a rather disagreeable laugh. "And you'll like the little chap. Everybody's sorry for 'im. But, say, you keep Mrs. Anderson—thet's Mr. Courtney's sister—outside. Thet's my advice. It was 'er made the trouble before."

Janet bade her a hasty good morning and walked out.

"And if you're dull or want a friend, come over 'ere. There's a pony for the little buggy, I know, up to Mister Courtney's place, and you'll soon learn to find your way about."

Janet was thankful to get outside. Even the mud and the slush of the roadway was preferable to the flowing stream of Mrs. Smithson's tongue. Yet the woman was good-natured and meant well. And she stood sufficiently in awe of Boss Courtney to be a little sorry for the woman who was going to be his housekeeper. Janet did not feel at all sorry for herself. She had nothing to complain of in the manners of her new employer. He was kind in a rough-and-ready fashion, and took pains to see that she was comfortably settled in the big, weird-looking waggon before they started out on their more or less perilous ride. It was the most astonishing experience Janet had ever encountered, and she had some anxious, even desperate, moments—notably when they essayed to cross a wooden bridge whose foundations were plainly shaking in the flooded current beneath.

"We must try it, Miss Fairweather, if you're game. If we don't, it means another six miles round. The water's come down a bit more since we crossed earlier in the morning. Just shut your eyes and hold tight. I promise you I'll get you out if we should go down."

Even the animals seemed nervous and shivering, but in response to a touch of the whip, and a coaxing word, they took the frail bridge at a swinging gallop. When Janet opened her eyes they were up the hill on the other side, and Courtney was laughing at her side.

"It's a bad bit, that, and we'll have to set about getting a new bridge. It's been a grand crossing all winter when the ice was holding. The sleigh took it in fine style. I haven't frightened you, I hope."

"I didn't like it," admitted Janet frankly. "But now I don't mind. I hope there are no more torrents to cross."

"Nothing to speak of, and soon I'll be able to point out to you the trees about Markyates. I'm rather proud of them. I planted five hundred, and they've all done well, and stand true to their name. There's some spruce like they grow in your country, and they're the healthiest of the lot."

Janet asked a few interested questions about the forms of vegetation that would flourish on the prairie, and, finding her intelligent above the average of her sex on such matters, Courtney was at great pains to answer her accurately. He was at home and even enthusiastic on the subject, and Janet found the journey pass very pleasantly. It was very hard and rather slow going, for the roads in any other country but Canada would have been pronounced impassable, but the upper air was delicious, and the sky, all pearly with mackerel-coloured clouds, had the softness of an exquisite spring in it. Courtney explained the warm Chinook wind to her, and told her other weather-lore of the plains, which interested her beyond measure. Presently, however, he jerked the reins a little bit, and pointed with the butt-end of the whip to a little dark ridge on the far edge of the horizon. "There's the place, see, Miss Fairweather? another ten minutes, and you'll see the house. It's only the little shack, but I've got the plans out for the new house. I hope you'll take an interest in it, then we'll start building as soon as the seed's in."

He was very boyish in some ways, and seemed glad to chat familiarly with a woman who would take the slightest interest in him and his concerns. But, in spite of herself, Janet's spirits sank as they came within discernible distance of Markyates. It seemed to her to mark the limit of the world. A handful of wooden huts clustering round an old log shack with a painfully new addition stuck on haphazard at the back, a few emaciated and sadly battered-looking trees, and a little lake which had an odd, detached, even a weird appearance in the strong noonday light, comprised the outward features of her new home. When the waggon was driven across the rough grass which stretched with some attempt at a lawn in front of the small verandah, she was even more dismayed. There was not a blind or a curtain at any of the windows. The whole place had an unfinished and unkempt look which contrasted painfully with the up-to-date suburban mansion she had left.

"Wonder where Denis is," observed Courtney cheerfully, not at all observant of the blank change in Janet's face as he offered his hand to help her to alight from the waggon. "I told him to come in from the plough at eleven, and see to the dinner and the stove. You'll sample man-made pie to-day, Miss Fairweather. Whether you eat it or not will depend on your appetite and digestion. Denis and me have learned not to be too mighty particular after nine months' batching."

An unlovely vision in a slouch hat, a pair of dilapidated trousers, and a woollen shirt which was either black naturally, or by actual dirt, came whistling across the grass with a broad smile on his pleasant Irish face.

" Your new mistress, Denis. Are the potatoes on ? " said Courtney lightly.

" Shure, sor ; and it's plazed to see yez I am, Miss," answered Denis, touching his hat as he stepped forward to take the horses.

Janet responded to his greeting as she best could, and mounted the verandah steps, the withered trails of the creeper slapping her face as she made through them to the door.

" It isn't open," Courtney explained. " We use the back door mostly. It's just here. Step right in, Miss Fairweather. You're welcome to Markyates."

Janet never forgot her first introduction to the kitchen, which she afterwards discovered had been the living-room for the two men all the winter. It was of a fair size, plastered white, but very grimy with smoke and dirt, and the strip of common oilcloth on the floor had evidently not made acquaintance with soap and water for a long time. The stove stood out in the middle of the floor, and on it were several saucepans boiling merrily. It was domesticity in the rough, beyond a doubt, and her heart sank in contemplation of what was expected from her.

All that Ellen Dunnet had told her now flashed back upon her memory, and she realised that there had not been an atom of exaggeration in it. Courtney, all unconscious of what was passing in her mind, and mightily pleased with himself at having actually brought her there, invited her to come and see the rest of the house.

Janet followed rather bl ndly, and in the little passage which divided the kitchen from the new living-room that had been built on at the back, she paused for one desperate moment, to dash away a very bitter moisture from her eyes.

CHAPTER XIII

THE NEW HOME

It just sufficed to relieve the tension of the moment, and when she passed into the inner room her spirits slightly rose. It was a bleak place, too, but large and airy, and the clean boards, covered with oilcloth of inoffensive pattern, were relieved by two or three warm-coloured rugs. A round table in the middle of the floor (on which stood a gramophone), a few bent-wood chairs and two rockers, upholstered in crimson plush, and an American organ against the wall, comprised the furnishings. There was nothing beautiful in the whole room except two water-colours of English scenery hanging above the organ, and one or two old china cups and saucers in a tiny corner cupboard behind the door. But it had possibilities. It could be converted into a homely place.

"Your bedroom's above this, Miss Fairweather. My sister Louie came over the other day and shifted my things. No, I'd like you to have it; the small room's all right for me. If you can persuade Billy to sleep in your room in his little cot, I'd be glad. The little beggar has never left me at night since his mother died."

"Is he here?" asked Janet with interest.

"No, he's up with my sister, but she'll fetch him to-morrow. She'd have been here to-day to receive you, only she has a three-months-old baby that has been sick, and I wasn't sure you would be here to-day. Just go up now and have a look round. It's a poor enough little place, after what you've been used to in Scotland and in Winnipeg; but I hope you'll take to it. I'll go and see about dinner, and after it we'll take up your traps."

Janet nodded and mounted the narrow staircase to the upper floor of the odd, quaint little house. She found three rooms there, two small ones, both in a state of disorder, and the one evidently occupied by the hired man, which exhibited an unmade bed and a lot of working clothes lying about the floor. It was totally destitute of furniture except for the bed and the Irish boy's battered tin box in the window. The other room, to which Yates had removed himself in view of her coming, was bare too, without a floor covering, but it had a dressing-chest across the window on which lay the ordinary equipments of the Englishman, among them two ivory-backed brushes with monograms in silver on them, an incongruity which caused Janet to smile suddenly but a little dismally. A small table against an empty wall had a lot of photographs set out upon it, and above them hung a large photograph of an old English country house with a wedding party assembled on the lawn.

The new bedroom, built above the living-room, was a spacious and pleasant place. It had two big windows, and though the drugget on the floor was cheap and ugly, the bed was good and the other furniture convenient. There was no wardrobe, but a cretonne curtain run on rings made a hanging cupboard across one of the corners. The view from it was heavenly, stretching for miles across the open prairie to the foothills of the Rockies, and then melting into illimitable space. It was a poor, mean, bare place, but it had possibilities. For a moment, however, the prospect of the actual physical work she had in front of her appalled Janet. She had a lady's instincts, and the idea of clearing up after the cheerful, friendly Denis was not inviting. She decided to have a very plain, frank conversation with Courtney that night before she slept. She knew that she was physically perfectly able for the drudgery, but she had no mind to undertake it unless it was absolutely necessary. It was characteristic of Janet Fairweather not to shirk any part of that which she had undertaken. From the lid of her box, which the two men carried up to her, she took out an overall, which she tied above her plain serge travelling frock before she descended to the kitchen. The meal was now spread there in the rough-and-ready fashion of the men who batch. A large piece of cold boiled beef, a glass jar of sticky pickles, and an immense bowl of potatoes boiled in their jackets, was the fare, accompanied by strong tea out of a tin teapot, hissing cheerfully on the side of the stove.

On the side table stood the man-made pie, which Courtney had promised her, and regarding which there were plenty of jokes. Ellen Dunnet had prepared her for sitting down with the hired man, and Courtney taking it as a matter of course, offered neither explanation nor apology as he set a chair for her.

Janet sat down, and, having received a slice of beef on a plate, helped herself to a potato, and discovered that it tasted good. She had only made a pretence of sharing Courtney's breakfast at the Fort Purbeck hotel, and it was six hours since she had partaken of a cup of coffee and a buttered biscuit in the train.

She tried not to observe the table habits of Denis Rourke, but she did wonder how Courtney, undoubtedly a gentleman, had been able to put up with them for so long. There was nothing offensive about the lad, however; his manner, if friendly, was respectful, and he did not obtrude his remarks into the conversation. Janet sampled everything, pronounced the man-made pie to be good, and even drank two cups of the liquid from the tin teapot. After it she felt ready for further adventure. Courtney, with the air of a man who has accomplished some cherished task, lit his pipe after dinner, and retired with the hired man to the work of the farm, leaving Janet mistress of the situation. The first thing she did was to sit down and laugh a little hysterically. She had often heard and read of the primitive conditions of domesticity in the Far West; now she sampled it for herself. Her mind was a curious medley. The more refined part of her revolted from everything she saw, and the mere idea of clearing away the *débris* of the meal and setting the place straight disgusted her. But the more virile part of her rejoiced in the undoubted fact that if ever a woman's presence was desperately needed in a house, then hers was. And she was free even in a truer sense than she had been at Winnipeg to do what she liked, to set her impress on the place. Out of the raw material lying to her hand it was open to her to create a home. There are very few women whom such an appeal would not touch. It touched Janet so mightily that after that one small hysterical outburst she simply turned up her skirts and her sleeves and set to work. She set on a huge pan of water for her washing up, and, piling the dishes on the tray, she retired upstairs to take out some of her belongings while she waited for the water to get hot.

She was careful and thrifty enough to dive to the very bottom of her trunk for her oldest skirt and a washing blouse. When she had donned these she felt readier for any emergency, and attacked the washing-up with a will. In the course of the afternoon she made a comprehensive inventory of the cellar, which was used as a larder; of the small dairy where the milkpans stood; and inspected the meagre household stores. Then she poured two buckets of hot water over the floor, swept it out with a long brush, and mopped it with a cloth, and then set the door and the windows open, so that the Chinook wind might dry and make it sweet. Then she investigated the working of the stove, found its guiding principle, and also discovered that it possessed a roomy boiler filled with hot water. The stove itself was sadly in need of polishing. She beheld herself in a mental vision getting up early next morning, and, with a duster over her hair and a pair of old gloves on her hands, working at it with a will. In such housewifely labour and planning, the afternoon simply flew by on wings. Six o'clock the supper hour arrived before she realised it. She was ready, however. She unearthed a clean cloth from a big trunk on the landing, and the table presented a very different appearance from what it had done at the midday meal. Courtney smiled as he stepped across the threshold.

"You haven't lost a bit of time, Miss Fairweather; but there was no need to hurry. You should take it easy for a day or two."

"I couldn't be happy in the middle of chaos," she answered candidly. "You went out without saying anything about supper, and all I can find is the remains of the cold beef and a few eggs. Would you like some scrambled eggs?"

"Indeed, and I would; I've forgotten the taste of them," he answered readily. "No hurry, Miss Fairweather. Denis and I will just go outside and have a wash up before we sit down. You're so neat, we'll have to buck up a bit in your honour."

The arrangements for washing were a tin basin set on a bench by the door near the pump in the yard, which Courtney explained had never been frozen all winter, even when the thermometer was thirty below zero.

"We've had a harder winter than usual, but this is a real artesian spring, and the water is delicious. No man knows the value of water till he can't get it. At my brother-in-law's place, though it's only nine miles away, they're practically dried up three months in summer, and have to cart it all, both for washing and drinking. Markyates's all right for that."

The supper was quite a cheerful meal, and when the hired man offered to clear it away, Courtney beckoned to Janet to come into the inner room, where he lit the hanging lamp and closed the door.

"You must make use of the boy as much as you can. He's willing enough, though a bit awkward. Of course, in a week or two I shan't be able to let you have him much. We'll have to tear in at the ploughing and sowing like madmen to get the stuff in. You never saw anything like the miracle of spring here. Almost literally you put the seed in one day, and it's showing the next. We have to hustle a bit, I tell you, from now till the beginning of June."

Janet smiled a little as she dropped into one of the rocking-chairs, glad to rest now after her undoubtedly strenuous day.

"May I speak quite plainly to you, Mr. Courtney, now I've seen the place?"

"Why, yes, of course; but I hope that doesn't mean that you're fed up with it already, and want to go off first thing in the morning."

"Hardly that; but I want to tell you that I don't like the idea of doing the roughest of the work, the scrubbing and the washing. I don't mind the cooking. I like it, and I think I can do it moderately well."

"I'm sure of it, but I'm disappointed, Miss Fairweather; I don't think I misled you that night at Winnipeg. I told you that, except for a few outside chores, you would have all the work to do."

"I know that you were perfectly honest, and did not mislead me at all. Only I didn't realise it quite, until I was up against it, as you Canadians say."

"Then what do you mean to do?" he asked ruefully. "I can't spare Denis to do house-chores, besides which, he's no hand at it. I could do them better myself, but——"

"But you don't propose to pay a woman forty pounds a year and do them," put in Janet with a perfectly good-natured comprehension.

"You've struck it, so what's to be done?"

"Well, I don't want forty pounds a year. I shouldn't be able to spend it here, and if you'll allow me to get a rough help, I shall be quite pleased with the half of it."

"You might just as well ask for the moon at once, Miss Fairweather. Didn't I tell you we hadn't had anybody here for nearly twelve months? It just means that we'll have to go on batching through the summer and trust to good luck to get someone to help us through with the press of the harvest cooking."

"Oh, but I think there's a way out. I had a woman at Mr. Nelson's house, an

Irish charwoman, really quite capable. She wants to come out west, and she'd come to be with me for a small wage. If you care to divide the money between us, her keep would never be missed. I'll make it up to you, for I think I am a careful manager; then I'm sure I should be happy here, and, what is more important, I could make you comfortable and make a home for you and your little boy."

Courtney's face brightened.

"Why, that's the very thing; why didn't you bring her right up with you yesterday?"

"Well, you see, I couldn't very well do that, because I hadn't seen the place, and didn't even know what your views might be. But I can write to her to-morrow, and she'll be up within a week. But what about her sleeping place? There isn't another room."

"Oh, we can fix up Denis in the stable-loft, now the warmer weather's coming. I'll ride into Purbeck to-morrow and mail the letter, or, better still, wire her to come, if you'll give me her address."

"That wouldn't do, for we'll have to send dollar bills to pay her way up," Janet reminded him. "But are you sure you don't mind? It's worth a trial, anyway, and though I'm not afraid of work, I'm nearly certain I shan't be able to tackle all this single-handed. You see, I must have it right or not at all. But if it's a question of money, I'm willing to do with a merely nominal salary, not forgetting the fact that I'm getting a home."

"It isn't a question of money," answered Yates, with rather a musing expression on his face as he began slowly to refill his pipe. "I've got it, and it's precious little use to me now. Queer thing how the dust is apt to roll in on a man when he hasn't the same use for it. Now, if I'd been as independent when my wife was alive as I am now—well, things would have been different. Poor thing, she hated this place. She thought she had been deceived; I suppose she had; but, of course, things don't affect a man in the same way as they do a woman. I shall never forget the night I brought her home. My God! if I'd ever done anything off the straight, I paid for it that night."

The intensity of his tone, the working of his face, the sudden unrest which took hold of him and caused him to rise and roam to and fro the room, struck Janet painfully. It surprised her as well. She had not expected to probe so soon beneath the surface of Courtney's nature, and she saw that he was capable of very deep feeling.

She was conscious of a deepening interest, and of a sympathy and compassion she could not have believed it possible to feel for a stranger.

"I don't know what makes me talk like this to you. Suppose it's because I haven't had a woman about the place for so long. Wait till you see my sister Louie. She'll tell you all about it. She was through the whole tragedy with me. My wife and she were school friends, and Louie told her everything about the life here. But it's just as you said. Women don't realise it till they're up against it. She ought to have come out first on a long visit."

It was all clear to Janet's mind; she saw the gradual unrolling of what had been the tragedy of Courtney's life, the tragedy which had aged him before his time, and brought him grey hairs and deep lines, which he need not have had for another ten years to come.

"I'd like to tell you it all right here, if you don't mind, then you'll understand. She stood it for just three years, then she went off home, taking the boy with her, and she stopped in England for over eighteen months. I was getting desperate, and at last I wrote and told her if she didn't come she could stop at home for good. She did not answer that letter, but started out in about a month's time, and the first intimation I had was that she had died on boardship, and been buried at sea."

He stopped there, and Janet held herself very still, for the poignancy of his tone told that the deeps of his being were stirred.

"That was a horrible thing for a man, and, of course, I blamed myself. I've never ceased blaming myself, because if I had left her in England she probably would have been alive still. The mistake was mine from the beginning. She was not suited to the life, and I ought to have seen it."

"But what could you have done?" asked Janet rather faintly. "If this was your home and your future bound up in it? She was your wife; her place was here."

"That's what Louie says; but she's made of different stuff. Forgive me for telling you all this, Miss Fairweather. I don't know what came over me, but when I saw you sitting there looking so friendly and so kind I felt I wanted you to know so's you could understand things. I don't want you to have any false ideas about me. I'm just a plain, blunt chap, with a brute of a temper that I do my best to keep under. Now I think that's all, and I think you'd better go to bed soon, for I'm sure you must be dead tired. Maybe I'll be off before breakfast with that letter; if so's you could just write it to-night, before you turn in."

"I can do that, of course. But I'll see you in the morning at breakfast. When do you have it?"

"Between six and seven just now, when every minute's precious on the land."

"Well, if it is so precious as that, isn't there a quiet horse of some kind I could drive into Purbeck to-morrow myself? I've been used to horses. I used to drive my father sometimes on his rounds."

Courtney looked at her with growing admiration.

"Now that's uncommonly handy. My sister can't handle a horse yet, though she came out of a hunting county. You'll see the sorry old crock she'll drive the youngster over with to-morrow. It'll make you laugh. No, there isn't anything on the place you could manage at present, and you saw the state of the roads yesterday. I can spare the time; indeed, I must; because it's important to get hold of that Irish help before she's snapped up by somebody else. It'll please Denis; he'll think he's got his old mother with him. He's a good sort of a boy, and I want to keep him, though he has a homestead of his own this side of Saskatoon."

Janet wrote the letter to Biddy Flanagan, and then she went to bed, thinking she was too tired to sleep. But before she knew where she was, sweet sleep descended on her and kept her in dreamless thrall until she was awakened by the sun across her bed. When she looked at her watch and found it was half-past seven, she sprang up in dismay, acutely conscious that on the very first morning she had failed in her duty.

There was not a sound in all the house, and when she had finished her hasty dressing she ran down the stairs to find an empty kitchen-place with the remains of an early breakfast on the table. The kettle was singing merrily on the lighted stove, and she was able to get her own breakfast quickly, still feeling ashamed that she should have fallen so far short of her duty. She was half through her meal before she observed a small piece of paper pinned to the table-cloth. It was a note from Courtney merely saying he was off to Fort Purbeck, and had taken the list of stores she had given him, together with the letter for Mrs. Flanagan. He also hoped she had slept well. It was an odd experience for Janet to find herself utterly alone in this small prairie house, apparently out of hail of all living things. It was quite a relief to her to hear the cluck-cluck of the poultry in the yard, and when she had finished her breakfast she went out to have a look round. There was none of the symmetry or compactness of a Scotch farmsteading about the place; it seemed as if a building had been stuck down wherever it was needed at the moment, and with no consideration for the symmetry of the whole. Space being no object, the big farmyard sprawled on three sides, right down to the wide, deep track that did duty as a road. Beyond it, the fields stretched away as if to the edge of some outermost sea.

About a quarter of a mile distant she could see a black object moving in the open field, and, after concentrating her gaze on it for a few seconds, discerned that it was Denis with his ploughing team. Then she felt less lonely.

The air was delicious beyond all telling, and the mackerel-tinted sky, a dream of beauty, promised all sorts of heavenly conditions to make glad the heart of the tillers of the soil. The miracle of the spring had begun. But there were still streaks of snow here and there, and even from the eaves of the outbuildings hung remnants of the giant icicles which had held them in firm grip the winter through. It had been one of the hardest winters ever known in that comparatively milder region, but the weather-wise predicted an abundant harvest from the well-watered ground.

It was with a singular lightness of heart that she re-entered the house and addressed herself to the duties of the day.

Methodical in all her habits, she set about them purposefully, and with a quite clear and definite idea what she wished to do.

Next day being Sunday, she must prepare some of the food, as had been the invariable custom in her father's house. She had made all the beds and put straight the upstairs rooms, and was busy at the baking-board when she heard through the open door the low, sweet jingle of harness bells. Wiping her hands hastily, she ran out, scarcely expecting that Courtney could have returned yet. A small covered buggy with a long-tailed piebald pony was climbing up the gentle slope from the roadway to the house.

A lady was driving, and a small boy in a blue overcoat and a red woollen cap sat by her side. Janet caught the gleam of his gold hair under the cap, and felt a curious stir at her heart.

The lady in the buggy waved her whip cheerfully, and smiled all over her plump, kindly face.

"At it already, Miss Fairweather?" she called out cheerily. "My brother hardly expected that you would get here till to-day. I came on chance. I'm Mrs. Anderson."

"Yes," said Janet, smiling all over her face, for Mrs. Anderson's look and manner were reassuring. "And this is Billy."

"Yes, this is Billy fretting so dreadfully for his daddy. I couldn't keep him over Sunday. My baby's been sick, or I would have been here yesterday. Well, and how are you? May I take a good look at you?"

"Yes, of course. I hope I'll do," said Janet, entering into the humour of the moment. Then she became conscious of a very keen, rather wistful pair of childish eyes, and, stooping down suddenly, lifted the small, sturdy, blue figure in her arms.

"Do you think I'll do, and that you'll like living with me, Billy?" she asked tenderly, and Louie Anderson, noting the expression of her face, nodded softly to herself as she drew off her big driving gloves.

"George has struck ile," she whispered under her breath and with a very great surprise, for there was no doubt that the new housekeeper was a lady. It was written all over her, and even a dab of flour on her nose could not destroy her natural dignity.

"He'll have to marry her, of course he will," she added under her breath. "And then I'll get time to attend to my own show."

Aloud she asked where Courtney was, and Janet explained, as, leading Billy by the hand, she turned towards the house.

"So you're not frightened or disgusted. When George told me what sort you were, and where he had found you, I had my doubts," said Mrs. Anderson, gazing with approval round the warm, tidy kitchen. "He's had such a bad time, poor chap, and so much of it. I really thought his luck had departed for ever. I'm nine miles away, and I've five children, and a husband that thinks the deluge will descend the moment I'm out of the house. Besides, I haven't had a help myself till three months ago, so my hands were too full to run two shows. Oh, I'm mighty glad to see you! I'd kiss you if you'd let me, and if I though it would help you to stop.

"I wish you would," said Janet, and her face flushed a little under the steady gaze of those very shrewd grey eyes.

"Well, then, I will," cried Mrs. Anderson, and accomplished the deed without more ado. "And I hope you'll stop a bit and make things comfortable for poor old Geo. He's one of the best. He has a temper; all the Courtneys have; but it doesn't last. You won't mind it when you get used to it.

"Well, and how have you found things? I did my best the day I was over, but one pair of hands can't do much in a day, in a place where two men have been batching a whole winter. But you look as if you were capable of anything in the housewifely line. Is it bread you're baking?"

"No, scones. I'll have to learn the breadbaking. Perhaps you can teach me."

"Oh, sure. Get me a cup of tea, Miss Fairweather, and let me sample the scones. They look as if they'd melt in your mouth. We call them biscuits here. Silly—well, a lot of things seem silly because they're new. Oh, I do hope you'll stop. It's the curse of the West that the women we need won't stop. They don't give us a chance; they keep moving on."

Billy, standing very close to Janet, waiting on his buttered scone, lifted lovely eyes of appeal to her face. And when Janet bent over him her heart was in her mouth. But she knew she was going to stop, if need be, for ever and a day.

CHAPTER XIV

NANCY INTERVENES

Bella Fairweather was pulling gooseberries in the garden at The Croft on a hot July afternoon. After a long, cold spring, summer had come with a rush, and, flowers and fruit quickly responding, brought some fresh harvest every day. Bella was far too economical a housewife to neglect anything, or run the risk of the smallest waste. In her thin black delaine frock, and white housewifely overall, with a mushroom hat of black straw to protect her complexion, and a pair of her father's old gloves to keep her hands from the thorns, she made rather a picturesque figure. But her expression as her fingers flew in and out the green bushes, adding to the weight of the basket on her arm, was not very amiable. Things were not going quite as Bella had expected in Balgarnie. Bobby Ludlow, installed seven months ago in her father's place, and now fully established in the district as his respectable successor, had not hitherto appeared to be as appreciative as might have been expected of the influence that had placed him there. Had Bella chosen, she could have sold the practice to someone else, and put a good many spokes in Ludlow's wheel. Two conclusions she had come to in the last six months, and now knew that her father had been so far right concerning Ludlow. He was lazy, and was not quite a gentleman. Not that he had any offensive ways; outwardly he conformed to all the requirements of everyday courtesy, but he failed in the little things, which Dr. Fairweather, with all his brusqueness of manner, had been punctilious about.

The old doctor had been as gallant to the poorest shepherd's wife from the hills as to his richest patient, and had showed them all equal attention. Ludlow, once fully established, committed the grand mistake of being off-hand and domineering with the poor. And as it is the travelling thirds who talk, so the men and women and little children in the cottages weighed up Dr. Ludlow and found him wanting.

With them, however, it was Hobson's choice. There was no doctor nearer than six miles, and when emergencies arose they sent to The Croft as aforetime, though sadly bewailing the change.

Bella had no fault to find with Ludlow in the house. He kept his distance. They met at meals, but his leisure time in the house he spent chiefly in his own room, which was study and consulting-room combined.

So far as Bella's private ambition was concerned, she was no further forward, and she felt her position to be rather a trying one.

Nancy was a good deal out of the house. She was greatly beloved in Balgarnie Manse, and, since Captain and Mrs. Frew had come home on six months' leave, she had been there more than ever. Even her Saturday half-holidays had been taken possession of at the Manse. If they had not, she would have been picking gooseberries now beside Bella in The Croft garden.

Scarcely a year had passed since Dr. Fairweather's death, and Bella was thinking of the changes as she was busy at her housewifely task. From the two who had sought fortune across the seas, Janet was far and way the best correspondent. She was still on the farm in Alberta, and, from her own accounts, seemed happy enough, though Bella certainly thought her accounts of what she had to do exaggerated The Irish help had not been able to accept the invitation out West, and all summer

Janet had been alone, baking and cooking and washing for her new employer and his household. Madge was still at Ravelston Springs in California, and did not write often. When she did, her letters were obscure and unsatisfactory. She said less about herself than Bella could have thought it possible for any ordinary woman to say in a letter.

It may have been imagination, but there were times when Miss Fairweather felt that her social position had not been improved by the new arrangement with Dr. Ludlow. People certainly called less frequently than they did, and invitations, particularly those in quarters which Bella prized, had been conspicuous by their absence of late. This was sufficient to cause her much secret heart-burning, for she was neither so contemptuous as Madge, nor so independent as Janet had been regarding such matters.

She was a smaller-minded woman altogether, and one whom pin-pricks seriously incommoded. All these she visited wrathfully on Bobby Ludlow's head as she picked her green fruit, and pondered what she could do to improve the situation. If she could marry him, she told herself, things would be different; indeed, she would make it the business of her life to see that they were. Certain things she suffered now would be sharply altered, and Bobby himself lifted to a higher plane altogether.

But so far Bobby had not shown the slightest inclination towards matrimony; he continued to behave precisely as if the arrangement, so convenient and advantageous to him, could last for ever.

Bella's thin lips ominously tightened as she filled her basket, but, busy though her brain was, she could not evolve from its recesses any scheme likely to mend matters. She could not propose to Dr. Ludlow, but she felt that something must be done either to bring matters to a crisis, or make some drastic change. She had even wondered whether she would have the courage to emulate Madge and Janet and take a flight into the unknown. For her, however, it would be the last desperate move; she had no love for change. She could live and die in Balgarnie with an absolutely contented and happy mind, provided things were equal and the environment favourable. At the present moment they left much to be desired. Just then she observed the white flutter of Ellen's cap streamers across the shrubberies, and, disentangling herself from a particularly thorny branch, she went to meet her.

"What is it, Ellen? I told you I wasn't at home this afternoon."

"Yes, Miss, I know, but it's Mrs. Frew, and she very particularly wants to see you."

"Mrs. Frew!" quoth Miss Fairweather, and a little flush rose to her face. It was the first time she had deigned to call since her return from India in April, and, having known her as a girl in Balgarnie, Bella had resented the neglect with all her might. She had put it down to the fact that Nancy had been obliged to accept money for teaching Mrs. Frew's children. Little things like that make a difference in social relations, of course, and when one gets poorer one is perhaps more sensitive.

"I've a good mind to say I can't see her, Ellen. Did you tell her I was at home?"

"Yes, Miss, for she was so very particular," said Ellen. "I very nearly brought her out here."

"Is she in the drawing-room?"

"Yes, Miss."

"And is Dr. Ludlow about?" she added as she signed to Ellen to undo the buttons of her overall. On second thoughts she told her to put them in again. "I'll just take my basket in with me and show her what I've been about. After all, though she's Mrs. Captain Frew now, she was only Elsie Dempster once, and if she hadn't kept Miss Nancy this afternoon, I needn't have been out in the blazing sun so long. Just fasten it up again, Ellen."

Ellen obeyed, thinking her own thoughts. Had she been a less staid conservative person, Ellen would have left The Croft any time within the last six months, for she did not like the new *régime*, and Dr. Ludlow himself she mortally hated. Yet he managed to get a good deal of service out of her. That was his way. He managed to get what he wanted by a sort of quiet persistence it was not easy to withstand. He had even caused Miss Fairweather to alter certain household arrangements which had once been as fixed as the laws of the Medes and Persians.

" Bring tea in ten minutes' time, unless I ring, and tell Mary White to put the gooseberries in the outside larder, then they'll keep perfectly right till Monday. If I'd left them in the sun another day, they'd have been too ripe for good jelly."

" Yes, Miss," said Ellen primly. " But I thought you wanted to take the basket in."

" I needn't. I can tell her what I've been doing. The drawing-room, you said? Did you attend to the flowers this morning ? "

" Yes, Miss, everything is right, and the new scones are just ready. Shall I butter some for tea ? "

" Yes, and bring it soon. Take out the best cups—the old china, I mean—and the old silver teapot. You'll find my keys in the basket on the parlour table."

Thus talking, she entered the house, just paused to wash her hands in the little cloakroom, and then proceeded to the drawing-room with a hint of aggressiveness in her manner.

On the way she decided that she would call Mrs. Frew Elsie, just to show that she at least recognised no social distinctions between people who were friends of old standing. But when the tall, elegant figure rose from the sofa to greet her, she could not be familiar, even though Mrs. Frew was smiling in quite a friendly way.

" How do you do, Miss Fairweather ? I hope it isn't inconvenient. It was rather important I should see you this afternoon ; in fact, I had to."

" It's all right," answered Bella a trifle ungraciously. " I've been picking the gooseberries. They couldn't wait another day, and I had counted on Nancy helping me this afternoon."

" Nancy, I'm afraid, is otherwise engaged," said Mrs. Frew, with her pretty smile, which disarmed Bella in spite of her efforts to be cold and stiff. There was no denying Mrs. Frew had charm, and that residence in India, where she was, of course, a person of importance at her husband's station, had wonderfully improved her and given her a self-possession which became her very well.

" Of course, I don't really mind," she remarked more affably. " I quite understand that when you have company at the Manse you don't want to be bothered with the children too much. Has Colonel Motcombe gone yet ? "

" No, he hasn't ; at the present moment he is driving Nancy to the Linn of Cabrach, and, I expect, enjoying himself very much."

Bella stared in complete bewilderment.

" Nancy gone to the Linn of Cabrach with Colonel Motcombe ! Why on earth should she have done that, and why did you or Mrs. Dempster permit it ? "

" Well, we had no just reason for preventing it, Miss Fairweather."

" But I don't understand even yet," said Bella in the same slow, bewildered voice. " What was the object of it? Had you or Mrs. Dempster any message for Nancy to take to Cabrach ? "

" No message. Can't you guess what has happened, Miss Fairweather ? "

" No," said Bella, for once in her life densely stupid, " I can't."

" Well, Colonel Motcombe is in love with Nancy, and he's taken her to the Linn of Cabrach for the purpose of telling her so."

" Merciful goodness ! " said Bella, and the colour rose in her cheek and a curious light came into her eyes. " It can't be true."

" It is true," said Mrs. Frew, and looked as if she enjoyed the telling. " Haven't you even suspected anything ? "

" No, that I haven't ! Nancy has never spoken the Colonel's name to me, though one day I saw her walking through the Three-mile Wood with the children, and he was alongside. I though it queer at the time, but when I spoke to her she only gave a queer bit laugh, and said he was very fond of the bairns, and they of him."

Bella was visibly excited. Mrs. Frew observed it in both looks and manner.

" I think Nancy is a very lucky girl. Colonel Motcombe is a splendid man and my husband's greatest friend."

" He's a lot older than Nancy, surely. He looked to me that day to have grey hair ; in fact, it is grey, for I noticed him in the church too."

" His hair is grey and his age is thirty-six. He's fifteen years older than Nancy, for I asked her age the other day."

" Isn't that very young for a Colonel ? Then do you mean that he will ask her to marry him, Mrs. Frew, this very afternoon ? " asked Bella in an awe-stricken voice.

" I do ; he may be asking her this very minute."

" Has he—has he spoken to you about it ? "

" Oh, often. He was afraid he was too old. It was I who assured him the difference was on the right side. And he's a perfect dear, Miss Fairweather. If I wasn't so much in love with Jack, I should like to marry him myself."

" But Nancy, Nancy ! Elsie, I can't take it in," said Bella with something like a little gasp.

" It's quite true, I do assure you."

" I hope she'll behave properly, that she'll grasp her good fortune and give him the right answer," said Bella with a note of painful anxiety in her voice. " If only I'd had an inkling. I might have pointed out things to her. As we are situated now, Mrs. Frew, and everything so sadly changed, we can't afford to be so particular as we once were."

At this naïve remark Mrs. Frew's happy laugh rang out.

" I assure you there is nothing to be doubtful about where Colonel Motcombe is concerned. He's a very rich man ; his antecedents are irreproachable. He's heir to an estate and a title in Suffolk."

" Mercy me, do you say so, and our wee Nancy ! It can't be true, Elsie Dempster —I beg your pardon, Mrs. Frew, but you'll excuse me. Of course, this has taken me quite by surprise, and I hardly know what it is I am saying."

" I quite understand," said Mrs. Frew rather gently, for there was something in Bella Fairweather's manner, about her whole personality, which struck a pathetic note. She was so pitifully sordid in her views.

" That would have spoiled everything. Bella, believe me," she said kindly, " I don't think Nancy will refuse him. I was talking to mother about it this afternoon, and she advised me to come round and have a talk with you about it. She was sure you had no idea."

" No, I hadn't, and I don't think Nancy has treated me quite fairly in the matter."

" Oh, why do you say that ? What could the child say ? She was not even sure, though the signs were pretty unmistakable. Don't be foolish, Bella, but just be as pleasant and kind to Nancy as you know how. Everybody loves her, and will, if she goes to India. She is the sort that will make friends everywhere, and if the Colonel has his way, you won't have her long."

" What ! " gasped Bella. " Do you mean to say he would ask for a marriage soon, in less than a year, maybe ? "

" Sure. His leave expires in October, and he's dead sure to want to take her with him. He came here only for a week, and he's stopped three, which shows how hard he is hit. I am surprised he has not been here before now, but, being able to see Nancy every day at the Manse, and on Sunday at the kirk, I suppose he postponed it. But you'll have him to-day, Bella, as sure as fate, and I thought it would be only kind to prepare you."

" So it was, so it was. I appreciate it very much, Elsie," said Bella warmly. " But Nancy ! I just can't get over it. Hush ! this is Ellen with the tea. Not a word in front of her, in case there should be any disappointment."

Ellen came in, and in her quiet, efficient way set the tea-table, and was quickly gone. The moment the door closed behind her again Bella sat forward with an air of excited eagerness.

" Did I hear you say he was heir to a title and estate, Elsie ? "

" You did ; but I've no doubt you'll have the pleasure of hearing Colonel Motcombe's credentials from his own lips before very long. Now tell me how Madge and Janet are getting on. Nancy seems to know a good deal about Janet, but not so much about Madge."

" Oh, they've both been very successful," said Bella primly as she put hot water in the cups. " Janet particularly has a good place, keeping house for a very rich *gentleman*-farmer," she added with much emphasis on the foreword. " She seems to be mistress of everything, and to be very happy. Madge is not one of the kind that settles down. She's been in several places already, but she said when she went away that she wanted to see a bit of the world. And she seems to be liking it fine. Do you and Captain Frew go out again in October, then ? " she added as if unable to keep off the one engrossing theme.

" Yes, and we are taking the children, for we shall be at the Hills for the next two years, and it will be delightful if we have Colonel Motcombe and Nancy beside us, though, of course, she will be socially my superior, don't you see, my husband being only second-in-command."

" Oh ! " said Bella, with a small gasp, and, in her nervous excitement, suffered a thin stream of tea to trickle across her best lace afternoon teacloth.

Mrs. Frew, not without a sense of humour, was keenly enjoying the sensation of the afternoon. She knew Bella Fairweather very well, and remembered all her little idiosyncrasies, which time had but served to accentuate.

" Mother was wondering what you would do when Nancy has gone if everything arranges itself nicely. And I'm sure it will, for Colonel Motcombe has the knack of getting his own way in most things," said Mrs. Frew as she contemplatively stirred her tea, at the same time keeping her eye on Bella's face. She saw the pale colour deepen again, and a peculiar line of hardness come about the mouth.

" It will complicate my life, of course, but nobody considers me much," she said rather hardly. " I've had to stand pretty much alone all my life, even when my father was here. But, of course, I would never stand in Nancy's way."

" Of course not ; but what will you do ? " inquired Mrs. Frew with quiet persistence. " You can't possibly stop on here with Dr. Ludlow, unless you marry him. Mother thinks that's the only way out of the difficulty."

Bella did not speak for a minute ; then she gave a small, nervous laugh.

" Oh, well, such a thing might happen. I've—I've had to keep him at arm's length, of course, but now it will be different. I don't mind telling you that probably that will be the end of it, Elsie. But I rely on you keeping it very quiet. You know what Balgarnie is, and how they can tear folk to ribbons. One can't be too careful about one's doings. I've had to walk very circumspectly, I assure you, in a most difficult situation. I should never have put myself into it if it had not been that I had to keep the home together for Nancy."

Again a faint sigh of pity for this plain, unattractive, middle-aged woman stirred Elsie Dempster's heart. She was so happy herself, and she was quite aware what hard things—nay, uncharitable things—were said about Bella Fairweather in the town. " I hope everything will be settled comfortably, and that you will be happy too, Bella," she said very kindly as she rose to go. " No, I can't stop any longer. I must be getting back to mother. She isn't so well to-day. She's beginning to fret already about the children going away, but she really hasn't been able to care for them in the last year."

She shook hands very warmly with Miss Fairweather when she accompanied her to the door.

" You're sure there's no mistake, Mrs. Frew. You see, I haven't taken it in yet," said Bella at the door.

" There's no mistake, you'll have to interview Colonel Motcombe presently, I feel sure. Don't look so alarmed. He's a very harmless and quite charming person."

Bella's face wore a very odd expression as she slowly walked back to the drawing-room after seeing her visitor to the shrubbery gate.

Then she remembered her ridiculous overall, and sharply rang the nearest bell.

" Unbutton my pinafore, Ellen, and take away the empty cups and bring clean ones, and a clean cloth as well. Miss Nancy may be back any moment, bringing a very important, particular gentleman with her. Mrs. Frew? Oh, yes, she has improved. I would hardly have known her again. That's what marriage can do for folk, Ellen Jeffreys."

CHAPTER XV

AN EVENTFUL AFTERNOON

BELLA FAIRWEATHER went back to the drawing-room in a perfect ferment of agitation. Hitherto Nancy had been the one member of the family who did not count. Nobody troubled about her; she never made any fuss or claimed consideration, but just slipped about like a wandering sunbeam, giving forth brightness, and asking nothing for herself. The world was a good place, and all its inhabitants kind to that sweet soul, born without selfishness or guile. None of the sisters, except perhaps Janet, had fully appreciated the deep sweetness of Nancy's nature. To think that she of all the four should be the first to obtain settlement in life, and such a settlement, filled Bella with a surprise that was almost consternation.

She walked up and down the ugly early-Victorian drawing-room, working her hands in front of her, trying to take in the stupendous news, and to face it in all its bearings. Nancy to be married before the year was out, to become a person of importance, the great lady of a station, and to have a title in front of her! It was all tremendous, unthinkable, just like a fairy-tale. In about half an hour's time, when she heard the swing of the front gate and the sound of approaching steps and voices, she was in such a ferment that the red burned in her cheeks.

But she controlled herself sufficiently to hasten to the window, and from behind the curtain watch them as they came to the door. Sht thought she would be able to tell from Nancy's face what had been the issue of that momentous drive. It was a good omen that the Colonel had returned with her; a man whose offer had been refused would have found some pretext for not bringing her home. Nancy's sweet face was softly flushed, and her eyes shining. Her beauty suddenly struck her eldest sister with something like a pang. Why had nobody noticed it before? why had nobody guessed that Nancy possessed in her own personality the most valuable assets in the family, that hers were gifts that no money has the power to buy? She was the embodiment of youth at its sweetest and best, of maidenhood in all its first appealing charm, so sweetly unconscious, so entirely simply and natural, that the lean, brown-faced man with the soldier's carriage and the air of breeding thought she was the most peerless creature his eyes had ever rested on. He was a handsome man, a little past his first youth, but if he had been sixty instead of thirty-six, he would still have been eligible in Bella's eyes. She turned to meet them at the drawing-room door with a beaming smile. She heard them laughing together in the hall, though when the Colonel opened the door Nancy hung back shyly.

But when she saw only her sister, she recovered herself.

"We were afraid you had folk to tea, Bella," she said simply. "This is Colonel Motcombe, who is staying at The Manse."

"Yes, of course. I've seen him about the town and at church," said Bella graciously. "Very pleased to see you, indeed, Colonel Motcombe. Please sit down, and we shall have tea immediately. You will want it, perhaps, after your walk."

"We have been driving most of the afternoon, Miss Fairweather," said the Colonel after they had seated themselves. "Your sister was so kind as to let me take her to Cabrach after lunch. It is a beautiful drive, but there are many in this neighbourhood."

The Colonel, though a man of the world, was a little nonplussed by the contrast between the two sisters. Miss Fairweather's gauche, stiff manner was so different from Nancy's simple charm. And he was a little shy of his errand in spite of his happiness. He wondered how he would ever get the words out. Ellen, acting strictly upon instructions here, appeared with the tea, and lingered longer than she need have done, her mistress thought, out of pure curiosity, about the unexpected caller. Ellen had been long enough a servant at The Croft to take a personal and proprietary interest in all its concerns. Her pride had been hurt no less than Miss Fairweather's at the changed social conditions consequent upon the upheaval in the Fairweather family.

She was satisfied that, as a lover for Miss Nancy, the Colonel left nothing to be desired, and she was very important with her news in the kitchen, being in no doubt whatever as to the errand on which he had come.

"You admire this countryside, Colonel Motcombe?" said Bella, as she began to warm the cups for the second time that afternoon. "I have heard from Mrs. Frew that you have prolonged your stay much beyond its original intention." Never had poor Bella made use of more dignified and conventional language, and never had she appeared so obviously ill at ease.

The Colonel gravely smiled.

"I am afraid the country has little to do with it, Miss Fairweather; this is the attraction," he said moving quite openly to Nancy's side. "I may as well out with it. Nancy has promised to be my wife, and I'm here this afternoon to ask your consent, as you are her guardian."

"Oh, yes, why not? Very pleased, I am sure," said Bella rather hurriedly. "Oh course, it's a very great surprise, and we haven't known you very long, Colonel Motcombe. Indeed, this is the first time I've spoken to you, but, of course, any friend of our dear Manse folk, and acquainted with Captain Frew, must be—well—all that we could desire."

She paused, quite breathless, and Nancy felt sorry for her.

"Then you won't refuse your consent, Miss Fairweather?" said the Colonel with evident relief. "But you don't know yet the extent of my presumption. I have only three months' more leave, and you won't ask me, I hope, to go back to India without Nancy."

"Oh, no, surely not—that is, I hardly know. Of course, it's all very sudden," said Bella, putting five lumps of sugar steadily into the cup one after the other. "What does Nancy think?"

"Oh, Bella, I hardly know," answered Nancy. "I haven't thought about it yet, but—but probably it will be as Colonel Motcombe likes."

She smiled up at him with an expression of perfect trust, such as sent another and very unusual pang to Bella's starved heart. It was the most beautiful thing she had ever seen in her life, though she was not sure whether she ought to approve of it. She saw the soldier's keen grey eye soften into an extraordinary tenderness.

"Of course, I understand that it is all very sudden, and that I have to lay my credentials before you, Miss Fairweather. You don't know anything about me, but you are at liberty to ask Jack Frew for my character. As to my people, it is my hope that you will spare me Nancy for a week. My mother lives in Suffolk, and she will, of course, want to see a great deal of the dear little girl I am going to marry."

"Oh, yes, of course—why not?" repeated Bella in her rather helpless fashion. "Oh course, it will be terrible for me when Nancy goes away, Colonel Motcombe, for only she and I are left. If only our dear father had been alive to meet you and settle everything. You quite understand that everything is very sadly changed for us since his death."

"Oh, quite," answered the Colonel quietly and sincerely, though he had a queer feeling that the woman speaking to him was not herself altogether sincere. Again, he wondered at the vagaries of nature that had cast these two sisters in such different mould.

By and by, under the spell of his quiet, kindly manner, the strain gradually left Bella's face and manner, and she became more normal in every way. After about an hour the Colonel said he must be getting back, and asked Nancy if she would walk a little way with him. Nancy smiled and looked at Bella, who primly smiled back.

" Why, certainly, my dear—whatever Colonel Motcombe wishes in reason—and, of course, Colonel, you understand that so long as you are in Balgarnie, you are very welcome to this house and all its contains. I hope you will make yourself at home in it, as you are to become one of the family. Perhaps I don't express myself very well; I am a plain woman, but sincere. I think you will find that is a characteristic of the Fairweathers, outspoken sincerity, and even if our tongues are sharp sometimes, our hearts are in the right place."

It was quite a long speech for Bella, and it astonished Nancy very much. The child was happy, and made no attempt to hide it; her love had gone out to her soldier-lover, the first that had ever knocked at the door of her young heart. It was one of the most beautiful love-stories Balgarnie had ever seen. But it would not have long to study it.

Bella accompanied them to the door and then ran in and pulled the drawing-room bell with a force which brought Ellen Jeffreys running to answer it.

" Ellen Jeffreys, look out of that window, quick ! "

" Yes, Miss Fairweather ! " said Ellen a little breathless but nothing loth.

" Do you see that splendid gentlemanly man, Colonel Motcombe, a friend of Captain Frew's, and his superior in the regiment ? Well, he is going to be Miss Nancy's husband. What do you think of that ? "

" I expected it, Miss Bella, the moment I set eyes on them in this room," said Ellen with great calmness.

" And it's a great lady she's going to be some day, my lady, indeed ! And at the station in India she'll take precedence of Mrs. Frew. And almost immediately she's going into Suffolk to a great castle of a house," said Bella, drawing on her imagination, " for the purpose of being introduced to his folk. That's the next chapter of the Fairweather history, Ellen Jeffreys, and it will be very good for some folk to hear it. I do not forbid you to mention it with discretion where you think fit."

So saying, she swept with great dignity from the room and into the hall. As she stepped into the hall, Dr. Ludlow came in by the front door, and, with his careless nod, was about to proceed along the passage to the consulting-room. Bella felt unable to let him pass without challenge.

" Did you meet Nancy, Dr. Ludlow ? "

" I passed them in the lane as we drove up to the stable gate," he answered. " That tall chap was with her, that's been living at the Manse for so long."

" Colonel Motcombe," Bella explained with great dignity and importance. " They're engaged."

" What ? " cried Bobbie, exhibiting surprise sufficient to satisfy Miss Fairweather, who nodded delightedly.

" Have you had your tea yet ? No ? Well, come into the drawing-room and have some with me. It isn't cleared yet, and Ellen will bring a fresh pot."

At an ordinary time Dr. Ludlow would have invented any excuse to escape such an ordeal, but at the moment his curiosity happened to be aroused, and he wished to hear the particulars. He accordingly followed her into the drawing-room, at the same time making a joke about the rarity of his visits there.

" I don't believe I've been more than a couple of times in this room since I came to The Croft, Miss Fairweather."

"That isn't my fault, Dr. Ludlow," said Bella with a touch of archness. "We always sit here on Sunday afternoons."

"You don't invite me to sit with you, though," he answered readily enough. "It's a fine room; the best in the house. It would make an uncommonly good consulting-room. I wonder Dr. Fairweather didn't annex it himself long ago."

"Oh, it is much too good for that," said Bella reproachfully. She regarded the practice with very little respect. It was merely a means to an end. The idea of putting her cherished drawing-room to such base uses would at another time have horrified her. But her mood was too uplifted to be jarred by such a trifle.

"So they're engaged? Well, I congratulate him," said Ludlow with such heartiness that Bella looked at him with a sudden, quick, jealous glance.

Why he should say that, when it was perfectly obvious that all the benefits, all the congratulations, were on the other side, she could not imagine, but something prevented her from asking why he said it.

"*We* are to be congratulated, I think, in getting such a brother-in-law. He is very rich and well born. Mrs. Frew has been here this afternoon pleading his cause with me," said Bella with great unction. "He is the heir to great estates, and even to a title. Just think of that for our little Nancy. Could you have believed it possible?"

"It's no more than she deserves," said Ludlow, and there was no doubt of the sincerity with which he spoke. He, too, had been touched and uplifted by the sweet wholesomeness of that beautiful nature, and there was even a ring of genuine regret in his voice.

"I can't think what everybody sees in Nancy; she's so young, and her mind so unformed," said Bella with a sudden plaintiveness. "It is a very good thing for her that Colonel Motcombe is so much older, and also that she will have the benefit of Mrs. Frew's friendship and advice in India, though, of course, socially the Colonel's wife will have to take precedence." Here Bella preened herself like some conceited bird. "But Mrs. Frew was very nice and sweet about it, and, of course, Nancy is far too well bred to give herself any airs."

"And when is it going to be?" inquired Ludlow; but Bella, with her natural secretiveness, put her finger on her lip at the entrance of Ellen with the third pot of tea for the drawing-room, a most unprecedented occurrence at The Croft.

When they were alone again, she assumed an air of great importance.

"It will have to be very soon. Colonel Motcombe is determined to take Nancy back to India with him in the late autumn."

Bobby Ludlow gave a low whistle of astonishment.

"Seems pretty hot work," he said with one of the vulgar touches which refined people did not like; but Bella was too excited to notice it.

"It's inevitable; and before the wedding can take place she will have to go to the Colonel's estate in Suffolk, to make the acquaintance of his people. Oh, Nancy has her hands full enough for the next three months."

"She has that," assented Dr. Ludlow, and as he drank his tea with relish he glanced with a certain furtiveness at Miss Fairweather.

A frankly selfish man, he immediately began to wonder how this event in the Fairweather family would affect him.

"It's rather rough on you, Miss Fairweather, isn't it? You'll be left stranded here."

"Yes, I will," assented Bella, keeping her eyes demurely on the tray. "But, of course, one has to sacrifice one's feelings in a case like this. It would never do to stand in my sister's light."

"Very good of you, I'm sure," murmured Dr. Ludlow, and the same furtive look lingered in his eyes.

"I shall be very busy, of course, for a good long time getting Nancy's things ready," said Bella with a little confidential touch. "But at the same time I shall have to be thinking about myself and what I shall do afterwards."

"I suppose you will," assented Dr. Ludlow rather heavily. "I hope—I hope that doesn't mean that you will be thinking of leaving The Croft."

"It will mean just that, Dr. Ludlow," said Bella with great clearness.

"Probably I shall go to Canada or to California to join one of my sisters. I shall not be able to make up my mind finally until I have written to them and heard their opinion. Of course, they will be as much surprised as I was."

"And what will you do with this house?" inquired Ludlow bluntly, now thoroughly awakened.

"I don't know. Either it will have to be let or sold. I shall, of course, have to consult Mr. Maclaine. The furniture will have to be divided. I don't suppose my sisters would agree to selling it."

Dr. Ludlow set down his empty cup, declined a second, and began to walk about the floor in rather a perturbed manner.

He did not like the prospect; it meant the setting of a limit to his personal comfort, which, under Miss Fairweather's roof, had been assured. Then his professional position had been consolidated, and he did not at all relish the prospect of going back to nondescript housekeeping with a person who had nothing at stake. Bella had really befriended him, she had been at considerable pains to keep the practice together for him, and he was fully aware of the value of such a service. Again he looked at her, and though he neither admired nor loved her, he admitted to himself that it might have been worse. Suddenly he stopped midway between the window and the sofa on which she sat, and regarded her with an intentness which made her colour rise.

"You must know that all this will be a serious business for me, Miss Fairweather. Somehow, I've got to imagine myself rooted here. You talk of selling or letting the house and dividing the furniture, just as if I didn't exist."

"Oh, no, Dr. Ludlow," she answered, with a faint laugh. "I assure you I have thought of you a good deal, even this very afternoon."

"I don't see any sign of it. If you had, you couldn't speak so calmly about kicking me out—that's precisely what it amounts to," he said ruefully. "I think it's too bad, myself, and it just shows what you must think of me."

"Oh, no!" she repeated again with as much emphasis as she dared. "I assure you I am very sorry, but you must see for yourself that the existing arrangement, which, after all, was only an experiment, could not possibly go on after my sister goes away."

"I see that, of course, but—but it is possible another arrangement might be made. I needn't beat about the bush. I don't want to leave The Croft, and I don't want you to leave it. Will you marry me, Miss Fairweather? I believe we could be happy enough together. We are both sensible, middle-aged people, and we have got to know one another pretty well in the last nine months."

"Have we?" asked Bella under her breath; but aloud she answered quite steadily. "Yes, I suppose we have."

"Then will you?" inquired Bobbie Ludlow with undisguised eagerness. "I'll do my best to make you a good husband, and we needn't wait. We might even get married before the Colonel and Miss Nancy, and be in a position to send them off with our blessing."

At this Bella laughed very happily, and answered, "Yes."

CHAPTER XVI

ON THE BRINK

JANET FAIRWEATHER was very, very tired. She felt her limbs and her back aching as she crossed the big, wide farmyard with the egg-basket over her arm, the child Billy in a cotton overall, and an old linen slouch hat trotting happily by her side. Physical weariness, however, is no hardship to a happy woman, and Janet undoubtedly was that.

Every morning she rose on the stroke of six o'clock and was pretty hard at it all day till nine o'clock at night, when she went to bed.

Biddy Flanagan, though full of specious promises, had never been able to cut herself adrift from the doubtful joys of Winnipeg, and all the summer through Janet had done the work at Markyates single-handed. While the men were slack and waiting for the harvest, Denis had been able to help, and even Courtney himself was willing to lend a hand; but now, since the middle of August, when the first sheaf was cut, till now, when the threshers were busy with the grain, she had been without help.

The hard, physical labour had told on her; she was very thin and brown and eager-looking, but her face wore a happy expression, and her grey-blue eyes were as clear as the sea. She had on a frock of grey linen, turned well back at the wrists, and very low at the throat, and a white apron above that to protect it. For when a woman has to be her own laundress, she learns to be careful about the wear of washing-frocks.

"Auntie," said Billy's thin treble, "is it to-morrow we're going to Fort Purbeck with Daddy?"

"Yes, darling, if the threshers get away to-night, and I do hope they will," she answered, glancing across the slope to the further field, where the whirr and song of the threshing-machine could be clearly heard.

Courtney had told her they would be gone before sundown, and that she need not prepare them another meal. For more than a fortnight she had cooked three solid meals per diem for seven men, and she was getting very tired of it. Indeed, her longing for the quiet of the winter, which Mrs. Anderson had assured her would compensate for all the rush of the short summer, had during the last days become almost unbearable.

Also she was just a little homesick, and to-morrow was Nancy's wedding-day. All day she had been thinking of the dear child whom they all loved, and of the wonderful adventure of her life, and of what lay in front of her. She had had several letters, including one from Colonel Motcombe, which had entirely satisfied her. Beyond a doubt the man loved Nancy, and seemed to have no desire but to make her happy. It had been the letter of a simple, sincere, manly man, who had managed to carry with him into middle life the heart of a boy. Bella had been married to Bobbie Ludlow on the first day of September, so that Nancy's wedding was taking place comfortably, as it should, from the old home. The announcement of Bella's intended marriage had not affected Janet at all. It was merely an arrangement of which she had expected to hear any day. But her heart was yearning over Nancy, and her thoughts had wandered very far from the Canadian prairie back to the old garden of The Croft, where the red rowans were blazing at the gate, and all the autumn tints glowing brown and yellow in the Balgarnie woods.

The child, with his quick perception, detected something amiss in the dear companion of his days. His little warm hand stole into hers as they approached the back door, and when she sat down suddenly on the verandah steps he stood in front of her and looked into her face with a wistful expression on his own. Then he saw, and great was his consternation, that her eyes were full of tears.

"You're crying, Auntie! does it hurt somewhere?" he asked almost tenderly.

Janet caught the child's hand and pressed it to her heart.

"It hurts just here, Billy." Then, seeing the child's puzzled look, she added with a faint half-smile: "You know how you used to feel when you were left a long time at Auntie Louie's without seeing Daddy? It's just like that."

"But Daddy's here," he answered, still looking puzzled as he turned his eyes in the direction of the threshing-field.

"Yours is, but mine isn't. I'm homesick, Billy," she answered, and, pulling the child closely to her, she rested her cheek for a moment against his.

"They've stopped!" he cried suddenly, with all the inconsequence of youth which cannot happily concentrate long on any given theme. "Look, there isn't any more smoke, and all the sheafs is gone."

"Thank God!" muttered Janet under her breath. "Well, little one, we'd better go in and get supper."

"May I run over to the field and come back with Daddy, now they've stopped, Auntie?"

"Surely, if you don't get in the way and worry him," she answered, and at this permission the child danced off down the slope, a flying figure in blue, very dear to Janet Fairweather's heart.

It was only physical weariness that had made the sudden wave of feeling sweep over her; she knew that she would not like to go back to Balgarnie, that nothing on earth would induce her to go. She would not change places with Bella, now absolute mistress of The Croft and of Bobbie Ludlow's destiny; nor even with Nancy, to-morrow to wed her gallant soldier-lover. Janet had found her niche; she was needed and loved on that lonely prairie homestead, where she had made home for Courtney and his little son. She made herself busy indoors, removing the trestle table which had been fitted up for the accommodation of the threshers, and with an odd look of relief she pulled back the little old one from the wall, the cosy family table that was just big enough for their needs.

Then, as it was only half-past five, she went upstairs to put on a clean frock and brush her hair, feeling that the occasion was one for to mark by special attention. From her windows, which opened on the balcony above the verandah, she could see the big lumbering train of the thresher and its waggons getting up steam again to move off to the next homestead. And about fifteen minutes later the menfolk and little Billy returned to the house. She met them at the door with a smile.

"They've really gone, haven't they?" she asked brightly, as she looked at Courtney's sun-browned face. "I can hardly believe my luck. Oh, I am glad! But I feel rather mean not having given them supper first. Are you sure they didn't expect it?"

"No, they wanted to get to Schreiber's before dark. Don't worry about them. I'm glad to get quit, too; now we'll have the place to ourselves."

He noted with approval, though Janet did not think he observed at all, how trim and immaculate was her white frock, how soft and winsome her face. Something crept over Courtney's heart: a sudden thrill of thankfulness for his mercies, for the priceless gift of this woman's willing ministry for him and his.

"I'd speak to-night," he muttered to himself as he made his hasty toilet in his own room, "if I wasn't afraid it would spoil things. I'm mightily afraid of that. I daren't risk it."

Janet was conscious of something in the air; she could not tell what; something which stirred her pulses and set her heart beating oddly, which brought something in her throat and made it difficult for her to eat. And with it all there was an ever-deepening sense of happiness and mystery ; she felt as if she were on the brink of some lovely land over which a veil hung which might be lifted at any moment. After supper, Denis, who had been kept hard at it for two weeks, went off for a pow-wow with a neighbour at the next homestead, and after Janet had cleared the table, she put Billy to bed.

" I told Daddy you was hurtin'," said Billy as she began to undress him. " He asked where it was, and I showed him, but he didn't say nuthin'."

" Oh, Billy, you ought not to have done that ! " said Janet, and hid the flame of her face in the child's brown, sweet neck. " You and me can't have any more little secrets if you tell them to other people."

" Not uzzer people," he said wistfully. " Only Daddy. And he knows everything. He's thinkin' of something to make you well. When he's not sayin' much, like to-night, he's thinkin' about makin' people well, I know."

Janet laughed as she sprang to her feet.

" You're a foolish, fanciful little boy. Now do you know that Monday you and I are going to begin lessons in earnest, A B C, and counting up little sums, so that you'll be ready to trot off to school with Rosie and little Elgar in the spring ? "

The child nodded and yawned deeply, and when he knelt down presently to say his prayers, his voice began to grow rather faint, and before he had got to Amen, he was fast asleep.

" Bless him," said Janet as she lifted him up and laid him in his cot, which stood at the other side of his father's bed, into which he would creep sometimes in the night if he happened to awake.

He did not wake up, and before she left the room she stood just a moment by the cot shading the candle with her hand and looking down upon his face. He was not in the least like his father. Mrs. Anderson had assured Janet again and again that he was the image of his mother, who must, Janet thought, have been a beautiful woman. She wondered, as she stood there in the flickering light, whether his mother knew that another woman was doing her best to mother her child. That wonder was still on her face when she descended the creaking stair and passed once more into the living-room. It was a very still and beautiful night for the late October, quite warm and delicious, with a star-gemmed sky above, and a big red moon rising up on the far horizon, away, Janet sometimes said, at the back of beyond. She could feel the whiff of Courtney's tobacco smoke, and knew that he was sitting on the verandah chair in front of the windows ; indeed, she could just see the broad outline of his back through the panes. She had some little things to do in the kitchen, but presently he pulled his chair along and looked in.

" Don't do any more ; you look dead tired. Come out here and sit down a bit. It's glorious out here. No, don't bring your knitting ; if you do I warn you I'll chuck it into the well."

She laughed a little.

" You won't. It's a merely mechanical exercise, and my fingers are uneasy when they're idle." She stepped out as she spoke, and Courtney rose from his chair, because it was the most comfortable one, and having set it at an angle where the light from the lamp on the kitchen table could shine on her face, made her sit down. Then he planted himself on the topmost step of the verandah, not very far from her feet.

" I must rig up a lamp out here if these fine evenings are going to last."

" When does your winter begin ? " she asked, leaning back on the comfortable lounge, conscious at once of her great weariness and a delicious sense of rest.

" Oh, it depends. I've seen weather like this right on into November and even early December, but when all the flame is off the maple, we begin to look out. Now we can have a minute to breathe, and to get about a bit. Tell me, are you fed up with things generally, and with Canada and Markyates in particular ? "

" No," said Janet in surprise. " I'm tired, that's all. Do I look fed up, as you call it ? "

" You look——" said Courtney quickly, and then suddenly stopped as if afraid to let himself go. " Say, what was that Billy was telling me about your being homesick ? Is that really so ? I've been hoping all night it isn't."

Janet let her hands drop on her knee a moment, and looked away beyond him into the dusky night.

" I'm thinking a good bit of them at home, that's all, principally about my little sister Nancy. She's to be married to-morrow at half-past two o'clock. I'd give—yes, I believe I'd give ten years of my life if I could be spirited away just for twenty-four hours back to Balgarnie, so that I could be at her wedding."

" Ten years of your life—that's a goodish slice ; and I don't think we could spare it," he said frankly. " To-morrow, at half-past two, is it ? Well, what do you say for you and I to get up early to-morrow morning and have a ride into Fort Purbeck, and send them a cable ? If we got there by half-past eight we'd just manage to hit it, I do believe. It took a cable just seven hours to get through to my mother once. Would you like to do it ? "

" Yes, I should. I've been thinking about it," said Janet, flushing a little at his kind thought.

" Well, if you're not too tired, we'll start at half-past six. Or I could take it myself, if you like. There's nothing pushing now for a bit, and we can take a little breathing space and live like Christians."

" Oh, thank you very much, but I think I'd like to come. It's lovely in the early mornings. I daresay Denis could see to Billy when he awakes, which won't be before nine, at least. He's such a little sleepy-head in the mornings. But don't you think he looks a lot better just lately ? To-night, when I was undressing him, I thought he was quite fat."

" Fat—of course he is fat, and as happy as a king. And so the little beggar ought. What do you think he said to me as we crossed from the field to-night ? "

Janet made no answer, but began to knit as if for dear life.

" He is a great chatterbox, and nobody must pay any heed to him."

" He said, ' Don't let Auntie be homesick, Daddy, for fear she goes away. What did we do before she came ? It was horrid, wasn't it ? ' That was a poser for me, and I didn't give him an answer. What do you suppose we did do, or could do if, by any appalling chance, you should happen to go back on us ? "

" There are other people," answered Janet ; but the words fell faintly, very faintly, from her trembling lips.

" There isn't anybody else for Billy and me," said Courtney as he rose to his feet and put out his pipe. Then he began to walk to and from the verandah, as if pursued by some spirit of unrest.

" I don't know how to thank you for all you've done for us this summer, and particularly since the harvest and the threshing began. You must know how I wish I could have spared you. You see how it is here. Money can't buy things we want. My sister Louie had been going through precisely the same experience. But there are very few who do that horrible drudgery so willingly and so efficiently as you."

" Don't call it that," said Janet with a quite cheerful note in her voice. " I enjoy it ; and just see how well I am ! Hard work never killed anybody yet. It's only worry and anxiety and other horrid things, and I'm looking forward to the long, quiet winter Mrs. Anderson has promised me when you and Denis do all the chores, and I shall be a lady at large, only cooking an appetising meal for you occasionally as a reward for good conduct."

She laughed, and so did Courtney, but there was a vibrant note of feeling in his voice.

" It's a lovely prospect, and I wish to God I could have it in front of me for the rest of my life. Could you——"

At the moment an unexpected sound interrupted them and brought Courtney to an abrupt stop, while Janet sprang to her feet.

" It's a buggy, or a team, Mr. Courtney, and it's coming here."

" So it is. What can be up, I wonder? Surely something wrong at Schreiber's or Willy Kerr's. I'll see. Why, here it is, close on us."

The heavy breath of a tired horse and the jingle of its harness beat upon the immediate air, and on the track a few yards away they saw the gleam of the lamps. Courtney stepped forward, and Janet, oddly excited, leaned over the low rail. Presently something strange gripped her as a loud, clear, half-laughing voice smote the stillness of the air. " There you are at last, Janet Fairweather. Sure, and it's the back of beyond, and no mistake. Yes, it's me, Madge, in the flesh, and mighty glad to see you, I can tell you, and to get to the end of the most ghastly journey on earth."

CHAPTER XVII

THE INVASION

MADGE in the flesh, Madge, radiant and beautiful, laughing from under the brim of her fascinating travelling-hat, and taking possession of the situation all in a moment. It was Janet who looked stupid and put out. Madge appeared triumphant, sure of her welcome. She kissed Janet lightly, but it was at Courtney she looked.

" I suppose I ought to apologise, Mr. Courtney, for taking you unawares like this. But I've heard of the big hospitality of your big country, and I've come to put it to the proof. I'm down on my luck, and I've come to see my own sister, and to get a little advice from her. She always has been the seer of the family. May I come in ? "

While she listened to these words, Janet thought of everything : of the upset Madge would be in the house, of the fact that she would have to share her room, sit at the board with them, be there all the time.

And something in her heart said dismally that there was nothing else she wanted less in the whole wide world.

But she drew herself up sharply, for, after all, Madge was her sister, and they were both stranded in a foreign land, and blood ought to be thicker than water.

" Why didn't you write, Madge ? Then we could have arranged everything and met you properly. I'm sure Mr. Courtney won't mind you paying me a little visit."

" No, indeed, Miss Madge, any sister or friend of Miss Fairweather's can never be otherwise than welcome to Markyates."

" Thank you. I felt sure you would speak like that. I gathered that impression of you from Janet's letters," said Madge graciously as she began to unswathe the folds of the mist-grey veil in which her head was enshrouded. " What about the man, Mr. Courtney ? he has driven me from Fort Purbeck station. Perhaps you would kindly settle with him. I am so tired, I only know now I've got here how tired I am."

She threw herself as she spoke into the lounge chair which Janet had vacated, and leaned back with a little air of abandon Janet remembered of yore. She was changed, had grown thinner, a little less ruddy of colour, but the old subtle, odd charm was there, in greater degree.

Janet suddenly felt herself a homely, uninteresting, everyday sort of woman, for whom an apron was the fitting dress.

" You look well, Jen, though thinner. Comfortable here ? I never could do it myself, if it's true you're doing all the work. But for that sort of man, well, perhaps I might even try."

She laughed as she spoke, and the flame leaped high in Janet's cheeks. Courtney was not more than a few paces away, quietly paying the driver of the buggy out of his own pocket, Madge not so much as offering her purse.

" I say, Madge, you'll have to pay, of course," she murmured in a low voice. " We simply can't let him. I've got change. I'll get it."

" Oh, don't trouble. I haven't change, and, anyway, we'll settle to-morrow," said Madge, smiling serenely. " Always the same old Jen, worrying over trifles like the split infinitive. He's got it, let him pay; it's what men are for, anyway. All the chances are theirs; we have to get along by our wits as best we can."

The undertone of bitterness in her voice immediately died away, and the cloud from her face, however, when Courtney stepped on to the verandah again and suggested to Janet that the man should have a sandwich and a drink.

"Yes, of course," murmured Janet, and disappeared into the lighted kitchen to procure the necessary refreshment.

"You've had a long journey, Miss Fairweather," said Courtney, leaning against the post of the verandah and regarding her with undoubted interest.

"Yes, from Seattle. It's a ghastly journey, isn't it? so many changes and stops; and, oh, these Canadian hotels, the little ones, I mean, at side stations. I really tried to stop the night at Fort Purbeck, but after I had eaten my supper, my spirit qualified."

Courtney laughed with her, knowing so well just how it had struck her. She had now removed her hat, and the light streamed through the kitchen window on to her red-gold hair, which she began to smooth with a little apologetic movement of her hands.

"I feel a fright after all these interminable hours on the cars, and the wind was blowing free as we drove over here; but how glorious it is! Oh, I think I should like this life. Don't you love it, Mr. Courtney?"

"Yes," he answered heartily. "I do."

Janet passed them by at the moment, went down the steps, and asked the man whether he could not leave the horse and come inside for his refreshment. But he answered that he was in haste to get back, so she brought out a plate of pie and a glass of milk, which he said he preferred to anything else. While he was eating Courtney stepped down to see to the horse, and himself brought him a bucket of water from the well.

"I can't believe, yet, it's you, Madge. Whatever made you come all of a sudden? and it might easily have been inconvenient," began Janet breathlessly.

Madge merely smiled wearily.

"I had to go somewhere, and I hadn't anywhere but here. I'll tell you about it later, as much as is necessary. You don't know anything about what it is like out in the big world for women like us; nobody does, except the women themselves."

"I faced it too, Madge," said Janet with an odd little note of bitterness. "And I didn't find it so very hard; but, then, I was willing to take what came along, and I knew my market value."

"Did you? Then you had learned the most valuable of all the lessons of life," answered Madge. "I haven't learned mine yet, but I'm on the way to it. I want to sleep soon. No, thank you, nothing to eat, though I wouldn't mind a glass of good milk. I'm tired, my dear—dead beat. I feel as if I could sleep for ever."

But upstairs, in Janet's pleasant bedroom, she revived again, after she had bidden Courtney good night, and oddly thrilled him by a glance from her mysterious eyes. She was certainly a beautiful woman, with a sort of uncanny beauty, which her experience of the last six months had oddly accentuated. She was the sort of woman who made her presence felt in a house instantly, as a sort of disturbing influence. She sat down on the edge of Janet's bed, and, throwing off her coat, revealed the slender lines of her figure in its well-cut blouse, the trimly belted waist, a simple garb she wore with her own distinctive and individual air.

"Queer we should be here together again, isn't it, Jen? I've been through lots since I saw you, but we won't speak of that just yet. What I want to know is whether your boss would let me stop here for a week or two till I get rested, and then allow me to prospect from here. I gathered from the two letters I've had from you (I didn't answer them because I hadn't anything to tell about myself you'd be particularly glad or interested to hear). Well, I gathered from your letters that a woman's hands seem to be a scarce commodity in these parts, judging from the multiplicity of chores you have to do. So I thought perhaps you or Courtney would put me on to a similar berth."

Janet inconsequently smiled, and her glance at Madge's long, slender, white and carefully preserved hands was significant. For an answer she spread her own out.

"Look at them; that's what has to go first with other things. You can't do the work on a Canadian farm and keep your hands right, or take any pride in them—at least, not that kind of pride."

"Well, and what do you get in exchange for this sort of white slavery?" asked Madge, drawing up one foot under her on the bed, and beginning to take down her hair.

Janet did not immediately answer. What did she get out of it? Something now she would find it difficult to put into words which she would never be able to forgo again. The thrill caused by Courtney's words on the verandah little more than an hour ago was in her blood yet. But that was the last thing in the world she would even mention to Madge.

"I've got a home," she answered quietly. "I'm needed here. He has been very kind to me, and there's a dear little boy."

"He looks like a gentleman, and he's awfully handsome, Jen."

"He is a gentleman," Janet assented. "They belong to an old English family. Their place there is called Markyates; there's a picture of it in the parlour. His brother was the eldest son, and there wasn't much money. The only daughter, Louie, is married to a Scotchman called David Anderson, living on a ranch about nine miles away in the opposite direction from Fort Purbeck, so now you know all there is to know about them," said Janet in a low, rather listless voice.

"I see; well, and what news have you from home? I haven't had a letter for ages. You see, I've been knocking about for the last two months, and had no settled address. I left Revelstoke Springs on the eighteenth of August."

"Haven't you heard, then? To-morrow is Nancy's wedding-day."

Madge gave a little shriek.

"Nancy's wedding-day! Don't you mean Bella's, Bella's and Bobby Ludlow's?"

"No, that's ancient history: *they* were married at the beginning of September. Nancy by to-morrow at this time will be Mrs. Colonel Motcombe, probably *en route* for the Punjab."

"You don't say so? Why, it's like a fairy tale! Please tell me every single thing about it instantly. This is most exciting."

Janet quickly put her in possession of the facts, Madge listening with her knees drawn up under her chin, and her big eyes glowering uncannily across the intervening space to where Janet sat beside the flickering candle.

"So Nancy has taken the bun," she said flippantly. "Who would have thought it! Demure little cat! You never know what's inside that kind. Why, one even felt that she was a baby that never would grow up. But that's the kind men like, young and pliable, so they can mould them in their own pattern. How old is this Colonel Motcombe? He can't be very young, as there are no youthful colonels."

"He's thirty-seven. He wrote me the most beautiful letter. I'll show it you to-morrow. I'm glad he has got Nancy. I should have hated the idea of her living on at The Croft with Dr. Ludlow and Bella."

Madge's red lips parted in a little smile of amused scorn.

"Bobby and Bella—it's too delicious! It'll be a very pretty little comedy to watch the gradual unfolding of Bobby. There's more in that little rat than meets the eye, and Bella will perhaps find that she has met her master."

"Don't speak like that, Madge, and call people such horrid names," said Janet hastily.

Madge continued to smile, but a little bitterness crept into her scorn.

"I've been out in the open, where there isn't any paint or varnish, my dear," she said calmly. "And I say that Bella has met her master, and that if we should ever find ourselves back in old Balgarnie again, we'd find a new Bella and a very decidedly new Bobby Ludlow. Heavens, can it be only ten months since we left Scotland ? It's like ten centuries."

" I want to hear about you now, Madge. Your letters couldn't be said to be satisfactory. Please begin at the beginning, when we parted that day at the Central Station at New York. How did you find Chicago ? "

" We *don't* think," said Madge, dropping her eyes. " I couldn't possibly go back so far. Chicago was disappointing. It's a horrible place, Jen, the nearest approach to the lower regions I should imagine to be found anywhere. A hateful, sordid place, and the people——"

She spread her hands out with a gesture of infinite loathing and contempt.

" You didn't get on well with Mrs. Ronderbusch, then ? "

" No, she was unspeakable ; she gave herself airs, and she didn't know how to treat a lady. Oh, yes, I went out to her place and took it on, but she treated me like an upper servant. Fact is, she was jealous of me, and mortally afraid her brother was going to marry me."

" Did he ask you ? " inquired Janet, wondering at her own temerity.

Madge was silent a moment.

" Yes, ultimately he did, but—but other things were not equal, and I refused him, and the happiest moment of my life was when I told Frau Ronderbusch that I had refused her paragon. My, it made her sit up ! I believe, if she could have killed me just then, she would. You see, there was Ronderbusch, a big, stolid Dutchman, immensely rich, and he enjoyed talking to me, and she didn't like it. Neither did I, though I had no complaint to make about him. He was very kind to me while I was there. She dismissed me at a moment's notice one day when she came back from Chicago and found I had been out on the automobile with Ronderbusch. It was then I told her I had refused her precious brother."

" But why did you refuse him ? " asked Janet, and her face was flushed a little, for there was something in Madge's way of speaking, in the whole story, indeed, which jarred upon her and made her feel as if she could shrink away from her sister.

" He wasn't rich enough. It's a millionaire I'm on the outlook for, and mean to have, Jen. I very nearly managed to pull it off at Revelstoke Springs, but again an old tabby intervened."

" You were in the hotel at Revelstoke, weren't you ? "

" Yes, I looked after the entertainment of the visitors, and saw to the flowers and the tit-bits. It wasn't hard work, but there was no salary attached. But as Revelstoke Springs is one of the haunts of the idle oof-birds, I thought I might get my chance there, and I very nearly did."

Janet rose rather suddenly, and snuffed the flame of the candle, which was burning unevenly and beginning to smoke.

" I don't think I want to hear any more, Madge ; it's horrible ! I don't know why you should speak or think like that. You were brought up just the same as the rest of us. If father could hear you, it would make him turn in his grave."

Madge merely laughed.

" I'm only a trifle more honest than the rest of you, that's all, my dear."

" Well, and if it's a millionaire you're seeking, why did you come here ? There are very few millionaires yet in the north-west of Canada. This place strikes about the average of a man's success ; and it isn't anything to boast about ; just a little more than comfort, that's all. It would never satisfy you."

" Well, I got very tired physically, don't you know ; the heat was so appalling across these plains in July and August. And I thought my looks were going off, and that I had better get a rest and a purer air without delay. Then I really wanted to see you, though you don't look as if you believed it."

" I don't know what to believe about you," said Janet soberly. " Were you paid off from Revelstoke too ? "

"Yes, I was; but the season was at an end, don't you know; it doesn't begin again till spring. Then I went to Los Angeles, and hired myself to a boarding-house as lady assistant. I did the cooking there, and did it well. It was ghastly, though, but they wanted to keep me on all winter. But the class of folks I met there were not good enough. After I've had a bit of rest here, I thought I'd try San Francisco. I hear it's very lively in winter, and I've got some addresses. Now I think I'll go to bed. I'm dead beat."

She began to undress, and let her hair fall round her lovely shoulders, and brushed it in the yellow gleam of the candle till it shone again.

Janet was at once attracted and repelled by her uncanny beauty, by a sort of weird charm she possessed, unlike anything she had ever met before. So tired was Madge that she fell asleep the moment her head touched the pillow, and Janet, before she blew out the candle, bent over her and looked at her beautiful face with its clear pallor and its sweeping lashes on her cheek. She blamed herself because she could not honestly say her heart stirred in tenderness to her who had had the same father and mother, who had shared with her so many years of the old home.

In her heart of hearts, in her sanctuary of secret and unutterable thoughts, Janet Fairweather was afraid.

CHAPTER XVIII

LOUIE INTERVENES

David Anderson, riding slowly the last field-breadth which separated him from his home, had a more than usually serious expression on his face. He was a big, stolid Scotchman, not given to unnecessary speech, and, like most silent persons, a very keen and generally correct observer, both of character and the actions of others.

He had observed something that afternoon at his brother-in-law's place which had disquieted him a good deal.

While he was putting up his horse, his wife, with the baby in her arms, came out to meet him. She lifted up her face to be kissed, for they were lovers yet, after ten years of married life, and Louie thought there was nobody in the world like her big Scotch husband.

He smiled as he patted her cheek and took the baby from her arms. Then they crossed the yard together.

For the first time for several years Mrs. Anderson had secured efficient help in the house, and had gone back to pretty afternoon frocks and to more dainty ways than are possible to the woman who has to do all the drudgery of a house.

" You're surely dressed up to kill, Lou ? " said David teasingly, yet with a glance of open admiration as they entered by the front verandah door into the pleasant, warm, and cosy sitting-room.

" I'm dressed up for *you*, my lord ; no, it isn't a new frock, though it's going to be. I've mailed ever such a big order to Eaton's in Winnipeg for finery, so look out for the bill. Well, how are they at Markyates ? "

" Oh, fine in health," said Anderson a trifle heavily. " But there's things there I don't like, Lou. The game's been completely spoiled. That sister of Miss Fairweather's is nothing but a cutty."

" What's a cutty ? " asked Louie.

" A cutty's a limmer, and if ye dinna understand that, my woman, your education's been neglected, and I canna help ye, for there is no word in the English tongue to explain it."

" I think I know what you mean," said Louie, with her head on one side like a saucy bird. " You mean that she's—she's the wrong sort."

" Indeed, and she's all that," said Anderson emphatically. " An' Geo, he's a making a perfect fool of himself. I've no patience with him. I could have shaken him to-day, him and her both." Louie's face expressed the undoubted horror she felt.

" Oh, but, David, you must be exaggerating. Why, he was openly in love with Janet before she came, and I was every day expecting to hear that it was all settled between them. I'm sure Janet expected it too. Not that she ever said anything, but a woman knows, and I'm sure she felt like that."

" I can't help what she felt. I'm telling you what I've seen. She's doing her best to haul Geo into her toils, and she's succeeding. What for ? The Lord only knows, since it's a certain fact that he's not half rich enough to keep a daughter of a horse-leech like Madge Fairweather."

" What did you see to-day, David ? Sit down and tell me every single solitary thing," cried his wife, with all a woman's eagerness. " I'm simply dying to hear."

" I'm not sure that I can put it into words. It was the kind of thing a body feels rather than sees. And Janet, she looks miserable. Oh, I tell you something will happen there before long, and when it's done, Geo will know what a fool he's been. He'll never get the chance of a second Janet Fairweather, never in this world."

" He wouldn't deserve it, if he let her go. You think he's in love with the sister, then ? "

" I don't know about love, but she's cast some kind of a glamour over him," said David moodily. " I'm not wanting to speak about it. What I do want is for you to go over to Markyates and tell your own brother what a confounded ass he's making of himself, and the sooner you go the better."

" I'll go to-morrow."

" Aye, do. Janet asked me with a bit pitiful look when ye were coming. I very near brought her back with me the day, only she couldn't very well have left Geo with the limmer."

" Did she say that, David ? "

" No, wifie, she did not. Do you think it likely, now, that Janet Fairweather would give the show away like that ? I'm surprised at you. I'll tell ye what it is, my dear. Madge Fairweather is one of those women that must have every man they see dangling after them, and they just lay themselves out for it. You think she's handsome ; well, if she's your taste, it's all right. She never would be mine. I'm not civil to her. I don't try to be. She called me the grizzly bear to-day, and asked me why I didn't have a card printed round my neck with ' Wha daur meddle wi' me ? ' on it."

" That was very rude and cheeky, David," said Louie indignantly. " I hope you gave her a good one back."

" I just turned my back on her. She's not worth my powder and shot, or any man's. But Geo ! he's all eyes for her ! I tell ye I could have shaken him."

" Well, and supposing I go and see Janet to-morrow. What am I to say to her ? "

" You're not needing me to tell you, for you and her understand one another, and the right word will come, my dear. What I am particular about is that you should not spare Geo. The thing that would bring him quickest to his senses would be if he were left at Markyates with nobody but the limmer to do for him. But in that case we should lose Janet, and we were set, weren't we, on having her for a sister ? "

" We're set on it yet, and I'm going to fight for it," said Louie, setting her small, determined mouth in a line in which her good man secretly gloried.

" I feel better now I've rolled it on to you. Now I can eat my supper." Then he spoke to the baby in his arms.

" Yes, my wee lad, when you grow up to be a man, it's cutties like Madge Fairweather you'll have to keep in their bit if you want to have any peace of mind."

There was a good deal of further talk about Markyates' affairs between the Andersons that night, and soon after breakfast next morning Louie set out with the old piebald pony in the single buggy to drive over.

It was now the fourth week in November, and the weather continued mild and even sunny, with never a hint of winter severity in its breath.

All the leaves had fallen from the maples and the sumachs, and the prairies were grey and desolate, as if they were ready to welcome their pure winter covering. The long spell of dry weather had kept the summer dust on the soft tracks, and Louie found it very easy going across the pleasant fields. She had not seen very much of the new inmate of her brother's household. Her little family kept her hands fully occupied, and there had been less coming and going than usual that fall between the two places. Louie, trying to count, was surprised to find how few were the times she had seen Janet Fairweather since the harvest.

They had met just very occasionally at Fort Purbeck, when they had both driven in for stores. One Sunday Courtney had driven both the sisters and his little boy over to the Andersons' place, and had spent the afternoon. But on that day Madge had behaved with great propriety, and had left rather a favourable impression than otherwise on Mrs. Anderson's mind. Never had she heard her big, slow-going husband speak with such vehemence, and she was conscious of a very lively anticipation as she came within sight of the snug little homestead, in which they had such a deep interest. She could see a small, red speck in the yard, which she surmised to be Billy at his play. He ran in to warn his aunt (he had begun to call Janet auntie of his own free will soon after her arrival, and Janet had loved the name), and by the time Louie guided the buggy to the foot of the slope, Janet was out on the verandah to welcome her.

Mrs. Anderson, observing her garb and the soap-suds on her bare, shapely arms, guessed that she had come from the wash-tub.

"I'm just done. I took the chance when they were away," she explained as they kissed one another. "Somehow, when one has a visitor, things get out of order and seem to accumulate."

"I suppose so; but where's your sister? Why isn't she helping you to-day? You don't mean to say you're washing her white skirts and blouses? I would see her far enough first," observed Mrs. Anderson with a very firm setting of her pretty lips.

"Oh, there aren't many, and Madge is a poor hand at anything of that sort. They've gone to Fort Purbeck. Mr. Courtney has to bring back some young pigs in the back of the rig. I hope Madge will enjoy her drive. I don't care about live stock at such close quarters."

Louie Anderson made no reply, but marched into the kitchen and looked round with rather stormy eyes.

"Sit down, Janet, and never mind the rest of the washing."

"You wouldn't leave the tail-end of it yourself, Louie, and I've only these few towels to wring out of the blue water. I'm anxious to get them out while there's a blink of sun. It's rather scarce in these days. Then I'll put on the potatoes, and we'll enjoy our dinner together."

"Where are the potatoes? I'll fix them."

Janet accepted the help as it was offered, and over their respective tasks the two women talked a little in desultory fashion about things which did not interest them very much. In about half an hour's time the towels were out on the line blowing in the wind, and the tubs removed from the scullery floor.

"Now I'll just run up and get a clean apron, and we'll enjoy a good talk," said Janet, nodding a little breathlessly, for the last tub had been rather heavy, and when Louie's back was turned she had carried it out unaided.

While Janet was upstairs, Mrs. Anderson set the table, and held a little conversation with Billy, of whom she was very fond. She learned from him that he at least had no love for the strange lady, but he refused to give his reasons for disliking her. Louie had great faith in the verdict of a child, and invariably distrusted the man or woman from whom her own children instinctively shrank.

"You look tired, Janet, and I'll tell Geo first time I see him that he's wrong to let you do too much drudgery. I suppose your sister has made a lot of extra work?"

"Oh, yes, of course, Madge is a bit dainty about her food."

"And do you mean to say you consider that?" asked Mrs. Anderson flatly.

"Yes, I do, a little, of course; you see, she's been used to a different life in California."

"Well, let her go back to it," said Louie shortly. "It makes me clean wild the way she carries on here, and you are just a big, soft baby, Janet, to give in to her as you do. It makes David mad, too. He came home in such a rage last night. I had the greatest difficulty in smoothing him down."

"Did he? Well, I'm sure Madge was as sweet as she could be to him," said Janet, but her eyes did not meet Louie's unflinchingly observant orbs.

"That was the head and front of her offence. David has no need for sweet women. He has all he wants of that sort of thing at home, my dear. So she may save herself trouble. Honestly, now, do you like having her here?"

Janet hesitated a moment, and then swallowed something hard in her throat.

"Honestly, Louie, I pray every night when I lie down that she may elect to go away in the morning. But I don't think she means to go very soon. Mr. Courtney likes to have her here; and I heard him telling her last night about the sleighing."

Louie Anderson carefully removed the brown jacket from a very floury and enticing-looking potato, cut it up carefully on her plate, and, mixing it with a bit of butter, ate it with relish.

"That's a lovely potato, Janet; we can't grow them like it at our place. It's astonishing what difference a nine-mile breadth of country can make in the quality of the land. Well, my dear, it just resolves itself into a question which of you is to be mistress here. Does your sister want to settle down on a Canadian farm? Would she do the chores you have done so cheerfully and so splendidly all these months?"

"No," said Janet. "That she wouldn't; and I would be sorry for the farm unless she had somebody at her beck and call to keep her place from rack and ruin."

"Precisely."

Mrs. Anderson pushed back her chair, asked for another cup of tea, and sipped it in silence.

Quite suddenly she leaned her arms on the table and looked across it at Janet's sweet, womanly face, which was beginning to show a good many tell-tale lines.

"I suppose you've guessed—for you don't lack sharpness, my dear—that David sent me over here to-day."

"I knew you came for something, Louie, though I didn't get so far as that. But whatever you have come to say, don't say it. It'll hurt, my dear. I don't think I could bear it to-day."

"It is sometimes good to hurt," said Louie in a low voice. "I came here to see Geo. What time do you think he'll get back from Fort Purbeck?"

Janet shook her head.

"It's a question of whether they enjoy their ride. You can make a long or a short job of going to Purbeck; you know that as well as me, Louie."

"But you privately expected it to be a long job to-day?"

"I shouldn't be surprised."

"Now, I'm going to ask something, and if you think it impertinent, don't answer, and I'll quite understand. Did George never say anything to you before your sister came which would let you know he hoped you would stop always here?"

Janet was silent a moment, very busy at the stove. Louie could just see the red tip of her ear, and knew that she had hotly flushed under the question.

"After all, I have a sort of right to ask it, Janet, because he has said heaps of things to David and me about it, and we both expected and hoped—indeed, I've prayed with all my might that you would care enough for him to marry him when he asked you. I made sure more than once that he had done it."

Janet, still silent, put some fresh wood on the stove, and then turned round quite quietly with her hands folded under her apron.

"I'm not angry, and I quite understand. I—I hoped it, too. There isn't any harm in telling you that, because you've been so dear to me, both you and Mr. Anderson, since the very first moment you set eyes on me. You're just the very best friends I've had in the world."

"But we want to be more," pursued Louie mercilessly. "So he never said anything?"

"Yes, he did, the very night Madge arrived. In fact, I do believe that she interrupted his offer of marriage," said Janet a little shamefacedly, but very quietly and bravely.

"And he's said nothing since?"

"No; well he hasn't had a chance."

"No, of course not; she takes up all the side-walk, and the front steps, and the best of everything," said Louie with a little vicious snap.

"Well, and what are you going to do now?"

Janet drew herself up with such pride that Louie Anderson secretly gloried in it.

"Do? Nothing! Don't you see that if—if he's turned away from what he thought he wished just because Madge has come, don't you see that what he has to offer isn't worth my while, or any other woman's? I don't make myself cheap, Louie, to George Courtney or any man, and very well he knows it."

"Oh, you blessed woman! that's the right spirit to bring that fool brother of mine to his senses," cried Louie in a great burst of rapture. "Well, what you have to do now is to go away and leave him to the tender mercies of your sister Madge. That would bring him to his senses quicker than anything."

"No, I don't do that, Louie. I'd chop myself into little pieces first. Why, that would give everything away with a vengeance! I'll just dree my weird; the thing is getting on finely; and when they come in some morning and tell me they're engaged, why, then it'll be time for me to quit, not a minute before."

"But wouldn't that hurt you, dear? Don't you care for him, after all?"

Janet was silent a moment, looking out through the open door across the verandah to the great open wideness of the prairie, rolling like the sea in front.

"I care so much, my dear, that I can stand aside if he's going to be happier with anybody else," she said at last quite quietly. "Now do let us talk of something else."

CHAPTER XIX

THE TRAIL OF THE SERPENT

MRS. ANDERSON spent the greater part of the day at Markyates, and when she left at last after an early cup of tea so that she could get home before dark, the pair had not returned from Purbeck.

She had gained very little by her visit, only got a little nearer in heart to Janet Fairweather, whom she already dearly loved. These two women, who had come close to the absolute reality of things, which is sometimes sordid unless the high spirit is brought to bear on it, had very few illusions left. And both were agreed, though it had not been put into naked words, that Madge, like the serpent, had come into their little world just at a moment when it had promised a great deal of happiness for both. Circumstances had prevented Louie Anderson from making any intimate friends in her prairie home ; for one thing, her upbringing had removed her a good deal in thought and feeling from many of these whose one idea was the labour of their hands, and no one knows, save those who have tasted it, what can be the loneliness of a woman on a western homestead. Many of them go under, break down in health both mentally and physically ; it is the inevitable toll to be paid to a country in the making. In Janet Fairweather, Louie had found a friend, a woman of her own class who was not ashamed to work with her hands, but who could preserve through it that nicety of soul, that innate refinement which adds so much to the grace of life. And she could not face the idea of letting her go without making some big effort to keep her. That she would go unless Courtney came to his senses quickly and realised the position, there was nothing more certain. Louie had seen it that day in the poise of her head, in the quick drawing up of her figure, the momentary hardening of her kind, true eyes.

And it was equally certain that Madge would never take her place. Even if George should go so far as to offer marriage to her, and she accepted it, she would never do for him and his what Janet had done and was willing to do. Madge was like the lilies of the field—she toiled not, neither did she spin, but she managed, nevertheless, to get the best of everything. Other people paid, that was all. And Louie Anderson feared very much that it was Janet who was going to pay. It is so often the good who have to bear the brunt of things. But in the long run things even up, and Justice has her innings, though sometimes very late.

" Now, my dear," she said as she pulled on her driving-gloves ready to depart, " you'll promise me not to do anything foolish. This thing will right itself. And remember that we can't any of us afford to lose you."

She dare not say any more, but her kiss was warm and close, and the grip of her slim hands told everything. Janet's eyes were dim as she watched the buggy until it became a little speck on the distant horizon.

How happy they had been together before Madge came ! Janet knew that in her heart of hearts she had asked nothing better than to become one of these dear people, making all their interests her own.

Both Louie and Janet would have parted with their last hope of a happy settlement could they have occupied the back seat of the rig in which Courtney and Madge were returning in very leisurely fashion across the wide level stretches of the bare wheat fields.

Madge had enjoyed her day, because she had a man in close attendance on her, and knew she had his sole admiration and his interest. But at the same time she had made up her mind that she must not go any further, for two reasons, that she had not the remotest intention of letting things become serious between her and George Courtney, nor did she actually wish to spoil Janet's future. She rather wished, on the whole, she had not come. Life on a western farm was a mighty slow thing, and she had had enough of it.

"This isn't the way we came, surely," she said, shading her eyes from the blood-red glare of one of the wonderful prairie sunsets. "Is that your place over there?"

"No," answered Courtney. "We're nine miles from it yet."

"Nine miles! that's a long way. I believe you've taken the longest way on purpose. It's all so monotonous and so much alike. Do hurry up a bit, and let's get back. Janet will be quite uneasy."

Courtney did not make the smallest effort to smarten up the horses.

"And we haven t got any little pigs, worse luck," said Madge, with a little wicked smile. "Were they any little pigs to be got really, or was that a fairy tale?"

"Anything sufficed so long as I got a long day with you, Madge," said Courtney recklessly. Madge shook her head demurely and laid a reproving hand on his arm.

"Now, what did I tell you over that weird dinner at Purbeck, that you weren't to talk any more nonsense. We've had our bit of fun, but it's over for the time being—for altogether, indeed—between you and me."

"Is it indeed?" said Courtney rather hotly. "I rather think not."

"Oh, but yes. I've really outstayed my welcome. My dear sister is beginning to look askance at me. Poor Jen; she always did take things rather seriously. I've really made up my mind to depart. I'll go on Monday, I think."

"Where to?"

"Well, since you're so very anxious to know, I'm bound for Vancouver in the first instance. Probably, if the Fates are propitious, I'll wait there until I've heard from my sister Nancy. I wrote her about two weeks ago offering a visit in India. I'd like to see that part of the world, and I hear it's possible to get round through China and Japan."

"It's a pretty long round, and an expensive one," said Courtney gloomily.

"Oh, but to the adventurous all things are easy. I'll get my expenses paid somehow. I can be a travelling companion to some rich old lady. Everything comes to those who wait."

Courtney was silent, but a slow passion was gathering in his eyes.

He had been swept off his feet in a whirlwind of passion for this elusive, fascinating woman who took everything as her right, and gave nothing, and her cool way of talking maddened him.

"I won't let you away," he said fiercely. "I've got you fast, and you've as good as said you wouldn't mind stopping here with me. You've got to be my wife, Madge, after all you've said. You've as good as promised."

"No, no, my dear man," she answered with the most provoking coolness. "I don't mind a mild flirtation, that oils the wheels anywhere. It's been rather sweet, and I don't mind saying that if you'd been a millionaire I should have asked nothing better than to spend the rest of my life with you. But such luxuries are not for the poor. You and I have our living to get, and we are both far too wise to take on anything that's going to get in the way. Do you fancy me doing all your chores for you? I'm always telling Janet she'll get all her thanks in one day, but she's got a conscience, a Nonconformst one, and a Scotch one to boot, so she goes on making door-mats of herself. She'll get wiser some day, perhaps, but I'd advise you, my dear, to stick to Janet. That way peace lies."

Courtney's mouth became very bitter, and his eyes flashed again.

"You're a kind of fiend, I believe, Madge Fairweather. You can drive folk to the verge of desperation," he said savagely, for what she said about Janet cut home.

"Oh, no, dear boy, only a Scotchwoman on the make, and that's a more inspiring and intricate sight than a Scotchman. By the by, how your David Anderson hates me! Yesterday he looked at me as if he could cut my throat."

"David? Oh, nonsense! he's far too stolid even to think of such a thing. He sees nothing."

"That's just where you English make a mistake about us," said Madge, with her provoking little smile. "We see everything, and when the time comes we do things which make the world wonder. David Anderson sees everything, and he wants to chase me away from Markyates with a scourge of whipcords."

"Then all the things you've said to me have been lies," he said in the same savage undertone.

"No, no, dear boy, not lies exactly. Don't be so crude. They served their purpose, *pour passer le temps*, don't you know? It's been quite good for you. You won't make Janet any the worse a husband because of anything you've said to me. You ought to be grateful to me for bringing a little diversion into your life. Heavens, isn't it deadly dull?"

Her face clouded, and such contempt was in her eyes as they swept the far horizon that Courtney was fascinated by it.

"I can't think how any self-respecting woman can stop here year after year. I suppose, after a while, they get a sort of mental atrophy, and become like automatons wound up to do chores. It's the only conceivable explanation. People weren't born for that—at least, I wasn't. Are we going home now?" she added suspiciously.

"Oh, yes, straight ahead. There's only one thing makes life tolerable here, Madge, and the happy few that have it don't mind. I thought I was going to get it. I've a good mind to keep you against your will."

"That wouldn't pay; no, no, my boy; you take my advice and stick to the housekeeper you've got. She's the right sort; I'm a wrong 'un. But I'm not a hypocrite, and even if every solitary word I've ever spoken in answer to your injudicious speeches was written down in black and white, it wouldn't amount to half a promise or even a quarter. It was just play, and surely if we can't have a bit of play as we go along, it's a mighty poor, dull business we'd be making of life."

At this Courtney relapsed into gloomy silence, and his jaw was set so hard that once or twice Madge glanced at him in secret admiration. She liked Courtney very much, and was perfectly honest in her assurance that, had he possessed the necessary means, she would have married him cheerfully. Incapable of any deep feeling herself, she was therefore incapable of gauging the extent of the injury she had done both to Courtney and to Janet. Certainly Janet had closed the door of her heart to her sister, and with a pride and strength inimitable, had kept her face to the weather so that neither Courtney nor Madge guessed the depth of her hurt. But it had hardened and soured her. She was not the woman she had been a month ago, nor perhaps would she ever be quite the same again.

There are some experiences that sear the heart too much. And it must be remembered that Janet's was touched for the first time. Courtney had no idea of the priceless value of the treasure he had belittled and passed by. She was standing on the edge of the verandah when the rig drove up in the quickly falling dusk, and Madge waved to her cheerily. "No luck! not a single solitary little pig to our name, Jen!" she called out banteringly. "How many homesteads have we visited in quest of the pig, eh? I think we've lost count. Well, what sort of a day have *you* had?"

"The usual kind of day. Mrs. Anderson was here for most part of it, but in spite of it I've got my clothes washed, dried, and ironed, and now they're being aired."

"Good little *haus-frau;* but don't do it, my dear," she said significantly as she ran up the steps. "They don't think any more of you for it."

"You forget I am working here for a wage," said Janet coldly.

"Oh, Lord, yes; but why mention such a disagreeable fact? I'm fed up with Canadian prairies. I've told the boss I'm going off on Monday."

"Oh!" said Janet, and Madge observed as she quickly turned away that she pressed her hand to her side, as if to still some beating there.

"Yes, I'm fed up; besides, I rather think I've outstayed my welcome. You've been most awfully good to me, and I'm feeling really rested, so now I must take the next stage of the journey. Did I tell you I had written to Peshawar offering Nancy and her Colonel a visit?"

"Oh, Madge, I do hope she'll say no!" cried Janet, and when she turned round quickly from the stove the colour was high in her cheek.

"She won't have the chance, my dear," said Madge drily, "because I don't intend to wait for her answer."

"But how are you going to get there? It costs oceans of money!" asked Janet, and there was a rasping note in her voice which told of nerves unstrung.

"Oh, I'll get there, never fear! I generally do when I set out armed with what the books call a purpose."

"But it doesn't seem decent, hardly, Madge. None of us know Colonel Motcombe, and we might at least wait until we are asked to visit at his house."

"Why? It's what brothers-in-law in India are for, to give their wives' sisters a chance," said Madge with her provoking smile.

She often said these outrageous things, but somehow until the last month Janet had never taken her quite seriously.

"I think the way you speak is horrible, Madge," cried Janet passionately, while Billy, disturbed by the look on her face and the unusual note in her voice, clung rather anxiously about her skirts.

"Run out, darling," she said unsteadily as she bent to his sweet, eager face. "Daddy is taking out the horses, and we want to know how long before he can come in to supper."

Billy, obedient as usual, and rather pleased at the prospect, darted off. "I can't think why you won't settle down and earn your living like the rest of us without trying to sponge off people," continued Janet with the same high note of passion in her voice. "Oh, I know it isn't a nice word nor a very polite one, but there are some things that have to be called by their right names. I don't want you to go to India. I'm—I'm afraid."

"Afraid of what?"

Madge sat down on the edge of the end of the couch, and looked quite straight at her sister's disturbed face.

"Afraid that you will be a disturbing element in Nancy's life. She's very young; she ought to be left to find her feet. And her husband is so wise and good that she will be quite safe and happy with him."

"Until I creep in upon their Eden like a serpent—that's the inference. I'm much obliged to you, Jen, for your very high opinion of me. Of course, I can understand what is at the back of it, but I do assure you I haven't hurt your big, stupid Viking. He's quite ready to be as devoted to you as ever, and instead of waiting until Monday, I'll go to-morrow. But I never thought you could be so vulgar and so horrid, Janet, you of all people, who always aspired to set an example to the non-elect."

Madge's lips wore a mocking smile as she left the kitchen and began to mount the stairs, humming a scrap of song just to show how little she cared. Poor Janet, trembling in every limb, ashamed of her own outburst, yet powerless to have kept it in check, turned towards the stove to the humble duty which, though the heavens should fall, is ever lying ready to the housewife's hand.

The high colour had not died out of her cheek, nor the passion from her eyes, when she heard Courtney and the boy on the verandah steps.

CHAPTER XX

AFTERMATH

WHEN Madge was called to supper she came downstairs with her hat still on, which surprised Courtney greatly.

Usually she made some little change of toilet of an evening, when she would look her best. Of late Janet had grown disheartened, and consequently more careless about herself. In very scorn of Madge's attractive guise she would often now wear the blouse suit and the apron in which she had been about the house all day.

" Helloa ! " said Courtney as Madge drew in her chair and sat down, without so much as a smile on her face.

She nodded defiantly across the table.

" I'm busy packing. What time does the Limited Imperial stop at Fort Purbeck to-morrow ? What a pity I didn't think of it to-day ; it would have saved the rig another journey to-morrow."

" But why," said Courtney, rather dazedly, " are you going to-morrow ? "

" Yes, please. Don't ask me any questions. No, I won't take any meat, just a cup of tea, and please make it strong, Janet, and you'll excuse me if I hurry away. I mustn't miss that train to-morrow."

Janet filled up the cup and passed it grimly to her.

Courtney, conscious of the under-currents, thought he had better hold his tongue. Five minutes passed in dreary silence, which Madge ended by rising and retiring upstairs.

" What's happened to upset your sister, Miss Fairweather ? " inquired Courtney the moment the door closed.

" Nothing particular. She has tired of this place just as she has tired of every other place."

" But to go to-morrow ! She said Monday," he said forlornly.

" Perhaps it will be as well. If the snow comes, as you expect, it might be difficult for her to get away, and she would be very discontented if she were storm-bound. Mrs. Anderson told me the first blizzard often lasts for several days."

Courtney made no comment on this remark, but finished his meal in silence.

" It will not be the same place without her," he said abruptly.

" No," answered Janet clearly. " It certainly won't."

He looked at her with an odd beetling of the brows.

" A woman's quarrel," he said to himself. " I'd dearly like to be at the bottom of it. But I daren't ask a question. Perhaps Madge will tell me to-morrow as I drive her over. There's always that in front. Perhaps I'll be able to make her change her mind."

His eyes as they followed Janet's oddly restless figure about the room had lost their kindly gleam. It was not so long ago since it had mattered greatly to him whether she was in a room or out of it, when he had watched keenly every passing play of the features which had become dear to him. But now all was changed. She seemed dull, uninteresting, positively plain. And he had no doubt that it was owing to her that Madge was leaving. Women could be very nasty to one another on occasion, though he had thought this particular one above the ordinary failings of her sex. If only good luck had sent him the younger sister in the first instance, well, things would have been very different! So he reasoned, entirely blinded by a brief infatuation, and totally unable to arrive at any just conclusion. He had long since thrust into the far background of his memory certain significant words he had spoken to Janet Fairweather on the very night of her sister's arrival, and which she had never forgotten.

Only once he had permitted himself to recall them, when he felt that the spell of Madge was becoming too strong for him, and then he had decided that they didn't amount to anything, and that no reasonable woman could possibly have construed them into an offer of marriage. He ignored the fact that they had been spoken by him with a quite definite purpose, and that a marriage with Janet Fairweather had then seemed to be the most desirable culmination of his hopes.

He went out on the verandah to smoke a pipe, and after Janet had cleared the table and washed up, she went upstairs to put Billy to bed. Then Madge ran down for a minute to seek Courtney, and presently the sound of their mingled voices floated up on the still and heavy air to Janet's ears, and it embittered her heart and her face.

As she listened to the child's sweet voice, saying his prayers at her knee, the prayer she had taught him, her own rebellious heart felt like a weight in her breast. Once she had believed what Billy was saying, had left herself and her outgoings and outcomings trustfully in the hand of the Father Who knows best. But He had forgotten her. He had no reward or recognition for those who do their duty faithfully in the place to which they were called. It was the butterfly women like Madge, who took care never to soil their fingers, or to engage in a single dreary or unbecoming task, who had the best of everything. It was not fair, it was not just. Janet had no use for a God, Who, if He had the power, could so misuse it. She, too, had lost her sense of proportion; she was so utterly miserable that her heart turned in a passionate longing to her "ain folk." She laid her head for a moment down beside Billy's on the pillow, and even his nestling arm about her neck failed to comfort her.

"Is your head bad, Auntie, like Auntie Louie's used to be?" he asked sympathetically, easily conscious of some flaw in her ministry to him.

She only kissed him a quick good night, and rose to shade the little lamp from his eyes and fold away his clothes. Who would do that after she was gone, she wondered, for she resolved that she would not stop much, if any, longer at Markyates. Her heart had lost its haven, and it would not be possible to live on under the same roof with Courtney with the spectre of Madge between.

She was terrified at the bitterness of her own feelings, at the violence of her anger against her sister. Words she had heard long since in Balgarnie Kirk rose up accusingly in front of her. "He that hateth his brother is a murderer!" Undoubtedly she hated Madge, therefore she was outside the pale of all decent and kindly things. There was very little refreshing sleep in the house of Markyates that December night, and Janet was astir before the dawn, feeling that nothing but work, hard, constant work, was the thing for her just then. Breakfast was a wretched, uncomfortable meal, at which very little was eaten. In the middle of it Courtney flung himself out of the house to get the horses in; then Madge went up to put on her big coat and to swathe her veil about her travelling hat.

When she came down, the rig was coming out of the shed, and the time for the last word had come. An odd look flitted just a moment across Madge's face, born of some faint realisation of the havoc she had wrought.

"I haven't been a success here, Jen, and I'm sorry I came. I didn't mean anything, and whatever happens, don't blame me. It is always the man who is to be blamed. Foolish, inconstant creatures, and the women who laugh at them and never take them seriously have the best of it. Remember that, my dear. I'm sorry."

Janet could not respond. What she did long to do was to cry out to Madge to take care in whatever place she might find herself next not to repeat the experience, to try and not stir up the depths and destroy the symmetry of other lives.

But her tongue merely clove to the roof of her mouth.

" Good-bye. I'm sorry it hasn't been a success, as you say. I never thought it would when you came. It's not the life you would ever care for. It's too drab and uninteresting. Yes, I've had about enough of it. I think I'll go back to Scotland."

Madge started at this speech, but at the moment Courtney called her that they would need all their time. She kissed Janet hastily, ran out through the open door, climbed into the rig, and in another moment Janet heard the clang of the harness bells and the smack of Courtney's whip.

She sat down drearily on the edge of her chair, and dropped her face on her hands, too miserable even to cry. She had not the faintest desire to go out and wave her hand to the parting guest. That undoubtedly was the very darkest hour that had ever come into Janet Fairweather's life. The awfulness of her attitude and feeling towards Madge was uppermost. She felt that God could never forgive her for it. They were children of one mother, had shared a home all the years of their lives till now, and yet there was nothing but relief at her heart, because she had gone away. How terrible it was that the human heart was capable of such thoughts, that such passion could ravage the whole being and turn the pleasant places of the earth into the desert! After a bit, Billy came sleepily down the stairs in his flannel suit, begging to be dressed, and Janet rose heavily to the duties of the new day. Never had she worked as she did that day. Beginning at the top of the house, she simply swept and scrubbed and polished as if she desired to obliterate every sign of Madge's presence from the house. Such was not her desire, however; it was only to keep her from thinking, perhaps to shut out the vision of Madge and Courtney together, alone, as they crossed the lonely plains, to prevent her brooding on their possible farewell.

By noon she was tired out physically, and after dinner persuaded Billy to lie down with her on the big couch near the stove. In the midst of telling him a story they both fell asleep, and when they awoke it was quite dark in the living-room, and cold too, the stove having nearly burned out. She rose hastily, and, glancing through the uncurtained window, saw the moving figure of Denis in from the fields crossing the yard. He seemed to be enveloped in white, and she saw that the blizzard had begun.

The Andersons were sitting down to their midday meal when Courtney's rig drove up to the verandah. The hired man rose and went to relieve him of it, and he came in looking blue and cold and excessively depressed.

" Where have you been, Geo?" Louie asked as she made him welcome.

" Fort Purbeck, seeing off Miss Fairweather—yes, she went to-day."

" To-day!" cried Louie, and made no effort to hide the satisfaction the news gave her. " It was very sudden, surely. I was at Markyates yesterday, and her sister said nothing about it."

" She wouldn't because she didn't know," answered Courtney gloomily. " I think they had some kind of a quarrel; at least, there was something. One felt it in the air all last evening. Anyway, she's gone to-day."

" A good riddance too!" growled David candidly. " Where has she gone?"

" West," answered Courtney briefly as he drew in his chair to get some dinner. He had come round that way simply because he did not feel equal to facing Janet Fairweather just yet. He was too sore all over, likewise his conscience was not very easy. Louie, watching him with unaccustomed furtiveness, saw that his spirit was perturbed, and prepared herself to render him more miserable still. He deserved it. He was a sick man, who must be made worse before he could get any better.

" She's stopped a goodish while, Geo; nine weeks yesterday since she came."

" You've kept account, have you? It doesn't look more than nine days to me, and I wish she would have stopped altogether," he said recklessly, just in the mood to quarrel with anybody who conveniently offered.

" You ought to be ashamed to say such a thing in front of me, Geo Courtney," cried Louie hotly. " I think she had a cool impertinence to stop so long, and to let her sister wait on her the way she did."

" That was their concern, my dear, not ours."

" It was yours, though, maybe, you'll find it out to your cost, George," said Louie. " I don't believe Miss Fairweather will stop long after her sister. She seemed yesterday as if she had had about enough of it. So poor Billy and you will have to face another winter's batching. I'm not a bit sorry for you ; you'll deserve all you'll get. But it's a shame for the little chap."

" You don't know what you're talking about, Lou. Miss Fairweather has no intention of leaving, or hadn't until you put it into her head. Was that your business at Markyates yesterday, may I ask ? Did you suggest that she should leave ? "

" Did I what ? " inquired Louie in wrathful tones. " Wouldn't I give my right hand to keep her always ? But you've lost her, Geo ; we all have ; and I won't forgive you for it in a hurry."

" It's stuff and nonsense you're talking, Lou," said Courtney, but in his voice there was an uneasy note.

" You'll see," said Mrs. Anderson with a wise nod. " All I have to say is that I'll wash my hands of you. You've had your chance, the best ever a man had to make a home, and you've thrown it away. So don't come over here when the abomination of desolation overtakes Markyates again, for I won't give you a bit of sympathy. In fact, I'll be glad, because it'll be nothing but your deserts."

" Wheesht, Lou," said David warningly, and at the moment the hired man returned to his place at the table, and Louie perforce had to be silent. Courtney bent over his plate and wrestled with his food, looking like a man into whose soul the iron had entered.

CHAPTER XXI

HIS DESERTS

COURTNEY, after a long day hauling a double team of wheat to the elevator at Fort Purbeck, got back to Markyates about four o'clock. It was a brilliant winter day. An intense frost had crystallised all the snow-covered prairies into one vast jewel, and the sun shone overhead from a cloudless sky without disseminating much heat. The cold was intense. Courtney thought, with longing, of his comfortable fireside and his evening meal, which never failed to be ready when he was ready for it. Madge Fairweather had now been gone five weeks, and apparently the household at Markyates had relapsed into its former peaceful state. But there was a difference, of which no one was more conscious than Courtney himself. He had expected that Janet Fairweather would leave him at once, but now that five weeks had gone by, he had begun to be a little easier in his mind. Probably now she would stay as long as he wished. The old comradeship, however, had totally disappeared. Janet did her duty for her employer, and no more. On the few occasions when he had tried to go back to the old friendly way, she had simply looked at him with something in her eyes which made his colour rise. She was very quiet, very reserved, and very, very distant in her manner. But with the conduct of his household affairs it was impossible for him to find fault. He had not forgotten Madge, the brilliant creature who had flashed like a meteor across the quiet horizon of his days, but certainly the memory of her had become dim.

Janet's old charm reasserted itself, and her very aloofness made her more desirable in his eyes. But he was afraid to say a word. He felt precisely as if a new person had come in Janet's place, whose acquaintance he had to make. And he found it a most difficult task.

She came out to speak to him when he came to the house door, asking whether he was cold, and even volunteering to help him off with his fur robe.

"Thank you. I don't remember such a frost here. It was forty below zero last night—as bad as Manitoba," he said cheerfully, for the little attention pleased him mightily. "Where's Billy?"

"His aunt was here to-day, and took him away for a few days. She thought it better."

"Better! Why?" asked Courtney suspiciously.

"Come inside and take off your frozen boots, and I'll tell you," said Janet a trifle hurriedly. "And I think you would like tea now."

She made haste into the inner room, while in the scullery Courtney hung up his buffalo robe and began to undo his heavy boots.

There was a stove in the scullery likewise, and before its cheerful blaze his slippers were warming. He thrust his feet into them, washed his hands and face, and finally appeared in the inner room.

"Well, what's up? What did Lou want to-day, eh? She might have waited for my leave to take away the kid."

"She came to say good-bye to me, Mr. Courtney. I'm going to-morrow."

Courtney stared at her stupidly.

"You're going to-morrow!" he repeated. "Oh, come, this is too much! You can't, you know; it isn't fair to a chap. You can't say it is!"

"I thought you must have guessed. I just waited to hear from my sister in Scotland, Mrs. Ludlow. The letter came yesterday, but I've been getting ready all the time. Even if I could not have gone to her, I should have left Canada."

"Oh—and has Mrs. Anderson known this all along?"

"Yes, she has."

"I suppose I'm not permitted to ask the why and wherefore of this mystery?" he said, trying to speak lightly, but failing miserably.

"The explanation is quite simple. I am rather tired of the life. It is a very hard one for a woman. I know of posts in Scotland I could take where the work would not be so hard."

"You've done too much. I've said so all along," said Courtney rather harshly.

"The work was there and had to be done. I have not exceeded my duty," Janet answered stiffly.

Courtney looked round crossly.

"So you've made it up between you, Lou and you, to leave me in the lurch, and Denis away homesteading! Oh, you've chosen your opportunity well so that I get my full punishment for my sins."

"There won't be any punishment. Mrs. Anderson has got somebody else for you. She's at their place, and will bring back Billy whenever you like. We arranged it like that, because I did not wish to say good-bye to Billy, or to let him know I was going," said Janet, trying to speak bravely. "I wanted to go to-day. I begged Mrs. Anderson ever so hard to drive me to Lincot station before you came back, but she wouldn't do it."

"I should think not. So to-morrow you're going to chuck me, and Billy, and Canada. Well, I suppose we've got the gruel we deserve, and must just swallow it. Please pour out the tea."

His face was a little white, and his eyes were blazing hard.

Janet, who knew these signs, having seen them on the rare occasions when Courtney's anger had been roused by things outside, obeyed him without a word. She brought the hot dish with its savoury contents out of the oven, set it in front of him, and made herself scarce. To sit down with him and make a ghastly attempt at eating would be to court disaster, and she was determined not to make a fool of herself.

She wished with all her heart she had made an arrangement with some outsider to drive her somewhere to meet the train, so that she could have escaped the look in Courtney's eyes, and the horrible, dreaded good-bye.

Courtney, in a white heat of passion, forced himself to make a good meal, and then smoked mightily. Janet felt the whiff of the smoke in her upstairs room, and it comforted her oddly. But, oh! how she wished she was away!

About an hour later he came to the bottom of the stairs, and called to her by name.

"I'll be there directly," she answered. But it was at least ten minutes before she appeared.

"I wish you had given me a little more notice. I ought to haul another load of wheat into Purbeck to-morrow. They're waiting for it."

"Oh, do! I could take the sleigh with Minchu in it. She's so quiet, and she could be stabled at the hotel till you have time to bring her back. I thought of all that, and my big trunk has already gone. I sent it in with Denis the day he went away."

"So you wanted to make sure," he said, and his strange eyes mercilessly covered her face. "Well, have it like that. No doubt it would be a trial to you to sit it out with me to Purbeck. Come to think of it, it must be three months since we rode that way together."

"It was five months yesterday," she answered clearly.

"So! I knew it was a goodish while. Well, and about the money. Are you going right through to the coast, to Quebec or Montreal, or how——"

"No, I shall stop at Winnipeg—I have a friend there—and again at New York. You forget the only Canadian boats are running from St. John's now, and I prefer to sail from New York to Glasgow. I have friends there too, and can wait till a good boat is available."

"You've left nothing to chance. Well, that's the way, when your heart's set on a thing. I'm glad you are to stop off at Winnipeg. I'll give you my cheque on the Merchants Bank there."

"It doesn't matter about that. You can send it to Scotland after me if you like."

"You would trust me that far, then ?" he asked, with a small smile that was half a sneer. "I can't blame you for going. I suppose we'd better not talk about it; but I'll tell you what —I wish to God you had never come."

Again the passion blazed in his eyes, and Janet fled from it, half fearing, half repelled, half fascinated by it. She did not come down again, nor see him that night, and there was very little sleep for these two alone together under one roof at the back of beyond, and with the yawning gulf of memory between.

Towards morning Janet, worn out with thinking and with the tears she had shed, fell into a sound, heavy sleep, and when she awoke, the sun was across her bed. She sprang up, and, looking at her watch, found it was half-past eight. Quite horrified, she dressed quickly, yet thinking with relief that probably by this time Courtney had got his own breakfast, and departed with the wheat. He had. When she entered the kitchen she found the table laid for her breakfast, the remains of his having been carefully removed to the scullery. She had taught them all habits of neatness and daintiness during the months she had been in the house. A letter addressed to her was on the end of the table, and she swayed a little as her fingers closed over it, remembering the first morning she had awakened in Markyates, and had found Courtney's scrawl pinned to the tablecloth.

It was a thick letter, and she decided to eat her breakfast before she read it. But her appetite sadly failed her, and at last she drew the envelope to her plate and broke it open. A pink-coloured cheque dropped out first, filled up for five hundred dollars, a hundred pounds in English money. On a sheet of notepaper, folded twice, these few words were written :—

"This does not pay you for what you have done for me and mine—nothing ever will. I'm glad you didn't come down this morning. I could not have said good-bye. But I do say here and now that there is no sea broad enough or deep enough to bear you clean away from me. Some day, somewhere, we shall meet again. I don't ask to be forgiven, for there are things that are better left in the limbo of forgotten things. But if it is any satisfaction to you, you can be assured that you have dealt out the swiftest and most condign punishment in the world to

"George Yates Courtney."

Janet's proud mouth quivered just a moment as her eyes once more devoured the words. They might mean so much, and yet said so little. But they comforted her. At least she need not go away with the memory of a mocking smile and a harsh note from the place where she had once been happy.

It seemed to her, as she moved about the house quickly, setting it to rights for the last time, that the old comradeship had somehow come back, in the spirit if not in the flesh. Her thoughts of Courtney were very tender as she looked for the last time round the little homestead where she had done her best. Perhaps she had failed, but at least no honest effort is ever lost. Her father had often said that to her when he would return sometimes disheartened over his fight with death. But it never occurred to her for one instant to take the full meaning out of Courtney's letter. Another woman would have read in the words an invitation to stay, but even had Janet believed that was the innermost significance of these hastily written words, her pride was too high and fine to permit her to recognise it. No, if she was worth anything at all, she was worth seeking. She would prove him at least. And if, as he said, there was no sea deep enough or wide enough to keep him away, why, then, she could wait. But she went happier than she had expected to go, though her eyes were blinded as she stood ready to step into the sleigh, and looked for the last time round the strange, remote, desolate-looking spot, which she had long since written of as the back of beyond.

Well, anyway, it had held her heart, and she could never, never be cold or forgetful of it any more, even if her eyes should never in life behold it again.

Wonder of wonders, the train was on time at Fort Purbeck station, and, to her intense relief, Janet saw nothing of Courtney.

" Lef' about an hour ago to go round by Anderson's," the voluble Mrs. Smithson informed her. " So you're quitting, Miss Fairweather ? Well, I don't blame you. It ain't no great shakes on a prairie farm in weather like this. My, ain't it cold ? But you'll be warm enuff on the cars. Thet's one good thing about the C.P.R. They don't grudge the coal. East is it you're goin', or west ? Arter that pretty sister of your'n ? "

There was a subtle suggestion in her last inquiry which Janet promptly ignored.

" It's the east-bound train I'm waiting for, Mrs. Smithson, and do you understand that the sleigh and Minchu are to stand here till Mr. Courtney calls for them ? "

" He tole me thet. Down on his luck, he seemed, and I don't wonder. Your sort ain't picked up any day on the prairie track, and so I told 'im. A little bit o' the hard again won't do Boss Courtney no harm. Well, must you be goin' ? Good-bye, then ; I wish you well. I'm sorry you're goin', though you ain't ever bin as neighbourly as one lone woman oughter be to another in this God-forsaken land."

With this little dig for her comfort, Janet made her way to the station to wait in the little stuffy booking-office, from which every particle of air was carefully excluded. But ere long she saw through the grimy window the puffing smoke of the approaching train, and in a few more minutes the next stage of the journey was begun.

Once more Peter Rose waited with all the heart in the world for the arrival of the train bearing a beloved and honoured guest to his home. Janet's eyes filled with tears when she saw his honest face beaming upon her from the side track. It was two o'clock in the morning, and the thermometer fifty below zero ; but these were items of no account to Peter on such an occasion.

" There ye are, Miss Janet, an' prood we are to see ye ! Late ? Ay, but I've had five hours in my bed. I'm on the nicht shift the noo, and I gang on at eight o'clock. Dinna you bother your heid aboot me. We'll jist leave the stuff to be brocht ower in the morning. An' we'll walk, if ye dinna mind. We've moved into a new hoose, an' it's only ten minutes' walk. It's better nor a cab on a nicht like this."

Janet gladly consented, and over the hard, frozen roads of a city gleaming white under the gem-studded sky they made their swift way to Ellen's house. Janet found it delicious after the close air of the train, though her very breath seemed to freeze on her lips, and their voices had an odd metallic ring in them. Peter asked no questions, but incidentally gave her a good deal of information about his own little *ménage*.

" We was gaun hame for Christmas, but there's a new bairn comin' in February. Oh ay, Ellen's fine and as cheery as ye like. I think she likes the country better than she did, and she's fell prood o' her new hoose. It's bigger—an' what do ye think ? She wad like a drawin'-room. She's for you to help her to buy the furniture. Fancy Ellen wi' a drawin-room ! Weemin are queer craters ! " Ellen's ambition seemed to amuse Peter mightily, but under it there was both love and pride, and all the tenderness a good husband has for the wife he thinks the world of.

By the time Janet stood with proper awe and admiration before Peter's double-fronted house standing in its beautiful piece of garden ground, she was in rather an exalted state.

For, in spite of Louie Anderson's friendship, she had been very lonely often at Markyates, and there are no friends like the old ones.

But Ellen was not prepared to see her so much changed, so much thinner, and all her pretty colour gone.

" Sicht—what hae they dune to ye on thae wicked prairies, my dear ? " she asked when she had taken her into the big, splendid best bedroom which she had prepared for her with such loving pride. " Certy, but they have taen it ooten ye, my dear. But I wairned ye. Eh, if I had but keepit ye here ! "

All the answer Janet made was to throw herself suddenly on Ellen's broad bosom and burst into tears.

Ellen was far too wise to ask a single question, but she needed no telling. The prairies had done more than rob her dear Miss Janet of her bright looks and sweet colour ; they had taken the heart clean out of her. In the privacy of their own room she shook her fist darkly at Peter, and said she would get even with them yet.

CHAPTER XXII

THE REWARD

It was April before Janet Fairweather arrived in Scotland. A month had quickly passed in Winnipeg, Janet having been easily persuaded to await the arrival of the new baby. Then she had spent two weeks with the Nelsons in New York, where she had been made much of both by Nelson and his wife. Having obtained her desire, Mrs. John P. Nelson was in the best of good humours, apparently in rude health, and without a fault to find with fate. Nelson appeared contented enough, the quality of his brain ensured his ultimate success in whatever business he addressed himself to, but he had liked the new West, and frankly expressed to Janet his regret at having had to leave it.

It was a grey and rainy day when Janet sailed up the Clyde to the Broomielaw, and entrained at Glasgow for the north.

Telegraphing to Bella, she expected to be met by her at Balgarnie station, but was disappointed. It was a lovely spring evening, with a delicious mackerel-tinted sky overhead, and the feeling of teeming new life in every air that blew. Janet was conscious of a bursting heart as she neared the place of her birth. Only a year and a half since she had left it, yet so crowded had these brief months been with new experiences that she felt as if it must be ten years! There was no change in the little old-world town on the edge of the moors and the great mountains. It looked precisely as it had done that fateful morning when she and Madge had said their good-byes. She stepped from the train and gave a swift look round, but the only person in view was Bobby Ludlow, very spruce and smart-looking in his well-cut tweed suit and slouch hat, with a setter at his heels. He was so vastly improved that Janet inwardly congratulated Bella on her work.

He came forward smiling with the utmost cordiality.

"Sorry Bella wasn't able to come. Yes, she's fairly all right. You'll see her presently. Had a good voyage? You look rather pale. We're glad to see you back."

Bobbie spoke with a perfect sincerity, for he had always liked Janet the best of all the Fairweathers, though he would have married Madge had she been willing.

"The trap's outside. I brought the brougham in case you would be tired, and the trap will take all your stuff."

Janet smiled, and when she saw the very smart green *coupé* with the man in livery on the box she thought things must be prospering greatly with the Ludlows. Bella had never been very communicative in her letters, and Janet felt her interest in all the old places and people springing into newness of life. But she did not want to talk much.

"Lots of changes since you went away, Janet. I suppose I may call you that now? There's been a letter from Madge. She's married too, so you're the last leaf on the tree."

"Madge married! Oh, it can't be true, Dr. Ludlow! I've never heard a word about it."

"Well, it's true enough. The letter was for you, sent on from your old place. Bella knew the writing, so she opened it, thinking it didn't matter. I don't think it did, as a matter of fact," he added, though Janet felt her colour rising, " as its chief import was her marriage."

" Who to ? " asked Janet drily.

" Chap of the name of Ronderbusch—something in wheat and soap. I believe, anyway, he has the necessary oof, and they're off for a voyage round the world."

" I knew of a Ronderbusch," said Janet stupidly. " But he had a wife already."

" Oh, that's a commodity easily shifted in the States," remarked Bobby facetiously. " Seems he divorced his wife, or she him. I believe it was the first named though, and he and Madge ran across one another in Vancouver, and fixed up things with the rapidity characteristic of the Free West. So she's got what she went out after. Let's hope it'll content her."

Janet listened but somehow she could not discuss Madge with this man, who, though Bella's husband, was still to her a stranger.

" I hope you have had a prosperous year, Dr. Ludlow," she said rather stiffly as they turned up the station road, and began the ascent to The Croft.

" Oh, yes, most things are coming my way. There is a tide in the affairs of men. You know the rest. I've nothing to complain of."

" And Bella, I suppose, is very jolly. She never wanted to leave Balgarnie, and I believe that, after all, she was wise."

" Bella's all right. Why shouldn't she be ? She's got a good husband, and she knows when she's well off. You'll find a few changes at The Croft perhaps, but I hope it won't be changed out of your recognition."

The first thing Janet saw was that the shrubbery which her father had planted, and whose growth he had watched with almost a father's pride, had been cleared to leave the gable end of the house almost naked.

" Had to clear the way for the new surgery," Bobby explained as the horse turned in at the gate. " People don't like to grope their way in the dark."

" But why did you build it at this end, so near the drawing-room ? Doesn't Bella find it awkward ? "

" Not at all. I gave her the other room, the little one. I wanted the big one for my consulting-room. If one wants a business to pay, it must be treated with respect."

Janet had not a word to say. She seemed to realise all in a moment that Bella had not only got a husband, but The Croft a master. Remembering the old order of things, she wondered how Bella liked it. But when she saw her precise little figure standing in the doorway presently, she saw that Bella appeared happy enough. She was obviously pleased. In fact, there were real tears in her eyes.

" I was so sorry not to come to the station, but Robert said there wouldn't be room for three, and he particularly wanted to go himself. I'm real glad to see you."

Janet gave a little sob as she entered the house clinging to Bella's arm. There was something about this new Bella that appealed.

She had entirely lost her little air of command, her slightly domineering way. Long before the evening was over, Janet grasped the fact that Bella was now a person under authority, and that the house existed and was run primarily for the benefit of Mr. Robert Ludlow. He was entirely urbane, and smiling and attentive in a kindly way to his wife, and the wonder of it sank into Janet's soul. She even conceived an odd sort of respect for the man, because the person who could dominate Bella must have something in him. Everything seemed altered at The Croft.

The Ludlows themselves occupied the spare bedroom, the dressing-room of which was elaborately fitted up for the doctor's use.

Also the meals were changed, and there was now an eight-o'clock dinner instead of the cold supper at any hour, which used to follow the substantial sit-down tea.

" The doctor likes it better, and he generally tries to get his work done by then," said Bella with a sort of prim pride. " Yes, he is always busy ; in the last six months he got no less than twenty new patients. He will get an assistant before another winter, because he would like to have a little hunting, and now he has not the time."

"It's astonishing what changes even a year can bring," said Janet, sitting down on the front of her bed, ready to talk. Bella had accompanied her to her room after they had said good night downstairs.

"I was sorry about Madge's letter, because it was really a private one from her to you. But it was Robert made me open it. He seemed quite as curious as a woman over it. Can you believe that three of us are married out of four? and what do you think of Madge away round the world with a millionaire?"

Janet did not say what she thought, nor did she even read Madge's letter. Bella was surprised to see her stick it unread in the fire, with rather a strange look on her face.

"She seems to have stopped a good bit with you on the farm. Why did you leave, Janet? Did you get tired of the hard work?"

"Partly, but I don't want to talk about it just yet, if you please. I'll tell you bit by bit. There's just one thing to say about Madge, Bella. Something or somebody has got to teach her and put a bit of real, genuine feeling into her. She hasn't any yet."

"Oh, life will teach her, and matrimony," said Bella, pursing her lips oddly. "It's surprising what a difference a man makes in a house. I wouldn't have believed it. I daresay she'll become quite a meek, stay-at-home sort of person after she has lived with this Ronderbusch man for a while. She's had some luck, hasn't she? Fancy one of us married with such prospects in India, and Madge a millionaire's wife! What are you going to do for the credit of the Fairweather family?"

"Remain single—and look here, Bella, you needn't be afraid of my outstaying my welcome. I should like about a month, just to see some of the old places and the old folk. Do you think your majorful doctor could stand me for a month?"

Bella laughed.

"You soon weigh up folks, but Robert's very kind to me, Jen, and, after all, I suppose it is better for women to be in a little subjection. It's what the Bible teaches, anyway, and I'm quite happy."

"You look it, and there is no doubt marriage with you has made *him*," said Janet quietly.

"And in September there'll be another one in the house," said Bella with a queer, far-away look on her hard little face. "Yes, honestly, and, of course, we're both very glad about it, for the doctor loves children, and I don't believe he would have been pleased if there had been none."

Janet's face instantly softened, and in that moment they drew nearer in heart than they had ever been, and when Janet lay down on her bed that night it was to ponder afresh on the mystery of life, and the astonishing variety of the lessons it could teach.

She spent a quite happy month at The Croft, and was made much of in a quiet way both by Ludlow and Bella, and by all the old friends. Then, in the month of June, she accepted a post as far north as Shetland, to live in a castle on an island, and look after the four children of a London M.P. until their parents should be at liberty to join them.

That was a life after her own heart, and the fresh affectionate companionship of these delightsome creatures did much towards restoring her to her normal state.

Janet Fairweather, however, was the type of a woman who does not easily or quickly forget. She had frankly left her heart on the Canadian prairie, and many a longing look she cast back to it, living over again its incomparable mornings and all its bitter-sweet memories. She remained in Shetland till the beginning of December, and then came down to The Croft to spend Christmas, and make acquaintance with the son and heir who had arrived at the expected time, a fine, strong, sturdy baby with the grey-blue eyes of his mother's folk. But his hair was black, like Bobby Ludlow's, and he featured him likewise, and was altogether as fine a baby as the most exacting could desire. Parenthood sat finely both on Bella and her husband, giving to them the needed little human touch. Janet slipped easily and naturally into her place as maiden-auntie, and sometimes Bella would look at her as she sat nursing the baby, and think what a beautiful mother she would make.

"You must get married yourself, Jen, for I never saw a woman handle a bairn like you. I wish I had your hands. Whenever you lift him, look, he is quiet. There's something about you that makes him feel safe."

Janet laughed and pressed her lips to the little wrinkled face on her lap, and finally carried him to his mother's lap.

"Take your bairn, or I'll never be able to go away from him. Now, I'm going up to the kirkyard with a bunch of rowans and these big white chrysanthemums for father's Christmas. Don't you mind how he loved the rowans? He was hardly ever without a little sprig in his buttonhole all the time they were in season."

"You do mind things, Jen. My memory seems like a sieve. You think of everything that used to happen. I only remember them when you speak."

"You have to go out of Scotland, my dear, to learn how sib you are to it. It's in the very marrow of your bones," answered Janet as she rose to go.

She enjoyed her walk across the hills to the old kirkyard, and, lingering there, she wondered whether the father, who in his own way had loved and cared for them greatly, had knowledge, where he was, of how it was with them now. And, above all, did he know about her empty heart? The sight of Bella with her baby had stirred in Janet all sorts of feelings and thoughts of which she thought she had got the mastery. All her thought, as she wandered back from the old kirkyard with a sprig of the dead heather against her lips, was of a little green-and-white frame house standing on the edge of the prairie at the back of beyond. It would soon be a year since she had turned her back on it. How was it faring without her? she wondered. Had another quickly and efficiently filled her place?

It was gathering dusk when she turned in at The Croft gate again, and there, before the door, beheld an astonishing sight. It was merely a small boy in a blue jersey buttoned close up to his throat, his golden head bare to the setting sun, playing round with the setter and her two puppies, his sweet shrill voice addressing them in the most endearing language. Presently he raised his head and saw her come in at the gate. Then he gave a great cry, and came running, but not faster than Janet herself, and the next moment Billy's arms were tight round her neck, his face pressed to hers, his eyes dancing, his whole lithe, sweet little body vibrating with joy.

"Oh, my auntie! oh, my auntie!" was all he could cry, breathless. "Come in quick. Daddy's here. He bringed me to you for Christmas. Come to him, quick."

She was borne in, as it were, on a whirlwind, and presently, at the consulting-room door, appeared Bobby Ludlow, side by side with a man beside whom his figure seemed to shrink into insignificance.

"A friend to see you, Janet," said Bobby facetiously, having jumped immediately to the right conclusion. "Supposing the little chap comes with me. There are some more puppies in the stable, and after we've seen them it'll be time for tea."

Billy was divided between longing to see the puppies and his new-found joy, but Bobby quietly lifted him and disappeared through the swing-door, and Courtney drew Janet into the consulting-room and shut the door.

For a moment they looked at one another, then Janet laughed an odd, trembling little laugh that was all sweetness.

"My breath is taken away! When did you come, and why?"

"We arrived at Liverpool yesterday—why, because we need you, Billy and me. Oh, my dear, my dear! how badly we need you you'll never know in this world, though I'll try to tell you if you'll give me a chance."

" I was thinking of Markyates as I came over the hill this afternoon. I don't know what brought it back—not the hills, surely, because there are none just near you," she said in a low, halting voice.

" Perhaps something told you we were here," hazarded Courtney, and his eyes devoured her face.

" Oh, no, I never thought that possible."

" It was Billy I meant to make special pleader, but he has basely deserted me," said Courtney very humbly. " I don't know what to say. Perhaps it would be best to say nothing. I—love you, Janet, with the best that is in me, with the only manhood that is worth any woman's acceptance. You can lift me up. Forgive all that went before. It was madness. I don't seek to explain or excuse it. I only ask you to forgive, and give me another chance, for the kid's sake."

Janet had not much pride. The woman who loves seldom has.

She just smiled on him, and held out her hands.

" I'm homesick too," was all she said. " And I'll come not only for Billy's sake but for yours."

THE END

THE INHERITANCE

THE INHERITANCE

BY

ANNIE S. SWAN

SUNDAY MAIL EDITION

1933

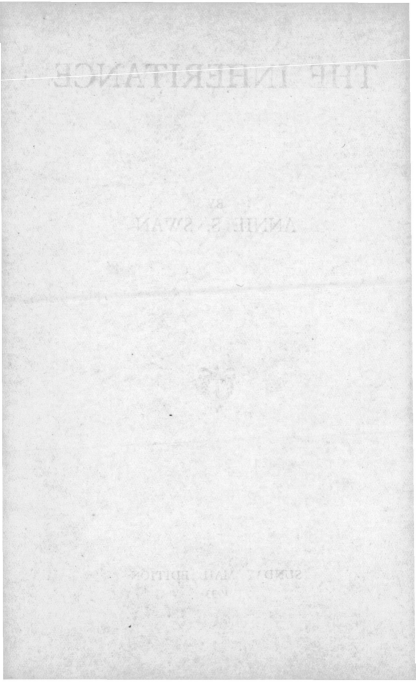

CONTENTS

CHAPTER I

THE PROMISE

OLD George Speed lay dying in an upper room of his beautiful home at Newport. Men who spoke of him in the great and busy city whose spires and chimney-stalks could be seen, veiled in an elusive mist, from the windows of the sick-room, said it was the close of a well-spent life.

He did not suffer much ; he had only a great weakness, and as he sat propped up in his bed with his pillows about him, a little skull-cap on the bare head above the fringe of his white hair, he made a pathetic picture.

In his prime he had been a fine figure of a man, but for a good many years now he had been creeping gradually down, and had become " little boukit," as the expressive Fifeshire phrase has it. His face was clean-shaven save for straggling side-whiskers, and that very day—his last upon earth—he had gone through the routine of his toilet, his faithful man Jarvis shaving him with a hand that trembled more than his master's. This personal fastidiousness had been characteristic of George Speed from his youth up, ever since the time when he ran a barefoot laddie in Rattray parish, in the Howe of Strathmore, and fought his brother Jamie for daring to use the bit of rag he called his towel. His mother had sympathised wholly with Jamie, and clouted Geordie's ears for being " finicky," as she termed it, asking him " where he thocht he had been brocht up and where he intended to end."

Where indeed ? The question must ever remain unanswered. You find this quick, keen sense of personal delicacy in unexpected places, and are often puzzled by it. Why there should be such differences in the one brood will ever continue to be one of the deep and unsolvable psychological problems with which the thoughtful torment themselves.

There was no onè with the old man in the room, the nurse having taken the opportunity of going downstairs for her tea while he was supposed to be asleep. He sat with his face turned towards the windows, a curious expression of wistfulness on it. He looked like a man who saw visions and who yearned towards impossible heights.

Tired of his waking thoughts, or, it might be, impatient for the final setting of his house in order, he pulled the bell. The trained nurse, in sudden alarm, ran up, full of apology.

" I'm all right, nurse ; only I want Jarvis. Where is he ? "

The old man always pronounced the name of his attendant as if it had been spelled with an " e."

" Coming, sir," replied the nurse. " Are you sure I can do nothing for you now ? It is not time for your medicine yet."

" I am sure, thank you, nurse. I thought I heard wheels on the gravel a minute ago."

" Yes, sir ; it was Miss Lundie, who called to inquire for you."

" Has she gone yet ? " he asked eagerly. " I should like very much to see her."

" Jarvis is speaking to her, sir. I said you were asleep. I'll run down and ask her to come up—if you are sure you are able for it," she added with a hesitating anxiety.

" I am quite able. Go at once, nurse," he said, with a touch of the old imperious manner that had been wont to make subordinates tremble.

She disappeared, but in a few minutes returned, and stood aside at the door to permit the visitor to enter.

Miss Katherine Lundie was a tall, slim girl, wearing a gown of soft, ruddy-brown material, and a big picture hat, which was tied under her chin with flowing chiffon strings. It was a costume which suited her to perfection and gave to her figure a rare distinction. She was well bred; you could see it in the poise of her head and the carriage of her beautiful body. Her face was very sweet, albeit it was easy to imagine it haughty. It was very soft and lovely at the moment, however, as her eyes fell on the wasted face and figure of the old man on the bed.

"Oh, pray don't lean forward; I am sure it will tire you, Mr. Speed," she said in her soft, kind voice. "It is very kind of you to see me to-day."

"The kindness is on your side in coming, my dear. Sit down won't you? I want to talk to you."

She looked a little uncertain. "Are you sure that it is wise? You look so tired and worn. You ought not to be talking, I am sure. I brought you some flowers—just a handful from the garden at Lunan. We came back only this morning."

She laid her bouquet on the bed. It was a beautiful thing, plucked with a careless grace: a few hardy outdoor chrysanthemums, some sprays of the Michaelmas daisy, a branch of bramble, and one of wild rose with the hips flaming on it. It was like Katherine to remember him and to bring such a simple offering as her own soul loved, though the glass-houses at Ravenscraig were full of rare specimens costing money to produce. Katherine did not care for costly products from glass-houses. She loved the children of Nature, and the bunch on the bed was wholly typical of her taste.

"Hips and haws," murmured George Speed as his frail fingers touched the bouquet for a moment. "Eh, lass, it's a long time since I ran wild between the hedges in the Howe o' Strathmore seeking them to fill my empty stomach."

"I'm glad you like them," she answered brightly. "They're lovely, I think. Where shall I put them?"

"On the near table, where I can see and touch them when I want. So you came up from Lunan only this morning. I suppose your father's gone to business?"

"Yes. But if you would like to see him I shall tell him, and he will come across immediately."

"To-morrow will do," said the old man quietly, and all the time his eyes did not leave the girl's fair face.

"You are very fond of the sands at Lunan and that queer little house of yours, aren't you? I wish you could give them a bit of your simpler taste at the Ferry."

Katherine laughed, understanding him perfectly, but having nothing to utter in reply.

"And what visitors had you over the Sunday? I have heard that you are never there alone. What waifs and strays from the Overgate or the Hilltown had you this week end?"

"Nobody, Mr. Speed—only Tom."

"Only Tom."

A little smile crept about his mouth, and he leaned forward and fixed his deep eyes full on her face so that her colour rose under his steady gaze.

"He spends a good many week-ends at Lunan, that same lad, doesn't he?"

"He has been a good few times. He likes the place. Some day he would like a house there himself, he says."

"And all the rest swear by St. Andrews. Eh, well, I don't wonder at his choice."

There was a moment's silence, then suddenly he leaned forward again and spoke significant words.

"My dear, I'm an old man, and my time's at hand," he said with a kind of quiet eagerness. "You won't mind if I speak out plainly?"

"No," she answered, but with some confusion, and her sweet eyes turned away a little quickly.

"It would please me well to hear that my grandson Tom and you will be man and wife. Is it to be, my dear?"

She shook her head and rose a little quickly, with some sign of distress.

"How can I tell, Mr. Speed? We are very good friends—nothing more."

"But you would make him a happy and a good man, Katherine. You have simple womanly tastes. I could wish that my granddaughters shared them."

Katherine made no reply. The subject of the conversation distressed her, and, but for seeming unkind, she would have abruptly changed it.

"But friendship is the best basis, lass," he said dreamily. "I've dreamed my dreams about you two. It isn't too much to say that most of my hopes are built upon you. You won't disappoint them."

She was silent a moment, standing by the window, her eyes sweeping the beautiful expanse of the Firth, then illumined by indescribable sunset effects. Her pride rebelled, her womanliness was abashed, and it was only her kindness of heart that prevented her from returning a churlish answer. She turned to him suddenly and spoke quickly.

" Mr. Speed, can't you see it is a subject on which I can't make any promise, and cannot even discuss it with you ? What woman could when the man has not said anything—not the faintest word. I do assure you we are good friends and comrades interested in the same things—and that is all."

" I beg your pardon, my dear. I see I had no right to question you," he said apologetically. Yet with the persistence of old age, which is precisely like that of childhood, he continued to harp on the same theme.

" It would be the right marriage, the best of its kind I've ever seen, and you would live in this house, Katherine. I'd like to think of you and Tom and your little bairns in this house, my lass. I built it as a monument to my prosperity, but it has been a white elephant to me ever since the day my wife died. Since then everything has been like dust and ashes in my mouth."

Her face was full of sympathy and compassion, for never had she dreamed of such depths in the hard old man's nature. She had come merely to pay a duty call, having been sent by her father, and this little interlude was wholly unexpected.

" It would have been better to have left it, Mr. Speed, and let ' The Rowans ' folk come into it. They would have enjoyed it to the full."

She was astonished at the sudden hardening of his face.

" That's what they would like, lass—what they've been plotting and scheming for all along. But no ! My son's wife has never considered me but as a kind of milch-cow, and she'll be cheated yet. I've never seen her face since I've been ill."

" Hasn't she called ? " inquired Katherine, helplessly, pained by the tone of the old man's remarks, yet sympathising with it to a certain extent, for she did not admire the wife of the younger George Speed in spite of the fact that she was Tom's mother.

" Been here ! Yes, every day of her life. She's like the corbies, at hame when there's ony chance of a buryin'. Don't look so distressed, lassie. I'm no' blaming you."

When she made no response he went on again.

" Tom's an ootlin' in The Rowans nest, lass. He's like his grandmother, an' for that reason my very soul cleaves to him, and it's for that I would see him and you happy. May I ask one more question before you go, my dear ? And, when you are going to answer it, forgive an old man—a dying man—his persistence. You can never understand how he wants things put right until ye come to this pass yourself. You are not angry ? " he added, almost pleadingly, when she turned away again.

" No, no—not angry, but I fear you are distressing yourself," she said quickly. " I wish you would not talk any more now. I shall come again to see you to-morrow if you like."

" To-morrow may be too late. What I want to hear must be said now to do me any good. Stoop down, lass, and tell me. When Tom seeks you, you will not say him nay, and I can die thinking that you will be mistress of this house which my wife—my Mary—hardly lived to see."

There was no escape, and, to satisfy him, she spoke the words he craved to hear. Then he blessed her with words of solemn joy and satisfaction which she never forgot. Her cheeks were aflame, her eyes shining as she descended the stairs, where she met the faithful Jarvis hurrying to answer his master's bell.

" Is that you, Jarvis ? "

" Yes, sir ; you're fair dune. Let me get ye a spunefu' o' brandy."

" Very well. Then to the telephone—first to James Gilfillan, the lawyer. Tell him to be here within an hour ; and syne to The Rowans, and, if my son be at home and come back from business, tell him I want to see him here at six o'clock."

CHAPTER II

THE CORBIE

THE telephonic message from Ravenscraig was received by George Speed's daughter-in-law in the morning-room at The Rowans, where she was replying to some cards of invitation. She was a large, fair woman, with masses of red-gold hair arranged high, giving to her face unusual length. A certain handsomeness distinguished her, but the face was hard, and the cold blue-grey eyes had at times quite a steely gleam in them.

Her second daughter, Netta, a somewhat pale but rather attractive-looking girl, was busy with a piece of embroidery by the table, which was laid for afternoon tea.

"Just as I expected, Netta," said her mother severely as she laid down the receiver. "Your father is urgently wanted at Newport. I warned him that he ought not to go to golf to-day—that something would be sure to happen."

"But we've had so many alarms with grandpa, mother," said the girl quietly. "Couldn't you telephone to the Golf Club?"

"You do it then, at once. I must get these letters out by the five o'clock post. It's very tiresome having to refuse every invitation."

"Poor grandpa takes too long to die," said the girl with a curious little curve of the lips. "But he never has been accommodating to us."

"He has never liked us—at least me, my dear," said Mrs. George calmly. "And it says a great deal for my tact and amiability that there never has been an open rupture. I flatter myself I can manage Grandpa Speed a good deal better than any of his own relatives."

Netta remained silent with the receiver at her ear, waiting for the answer from the Golf Club. It came in a moment.

"He's gone to the train already, mother. So he will be here in about half an hour."

"Ring up Ravenscraig, then, and say that he's on his way to Newport."

Netta obeyed, and then returned to her interrupted work. She was a very silent, reserved girl, but her mother did not trouble about her.

The Speed girls were what their mother called "well brought up," that is to say, they had been moulded by her on the conventional pattern, and were amenable to parental authority in all matters pertaining to their welfare.

Mrs. George Halliwell Speed, as she styled herself, was autocratic in her household and all its ways, and so far had not had much trouble. The elder daughter had married—satisfactorily in her mother's eyes at least—a middle-aged captain in the Engineers, who had been attracted at Homburg by her dashing looks as well as by exaggerated reports of the wealth of the Speeds.

George Speed's wife had been a Halliwell of Broughton—an old Manchester family, and had brought some money to her husband and a great deal of personal ambition. Her sole endeavour since she had come to the North was to get herself attached to the county, but after five and twenty years she found that she had barely touched the fringe. For this she blamed old George Speed in that he had never allowed them an income adequate to their position and his means. She therefore waited his demise with an impatience she did not disguise from herself or her own family. She said rightly that old George did not like her—that he had never even pretended to do so.

At heart he was a simple, kindly old man. Some of the failings of the self-made man were his, but he was altogether free from the unsatisfying ambition which was the mainspring of his daughter-in-law's life, and which she had succeeded in strengthening in his son. Of late years the gulf between the two houses had widened, and though Mrs. Speed went a great deal to Ravenscraig, " doing her duty," as she expressed it, she always left with an irritating consciousness that she was kept on the outside. She had a good house at Broughty Ferry, but it was a hired house of the suburban type, and she was longing for the day when she should enter into the possession of Ravenscraig and all its treasures. In his later years the old man had been both traveller and collector, and Ravenscraig was a veritable treasure-house.

" Do you happen to know where Tom is this afternoon, Netta ? " she inquired as she shut down her last letter. " He might be wanted too, and he never is at hand when he ought to be."

" Why, you've forgotten, mother ; he's at business. This is Monday afternoon, not Saturday."

" Why, of course it is. That comes of your father taking a half-holiday. I asked him at lunch whether it was safe to go off on a Monday afternoon. He said he was tired and would have his game. I wish I saw Tom keener on business, dear, now your father shows a desire to slacken off."

" Oh, dad isn't really slackening off, mother. As for Tom, he'll never be what you call ' keen.' He's interested in too many things outside of business. You should have heard Katherine and him one day when I was out at Lunan last week. They were discussing a plan to reorganise the world, according to which all would be on the same level, and there would be neither poverty nor riches. It was most amusing, but they reproved me for laughing."

Mrs. Halliwell sighed quite plaintively.

" I can't think where Tom has got his extraordinary ideas—certainly not from me, or your father. He is very disappointing. I wish you had been a boy, Netta."

" So do I," said the girl with a sudden flash. " It's sickening to be a woman. I think one can do nothing. It is all so horribly monotonous living as we do. I am not sure, mother, whether Katherine hasn't the best of it."

" My dear Netta, although Katherine is, I hope, going to be my daughter-in-law, I assure you that in some respects she is impossible," said Mrs. Speed with sudden asperity. " She presumes on her position as Mr. Lundie's daughter. And after all, who are the Lundies ? They are only a remote branch of a decent family, and as poor as church mice, or were until your grandfather bought your father the partnership in the mills."

" But they belong to the county, mother," was all that Netta said. " And because of that Katherine doesn't care what she wears or what she does, and she associates with all sorts of people in Dundee. If you saw her drawing-room on a Sunday afternoon you would be positively horrified."

" I don't want to see it. It's very silly, and it's a mere pose which will pass. This socialistic craze is really one of the most sickening Society fads I have ever come across. But I hope it will pass—in Tom's case, at least—and that shortly he will settle down in earnest. Your father is getting sick of his slackness, and has even spoken of sending him out to Calcutta to be taken in hand by your uncle Mouat, who has turned out so many splendid young men."

" Katherine has an interesting life, though, mother," said Netta, with her chin on her hands. " It is much better, I think, not to care what people think or say, but just to please oneself."

Mrs. Halliwell Speed did not vouchsafe any reply to this treasonable observation. She had not hitherto had any trouble with either of her daughters, and she did not anticipate any. Netta would marry when the suitable person came along ; she had no doubt about it. And that person would in the primary instance be selected by her mother.

" I'm very sorry to refuse the Melvilles' invitation to meet Sir Rafe Fletcher. He is quite delightful, every one says. How would you like to be Lady Fletcher, Netta ? Then you would walk in front of Tom's wife."

Netta laughed.

" There's father coming up the drive. You are very sure about Tom and Katherine, mother, but honestly I don't think Tom is one bit in love with her, even if she is with him—which I don't think she is. Don't you see they pride themselves on their Platonic friendship. It is one of their ideals that there should be friendship between men and women like that, undisturbed by the eternal bogey of matrimony. I'm only quoting from Tom, now, mother. So you needn't look so severe."

" Fiddlesticks," quoth Mrs. Speed as she rose to meet her husband in the hall.

" That's a message from Newport. Your father wants you at once, George. Didn't I tell you you shouldn't be farther than the mills just now when we never know what will happen ? "

" How long is it since the message came ? " inquired Speed as he put his cap on the table.

" Only a few minutes ago. I think I'll go with you, George. I haven't been across since Friday."

" Very well," he replied. " I suppose you won't be long in getting ready ? " He took up some letters that were lying on the table and looked at them casually. George Speed the younger was a handsome figure of a man. Tall, well-built, and well-preserved, he by no means looked his fifty years. His tweed golfing suit was eminently becoming, and his ruddy face suggested the outdoor life. He was a prosperous man and looked it.

Netta came out when she heard her mother moving about upstairs.

" Grandpa must be a lot worse, dad," she said. " It was Jarvis who telephoned, and he said that both Gilfillan and Dr. Alister were coming."

" Gilfillan ! " repeated her father with a sudden alertness in his looks. " I thought everything had been finally settled by Gilfillan more than a month ago."

Netta made no response. She was not greatly interested in the disposal of her grandfather's wealth. She did not suppose it would make very much difference to her.

Mrs. Speed took but a short time to dress. A long handsome cloak covered her house attire, a neat toque was pinned to her abundant and really beautiful hair, a veil and gloves were quickly donned, and the pair left the house to walk to the station only about five minutes distant.

" Netta tells me Gilfillan has been sent for to Ravenscraig, Marian," said Speed as he guided his wife's steps down the steep garden path which gave a short cut to the station. " What do you suppose it can mean ? We don't want any codicils at the last moment."

" No, certainly not. You'll make inquiry, won't you ? It would be too disappointing if anything happened. You never can be sure with old men. Just look what my father did at the last, leaving all to his second family."

" What I'm afraid of is a sudden philanthropic impulse," said Speed gloomily. " He's been harping a good deal on wasted opportunities and the like, the usual mood of a man coming near the end of his life. But I pointed out to him how much he had given away in his lifetime. Why, his benefactions to Dundee alone can't be much under thirty thousand. I shall be glad for some things, Marian, when it's all over. This sort of thing is a strain."

This kind of talk, betraying considerable misgiving on his part, occupied them during the quick journey to Newport. They were fortunate in finding a boat waiting, and they were at Ravenscraig before the brief October twilight fell.

Jarvis met them at the door.

" Mr. Gilfillan's just left, Mr. George. Ye would meet him going to the boat."

" No, we didn't," said George Speed sharply. " Any one with your master now ? "

" Yes, the doctor. He's just gane up."

" How is he now ? "

" Sair failed," answered the old man sadly. He had been a lifetime in the service of old George Speed, and there was no doubt about his allegiance, which was that of devoted love.

" I'll go up. You'd better wait here, Marian," he said to his wife.

" But I want to see him, George," she said, acquiescing only ungraciously. " I shouldn't always be kept out. Give him my love, and tell him how many times I called and was denied last week."

George Speed passed upstairs. Jarvis helped his wife off with her coat.

" I suppose you have a lot of callers still, Jarvis ? "

" They keep drappin' in, ma'am. Miss Lundie was here this afternoon."

" But Mr. Speed didn't see her ? " she said with a quick, jealous note in her voice.

" Oh yes, he did. She brocht him up a bunch of flowers from Lunan, and she was up the stairs the best pairt o' half an hour. He's very fond o' Miss Katherine, ma'am, and has aye been."

" And who else ? "

" Yesterday, Sir Rafe Fletcher."

" Did Sir Rafe actually call ? " she asked with interest visibly quickened. " Did Mr. Speed receive him ? "

" Yes. He kent his faither, and he was very pleased to see him. Besides, they had met somewhere—in India, I think, but I'm no' sure."

" And who else ? "

" The usual folk that come every day—the Spences an' the Woodheads an' the Martins. They come or send every day."

" Tell me, Jarvis, do you think he'll last much longer ? "

" Ma'am, he canna," said Jarvis with a rising tear. " The doctor said this morning he thocht it could only be hours."

" It's very sad, but after all, he's had a good innings, Jarvis. Seventy-six is a long age."

" Ay, but his kind canna be spared, ma'am," he said as he turned away.

Mrs. Speed stepped into the dining-room and took a careful survey of its furniture and arrangements, picturing the entertainments which she would be able to give in that handsome panelled room. She liked the picture inlet above the mantelpiece on the whole, though the subject—that of an extremely plain and homely woman—did not much appeal to her. It was a portrait of George Speed's wife, and had been to him a shrine.

Mrs. Speed had never seen her husband's mother, who had died the year before her marriage into the house of Speed.

She liked the house. After her own suburban place it seemed quite palatial. Wandering out into the hall she admired anew the gallery staircase, and the beautiful soft colouring of the painted windows. Yes, in a year or two from now she would be able to hold high revels in Ravenscraig. She could picture the place aglow with electric lamps, the shimmer of silk and satin, the flash, perhaps, of coroneted heads. Mrs. Speed was very ambitious. She fully believed that the realisation of her most cherished hopes was at hand.

CHAPTER III

THE CHARGE

George Speed could perceive a change in his father's face when he entered the sick-room. The grey shadow of death was there, and the sharpened outline which can never be mistaken. But all his faculties were alert, and though his voice was passing weak, almost a whisper, his words were perfectly clear and definite. The doctor who stood by his bed stepped back at the entrance of the son, and with a brief salutation turned to leave. His work was done. He was a very young man to have the responsibility of such a valuable life; but on this point old George Speed had remained obdurate. He had dismissed the man who had been his nominal medical attendant for a good many years, because he imagined himself to have been deceived by him in a certain matter, and had called in David Alister on the recommendation of his grandson Tom, whose College chum he had been.

The younger Speed had a very curt recognition for Alister, whom he did not like and whose presence there he resented. The door softly closed, and he approached the bed with serious looks.

" Are you feeling worse, father ? "

" No, better," said the old man in a laboured whisper. " I'll soon be quite well in the place where there's no more pain, and where we can cheat all the doctors."

He would exercise his grim humour even in his extremity, but his son did not smile.

" I'm sure we're wrong to leave Alister in charge, father. Afterwards, perhaps," he added, with a slight hesitancy, " we shall blame ourselves."

" The dirdum maun be mine, then, George," re replied airily. " I'm quite content wi' Alister. He knows his business—and does it, and he's as straight as a die. Sit down, George, and don't fidget on your legs like that. I want to speak to you."

George obeyed, and he drew a chair forward so that his father's face could be clearly seen, while his own—perhaps purposely—was left in the shadow.

" There's two or three things to redd up before the final balance is struck, George," said the old man, and would have leaned forward had not his great weakness prevented him. " Tell me, have you heard ocht o' Helen Drever ? "

George Speed's face flushed.

" That's a far cry, father. I heard that she had got married not so long after I did."

" Did ye take steps to verify that ? "

" No. I believe in letting sleeping dogs lie," he answered drily. " It was Dempster that told me. You remember Alec Dempster, the traveller for Carstairs, whose folk belonged to Rattray."

" I never saw him, but I mind his folk, an' they were a' leears. I'm not easy in my mind about her, George, and I want you to promise that you'll seek her out and do something for her, if she's in need. which I think she is."

" What reason have you for thinking that ? I'm sure it's pure imagination. And there's no cause to doubt that she did get married and that she's now quite comfortably off."

" She's not, I tell you," said the old man a little irritably. " I've got her on my mind. Promise me that you will seek her out, and if she needs anything, that you'll help her."

" If it'll make you any happier I can make a few inquiries next time Dempster comes around. He's a kind of a ferret. He'll soon find out for me. I didn't give him much encouragement when he did speak her name. He was trying to trade on a bit of Rattray gossip."

" But it was a cruel thing, George, and if I had kent that you had promised her marriage and that she was getting ready for it, I would have seen that you kept your promise."

" You appeared to be quite pleased with my choice, father, and it was by your own advice that I looked where money was," said Speed drily.

" Ah, that's right enough if there's no entanglements. But I dare say you've paid for your sin," he added with significant dryness.

" Sin ! Don't call it by such a name, father. How many men have you known that have broken unsuitable ties when they discovered their mistake ? There's hardly a man in Dundee, I could almost take my affidavit, that has not come through some experience of that kind."

" Aweel, so much the waur for them," said the old man grimly. " Two things I have never done in my life, George, broken faith with a woman and lied to a man in the way of business. My slate is clean of these two counts."

His eyes beamed the satisfaction which the consciousness gave him, but his son's face continued gloomy and troubled. His father's unexpected charge had started a rather painful train of thought.

" You'll inquire onyway and mak' it up to her, as far as money can mak' up for a broken faith. It's a simple act of justice, for if she had been another kind of woman, she would have sued you for breach of promise, my lad, and would have won her case."

" It's hardly fair to Marian, father," protested George Speed. " As the other woman married, and I maintain that there isn't the smallest reason to doubt it, I am wholly absolved."

" You have promised, and I expect you to perform," said the old man quietly. " That's the main thing I wanted to say. The rest has gane awa' clean from my mind."

George Speed saw the weakness increasing, and casting about for some stimulant espied a brandy bottle and proceeded to administer a few drops, which revived his father's fleeting strength for a brief moment.

" My wife is downstairs, father. She sent her love and would like very much to see you. She has been very faithful in her attention. Won't you see her ? "

The old man shook his head.

" I canna. I was hardly able for Mrs. George in my best days—I couldn't thole her now," he answered frankly. " She may be a guid wife to you, my son—I'm no' seekin' to deny it—but she's a different stamp of woman from your mother. She set me a pattern, ye see, and I canna get beyond it."

What could be said against such an argument ? Speed felt that it was useless to plead.

" Is there anything else, then, father ? " he asked, very softly for him, for the pathos of that lonely deathbed appealed to a side of his nature not often touched.

" Yes, there were other things. It was Tom I wanted to speak aboot, but I've forgotten what it was I wished to say. Oh, ay ! He's not needin' to be sent to James Mouat at Calcutta ; that's what I wanted to be at. He's a good lad. Leave him alone and he'll come out right in the end."

" I wanted to cut him off from his fads and his undesirable acquaintances," said Speed soberly. " And Mouat would put him in the right way."

" Let him alone. He'll never tak' up wi' onybody that will harm him ; you tak' my word for it. I want Jarvis, noo, George ; I'm very tired."

His head fell on his breast. In sudden alarm George Speed rang the bell, which brought the nurse and Jarvis to the room. Speed passed out, meeting on the stairs his wife, who, having heard the bell, ventured up, half expecting that the summons might be for her.

" What is it ? Is he worse ? "

" He's far through."

" Won't he see me ? "

" He really isn't able, Marian. He hardly knows what he is saying now. I think you had better go home, dear. I'll need to stop till the end comes."

" Is it so near as that ? " she asked. " I met Dr. Alister as he came down, but he didn't give me much satisfaction. I don't believe he knows, George ; he's much too young. It really isn't right that a lad like that should be absolute here."

" He's got the right side of my father, Marian, and nothing I can say will alter his opinion ; but it won't make any difference now. He's through : anybody can see that."

A little silence fell upon them as they entered the dining-room, where Mrs. Speed had left her cloak.

"Don't you think I'd better stop too, George? There will be a lot to do, and it would certainly look better. I can telephone to them to send our things."

"Please yourself, Marian," he answered a trifle abstractedly. He was not overwhelmed with sorrow, nor did he seek to affect that he was, but a deep depression held him. His wife's shrewd eye could see that, and, so far as was in her nature, she sympathised with him. She had no very deep feelings, but George Speed had been a good husband to her, and she cared for him now as much as it was possible for her to care for any one except herself.

"Don't worry too much, dear," she said, quite gently for her. "It was inevitable. He's an old, old man, and has had a good innings, as I said to Jarvis. And I am sure he does not care now whether he lives or dies. I have often heard him say that."

"It isn't that, Marian. All that you say is true, but there's something about death which sobers one."

These words decided Mrs. George to stay, and she went out to telephone to The Rowans for their things to be sent over. When she returned, her husband was standing in the great square window, looking across the noble sweep of greensward that sloped to the shore of the estuary. It was a lovely situation for a house, and the amenity had been most carefully considered. Ravenscraig was certainly the gem among the many beautiful homes scattered on the fringes of the Firth of Tay.

"It's a bonny place, Marian, but my father never got the pleasure out of it he ought to have had, considering its cost."

"What did it cost?" she asked interestedly.

"I don't know the actual figures, but certainly not less than fifteen or twenty thousand."

"Absurd! Why, he might have bought a place in the county for that," she said quickly. "I am always astonished at the shortsightedness of self-made men in building big castles like this, which after all are only suburban houses, and go down in value instead of up."

"My father never had any county ambitions," replied Speed somewhat drily.

"It would have been better for us and the children if he had had," was her reply. "If there are no restrictions we could sell it, George, couldn't we, and buy a country place?"

"There will be restrictions, Marian, sure enough. This place has been the apple of his eye, and he'll want somebody to live in it that will appreciate it."

George Speed voiced his own conviction, little guessing that his words were not only true, but prophetic.

"Well, we can only wait and see," she said. "I'll go and find out about our room. All the servants here give themselves airs, George, and want setting in their places. Mrs. Robertson, the housekeeper, is insufferable."

Speed made no answer, and when his wife left the room he continued to stand at the window, looking out with an absent expression on his face on the fair picture over which the dusky night shades were stealing.

In spite of himself his thoughts went back to the little Perthshire village, the place of his boyhood, and, it must be added, of his happiest days. There the first dreams and visions of young manhood had come to him, visions wholly fair. He saw himself once more an ardent lover on the bonny Perthshire braes, vowing eternal fealty to a gentle heart that had trusted him. Then, slowly, the lure of the world had got him in thrall, and the early visions had faded into nothingness. Broken vows, forgotten promises followed, then the final drifting apart. Yet hither, across the misty bridge of the intervening years, some spell was wafted, and he was back once more, looking into trusting eyes under the lover's moon in the Howe o' Strathmore.

A sudden bustle and hurrying of steps above arrested his attention. There was the swift, loud shutting of a door and the hasty peal of a bell. He hastened upstairs. His wife, on her way to select a bedroom for their occupation, was before him in the sick-room, now the chamber of death.

"He's just slippit awa', sir," said Jarvis through his tears. "He said he was very tired an' wad sleep. I turned him ower and covered him, and when I lookit again he was awa'."

CHAPTER IV

THE BLOW

A LITTLE later in the evening George Speed telephoned to the house of Mr. Gilfillan, the lawyer, at West Ferry, only to be informed that he was dining out. He had therefore to content himself till next day regarding the will which he expected to make such a difference in his future.

Although there had not been a great deal of confidence between father and son, George Speed knew his father to be a rich man. Ten thousand pounds had been paid for the partnership in the Eliot Mills—formerly Lundie, Raith & Lundie ; now Lundie, Speed & Co. It was a very good portion, and no man need have grumbled had it been his only one ; but then George Speed was an only son, and naturally expected that the bulk of his father's property would accrue to him. His wife, more than he, had resented the old man's benefactions to the town of his adoption, and he had inclined to the belief that there must be plenty behind to justify them. Yet somehow of late he had felt a little uneasy regarding the future. Depending upon something substantial at his father's death, they had lived up to the uttermost farthing of their income.

The Eliot Mills had been a losing concern when the partnership had been bought, and, though the infusion of fresh blood had helped the business considerably, it was by no means so lucrative as its size and importance seemed to indicate.

George Speed was a first-rate business man, and had put abundance of energy into it, but he had had a good many lean years, and was only now beginning to recover himself. The twenty or thirty thousand pounds, however, he fully expected to receive by his father's will would make a great difference, and, as mistress of Ravenscraig, his wife would be more contented than she had been of late years. He could see how she had built herself upon occupying this position by the way in which she comported herself in the house that evening. The half-deprecating, half-conciliatory manner which she had deemed it prudent to adopt towards her father-in-law disappeared, and complete assurance took its place. They dined alone there, and she took her place at the head of the beautiful, massive table with an air of subdued satisfaction not lost upon Speed. He did not mention to her, therefore, the qualms which visited him—qualms which had not disappeared by next morning.

He crossed by an early boat and went straight to Gilfillan's office in Reform Street. The death of old George Speed, as he was called, was of course already known to the majority of Dundee folk through the medium of the morning papers. Gilfillan was therefore not at all surprised to see Speed, although it cannot be said the visit gave him any pleasure. They were not intimate, nor did Gilfillan transact any business for the younger Speed. In all their ways the two households had differed, the younger Speed even attending the English Church, while the old man remained true to the Presbyterian faith in which he had been reared. For this lapse from old tradition the old man had blamed his daughter-in-law. He liked her so little, indeed, that he had seldom been just to her.

" Good-morning, Mr. Gilfillan," said Speed a trifle formally. " I suppose you have heard."

" Yes ; I can't say I was surprised. I saw yesterday afternoon that he was very far through."

" You were there yesterday, I heard. Was he making any alteration in the will you drew up for him five years ago, a copy of which he let me see ? "

The lawyer fidgeted ever so slightly in his chair.

" There has been another will since then, Mr. Speed—in ninety-five. I can give you the exact date, if you like," he said, rising with relief—perhaps to get away from the startled look. "Yes—the nineteenth of March, ninety-five."

"March, ninety-five! The year I went to India—the very day of my return, I believe. I came back to Dundee on the eighteenth."

Gilfillan nodded, stroking his thoughtful chin.

"It was the day after. Now that you have mentioned it, I may as well say that your Indian visit influenced him a little; that was the indirect cause of the new will being made."

"Why?"

"Well, he was so completely satisfied with the results of your trip and the business prospects it ensured that I suppose he thought you would not need the money so much."

"What money? In Heaven's name, what are you talking about, Gilfillan? Get the thing out and let me see it, can't you?—the new will, I mean. Why should I be kept on tenterhooks like this? It's intolerable!"

The lawyer took the rebuke mildly, realising fully that Speed's irritability was excusable in the circumstances. And since yesterday evening he himself had not been a very happy man concerning the Speed bequests.

He opened the deed-box with the name of Speed printed across the lid, and drew out the sheet of foolscap containing the last will and testament of the deceased master of Ravenscraig.

"Shall I read it out to you, or merely tell you the main items?"

"What are they?"

Speed's voice sounded thick, and he cleared his throat and sat back in his chair with a look of sudden apprehension which quenched his anger.

"There is only one bequest of any importance, and that is Ravenscraig and a sum adequate to its upkeep—to Mr. Tom."

"To Tom!" repeated George Speed, aghast.

"And to that there is a condition attached—that he marries Miss Lundie within eighteen months," went on the lawyer, steadily keeping his eyes on the closely-written foolscap.

"They are practically engaged, of course," said Speed in the same strained voice. "But what happens if by any chance the engagement should fall through? Such things have happened, Mr. Gilfillan, and my father ought to have known better than to attach such a condition, which to certain temperaments is likely to prove a too irksome bond."

"I pointed out that to Mr. Speed," answered the lawyer. "In fact," he added as he glanced for a moment over his broad, gold-rimmed pince-nez, "I disapproved of the whole disposition of the property, and tried to reason with him. But I dare say you don't need me to tell you that your father was a man who at all times not only knew his own mind, but adhered to his purpose in spite of all obstacles."

"The alternative about Ravenscraig?" cried Speed feverishly. "What happens if the condition is not fulfilled?"

"It becomes a Home of Rest for the old people of Dundee—for respectable men and women who, through no fault of their own, are left stranded when they are no longer able to work. It was a form of charity which particularly appealed to him, as I dare say you know."

George Speed's face became ghastly pale, and his hands involuntarily clenched.

"It's a shame, Mr. Gilfillan. Ravenscraig was never built for that purpose! If by any chance it should have to be used for such a purpose it would be monstrous. Have you any explanation to offer of the fact that my father has not bequeathed the place to me? I ought to have had it. I always understood—and my family have understood—that it was to be our future home."

Gilfillan remained silent. His client had made no secret of his reason to his old friend, but it is never wise to fan the flame of a bitter indignation.

He had expected this painful interview, and had done his best to prepare himself for it, but he wished it would quickly end.

"How much money did he leave altogether?"

"There is surprisingly little, for a man in his position, Mr. Speed; but, as you know, his benefactions in his lifetime were enormous. There is a sum of one thousand pounds to each of your daughters, five thousand pounds to yourself, and a thousand pounds to Dr. Alister to enable him to marry soon. He was a great believer in early marriage," he added with a slight smile. "He believed early marriage, even when a little imprudent, to be the salvation of every man."

George Speed almost ground his teeth. He was too much agitated to make a single comment. The lawyer went on rapidly to cover the contents of the will.

"All the servants are remembered, of course. Jarvis and Mrs. Robertson have each an annuity left to them, and all the charities in which your father was interested in Dundee benefit. But the best plan will be for me to have a copy of the will made and sent out to you, Mr. Speed. Shall I do this to-day?"

George Speed rose to his feet. The pallor of his face, the working of his lips betrayed his inward agitation. He turned with a sort of suppressed fury on the old lawyer who had dealt him such a blow.

"Gilfillan, don't you think it might have been your duty to have informed me as far back as five years ago of the existence of this will?"

Gilfillan betrayed no perturbation.

"There was no precedent for that, Mr. Speed, because the will, though a little out of the ordinary, is not an unjust one. Your father started from the premise that you had had your full share."

"But I'm his only son. I am entitled to it all, bar a few legacies which nobody would dream of disputing."

"Your father did not take that view. After your successful journey to India he decided that your fortune was made. He then proceeded to dispose of his own to please himself."

"Without the smallest remonstrance from you?"

The lawyer shrugged his shoulders.

"I ventured to remark that probably you or Mrs. Halliwell Speed would be disappointed about the house. But he paid no attention to me. He took the greatest pains in working out all the details of his bequest, and his instructions in each case were most explicit. There is an additional thousand to you on condition that you seek out a lady in whom he seemed to be specially interested, and see that she is not in want. That was his business with me last night."

George Speed turned to go. What end could be served by futile discussion with the man who was after all merely the instrument of his father's strange animosity? Speed guessed the reason why Ravenscraig had been put past him. His wife's proprietary interest in the place—her way of appraising its value and its contents every time she visited it had always irritated his father, and he himself had warned her against it.

What would she say now? His face grew a trifle greyer at the thought. He was a hard man, but he cared for peace, and greatly feared the bitter edge of his wife's tongue. She could be very bitter, as he had on more than one occasion proved.

"I needn't stop to say anything more," he remarked heavily. "Though some men in my place would contest the will, I shall have to wait my family's verdict."

"You would be very ill advised to do any such thing," said the lawyer sincerely and emphatically. "It would be perfectly futile—in the first place, because your father was of sound mind and clear judgment, and in full possession of his faculties up to the last; and, secondly, because it would create a scandal in Dundee, surely much better avoided."

Speed neither denied nor affirmed. He put his hat on his head and walked out, a miserable and an angry man. At the very back of his mind there was a sore, hurt feeling that his father should have done this thing to him, his only son. It did not look well, and it left a bitter sting. He wanted some one to blame, but did not quite know where to turn. Tom seemed the natural scapegoat, and if by any chance he should make any difficulty about fulfilling the conditions of his grandfather's will where it concerned him, he would be anathema to them all. Yet he felt by no means sure. Tom was a free-lance, and had always been, and nobody had ever been able to anticipate his course of action in any circumstances whatsoever.

Those who met George Speed that morning as he traversed on foot the distance between Reform Street and the Eliot Mills, noting his changed looks, offered him in their hearts respectful sympathy, in no doubt that he felt his father's death acutely.

Ten o'clock rang as he climbed the last steep ascent to the mills, and a thousand whistles blew. The air was alive with the patter and haste of myriad feet as the multitudes of toilers hurried back after the breakfast hour to the next span of labour. He passed through the gates among the throng, taking no notice of any. At the door of the handsome offices that had been built at his own expense he stood still with the same absent look upon his face. The women were hurrying past in twos and threes, or singly, all intent on getting to their appointed niches in time.

Suddenly a face arrested him—a face and a figure which did not accord with those of the others, but proclaimed their possessor of a different order of woman. A tall, slim girl, shabbily dressed in a blue skirt and a black jacket, with a small, neat hat on her glossy hair and a pair of old darned gloves on her hands, walked alone. Her face was pale, but not unhealthy, possessing that singular clear pallor which goes with certain types of beauty. Great sweetness was there in conjunction with a pathetic sadness.

She walked with a certain grace of mien, looking neither to the right nor to the left, and disappeared up the wide ladder leading to one of the spinning flats. A strange look came upon George Speed's face, as if he had suddenly beheld a face from the dead.

Walter Soutar, the manager, a dapper individual, well dressed and fully conscious of the value of his services to the firm, crossed from the engine-room door at the moment, his expression adjusted to the seriousness appropriate to the occasion. He was about to utter a few words of commonplace sympathy when his employer anticipated him by asking : " Who is that girl, Soutar, the one who has gone up the stairs behind all the others ? "

CHAPTER V

THE HAUNTING FACE

SOUTAR looked across the open courtyard at the vanishing skirt. "I didn't see her face, sir, but I think I know whom you mean," he answered. "A superior-looking girl—looks almost like a lady, rather tall, not much colour in her face."

"Yes, that's the woman I mean."

"A new hand, I think. I don't know her name; Lonie could tell you. Shall I go and ask him now?"

"No, no, never mind. Where's Mr. Tom?"

"There he is now, sir; just coming down the stairs."

"What's he doing up there just now?" said Speed, with a strong note of suspicion in his voice. "He has no business among the women at this hour."

"Mr. Tom's like lightning, sir—all over the place a dozen times in a day," answered Soutar easily. "You never know in what unexpected corner you'll see him next."

"Far enough away generally from his proper work," said Speed so irascibly that Soutar regarded him with fresh surprise. His was not the subdued manner of a man plunged in personal sorrow, but rather the hasty irritability of one whose nerves were on edge. Soutar naturally wondered what had happened.

"We are very sorry about the old gentleman, sir," he said, sincerely enough. "He'll be a loss to Dundee."

"Tell Mr. Tom I want him inside at once," he said ungraciously, turning on his heel even while Tom was waving his hand in genial morning greeting. Soutar nodded, and stood waiting while the youngest member of the firm came lightly and quickly across the open courtyard. He had a fine, tall, lithe figure, slenderly built, but giving the impression of strength and muscle. His bare head, ruffled by the cold October wind, was beautifully moulded. It was an intellectual head, and he had delicate, clean-cut features, lit by eyes at once dreamy and keen. He looked like an idealist, and there was little to suggest the alert business man, eager to grasp the main chance and to create it in unlikely quarters. Whence had Tom Speed derived such an unusual cast of mind and looks.

Not from his worldly mother, or his weaker, but still worldly, father. Partly from his grandfather, perhaps, whose outward man had been of common texture, through which, however, were woven the threads of that innate refinement which in the old Rattray days had singled him out from his family and fellows. Old George had taken an inordinate pride in his handsome grandson, and there had been a good deal of sympathy between them. To the old man Tom had never been shy of unburdening himself regarding the problems of life which had perplexed him early in his boyhood, and now pursued him in young manhood, demanding solution.

A dreamer and a visionary Tom might be, but he was universally beloved in Dundee, where they had already christened him "the poor man's friend." Tom mourned his grandfather deeply in the sense that he would miss his bodily presence, but his attitude towards death was as startling to some conventional minds as his theories of life.

He held that undue grieving over the close of a well-spent and rounded life, and its subsequent preferment to the fuller existence beyond, was not only wrong, but wholly illogical, for which reason he condemned the wearing of mourning, the tolling of bells, the drawn blinds and closed windows—in a word, all the forbidding trappings of death which make it so hideous. Consequently he had not changed his bright red tie, though his mother had taken great care that his father went forth in the customary black.

"The maister wants you, Mr. Tom," said Soutar. "He's feeling bad. It's very natural. Everybody will miss your grandfather."

Now Tom did not like Soutar. His keen perception had convinced him that the manager was a time-server, keeping an eye on both worlds. Soutar was religious or profane as occasion demanded, and the note of insincerity always struck Tom acutely, on which account he avoided him as much as possible. He was obliged, however, in the prosecution of his daily duties to come a good deal in contact with him, and to show him a certain amount of deference, because he possessed the entire confidence of the heads of the firm, and in the course of a few years would in all probability be admitted to a small partnership.

So Tom merely nodded and passed on through the outer office to the room where his father usually sat, and where he transacted all the business requiring his attention. It was comfortable, but by no means luxurious, though the bright gleam of the fire made it cheerful on a cool morning.

Speed was turning over the morning mail at the long desk that stood between the windows.

"Shut the door," he said curtly, without turning round.

"Good morning, dad. What's up?" asked Tom, in a mild wonder.

Usually his father was cheerful of a morning, and Tom, like Soutar, was struck by the extreme irritability of the tone.

"You may ask. I've been to Gilfillan this morning, Tom, and got a nice little *billet doux* in the shape of your grandfather's will."

"Yes," said Tom interestedly. "Did he leave a lot?"

"I didn't hear the amount. Gilfillan's close, Tom, but there's precious little for me—in fact, nothing to speak of. But the thing that troubles me most is your mother's disappointment about the house."

"Ravenscraig, do you mean? Hasn't he left it to you, as we all expected?"

"No, it's left to you."

Tom whistled, by no means elated or even moderately pleased.

"To me! What do I want with a great barn of a place like that? I shouldn't know what to do with it. But it will be the same thing, won't it, dad? If it's mine we can all go there just the same."

"It's not quite the same, unfortunately. There's a drastic condition attached even to your possession."

"What's that?"

"That you marry Katherine Lundie within eighteen months."

Tom stared, absolutely aghast. His cheek even paled a little, and his brows contracted.

"You don't mean to say that! Why, it's preposterous! Nobody wants to be hounded to matrimony like that. I am not in the least matrimonially inclined."

"Well, you'll have to be, if you're to inherit your grandfather's gift," said Speed drily.

"What happens if I don't fulfil the condition?"

"The place is to be handed over to a Committee to be formed into a Home of Rest for the deserving old men and women of Dundee," his father answered with a sarcastic note in his voice.

Tom whistled again.

"Well, it's what it would be fitted for. A fine scheme! The Committee must take it then," he added serenely.

His father looked at him with a sudden incredulous expression on his face.

"I am not surprised that you resent the terms of the bequest. Certainly they are arbitrary, but surely you would never be guilty of such transcendent folly as to refuse to fulfil them."

Tom shifted from one foot to another. He was in no doubt as to the reply he wanted to give, but was only reluctant, as fine natures are, to inflict disappointment or pain. He understood also that a bad quarter of an hour was in store for his father—for them all, indeed—when his mother should learn that she could not immediately become mistress of Ravenscraig.

"I hope it will not be necessary to tell Katherine about this, father," he said. "It would make her desperately uncomfortable, and would altogether ruin our comradeship. We've been very good chums all these years. It will be horrible if this puts an end to it——"

" Tom, I do believe you are the biggest ass I've ever met, interrupted his father.

This perfectly spontaneous tribute caused Tom to smile.

" I know you think that, and you've all expected the usual engagement which is understood to follow when a man and woman become good friends. But I assure you there is nothing of that kind between us, nor has there ever been. We are friends and comrades—nothing more."

" Are you sure about Katherine, Tom ? " his father asked significantly.

" Yes, of course—dead sure. I do hope this impossible whim of my grandfather's won't be made public, or it will spoil everything."

" Do you realise what you propose to do, Tom ? Do you mean thus lightly to refuse a place worth perhaps twenty thousand pounds—certainly fifteen in the open market—and the sum to keep it up that goes with it ? "

" I don't want it. I shouldn't know what to do with it. If I ever have a home of my own it will be right here in the heart of the city among my fellow-workers," said Tom quietly.

His father was silent a moment, totally at a loss. To storm and rage was useless, to argue seemed equally profitless. He could only suffer. And he did suffer more acutely than Tom had any idea of.

The things that matter in this life are largely a question of temperament. Tom could airily cast aside a fortune which seemed almost sacred in his father's sight.

" I wish I knew where you got such suicidal ideas, and how I could rid you of them," he said in a troubled voice. " You can picture your mother's indignation—her just indignation ! I hope you are prepared to meet it ! "

Tom was silent a moment. He loved his mother, but she had very little part in his life, and absolutely no sympathy with his views. They had had many stormy arguments, and at last for the sake of peace they had agreed not to discuss certain subjects any more. Mrs. Halliwell did not like Katherine Lundie, but she hoped great things from the marriage which she had no doubt would take place. She was fond of saying that nothing would more quickly cure a Socialist of his heresy than to give a few hostages to fortune in the shape of children. Yes, certainly marriage and family life would cure Tom of much of the folly that vexed her now.

" She'll cut up rough, I don't doubt, but after all a man has a right to live his own life, and I am twenty-four."

" You are, and quite time you had got some common-sense knocked into you. You had better go and send the clerk in to the letters. I don't want to talk any more about it, but I've never been so upset in my life. I don't think I deserved this. My father has not treated me fairly."

Tom's quick sympathy went forth to his father, though he did not honestly consider the trouble a serious one. They had a comfortable and luxurious home at The Rowans—much superfluous comfort indeed, wholly lacking in many of the hard lives with which he came into contact. Everything is measured by comparison, and Tom drew his philosophy of life largely from the poor, while for his mother the poor did not exist. She did her share of charitable work after the lukewarm fashion of the worldly woman, but she had no wish to come into actual, personal touch with the poor.

" Don't worry too much about it, dad. It isn't worth it—hardly anything is in this world," he said affectionately. It was not the philosophy of the pessimist that prompted these words, but rather the cheerful confidence of one who had shaken himself free from extraneous things.

For a brief moment George Speed almost envied his son for his outlook, albeit it was disastrous to all wordly success.

" I don't know how I am to tell your mother," he said gloomily. " She'll be furious."

He put his hand on the electric bell, and his clerk immediately answered the summons. For an hour he was occupied with his correspondence, and when at leisure he immediately left the office, half-determined to go home, yet reluctant to face the inevitable scene.

At the door he met his partner Henry Lundie, who, since Speed had entered the business, had become practically a sleeping partner. By his slackness, however, the interests of the firm in no way suffered. Henry Lundie was an aristocrat, a patron of the fine arts so far as his means allowed him, a reader and a collector of books, a fine musician—anything and everything but a business man. One of the younger cadets of an impoverished Forfarshire family, he had as a last resource entered the business of an uncle on his mother's side. By a series of unexpected family bereavements he had been left sole head of the Eliot Mills, the result being that the profits steadily declined. It had been at a crisis that old George Speed had stepped in and bought the partnership for his son.

There was a great contrast between the two men, but they were fairly good friends, because none of their interests clashed. Lundie was the ornamental part of the concern, and his name was one of its assets, but as a practical or active member he did not count. They shook hands, and Henry Lundie spoke a few words of condolence, in his case perfectly sincere, since he had entertained a warm liking for old George Speed. For a moment Speed wondered whether he should take Henry Lundie into his room to acquaint him then and there with the terms of his father's will, so far as Katherine was concerned. But he decided against it—the wound was too raw yet, and he needed more time for reflection. So he simply replied in subdued tones to the well-expressed condolences.

He stood irresolute a moment in the open space from which all the wings of the mill buildings radiated like the spokes of a great wheel. Then, as if drawn by some magnet, he crossed in front of the engine-house and ascended the stair which was largely used by the women workers.

It was not unusual for him to take a walk through the various departments, and his presence therefore occasioned no remark.

Through one long room after another he went amid the noise and the clank of machinery until he found the object he sought, the face of the girl that had drawn him irresistibly to the spot. She was working at one of the big spinning frames. He stood a little way back and watched her for a moment in silence, noting the grace of her figure, the little flush on her cheek, brought thither by the continuous exertion required to meet the turn of the wheels. He observed among other things that she had a small veil tied over her hair to protect it from the flying dust that permeated everything—a precaution which none of her neighbours ever thought of taking.

Yes—the profile was strangely, aggravatingly familiar, only it was a finer profile, more clearly cut, more sweetly winning than that he had in his mind's eye. But the likeness was undeniable. Could such a likeness possibly be accidental? He stepped forward and said in a clear voice which sounded above the mighty din: "Surely you are a new hand. What is your name?"

CHAPTER VI

MRS. SPEED SPEAKS

THE girl gave a little start, and her apron slipped from her hand, so that the bobbins it contained fell on the floor.

"My name is Mary Durie," she answered clearly and quietly, but without adding the "sir" usual from the employee when speaking to the master—a practice not quite fallen into disuse even in these levelling days.

"Mary Durie!" he repeated. "And are you a native of Dundee?"

"No."

"How long have you been here?"

"Only three weeks."

"You find the work hard?"

"Yes."

"Any complaint to make?" he suggested, knitting his brows, while his eyes met the clear grey orbs bent so unflinchingly on his face. Her whole manner and bearing differed from those of the ordinary millworker, who, when addressed on any subject by the authorities, usually manifested signs of panic.

"No."

"You haven't got any superfluous words at least. Where do you live, may I ask?"

"In Dundee."

"I should suppose so, as you work here," he observed grimly. "But in what part or street of the town?"

"I prefer not to say," she answered, and she stooped to gather up her bobbins as if she wished the conversation to terminate. It was being eagerly listened to by such as could overhear, notably by her immediate neighbour, Betsy Baxter, a small, dwarf-like creature with a weary, wizened face, on which years of sordid life had left many unlovely lines.

"Do you live with your own family?"

"Yes."

He could not inquire their number and vocations. Obviously his dignity required that he should now pass on. But the large, lovely eyes continued to hold him and to make strange, stirring demands on his sympathy.

"Well, if you have any complaint to make, or if I can do anything for your people, you can come to my office."

She made no reply, not even so much as a "Thank you" passed her impassive lips.

The master moved on, and he took a walk through the great room and to theone beyond, returning by the same passage. By this time Mary Durie had left her post.

"She felt a wee fent, sir," said the voluble Betty Baxter. "She'll be back the noo."

"Do you know anything about her, Mrs. Baxter?" enquired Speed.

Betty was an old hand, who had worked girl and woman in the Eliot Mills for twenty years.

"No much. She's never telt me whaur she bides, but she has a mither," she said confidentially. "She's a leddy—onybody can see that, but my! she's a grand worker. She gets through mair in a day that some o' them that ha'e been here for years."

"She looks as if the work were too hard for her."

"I dinna think it is, sir. She says she likes it because ye canna think when ye're at it. A queer reason for likin' a job, I say, but I like the lassie, sir. She has a kind heart. She cam' last Sunday efternune and took every ane o' my weans to the Baxter Park and let me get twa oors' sleep. An' they're no' easy herded, I can tell ye; Tammy an' wee Liz are perfec' deils."

Speed faintly smiled and passed on. The face and the story haunted him. He must find out more about Mary Durie. Meanwhile, however, he thought he would go back to Ravenscraig for lunch and talk things over with his wife. The sooner the interview was over the better. He telephoned first to inquire whether she was there, and found that she had come into town to see her dressmaker, and that she was not expected back to lunch. He left the mills, and sauntered slowly down town, meeting a good many who knew him and receiving numerous condolences. The name was naturally much respected in Dundee, though it was common opinion that old George would not have in his son an altogether worthy successor.

Certainly the dead man's good deeds would not be perpetuated by him; he was cast in a harder mould. The general opinion was that the Halliwell Speeds would now come into a fortune which would enable them to make a great display if they liked. It was certain Mrs. Halliwell Speed would enjoy that.

It added to the bitterness of George Speed's thoughts to gather from the nicely-adjusted manner of certain persons that he was now considered of greater importance than he had even been in his father's lifetime. He saw his own carriage at the door of an establishment in Reform Street, and stopped to speak to the coachman.

"Yes, sir, I think we're gaun hame to lunch."

"Did you go to Ravenscraig for your mistress?"

"No, sir. She telephoned me to meet her at the ferry."

"Is Miss Netta with her?"

"No, sir."

"I'll come back in twenty minutes' time, Roberts. Perhaps your mistress will be ready by then."

As he spoke, however, the swing door of the shop was opened, and his wife appeared, waited on with great courtesy by the shop walker. Speed raised his hat, his wife smiled to him, and they entered the carriage together.

"I'm glad you have turned up here, George. I was going to fetch you after I had seen the dressmaker. Netta has gone to St. Andrews to spend the day with Beata Ramsay. She has no sense of the fitness of things. I was much annoyed when I rang her up just after you left to find that she had gone by the early train. She ought to have understood that death cancels every engagement."

The words, uttered to express a merely conventional commonplace, struck George Speed. If it were indeed true that death cancelled every engagement, what latitude it would give to many perplexed souls, his among the number!

"I've changed the day of the funeral because of Mrs. Morgan's at The Mount, which is fixed for Friday. They would clash, and people could not go to both. Saturday afternoon at half-past two—a day more doesn't matter, especially with an old man," was her next announcement.

She reduced everything to the most commonplace ground, leaving nothing for the imagination to cling to. Speed rather furtively studied her fair and still youthful profile, the abundant masses of her hair which shone in the sun, her well-groomed, well-cared-for appearance, and, above all, the satisfaction that beamed upon every feature. Old George Speed's death was to his daughter-in-law a long-deferred relief.

"Did you have time to go to Gilfillan, George? I once thought of paying him a call myself, but thought it would not look well. I do so want to know what your father has left."

"Not much, Marian, so far as we are concerned," he replied quietly. The horses took a swift curve at the moment to avoid a passing dray, and she clutched his arm. She was nervously apprehensive of road accidents, for which reason horses of sedate manner and substantial age were always chosen. When they were quietened again and their heads had been turned away from the town, she looked at her husband with a sudden apprehension.

"What do you mean, George? He hasn't put anything past us, I hope?—that would be too terrible."

"The house, Marian. You'll be disappointed. Ravenscraig and all it contains goes to Tom."

"To Tom?" She repeated the words in undisguised dismay.

"Yes, to Tom; and that only on condition that he marries Katherine Lundie within the next eighteen months."

She sat silent a moment, simply because words were wholly inadequate to express her feelings.

"The fulfilment of the condition will be a foregone conclusion, I suppose?" she said at last. "But it isn't right, George. In fact, it was wicked and mean of your father, and though he is dead I must say it. He never liked me, and he has taken the best way to punish me, though why he should punish me I don't know. I have never been anything but a dutiful daughter-in-law to him."

"I think you made a mistake in showing him how keen you were about Ravenscraig," said Speed a trifle helplessly.

"Why, I only admired and appreciated the place. That ought to have pleased him. I feel as if I couldn't give it up even now to Tom and that Kate Lundie, with her high and mighty ways. She tries to patronise even me. We ought to come to some arrangement. Do you think it would be seemly for these children to be reigning at Ravenscraig while we grub along at The Rowans?"

Speed didn't immediately reply. Personally he felt very comfortable at The Rowans, and his ambitions of late years had slightly waned. But his wife's remained a consuming and unquenchable fire.

"But perhaps there's enough for us to buy a country place? How much did he leave altogether?"

"Not so much. He gave away most of it in his lifetime. We are richer only by five thousand pounds. It will buy a better house—The Mount, perhaps, if it comes into the market now—but that's all."

"Five thousand pounds!"

Mrs. Halliwell's face was a study in blank dismay and in a thousand inexpressible emotions. Was it for this that she had toiled and struggled and tried to possess her soul in limited patience?

"A thousand to each of the girls, and, of course, the old servants are provided for, and there are a few minor bequests to the charities he was interested in. But, of course, Ravenscraig is the plum. If Tom fails to fulfil the condition the place passes into the hands of a Committee—named, I believe—who are to convert it into a Home of Rest for the respectable aged poor of Dundee."

George Speed recited the main counts of the will in an even, judicial voice, glad to unburden himself of them.

"You take it very quietly, George," said his wife in a stifled voice, though the flame burned in her cheek. "I can't realise what you are talking about. Your father must have been deranged to have made such a will. It's open to you to contest it."

"Open?—yes, but perfectly futile, Marian. I forgot to mention, too, a legacy of a thousand for Dr. Alister to enable him to marry. For a widower of so many years' standing," he added with a slight, dry smile, "he seems a little inconsistently to insist on matrimony."

"What does Gilfillan say about this horrible will?"

"Well, nothing much. I suggested undue influence, mental aberration even, in the first flush of my anger."

"Then you were angry?" she said a little scathingly. "Nobody would guess it from your manner now, and you don't seem to realise what I feel about it."

"I do. I was afraid to tell you, Marian, but we are quite helpless. The obvious thing is to take it quietly and with dignity, and let nobody know that we are disappointed."

She was silent, and as the vista of her mighty disappointment opened out before her, her indignation grew. She had made no secret to her intimates of what she intended to do as mistress of Ravenscraig, and her humiliation now would be particularly galling.

"Have you seen Tom? Is he elated, as he ought to be, over his good fortune?" she asked, trying to steady herself.

Speed was silent a full minute.

"Yes; I told Tom. You'll have to take him in hand, Marian. He's inclined to kick."

"Against what? He has the best of it—the best of us!" she cried passionately.

"True, but he doesn't relish interference with his individual liberty, and he says he doesn't want the place, and won't marry Katherine. So I've had my two bad quarters of an hour already, Marian ; don't give me another."

She bit her lip, and two tears of genuine mortification trembled on her eyelids.

"I don't know what my sins have been, George, but the punishment hardly fits the crime this monring," she said unsteadily. "Don't let us speak any more about it. Marry Katherine ! Of course he'll marry Katherine. You may safely leave that to me. I've given him a good deal of rope in the last two or three years—probably too much—but I'll talk to him now."

"Both Katherine and he hold quixotic views," he observed absently. "If she gets to know of the condition I'm afraid she'll back out, even if she had been keen before. And apparently she is not keen either. Tom insists that they are merely chums."

Mrs. Halliwell shrugged her shoulders in ineffable scorn.

"Tell me another one," she said hardly. "She's in love with Tom and always has been. You can't deceive another woman on that score. All this comrade business, so far as she's concerned anyhow, is perfect rubbish."

CHAPTER VII

TWO DAUGHTERS

KATHERINE stood at the door of the offices waiting for the whistle to blow, the signal which would, as if by magic, still the mighty, throbbing heart of the great machine and bring the long working day to a welcome close. Her face was eager but a little sad as she watched the stream of humanity flow from every doorway. The dispersal of the millworkers always interested her, because she was so deeply interested in human things. Yet to the casual looker-on there was nothing to depress in that eager crowd, chatting and laughing together and indulging in mild horseplay, which indicated that the day's work had not been long enough or hard enough to damp their spirits completely. The women were for the most part neatly dressed, the day of the little shoulder shawl and the soiled apron, except in very few instances, being now happily past. Many of them returned Miss Lundie's interested, friendly glance with a smile and a nod, for she was well known and greatly beloved among the millworkers of Dundee.

She made a striking picture as she stood there in the clear October light. Distinguished was certainly the epthet to apply to her appearance. The simplicity of her dress, with its extreme daintiness, struck the keynote to her whole nature. She was the first and only child of parents who had loved one another with a great love, and her nature was pure gold without alloy. Her lovely unconsciousness of her charm was part of her gracious personality. Happy herself, she was anxious that others should be happy, and she did her utmost to make them so. There was yearning in her eyes as they swept the hurrying crowd of women and girls, noting the large proportion of very young girls among them. All sorts of faces were there, all sorts of possibilities for good or for evil. She sighed a little, thinking of the woman's destiny awaiting most of them—" to live, to suffer, and to weep." But better to suffer and to weep than not to live, she might have said had she been asked her philosophy of life.

A face suddenly attracted her, a new face, which, indeed, was not surprising, for, though she was a frequent visitor to the mills, hands were constantly being dismissed and taken on. Under the shabby, dusty hat there shone a face so pure and attractive, so hall-marked by refinement that it made an instant impression. She came out with a bevy of the younger girls, which seemed to indicate that she occupied a subordinate position. At the master's daughter standing in the doorway she did not look, but hurried on as if her chief and only object was to get away from the place and its associations. Katherine's eyes followed her interestedly, conscious, perhaps, with that subtle intuition which is the heritage of the spirit finely wrought, that destiny had something in store for her concerning this woman.

At the moment, Soutar, the manager, who had been watching Miss Lundie for some time from behind the gauze blind in the office, stepped out. Katherine, who did not like the man, acknowledged his presence by a rather distant bow.

" Good afternoon, Mr. Soutar. I am looking for my father. Have you seen him this afternoon ? "

" No, Miss Lundie. He left before luncheon to-day, so did Mr. Speed."

" Ah, then, I may go too," said Katherine, gathering her skirts in her hand.

" I think Mr. Lundie mentioned that he was going on to the platform at the meeting in the Kinnaird Hall about the Social Service Board," said Soutar, anxious to prolong a moment which could not be all pleasure.

He greatly admired Miss Lundie. It would not be too much even to assert that he had personal ambitions in her direction, especially of late, when in temporal affairs he had felt himself on the crest of the wave. Dreams are not forbidden to any man. A slight expression of chagrin crossed Katherine's face.

"How could I possibly forget the meeting of the Social Service Board? I ought to have been there. I suppose the sad news about old Mr. Speed has put things out of one's mind."

"He will be a loss to the town," observed Soutar casually.

"A loss everywhere; he was a dear old man," said Katherine quickly. "I suppose Mr. Speed is very much upset."

"Yes he is. I have never seen him more so; he couldn't give his mind to anything this morning."

"It should not have been required of him." said Katherine shortly.

Neither, of course, knew of the additional and serious cause for George Speed's perturbation of mind. The idea that there would be anything disturbing or disappointing about the will did not occur to either. Before Katherine bade the manager a brief good afternoon she put a sudden question.

"Mr. Soutar, do you happen to know the name of a girl I watched go down just now? I can't describe her very well to you except by saying that she stands out from the rest. She looks like a lady."

"I think I know the party you mean," said Soutar, whose choice of words did not always reach the standard required by Katherine's rather fastidious taste. "Rather white in the face, big eyes, pretty little woman."

"That description might answer," admitted Katherine. "Do you know her name?"

"No; but I can get it from Lonie, the cashier, in a moment if you'll wait. You can understand it isn't possible for me with all I have on my mind to remember the names of new hands or to take much notice of them."

"Yes, I understand, and her name is a matter of no consequence, thank you."

"Mr. Tom would probably know. He has a good memory for spotting faces, and you know the interest he takes in the hands; but Mr. Tom has gone home. His mother 'phoned to him from The Rowans. They seem to be all upset there."

"Naturally."

"I wonder how much he has left? He has given so much away there can't be a very big fortune now unless he was a millionaire. But old George was the kind of man who kept his thumb on his own affairs."

"Good afternoon, Mr. Soutar," said Katherine, a trifle coldly as she turned away.

Soutar returned her not very cordial farewell, at the same time hesitating a moment, knowing quite well that as a gentlemen he ought to see her to her carriage, but he was not sure how such an attention would be received from him as one of her father's employees. Katherine decided the question for him by simply walking away, and he did not presume to follow her.

"There's pride enough there to sink a ship, my lady," he muttered under his breath. "But maybe we'll get even yet."

Katherine had no difficulty in dismissing Walter Soutar from her thoughts. He was a person whom she remembered only when, as now, she accidentally came across him. The carriage with the pair of beautiful bays—Henry Lundie's one extravagance—was waiting in the narrow defile outside the gates. Katherine stepped in, the horses started forward, and took the sharp incline towards the town. She was not in a good mood. The day was out of joint.

She supposed it was the return to the grey city after the light and colour and beauty of life at Lunan which affected her, and she began to ponder seriously whether it would not be possible for them to live entirely at Lunan. Such a change could not very much affect her father's business, since he was little more than a sleeping partner, the details of the great machiue, which had always wearied him, and which even in his best days he had never fully mastered, having now passed into far more competent hands.

The streets were thronged, all the great labour centres having, as if by one simultaneous impulse, disgorged their units, like sands of the sea for multitude, and scattered them broadcast. In some of the narrower parts and at sharp curves and corners the carriage was brought very close to the hurrying stream. Katherine's kind eyes, ranging with sympathetic interest in search of familiar faces, found many, and never neglected the cheering beam of recognition. The toilers appeared a happy, careless crowd, laughing and talking, humming snatches of ballad music or the latest pantomime ditty, all of which surprised Katherine.

In common with many of her class she cherished the mistaken conviction that the lives of the working poor are uniformly monotonous, drab, and sad. She knew nothing of the homely joys and simple pleasures, the immense reserves of jollity and fun, the singular freedom from care possible to those who have very few responsibilities to burden them. Given good health and steady occupation, the lives of the working folk certainly compare not only favourably but enviably with others cast apparently in more pleasant places.

Presently she saw the face which had already that afternoon attracted her. As the carriage came close to the solitary figure walking apart amid the general throng, Katherine gave the coachman the word, and when he pulled up sharply she called to the girl in her clear, beautiful voice: " Excuse me. I am Katherine Lundie, and I should like to speak to you for a moment, if you please."

The girl stopped, but that was all. Her face expressed, not response, but rather a dull resentment.

" Don't look so ungracious," said Katherine, smiling as she held out her hand. " I should like to know you. Won't you come and help me at the Girls' Club ? We meet every Saturday evening at eight o'clock in White's Hall, in the Foregate."

The girl shook her head. " I have my mother to think of. She is mostly an invalid. I have to be away all day, and I never leave her at night."

" I am sorry to hear that, and I imagined you looked forlorn, walking all alone. Are you a stranger to Dundee, then ? "

" Yes ; we have not been here long."

" And how long at the Eliot Mills ? I was sure your face was new to me."

" Not long either. This is only my second week."

" Oh ! " said Katherine interestedly. " And do you—do you like the work ? "

She put the question somewhat hesitatingly, almost anticipating the answer.

" No, I don't like it, but it means our daily bread."

" Some of the workers are happy enough in it," said Katherine quickly and somewhat sensitively. " But certainly it is not the work for you. Won't you come up to my house, then, and see me one evening, or on a Sunday afternoon ? I live with my father at 78 Albion Terrace. We might together find a way out for you.

" I would rather not, Miss Lundie," replied the girl, but in a moment she added more graciously, " Thank you all the same."

" But why ? " asked Katherine, leaning further over the carriage door. " I am a very harmless person, and there is nothing I am more interested in in the whole world that women and girls."

The girl made no response.

" Won't you tell me your name ? " she said disappointedly.

" Yes—Mary Durie."

" And where do you live ? "

" I would rather not say."

" But you forget ; they must have your name at the office, and I could get it there."

" They did not ask me for my address. At least, when I said I would rather not give it, the foreman did not insist."

" I suppose I also must repress my curiosity then," said Katherine with a little sigh. " But I do assure you that it is interest and not curiosity which is my motive for asking it."

" I am sure of that, Miss Lundie," said Mary Durie a little more softly. " I have heard of your kindness, and I felt glad that you took so much interest in the women and girls who work. But can't you do something more ? " she added with a swift touch of passion. " It breaks my heart to see so many little girls—to see how they have to toil when they ought to be feeding and to be growing in the sun."

The words found a quick enough echo in Katherine's heart.

" Look here, my—my dear, we must meet. We are going to meet. Something tells me the fates have decreed that. If you don't give me the opportunity I must make it. You have no idea how clever I am, or how many doors I can open when I want a way out or in."

" It will be better to leave us alone, Miss Lundie," replied Mary Durie in the same quiet but resolute tone. " There are plenty who need your kindness more, and I have heard from Betty Baxter how kind you can be."

" I question whether there is anybody in the whole of Dundee at this moment who needs a woman friend more than you. Good-bye, then, if you will go, but remember that I won't lose sight of you, and that you will always find a friend in Katherine Lundie."

CHAPTER VIII

MY LEDDY

THE eager horses strained forward, and as the carriage passed Katherine waved her hand with a significant smile, intended to emphasise her parting words. The girl interested her deeply, and she felt keen to discuss her new acquaintance with her comrade, Tom Speed, whose duty it would certainly be to help her with the case. When she reached the Kinnaird Hall the meeting was dispersing. Her quick eye discerned her father standing on the kerb, talking earnestly with a man whom she did not know. He had an interesting face—not young, but clear cut and strong, with a very winning smile.

Henry Lundie saw the carriage stop, took off his hat to his daughter, and spoke a word to his companion, whereupon they both came forward.

" I did not expect you to meet me, my dear," he said perplexedly. " Have I forgotten anything ? "

" The marriage call at Drummearn. But it was my fault, papa, for I forgot that the meeting was to take place to-day. Was it successful ? "

" Fairly. Let me introduce Sir Rafe Fletcher to you, Katherine. My only girl, Sir Rafe, and I assure you that she keeps me up to the high-water mark of public and private duty."

" Having first reached it herself, I don't doubt," said Sir Rafe as he took Katherine's frankly outstretched hand.

Katherine enjoyed the second new sensation of the afternoon, for the Caddam succession constituted one of the romances of Forfarshire, and would in itself make no bad story.

" We are very glad to welcome you back to Scotland, Sir Rafe. It is a long time since you left it, isn't it ? But I hope your heart hasn't grown cold to the ' auld country ' yet."

He lifted his hat.

" Three and twenty years, and an exile every year of it, Miss Lundie, you may take my word for it. An exile without hope, too, which makes my good fortune all the more acceptable."

Katherine's lovely face glowed as the words touched her heart.

" Do ask Sir Rafe to come to dinner, papa, one evening. He must have so much to tell us," she said quickly.

The invitation, readily given, was as readily accepted, and they parted with the feeling that friendship would be possible to them.

" I do like his face, papa," said Katherine musingly as they drove away. " It is so interesting. What did he mean by saying he was an exile without hope ? "

" He was the third son of a second son without a copper to his name, my dear. His chance of succession was as unlikely as mine might be to the throne of England. But he's the right sort, and I'm glad we have got him in Dundee."

He stroked his chin, and a whimsical smile stole to his lips.

" He'll set all the match-makers by the ears. To be Lady Fletcher of Caddam would suit a good many of the young ladies, wouldn't it ? "

Katherine scarcely smiled, her thoughts being preoccupied.

" Did he speak at the meeting ? "

" No—there was enough speech without his, and none of it to the point. The spirit was lukewarm—the remedies suggested parochial in the extreme. Most people have only one idea of helping the poor—namely, to put their hands in their pockets and throw them a dole. But look at the blood-red trail on the water, Kate. We get occasional gleams to compensate for the sunsets at Lunan."

"Yes, it is lovely," assented Katherine absently. "Papa, I do feel so sorry to-day about old Mr. Speed. You can't think how sweet he was to me last night. I am so glad I went up to see him and took him my posy from Lunan."

"He was a fine old man, my dear. Ay, ay—a fine old man of a type fast passing away. It is certain that his son will never fill his shoes—though," he added after a pause, "his grandson may."

Katherine made no reply, and somehow their talk seemed to decline, so that the latter part of the drive was pursued in a long silence.

Meanwhile the girl in whom Katherine had been so interested had reached her poor home in Wilson's Court, one of the oldest and now, alas! most disreputable parts of Dundee. Wilson's Court was a cul de sac, terminating in a square open court, with tall tenements standing high and blocking out the sun. The old houses were very characteristic—some of them even beautiful in their decay. The doorway under which Mary Durie passed to ascend to her home was low and wide, and it showed traces of wonderful carvings, the gargoyles crowning the lintels being quite perfect and grotesquely beautiful. But the courtyard itself—once, doubtless, the vestibule to a noble house—was now a squalid place in which the gutter children played.

Mary spoke as she passed a civil word of greeting, to which the loungers at the doors responded with evident pleasure. They had christened her "My Leddy" in the Court, but there was no venom in the sobriquet, her gentle manners having won them all.

She passed them quickly, however, and with relief ascended the tumble-down stair. Up to the very top she went, the air growing purer and clearer, the footing more cleanly with each step. And finally at a door on the top landing—five storeys from the ground—she paused and fitted her key.

It slipped easily into the keyhole, being oiled so that no grinding or rasping sound might disturb a sensitive ear within. A little bare passage, lighted by four panes of glass in the roof, with a door on either side giving admittance to the kitchen and a sleeping-room, comprised Mary Durie's home. She hung her dusty jacket on a peg behind the door, gave her hair a hasty smooth with her hands, and opened the kitchen door.

A little gust of wind met her, and she ran forward, with a word of expostulation, to shut the window, which had been thrown up as high as possible.

"Mother, mother," she said warningly, "you're letting your craze for fresh air go rather far."

"No, Mollie; I like it, and the sunset has companioned me the last hour. Look, isn't it lovely yet?"

The words were not such as one would have expected to hear in a Dundee slum, and the woman who uttered them had surely no kinship with the slatternly atoms of humanity that Mary had passed on her way up.

She sat in an old wheel-chair as near to the window as it could be pushed, and the wind played with her faded hair. It was pretty yet, being soft and naturally waved, while her face, worn with much suffering, had great sweetness. It was even more refined than her daughter's, probably because she had been through so many phases of pain, both physical and mental.

A look of the deepest affection passed between them, and Mary bent over the chair and let her hand fall with a caressing movement on the soft hair.

"Yes, it is lovely from here," she said, as she stood a moment to watch the last radiance touching into indescribable beauty the roofs and spires of the city, which from that height were spread around them like a panorama.

"You look tired, my dear," said Helen Durie tenderly. "What kind of a day have you had?"

"Same as usual. I am getting used to the noise now—in fact I don't mind it in the least. The first day I never thought I should be able to stand it."

The mother's lips tightened in a rebellious line.

"I shall never get used to it for you, Mollie—never in this world."

"But think of to-morrow, when I shall have nearly thirteen shillings of my own."

She nodded brightly, and stirred up the fire so that the kettle on the hob began to sing.

"And what sort of a day have you had? You look better somehow—as if something had happened to cheer you. Has the doctor been here?"

"Yes; he was here a whole hour, Mollie, talking all sorts of things."

"Bless him," said Molly quickly. "If we had known him before perhaps you would never have been so ill."

"He thinks I need not go on being so bad, Mollie," said the invalid with a quick little breath. "We were to make a little secret of it, and not tell you till we were sure, but he did not know how difficult it is for us to have a secret from one another, did he, dear?"

Mollie winced a little as she opened the cupboard door to get out the tea things, but answered readily enough, "No, indeed."

"He's a splendid fellow, and so kind to the poor. I told him to-day he would never grow rich if he went on spending himself and his substance like this."

"We must pay him for what he does for you, mother. I certainly will," said Mary firmly.

"Yes, yes, when you are able; but it is not a debt that would weigh upon me. There are people in the world—only a very few—one feels like that with. Now, Dr. Alister might be my own son. I could not feel more at home with him if he were."

"Yes; but he is a young man with his way to make, and we must pay him," repeated Mollie firmly as before. "Tell me what he has been saying to you to-day. Tell me every single, solitary word."

"He talked a lot about you, Mollie."

"That doesn't interest me in the least," said Mollie rather shortly. "What did he say about you? That's what I want to hear."

"He thinks that perhaps I may be able soon to get up and walk about again."

"Yes—that's great news," said Mary playfully. "You know I have sometimes said you might, if only you would try very hard."

"Now, don't be unkind. You don't know how feeble and ill I feel," said the invalid, giving way to one of her moments of weakness, which, of late, however, had become fewer.

"No, no, not unkind. Well, if Dr. Alister achieves what we've both been trying for so long, it will be a great triumph."

"He is to try a new remedy, but you won't be angry if he fails, Molly?"

The childish, wistful look in the eager eyes touched a quick chord in the girl's sensitive heart and reproached her for more than one rebellious thought. She went quickly to the side of her mother's chair and kissed her fondly.

"Motherie, don't let us talk any more about it. I love you as you are. What would I do without my big baby? I shall never be a real mother, so I lavish all the love I have on you."

"Why do you say that?" cried Helen Durie jealousy. "You are not too good for the best. Dr. Alister is the best, Mollie, and I am sure——"

"Mother—not another word, or I shall go out and not come in till bed-time. Don't you forget that I am only a mill-hand, and that Dr. Alister is a gentleman. That's the way to express it, isn't it? I don't want to forget it, and I'm not likely to."

"Something has happened to upset you at your work to-day, Mollie."

"Only a trifle. A lady came to see the mills and tried to patronise me, and I resented it; that's all."

"Tell me all about it."

"There isn't really anything to tell, and it was silly of me after all, for how could she know the difference—if there is a difference?"

"If she didn't see the difference she must have been a fool," said Helen Durie, with extraordinary bitterness. "I never approved of your going to the mill; give it up to-morrow."

"That I won't! Having tasted the comfort of a steady wage, I can't drift back to the uncertainty of the needle again. I believe you are better, mother, because you have had better food. Now, come and have your tea, and let's talk about something outside of ourselves."

It was interesting to note the dominance of the stronger mind over the weaker one. Mary Durie was really older in mind and heart than her mother, double her age.

They grew merry, almost like children, over their meal. Then Mary washed up, made the fire steady and bright for the night, and, having changed her gown, said she must go and do a little marketing. She gave her mother the new *People's Friend*, and leaving her quite comfortable by the fireside, sallied forth into the now brightly lighted streets.

Her shopping, however, must needs be of the most meagre description, there being now very little of the week's money left.

Her chief errand, happily, was to a place where money would not be immediately required.

CHAPTER IX

THE STORM

A PEREMPTORY telephone message from his mother had summoned Tom Speed from the mills about three o'clock that afternoon, just as he was on the point of leaving to attend the Social Service meeting which he had been mainly instrumental in organising. He tried to explain over the telephone that it was almost imcumbent upon him to put in an appearance at least for a few minutes, but the answer came promptly back that the meeting was of secondary importance, and that he was required at home.

He did not anticipate any real trouble, yet he felt a little perplexed as he rode out to the Ferry on the bicycle that he kept at the mills for emergencies.

His father had gone home to lunch, and he supposed that his mother wished a family conclave to discuss the conditions of his grandfather's will. It was not a discussion to be looked forward to with any pleasure, and had Tom been able to talk to his mother over the telephone, he would have tried to reason with her. But she was either too much upset or too wary to give him the opportunity.

He left his bicycle at the gate of the little lodge, and walked up the broad, steep avenue to the door of the house where the blinds were all decorously drawn down, just as they were at Ravenscraig across the water. Tom's mouth took a displeased curve at the sight, and his one desire was to rush indoors and pull them all up to the very top so that the blessed sunlight might shine in.

He passed through the glass door, tossed down his cap, and walked into the morning-room. His father and mother were both there, looking the pictures of distress and indignation.

"You have been a long time in coming, and why did you make so many excuses to Mathieson over the telephone?" said his mother sharply. "Surely it ought to have been enough that I wanted you."

"I came as quickly as I could, mother," answered Tom mildly. "But I ought to have been at that meeting. At the last moment I had to send Soutar down with my notes to Mr. Rattray. It was very awkward——"

"Shut the door, Tom," she said, precisely as if he had not spoken. "Your father tells me you know about your grandfather's absurd and wicked disposition of his property. Did he make you his confidant about it beforehand?"

"No; it came as a surprise to me, mother, and not a pleasant one, I assure you. I suppose dad has told you I don't want Ravenscraig, and won't have it at any price."

"He has told me something of the sort, but of course you can't be in earnest about that, Tom. You never would or could be guilty of such tremendous and suicidal folly."

Tom gave a low whistle, and shifted somewhat uneasily from one foot to another. He perceived that his mother was much excited, and in one of her most headstrong and dangerous moods, a circumstance which accounted for the dejection of his father's looks.

There was a brief silence while the young man strove to adjust his thoughts. There was no dubiety whatever in Tom's mind regarding his course of action. The only difficulty was to put his decision clearly and plainly, but at the same time finally, before his mother.

His father would be less difficult and more reasonable, though his disappointment might be candidly expressed.

"Look here, mother," he said in a low, earnest voice, "I don't know what grandfather could have had in his mind when he did this. I never made any secret of my views of life to him, and up to a certain point he seemed to sympathise with me. But if there was one point I was clearer about than any other it was that I would not under any circumstances live in a big house, that is to say, after I was on my own entirely. In fact," he added with the slightest hesitation, "he knew perfectly well that as soon as the Settlement House in Dundee should become an accomplished fact I would go and live there."

"It shows that your grandfather realised to the full your stupendous folly," she said in a voice which seemed to cut the air, "and that he thought of the one way by which you could be steadied. He hoped to create in you a pride of home, seeing that you did not seem to take pride in anything else except in wounding your father and mother."

Tom winced. Every word went home.

"Play fair, mother. I have never tried to vex you, and at least I have not given you any of the particular anxiety which makes a good many homes miserable. How would you like if I had to be fetched home helpless from the Club most nights, like Arnold Graeme?"

She shook her head impatiently.

"Don't cite extremes, but listen to reason," she said shrilly. "Are you or are you not going to marry Katherine Lundie?"

"I am not," he answered clearly. "I don't care for her in that way, nor does she for me. She would resent being disposed of in this fashion even more keenly than I do. Don't look so desperate, mother. What difference can it make to you?"

She made no answer, but she wiped her hot face with the wisp of her lace handkerchief.

"You talk very glibly about Katherine," she said slowly. "But you have hopelessly compromised her in the last few years, running after her day by day, being seen with her everywhere, making visits of indefinite length at Lunan, giving people much occasion to talk. I could not tell you how many times I have been asked within the last month when the engagement is going to be announced. I am surprised that Mr. Lundie has not spoken to you on the subject. It will hurt his pride very much when he learns how ready you are to scorn her after all. From what he has said to me on more than one occasion," she added deliberately, "I know that he fully expects, as we have all expected, that you will marry her."

"Katherine herself does not expect it," said Tom steadily, though he visibly winced. "A marriage contracted on such grounds, merely to secure this bequest which nobody wants less than Katherine or myself, would turn out disastrously. Probably I shall never marry," he added quickly. "Life is too full of other interests."

His mother made a gesture of contempt, while his father, standing at the end window of the room looking down the steep slope of the garden to the sea, wondered how the scene would end. Presently he turned slowly and walked out of the room. Mrs. Speed then rose, and approaching Tom, laid her hand on his arm. Her face softened in response to the will that bade it relax, and the hard note left her voice.

"My son, this is a serious matter to us, but especially to your father, who has worked so hard and who has had to bear this very great disappointment. His father has not treated him well. As an only son he ought to have had Ravenscraig."

"But could no compromise be made?" asked Tom eagerly. "I have already spoken of it to my father. Couldn't Gilfillan make some arrangement by which you might become my nominal tenants, or something of that sort? It seems quite simple and fair——"

"It is impossible—the conditions of the will are exact and explicit. You inherit Ravenscraig on one condition only—that you marry Katherine Lundie. And she is charming, Tom. Most men would jump at such a chance. I cannot—cannot understand you."

Tom set his young mouth in a hard, determined line.

"No man likes his personal liberty interfered with, and marriage, less than any other affair, cannot be arranged like this. It must spring from impulse, and become a necessity because of the love that already exists. You don't know Katherine, mother. Her whole soul would revolt from such a cold-blooded bill of sale—it is nothing else."

"I know enough of Katherine to be certain that she is in love with you," she retorted. "And though I don't particularly like her, I think you have treated her shamefully. It is useless to discuss the matter any longer. I see there is no hope of making any impression on you in your present state of mind. I wash my hands of you. You have given me many an anxious hour, Tom, but never one like this. I am a baffled and disappointed woman. I hoped great things from—from the disposal of your grandfather's means. I had the right to expect that it would make a difference in my position. But he never was just to me. I've toiled and struggled for his son without a word of thanks, and I am repaid this day."

She swept from the room, tears of real vexation in her eyes.

They sent a pang to Tom's sensitive heart, but he had very little real sympathy with his mother's disappointment, nor did he realise its stupendous nature.

He hung about for a few minutes, inquired for Netta, only to be told that she had not yet returned from St. Andrews; finally he left the house, and, remounting his bicycle, set off for Dundee.

By the time he reached it the mills were closed, and the quick, mellow October dusk was falling. His thoughts as he rode along were much disturbed. His mother's words had left a sting. She had spoken very positively about Katherine, and what she had said gave him rather more than a passing uneasiness. He was in two minds whether to go up to Albion Terrace and have it out with her. With such good friends and comrades as they were it would be the straightest and the simplest way.

Yet something undefined and intangible held him back.

He felt the need of a little more light on the subject, and the longing to take counsel with a friend led him by natural instinct to a certain unpretentious house in the Foregate, where dwelt his friend and college chum, David Alister, who had commenced practice in Dundee solely to be near him, and who was slowly but surely carving a way for himself.

As yet, however, he was almost exclusively a poor people's doctor, old George Speed having been the first of the richer class to be on his list. At the Foregate he kept an open surgery in the evening and saw many patients, most of whom paid him nothing. To them all he was more than a mere physician—he was something of a guide, philosopher, and friend, to whom they brought all their woes.

He was snatching a meal when Tom Speed burst in upon him—enjoying a glorified tea which would serve him until the late hour when he would be free from the surgery.

"Hulloa, Tom, come and eat. What brings you here at this hour?"

They did not shake hands. Tom threw his cap on the floor and drew in his chair.

"I'm in a horrible mess, David. Help me out."

Alister smiled slowly, and, opening the cupboard door, took out another cup, which he proceeded to fill with tea.

"Drink that, and don't look so glum. I know the kind of messes you get into. Been taken in again, I suppose, by some fraud a baby could have seen through."

Alister had a kind of slow, drawling speech which surprised those who knew how much work he could get through in a day. He explained that he accomplished everything by never being in a hurry. Nothing could make him excite himself, yet his daily record would have put most men to shame.

In person he was tall and lanky, with a good-natured, somewhat vacuous-looking face, which in early life had been simply cherubic.

There was not much outward or visible sign of intellect about David Alister, nor was there dignity in his looks, yet the fact remains that he inspired both affection and esteem. Men took him seriously and believed what he said, and knew that he seldom or never made a mistake.

"It's worse than that, David. My grandfather has left me Ravenscraig tied to an impossible condition—that I marry Miss Lundie within eighteen months. I don't want to marry. I won't have the place on that condition or any other. I want to be let alone, to get peace to live my own life. But my people are furious, my mother especially. I have just had a jolly bad half-hour with her."

Alister neatly shaved a slice off the loaf, spread it with butter, and passed it on the knife to his friend.

"Eat, and let me eat in peace. I had no dinner to-day, and Heaven knows when I'll get any supper."

Tom, inwardly fuming, suffered himself to be calmed by his friend's large, imperturbable ease.

"You're wonderful, David. I wish I could swallow everything as you do. But, really, this is bad. I don't know how I'm to get out alive."

"Your grandfather has had his fun off us at the last, Tom. I suppose you have heard of his legacy to me."

"Yes, but that's quite simple. I'm jolly glad, old chap. It's no more than you deserve or had the right to expect. And there isn't any condition attached. You needn't even marry, unless you like."

"I'm very grateful for the money," said Alister soberly. "And I'm going to devote one-half of it to buying a cottage for my mother. I wish the old man had given me an inkling of his intentions, so that I might have thanked him. You did me a good turn, Tom, when you took me that memorable night to Ravenscraig."

"The old man was grateful, too. He liked you, David; how often he said it!"

'And I liked him. What I did for him was very little in comparison with what he has done for me. It was always a joy to go there."

"Yes, but why, oh, why, did he play me such a shabby trick at the last?" said Tom with a groan. "I didn't deserve it, and never expected it. What on earth could he mean by trying to punish me like that?"

Alister pushed back his chair, and, rising to his feet, reached for his pipe.

"Tom, your grandfather spoke to me once on the subject. I think I am at liberty to tell you now. It's just possible that it might throw a little light on his motive, and help you at the present crisis."

CHAPTER X

THE POOR PEOPLE'S DOCTOR

ALISTER filled his pipe and handed the pouch solemnly to Tom.

" We jawed a lot about you, Tom. In fact I may say that you were our staple theme of conversation."

" I don't know how you could fill up the time like that," said Tom, with a wry face. " But go on."

" He admired you immensely, lad, but always spoke as if you were not yet out of swaddling clothes. I suppose we hot-headed youngsters must appear in that light to men like your grandfather, who have lived their day."

Tom was surprised at Alister's choice of words. Inspired himself with a good share of the fine arrogance of youth, which accomplishes so much of the world's work and is purged of its mistakes by experience, he was inclined to be cynically tolerant towards those who did not see eye to eye with him on certain subjects.

" The old man, of course, was restricted in his action by his ideas regarding property, but I never thought he'd seek to restrain me in the same way. Well, what did he say ? "

" He thought you made a lot of mistakes and would make many more. He thought your heart stronger than your head, but loved you for it. And it was to prevent you making any sort of shipwreck of your own private life that he tried to safeguard you by attaching to his bequest the condition you complain of."

" Alister, you were in his confidence—you knew he contemplated this, yet you did not warn me or try to put him past it ! "

" No, old man. I knew nothing about his actual intentions, but I do know that he was extremely anxious for you to marry Miss Lundie."

" He told you as much ? "

" Often, and questioned me very closely about your relations with her. But on that point," he added significantly, " I was never able to give him any satisfaction."

" Why, pray ? You have known us both long enough," said Tom drily, " and I have never made any secret of my views on the subject of matrimony."

" You have a lot of views, Tom," said Alister drily. " But some of them won't wash."

" You're like the common herd, Alister, after all," observed Tom rather savagely. " You think there can only be one sort of relation between men and women."

" In my business I get down to the bedrock," was Alister's answer. " And in the main I guess it is so."

" I'm disappointed in you, Alister. Then I suppose you're on the other side in this ? You'd like me to be the tame cat, fall in nicely with all the wishes of my kindred, marry, settle at Ravenscraig, and in due course expire in the full odour of respectability."

Alister for a moment did not reply. His pipe did not seem to be drawing well, and required his full attention. He was really, however, bracing himself for a straight question.

" Tom, I'm wondering—I've been wondering for a good while—whether all this sort of thing is fair to the girl."

" What girl ? "

" Miss Lundie, of course."

Tom laughed hardly.

" There you are, Alister. You might be my mother with your worldly wisdom ! I can only say to you what I said to her, though it makes me very sick that you should need it said to you. There has never been any fool talk between Katherine and me. We are chums, I tell you—good, honest pals. Never have been, never will be anything else. And I assure you, though with your newly-developed pig-headedness I don't expect you to believe it, that nobody would resent this sort of thing more than Katherine herself."

Alister made no verbal response, and for a few moments they smoked in uncomfortable silence. Tom at least felt it uncomfortable. Alister appeared serene.

"I'll ask her—yes, I will. I'll tell her the whole story as I would tell it to a pal like yourself, and I dare swear that I'll find her a jolly sight more sensible about it than the rest of you. Why, there simply isn't an atom of that sort of nonsense about Katherine. She's the most level-headed woman I have ever met."

"That's what your grandfather thought, and also that she'd steady the compass," assented Alister.

At that moment the surgery bell rang.

"The deluge," said Alister, putting down his pipe. "I'll be hard at it for the next couple of hours, Tom, so what will you do? Sit here if you like, and I'll look in on you at intervals. There's a new book from America on "Socialism." Roebuck sent it to me only yesterday. It's rather interesting."

The housekeeper opened the door and announced a name.

"Miss Durie."

Tom pricked up his ears. "Durie," he said quickly. "We've a woman of that name at the mill—just come——"

"It's the same," said Alister as he rose to his feet.

"Is she ill?" asked Tom interestedly.

"No; her mother is."

"How long have you known them?"

"Some little time," answered Alister with a certain restraint in his voice. "They're very poor, but haven't always been that. They're gentlefolks, Tom."

"I thought as much. I have just spoken to her at the mills, arrested by her face. There's a tragedy there, Alister."

Alister nodded. "I don't know their past, but the daily tragedy is bad enough. The mother suffers from hysteria consequent on sorrow and privation. She is a handful for her daughter."

"A brave, uncomplaining, gentle soul—if faces don't lie," suggested Tom in a tone of quickened interest.

Alister assented, but did not appear anxious to pursue the subject. Afterwards, indeed, Tom wondered a little at the manner in which his friend had spoken of the Duries.

"Well, what are you going to do—wait or go? I shan't be free certainly much before nine. But afterwards I can go where you please. Are you going back to dine at home?"

"No; I've had all I want. I may stroll up to Albion Terrace."

"And thrash it out with Miss Lundie?" added Alister with a slight smile. "Yes, do, and come back with your eyes opened."

"Where's Miss Durie waiting?"

"In the surgery. I have told her to come to the front door, but she won't. She's a working woman, she says, and can only pay the lowest fee. I'd see her for nothing any day, Tom, only she isn't that kind of woman."

Again Tom was struck by the words, but Alister gave him no opportunity to reply. He simply gave him a parting nod and left the room. The surgeries were round the corner in a mean street, and there, night after night, the poor people's doctor ministered to disease both of body and of mind. He passed into the consulting-room, opened the communicating door which led into the outer surgery, and bade the waiting people good evening. Since Miss Durie's name had been brought in several other patients had entered. But at sight of the doctor she rose and came into the inner room.

"How are you this evening?" he said gently. "You look ghastly. Had a hard day?"

"Not more so than usual, thank you, doctor," she said, comforted at once by the sympathy of his manner. "I only came to speak to you about my mother, if you're sure you can spare me a few moments now with all these people waiting."

"You took your chance with them," he said with a smile. "And there is plenty of time for everything."

"Do you really think she is any better, doctor?"

"I think she is going to be," he admitted guardedly.

"What is her disease?"

"I thought you might have guessed. It is hysteria."

"Then her idea that she can't walk or move is purely imaginary?"

"Largely so. I surprised her to-day walking quite well, and had a straight talk with her."

"I am very sorry for her," she said quietly. "But I have suffered—we have both suffered a great deal through it."

"That is obvious," he assented.

"May I ask you something, doctor?"

"Yes, surely."

"Is it possible for a person suffering from hysteria to imagine wrongs—to imagine them so vividly that they become quite real?"

"Not only possible, but common as daylight, Miss Durie. I am meeting this sort of thing every day."

She hesitated a moment, colouring a little, yet moved to give him her full confidence.

"I've had to pretend a good deal lately. When things got so hard with us just before you came to see mother that first time, and when I saw that something desperate would have to be done, if we were to live at all, I suggested going into the mill. Of course, my mother was against it, but that I did not mind. I wanted to go into the Eliot Mills, for what reason, do you think?"

"I don't know, unless because of the reputation of the firm for generous treatment of their employees."

"No, that did not enter into my consideration. My mother told me soon after we came to Dundee an extraordinary story about her past acquaintance with Mr. George Speed. She says she was his wife."

"His wife!" repeated Alister in amazement. "It's impossible."

"His wife in the sight of Heaven—as she expressed it—and that he was bound to her by every tie of honour and fealty. But he threw her over for a woman who could forward his social and personal ambitions."

"That might be true enough. But she recovered—your mother I mean—seeing that she herself afterwards married."

"Oh yes, she did; but his conduct ruined and spoiled her life," said the girl, with a bitter look in her eyes. "I believe myself that she never cared for any other man. She certainly made my father very unhappy, so much so that he left us."

"It is a sad tragedy. Where is your father, then? Has he died?"

Mary Durie shook her head.

"We have heard nothing of him for many years. Once only he wrote and sent my mother a remittance. That was five years ago. Now we suppose him to be dead."

Her eyes filled with tears.

"He had a sensitive soul. He had been unfortunate all his life, and my mother's reproaches nearly drove him wild. I sometimes think that it is remorse that makes her so difficult to live with now."

"I am sorry for you, Miss Durie," said Alister simply, "sorry for you both."

She lifted her sad eyes to his face with a faint grateful smile.

"You have been more than kind. She has told me of your long visit to-day. You will not misunderstand if I say that such visits are luxuries for which we can't afford to pay."

Alister's face flushed slightly.

"You are very proud, Miss Durie. I suppose you would not give a man credit for wishing to do a kind act."

"I give you credit for that and more," she answered simply. "But you are a busy man and you have your way to make. My mother is exacting and thoughtless. You must not let her impose upon you."

Alister smiled. She might have been speaking to a child whom she wished to warn off debatable ground.

"Your mother's case interests me, and if by moral suasion, even a little diplomatic manœuvring, she can be restored to a normal state, don't you think I might be sufficiently repaid?"

"I can't take that point of view. Your time is money, Dr. Alister. But I do assure you that I appreciate your kindness. Shall I go on as I have been doing with my mother, then, sometimes scolding her, sometimes petting her? I am afraid I may have made many mistakes about her, but always I am so sorry for her."

"You do very well; don't trouble. I'll see the thing through. I think I see the light even now. Mrs. Durie has entered into a little conspiracy with me. May I put another question to you—why did you leave Edinburgh where you had lived so long and where you must have had many friends?"

"I did not know at the time what was my mother's idea in coming to Dundee. I know now that it was because Mr. Speed lived here."

"Has she ever seen or spoken with him, then, since you came?"

"Never. It is not many months since we came, and she has been ill all the time."

"May I ask why you chose his mill in preference to any other?"

"Not because I had heard that they were kind to their employees," she answered a trifle formally, then faintly smiled and looked him straight in the face. "No, I will be honest. I went because I wanted to know the Speeds and to understand, if possible, something of my mother's past."

"And have you succeeded?"

"I have learned nothing. Mr. Speed spoke to me to-day for the first time, though his son had already spoken to me several times. But I am sure it was a mistake. Please don't tell her I am working there."

"I won't, but I think you should give it up. Such work is too hard for you. I am sure you have lost weight since you went there. I'll try to find something more suitable for you."

She shook her head.

"I don't dislike the work, and the place seems to have a sort of fascination for me. But remember that I am particularly anxious my mother should not know where I am—in the meantime, at least."

Alister made no reply. He thought the position unwise and the motive unwholesome, but he did not like to say so. The sweet face appealed to him, the whole circumstances interested him more than he liked to own.

"I am keeping you," she said quickly. "Thank you very much. I feel better now I have seen you."

"Don't worry any more about your mother than you can help. We'll pull her through," said Alister cheerily as he opened the door into the hall.

"I'll let you out by the front door. The other place is packed to the door, and you won't like going through the crowd. Good evening, Miss Durie."

She thanked him and stepped into the outer hall. At the same moment Tom Speed, after having smoked his pipe out and decided what he was going to do next, stepped from the door of the dining-room on the opposite side of the hall.

CHAPTER XI

THE BEGINNING

Tom bade her good evening, but she hurried towards the door with a scarcely perceptible acknowledgment. Alister opened it, said " Good-night," and closed it behind her rather sharply.

" Are you going then, old chap ? " he said to Tom.

" Yes. Why did you shove her out like that, David ? I wanted to speak to her."

" She didn't look as if she wanted to speak to you," was all that David replied. " Are you going up to Albion Terrace, then ? "

" Yes, I think I will."

" Come back here later on ? I'll be through at nine."

" I'll say good-bye just now."

They dispensed with the formality of hand-shaking. Once more Alister opened the door, and before he suffered Tom to pass out he took a rather sharp glance outside. But already Mary Durie had disappeared.

For the moment there was between these two men a curious feeling of hostility, arising out of a psychological experience which neither could have put into words. A woman had entered into their lives, and their interests were likely to clash. Alister felt this almost as a certainty. He said nothing, however, but simply reiterated his " good-bye," and Tom passed out.

He took the sharp corner into the Foregate rather eagerly, and glanced round swiftly, but did not perceive the figure that he sought. He walked on a few paces, and presently descried the girl before a newspaper shop, evidently scanning something with great interest.

An overwhelming desire to speak with her took possession of him and he did not trouble to combat that desire. In such matters he was a law to himself, being undeterred by any fear of consequences or by any conventional scruples. Human nature being his study, it mattered little to him under what unusual circumstances he studied it.

Mary Durie turned away from the window, after having noted something on a small scrap of paper which she took from her purse—turned to meet the steady eyes of Tom Speed fixed on her face.

He slightly raised his hat, and once more bade her good evening.

" May I speak to you for a moment, Miss Durie ? "

" Certainly," she answered steadily, and stood still quietly with her eyes raised questioningly to his face. She betrayed neither surprise nor embarassment, a fact which gave a certain semblance of ease to the meeting thus forced upon her.

" You saw me at Dr. Alister's ? We had been talking of you just before that, and I felt very much interested in your story."

There he paused, for something in the girl's strained white face checked him. Her looks seemed to say that he had taken an unwarrantable liberty.

" If Dr. Alister has told you my story, or such part of it as he knows, he has betrayed a trust," she said clearly and coldly, " and I should not have expected it of him."

Poor Tom, reddening furiously, hastened to repair his egregious mistake.

" Oh, don't run away with that idea," he said hastily. " He told me nothing except what I could easily have guessed before he spoke. Any one could see that you were not accustomed to work in a mill; indeed it is an incongruity even to see you there."

"Has there been any complaint about my work, Mr. Speed?" she inquired quietly. "I have tried to do my duty, and the overseer has found no fault."

"Fault! Good Heavens! no; you work too hard at it, that's all," cried the impulsive Tom. "I hope you will excuse my talking to you like this. I only wanted to ask whether there was anything I could do to help you. You are a lady. There ought to be something better for you in Dundee than a millworker's place."

"There ought to be, but there isn't," she answered steadily. "I don't want any help, Mr. Speed. I am quite contended——"

She stopped there rather abruptly, her lips choking on the half lie. Contented! when her whole heart and soul were in revolt over the tryanny and injustice of circumstances. Contented! when she had not a moment ago taken from the newsagent's window particulars of a situation advertised in a paper which she was too poor to buy.

"Won't you walk a little way with me?" said Tom persuasively. "I will try to explain to you why I am anxious to help you."

She hesitated for a moment, looking at him steadily. His handsome face was earnest and sincere, his eyes had a kindly yet compelling gleam in them. And her heart was so starved of all that a woman has the right to expect. The moment was fraught with special temptation. What had she to lose, anyhow? Whom had she to consider? If he were brave enough to risk being seen with one of his father's millworkers in a public thoroughfare in his native town where he would most certainly be recognised, why need she care?

"I am not going home just yet, Mr. Speed. But it is a little unusual, isn't it, for you to speak to me like this without introduction?"

"There are cases where introductions don't count, and you forget that I know you quite well. I have watched you more closely in the last weeks than you think. How many times have I been in and out the spinning-room since you came?"

"I couldn't say," she answered. "I don't think I have noticed you very often."

"I've been there all the same," said Tom, as they turned to step across the street to the quieter side. He looked down from his tall height on the sweet profile of her face, noting its sharpened outline, and something stirred in his heart—something that was neither pity nor yearning, but a strange commingling of both.

"How is it you have come to straits like these?" he asked abruptly.

"The stress of life," she answered quietly, keeping her eyes fixed straight ahead. "We belong—my mother and I—to the great army of superfluous women."

"But what brought you to Dundee?"

"I can't tell you. It was my mother's wish."

"Had you any means when you came? Don't be angry. I'm not prying, but it is almost the business of my life to try and help people who need help. I make a lot of mistakes, but I always mean well. And I would help you if I could."

"If you could, I believe you would. I have heard of you in the mills and outside of them as the friend of the poor, but there is no way whereby you can help me, Mr. Speed—no way at all."

"That way must be found. I have women friends in Dundee who would befriend you if I asked them."

"That is the very last kind of help I want, believe me, Mr. Speed, and the very last I would accept. I know what ladies are. I've had some experience of them in my search for work before I came to the mills, and now I want to steer clear of them for the rest of my natural life."

"Don't judge all by your limited experience of a few," he urged. "I assure you there are women in Dundee worthy of the name whose greatest joy would be to help you if they knew about you."

"I should like it proved," she made answer. "I don't believe it now."

Tom walked on a few paces in silence. Then, by one of the fateful chances which do so much to disturb the peace of human lives, they met clear in the middle of the road Walter Soutar, the manager, walking with another man. The expression which instantly sprang to his face made Tom secretly writhe. He passed him with the curtest possible nod. Mary did not appear to have noticed him.

"Would it not be better for you to obtain a teaching post of some kind?" Tom suggested, when his momentary dismay had passed.

After all, if Soutar should say anything to him, he could effectually shut his mouth. There were others besides Soutar, however, who saw them that night in the busy Foregate, notably Betty Baxter with a large basket on one arm and a baby on the other, shopping for her numerous brood.

She rubbed her eyes to make sure that she had made no mistake, then she nodded to Mary with a kind of fierce exultation.

Both Soutar and Betty Baxter unfortunately cherished the most primitive ideas concerning the relations between men and women. In the eyes of both, therefore, the fact that Tom Speed and Mary Durie should be walking together could admit of only one explanation. Betty Baxter, though a very decent, hard-working woman, did not feel any moral qualms about the matter, and she determined to give her neighbour a bit of good sound advice on the morrow.

Meantime she was as pleased at the incident as if somebody had given her half a sovereign, simply because a little brightness was likely to be infused into the life of the girl she so much liked.

The sight of Betty, even her significant half-triumphant smile had no power to disturb Mary's equanimity. Conscious of no wrong, she was immune from suspicion. But they turned into a quieter thoroughfare, guided thither by Tom, before she answered his question about the teaching post.

" You forget, Mr. Speed. I'm neither a trained nor an educated woman."

" You may not be trained in the technical sense, but you are certainly an educated woman," was his quick response. " Why do you take such delight in belittling yourself ? "

She made no reply for a moment.

" I know my market value," she then said. " I have discovered it in a very hard school."

" There are situations outside the mere requirements of any Board. Couldn't you seek a place as nursery-governess to some children ? If I make inquiry, would you be willing to—to consider it ? "

She shook her head.

" I am not fond of children. At any rate," she added, quite conscious, though she did not look at him, of his dissent, " I would not in my present nerve-racked state have any patience with them. Besides, I would not leave my mother."

" Then every avenue seems to be closed," he said gravely. " All the same, I will not relax my efforts. Something must be done to get you away from your present unsuitable employment."

" Why do you think it is so unsuitable when so many women have to endure it ? "

" Well, but you are different and of a different class. I feel about it just as I should if my sister, through some stress, had to get her living by it. Can't you understand ? "

Her face softened, and half-involuntarily she turned to him.

So few were kind : her heart was quickly responsive. That timid, upward glance, the softening of the sweet, pathetic mouth, added so much fuel to the fire of Tom Speed's chivalrous determination. His interest dangerously deepened. To receive another such glance of confidence and gratitude he would do much.

" Look here, Miss Durie, can't you take this—this very small kindness in the same spirit in which I offer it ? My creed of life is to be of service each day to some fellow-man or woman. I've wanted to help you since the first day I saw your face."

" It is not easy," she said frankly, " for a man in your position to help a woman in mine. It would lay us both open to a great deal of misapprehension."

" But it ought not ! " he cried hotly. " It is one of these lying conventions I am trying to combat. I have a woman friend who will help me. Tell me where you live, and she will come to see you."

Once more she shook her head.

" My home is a very poor one, but I wish to keep it to myself. Don't think me ungrateful, Mr. Speed. Indeed, I shall always remember this night. But there is no common meeting-ground for us anywhere, you must understand that."

" I don't understand it. I refuse to accept that verdict. I shall see you again, and though you may withhold your address now I can easily get it."

"But we can always move from the place where we now are. People in the position of my mother and myself are easily hidden. The world does not chronicle our movements."

She gave a little mirthless laugh, and suddenly, at a dark curve in the road, without any warning, she bade him a hasty good-night and fled.

She was gone in a moment, folded in the night mists like an invisible thing, and he was left feeling a little foolish, but none the less determined to follow up his interesting adventure, and to improve his acquaintance with Mary Durie.

CHAPTER XII

THE LITTLE RIFT

EIGHT was ringing from all the town clocks as Tom stood for a moment irresolute on the edge of the pavement in the Lochee Road. Then he suddenly thought of Katherine Lundie and the business he had with her.

They dined at seven at Albion Terrace ; he would be certain to find her at home and disengaged.

He turned back, and in a quarter of an hour's time was on the high ground where the long sombre row of the Terrace houses stood outlined against the sky, and looked down with perhaps a certain hint of patronage, upon the toiling city. The Terrace—as it was familiarly called—represented a sort of half-way house on the Dundee business man's journey towards success. It was chiefly inhabited by junior partners and younger sons, who married early and who expected to spend a good few years within the actual precincts of Dundee before they should move out to the more pretentious, but perhaps less comfortable, dwelllngs in the Ferry suburbs or over the water.

The houses were tall, square, and solid, built by a man who had had an eye to stability rather than to beauty—good family houses where every inch of space was utilised and where there was no superfluous decoration or embroidery. The rooms were airy and lofty, everything pertaining to them being of the best, though not of the very latest design.

Number 78 had been Henry Lundie's town house from the time when he had entered the commercial world. To it he had brought his young wife from the sunnier south, and to him it was a home. Katherine, being free from so many of the petty ambitions of her class, had never urged him to leave it. After all they were Lundies, and it mattered very little where they lived. Her father was deeply attached to the house ; so also in a less degree was she. They had made a compromise with the demands of his position by building a cottage at Lunan, in which Katherine took the keenest delight, and in all things pertaining to which she was allowed to exercise her individual taste. It was called a cottage, but was in reality a very roomy bungalow capable of comfortably housing quite a large family. Quaint in design and perfect, though conspicuously simple in all its furniture and arrangements, it was to Katherine a real home. It was only her numerous philanthropic works that reconciled her to spending the winter in Dundee.

She and her father were sitting in the drawing-room when Tom Speed was announced. That he was a frequent and always welcome visitor to the Terrace was evidenced both by his reception and his own familiar ease of manner. Tom was really more at home in the Lundie's house than in his father's, in the sense that his real self, sure of finding appreciation and sympathy, could always find expression.

This stmosphere had perhaps been a trifle enervating for the young man, and there is no doubt that he had presumed upon it.

They talked for a little while on topics of common interest. Then Henry Lundie rose and said he would go to his books in the library, where they could join him when they felt inclined.

This procedure, by no means unusual, being in fact part of the routine of the evenings which Tom spent at the Tarrace, seemed perfectly natural to them all. It was never planned—it seemed just to be the right thing to do.

Katherine looked lovely. Tom could not help thinking so as he watched her beautiful head bent over her needlework. She wore a gown of soft black as mourning for his grandfather, he knew, for Katherine did not care for black, but preferred ruddy tints that suited the warm hues of her skin. Everything about her was dainty, and the film of black lace falling away from the elbow-sleeves revealed at once the perfect contour and the exceeding whiteness of her arm.

The harmonious and beautiful room, the flowers, the soft lights, all the accessories that so naturally surround the daughters of the well-to-do seemed to strike Tom with a fresh sense of contrast and a little resentment. The woman whom he had just left and whose circumstances had so touched and fired his heart was just as capable as Katherine of appreciating to the full the refinements of life, and yet its very necessaries were denied her.

" It's jolly nice in here, Katherine. All the same, it seems hard—— "

" What does ? " she asked softly, but without raising her eyes. A great well of content was in them. Tom's presence seemed to complete the picture she saw in her mind's eye—seemed to round off the ideal of her life. Katherine had been forced that day to some inward analysis as she recalled her conversation with old George Speed, and she had arrived at a fairly satisfactory conclusion. After all, her marriage with Tom would be the fitting consummation—perhaps the only possible one—to their perfect friendship. Certainly she could never spare him to another woman. A delicious sense of expectation, of personal happiness, gave a special lustre to her fine eyes and a soft colour to her cheeks which made her doubly attractive.

Tom saw all these charms, only to be hurt by them because of all that was denied to the other woman.

" The contrasts of life, Katherine," he answered as he sat down near her. " I've just been talking to a girl who would like all this sort of thing—one who has been born, I mean, for better things, but whom fate has decreed should be a mill-worker and associate with the common herd. Yet she's a lady, Katherine, as much as you are."

" Who is she ? " asked Katherine interestedly, letting her work drop into her lap, and looking across the soft light into his face.

" I don't suppose you would know her. She hasn't been long enough at the mills, and you weren't often there while you were staying at Lunan."

" I think I do know her. Her name is Durie, isn't it ? "

Tom sat forward eagerly.

" So you have seen her ! When, Katherine ? It hardly seems possible seeing that you came back only two days ago."

" I was at the mills yesterday at closing time. I saw the girl come out, and, being rather interested in her looks, drove rapidly after her and over-took and spoke to her, but she was most ungracious—almost rude."

" I can't imagine her rude, Katherine, but even if she were there is some excuse. Think for yourself of the position ; it's intolerable."

" She's certainly unsuited for the work, and I told her that."

" Did you ? " he asked eagerly. " And what else ? "

" Asked her to come and see me—first invited her to the Guild meeting on Saturday night, but she declined ; then I asked her to come here. She declined that too, and not very civilly. She certainly desires to be left alone."

" She must not be left alone," was Tom's almost fierce rejoinder. " She's got an invalid mother dependent on her. You must help me, Katherine, to get her a better place of some sort. Among all the women we both know surely something can be done. What about Mrs. Spence ? She has a lot of little children ; surely she might be able to give her something to do."

Katherine smiled. " You forget that the children are Mrs. Spence's special fad. Why, she has Norland nurses and all sorts of up-to-date products and appliances at Fairview. She would be the very last person to ask."

" But you'll try and think of something ? "

" I don't know what I can do now, Tom. You see, I offered everything I could think of, and she refused—not too courteously. Yes ; I'm quite sorry for her, but, after all, what is one to do ? "

" A little diplomacy and she'd be won, Katherine. I have counted on your help."

Katherine looked across at him, a little strangely, he thought. She had on a pair of pince-nez to enable her to see her fine threads. Tom had always said they spoiled her looks.

"You are getting two wrinkles by wearing those things, Katherine. Take them off," he said quickly. But she paid no heed.

"Why don't you speak. Then you won't go and see this girl for me when you get her address?"

"No; I don't think so."

"That's unlike you. She needs a friend, Katherine."

"Well, I offered to be one. She refused—and not graciously. She must come to me now."

In his present mood Tom naturally thought her decision hard. He had never heard Katherine thus assert herself. Usually he had but to speak and it was done.

"Very well," he said a trifle stiffly. "I suppose there isn't any use saying more on the subject."

A little smile rippled across her mouth, making her adorable. She was certainly a beautiful woman, and Tom thought so. But, after the wayward manner of youth, the winning of Katherine being all too easy for him, did not attract him. It was hardly an auspicious moment to broach the subject of which his mind had earlier in the evening been full, but Tom Speed was accustomed to blurt out what was in his mind without any regard to consequences. He certainly lacked that gracious tact which was one of Katherine's most delightful characteristics.

"I say, Katherine, they've made a muddle of our affairs among them. My grandfather has, I mean, with that absurd will of his. Has anybody told you?"

"Nobody. What has he done?"

She did not put down her sewing. Perhaps something warned her that she might need it as a guard.

"He has left me Ravenscraig—a thing I have no use for, and never will have any use for, in this world."

"Well, you can sell it. I shouldn't fuss about having such a fine house left to me," she said whimsically.

"But I can't; there's a condition attached to it. I had very nearly said a beastly condition, and if I had you would have known what I meant. They've done their best to spoil our friendship, and I'd dearly like to know who was the first to put the idea into my grandfather's mind."

Katherine did not ask another question, and Tom fidgeted about a trifle uneasily, half wishing he had not opened the subject. It was a little ungracious after all to repudiate the suggestion as absurd.

"I said to them to-day that I failed to imagine what you would say—that your indignation would know no bounds. For we have been proud of the fact, haven't we, that our friendship has been a real friendship, without alloy?"

"Yes, we have," she assented, and broke off her thread at a place where no break was necessary. Had Tom been watching her closely he might have observed that her fingers trembled.

"I'd better get it out, Katherine, and be done with it. I came to get it over so that we might condole with one another. The place is left to me solely upon condition that you and I marry within eighteen months. Absurd and—and annoying, isn't it?"

"Oh, very. And what happens when we both refuse to fulfil the condition?" she asked with a wholly admirable calm.

"Oh, Ravenscraig passes into the hands of a Syndicate or Committee, to be transformed into a Home of Rest for the aged poor of the town."

"An ideal scheme, but how much simpler if your grandfather had left the place unconditionally for that purpose alone."

"That's what I say. I am awfully sorry, Katherine, that your name should be dragged in like this. If I could have prevented it I would, but we'll do our best not to let the conditions of the will become known. I've been to Gilfillan already. He's an old fossil, but I managed to let him see my—our point of view."

Katherine sewed on. "Isn't your mother very much disappointed about Ravenscraig?" she said after a time. "Her heart has been set on it a long time."

"She's—she's simply furious. She hadn t an atom of reason in her this afternoon. I assure you, Katherine, I have had a miserable day."

"But it's over," she said quietly. "That's the joy of all days—that they have an end."

It was a curious speech.

"I'm glad and grateful that you take it so quietly. If you too had been furious, that would have been the last straw. You won't let it make any difference. I can't do without my friend and comrade, even when she won't stretch a point for me. Things will go on the same, Katherine?"

"Oh yes, quite the same," she said, and sewed on, tracing a pattern where none had been before.

"You're not very friendly to-night, and I'm out of joint myself. Let's go down to Mr. Lundie. I want to hear about the Service meeting. You weren't there?"

"No. I'm ashamed to say I forgot all about it. Yes, go down, Tom. I'll come presently. I have a note to write to Biddy Macleod about Saturday's Guild. She promised to sing, and I fear she has forgotten."

Tom, all unsuspecting, left the room, relieved that he had had it out, as he imagined, with Katherine Lundie, and grateful to her for having taken it as she had done. It was no more than he had expected, of course, but some girls might have behaved differently. He closed the door. Katherine dropped her sewing and sat very still, staring into space. The mask was torn away, and she saw her passionate woman's heart as it was.

It had gone irrevocably into the keeping of a man who did not care for the gift.

CHAPTER XIII

THE SCHEMER

On Saturday afternoon they buried old George Speed beside his wife in a little churchyard about three miles from Ravenscraig, and on a wind-swept hill looking out to sea. It was a calm and beautiful day, and all the proceedings were decorously and admirably carried out. A reverent throng, representative of the wealth and prestige of the flourishing city, attended the service in the drawing-room, and it was afterwards augmented by a great following outside. All the family from The Rowans were present, Mrs. Speed looking stately and handsome in her sweeping black frock, her fair face giving no hint of the undercurrents of feeling. She would do all things decently and in order, still cherishing the hope that Tom's folly might not prove irremediable.

No hint of the disposition of the old man's property had been suffered to leak out, but there was not a great deal of curiosity. In view of his generous benefactions in his lifetime it was generally supposed that beyond the house there could not be much left, and that that would in the ordinary course go to his son. The presence of the ladies from The Rowans on the funeral day, as of those already in possession, strengthened that belief. There was no formal reading of the will—that is to say, no invitations to return to the house had been issued, and the company, with one or two exceptions, scattered at the churchyard gates.

Two carriages only drove back to Ravenscraig. In the first, George Speed, his son, and his partner, Henry Lundie ; and in the second, Mr. Gilfillan, the lawyer, Walter Soutar, the manager at the Eliot Mills, and Dr. Alister. Alister, however, left the carriage at the nearest point to the Ferry. His treatment, especially on this occasion, by the Speeds, with the exception of Tom, left a good deal to be desired. Conscious of nothing in his own behaviour to warrant it, he was proud and quick of spirit to resent it, for he had done his duty absolutely by his patient, and had nothing to reproach himself with. As for the legacy, it had surprised him more than it had surprised them.

When Alister left the carriage, Soutar looked undecided as to what he should do. He had not been invited to return to Ravenscraig, but Mrs. Halliwell Speed had been very gracious to him, and it was his nature to take an ell when granted an inch. His curiosity was insatiable. So, after a momentary hesitation, he kept his seat. Speed had already given him in substance the contents of the old man's will, and had been duly condoled with. Soutar, however, imagined that he now possessed the key to Tom's persistent and suicidal refusal to accept Ravenscraig and fulfil the condition attached. He had found it in the Foregate two nights before.

" Ravenscraig's a nice place, Mr. Gilfillan," observed Soutar as the carriage rolled through the gates. " It'll be a down-right shame if it passes out of the family all through the folly of a young man who doesn't know his own mind."

" Mr. Tom Speed has always struck me as a person who knew his own mind remarkably well," replied the lawyer a trifle drily. He was not greatly enamoured of the specimen of the rising man who sat by his side immaculately attired in new mourning, and looking the part to perfection.

" Well," corrected Soutar affably, " a young man who can't see what side his bread's buttered on. But you know what young men are, Mr. Gilfillan ; in the meantime he has other fish to fry."

Gilfillan cast a keen glance at the smooth, smug face of the man by his side. The lawyer was not at any time curious, and he abhorred gossip, but he was not just then averse to getting any light thrown on a case which had occasioned him a good deal of anxiety and thought.

" You mean that his interest is engaged elsewhere—that, in fact, the case is one of *cherchez la femme ?* "

Soutar nodded delightedly, albeit the smattering of French he had picked up at the night-school had not included the trite phrase which Gilfillan used at the moment to express his passing opinion.

" It's a pity when a man makes a *mesalliance*, Mr. Gilfillan," he said, strongly emphasising the first syllable of the French word. " It's all up with him. It's always better for a man to aspire when his mind's set in that direction, don't you think ? "

" It depends on circumstances," answered the lawyer gravely. " Then there is another woman in the case ? I hear a good deal about Tom outside, but I must say, never a whisper of that kind. I thought he was above all that—that his ideals—fads, if you like—led him in quite other directions."

" Even the man with a fad, Mr. Gilfillan, is only human ; and a pretty face is always a pretty face."

" Then you know the lady ? "

" Oh yes, very well."

" She's unsuitable ? "

" Quite—in fact, impossible ! "

" Do they know about it at The Rowans ? "

" Nothing as yet. I happened to discover it by the merest accident, and, of course, I'm too sincerely a friend of the family to make it a matter of common gossip."

" But you are sure ? "

" Quite. The evidence was indisputable."

" Who is she ? "

" I prefer not to say, but if the whole of Dundee could be searched a more unsuitable person could not be found. She's practically on the lowest rung of the ladder—a working woman. But we needn't be surprised, considering how Mr. Tom spends his evenings and generally disposes of himself in Dundee. His sort of Socialism's only a fad, Mr. Gilfillan—must end in disaster. It's a pity for his family."

" I like young Tom," said the lawyer quietly. " And I don't believe he'll come to any grief. He's sound at bottom. If I were you, Mr. Soutar, I wouldn't attach any importance to the stories you may hear about him in Dundee. He's talked about, of course, as any man is who has a little courage attached to his opinions. Probably what you have told me would, if investigated, be found capable of some simple explanation."

" I've seen him with her, and others have seen them too, Mr. Gilfillan. Don't think I've gone out of my way to make up a cock-and-bull story. That wouldn't suit me at all. As I have said, I'm too sincerely a friend of the family to make mischief."

" Well, I shouldn't spread the story if I were you," repeated the lawyer warningly.

Soutar, thus snubbed, changed the subject.

" What's going to happen to the place in the interval while they're waiting for Mr. Tom to make up his mind ? "

" It will remain in charge of the servants," replied the lawyer absently.

" Seems a bit hard on Mrs. Halliwell, doesn't it ? There's no doubt she's keen on Ravenscraig."

Gilfillan did not reply, and at that moment the carriage drew up before the door. Tea was laid at the big dining table, where Soutar proceeded to make himself at home. He was specially attentive to Mrs. Speed, apprehending that she was the real mistress of the situation. Mrs. Speed rather liked Soutar, and was very gracious to him. The day had been very trying for her, but she was a woman who could rise to a crisis, and no one had been able to detect a flaw in her demeanour. There was some little talk on general subjects, conducted in the low, decorous tone suitable to the occasion. Tom was obviously the most restless and uncomfortable person present.

" Mr. Tom seems a bit uneasy," said Soutar to Mrs. Speed.

" He well may be, Mr. Soutar," she replied, with a sudden hardening of her lip. "He is occasioning us a good deal of anxiety at present. Couldn't you, with your sound commonsense and business acumen, manage to make some impression on him? You see him every day. I cannot understand how it is that with so many good examples before him he should come so far short of all he ought to be."

"I'm not very far in Mr. Tom's good graces," modestly replied Soutar. "I'm too keen on business, you understand, and we've come to loggerheads a good many times when I insisted on putting the interests of the firm in front of his fads."

"Right—quite right. I do wish you could imbue him with some of your commonsense."

"He'll learn only by experience. Meantime, if we could get him away from scheming and undesirable persons, only too ready to profit by his eccentricities, perhaps we could induce him to be reasonable about his grandfather's will."

Soutar advanced this suggestion warily, not certain how it would be received. But Mrs. Speed, only too eager to get some fresh light and to obtain some knowledge that she could use against her son to convince him of his folly, looked eagerly into the manager's face.

"I suppose that, living in the town, you must hear a good deal about Tom?"

"Yes; I both hear and see," he said significantly.

"You know that he has undesirable acquaintances? Are any of them women, Mr. Soutar? It has seemed to me during these trying days that there must be some motive other than mere caprice for his refusal to accept the conditions of his grandfather's will. Mr. Speed told me he had spoken to you. If you know of any entanglement, it might—might help considerably if we knew about it too. Of course, you understand there would not be any pressure brought to bear on him. In Tom's case that would be quite fatal. You know, I dare say, how hot-headed he is. It would simply drive him to still greater lengths."

"I quite understand that, but I can hardly go into the matter here, Mrs. Speed. I have already taken up too much of your time."

"And we may be overheard. Come and see me at The Rowans to-morrow afternoon. I shall be at home after four o'clock."

Soutar, greatly gratified, promised. To obtain Mrs. Speed's confidence—to become her ally—would be a great step gained in his career of self-advancement. Tom, seeing them deep in conversation, could not help wondering whether Soutar was informing his mother of the chance encounter in the Foregate. But as she did not frown upon him he concluded otherwise. Had she been told of his walk with Mary Durie her wrath would have known no bounds. Soutar left immediately after tea, as did Henry Lundie, though at different moments. Only Gilfillan was left, and he stayed behind merely to go through a few formalities connected with the winding-up of the estate.

"I feel sorry to think you will not remain in this house, Mrs. Speed," he observed quite sincerely. "It certainly seems a pity that it should be left to servants."

"But why should it be?" inquired Tom bluntly. "Although I may not eventually fulfil the condition of the will, doesn't it belong to me, at least until the time for doing so is up? Why can't my father and mother come here?"

"Because the terms of the will are most explicit. You may live here yourself, Mr. Tom, if you like, but you can't hand the house over to any one else."

Tom made a wry face. "He's dead, but I never knew a more idiotic thing in my life," said Tom impulsively. "He knew even while he was drawing up the wretched thing that I should refuse to fulfil any of the conditions."

Gilfillan shrugged his shoulders and shut up his brief-bag. He himself thought that the clause affecting the occupation of Ravenscraig manifested less than the dead man's usual acumen. It seemed a futile way of trying to force a desired conclusion.

Suddenly Netta, who up till now had said very little on the subject, made a suggestion.

"Why shouldn't you live here, Tom, and invite us to be your guests, at least until the time is up? There's always the offchance that you may change your mind, you know."

She showed her even white teeth in a little half-malicious smile, to which Tom could not help responding.

"Well, I'm sure I don't mind. It will make very little difference to me in the long-run, for as soon as the Settlement House is ready I am going there. And

March will see it occupied. What do you say, mother? Would you care for a year in the house?"

She shrugged her shoulders. "At least your property would be well looked after. I can't imagine what your grandfather could be thinking of to contemplate leaving it in the care of servants. We all know what that class is without supervision."

Tom looked at his father. The proposed arrangement was a compromise, but the last two days had been anything but happy ones for him at The Rowans, where he had been made to feel himself outside the pale.

"I think if your mother would care for that, Tom, you ought to agree," said Speed, who looked strangely haggard and worn. The nagging of the last two days had tried him hard, and his own private thoughts gave him little peace.

"Very well; I don't mind so long as I can come and go as I like, and it's understood that the arrangement doesn't bind me to anything."

His mother checked the glimmer of a smile which stole unawares to her lips. To her it was more than a compromise—it was a respite, and an opportunity which might be turned to the utmost advantage. In a year how much might happen! Even Tom himself might be brought to reason! And at least it would shut people's mouths and give her what her soul had so long desired. The public need not know the exact terms on which they entered Ravenscraig.

She decided to grasp the opportunity, and she returned to The Rowans full of plans for the transfer of her household to the mansion-house over the water.

CHAPTER XIV

PLAYING THE GAME

NEXT afternoon Walter Soutar, in place of going to church, walked out to the Ferry. He lived in rooms in Dundee, having detached himself from his own family and settled them in his father's native village of Ceres, where a pretty cottage had been available at a very modest rent. Soutar's father had been a jobbing gardener, and a very honest, capable man, highly respected in Dundee, and constantly employed. He had saved a little money, and having been presented with the house by Walter, he and his wife were most comfortable. Their one other child—a daughter, married to a ship carpenter at Whiteinch—sometimes came on a visit with her children, and the old couple were quite contented with their lot.

They had a certain pride and faith in their son, who had got on so well, but he was not now so homely with them as Mamie, who was still their ain bairn. Walter seldom saw his sister, as he could not get on with his brother-in-law, a plain-spoken person, who did not like Soutar's airs. Of late Soutar's ambition had mounted very high, and the suggestion that he should go to Calcutta on the business of the firm had, of course, helped to swell that ambition. He had been frankly told that if he engineered that delicate bit of business well a small partnership would be the reward. As partner he would be justified in aiming high—perhaps even as high as Miss Lundie, whom he immensely admired.

Her very aloofness charmed him, and now that Tom Speed had made his choice, or at least decided against her as his future wife, all things seemed possible to the aspiring manager. He had not a fine or sensitive nature, and rebuffs did not daunt him. A man cast in a different mould would long ago have understood Katherine's cool manner.

He thoroughly enjoyed his walk. It was a fine, clear, crisp afternoon, with a hint of the coming winter in the sharp edges of the clouds dipping to the horizon, and with a nip in the wind which ruffled the long, grey waves rolling up the Esplanade. A sense of importance and anticipation gave a pleasant excitement to the walk, and, though he might not be very hospitably received by Tom, still he came on the invitation of the mistress of the house.

Contrary to his expectation, he was taken, not to the drawing-room where the family usually sat on a Sunday afternoon when visitors often dropped in to tea, but to a smaller sitting-room belonging to Mrs. Speed, where she wrote her letters and interviewed persons with whom she desired to talk in private. While this privacy gave to their talk a sense of intimacy, Soutar would have preferred the drawing-room. He liked to feel that he was regarded as one of the family.

Mrs. Speed was writing letters at the old-fashioned bureau between the windows when he was announced, and without rising she turned and gave him a little nod.

" Just a moment, Mr. Soutar, please. I am finishing a rather important letter, and my thoughts just at present are rather difficult to keep in order. If I lose my thread I may never find it again. You will excuse me, won't you ? "

" Certainly ; don't mention it," he assured her as he took a chair.

She did not keep him waiting more than three minutes. Then, pushing the letter into its envelope, she turned to him with a smile.

" Now we can talk. I thought that here we should be undisturbed. Mr. Speed and my daughter have gone for a long walk, and Tom is, as usual, invisible. You walked out, I suppose ? "

" Yes, and it was very pleasant. I hope you are not too tired after the strain of yesterday ? "

"Oh no. I have a great deal of reserve strength. I am not one of the women who make occasions or who pose, Mr. Soutar. I am a straight person, who says what she means and means what she says."

Soutar laughed, and said he had never had any doubt of it.

"Therefore my object in asking you to come to-day is to get the fullest light on the matter we talked of yesterday. You have my husband's complete confidence in business. I am only following his example in trusting you where our family affairs are concerned."

"Thank you," murmured Soutar. "I'm sure I feel honoured, and I will do my best to deserve that confidence."

"Oh, I am sure you will. I seldom make a mistake in judging character," she said complacently, "and I am going to speak out quite frankly to you. I have really very few to whom I can speak. It is difficult for me to be quite frank to my husband about this matter, seeing that old Mr. Speed was his father."

"I quite understand," murmured Soutar, more and more delighted at the channel into which the conversation was drifting.

"Well, then, what about this woman? Is it a woman in Dundee in whom my son is interested—one of these dreadful, faddy, straight-haired persons who get carried away with enthusiasm, forgetting how unbecoming it generally is and how detrimental to their appearance?"

Mrs. Speed, when she liked, had a caustic tongue.

"It is even worse than that, I am afraid, Mrs. Speed."

"Oh, come, don't tell me there is any disgraceful kind of entanglement, Mr. Soutar. Tom may be bad enough, but I never should believe that of him—never."

"There is nothing disgraceful, but there is something. I mean that he is taking in one of our own workers an interest that he ought not to take."

"Nonsense, Mr. Soutar! I shall never believe that of Tom. I tell you he isn't that kind of boy. If he had been a little more human we might have made more of him. He's all fads, and doesn't give his natural impulses a chance."

Soutar did not say anything more.

"Who is the girl?" asked Mrs. Speed presently. "I can't imagine any one in our position taking interest in a girl of that class. The few times I have been in the mills I have always been struck by their unattractiveness. It is incredible that it can be as you say."

"About three weeks ago," said Soutar quietly, "we took on a new hand. I thought at the time she was unsuitable, but there was room and we thought we would give her a trial. She's a cut above the common."

"And that's the girl! What brought her there?"

"Ah, that I don't know."

"What's her name?"

"Durie. But the name doesn't matter much, Mrs. Speed," he answered shrewdlys "It might not even be her real name. We do now and again light upon bits o. comedy and tragedy among them. And there's certainly a story in this woman'f face."

"Which I should have thought the unpardonable sin. Is she young and—and pretty?"

"Yes and no. I hardly know how to answer. Perhaps interesting would be the better word. She's tall and pale and slim, with big dark eyes and a sort of way of looking at you. She's a girl you couldn't have the heart to find fault with even if she needed it. An uncomfortable kind of person to have about the place in that capacity."

"I should think so, yet the very woman to appeal to Tom. I wonder whether there's anything behind—whether she knew him before, and came there with the idea of preying on his sympathies?"

"Oh, I don't think that. It was several days before he saw her, and then he immediately asked about her. But I don't think he was able to find out much. She is not communicative but keeps herself to herself."

"But in a place like the mills is not the presence of a person of that sort resented, and is she not sent to Coventry, as the boys say?"

"Usually they bring folks to their level pretty quickly and without ceremony," admitted Soutar. "But in this case nobody seems to mind. She's very quiet, and, as I have said, she keeps herself to herself."

"Which I should have thought the unpardonable sin. There's no reserve in that class. Well, and do you say that Tom has found other means of getting acquainted with her?"

"Evidently, for I met them only the other night walking together up the middle of the Foregate."

"The Foregate? A strange place to choose for a lover's meeting, if it was that."

"They were going somewhere else. I watched them turn off into a quieter street."

"Did they look loverlike?"

"They were talking earnestly enough—at least, Mr. Tom was, looking at her as if her face was the only one he cared for in all the world. Of course, I haven't much experience of love-making myself—never could afford it," he added facetiously. "But to me and the man who was with me the thing could have but one meaning. The man was John Murray the ironmonger. I asked him not to say anything about it, and tried to make as little of it as possible."

The latter part of the speech was uttered upon the spur of the moment, and had no foundation in fact. Murray had merely smiled and passed on to the topic they were discussing, and had not given the matter another thought. Young Speed was known to take an interest in all kinds of waifs and strays, and his conduct could never be construed like that of other men. Murray had not even mentioned the matter to his wife. But it suited the manager mightily at the moment to pose as the friend of the house of Speed.

Mrs. Speed sat back in her chair, her finger-tips meeting, a perplexed look on her fair face. She was pondering on the next best step, and how she could most successfully engineer this difficult and delicate matter. Tom had to be handled with great skill lest he might be driven to the perpetration of greater folly.

"What would you advise, Mr. Soutar?" she presently inquired. She often asked for advice, but seldom took it. Advice had its place in the economy of things: it often shed fresh light on difficult problems.

"I don't know what to advise. You see, Mr. Tom's kittle cattle, isn't he? He'd get so angry if we dismissed the girl. It would give him a handle and a grievance, don't you see? which he'd never cease to use against us."

"Exactly what I think. Still, she must go. Would it be possible for you to dismiss her quietly without saying anything about it to Mr. Speed or to Tom?"

"Nothing easier, but I don't advise her dismissal, Mrs. Speed."

"If there's anything in the affair it is better that she should go, isn't it, before the millworkers begin to buzz over it?" she said shrewdly. "To-morrow try and find out what you can about her and her people—where she lives and everything else you can. In the afternoon I'll come up myself. I haven't been in the mills for over a year, but as I do go sometimes my visit won't create much remark. I'll be there about four, and will expect to see you about."

"Yes, I'll be there."

"And you'll take me through the room where she is and point her out."

"I think you'll notice her without that. She's a cut above the common," repeated Soutar.

The phrase rather offended Mrs. Speed, and though it was necessary to be friendly with Soutar, she did not care for his company. She reached out and pressed the electric button on her desk.

"Bring up some tea here, Beith," she said to the smart maid who answered.

"We mustn't wait for the rest. They may drop into some one's house for tea. You deserve some after your long walk, Mr. Soutar."

It was really meant to hasten his dismissal, and Soutar intuitively felt that it was so. His visions of an hour or two spent intimately and pleasantly with the family vanished, and a little later on he left with the feeling that he had been made use of—"squeezed dry" was the elegant phrase he iterated in his own mind.

"She's clever," he said to himself, with a slow smile as he descended the hill. "By George, she is. She's worth watching. But I can keep my eyes open too," he added to himself. "Two can play at that game, Mrs. Speed."

CHAPTER XV

THE BARRIER

AFTER lunch that Sunday Tom walked into Dundee, as if drawn by a magnet to his friend Alister. He found him stretched at ease on the old haircloth sofa in the consulting-room, trying to snatch a few moments of hard-earned Sunday rest.

"No, I haven't been to church. They hauled me a mile up the Lochee Road at three o'clock this morning, and the air was enough to nip the face off you," he said, turning to Tom with lazy good-nature. You may as well come in now. I'm wakened up, and if you don't somebody else will."

He did not offer to rise. Tom drew in his chair, stirred up the somewhat dull, smouldering fire, and took out his pipe.

"All well at home ?" inquired Alister.

"Yes, fit enough," he answered moodily. "But this business is going to upset things, Alister. More and more I am puzzled by the old man's motive in throwing such a bomb into an otherwise peaceful camp."

"Any fresh complication ?"

"Oh no. It's arranged, I think, that we're going to move to Ravenscraig. My father seemed to think I owed it to my mother to suggest that. And it can't make any real difference to the issue, though I don't see what difference there is between one house and another. They all serve the same purpose."

"That arrangement may complicate matters, if it doesn't altogether prevent the issue you desire. If you're determined, Tom, I honestly think the best plan would be to hand the place here and now to the syndicate—or whatever it is."

"We can't," said Tom, as he spat into the fire. "We are bound hand and foot by conditions. Oh, the old man has us properly, I can tell you—every one of us."

"But he has to give you half a chance. Eighteen months is time enough for any man to change his mind in. Honestly, Tom, I hope you'll change yours."

"Do you, and why, pray ?"

"It would be better for everybody concerned, but chiefly for yourself. As you say, the house a man lives in can't matter much. You can live your own life under any roof."

"You can't. Sometimes it crushes you, Alister."

"In theory, perhaps, but Ravenscraig wouldn't crush you, and it would always be open to you to devote a part of it, if you liked, to the alternative purpose your grandfather had in his mind," suggested Alister. "You certainly do look down on your luck, man. What's it all about ?"

Tom remained silent for a moment.

"Everything's out of joint, David." Then after a pause he added a trifle shamefacedly, keeping his eyes fixed on the fire, "I went after Miss Durie on Thursday night and spoke to her."

"You did ?"

Alister sat up, and an indefinable change crossed his face.

"For what object ? It wasn't wise, Tom. What could come of it but discomfort to the girl ?"

"I hardly see that. She's the only woman I shall ever marry, David. I know that."

Alister sat silent, chewing the cud of bitter reflection.

His own heart was tender towards Mary Durie, but he had thought there was no need for haste in telling her so—that he could bide his time. The legacy that had come to him so unexpectedly had opened up the way, and that very afternoon before he slept he had been dreaming of the day on which he should tell her what was in his heart. Slow of thought as of action—slow and deliberate he had lost in the race, while Tom Speed in his usual high-handed fashion had stepped in without a moment's warning and won. Alister, observe, had no doubt that Tom had won. That was Tom's way—his arrogant way. He could brook no interference. He had a kind of splendid selfishness that bore down opposition, that swept obstacles from his path.

" This is all very sudden, surely," he said, with a new harshness in his voice. " You've given me lots of starts and thrills, Tom, but surely this is a bit off."

" Of course, you will say that. I guessed you would," answered Tom, still glaring into the fire. " But this sort of thing is bound to come to a man suddenly, if it comes at all and is worth having. I knew the first time I saw her she was going to be a force in my life."

The phrase was a favourite one of Tom's, but this time it did not provoke a smile on the face of his friend.

" This will complicate things with a vengeance, and be a great blow to your people, won't it ? " he said, a little stiffly, sitting forward on the old couch with his knees drawn tightly together and his head well advanced.

" Oh, they wouldn't like it, of course, but she's a lady. Even you could see that. I suppose, Alister ? "

" The " even you " was good, but again Alister did not smile.

" Did—did you ask her point-blank on Thursday night, then ? " he inquired bluntly.

" Good heavens, no ! What do you take me for ? That sort of woman isn't to be picked up for the asking. She's got a pride high enough to reach the heavens. Can't you tell me more about her, David ? Where do they live ? "

Alister hesitated for a moment.

" I don't know whether I ought to tell you where they live."

Tom laughed in scorn.

" Don't then. As if I couldn't find her on short enough notice even if she were hidden in Dundee's remotest corner. Don't be an ass, Alister, but help me as you've always done. I tell you I'm hard hit this time."

Alister found it difficult to believe that. Cast in a different mould himself, he could not take these mental aberrations seriously. He believed that Mary Durie's sweet face had attracted most men who saw it, but he decided that in this case it was her circumstances, the halo of mystery, the possible story or tragedy behind, that had most appealed.

Alister had now known the Duries for about two months, during which he had seen a good deal of them, and had arrived at a very just estimate of them both. His immense compassion for the girl had paved the way for a warmer feeling, and he was now prepared to marry her. That very day, in fact, he had been planning how he could best let her understand his feelings and persuade her to respond. And while he had been planning, Tom, the impetuous and irresponsible, had rushed in and forestalled him. Alister did not feel very kindly disposed to him at that moment. Their warm friendship had received a rude shock.

His deep eyes positively glowered out upon Tom's unconscious face. In this matter Tom had shown the fine selfishness that had characterised his relations with Katherine Lundie. Yet how he would have opened his eyes had the sin of selfishness been laid to his charge !

" I'm wondering how I'm going to work it. You must help me, old chap. You see, as things go now, I daren't talk much to her at the mills. You know what a nest of evil speech and suspicion such a place is. Fact is, she must be got away from the mills—something else be found for her to do until things get settled a bit at home, and I see my way clear. What would you suggest, old man ? "

" I can't suggest anything. I think it's most unholy," was Alister's startling reply.

The word arrested Tom, and he looked for the first time straight and steadily into Alister's face, where he found an expression entirely new to it.

" Unholy ? What do you mean ? "

" What I say, of course. You try to take a grip of destiny with both hands, Tom but experience will teach you it can't be done."

" I suppose you mean that she won't look at me, but if a man sets his heart on a thing he can generally compass it somehow. At least, I must try and make her life easier for her. Her pathetic eyes haunt me now."

"I don't see precisely how it's going to be done," said Alister, in slow, rather measured tones. "As you remarked a moment ago, any notice you may take of her can only recoil to her disadvantage. The fault of our social order? Yes, but where a woman is concerned we have to be very careful, Tom. The last thing you would wish, I suppose, is that your name should be coupled with hers."

"Depends on what way it was coupled," Tom replied lightly. "I don't care though the whole of Dundee should know that I mean to marry her. But in the meantime it wouldn't be politic to say anything at home. I'm deep enough in the black books there already. We must let the Ravenscraig business simmer down a bit. But she must be helped, and you must help me to help her, David."

"It would need a woman to do that."

"But where are we to get one? My mother wouldn't, Netta can't, and—and Katherine won't."

"You've asked her?"

"Yes."

"Having told her first what you've just told me?"

Tom's face reddened a bit.

"Of course not. I went up to Albion Terrace after I had parted from Miss Durie on Thursday night, and I didn't know my own mind then. I only knew that she wanted a woman friend, and I made sure that Miss Lundie was the one."

"I should have thought the case would have interested Miss Lundie. What did she say?"

"It appears that she had already tried to befriend her in a way, but Miss Durie had resented it—I suspect, because Katherine didn't adjust her manner to the right point. She would speak to her as she speaks to her Guild girls—too familiarly, a familiarity which a woman like Miss Durie would, of course, instantly resent."

Alister sat still, glowering at his chum with a kind of slow wonder in his eyes. Tom was really great!

"But I can't think yet why she refused. When I asked her to go and call at the house, she simply declined rather ungraciously. It was very unlike her."

"Miss Lundie doubtless had her reasons," said Alister sympathetically.

Tom was silent for a moment, not noticing that his pipe had quite gone out.

"She was sound on the other matter, Alister," he said suddenly. "I knew I hadn't made any mistake."

"Did you actually speak to her about it?"

"Why, yes, of course. Didn't I tell you she was my very good pal, and that we thoroughly understood one another? Naturally she was a little indignant, but she'll see me through. She's as much annoyed as I am that our names should have been bracketed like this, but we'll take care that nobody outside the family knows. So you see you were wrong after all, Alister. How little you seem to know about women, though I suppose you see more in a day than I see in a month."

"I don't pretend to any great knowledge, do I?" said Alister as, with a queer, silent laugh, he lifted his big frame from the sofa.

"I think I'd like a walk now, Tom, before tea-time, if you don't mind."

"I'd like it, but you haven't suggested anything yet, Alister. Haven't you any ladies in your practice who would be interested in Miss Durie and make a post for her somewhere?"

Alister shook his head. "I haven't, and, honestly, I don't know how it's going to be possible for you to help her, Tom, except by leaving her alone."

The tone was so different from Alister's usual hearty one that Tom looked at him, genuinely aggrieved.

"I can't think what's come to everybody, David. Even you, who used to be like the shadow of a great rock in a weary land, have suddenly failed me. What's up?"

"Nothing particular, but I really think, Tom, you're proving a bit of a trial to your friends at present."

"Oh, well, if you're going to take it like that I can sheer off," said Tom, with a shrug of his shoulders.

Alister laughed, and let his big hand drop on Tom's shoulder as if he had been a little lad. At the moment, indeed, he felt himself to be years older than Tom Speed.

"Say, Tom, was it before or after the legacy story that you asked Miss Lundie to befriend Miss Durie?"

"After. I went to the Terrace for the express purpose of having it out about Ravenscraig, and I had it out," he answered virtuously. "But why—what difference could that make?"

"None, perhaps," said Alister. "As you say, I don't know much about women, but I can't help thinking—stupidly, of course—that in this affair you acted with even less than your usual perspicacity."

Tom plied him with questions, but not another word on the subject would Alister say.

CHAPTER XVI

MRS. GEORGE SPEED INTERVENES

DESIROUS of giving a natural complexion to her small plot, Mrs. Speed informed her husband next morning while they were dressing that she intended to go up to the mills that afternoon.

"I haven't been there for a long time—not since the new wing was opened."

"I have to go to a board meeting at half-past two," he said, "but I'll be back by four."

"Oh, that doesn't matter. Tom can take me round, or Mr. Soutar. He called yesterday when you were out. A very nice man—don't you think, George ?—and almost a gentleman."

"I don't know about the gentleman, Marian, but he has got a clear, shrewd head on him and he's worth a lot to us. And there's no doubt that he's the man we ought to send to Calcutta if I don't go myself."

"I shan't let you go, George," she replied decidedly. "You were not yourself for a long time after the last Indian journey. Why not send Tom ? It might be the very salvation of him just now."

"He doesn't want to go, Marian, and my father on the day he died warned me against sending him."

"I don't see what your father had to do with it. If he had minded his own business better we might have been the gainers. He has made a nice mess of Tom's future, anyhow," she said, with a warning snap in her voice.

Speed made no response. Then her anger seemed to cool. She was so full of scheming that one idea seemed to chase another through her brain, leaving time for none to operate successfully.

"Well, we needn't discuss it now," said her husband after a pause. "The matter doesn't press for a week or two, and anyhow we must wait for a reply to our last mail. I suppose you'll take Netta with you ? They'll get you tea, and I'll come back as quickly as I can."

"Netta's going over to St. Andrews again to-day."

"Why all this running to St. Andrews ?" inquired Speed quickly. "She seems to have developed a sudden fondness for the place."

"It's only her music-lesson that takes her there this afternoon," she answered equably. "I am glad she likes it so well. Marchesi seems to be a first-rate teacher. All his pupils enjoy their lessons. I have seldom seen Netta so interested in anything."

"I suppose it's all right," was Speed's reply, and the subject dropped.

Netta left after an early lunch, and Mrs. Speed drove into Dundee, arriving at the gates of the mills soon after three.

"You can put up in the town, Roberts, and come back about half-past four, when we may get Mr. Speed to drive home with us."

Soutar was waiting about for her, and he approached to meet her, raising his hat. He looked well in his homespun suit. The sober Sunday black in which he had appeared at The Rowans on the previous afternoon had seemed to give him something of the look of a menial. Clothes are more potent in certain directions than we fully understand, and can change the whole aspect of a man or woman to an incredible degree. We are yet very far from comprehending to the full the delicate art and philosophy of clothes.

Soutar was in the habit of placing himself in the hands of his tailor, who chose for him—without much regard to results, which were not always successful—the most expensive and presumably the latest modes.

In his tweed suit the manager looked what he was—a capable, alert man of business who could handle every detail of his work as an expert.

"Good afternoon. I'm a little late. Mr. Speed has gone to the Board meeting. Where is Mr. Tom?" asked Mrs. Speed affably.

"In his own department," answered Soutar, and she did not ask where that was.

"I'll go into Mr. Speed's room and rest a moment," she said, and he led the way to the door of the inner room, where he stood aside to let her pass, a little undecided whether to enter himself.

"Come in," she said amiably. "Is she here to-day, then?" she asked as he closed the door.

"Yes—been at her work with the others since six o'clock."

Mrs. Speed gave a small shrug.

"Six o'clock in these bitter mornings! Poor thing, I'm sorry for her. And has Tom seen her to-day?"

"Been through the room twice to my certain knowledge," he answered. "But I don't think he spoke to her."

"How does she look? Any sign about her of—of a secret understanding?"

"None. She's impassive of face, but active at her work, as she always is. My own opinion is that she's a deep one."

"I should imagine so, and it wouldn't surprise me to learn that her being here is all part of a deep-laid plan on the part of one who got to know my son and all his weakness outside. There is nothing easier than to trade on sympathy, and unfortunately his is often misplaced."

Soutar neither denied nor affirmed.

"Well, can you take me round now?" she asked, her usual restlessness seizing her. "We needn't go to her flat first, you know. We can get there by a circuitous route. Only don't let us stop too long in any of these horribly noisy and smelly places. I can't stand it."

"It's very noisy where she is," Soutar reminded her.

"I really do want to see the new wing. We can go there first."

Soutar nodded, and they once more passed out into the open sunshine of the great courtyard, which they crossed in silence.

"I hope Miss Netta is quite well to-day?" Soutar ventured to ask.

"Oh, quite. Gone to St. Andrews to a music-lesson. Would you like to go to Calcutta, Mr. Soutar?" she asked suddenly.

"I'm willing to go anywhere in the interests of the firm," he replied with an affectation of modest sincerity which caused her to smile. She simulated an interest that she did not feel in what he proceeded to show to her. The details of the great machine did not much appeal to Mrs. Speed, though the smoothness of its working affected the results which were her concern.

It had seemed to her all along that too much money was required for the perfecting of that machine, and that the profits were not proportionately large. George Speed liked efficiency in every department—up-to-date appliances, and certainly the outlay had been great. But he fully expected to reap a full return one day.

In about twenty minutes' time—for Mrs. Speed did not waste any superfluous moments on the way—they came to the spinning flat where Mary Durie was employed.

As the swing-doors rolled back, the dust and the smell and the mighty noise seemed to envelope them and caused Mrs. Speed to give a little gasp.

"What a horrible place!" she said, starting back involuntarily, not pausing to think of the women and girls who had to spend so many hours in such an environment. "It can't be properly ventilated. Surely there ought to be some method of consuming all that fluff and of mitigating the bad odours. Why doesn't some inventive genius apply himself to that problem?"

Soutar nodded.

"You won't notice it when you are fairly inside. I assure you it's not so bad as it seems."

The doors slipped back, and they walked up the somewhat narrow aisle between the frames finding it difficult to steer their course between the little boys with their trolleys and all the rush and tear of the working hours. Mrs. Speed of set purpose walked quite slowly and spoke to several of the workers on her way, pausing quite a long time by an elderly woman to inquire how long she had been in the mills and whether she found the work too hard. The reply was blithe and cheerful and reassuring. Mrs. Speed passed on smiling, looking to perfection the part of the master's wife kindly interested in the welfare of her husband's people.

" At the end of the room on the right, Mrs. Speed," said Soutar in a low voice. " The very last row, she's nearest the outside."

Mrs. Speed nodded, and she stopped quite near to Mary Durie to speak to a small mite of a girl bearing a basket full of empty bobbins. While she was speaking her eyes took in every detail of the figure which so much interested her, but she could not see the girl's face.

" Speak to Mrs. Baxter, won't you ?—just here," said Soutar in a purposely loud voice. " She's been in this place most of her married life. She began here in old Mr. Lundie's time, when she was about fifteen, I think. She's one of the oldest hands."

At the sound of her own name Betty Baxter turned round with a pleased grin. She liked to be taken notice of, and there was always the chance of such notice bringing grist to her mill. To her, with so many mouths to feed and a useless and lazy husband, any chance gift of the gods was welcome ; and Betty was not troubled with any false pride.

" How do you do, Mrs. Baxter ? I'm pleased to see you're here yet, hale and hearty," said Mrs. Speed, stepping forward so that she came in line with all the women in the row and could obtain a full view of Mary Durie's face.

Its expression did not alter, however, nor did she so much as look round. Having exchanged a few words with Betty, Mrs. Speed addressed her neighbour, Mary Durie.

" I don't think I know your face," she said in a tone of most admirably assumed pleasantness.

" No madam," answered Mary without lifting her eyes.

" You have not been here long, perhaps ? "

" No, madam ; a few weeks only."

" You find the work a little hard, I am afraid ? "

" No, madam. I can do it. I am getting used to it."

The tones of her quiet voice neither rose nor fell, and she went on steadily with her work while the brief colloquy lasted. Mrs. Speed, however, wished to get a good square look at her face, and especially to see the eyes which reveal so much of the personality within.

" You have not been used to the work, I think," she persisted, while Soutar, deeply interested in the little comedy, stood back, but near enough nevertheless not to lose anything that was said.

" I have always had to work, madam, though I have not been long at this—— "

" Where do you live ? I might be able to do something for you. I should like to come and see you, if I may. I try to take an interest in my husband's work-people."

The tone was the tone of the rich woman addressing the poor woman, between whom and herself there was a great gulf fixed. She saw the colour rise in the girl's clear, pale cheek.

" Thank you, madam," was all that she said.

" Won't you tell me where you live ? Before there can be any good done anywhere, even in business, there must be reciprocity. Isn't that so, Mr. Soutar ? "

At this speech, which certainly did not betray much tact, Mary Durie lifted her head and suffered her eyes for a moment to meet the hard, brilliant orbs fixed so relentlessly on her face.

" I must get on with my work, madam, if you please," she said, but in a tone that was full of resentment and rebuke.

" I'm sorry if I have interrupted. I meant well," said Mrs. Speed, with an air of offended dignity, and signed to Soutar to pass on.

She had seen all she wished.

" She must be got rid of, Mr. Soutar," she said a little breathlessly when the swing-doors closed behind them and they stood alone on the little gangway outside. " A designing minx, if ever there was one. I trust to you to see that she leaves the mills this week. You have the power, I think you said."

" Oh yes, but—— "

" But what ? " She stamped her dainty foot a little impatiently, not liking the hesitation in his tone.

" It is difficult to find a reason."

" Faugh ! A reason can always be found for everything—for everything, do you hear ? And surely, if you are the head of anything, you can exercise your prerogatives. Otherwise, why be a head ? Understand that I expect you to dismiss that girl this week."

Soutar for a second remained silent.

" Very well. I'll do it," he said at last.

" Who's going to question you ? "

" Oh, nobody, unless maybe Mr. Tom. But she needs the work, she needed it when she came ; and besides, there's just the off chance that her dismissal may hasten what we want to hinder. It's the sort of thing that'll make Mr. Tom's blood boil."

" You do it, Soutar. In this matter you have pledged yourself to me, and I shan't forget your willingness to serve me. As for Tom, he shall go to India ; that'll be the best thing for him meanwhile."

But Mrs. Speed was yet to learn that it is not permitted to any human being to be the complete arbiter of destiny.

CHAPTER XVII

DISMISSED

THE cashier at the Eliot Mills was one Andrew Lonie, who had been in the service of the firm for twenty-seven years. He was a gentle, small man, with straggling grey hair and rather weak eyes protected by a pair of spectacles. Though not particularly bright or clever, he was a very conscientious servant, and was a favourite with everybody within the gates.

To him had been relegated the task of informing Mary Durie that her services would not be required any longer.

She did not take her dismissal without a protest.

" Why am I paid off ? " she asked quietly, fixing the cashier with her steady eyes.

Lonie looked kindly over his spectacles at her, but shook his head.

" That's no' my business, my woman. I suppose they're gettin' slack—— "

He knew that the reason he had given was insufficient, for when he had asked Soutar what cause he was to assign for the girl's dismissal he had received—not a satisfactory answer but only a snub in the shape of the question, " Since when did it become necessary to give a reason to a servant for dismissal ? "

Lonie, with his old-fashioned code-standard of conduct thought that it was necessary to give one, unless the occasion flagrantly demanded dismissal.

" I want to know why I'm paid off," she repeated, with rising rebellion in her eyes. " Nobody has complained of my work or given me a hint that this was coming. It isn't fair."

" It seems like it, lassie, but the fault's nane o' mine. I get my orders, and a' my concern is to obey them. But the mill's nae place for you onywey. It's easy to see that."

" That has nothing to do with it," said Mary a trifle hotly. But at the same time grasping the silver firmly in her hand, she turned to go, for the waiting throng was pressing towards the outside. Lonie leaned over his desk and called her back.

" Here, lass, if I were you, I'd see ane o' the maisters. Maister Lundie's no' here, but Maister Speed's in the office. Try him."

She declined with a curt word and walked out with her head in the air. Looking neither to the right nor to the left, she proceeded towards the gates.

An immense bitterness surged in her heart. She knew that she was an efficient worker and, strange as it may seem, she had begun to like the routine—to even find a certain music in the roar and the boom of the machinery. Her work required no exercise of brain power, but rather quickness of touch and that steady application which tells in every walk of life. Busy all day, she had enjoyed a singular feeling of detachment from life. The purely mechanical exercise of certain physical powers bore no resemblance to life as she understood and had dreamed of it, yet in the meantime it sufficed. And the work meant her daily bread—was the only thing which stood between want and her mother and herself. To be thus summarily dismissed without reason or explanation given was not only a shock but a gross injustice. An untold bitterness surged within, making her feel that she could cry aloud to publish her wrongs to the world. It was so little that she had asked from life after all—only the opportunity to earn a living wage and peace to spend it.

These, so hardly bought, were now ruthlessly taken away. At whose instigation ? Well, perhaps, that mattered little. For the moment she did not attach any personal significance to what had happened. She supposed that if the demand for labour had slackened she, as the latest employee, must be the first to go. Her dismissal was merely the result of the operation of natural causes in the great-little world which represented so much supply and demand. The employees were just so many ants working busily on the heap. One more or less of the number crushed, what mattered it to anybody, except to the ant?

Betty Baxter, waiting for her neighbour at the gate, noticed from the girl's demeanour that something unusual had occurred.

Of late Mary had never failed to walk with Betty, though she was one of the most draggled and untidy of all the band. Mary had no false pride, and the courage and the endurance of the little woman had often inspired her.

"What's up? Been gettin' into the hat?" she inquired affably.

"No, out of it," answered Mary dully. "I'm paid off."

"No!" cried Betty in unfeigned surprise and dismay. "Noo, that's no' fair—no' it's no', for ye've workit like the verra deil. I've often said to ye to pit less intil it, that it didna pey to tear yersel' to bits for ither fowk."

Mary was not ready with a reply. She had had none of the guile of the paid worker about her. She had simply put into her task all the energy she could command.

"It's no' fair, but never mind, you'll get something else, sure's daith ye will, an' something better too."

"That isn't the point, Betty. I want to know why I'm paid off. They ought to give a reason. Even the lowest,"—she added bitterly—"is surely entitled to justice."

"Oh, there's nane," responded Betty airily. "You're better aff when ye dinna expect it. I dinna fash my heid, ye I get warstled through."

They passed out and crossed the road to the side where the throng was less dense.

"I'm sorry for ye, my lassie," repeated Mrs. Baxter kindly. "But things micht be waur. What wad ye dae if ye had a man like Bob that wadna work an' was aye ready to leather ye, if ye didna gie him enough?"

Mary's smile was very wintry. She could not imagine herself in any such plight, but to the primitive mind of Betty Baxter things were either bettered or worsened by comparison with other things.

"A tyke like Bob," she repeated, "and seevin weans, an' only wan pair o' haunds to work for them, but, bless ye, a body aye gets warstled through."

"I might warstle through," commented Mary, "but Bob, as you call him, would find himself left on the outside. I wouldn't give him a halfpenny-piece, but would try to get him shut up or punished in some way for neglecting to keep me."

Betty laughed.

"That's the wey fowk speaks that has never been mairrit. Bob's no a bad sort when he's sober, an' he never minds haudin' a wean. Besides he's aye a man aboot the hoose."

Feeling the last argument to be unanswerable, Mary held her peace.

"Hasn't he a trade?"

"No—that was the mistake. Dinna you mairry a man without a trade. Whenever the bad times come, it's the labourin' man that's thrown oot. An' when a man's been oot wance or twice, he's no carin' whether he ever gets in again. It spiles them, see. That's whit wey we've sae mony unemployed, as they ca' them. It's a disease."

This explanation of the unemployed problem interested Mary, and for the moment took her mind off her own wrongs. How much she had learned from this homely creature in these days! What lessons in life!

"We're gettin' them hauled up," went on Betty cheerfully, always ready after the guileless manner of her kind to hold forth on her private concerns. There is no doubt that this lack of reticence, this desire to take the whole world into their confidence, is one of the greatest joys of the poor. "Annie's makin' aicht shillin's noo and little Bob five. I dinna alloo him—auld Bob, I mean—to touch the bairn's money. He daurna. He kens it's the wan thing that pits my daunder up."

Betty looked attentively at the profile of the girl who walked by her side, and she wondered what she would do next.

"If I were you, lassie, I wad speak to Maister Tom. He's the puir fowk's freen'. D'ye no' see hoo nice he is when he comes roond, but of coorse ye ken him weel eneuch. I saw ye in the Foregate the ither nicht, though ye didna see me,"

There was a little touch of facetiousness in her tone which, curiously, Mary did not at that moment resent.

Yes, he had been more than kind, why not make more of the opportunity thus afforded? Something told her that no appeal made by her to Tom Speed would fail.

They came at that moment to the crossing where they usually parted. Betty's way lying in the opposite direction from Mary's.

" It's no' for you workin' in a mill, onywey, an' livin' in the Meal Vennel," observed Betty.

" How do you know I live in the Meal Vennel, Mrs. Baxter ? " asked Mary rather sharply. " I've never told you."

" I fand oot," replied Betty, not in the least abashed, though she did not add that she had sent little Bob to follow at a distance to discover where Mary Durie lived.

Betty would have found it difficult to explain her motive for doing this. It was not exactly vulgar curiosity, it was rather the feeling that the information might come in handy some day. She was primitive in this as in most of the affairs of life, acting on the first impulse, never stopping to analyse motives, or consider possible consequences.

He seemed awfu' ta'en wi' you," she ventured to say when her remark about the young master was not resented. " He's the puir fowks' freen', Maister Tom is, jist as Alister's the puir fowk's doctor. If ye play yer cairds weel, lass, ye micht be leddy ower them a' yet. My! whit wad I no gi'e to see it."

Mary bade her a hasty good-day, having heard quite enough. But the words had started a train of thought which was distinctly tempting to pursue. Her mind was in a whirl when she reached the Meal Vennel, which was busier than usual on a Saturday afternoon.

Out of the chaos she must bring some order before she faced the fretful invalid in the little kitchen near the sky. On the stairs she paused and pressed her hand to her heart and drew a long breath of perplexity—almost of pain.

She must concoct some story for her mother's benefit, for it would not do to tell her that she had been dismissed. In her dealings with her mother Mary had undoubtedly made mistakes. A stronger policy, the policy of honest straight dealing pursued from the beginning might have helped to strengthen the weaker will. Mary, for the sake of peace, had fallen into the habit of treating her mother like a child, and she always tried to banish the gloom from her mother's face, and to appear cheerful when she entered the house.

She was in no way surprised to find her mother in bed, as she had left her, some bright-coloured novelettes lying on the counterpane, and a small table with a tea-tray drawn up close to it.

" Lazy person," she said playfully. " I really thought you would be up by this time."

" I've had a bad day," came the fretful answer. " A splitting head and the noise is something awful! They've never halted off that stair for one minute since you went away."

" No, it's very bad, I know. I think we'd better leave the Vennel, mother; I've never liked it."

" But it's cheap. Where will you get two rooms cheaper? And it's airy and nice when you get up. Why do you want to leave it? You're never happier than when you are hauling me about. You forget that I'm not able for it."

Mary laughed a little hardly, and throwing off her hat and jacket, knelt on the hearthrug to rake out the fire. She was weak for want of food, but she could get none until she had prepared it. She had brought in two chops in her hand, and would cook them when the fire kindled. The smoke came down, and she went to the window and threw it up to make a better draught. The wind stirred her hair, and the sun caught its meshes till it shone like pure gold.

" It's a shame, Mollie, that we have to live where nobody can see you," said her mother fretfully. " You are far bonnier even than I was as a girl, yet I was a toast in the Carse of Gowrie, and they made a song about me."

Mary laughed lightly.

" I'm waiting to hear that song, mother. You might sing a verse of it to help the kettle to boil."

" Well, but it's true, though you don't believe it, and when I think of the women who get such chances without the half of your looks, I can't help being angry. I dare say if we go on living like this you'll never have bairns of your own, so you'll never know what I suffer on your account."

Mary's colour rose a little quickly.

"Don't speak like that, mother; you know it's the one theme I can't bear."

"Well, of course, you always are against me, but it's the truth I'm speaking. You never see what you don't want to see. Now there's Dr. Alister, I'm sure it's you he comes here to see——"

"I don't see how you make that out, seeing that he always takes care to come at an hour when I'm not here."

"Ah, but you should hear him! And he's a true gentleman, Mollie; he's not above taking an interest in an old faded woman for kindness' sake. How is it you've never told me about the Wellstoods at Lochee? There are two sons. Do they never take any notice of you?"

Mary looked round in amazement at this speech until she suddenly recollected that her mother was not aware that she worked at the Eliot Mills, but had got it into her head that she went to Lochee.

"I've never spoken to either of them in my life," she said truly enough. Then quite suddenly, and before she could check herself, she blurted out an unexpected question:

"Mother, will you tell me quite frankly and truly what really happened long ago when you knew the Speeds?"

CHAPTER XVIII

FROM OUT THE PAST

HER mother was silent a moment, not so much from reluctance to speak about the past as from surprise that Mary should of her own free will allude to it. She had never encouraged her to go back to the past, but on the contrary had always shown an impatience over her reminiscences and tried to turn the conversation away from her mother's young days.

" It's a long story, Mary, and will take some telling, but I should like you to hear the rights of it at last. It begins far back when I was a lassie at Rattray school, running on the braes with a heart lighter than yours has ever been."

" That could easily be, mother," said Mary, with a sigh. " I have never been a bairn."

" The Speeds belonged to Rattray, Mary ; you have heard that much, and I've heard my mother tell about the widowed mother and her two laddies—Jamie and old George that has just passed away. Jamie was never out of scrapes with his poaching, and was always in every kind of mischief. In the end he shot a gamekeeper in the leg, and he ran off—a stowaway—in one of the Dundee boats and never was heard of more. Mrs. Speed had a little shop, and George helped her to keep it, and was a comfort to her all her days. He was very keen on business, even as a lad, and he used to travel the country with a pack, selling inferior stuff to the puir folk at a high price. At any rate they said in Rattray that that was the way in which he laid the foundation of his great fortune. He aye had a heid above his station, they said, and had a job to keep his mother up to the mark of gentility he was aye aiming at."

" Did he make a grand marriage, then ? "

" No, he married the daughter of a farmer from Strathbraan, but she was a fine woman, and I think she made him very happy."

" Did they live in Rattray ? "

" Yes, above the shop. His mother died in the same year that they were married, and they saved money, and he went into the wholesale line, and had a lot of folk on the road trading for him. I've heard say it was a sort of co-operative society, and that he was the first to get folk to serve him well by paying them a share of the profits."

" And had he only one son ? "

" Only one—a year younger than me, and we went to Rattray school together and were like brother and sister, till—till we became something else. George was not like his father, he hadn't his ambitions, not at least as long as he was in Rattray. He went to school at the Perth Academy, and while he was there he wrote me a letter every week. He boarded with his aunt in Perth, and came up to Rattray on Friday nights. Ah, these were the happy days, Mary, when we were young and there was nothing to come between us."

Mary looked at her mother in secret amazement. The recital of the story that had so long been eating into her heart made her a changed woman. Her eyes shone, her cheeks softly glowed, there was a latent beauty restored to the faded features which brought back part of the charm of long ago. The mystery of it struck Mary Durie, and she felt that she had only partly really understood her mother and that, perhaps, had she allowed her to talk more about the past, they might have been happier.

" Then when he grew up, you—you were sweethearts."

"We were more than that, Mary," said her mother solemnly. "We were pledged to one another by every vow of fealty. For him I refused many a good offer because I cared about him, Mary. Ah, how I cared and—and care yet! There never was, and never will be but one man in the world for me!"

"Oh, hush," said Mary in a low voice full of pain.

"It's true, and the truth can never hurt. I lived but for him; I would have laid myself down in the road and let him walk on me, or followed him to the end of the world without asking a single question. But that's not the way to treat a man. You get all your thanks in one day."

"Then what happened?"

"He was sent away for a time to be with a firm that his father dealt with in Manchester, and it was there he met his wife. When he went first he wrote constantly. For some weeks I had a letter every day. If ever man cared about a woman, he did, I think, for me, Mary, though he afterwards changed so sadly."

"How long was it before he changed?"

"Oh, not long. They say that absence makes the heart grow fonder, but there's not a word of truth in that, Mary, so dinna you believe it. Absence is cruel, and where a man is concerned, never safe. For they are not like us, Mary, who make love the business of our lives."

"Had his father anything to do with it?"

"That I can't tell you. When the time came that he had to tell me he was married to another woman, I never knew of the marriage till she had been his wife for two months. He said that pressure had been brought to bear on him by his father, and that he had had very little choice in the matter. But I did not believe that, Mary, and I had a letter afterwards from his father which proved what he had said to be false. He was a hard man, old George Speed, but no one ever said that he was an unjust or a cruel one, or that he ever broke his word. George was more like his grandmother, who was "shiftless," as they said in Rattray, and who could say one thing to-day and another to-morrow, and think it was all right."

"But you thought he too cared, did you not, poor mother," said Mary, her heart made very tender by this old love story so simply told, yet throwing so much light on many things that had troubled and perplexed her.

"He did care, but he was keen to get on, and I was but a poor dressmaker who could not help him unless with her love. He had all that, Mary, and I never lifted my head after his heartless conduct. For a while I thought I would destroy myself or go mad."

"What a shame it was for you to marry when you felt like that," said Mary involuntarily. "It would have been better that you alone should have suffered."

"It's easy to speak, but my pride was hurt and sore, and when your father came to see me and asked me for the third time, knowing perfectly well how I felt and that I cared only for George Speed, married or not, the temptation to accept him was great. For in Rattray everybody knew how I had been jilted; and I had had a sore time of it between their pity and their scorn. But it broke my heart and my spirit; and it's a terrible thing to marry one man while your heart belongs to another, as mine did to George Speed, and will belong while I have life."

Mary was silent, unable to comprehend the strength of a passion like this, but fully alive to the devastation that it was capable of working in all the lives it touched.

"I married your father; yes, in that I was wrong, but at the first I tried to do my duty by him, and we were happy for a year or two. But he was unfortunate and my health broke. And when there is no real love in a woman's heart for a man there is no patience, so the tragedy grew and grew, till he went away."

"It was cruel—it was very cruel!" cried Mary, clenching her hands, "and I don't know whom most to blame."

"There is only one person in this world to blame, Mary, and that is George Speed. All our misery lies at his door, yet see how he flourishes, and how his wife rolls by in her carriage while we starve in the same town."

"But there is a Nemesis," said Mary, with a little catch in her breath. "And though it may seem to take a long time to do it, it makes things even at the last."

"I've never seen it. Old George Speed who made his money out of poor folk that never knew the value of the things for which he charged them so high, died in the odour of sanctity, and was praised in columns of the newspapers. And his folk are the big folk of Dundee, while we that never did harm to a living soul, starve in a garret."

"Knowing all this, surely you must have known, mother, that it was very unwise to come to Dundee."

Mrs. Durie sat forward in her bed, her eyes glowing strangely. "Lassie, I had to come. It was borne in on me for weeks before I even mentioned it that I had to come to Dundee. I think myself that the matter is not ended yet."

"Only beginning, perhaps," said Mary, with a strange, almost exultant note in her voice. "Mother, I ought, perhaps, to have told you that I have been working at the Eliot Mills all this time. I feared to mention it in case it should upset you."

"Working at the Eliot Mills as a servant to George Speed. And does he know it ?" asked her mother shrilly.

"Oh no, he knows nothing. But to-day I have been dismissed."

The first fact seemed to be enough for Helen Durie to grasp, and she did not seem to apprehend that of the dismissal or what it might portend.

"My girl working to George Speed ! It's the very irony of fate. Tell me, has he seen you, for you are very like me. Mollie, though your colouring is different, and you have your father's smile."

"He has spoken to me only once."

"Tell me how he spoke," she asked feverishly. "Was he kind ?"

"Quite. He asked me my name and where I came from ?"

"Your name ? And what did you say ?"

"I told him my name, but not where I lived. I have never told any of them that."

"But he seemed interested. Tell me quickly," she said, sitting forward with an almost painful eagerness.

"Not specially, but I hardly looked at him."

"Is it usual for him to come among the workwomen to speak to them ?"

"It was the only time I had ever seen him there."

"How did he look ? Tell me quickly. Oh, how I should like to see him again ! A woman never forgets her first sweetheart, lassie, and he was my only real one."

"Dear mother ! Poor mother !" said Mary with a tenderness that surprised herself. Also her eyes were full of warm tears. Never had she felt so keenly for her mother or seemed to understand her better. In that moment of confidence and sympathy all the bitterness of the intervening years seemed to be wiped away.

"I can hardly tell you how he looked. There is nothing striking about him, mother. He is simply a well-dressed, prosperous man ?"

"Does he look old ? Is he happy, do you think ? Oh, if I saw his face I could tell that ! How strange that you should meet, that he should talk to you, that you should go there at all ! It is like the finger of Fate !"

"I went there because it was the only opening," said Mary, trying hard to keep to plain facts and remembering her mother's proneness to exaggeration. "And now I have left it we need not talk any more about the Speeds. Mother, let us go back to Edinburgh, where we had one or two friends at least. We have none here."

Mrs. Durie did not for a moment reply. Her face wore the expression of one who communes with the past. It was a gentle, sweet expression, full of an indescribable pathos.

Mary saw that she was forgotten, and moving softly to the window, stood looking out, thinking over the story she had just heard. It was not quite the story that she had expected, and it had been told with a convincing simplicity which left her in no doubt as to the truth of the details. What suffering had been caused in their lives by the treachery of one man ! What irreparable mischief had been done ! She thought of the spoiled and ruined home, of her father who, desperate, had at last cut the bonds and was now a wanderer on the face of the earth, if he had not indeed already passed into the silent land, of herself without means, denied all the rights and privileges of other women, though possessed to the full of desire for them and capability to enjoy them. It seemed wrong—all wrong. The world was filled to the uttermost with injustice and cruelty and pain.

Something whispered to Mary Durie in this evil hour that, if she liked, she might be the instrument of revenge on the man who had wrought all this woe. At the very height of his prosperity she might wound him in his dearest part, through his son. She might make him suffer even as he had made her mother suffer. Remembering the light that had been in Tom Speed's eyes as they were bent on her face that night in the Foregate, and later as they walked in the quieter byways of the city, she felt the stirrings of her woman's power. There was no response in her heart to the anxious tenderness of his. But she could use her power!

For some inexplicable reason, perhaps, she had not mentioned the name of Tom Speed to her mother, who did not even know of his existence. She would not, therefore, be hindered in her design to pay off an old score. Through her her mother's wrong should be avenged.

CHAPTER XIX

THE SEARCH FOR WORK

On Monday morning after breakfast Mary Durie sallied forth in search of work. The prospect did not allure her, experience having taught her the bitterness that attended such a quest on the part of the superfluous woman.

To the idlers of the Court she was an instant object of interested curiosity.

"Ma leddy's left Lundie's," they whispered to one another, and sought the reason why.

"Ma leddy," had scant courtesy for them that drizzling November morning. Her own heavy anxieties monopolised her thoughts.

At the mouth of the Court she paused, uncertain whither to turn. A moment's thought decided her, and she proceeded towards the main street, where, at a small newsagent's shop, she intended to purchase a copy of the morning paper.

The rain had now begun to fall so heavily that before she left the shop she opened it out to the "Situations Vacant" column, the old woman behind the counter regarding her with kindly interest and pity.

"I hardly need take it, I think," murmured Mary, "there's nothing here I want."

"Then dinna tak' it or pey for it, my woman," said the old lady kindly. "It's nane the waur o' your lookin' intil it."

Mary smiled involuntarily at this little touch of unexpected kindness, which, however, did not surprise her. Her life among the poor as one of themselves had been illumined by many such rays.

"Thank you very much; but that isn't good business," she said brightly. "Suppose I pay a halfpenny—that would be fair."

"But I couldna chairge a penny to the next wan that wantit it. That wouldna be fair either," said the newsagent, with a shrewd smile. "Tak' up your bawbee, my woman, and come in anither day. May I spier if it's a job you're seekin'?"

She spoke with a slight hesitation, not being able even with her considerable experience to classify the girl who, while not well dressed, looked and spoke like a lady.

Mary nodded and lingered, being held by the genuine kindliness of the old woman's face, which, wrinkled with age, had still upon it a glow like a winter apple, brought thither, perhaps, by her loving kindness towards the whole world.

A stranger to Dundee, Mary was not aware that her she spoke with one of its best-known and most attractive characters, Nancy Gow, whose opinions on the burning questions of the day were often quoted, and whose little shop was visited by all sorts and conditions of people.

"What kind o' a job? In the governess line, maybe?" she asked, leaning across the counter in kindly inquiry.

Mary shook her head.

"Oh, nothing so exalted. I've just come out of the mill. I imagined that I might perhaps find a berth in a shop or in the domestic service line, though I'm not particularly well qualified for either."

"The mill! Ye dinna look like it, and I dinna wonder ye couldna stand it. The racket wad kill me in a week, and I never lat ony o' my lassies gang till it' though some of them were fain."

"You get used to it in time," observed Mary listlessly. "I liked it very well."

Mrs. Gow shook her head.

"Guid service is the thing. Gi'e me guid service! I was seventeen year in wan place mysel' afore I mairrit Gow. An' my lassies, at least what o' them's no' mairrit, are in service. Nancy, my youngest, is heid-housemaid at Caddam wi' Sir Rafe Fletcher."

The name spoken with such pride conveyed nothing to Mary Durie's ear, but she lingered to hear the old woman's tale.

"I suppose she is very comfortable there. Where is Caddam ?"

"Five miles oot the Perth Road. Yes, she's comfortable. She's the only wan keepit on. He's made a clean sweep o' the hale place since he cam' back, and I dinna wonder at it. There's been naething but wholesale robbery an' corruption at Caddam since his cousin de'ed—gairdners sellin' the fruit an' vegetables, an' the weemen ransackin' the hoose ! Ech, sirs, it's an awfu' warld !"

"Who lives at Caddam, did you say ?"

"Mercy me ! Ye canna be Dundonian, or ye wadna be needin' to spier. Ha'e ye never heard o' the Fletchers o' Caddam ?"

Mary shook her head.

"They're the guid auld stock—no' mony o' them left hereaboots noo since a' the money's rowed into the pockets o' them that's sprung up like. He was the third son o' a third son ; so ye may ken hoo far awa' his chance o' Caddam must ha'e seemed. But, wae's me ! They de'ed wan efter anither, jist slippin' awa' like snaw aff a dyke. They say that it's the curse o' Caddam come hame to roost, and that there'll never be ony peace nor health in the place till some guid woman lifts the curse."

"Quite an old legend," said Mary interestedly.

"Ay, and there's mair truth in thae auld stories than onybody kens. I've seen things—ay, have I. I was in service mysel' at Caddam in auld Sir Rafe's time jist for a few months afore I mairrit Gow. But my mither was hoosekeeper there frae the time she was made a weedy afore she was thirty."

She paused and looked keenly at the sweet face opposite to her.

"Ye micht dae waur than try Caddam. They're needin' fowk in the hoose, but he's that particler. He sees a' that comes aboot places himsel', and aye there's something he disna like aboot them. But Nance says he's the best maister that ever was born. She'd gang doon on her knees till serve him."

"But in what capacity could I serve ? I have been a dressmaker and a millworker, but I don't know the routine of work in a mansion like that."

The old lady put her head on one side like a bird.

"Unless I'm sair mista'en you're wan that could put your hand to onything. They're wantin' a ludge-keeper at Caddam. What for should ye no' try that ?"

"I should have no chance of such a place as that. You forget that I've neither qualifications nor—nor character."

"It's no qualifications he's seekin'—it's quality, and as for character, yours is writ on your face, lass," said Mrs. Gow heartily. "Nance was for me takin' the ludge. Sir Rafe wad ha'e gi'en it to me for her speerin'. But I've been ower lang in the public wey, and in the public wey I'll bide or they cairry me to Balgay."

"But don't you get tired now and then, and feel as if you'd like a rest ?" asked Mary sympathetically.

"Tired ! What for should I be tired ? There's ower muckle said aboot rest and far ower mony holidays needit nowadays. Even Nance tries to tak' her forty winks efter dinner. If they'd sup mair parritch, as I tell her, and drink fewer blashes o' tea, they wadna be needin' sae mony rests. I've nae patience wi' them."

Mary laughed with a spontaneous heartiness that surprised herself.

"How old are you ?" she asked suddenly.

"Sixty-nine last April, an' never a day in my bed 'ceptin' wi' the weans. I've reared seeven—ane o' them born efter his feyther de'ed. They're a' well-daein', and Wullie—that's my youngest bar Nance—is in Sooth Africa, whaur he's ane o' the chiefs o' the Mounted Police. But he's comin' hame to see me gin simmer."

"That's delightful ! I am very glad I came in this morning. Thank you—you have helped me very much."

"Helped ye, my lass ! It's very little I've dune. If ye wad leave me your name and address it micht be worth while. A'body comes in to Nance Gow, an' ye never ken whaur a blister micht licht."

"I'll come and see you again and tell you what luck I've had at the shops."

"Shops !" quoth Nancy in supreme scorn. "I watch the shop lasses gang by in the mornin' wi' their jimp black frocks an' their toosled hair an' their empty wames, an' I want to tell them aboot the guid meat an' the peace o' honest service. Dinna you try the shops, lass. It'll crush the soul ooten ye. You've gotten wan to begin wi'—onybody can see that."

Mary smiled slightly, bade the garrulous old dame good-day, and stepped out into the rain, sensibly cheered and comforted by the brief interview and the fresh light on life.

But the little glow quickly faded.

A certain diffidence and nervousness crept over her as she approached the region of the fasionable drapers' emporiums, where she would be most likely to find a market for her services. It required a considerable effort of the will to impel her to enter and proffer her request.

The dismal morning with a fine cold rain filtering from leaden skies through the murky air had its swift effect on business, and the huge emporium which Mary first entered was quite destitute of customers, though the assistants seemed as busy as usual, arranging and rearranging boxes full of finery which was to tempt the purses of the rich women of Dundee when the weather should become favourable for shopping expeditions.

A smart shop-walker, immediately on the alert, came forward politely to inquire how he could serve or direct the slim girl who came somewhat timidly through the big swing doors. "A cheap veil or a pennyworth of tape," he mentally decided, taking a swift inventory of her appearance, yet not abating one jot of his bland courtesy of demeanour. It changed, however, when she spoke.

"I don't wish to buy anything, thank you," she said in a low voice. "I came in only to inquire whether there is a vancancy in your establishment."

"I am sure there isn't, miss," he answered, his manner at once giving place to one of easier familiarity. "It's the slack time. I can inquire, however, if you like," he added good-naturedly, being rather struck by something above the common in the applicant's looks. "What experience have you had?"

"None of serving in a shop, but I have been fairly well educated, and I am not afraid of work."

The shop-walker shook his head.

"We don't take inexperienced hands, here, miss. Ours is a high-class business. After Christmas, perhaps, when the sales are on, you might have a chance, but not for a permanency. I would advise you to try a smaller place where they'd be willing to teach you the business, but I warn you the pay would be very small, perhaps you would get nothing to begin with."

He spoke kindly, because the deep grey eyes appealed to him.

"I am afraid I could not afford to work under these conditions," she replied in a rather hopeless tone, and she turned to go, whereupon he spoke again.

"I can inquire. They might want some one in the outfitting and the heavy drapery departments, and you might have a chance if you are a good needlewoman and the pay's better there than behind the counter, though why I should tell you this I don't know."

Mary thanked him and said she would wait.

She did not offer to sit down, though he indicated a chair as he walked away, for she was too much interested in watching the long line of black-robed figures behind the counters, trying to picture herself as one of them, sorting out endless rolls of ribbon, showing gloves and laces and other dainty confections to women who had so many of the world's goods that she so sadly lacked. She remembered old Nancy Gow's pronouncement regarding them as a class, and certainly some of them looked pale and tired, though all were neat and apparently well dressed. The hollowness of things, the futility of life for workers of a certain class, the desperate case of the superfluous woman once more came home to Mary Durie, bringing with it a sense of dull rebellion.

Several curious glances were directed towards her, and presently a girl, who was standing behind the counter nearest where she stood, and who had overheard part of her brief colloquy with the shop-walker, leaned over the counter and spoke in a confidential tone.

"It's hard work and poor pay. Don't you take it on. I've only eight shillings a week, and I've been here eighteen months."

"It doesn't seem much, and the hours are long, aren't they?"

" Yes ; it isn't much—it hardly pays for your frocks and for the shoe-leather you wear out walking back and forward every day. My feet are soaking now. I had to walk two miles in from the Lochee side this morning, for all the cars were full."

At that moment the man who had spoken so kindly came back, shaking his head.

" Just as I expected. They're not only full up, but they're paying off any casual hands they've got."

" Thank you very much for taking the trouble to inquire," said Mary dispiritedly as she began to move towards the door, the shop-walker following to show her out as politely as he had admitted her.

" I'm sorry for you, miss. You might try one of the smaller shops. They have vacancies oftener, though not so many, perhaps. I have a relative in Burgess Street —a Mrs. Crane, who keeps a ladies' outfitting establishment. You might inquire there. Say I sent you, if you like. My name's Braidwood."

" Thank you very much," said Mary gratefully. Her heart was lightened a little as she stepped once more into the cold, wet folds of the mist.

In one morning to find two kind hearts ! Surely the world was not quite bankrupt after all.

CHAPTER XX

THE CHAMPION

MARY stood outside irresolute in the rain, looking up and down the street. There were other shops in plenty, but, after her experience and the advice received from the kindly shopwalker, she had no temptation to seek further market for her poor wares. The rain was now falling heavily, and home seemed to be the natural refuge.

She had left her mother despondent and fretful, the exalted mood created by the recital of her story not having lasted beyond the day of telling. Her nature was really warped and poisoned by long brooding on what she called her wrongs, and she had now small consideration left for others. The prospect of spending a long day in her company, of counting the idle hours till the spirit should be strung up to the highest tension, did not allure Mary. Higher and higher mounted her indignant sense of injustice at having been dismissed from the mill without a word of explanation.

In spite of every reason for disliking it—in spite of the hard, unlovely nature of the work, she had become strangely attached to it.

She told herself she could have been happy there, living from day to day and giving to each hour its meed of appointed task. She thought of it now as one might think of some desired haven from which buffeting waves shut one out.

She was standing hesitating on the edge of the pavement, looking up and down, the rain dripping from her umbrella, her skirts held rather high to keep them from the muddy stones, when some one on the other side of the half-deserted street caught sight of her, and made a great stride through the traffic to reach her side.

"What are you doing here?" asked Tom Speed's voice, vibrant, masterful—even as she had heard it that memorable night in the Foregate.

"I am not doing anything, as you see," she answered coolly. "Watching, perhaps, for the rain to go off."

"Meanwhile you are getting wet through. But I don't understand what you're doing here at this time. It's half-past eleven! Haven't you been at the mills today?"

"No."

"Why?"

"Because I haven't."

"Did you give in your notice on Saturday?"

"No—I got it."

"You **got** it? Do you mean that you were—were dismissed?"

"Yes."

"By whom?"

"The cashier—in the usual way, I suppose. He gave me my wages in my hand and told me to go."

"What reason did he give?"

"None."

"And you asked for none?"

"Yes, I did. He did not seem to know, but said he supposed they were slack. Of course I was a novice, liable to be dismissed at any moment. I knew that, but they seemed pleased with my work. I did my share—some of my neighbours thought more than my share."

"By Jove, you did! I've watched you work, and I told you one day, if you remember, that it was not necessary to tear at it like that."

"I liked the work well enough; it was not too hard for me."

"And what are you going to do now?"

" I don't know."

She raised her eyes to his face for a brief moment, and once more his expression smote her with a sudden qualm. It betrayed an interest which could have but one meaning, and, though there was no kindred response in her heart, once more arose the fierce temptation to use his love for her own ends. Thus, perchance, would justice be satisfied, though two more lives might be spoiled in the process.

" Why are you out on this terrible morning ? "

" You can guess. I have just come out of that shop yonder, where I asked to be taken on, but there isn't room anywhere for the superfluous woman."

" There shall be room, and there ought to be no human being in the world superfluous ! " cried Tom fiercely, her words awakening all that was chivalrous in his breast. The spectacle of a solitary woman of Mary Durie's refinement wandering in the rain-swept streets of the city in search of the work denied her on every hand worked him up to a species of frenzy.

" I'll find out before I'm an hour older what's the meaning of this, and by whose authority you have been dismissed. Meanwhile promise me you'll go home, and I'll come to see you in the evening."

" You ought not to do that," she said weakly. " You mean well and kindly, Mr. Speed, but I question whether this will better my case. It will be far more prudent for yourself if you leave me to fight my own battle."

" I won't, and you know it ! " he answered with a kind of passionate significance. " My mother or sister or some one shall come to you. A way shall be found. Meanwhile, give me your address."

But Mary, with a scruple which did credit to her pride and her sense of right, once more refused it.

" I can't understand this. Then you'll meet me again to-night ? I must see you to tell you the result of my investigations at the mills. We can't walk about in the rain—will you meet me at tea-time, half-past four, or at six o'clock, if you prefer it, at Lamb's Hotel ? "

The boldness of this proposition almost made her smile. How much in earnest he was ; how little he cared for what people saw or said !

It was impossible not to feel a responsive thrill to his chivalrous championing of a beaten woman's cause. Her eyes marvellously softened, and all that was best and sweetest in her nature rose to the surface.

" Mr. Speed," she said softly, " I do appreciate your generous kindness, but again I assure you it will be better for us to go our separate ways. If you champion me you will get into trouble for yourself."

" What kind of trouble ? "

He planted his foot firmly on the edge of the kerb, and bent his head to look under the umbrella so that he might see her face. What cared he though the whole world should see and know that he was interested in this woman—that she was the one woman in the world for him ?

" Well, trouble with your people at home. They won't like it. How could they be expected to like it ? Better leave me. I will get through somehow. There must surely be a corner in Dundee into which I can creep and earn enough to keep the wolf from the door."

" You may talk and talk—it will make no difference to me. I tell you this is my business. Can't you understand that I want to see you again—that, apart from the mere question of helping you—which is the least of it—I must see you again."

Her colour rose, and the umbrella drooped over her face.

It was a strange place for a passionate love-making, and the dismal reality of a wet morning in Dundee might well have damped the most ardent wooer's enthusiasm.

But to Tom Speed's temperament obstacles merely acted as spurs.

" Will you come this evening, then, and let us talk things over ? I shall have thought of something by then—shall at least have cleared up at the mills the affair of your dismissal. There must have been a mistake. I've never heard of such a cruel thing being done. It's against all the traditions of the place."

Still Mary hesitated. She was confronted with a great temptation, and had her heart been really responsive, she probably would not have hesitated. But to lead him on for the mere purpose of getting things made even in her mother's lot and her own seemed mean and dishonest as well.

Therefore she hesitated.

"You must come!" he insisted. "If it's fine we needn't go inside unless you prefer doing so, but I must see you. Will you come?"

She hesitated just one more instant.

"Yes, I'll come. But, remember, I warned you. I am grateful for your kindness, but I don't want to see you get into trouble at home."

"And what about you?"

"Oh, I am accustomed to—to fight," she answered rather drearily.

"In future I will do the fighting for you," he answered, and the tears rose in her eyes in spite of herself.

She turned hastily away, and without another spoken word walked away.

Tom did not offer to follow her. After all he must for her sake be prudent, and even on a wet day there are prying eyes in the streets of Dundee.

A man has to be very careful where his love is concerned. His first precaution should be to guard its object from evil-speaking.

He had some business to do in town, and with difficulty he collected his wits. The fault of this young man, whose future promised him the headship of a great concern, was that he was apt to concentrate the cream of his energy on outside matters—matters quite foreign to his appointed sphere.

On this occasion, however, his impulsiveness was to entail consequences farther-reaching than either Mary or himself anticipated.

He accomplished his business at the City Chambers and then made haste back to the mills, his mind full of Mary Durie's dismissal, and hot indignation burning in his soul.

As he passed up from the gates he met Soutar coming out from the engine-room and, without a moment's hesitation or delay, broached the subject.

"Look here, Soutar. By whose authority was a young—a young woman called Mary Durie dismissed on Saturday?"

He hesitated in his choice of a term to apply to her, the ordinary mode of speech used in referring to the millworkers refusing to come.

Soutar stood still, looking at him with an admirable assumption of mild surprise.

"She wasn't needed," was all he replied, "and the rule is that the casual hands must go when there isn't room."

"Soutar, you're telling me a lie!" cried Tom hotly. "There's no slackness, and she was more than a casual hand—she was one of our best spinners. Any of them will tell you that. Ask Alec Mason, or Bell, or any of them in the place."

Soutar made neither denial nor demur, but continued to look mildly surprised.

"Why should you care because she has been dismissed, Mr. Tom? One more or less can't be anything to you, and you don't usually interfere."

"But this time I must interfere," interrupted Tom passionately, "for a gross injustice has been done. Neither my father nor Mr. Lundie would sanction it, I am sure."

"I don't see where the injustice comes in, Mr. Tom. Please explain yourself——"

"A helpless woman with no other means of subsistence," again interrupted Tom, "is calmly paid off without a fault found or an explanation given. Why, the injustice is as bare-faced as it possibly can be! Man, can't you yourself see it?"

"If we are to explain and to apologise every time that we give notice, Mr. Tom, we've got our work cut out for us," said Soutar grimly.

"You're begging the question," said Tom, more and more irritated by the manager's manner. "I want to know why this particular woman was singled out for dismissal. There are others—mere wastrels—who might have been sent off, if any weeding out were needed. There's something at the back of this, and I believe you've a hand in it, Soutar."

"Very well, Mr. Tom, is you ve got that idea into your head, nothing will put it out," observed Soutar tranquilly—even patiently, as one might have answered the argument of a child.

"You've had your knife in her ever since she came, and I noticed and understood the way in which you looked at me the other night when I met you in the Foregate. If only you had a clean mind, Soutar, you might be able to fathom a man who had an honest purpose—who can befriend a woman without—degrading her——"

Soutar broke into a laugh, and without a word of apology passed on.

CHAPTER XXI

THE REASON WHY

His brief colloquy with Soutar left Tom Speed in a furious passion. Always antagonistic to the man, he now conceived something like hatred towards him. He strode up the hill, crossed slantwise to the offices, and burst into his father's room.

"I say, father, has Soutar power to do as he likes here? He seems to be master. I can't stand him! I must be put where I can't come into contact with him!"

Speed turned round, mildly surprised. Accustomed as he was to vagaries of various kinds on the part of his son, he was now called upon to listen to Tom's first actual challenge against the existing order of things.

"What's it all about? What has happened now?" he asked.

"All I want to know is—can Soutar dismiss the hands as he likes without either rhyme or reason, but just to please his own caprice?"

"Whom has he dismissed?"

"That isn't the point. The question is—Can he do it? If he can, I won't go on working where he is. The man's a coarse brute! I can't stand him!"

Tom's language was the language of passion, but Speed suffered it to pass unrebuked.

"I can't give you any answer until you tell me what he has done," was all he observed, and that with a calmness contrasting sharply with his son's heat.

Tom was in no mood to appreciate calmness, his attitude towards things in general being at the moment revolutionary.

"He has sent off one of the women for no reason whatever as far as I can make out —except that he had determined he would send her away. I've my own views about his reasons, and all I've got to say is that, if he's allowed to do as he likes in matters of that kind, I can't stop here."

"You forget that you're speaking of a man who has earned his place, whose devotion to our interests has been tested and proved, who has our fullest confidence and appreciation. Really, Tom, your folly in these days transcends everything. A very little more of it will be as much as I—or any of us—can stand."

The tone was severe, almost threatening. Tom stood sullenly by with gloom gathering and settling on his brow.

"If you'd only listen to the particulars."

"I'm only waiting to hear them," observed his father drily. "You burst in here like a hurricane, trying to sweep everything from your path. I've had about as much to bear as I can stand. I warn you, and if there are to be any changes it is you who will have to look out for yourself."

"They haven't a fault to find with her! Even Soutar admitted that, and she's frightfully poor, with an invalid mother depending upon her. She has been thrown into the streets, and Soutar has the impudence to laugh in my face over it. It's sickening! I could have knocked him down! I will knock him down one of these days if he doesn't look out," cried Tom.

"He's a big, powerful chap," remarked his father in the same dry tone. "I'd advise you to mind what you're about."

"But you can't hold with him in what he has done. It's inhuman!" protested Tom hotly.

"There are other mills, and the woman, whoever she is, needn't be long out. There's no slackness in the trade——"

"That's what I say," broke in Tom. "We're busy here, and we can't afford to throw out so good a worker. Why was it done?"

" Soutar doubtless had his reasons—and good ones, if you had waited to hear them."

" Well, will you call him in and ask him his reasons ? "

" Before you ? Certainly not. It would be a gratuitous insult."

" It's all of a piece," said Tom gloomily. " There's a conspiracy of injustice, and it's no use fighting against it."

George Speed sat back in his chair, and laughed a trifle hardly.

" Who is the woman, and how does it come that you are so desperately interested in her ? "

" I know very little about her. I've spoken a few times to her—that's all. Her name is Durie."

" Ah, where did she work ? "

" In number five."

" I know the woman you mean. I did not like to see her there myself. It was no place for her."

" And for that reason you gave orders that she should be put out of it without inquiring what was going to become of her ? I suppose she offended your eye—made you think uncomfortable things——"

" Don't be impertinent, lad," said George Speed rather quietly, but in a voice which drew up his hot-headed son rather sharply. " Go back to your work. I'll inquire into the matter, and if the girl is in want she shall be relieved. Meanwhile, I think it will be in everybody's interests if we cable to Mouat that you'll go out to Calcutta at the end of the month."

" I don't want to go to India, father. Send Soutar."

" We can't spare Soutar. I'm not feeling very well myself, Tom. All this worry about your grandfather has told on me. You know what Mr. Lundie is, and I shouldn't care to be left here alone. That perhaps won't count for much with you," he added a trifle sadly. " But it is the truth."

It was very easy to reach Tom's soft, impressionable heart. Remorse immediately smote him—remorse as hot and unrestrained as his former rage.

" Forgive me, dad. I didn't mean to worry you, and I'm really sorry I can't see things as you do. It would be a lot easier for me if I could. I don't want to go to India, but, of course, if it's necessary I'm not going to stand out."

" Have you been to the Council Chambers this morning, then, and have you brought any reply from the Clerk ? "

" He's coming up, he says, after lunch—about three o'clock," said Tom rather shamefacedly, as he was thus reminded of the duty that had clean gone from his mind.

" That's all right. Go now, lad. I'll make inquiries about this dismissal, and you try to get a better perspective let into your view of things. This exaggeration of detail is going to work a lot of havoc among all of us."

This advice, quite sincerely given. had not much effect on Tom, but he departed, in a slightly more subdued frame of mind, to give a belated attention to his own particular duties. His father, at any rate, had some reason in him. Had he been detached from other influences he might have sympathised more keenly with his son's aspirations. Such at least was Tom's view. Speed himself was a little puzzled over this action of the manager's, and for his own satisfaction he despatched the office-boy for him in order that he might hear his version of the affair.

Soutar came into the inner room unperturbed. Strong in the consciousness that his action was not only sanctioned but commanded by his master's wife, he was prepared to justify his position, though undecided whether he should let his master know everything.

" Mr. Tom's just been in here like a whirlwind, Soutar," said Speed without looking round. " What's all this about what he calls a wrongous dismissal ? Who is the woman, and how does it come that he's so interested in her ? "

" Ah, that's the rub," said Soutar, with a slow grin. " Why is he interested in her ? I don't know, but he is, and though I wasn't thinking so much of him at the time, I believe that indirectly I may have done him a service."

" But why was the woman dismissed ? We've got to give him a reason. This is just the sort of grievance which he'll ride to its death, don't you know, and over which he'll have us all worried into our graves."

" She wasn't suitable for the work. Anybody could see that, and they didn't like it in number five. If I'd seen her when she came first I never would have taken her on. That was Bell's doing, and afterwards he was as keen as any one to get her away."

Soutar spoke glibly but far from convincingly. Speed, eyeing him steadily, decided that he was not telling the truth.

"It seemed a bit high-handed, and if the woman is in need, something will have to be done. Where does she live, do you know?"

Soutar shook his head.

"Better ask Mr. Tom, sir."

Speed sat round in his chair.

"You don't mean to suggest that there's anything of that kind between them? That would indeed be the last straw!"

"I don't suggest anything, sir, but I may think what I like. Is it usual for a young gentleman to champion a mill hand so hotly, if she doesn't happen to have a pretty face and a pair of beguiling eyes? Mr. Tom's worth watching just now. Excuse me, sir, but as you've put the question, it's no more than my duty to speak out."

"This is rather serious. Thank you, Soutar, I'll see what can be done."

Soutar, who would willingly have pursued the theme further, being thus dismissed, had no alternative but to go.

George Speed sat a few moments deep in thought. Then, sighing somewhat heavily, he rose to his feet, and putting on his hat, crossed the courtyard and began to ascend the stair leading to number five. Arrived there, he walked straight to the other end of the long room where Betty Baxter, bereft of her companion, now worked alone. She turned naturally when he came near, and he beckoned her to come out, taking care to step as far as the lift door so that none might overhear them.

"Mrs. Baxter, can you give me the address of the young woman who worked beside you for the last week or two?"

"She lives in Wilson's Court, sir," replied Betty, breathless with excitement.

"In Wilson's Court. Ah, thank you. I suppose you've been there to see her, have you?"

"No, sir, but she has been to see me mony a time. An' she never telt me she lived in Wilson's Court. I sent ane o' my weans to see whaur she lived," she said ingenuously.

"I suppose she's very poor?"

"Like the rest o's, sir,—waitin' on the weekly wage. She lives wi' her mother, wha's no' strong."

"Have you seen the mother?"

"No, sir, never. I dinna think she gangs oot. They're no common workin' folk, but it was a peety she was peyed off. She did her work verra weel. Better than some o' them that craws mair aboot it," said Betty, emboldened by her master's interest to put in a word for the girl she liked and about whose future she was really troubled.

"Ah, I'll inquire about it. There may have been a mistake. Have you seen her since she left the mills?"

"Yes, I saw her yesterday."

"Ah, Sunday! She would not, of course, have heard of anything else?"

"No, but she was thinkin' on tryin' to get intil a shop. It's a puir business that, sir, for ony lassie, unless she has a guid hame, an' it disna much maitter hoo little she earns. Aicht or ten shillings to begin wi'. Can a body live an' keep a mither aff that?"

"Hardly. Thank you, Mrs. Baxter. I'll inquire into the case," said Speed, while Betty, greatly gratified and bristling with her own importance, retired to her post.

George Speed stepped out into the open air again, where he stood still for a moment thinking deeply. His brows were drawn, his expression was that of a man face to face with a difficult problem. He had not now the slightest doubt but that the girl who thus strangely had come across his path was the daughter of his old sweetheart, Helen Drever. Strange how the working of destiny should have brought them once more in near proximity to ane another at the very moment when he had been charged to inquire regarding her ultimate fate.

It seemed as if some gleam of second sight must have been vouchsafed to the old man—which, indeed, is no uncommon occurrence in those approaching the confines of the other world. When the soul becomes prepared for the great change, some of the darkness surrounding human destiny falls away as a garment for which it has no further need, and there comes in its place a clearness of vision which has something almost prophetic in it.

Some such vision had undoubtedly come to old George Speed in the last hours of his life, causing him to leave a charge with his son concerning the girl whose heart had been wrung by his desertion.

Shall I go now? was the question his son asked himself, moved to act on the impulse of the moment, yet held back by a natural reluctance to lift the veil once more from the painful past.

While he hesitated, a carriage drove up to the office doors, and a county magnate, desirous of pressing George Speed into service at a coming political campaign, alighted. Thus was the opportunity lost. It never came again.

CHAPTER XXII

FINELY TEMPERED

KATHERINE LUNDIE had an aunt in St. Andrews, her father's elder sister, who lived in an old-fashioned house near the Cathedral Close. Miss Anne Lundie was one of the characters of the little city by the sea, much respected, though a little feared, by reason of her sharp tongue and somewhat eccentric ways. Between Katherine and herself, however, there was a perfect understanding. A peremptory reminder, couched in Aunt Anne's usual drastic language, that she had not been near her since her return from Lunan, took Katherine over to St. Andrews in the week following old George Speed's death.

Katherine loved the little city, worn and grey, for its incomparable associations, and also because it sat so royally on the windswept edge of the grey North Sea. She had kinship with the sea in all its moods, though the little glimpse of the Firth obtainable from the windows of her room at Albion Terrace did not much appeal to her, except as the highway of commerce whereby men garnered to a great port the spoils of the greater seas beyond.

Best of all did she love St. Andrews in winter when the sun dipped blood red to the edge of the horizon where, to her fine imagination, it would seem to make a weird dividing line betwixt two worlds.

There was something in the roll and dash of the long grey waves inshore, in the unrest beyond the tossing bar, in the wideness and the mystery, which always stirred her blood. And she was wont to say to her Aunt Anne that she greatly envied her the privilege of living in such an environment.

Miss Anne Lundie, of the caustic tongue, was very well pleased with her lot, albeit she had only a modest income saved from the wreck of the former fortunes of her family. She was a gentlewoman of the old school, not afraid to speak her mind, not ashamed of poverty, and having a pride so high that she would not stoop to a mean act, or suffer in her presence such as did not pass the bar of her critical judgment.

Miss Anne was one of the leaders—perhaps the acknowledged head—of the most exclusive set of St. Andrews society, for whose smile outsiders sighed in vain. Their blandishments were lost on Miss Anne.

" They're well enough," she said once in answer to a lady who had ventured to plead for certain newcomers. " I have no fault to find wi' the folk. Only I don't want to ken them. Why should I ? I've something better to do with the remnant of my time."

" Remnant " was a favourite word with Miss Anne, and sometimes she used it in rather incongruous connections.

She was genuinely fond of her niece Katherine and inordinately proud of her looks, her stately ways, her air of quiet distinction. In Aunt Anne's opinion Katherine was a real Lundie, worthy to be numbered with the fine old gentlewomen who had made Battledore once so famous.

For her brother she had an affection, slightly tempered with a good-natured contempt. It had been a blow to her when the family had ordained that he should take up commerce, a blow from which she had never actually recovered, though the subject was now relegated to the region of things that she did not talk about, but simply endured.

With Miss Anne dwelt a fearsome duenna—also of the old school—named Marget, who was the one human being of whom Miss Anne stood in awe.

Marget was the ubdoubted and absolute mistress of the little High Street house, according to her mistress only a limited amount of liberty of action, even of speech. Her prickly devotion, though invaluable, was oft-times a thorn in the side of Miss

Anne, and when she paid her rare visits to Dundee or to Lunan she was openly and confessedly envious of the raw material Katherine drew from the soil of her Girl's Guild and moulded into form to please herself.

"Do ye not think shame, eh?" she inquired sharply when Katherine, glowing from her battle with the wind, came fresh and bonnie into the little drawing-room. "Do ye not think shame to neglect your auntie like this? Eh what a colour, and how are ye, my dear?"

The thin voice vibrated with tenderness, and the coal-black eyes which could gleam with such disconcerting fierceness, were soft and kindly as they rested on Katherine's beautiful face.

"Quite well, thank you, Aunt Anne," replied Katherine, as she warmly pressed the old lady's hands in her warm, soft palms.

No kiss ever passed between them. The indiscriminate kissing, so prevalent at every street corner, as Miss Anne expressed it, was one of the modern manners which roused the old lady's ire.

"And how's your father? Not a line or a scrape have I had from either of you since I came from Lunan. I micht be deid for all you ken of care."

Katherine laughed and threw off her hat on the chintz-covered sofa. She loved to be there. The little room had been home to her through all her motherless girlhood. She took all sorts of liberties even with the prickly Marget, who never said her nay, and even went out of her way to concoct special dishes for the early dinner when Miss Katie came. On all other days she kept her mistress fed on a diet of Spartan simplicity.

"You smell good, and I'm hungry, Aunt Anne," she said gaily.

"I'll get a good meal the day, lass. That besom starves me; she thinks nothing of making a chicken last three days, and then making a drop thin tea o't out of the bones. Gi'e her a word, Katherine; I'm no' gettin' my meat."

Katherine smiled again, not crediting the statement of the old lady, whose speech was always strong. Yet it was the simple truth she spoke.

"Father's very well," said Katherine, as she sat back in her chair. "You look sweet, auntie, and where did you get that cap?"

"It's what you made an' gied me three years ago at the New Year, and I put it on the day in spite o' her. So you've gotten old George Speed awa' at last. What kind of an end had he?"

"Peaceful," replied Katherine, and like a flash, the brightness left her face. "I saw him on the day he died."

"You did? And did he ken he was nearin' his latter end, and was he ready for it?"

"I think so."

"He hasna left so very much, but of course he scattered it while he lived. Not a bad plan, Kate, for at least he had the satisfaction of seeing it do some good, but we never had a chance. Others scattered it for us."

"And how's that pelican at the Ferry?" she asked suddenly. "She'll have got the desire o' her een at last—to dwell in that great big barren place. I never could stand that woman, Kate, and I'm sorry for the folk that have to live with her."

It was no news to Katherine, but she did not answer for a moment. Her heart was still smarting with a keen sense of personal injustice, created by the terms of that portion of old George's will relating to his grandson, and a sudden desire to talk about it possessed her. The subject had never been so much as named between her father and herself, and she did not suppose he was aware of that singular bequest, and she hoped he would never know. But Aunt Anne was different.

"What's the long face for, Kate?" asked her aunt, quickly conscious of the change of the bright face she loved.

"Aunt, a horrid thing has happened to me through old Mr. Speed. He meant kindly perhaps, but it has—it has vexed me a good deal."

"Ay, what is it?" inquired the old lady, sitting forward with her hands on her knees and the eagerness of swift curiosity on her small, keen face. She loved news—it was her one weakness. She liked to know what was going on from one end of St. Andrews to the other, and over the water too—in such degree, at least, as it affected those in whom she was interested.

"The Halliwell Speeds don't get Ravenscraig," began Katherine; "it has been left to Tom."

" Well, he's an eident lad that'll come to his seevin senses by and by. Tak' it from me, Kate, he's the best o' the bunch."

Katherine did not gainsay this assertion ; probably she agreed with it.

" I like the lad, and have aye liked him since I saw him at Lunan last simmer," the old lady continued. " But it's a big house, and unless there be siller to keep it up, it'll be nothing but a stane about his neck."

" Oh, I think that part of it was all right, but there was a condition attached which he refuses to fulfil."

" Ay, what was that ? "

Katherine rose to her feet and walked to the narrow window and looked out for a moment on the quiet, grass-grown street. " It's conditional that he marries somebody named by his grandfather——"

The old lady rose too, scenting battle in the air.

" You, Kate," she said a trifle unsteadily.

Katherine nodded, and turning suddenly, she ran a little blindly to her aunt and fell upon her breast.

It was an action so entirely unlike the girl, so totally unexpected, and almost appalling, that for a brief second Miss Anne did not know how to act. But deep down in her heart there were wells of womanly tenderness, ay, and of womanly understanding too, and a glimmering of the truth came home. It was a moment of emotion so rare and so exalted that it seemed to lift them into another world.

" There—there, lassie, dinna greet. Dinna greet ! " she repeated with a sudden fierceness. " It—it tears me to bits. I canna bear it, lassie, dinna greet, d'ye hear ? " The tone was desperate, and Aunt Anne's lips were trembling, her eyes full of terrible pain.

Instantly Katherine recovered herself, bit her lip, and drew up her proud head.

" Forgive me, Aunt Anne, I don't know what came over me. It has hurt me because Tom and I are only friends and will never be anything else. We have been very happy, and I am afraid this will spoil everything."

" Ay, ay, of course, only friends," said Aunt Anne fussily. " And George Speed might have had more sense. It disna do to meddle with fowk's lives, Kate. I would like to cry that from the house-tops. And of course your pride was hurt—any woman's would, to be made a thing of barter like this. A ' condition ' ! bah ! The man's deid, but I would like a straicht word wi' him even yet."

Indignant fire burned in the old lady's eyes, but Katherine began to smile a little unsteadily through her tears. Aunt Anne had struck the right note, and how grateful she was to her, Katherine would never tell !

But neither of them was in the least deceived. Aunt Anne had never married, and it was long since she had left the world where young passions play havoc with peace of mind, but she understood—ay, full well—what was in Katherine's heart. But she would rather have died than have acknowledged it even to herself. Was she not a Lundie, whom tradition forbade to wear her heart upon her sleeve ?

" I am sorry for you, lass, and for the lad as well, and George Speed might have had more sense. And what does your father say about it ? "

" Father does not know yet, Aunt Anne. I hope he will never know. The least the Speeds can do for me is to try and keep that part of the will out of the newspapers, and it is a thing I will certainly never speak of to father, if I can help it."

" I'm glad ye spoke to your Aunt Anne, lassie, for if I had heard this outside not understanding the truth about it, I would have gane clean wild. Never mind them ! Dear me, what havoc fowk can play wi' tryin' to imagine themsel's God Almichty. But mow ring the bell, lass. Surely Marget should be ready for us now, and I'll gi'e ye the St. Andrews news. There's been a ball this week that has set them a' by the ears, and I have a story to tell ye about Charlotte Anstruther an' that whipper-snapper, young Fenwick o' Strathdrum. He's English, or it wad never be forgiven him in the kingdom of Fife."

Thus did the old lady strive to beguile her niece's wandering thoughts, and Marget, who waited on them somewhat grimly, betraying none of the pleasure it actually gave her, thought she had never seen them so gay.

Katherine left early, giving herself a good half-hour to get to the station so that she might have a blow across the Links. It was a very windy afternoon with a threatening of squally showers, and there were very few red-coats visible on the course.

Katherine left the Scores and took a slanting cut across the Links to a little strip of pebbly beach of which, as a child, she had been very fond. There the bank rose high and shut the dreamer off from the players on the Links. She walked softly, her cap pushed back, the wind playing with her hair, the salt sea-breath stinging eyes and lips, but giving out to her something of its fine strength.

She stood for a moment on the edge of the dune, and looked across the grey North Sea, filled with a sense of its immensity, an awe of its rugged strength.

Suddenly she became aware of two figures—a man and a woman—standing in the lee of the bank a few hundred yards from her, standing very close together, with their backs turned towards her so that they did not see her at all. The man's head was bare and bent towards the girl, who seemed to be listening rather unwillingly to some special and passionate pleading.

Katherine, interested for an instant, was suddenly struck by the fact that she knew them both. Something sharper than the rude caress of the north wind heightened her colour, and with a sudden sense of shame and shock, she stepped back to the level of the Links and turned away. She felt a little sick at heart, and wholly as a loss.

Her eyes had not deceived her—the two figures were those of Netta Speed and her Italian music-master, Marchesi, who has lately come to St. Andrews and was now the rage. And their attitude left her in no doubt as to the fact that they were lovers.

CHAPTER XXIII

SPECIAL PLEADING

KATHERINE made haste to the station, where she walked up and down the platform in a fever of thought. For the moment she forgot her own trouble in the contemplation of possible contingencies arising out of the incident which she had just witnessed.

Surprise, of course, was uppermost in her mind, Netta Speed being the last person whom she would have thought likely to carry on a clandestine affair of any kind. She began to ponder on the girl whom she had known since they were both children, but with whom she was not even now intimate. Netta had never interested her. She had seemed colourless and conventional and too entirely submissive to the will or her worldly mother. Mrs. Speed had refused her request that Netta should come and help her at the Girls' Guild or learn the dispensing at the Medical Mission on the plea that, not being so robust as Katherine, she might be liable to infectious disease—a very thin excuse which Katherine had been able to appraise at its true value.

Netta had seemed indifferent, indolent, quite willing to be guided by her mother and kept in the conventional path of calls and of dinner parties and mild entertainments given by the right people. At least she had made no demur. Yet all the while there must have been rebellious depths and possibilities in the girl, who had found some outlet for them all in this very dubious and perilous fashion.

Two minutes before the train was due to leave and just as Katherine had taken her seat, the door of her compartment was suddenly opened by the guard, and Netta almost tumbled in.

" Thank you very much. I'm so glad I got it," she stammered as she slipped a sixpence into the man's hand. Then she dropped into her seat and looked at Katherine, whereupon she blushed and gave a nervous laugh.

" How awfully fortunate, Katherine! I didn't know you were coming across to-day. When did you come? Not at one-ten?"

" No, at twelve—to lunch with Aunt Anne," replied Katherine, and, in order to relieve the embarrassment of which she was quite conscious she rose to close the window on the windward side.

" Very stormy, isn't it? There will be a gale in the Firth to-night."

" Will there? I didn't notice. I've been having my music lesson. I'm getting on splendidly, Katherine. I think it's a pity you don't go to Signor Marchesi. He really is a splendid teacher."

" You like him?" Katherine said, the question seeming to force itself from between her lips.

" Oh, yes. He is so interesting! He is far superior to the kind of teacher one gets in Scotland or even in England. He simply lives for his art, and he makes you see it like that too."

Katherine was silent for a moment, looking out of the window as the train gathered speed over the sand dunes. Netta was looking lovely. Certainly she had awakened—something had touched her phlegmatic being into life. Quite suddenly Katherine, as if moved by an uncontrollable impulse, turned round and looked her full in the face.

" Netta, I ought to tell you—I must tell you—that I saw you and Marchesi on the sands."

Netta paled on the instant, and a look of terror sprang to her eyes; but it passed, and she sat up with a touch of defiance.

"You did? Well, what then? He asked me to go for a walk with him after the lesson. His head ached, as he had been teaching since half-past eight, and went. There was nothing much in that, seeing I had nothing else to do with my last hour. Though, if I had known you were at Miss Lundie's, I might have called there."

"It was more than a walk, Netta," said Katherine with difficulty. "I stood on the bank just above you, and—and he was making love to you. I hate to speak about it, but it is better you should know that I saw you and that I understand."

"Well, and if he was, I don't care! He knows how to make love, Katherine," she added with a malicious little smile. "We don't know anything about it here. That's—that's—life."

Again for a moment Katherine was silent. She wanted to help Netta and to save her, if possible, and if not too late.

"But, Netta, nothing but misery can come out of it. I don't want to say anything about Marchesi, though one may be justified in thinking that he has basely betrayed a trust placed in him by your people. What would they say, do you suppose, if they knew?"

"They will know soon. I am going to marry him, Katherine," said Netta in a low voice, which, however, vibrated with determination.

"Marry him! No, you will not do that, Netta, if I or any one else can prevent it! You know nothing about him. He may be—and probably is—a mere adventurer. He may even have a wife in Italy. Who is to know or tell us anything about him?"

"That is just how one would expect you to speak, Katherine. You are as conventional as any of them in spite of your great pretensions," said Netta rather bitterly. "I suppose you will go or write to mamma now and tell her what you have seen."

Katherine was not angry. She sat forward and looked very earnestly across at the flushed, rebellious face.

"I only want to do what is right, Netta, and what will be best for you," she said simply. "I do sympathise with you up to a certain point."

"I tell you I only now know what it is to live! I've been in prison all these years since I grew up—prison, though they call it home. I haven't had the liberty of an ordinary prisoner. But I can tell you, though I haven't said much, that I'm not going to be sold to the highest—or any bidder—as Florrie was. I'll live my own life and be happy in my own way. It's no more than my right, anyhow! People forget that. I do think, Katherine, that the rights of children are as important, and ought to be as sacred, as the rights of parents—more so, indeed, since we are here without having had any voice in the matter. They even owe us an apology for that."

All this was so foreign to Katherine's former estimate of Netta Speed that for the moment she felt distinctly baffled. How little, after all, do we know of the inner sanctuary of the lives being lived very closely to us until some sudden spark reveals the hidden fire!

"Netta, you surprise me very much!" she said not dictatorially, but in a gentle, sympathetic voice which went instantly to the girl's by no means hard heart. "I've often been sorry for you, my dear, because you seemed to take so little interest in the real things of life; I should have been even sorrier had I dreamed of this."

"You can't know what I've often felt like, for you have always been allowed to live as you please. My days have been so colourless, so dominated by mamma! She had simply crushed me in everything. Do you wonder, Katherine, that I should be ready to respond to the warmth and light and colour of the life in the South which Marchesi promises me?"

Katherine shook her head, realising to the full how far more serious was the affair than she had suspected or dreamed. She prayed for wisdom to speak now the word in season which might help Netta at this tremendous crisis in her life.

"I don't like to say too much, dear, for I haven't the right, nor have I perhaps the requisite knowledge of Signor Marchesi. He may be all right—he may even be what you say, but I cannot, cannot think he has the soul of honour or he would not ask you to meet him in secret as he has done. It is betraying a very great trust that has been committed to him. Here in Scotland we call things by their right names. Signor Marchesi is not behaving like a gentleman."

Netta could not gainsay these words, though she resented them. Katherine saw that she did so by the ominous tightening of her lips and the flash of rebellious eyes.

" Well, what are you going to do—write to mamma or go home with me now and tell them ? " she asked sullenly.

" I don't want to do either," replied Katherine quietly. " It is no immediate business of mine, but—but I should not like to see you unhappy, Netta, or hear of you doing anything rash. It is so easy for a woman to make shipwreck, and—and so difficult for her to retrieve."

" You say what is quite true. It is worse than difficult—it is impossible ! " replied Netta with quiet bitterness. " But if I choose to marry a little out of the beaten track—to choose love and light and colour for my life rather than the drab path of duty and conventionality, who is to blame me ? After all, every one has the right to say what her life shall be, if she likes to make or mar it for herself."

" Yes, dear, and if Signor Marchesi will go to your parents, lay his position before them, and win you in spite of the opposition which they may at first advance, then you will have a right to your happiness and some surety for it. But as it is——"

She leaned forward suddenly and touched Netta's arm, her grave eyes full of a searching tenderness.

" Dear, what was he saying to you ? He seemed to be urging something upon you. His looks terrified me ! It is not curiosity that makes me ask, but if it is further concealment that he was urging—if he wishes you to take some irrevocable step in secret, don't agree to it, don't, dear Netta ! Remember that marriage is not like anything else—it is final ! "

" If you had ever been in love or had had the faintest experience of being loved you would not talk like that," said Netta pettishly. " But you need not be afraid. I am not going to do anything foolish. Believe me, I have been too well trained for that."

" Then you will not meet him any more as you did to-day ? Tell him, dear, that if he wishes to see you he must come openly to your father's house. And surely after to-day you won't take any more lessons at his house."

Netta sat back and laughed.

" Why, this has been going on quite a long time—since Easter ! " she said with a ring almost of exultation in her voice. " He has always cared about me, he says, since the first day mamma took me to him to make arrangements about the lessons. I can't stop everything at once."

" Then you will tell them at home ? "

" Why should I ? You know as well as I what the end of that would be. I should simply be forbidden St. Andrews, and Marchesi would have his cheque for the lessons by the next post. No, no ! I won't do that. It means too much for me."

" When do you go back ? "

" Next Wednesday, but he writes to me every day."

" Every day ! Do the letters come to The Rowans, then ? "

Netta did not reply, and Katherine understood that there was some other arrngĕment—that the whole intrigue was being conducted on the stereotyped lines of such escapades. Probably Marchesi was a past master in the art. In the fierceness of her anxiety concerning Netta, Katherine was hardly just to him. She would not even concede to her own mind that he honestly cared for the girl. Where did her duty lie ? She looked at the bright face, at the rebellios eyes, at the mouth set in a new firmness, and acknowledged that Netta Speed would probably, in the end, have the courage to live her own life.

" He has talked about seeing papa," she presently said. " So you need not think that he is quite a stage villain. Next time we meet I will tell him that it is necessary to see papa. Meanwhile, promise me you won't say anything, Katherine. You know what mamma is—quite capable of shutting me up in my room, and feeding me on bread and water or of sending me to Colchester with strict instructions to Florrie to play the dragon. I'll promise you nothing shall happen, if you don't give me away."

Katherine was silent.

" And after all it isn't any business of yours," went on Netta when her appeal brought forth no response. " You don't like being interfered with yourself. Nobody ever does interfere with you. And though I may see things a little differently from you, it doesn't follow that my point of view is bound to be absolutely and entirely wrong."

They were crossing the Tay Bridge at the moment, and Katherine gazed out on the seething expanse of the Firth with shadowed eyes.

Netta was right so far, yet her mind was not at rest.

She greatly feared catastrophe. Where did her duty lie ?

" I'll promise to say nothing just now, Netta, if you give me a promise as binding that you won't see Marchesi alone again."

Netta laughed loudly and shrilly.

" That I will never promise—never in this world ! Why, you would take the only little bit of sunshine clean out of my life ! Do you know that these hours in St. Andrews and my daily letter are what I live for, and I don't care who knows it. I've only just begun to live, and it's too, too precious to give up. You're not built on these lines, so you can't understand. But I tell you it's life, Katherine, and I wouldn't change places with any queen ! "

Katherine gave a little shiver and turned her face away.

Netta's wild words were unanswerable. Of what use was it to argue or reason with a woman in the thrall of passion ? She must wait and ponder and finally decide what would be the best thing to do in Netta's interests.

CHAPTER XXIV

TÊTE-À-TÊTE

KATHERINE took a cab from the Ferry to Albion Terrace, and, as she drove up, she beheld a carriage before the gate. She recognised the horses at once—even before she saw Mrs. Halliwell Speed coming away from the front door.

Katherine hastily paid her cabman, and ran up the steps, feeling at the moment quite glad to see a sometimes unwelcome caller.

" Oh, how do you do ? I'm so sorry I was out. Won't you come in and have tea ? it will be quite ready," she said breathlessly. " I have been at St. Andrews lunching with Aunt Anne."

Katherine had put on slight mourning for old George Speed, and was one of the few women who could wear it becomingly. Mrs. Speed thought how distinguished she looked, and admired the unusual colour in her delicately-rounded cheek.

" Thank you, I should like to. I'm fortunate in arriving at the psychological moment," she said smilingly. " I was sorry to miss you the other day when you called. My dear, how well you look ! "

" I'm quite well, thank you," said Katherine, and then a kind of panic seized her. Should she or should she not give Mrs. Speed a hint of the possible tragedy that might happen at St. Andrews ? Once more she asked herself where duty lay.

" I have had a good deal to do and am out more than usual just now," said Mrs. Speed, as she followed Katherine into the cosy library, where tea was usually served when Katherine was alone. " I suppose you have heard we are going over to Ravenscraig next week ? "

Katherine had not heard, and expressed her surprise.

" You haven't heard ? That seems impossible ! Haven't you seen Tom, then ? "

" No, not for several days," replied Katherine very calmly as she stooped to break up the fire. A ruddy glow immediately suffused itself over the room and showed up her beautiful face to the best advantage.

" I am surprised. And how is dear Miss Anne Lundie ? I haven't had the pleasure of seeing her for a long time."

Katherine smiled rather faintly at the remembrance of what " dear Miss Anne " had said concerning Mrs. Halliwell Speed.

" She is very well indeed, thank you."

" Did you come across with Netta ? "

" Yes," answered Katherine, and she felt thankful that the servant came in at the moment to draw the curtains and lay the table for tea.

" That was fortunate for her. I don't care for the journey for her now the afternoons are getting so short. It would certainly be a very great advantage if Marchesi would give his lessons in Dundee, but I suppose that couldn't happen. He gets enough to do in St. Andrews, and I suppose he finds the atmosphere more to his liking."

" How long do you intend Netta to go on with the lessons, Mrs. Speed ? "

" I haven't really thought about it. She enjoys them so much, and she has not so very many pleasures. I don't think of cutting them short. When we are at Ravenscraig she will find the railway journey shorter."

" I shouldn't let her go on, if I were you, Mrs. Speed—not in the meantime at least."

The words were out before Katherine could stop them.

Mrs. Speed naturally looked surprised.

" Why dear ? Don't you think Netta likes them ? She has always seemed to."

"Oh, yes, she likes them. Pray, excuse me. I spoke without much thought," said Katherine, rather confusedly. "I am surprised that Marchesi has been such a success in St. Andrews, though. Some people don't care for him at all. Is anything known about him?"

"He came under the auspices of Lady Barter. Don't you remember her musical parties last winter? Did Miss Anne never go to them?"

"Oh, no. That is the very last thing Aunt Anne would do. She does not even know Lady Barter," replied Katherine with a little laugh. "What will you do with The Rowans?"

She broke off suddenly, feeling the necessity for a change of subject, so that she might the better collect her thoughts.

"My dear, I have had a piece of the most extraordinary good luck," said Mrs. Speed. "Do you remember Ethel Macnaughton, who went out to India to be married three years ago?"

"Of course I do—perfectly. I was at the wedding."

"Well, she's coming home with her little girl and expecting another child. Her mother, hearing that we might be going to Ravenscraig, came to me yesterday and asked me if we would let The Rowans to her furnished for six or nine months. Could anything be more opportune?"

"It certainly is very nice," assented Katherine readily. "A house gets so soon out of repair when it is not inhabited."

"In six or nine months," pursued Mrs. Speed, "we shall probably know where we stand. Have I your permission to speak on a forbidden subject, and you won't misunderstand me, dear, will you? It has occasioned both Mr. Speed and myself acute pain, I do assure you!"

"I think it will be better if we do not speak about it, Mrs. Speed," said Katherine, clearly and rather coldly.

Mrs. Speed sat forward a little on her chair with a very anxious expression on her face.

"My dear, you will forgive me, but it is better that we should speak about it. Frankness in family matters is always best."

Katherine neither denied nor affirmed. Her anxiety concerning Netta had caused her to forget for a moment the dire possibilities of a *tête-à-tête* with Mrs. Halliwell Speed.

"It is our hope—I had almost said the one hope of our lives—that the condition of grandpapa's will may yet be fulfilled."

"It never will be, Mrs. Speed," replied Katherine steadily. "It is better that you should understand that at once."

A woman with a finer spirit would have understood that the subject must then be barred, but Mrs. Speed, notoriously lacking in tact, blundered on.

"Don't say that, Katherine. Such a tremendous sacrifice would be really iniquitous. What has come between you and Tom? During the last year we expected that any day we might hear of your engagement."

"You were mistaken then, Mrs. Speed. There never was or has been the remotest chance of that."

"Then why?" she persisted. "Everything is in its favour. It would please us all. In fact, you were made for one another. I wish you young people would not be so headstrong."

Katherine faintly smiled, toying with a morsel of bread and butter. Now that the worst was over, there was something infinitely amusing in Mrs. Speed's persistency, the reason for it—namely, to keep Ravenscraig—being so very obvious.

But behind Katherine's smile there was a mask of impassiveness which her tormentor, with all her assumption of cleverness, could not penetrate.

Mrs. Speed suddenly determined to push the matter further, to take Katherine into her confidence, and then perhaps arrive at some conclusion as to her feeling for Tom. She sat back with a little sigh, dropped the aggressive, and passively sipped her tea.

"The woman who doesn't marry, Katherine, certainly escapes the life of harassing care that is the lot of a married woman, if she has a family, and the worries of another kind that fret the wife who has only herself and her husband to consider. Would you believe that I have toiled for my family, never thinking of or sparing myself, and, with the exception of Florrie, I have very little comfort in them. I married Florrie very young to a man much older than herself, and she has developed into a splendid woman. She is the very life and soul of the best society in Colchester, which, as you may understand, is very exclusive, as in all military places. Now, with Netta I've been able to do nothing. She's phlegmatic, and she has not Florrie's spirit, and she is very dull and unresponsive."

"Oh, I think you are entirely mistaken regarding Netta, Mrs. Speed. And do try to gain her confidence," cried Katherine a little wildly.

Mrs. Speed, however, did not attach any importance to these words. Bent upon a different purpose, she scarcely even noticed them.

"Then Tom gives us a good deal of anxiety. He is really of very little use at the mills, and does not save his father at all. He is entirely taken up with outside things. It's all very well for a young man to have a hobby, but Tom rides his beyond all bounds. And, of course, the inevitable has happened, as it always does when a young man of position goes out of his own sphere and mixes familiarly with all sorts of people."

"What has happened?" asked Katherine politely, but betraying no sign of perturbation.

"He's carrying on with some one outside—one of our own mill-workers."

"I don't believe that," said Katherine unexpectedly. "That is the last thing he would do."

"So we all have thought, or we should not have suffered his folly so long. He would have been shipped off to India in his teens. That is where the mistake has been—in not removing him from associations here. I know the interest you take in the girls. Do you happen to know this one? She has not been long at the mills; her name is Durie."

"I have spoken to her, but Tom has known her only a little while, Mrs. Speed. I don't think honestly that there's anything in it."

"My dear, I have proof positive. Some one from the outside brought it to me. I have done what I could: she's been dismissed from the mills, but I am very uneasy, not knowing what I may hear next."

Katherine sat silent, amazed at the woman—at the mistakes she could make, while yet wondering at the failure of her scheming. Once more Mrs. Speed sat forward.

"If you have not sufficient interest in Tom to take his future in hand," she said, hesitating for a suitable phrase which would convey what she meant without giving offence, "at least you are his friend. I wish you would try and help me here, or we shall be having a pretty scandal one of these days—a clandestine marriage or something of that kind."

"What can I do, Mrs. Speed? You ask the impossible. We are very good friends, but in that I could not possibly intervene. Ah, there is papa! I hear the sound of his key in the door," she said, rising with evident relief. "Excuse me; I must go and meet him."

Mrs. Speed nodded and continued to sip her tea, fully conscious that she had failed. She was not happy concerning her family. For the moment all the affairs of her life were out of joint.

Henry Lundie, gravely courteous always, bade her welcome, and, to Katherine's immeasurable relief, took the burden of entertaining the visitor for the next ten minutes.

"And how is Aunt Anne, my dear? But first, how are you?" he said when he had hastened back to the library after having seen Mrs. Speed to her carriage.

"Aunt Anne's lovely, papa, and I am a little tired. Mrs. Speed is rather tiring, don't you think?"

"She was less overpowering than usual to-day, I thought. Has she been here long?"

"About half an hour. Do sit down, papa, and let me sit at your feet as I used to do when a little girl."

"Why not on my knee, little girl?" he asked, with a touch of whimsical tenderness which nearly broke Katherine down. She had had a trying day, and the effects were visible on her face. She sat down on his knee, curled her arm round his neck, and laid her cheek to his.

"Now I will tell you about St. Andrews and the exciting adventures I had there. I need your advice, papa. I don't know what to do in a crisis like this."

Then she told him what she had seen on the sands and of the talk she had had with Netta in the train. Contrary to her expectation, her father became excited over the recital.

"Something must be done, my dear. I've a good mind to go out to the Ferry now and speak to George about it. If it were my girl I should thank any man to put me on my guard. With these foreign rascals one never knows what will happen. They are past masters in deceit and intrigue, and Netta seems to have become an apt pupil."

"She's very headstrong, and the trouble has all arisen out of her unhappiness at home. Oh, darling, how thankful I am that I have you! If I had been brought up by Mrs. Speed what a dreadful creature I should have been—capable of any crime, I am sure!"

He stroked her hair and patted her cheek, just as if the years had rolled back and she was the motherless child in pinafores once more coming to him with all her troubles.

"I'll speak to George to-morrow morning, dear, so you may roll that burden off your shoulders. It will take a man anyhow to deal with it. Now, what else did she worry you about?"

"I have forgotten already," said Katherine, but she continued to gaze into the fire with a far-away look in her eyes.

CHAPTER XXV

THE TRAVELLING BAG

NEXT morning Katherine walked with her father to the mills—a proceeding which neither surprised him nor occasioned remark elsewhere. Since her return from the school at Lausanne, kept by an old governess of the Lundie family, she had made it a habit to call at the mills at any time that was convenient to her. Knowing that her father was always glad to be relieved from the duties in which he had no real interest, she would, when she was finding the day too long, fetch him out for lunch or for an afternoon walk.

The vagaries of the pair had ceased to evoke any comment at the mills, where Henry Lundie was called by some of the smarter understrappers The Figurehead.

Katherine left her father at the office door and crossed to the stairway leading up to the spinning flat in which she was just then specially interested. She was some time in reaching the farther end of the long room, having many *protégés* to give a kindly word to on the way.

But at last she reached Betty Baxter's side, and after an inquiry for her numerous brood, asked for Mary Durie's address.

" Wilson's Court, ma'am," replied Betty promptly, feeling herself elevated to a position of great importance as the only friend of the girl in whom all those in authority seemed to be for the moment interested.

During the intervening days Betty's tongue, alas ! had not been silent or conspicuously prudent, and already the affair had attained the most exaggerated proportions among the mill-workers, who, scenting a romance, were on the *qui vive* for the latest detail. A sort of subdued excitement spread with the swiftness of lightning over the busy hive at Miss Lundie's entrance, and, had it been possible to give pause to the mighty din, it is certain that every ear would have been strained to catch the slightest word of the brief and quite unimportant conversation that ensued.

" Wilson's Court ! " repeated Katherine perplexedly. " Where is that ? "

Betty proceeded volubly to explain, which she did with so much wealth of detail that it confused instead of enlightening her listener.

" Thank you, yes. I think I understand, Mrs. Baxter. Have you seen her since she left ? "

" I havena seen her, ma'am, and I dinna ken whether she's gotten anither job. Ye think she'll come back, maybe ? "

" I don't know, I'm sure. I am afraid that she didn't like the work."

" Oh, it wasna that, Miss Katie. She was payed aff," said Mrs. Baxter significantly.

Katherine nodded and passed on, hastening her step a little, as she did not then desire to come into contact with Tom Speed. A cloud had fallen on their happy relationship, and now the whole atmosphere seemed charged with suspicion and distrust. Katherine had suffered some uneasy moments regarding Mary Durie, and her always tender conscience had pricked her for her refusal to befriend her simply because she had been once rebuffed. It is possible, however, that a certain curiosity now mingled with her qualms, and that she desired to follow for herself, step by step, the windings of the story.

She had no difficulty whatever in finding Wilson's Court, and when she saw that squalid place and the types that peopled it she felt sorry for the girl who had had to make her home among them.

Her advent was naturally the signal for an immediate quickening of interest in an otherwise idle crew.

"Durie, mum? Yes, she lived here. 'Ma leddy,' we ca'ed her, but she flitted the day afore yesterday, cleared oot, stock, lock, an' barrel," said the portly dame to whom Katherine had put the question. The answer naturally dismayed her.

"You don't know where she has gone, I suppose?"

They simultaneously shook their heads.

"The cairt, it was a green-grocer's cairt, an' didna belang to onybody hereaboot, an' they hadna muckle furniture, puir things, it went wast."

The vague direction did not help Katherine in her quest.

She thanked them and turned once more to the low gateway which gave admittance to Wilson's Court. Just under its shadow a tall figure appeared from the outside, and Katherine stopped short in genuine pleasure.

"Dr. Alister, I am so glad to see you! I believe you are the very man that can help me."

Alister raised his hat, smiling in response to the heartiness of her greeting.

"What is it I can do?"

"I am seeking some people who lived here. If you are in the habit of visiting in these parts you may perhaps know something about them. The name is Durie, and the girl works in our mills."

A gleam of enlightenment brightened Alister's eyes.

"I did know them. I used to visit the mother here regularly, but they have disappeared, and nobody seems to know where they have gone."

"Strange!" she said musingly. "And they seem to have taken precautions against being followed. The women in the Court whom I have just been questioning said that their furniture was removed in a strange cart with no name on it. Looks as if they wish to hide."

Alister nodded. It was precisely his own opinion, and he had spent two miserable days brooding over the possible hardships of the woman he loved. Katherine, not aware, of course, of the undercurrents which one woman had quite unintentionally set in motion in so many lives, talked on frankly.

"It is very tiresome. I particularly wished to see her. It seems that she has been dismissed from the mills through some mistake or misunderstanding, and, of course, one would wish to help in a case like that."

"There was no mistake, I think, Miss Lundie," said Alister with a candour for which he afterwards blamed himself. "I am confident that her dismissal was intended and arranged by those at headquarters."

"Whom are you talking of?"

"Mrs. Halliwell Speed."

Katherine looked beyond him into space, and things began to clear.

How short-sighted she had been not to grasp the truth!

"Well, if that is true," she said with a sudden sharpness in her voice, "it is all the more necessary that I should find her. Something ought to be done in circumstances like these. The girl may be quite innocent."

"Innocent!" repeated Alister with a thickening of his voice, while his colour rose. "Of course she is. Why should she not be innocent? She has been the victim of misfortune, that is all, and of Tom Speed's imprudence."

Alister, worked up into a state of rage and indignation, could not restrain himself. He did not pause to consider that his words might wound the woman to whom he was talking.

"Speed's a fool, an utter fool, Miss Lundie. I've known him for over ten years, so I know what I am talking about, and in spite of his pose as the friend of mankind in general and the suffering poor in particular, he's too selfish for words to express. He ought to be shut up. Upon my word, it is neither fitting nor safe for him to be at large."

Katherine listened to this grim outburst with cheeks slightly blanching. She respected Alister too much to believe him capable of treachery to a friend. She perceived that Tom had alienated his friends one by one.

"I don't quite understand what you mean," she said faintly, though she understood too well.

"It's quite easy to understand," pursued Alister ruthlessly. "He took a fancy to this girl—it's a brutal way of stating the fact, but it puts the thing in a nutshell. Then he proceeded to make her conspicuous to the best of his ability. His attentions, of course, attracted the notice of evil-speakers. That was inevitable. He talked to her at the mills, he walked with her in the street without making the smallest attempt to disguise his interest, and when I remonstrated with him he talked a lot of high-falutin' which made me sick. I wish you would talk to Tom! It is possible that he might be influenced by a few words from you. We're at daggers drawn at present."

Katherine's lips curled.

"I shouldn't dream of doing such a thing. A great deal of what you say is true, Dr. Alister. Tom does not pause to think of consequences."

She hesitated just there before expressing her next thought. "Do you think he knows where she has gone?"

"I can't say. I haven't seen him. Probably he knows, but if he does, then I am disappointed in her."

Katherine turned to walk away.

"You are going into the Court to visit some of your poor patients, perhaps?" she remarked with the manner of one who wishes the subject changed.

He nodded.

"I'm glad I've been fortunate enough to meet with you," he said sincerely enough. "It is a relief to speak out, and as we both know Tom Speed so well and give him full credit for his good qualities, we have not been in the least disloyal, though I confess that I was a bit hot over it," he added with his appealing, boyish smile.

"Oh, no!" What a quaint old place this is, but what a slum! It makes one quite wretched to think that such places exist in Dundee. Now, an old, historic relic like the Court ought to be preserved, and kept up as a sort of national memorial."

Alister smiled again.

"We are utilitarian in Dundee, aren't we? We might start an antiquarian society, which would have for one of its objects the preservation of old buildings."

He raised his hat to pass on, whereupon Katherine detained him another moment.

"If you should happen to hear anything about these people, Dr. Alister, will you let me know?"

"Yes, surely."

"I can do something for—for Miss Durie, I am sure," she said, hesitating a little, "though it will be difficult. Do you know their history?"

"Only in part."

"Who are they and where do they come from?"

"They come from Edinburgh. Mrs. Durie's husband was originally a farmer, I understand, in the valley of Strathmore, but gave up his farm and went to Edinburgh, where they were unfortunate. He is now abroad, I believe."

"She is not a widow, then?"

"I understand not. I have only gathered fragments of their history, and have pieced them together."

"I see. It was obvious, of course, that the girl was not born to such work as that of the mills. And she seemed naturally proud."

"She is, and I admire her for it," said Alister a trifle warmly, imagining Katherine's tone a little contemptuous.

She inclined her head.

"I dare say, but there comes a point when pride ceases to be a virtue. I had no idea of patronising her. I hope I am not that sort of person."

She tapped the point of her shoe a little coquettishly on the edge of the broken pavement at the Court mouth, and she looked straight at him rather defiantly. How dreadfully in earnest both Tom and the doctor were in their championship of Mary Durie, and how ready to blame her! She could put only one interpretation upon it.

They parted just then, Alister continuing his progress through the Court, while Katherine returned to the Foregate and walked thence on to Reform Street, where she had intended to do some shopping.

She was so much preoccupied, her mind being full of Mary Durie and her affairs, that she passed several of her acquaintances without recognising them.

As she approached the windows of the shop where she usually made her feminine purchases an incident happened which gave her a sudden chill of alarm. One department of the large shop was devoted to travelling accessories, and a window displayed them in tempting profusion. This department had a separate door. Katherine merely glanced at the window, her thoughts just then being far enough from mundane things.

At this moment some one passed in front of her—a man wearing a peculiar but very becoming cloak and a slouch hat of distinctly Continental style. He raised his hat with a word of apology, and a smile in his dark eyes for having brushed her skirts as he passed. Katherine scarcely acknowledged his politeness, being struck by the man himself—Marchesi, the Italian Professor of Music from St. Andrews.

A sudden, swift thought passed through her mind, and acting on an incontrollable impulse, she immediately passed through to the travel department, where she saw Marchesi inspecting some kit bags.

She felt her face flame and then pale as she hastened back, and, lest her demeanour should be noticed, she stopped at one of the counters to make a trifling purchase. Then she inquired whether she might use the telephone provided for the convenience of customers.

CHAPTER XXVI

THE FLIGHT

KATHERINE's call to The Rowans was answered by one of the maids.

"Has Miss Netta gone to St. Andrews to-day?" she asked, remembering that it was the day of the music lesson.

"No, Miss Lundie," promptly came back the answer.

"Is she at home?"

"No, Miss Lundie. She has gone with Mrs. Speed to Ravenscraig, and they will not be home to luncheon."

Katherine hesitated yet another moment, loth to question a servant, yet goaded to do so by some inward fear.

"Do you know why Miss Netta did not go to St. Andrews to-day? Was it on account of the visit to Ravenscraig?"

"No, ma'am," came back the answer clearly.

"Oh, thank you," said Katherine, and dropping the receiver she stepped back into the shop.

She felt partly relieved, yet Marchesi's appearance did not suggest illness, and the purchase of the kit bag continued to haunt her.

Why should he want a new bag in the middle of his working season when it would not be possible for him to get away. Then the plea of illness—could it have been assumed for some underhand reason?

Katherine, unversed in intrigue, hated herself for her horrible suspicions, and tried to banish them. Netta being safely at Ravenscraig under her mother's care, surely nothing could possibly happen.

Later in the day she would telephone to Ravenscraig and make an appointment with Netta, ask her perhaps to come out to tea on her way home.

Neither she nor her father had a second time alluded to the subject of Netta and Marchesi, and she wondered whether he had spoken to George Speed about the Italian. Probably he had already forgotten the incident. His dreamy moods had become more absorbing of late, and he forgot many things. Katherine felt the need of some one to share her anxiety, but she did not know where to find the right person.

She reached home to find that her friend had come in from Monifieth and would stay to luncheon, which diverted her mind from Netta and her affairs. When she was again left alone she made haste to the telephone and rang up Ravenscraig. Mrs. Speed answered her, and told her that Netta, on the plea of a headache, had just gone home.

"I am stopping here all night," she explained. "The bulk of our personal belongings are coming over in the morning, and I must be here to receive them."

Katherine had made some commonplace remark and rang off. Then she hastily dressed herself, ordered the carriage, and drove out to the Ferry.

She could not be at ease concerning Netta Speed. The vision of the cloaked foreigner and the kit bag haunted her, and every trifling incident became magnified into something significant and important. The feeling of strain, the prevision of trouble seemed to be in the very air.

When she rang the bell at The Rowans and asked for Miss Speed she hardly expected to hear that she was in the house.

"Yes, ma'am, she's just come over from Ravenscraig, very tired and with a bad headache. I think she's gone to lie down, but if you'll come in I'll go up and see."

"Don't disturb her," said Katherine hastily, "unless she would let me come up for a minute. Ask her, will you?"

The servant closed the door, and Katherine sat down on a low chair by the hall fire to wait. It was very still in the house—the ticking of the clock on the upper landing could be distinctly heard.

It was warm and pleasant too, and the atmosphere was heavy with the scent of many flowers. Mrs. Speed was inordinately fond of flowers, and she often had her room too crowded with them for comfort.

The garden and the hot-houses were the special attractions for her at Ravenscraig.

The maid was not long gone.

"Miss Netta will see you in a moment, Miss Lundie. She was asleep, I think. She says that perhaps you will not mind if she doesn't get up or have much light in her room, her head is so bad."

"I feel I ought not to go up at all," said Katherine apologetically. "But I am very anxious to see her."

She sat for a few moments longer until the maid came again and asked her to go up.

She had never been in Netta's room, for they had never been intimate or inclined to exchange girlish confidences. Katherine indeed felt that she was intruding now, and wondered how she would explain her importunity. Netta, however, seemed to take the visit as a matter of course.

The room was darkened by the soft blue curtains, and Netta, lying on her bed in a loose dressing-gown, merely turned her head.

"I'm so sorry I couldn't get up to come down to you, Katherine," she said apologetically. "We've had a hurricane of a morning at Ravenscraig, sorting out the china. Mamma never seems to tire, but she let me off after luncheon. I'm quite stupid with one of these dreadful sick-headaches."

Katherine expressed her sympathy, and coming nearer, was actually relieved to see that Netta's appearance confirmed her words. Her face was feverishly flushed, her eyes heavy, her hand when Katherine touched it hot and restless.

"I ought not to have come up, but it's a good drive, and I wanted to see you."

"Yes," said Netta languidly, "I'm glad you came. You can stop to tea? I told Beith to bring it up at once. What o'clock is it?"

"Only twenty minutes past three."

"Ah, well, I'll be glad of it. It may do my head good. How is Mr. Lundie?"

"All right, thank you," replied Katherine. Then there was an awkward pause. They had not met since that day in the St. Andrews train, and both felt a little embarrassed, though Katherine showed it most.

"You weren't able to go to St. Andrews to-day," she said casually, yet with her eyes fixed on Netta's face. Netta moved up her hand and pushed it through the masses of her fair hair.

"No, Signor Marchesi could not take me to-day," Netta said quietly. Then after a moment she leaned forward and looked quite steadily at Katherine.

"I am very much obliged to you for not having given me away. I should have had a dreadful life if you had. It would have been needless besides, for I shall not be taking any more lessons after this term. Signor Marchesi is tired of Scotland, he says, and will leave St. Andrews. It is too bleak and grey for him. If you heard him talk of his own land you would wonder why he has stayed away so long."

Katherine was wholly deceived by this seemingly natural and spontaneous talk about the music-master, and she sought in vain for any sign of perturbation or even consciousness about Netta. She began to wonder whether she could have dreamed the incident of the sands.

"I saw him to-day," she said suddenly.

"You saw him! Where? Are you sure, Katherine? I thought he was ill and unable to leave the house. He certainly wrote so to mamma."

"I saw him in Stewart's, dear, buying a travelling-bag. I was in the shop myself at the same time."

Netta pushed her fingers through her hair again, and gave a short laugh.

"How awfully funny! I can hardly believe it, and yet you could not be mistaken I'm sure. There can't be two Marchesis. Here comes tea! Do tell me how you like Sir Rafe Fletcher. I heard from mamma that he had been dining at your house."

"We liked him very much," answered Katherine, and for the next ten minutes their talk was that of acquaintances interested in the various members of their circle. Katherine left soon after four o'clock, partly reassured yet perfectly conscious that she had a load on her spirit for which she could not account.

That evening she and her father were to dine at Caddam, an occasion to which she had looked forward with much interest, and the charm of which succeeded in banishing other and more unpleasant thoughts from her mind.

Could she have looked back, however, into the room which she had left how great would have been her surprise, how vast her apprehension!

Netta waited until the roll of the carriage wheels on the short avenue had quite died away and been swallowed up in the traffic of the road beyond. Then she rang for the maid to clear away the tea things.

"I won't see any one else, of course, Beith. I'll try to get a little sleep before dinner. It's quite early yet."

"Yes, Miss Netta. The mistress has just telephoned to ask if you got home all right, and to say that master also is going over to Ravenscraig to dine and sleep. So there will be only Mr. Tom and yourself at home."

"And we're never sure of him," said Netta with a languid smile which hardly covered the intense relief and satisfaction which she felt. "Well, don't disturb me. I'll ring when I want anything. I may go to sleep for the night."

"Very well, Miss Netta," said the girl, and she only waited to build up the fire and to arrange the screen so that the light should not be too glaring in the eyes of her young mistress.

It happened to be Beith's night out, and she departed an hour earlier than usual, leaving her duties to the housemaid, with special instructions that Miss Netta was not to be disturbed.

When a few moments later the girl had gone downstairs Netta rose and turned the key in the lock. Then she turned up the light near the fireplace, and looked round with a little, nervous laugh.

"The fates must approve," she said to herself, "or every obstacle wouldn't be removed from the way."

She sat down for a moment before the fire to put on her stockings, and instead of the dainty boudoir slippers which would have been suitable to the occasion, a pair of high, strong, walking boots.

Her room was above the drawing-room, which nobody was likely to enter that night. She could therefore move about freely without being heard.

Her preparations did not take very long. A dressing-bag and a very small hold-all, containing only such articles as were absolutely necessary—these filled and locked, Netta proceeded to make her own toilet. A warm, cloth dress, which was very plainly made, but whose lines showed her graceful figure, and whose rich colour became her paleness, a neat, close-fitting straw toque, and a long, dark coat lined with fur constituted a very suitable and becoming travelling garb. About her hat she swathed a long, soft motor veil of grey chiffon, in the folds of which she could, if necessary, hide her face. Then she was ready.

A well-filled purse taken from the locked drawer of her escritoire gave her some satisfaction, and as she counted out the money she smiled with pleasure. She had forty-eight pounds—a large sum to Netta, who was accustomed to have her clothes ordered by her mother, and to have her pocket-money doled out willingly enough, but never generously, by her father. But Netta had never been a spendthrift. Nay, she had taken a certain delight in hoarding all sorts of things from her childhood up, and her drawers presented a strange mosaic of articles, old and new, which she loved to gather about her.

Netta Speed was not a sentimental person. Perhaps, also, she recognised that to give way to emotion even for a moment would be detrimental to her courage. So when she was quite ready and her things stood on a chair waiting to be lifted, she unlocked the door.

Standing expectant and alert on the landing she listened, but there was not a sound. Far away in the servants' quarters they would be at their tea, from which they did not rise till six o'clock. It was now twenty minutes to the hour, and the coast was clear.

Two ways of leaving the house were open to her—the ordinary exit by the hall door, and that at the end of the corridor by the fire-escape, which had been installed by her father because he was himself extremely nervous regarding any possible outbreak of fire. Netta had carefully examined the fire-escape, and had decided that it would be possible for her—with some difficulty—to get down with her slender luggage. But for many reasons she preferred the door as a means of exit, and she resolved to risk it. She was nearly an hour too early for her appointment, but in her feverish haste to get outside she determined to go at once. She brought out her bag and hold-all, then paused to lock the door from without and put the key in her pocket in order that, if any of the household should come up and try the door, they might surmise either that she was asleep or that she was unwilling to be disturbed.

Then with a catch in her breath and a wildly-beating heart she ran down the broad stairs. On the first landing she paused and heard a trill of distant laughter from the servants' hall. Yes, they were all safely occupied, and would not be likely to trouble her. The morning-room had a window to the garden, leading across the lawn to the path which led down the hill to the station. Netta softly undid the bolts, waited to draw the curtain after her as closely as possible, then stepped gently out upon the well-rolled gravel of the broad walk. It was very soft with much rain, and the night was so dark that she had to grope her way across the lawn till she found the firmer footing of the path through the little wood. Once safe within its sparse shelter she gave a little hysterical laugh. Her ruse had completely succeeded, and she had now only to reach the place appointed for her meeting with her waiting companion.

Marchesi, skilled in the arts of intrigue, had been over the ground, and had himself sketched and arranged the whole plan of her escape, giving her several alternatives. But the first venture had succeeded beyond all her hopes, for when they had fixed the date and settled the details they had not expected that all the members of the household would be conveniently absent from The Rowans.

At the end of a certain quiet and unfrequented road about half a mile from The Rowans, Marchesi waited with a cab in which he had travelled from Dundee. He received with words of passionate love the girl who had yielded to his entreaties, and a few moments later they were rolling smoothly along the road towards Monifieth, where they joined—not the South, but—the North-going train.

All unconscious of the catastrophe which had desolated their home, George Speed and his wife sat at dinner in the big, gloomy dining-room at Ravenscraig discussing their prospects.

Tom, after dining at his Club, reached The Rowans about eleven o'clock, and after a quiet pipe he went upstairs to bed.

CHAPTER XXVII

IN THE MORNING

Tom Speed rose about his usual time next morning, and after having made himself a cup of tea on the spirit-lamp in his bedroom he left the house by seven o'clock to ride on his bicycle to the mills. Tom was slightly Spartan in his habits—as befitted a person professing his extreme views, which included a rule that no servant should be asked or even allowed to wait on him to a greater extent than was absolutely necessary.

The servants rose early at The Rowans, and all took tea in the kitchen before setting about the morning's work. It would have been a pleasure to any one of them to have taken up a tray to Mr. Tom, but such service was absolutely forbidden.

Soon after he had left the house Beith went softly up to Miss Netta's room and knocked lightly at the door to inquire whether she would like a cup of tea after her long fast. The girl had, of course, heard that nothing had been served to her the previous evening and that she had not rung to ask anything.

There was no response, and she tried the door softly. Finding it locked she had no alternative but to go down again, feeling, however, not altogether easy in her mind. At the bottom of the stairs she met the housemaid with her box returning from doing up the fireplace in the morning-room.

" Ye forgot to lock the windy, Jean," said the latter with a nod. " Guid thing for you the mistress didna catch ye."

" I didn't forget the window, Bella Kitson," answered Beith shortly. " Somebody must ha'e come in or gane oot efter me."

Bella laughed and passed on. There was a good deal of sparring below stairs at The Rowans, and changes in the staff were frequent.

Beith proceeded with her work of cleaning the dining-room and getting it ready for breakfast, but before laying the cloth she decided to go up again to her young lady's room and inquire whether she would come down or have a tray sent up. She knocked several times clearly, and getting no response she called Miss Netta rather loudly. Then she began to tremble with apprehension.

She ran down to the kitchen, from which the appetising odour of bacon on the grill had already begun to ascend, and confided her anxieties to the cook. The latter rested her hands on her substantial sides and put her head a little on one side.

" We'll ha'e to break open the door if ye canna get ony answer. Sam Petrie's in the gairden. Bring him in."

Beith, however, looked undecided.

" Don't you think I had better telephone first to Ravenscraig and ask the mistress what to do ? "

" Wait a jiffy or I tak' aff my ham and I'll gang up wi' ye."

By the time they reached the second landing they were joined by the housemaid and Tweeny. The laundry-maid, the only other member of the domestic staff, had gone out to get her copper alight in the laundry for the day's work. Cook put her eye to the keyhole.

" Mercy me, the key's no in it ! Rin doon, Tweeny, an' tell Petrie to come up wi' a hammer and a chisel."

The women looked at one another in dismay, mingled with growing excitement.

" I'll get into trouble for going out, and you, Bella, for not taking up something to Miss Netta before bedtime," Beith said dismally.

" Whatever we dae, we'll get into the hat ower it, Jean," replied the housemaid equably. " So we can a' keep oor hair on."

Presently Petrie appeared in the wake of Tweeny, without, however, having the implements he had been desired to bring.

" The fire-escape, ye fushionless crew ! " he said, grinning delightedly. " I'll be at the windy in a jiffy, and—if it's open—inside the room, though, if she's there, what she'll say guidness kens."

" She's no there, Sam," said Beith confidently. " And, look, the key's away ! "

" Well, I can satisfy mysel' whether she's in the room or no."

" Oh, oh ! " said Tweeny in a dread whisper. " She micht be deid—murdered in her sleep."

Tweeny was much given to the consumption of red novelettes, and had in consequence a highly coloured imagination.

" Shut you up, Tweeny, and speak when you're spoken till," observed cook, bending her massive brows with the utmost severity on the long, lank slip of a girl who was drudge to them all.

The gardener was not long in making his way to the bedroom window, which, being open about twelve inches from the top, lifted easily. Drawing aside the blind, he satisfied himself that the room was empty, though the bed was as its occupant had left it, the blue dressing-gown thrown carelessly across the pillow. He came back with this information, and they stared at one another in mute dismay.

" Some o' ye had better telephone to the maister, and I'll get the door opened. Evidently she's ta'en awa' the key," said Sam. Then, when half-way down the stairs, he looked round and added, " She never walked in her sleep, did she ? "

" I never knew her to do that," replied Beith. " Wha's gaun to the telephone ? No me."

" You're aye at it, and it's no my business," observed cook as she proceeded downstairs behind Petrie. Bella and Tweeny followed suit, and the performance of the unpleasant duty was left to Beith.

It was now half-past eight, and George Speed was sitting down to a solitary breakfast at Ravenscraig, his wife, tired with her long day, taking a morning in bed.

" They're at the telephone, sir, frae The Rowans," said Jarvis, who was still in the house, though he and Mrs. Robertson, having decided to spend the remainder of their days together and to share the provisions left by the old master, were going to marry immediately, and take a house at Carnoustie suitable for letting in the summer.

" Ask them what they want," said Speed rather shortly.

He had risen not in the best of humours, and he was missing the cosy comfort of his accustomed place at home. He was not fond of changes, and the prospect of spending one troubled and uncertain year in his father's house, and of then clearing out seemed to him both absurd and unnecessary. But his wife's strong determination had, as usual, borne him down.

" It's Beith, sir, and she seems in a way, as if something had happened," said Jarvis, returning after a few moments.

Speed threw his serviette on the table and stalked out to the hall.

" What ? " he shouted in a voice which startled Jarvis in his pantry and made him hold his breath.

Beith repeated her information in a trembling yet perfectly clear voice.

" Miss Netta not slept in her room—gone and taken the key, girl ! You've taken leave of your senses. Have you looked through all the house ? "

" Yes, sir."

He threw down the receiver, and after a moment's bewildered hesitation mounted the wide stairs to his wife's room. She was sitting up in bed, her breakfast tray in front of her, a white wrap about her shoulders, and was looking very comely and well pleased. The morning sunshine lay like a golden flood on the beautiful and spacious room, which looked across the Firth and commanded a magnificent panorama of the opposite shore.

" Something's happened at home, Marian, to Netta," said Speed thickly. " That's Beith at the telephone. She says that Netta's bed has not been occupied, and that she has evidently left the house, taking the key of her bedroom door with her."

Mrs. Speed's face blanched.

" There must be a mistake somewhere, George. Netta's not that kind of girl. She was very unwell last night, poor thing, with her bad head. I'll get up. No sooner is one worry over than another comes into my life. I'm sick of it ! "

She was not even yet wholly anxious, but in the father's heart hope had already died.

" Supposing it's true that she's gone away," he said in a low voice, " have you any explanation ? Is there a love affair of any kind ? Did Netta know any undesirable person ? "

His wife flashed a glance of scorn upon him. " Netta has been well brought up, George. Neither of my girls would be capable of such a thing. Besides, how could a love affair possibly have got to this without my knowing anything about it ? Are you going ? You must wait for me, George. I'll be ready in a quarter of an hour."

They left the house together, and they arrived at The Rowans inside the hour, when they found everything precisely as Beith had told it over the telephone.

Mrs. Speed, white enough now with anxiety and unspeakable dread, stood in the middle of the dishevelled room, looking round in blank dismay. Without speaking a word she opened the wardrobe, and her practised eye at once detected what had been taken and what left. Then she stepped across to the box-room at the opposite side of the landing and examined the travelling gear, neatly stacked there after the methodical system which her soul loved. Her husband had followed her, and he stood within the doorway, gazing helplessly, and hoping for some crumb of comfort from the strong spirit that had so long dominated his life.

" Her dressing-bag and the brown hold-all," she said in a very calm voice. " She had on her crimson dress, and she has taken a silk skirt and some blouses. Yes, there's no doubt that she has gone, George. Where ? "

She leaned against the lintel of the low doorway, her eyes big and pathetic with terror and misery. So in silence did they both stand for a moment regarding each other.

Then George Speed awoke to an agony of activity. He plunged down the stair, and for the next twenty minutes the telephone was never still. First he rang up the Police Station to make an appointment and to ask that one of their cleverest officers should be placed at his disposal when he called in an hour's time. Next he called up Tom at the mills to inquire what he had been about all the previous evening, but, as usual, Tom could not be found.

The carriage was ordered, and both husband and wife drove into the town and direct to the Police Station, where the matter was taken in hand by a grave-faced officer, who proceeded to make his notes of the case. He put a few leading questions to Mrs. Speed, which made her very angry.

" I tell you there is no man, no love affair—absolutely nothing whatever of that kind. It's impossible ! I know my daughter too well, and there never was a day on which I could not account for all her movements. She knew no undesirable people. No, the explanation must be found elsewhere. She has either committed suicide," she added brokenly, " though why she should I don't know, seeing that she was perfectly happy ; or out of some whim or other she has gone away from home, perhaps with the idea of earning her own living or doing something out of the ordinary."

" She had sometimes expressed discontent with her life, then ? " said the officer.

" Occasionally, as a girl might when things were dull," said her mother. " But I did not attach any importance at the time to her grumblings. Her father and brother will tell you that she was perfectly happy."

" She said very little about herself at any time," said George Speed, and his grey face and still manner impressed the officer far more than Mrs. Speed's noisier demonstration.

" I'll at once put into operation every means of tracing her movements," he said sympathetically. " The stations shall be inquired at, and I shall be in communication with you throughout the day."

" Where now ? " asked Mrs. Speed as they turned to leave the room.

" The mills, so that we may hear where Tom was last night," said Speed as he took her arm.

" Ah, Tom. Yes, of course. He was not at home : he never is when anything is wanted of him. Let us go and see what Tom has to say."

She was rapidly losing control of herself. The first real calamity of her life found her totally unprepared to meet it. In silence they drove along the familiar way through the busy streets, and up the steep ascent to the Eliot Mills. In the office they found Henry Lundie alone, wondering what had occurred to detain his partner so long past his usual hour. When he saw them both enter, and noted the expression on their faces, he guessed that something had happened to upset them.

" Where's Tom ? " asked Speed abruptly, not even bidding him good-morning.

" I haven't seen him. Send Richards. He's a sharp little chap, who will find him if he is on the premises."

He put his finger on the electric button, but he forebore to press it as he looked at his partner's face.

" What is it, George ? " he said, half rising from his chair.

" My girl ! " said Speed with a gasp. " Something has happened ; she has left us, Henry. She has been out of the house all night."

Henry Lundie fell back, and his face whitened, too, as the memory of Katherine's warning and his own remissness swept over him.

" Marchesi ! " he said, with a kind of gasp, but that name was enough for Mrs. Speed.

In an instant of time the whole matter was clear as noonday. Unconsidered trifles, now seen in their true significance, started up before her. The next moment she had sunk unconscious on the floor.

CHAPTER XXVIII

AT CADDAM CASTLE

SINCE his romantic accession to the estate, Sir Rafe Fletcher had found no lack of persons anxious to show him kindness and become his friends. He had accepted several invitations, and in the way of hospitality had casually met the best that Dundee and the neighbourhood could offer, but he was a silent, reserved man who did not easily make friends.

Of all the houses he had visited he had found the simple domicile in Albion Terrace, with its atmosphere of freedom and sincerity, most to his liking. Father and daughter alike had charmed him, and it came quite naturally to him to try to cultivate their friendship.

Henry Lundie, by reason of his tastes and somewhat Bohemian personality, had always felt himself a little alien to the prosperous, commercial atmosphere of Dundee, and, though respected, he was not in any sense of the word popular. He possessed few popular gifts, though to his intimates he was that rare acquisition—a perfect friend.

He had been greatly drawn to Sir Rafe and delighted with his stories of life in the remote Continent, which swallows up so many younger sons. He had accepted the invitation to dine at Caddam with a delight which had affected Katherine, and they started on the drive with the most pleasurable anticipation.

On second thoughts Katherine did not convey to her father the fears concerning Netta Speed that had assailed her in the afternoon, and that she had almost convinced herself were, if not groundless, at least exaggerated. She supposed that Netta had taken to heart her words spoken in the train, and she congratulated herself that she had been given the opportunity to speak them.

The lands and woods of Caddam stretched away back from the highway, whence the castle was approached by a private road, which, with the avenue itself, shut the house off most completely from the traffic of the public roads.

The night was intensely dark, and the lighted carriage lamps seemed only to intensify the gloom. It was very still and warm, however—a typical November night, with a fine rain filtering down from the mist-enveloped sky. Katherine opened both the carriage windows and peered out.

"How dark, papa—one can almost feel it, and the gateway at Caddam is very narrow! I hope Reid will be careful. Here we are, but there doesn't seem to be any one at the lodge—at any rate there is no light."

Mr. Lundie himself got down to make sure of due caution being observed, and he walked by the side of the carriage while the coachman guided the horses between the old moss-grown pillars of the gate. The lodge—a very small, low house with latticed windows and a thatched roof—was in perfect darkness.

"There's naebody into the lodge, sir," said the coachman. "They send somebody doon frae the hoose to open the gates when onybody is expected."

"A primitive arrangement, surely," observed Mr. Lundie as he re-entered the carriage.

In a few more minutes they reached the wide sweep of gravel before the quaint, low doorway of the castle, and their host himself in a quiet, unconventional way came forward out of the ruddy glow of the lighted hall to receive them. Katherine thought how well he looked in the conventional evening-dress, though she fancied it made him look older. The hair at his temples, she now for the first time noticed, was quite grey.

"I hope you got through the gates all right. I'm looking for a lodge-keeper, but I want to get the right person, and at the same time do a good deed. I think I heard of some one this afternoon. I am glad to welcome you to Caddam, Miss Lundie, though I wish there was some one fitter to do the honours than myself."

Katherine smiled back at him her frank, delightful smile, which not only beautified her face, but seemed to envelop in a warm glow the person on whom it was bestowed.

"Nobody could be more delightful than you are," she replied. "Oh, what a charming old hall! Look, papa, at that picture let in to the fireplace. Sir Rafe, I shall not want any dinner, I assure you. If only I am allowed to wander as I like through this beautiful old place I shall be satisfied."

"Afterwards," he said genially. "Will you let the maid take you upstairs? I believe ladies always go upstairs—at any rate Nancy has told me so. Nancy, come and wait on Miss Lundie."

Nancy Gow, smiling and important, came forward, and Katherine handed the girl her cloak and scarf.

"Thank you. I need not go up now," she said as she advanced to the fireplace, her white skirts trailing softly over the faded carpet.

Katherine Lundie never wore rustling robes of any kind. To her perfection in dress did not consist in the stiffness of the silk which could noisily proclaim its existence—perhaps its price—to every passer-by. She preferred soft materials and graceful draperies. Her dinner-gown was of white cloth trimmed with Irish lace, and made high to the throat, where, however, the lace was transparent and finished by a string of her mother's pearls.

Henry Lundie felt a fresh pride in his girl as he saw how well she accorded with her surroundings in that beautiful old family house, how naturally indeed, she seemed to complete the picture. Undoubtedly it was the fitting background for a gentlewoman of her refined type. Being debarred from any chance of ever possessing Battledore, he felt that, if he could only behold her permanently in such a setting, he could, like Simeon, depart in peace.

As Sir Rafe and she stood together amid the dancing shadows of the firelight they looked a handsome, well-matched pair. These thoughts chased one another unbidden through Henry Lundie's mind, surprising him greatly. It was the first tinge of worldliness to reveal itself in a mind singularly detached from worldly things.

The dinner was simple, but it was exquisitely served to all the accompaniments of a well-appointed house belonging to a man who hated ostentation, but who knew what was necessary and fitting. The softly-shaded lights from the old candelabra fell on Katherine's beautiful face, accentuating the refinement of every feature. Sir Rafe regarded her with increasing admiration, and the hour spent at the table was one of perfect ease and enjoyment for them all. Henry Lundie plied his host with questions regarding his life abroad, and they were all so deeply interested that they lingered longer at table than was customary.

"How hard it must be for you to settle down here after such a life, Sir Rafe!" said Katherine with a little sigh. "And how you must hate it!"

"Not necessarily. There are compensating circumstances. The mere possession of a home, for instance, to a homeless man is something."

"Yes—and of a home so beautiful," said Katherine, with an admiring glance round the sombre, harmonious room. "You have told us a great deal about the roughness of your life abroad, but you have not forgotten any of the things that go to the making of a home."

"I have to go back in memory to what my mother made of a small house in Edinburgh," replied Sir Rafe. "But it has not been easy getting the right people to carry out one's ideas."

Suddenly he went off at a tangent. "I was very much interested to meet your partner's son, young Speed," he said, addressing Mr. Lundie, "at the meeting of the Housing Committee this afternoon. He spoke remarkably well. An able chap, and one with ideas. He is, I suppose, one of the mainsprings of the business."

Katherine and her father exchanged smiles, and Sir Rafe observed that her colour seemed slightly to heighten.

"A very good fellow is Tom," answered Henry Lundie indulgently, when he found that Katherine did not speak. "So he spoke on the housing question? Well, he is more at home in that, I dare say, than in the details of the business of the Eliot Mills."

"Indeed! I am rather surprised. I thought he seemed shrewd and far-seeing.

We walked together after the meeting, and I had some talk with him. I liked exceedingly what I saw of him, and asked him to come out and dine with me to-morrow night for the purpose, really, of seeing the lodge. He has some poor friends whom he is very anxious for me to instal there."

"Who are they?" asked Katherine, and in spite of her effort to the contrary, a certain coldness crept into her voice, and her eyes seemed to harden.

"He did not mention the name, but they are a widow and her daughter—very superior people, I believe. I told him I would be only too glad to take any one on his recommendation, and he is coming out, as I have said, to-morrow evening to arrange about it."

"Shall we go out into the hall? The atmosphere may be purer there and they will bring the coffee," asked Sir Rafe when Katherine made no remark.

He felt conscious that some slight but subtle change had taken the bloom off that exquisite hour—certainly one of the happiest he had spent under the roof of his new home.

Katherine rose at once, and they passed out into the subdued glow of the warmly-lighted hall, where the scent of flowers was so sweet as to be almost overpowering.

"They have put out too many azaleas, I'm afraid," said Sir Rafe, imagining Katherine to be affected by the strong perfume. "In our anxiety to do honour to the first lady who has dined with us we have been too lavish in our display. Shall I tell them to remove some of them?"

"Oh, pray, don't," said Katherine quickly. "I assure you I can never have too many flowers."

"Yes, I was quite taken with young Speed," resumed Sir Rafe as he lit another cigarette. "It is so unusual in these utilitarian days to find any of our young men interested in the bigger things of life. I am quite looking forward to his coming to-morrow night."

"He'll haul you into all sorts of outlay both of time and money if you are sympathic, won't he, Kate?" said Henry Lundie with an amused laugh. "We don't take him quite seriously, but I agree with you that he's an honest, straight chap, and that he gives to good, public work the time he might very easily waste. He makes his mistakes, of course, as we all do—but his heart's in the right place."

Sir Rafe then changed the theme, fancying that somehow it was not so congenial as some of the others which they had discussed.

Katherine and her father left soon after with many expressions of appreciation of the happy evening which they had spent, Henry Lundie being especially demonstrative.

"You liked him, Kitty, didn't you?" he inquired anxiously as the long, dark shadows of the wood once more enveloped them.

"Oh, yes, papa, very much," she answered readily enough.

"He's my beau-ideal of what a man in that position should be. He has been tried in the furnace of real life, and that experience has given him sympathy and common sense, and he's personally most lovable. Don't you think so, Kitty?"

"Yes, papa, he is certainly all that you say."

"He will be a prize for some woman," said Henry Lundie with a sigh that came up from the very depths of his fatherly heart.

"Stranger things might happen, and if—if I could leave you at Caddam in Rafe Fletcher's care, Kitty, I could die easily and could go to your mother with a happy heart."

"Don't, papa," was all that Katherine said.

CHAPTER XXIX

SYMPATHY

THAT evening at Caddam Sir Rafe Fletcher waited in vain for his expected guest. At half-past eight he had dinner served, and he had nearly finished it when Tom Speed was announced. He gathered at once from his face that something untoward had happened.

"I'm very sorry," stammered Tom. "An awful thing has happened in our family. I've just come from seeing my father and mother off to London."

"What is it?" asked Sir Rafe kindly, laying at the same time a sympathetic hand on the young man's shoulder.

"My sister!" faltered Tom, and his sensitive colour rose. "She's run away from home. I'm almost ashamed to tell you."

"Has she gone with some one?"

"Yes, her Italian singing-master, a scoundrel of the name of Marchesi, who gave lessons at St. Andrews."

Tom, overcome by the strain of the long day and by his genuine misery, dropped into a chair and covered his face with his hands.

He had not escaped severe blame for the family calamity, his mother having been specially reproachful concerning his lack of interest in his sister, upbraiding him with the fact that he had not even taken the trouble to inquire how she was when he got home. Tom had accepted the blame meekly, feeling that it was not altogether undeserved. He had certainly of late lived very much detached from his family.

"I am very sorry to hear this, my lad," said Sir Rafe very kindly. "Tell me how it happened, if it will relieve you. But I don't want to seem to pry into your intimate family affairs."

"Oh, there's nothing very intimate about this," said Tom gloomily. "It will be in all the papers to-morrow—nothing on earth can keep it out. There isn't almost anything to tell, beyond the fact that she's gone—took the opportunity last night when my father and mother were sleeping at Ravenscraig. She must have been gone before I got home at eleven o'clock, because they've found out to-day that she and Marchesi travelled north from Monifieth by the six-forty. That, of course, would be to put people off the scent, since they are both known at the Ferry and in Dundee. They've gone south by this time, no doubt, and my father and mother are following them up, though what good it's going to do, I can't say."

He groaned again.

"It's too beastly that one's sister should do this, and with a foreigner too, whom nobody knows anything about! He may even have a wife already."

"We must hope for the best," said Sir Rafe, trying to speak cheerfully.

"Is nothing known in St. Andrews about his antecedents?"

"Nothing. He came in the train of Lady Barter, who is herself a little of an outsider. He belongs to Milan. Perhaps my father and mother may have to follow them there."

"It was not even suspected that there was an affair going on?" said Sir Rafe.

"Suspected! Good Heavens, no! it was the very last thing any of us would have suspected. And Netta was the very last person one would have thought likely to do such a thing; a reserved, self-contained girl, no one ever knew what she was thinking. Where we have all erred is in assuming that she had not much strength of character. She's had enough, anyhow, to take the bit between her teeth. I tell you the whole thing has bowled me over. I really forgot till the train had left that I was due here. I hope you'll excuse me—"

"Don't mention it, my boy. Have something to eat now. Have you had dinner?"

" Oh, yes, at home. At least there was a pretence of dining ? Nothing more to eat, thank you ; but I'll take a cup of black coffee, hot and strong, if you please."

" Come to my den, then, and they'll bring it there."

Tom rose and followed, too crushed to take notice of the beautiful old house which only last night had been illumined by Katherine's presence.

Sir Rafe's experience among all sorts and conditions of men guided him in his dealing with Tom Speed in his hour of distress, and in half an hour or so the world seemed to the latter less black and hopeless than it had been.

In that half hour Fletcher learned all that he desired to know concerning the house of Speed, and he arrived at a very correct estimate of its various constituents. Tom, sure of sympathy, was quickly won to an unusually confiding mood, and the time passed on the wings of the wind.

" You see it's like this, Sir Rafe, I've been pulling the wrong way, I think, and now I'm in a worse fix than ever, because—because I've got a love-affair of my own, which can t be acceptable—in fact it will make my mother furious. After this affair of Netta's I shall have to keep very quiet. In fact, I don't know what I am to do."

" You're pledged to some girl not—not quite in your own station. Knowing your views, it's no more than I should have expected to hear," said Sir Rafe with a good-natured smile.

" She's not so impossible—she's really a lady," said Tom, sitting forward eagerly. " She has worked in our mill, but that was because every other door was closed against her."

" She's the daughter of the lady you spoke to me about yesterday afternoon ? "

Tom nodded.

" Yes, and if you could see your way to let them have the lodge, it would be a true kindness to them first, and then to me. At present they are living at Lochee, not more than half a mile from your gates."

" Then I can call on them to-morrow. But they would not be able to live on the small sum that I would pay to a lodgekeeper."

" Miss Durie would earn something. In fact she has some work now in a shop in Burgess Street. It's very humble work of course, but it brings in something. If they had a home such as your cottage would be to them, they would be able to live. They have known poverty in its most acute form, and they can make the best of the smallest things— "

" I will see them to-morrow without fail," said Fletcher as he took out his note-book to jot down the address.

" Then I take it that your parents are not aware of your interest in this young lady."

" I think they suspect something, and that that is the reason why she was dismissed. It was a most cruel and unjust dismissal, for at that time I had only spoken to her twice, and I assure you that it hastened the very catastrophe which they wanted to prevent."

" Seeing the damsel in distress, you at once proposed, I suppose," said Fletcher with a half smile. " That would be in keeping with your impulsive way."

" Why do you all call me impulsive ? I assure you I think out all the actions of my life, and I am always making fresh rules for my conduct."

" A mistake surely. It is easier to live naturally than by rule."

" But then, you see, I hold strong ideas on certain points," said Tom naïvely, " and I have to regulate my conduct accordingly. Women, I think, have hard lives. I consider that working-women suffer from too many disabilities, and that they, like men, should be properly organised. I was bound, therefore, to stand up against such obvious and glaring injustice as Miss Durie's dismissal from our mills— "

" Durie," repeated Fletcher musingly. " Is that a very common name in these parts ? "

" It is not unusual, though I don't think there are many Duries in Dundee. It's a Fifeshire name, I believe."

" I met a man of that name out west, a very decent chap."

" Couldn't belong to them. So far as I've been able to gather they have no people, and the mother is a widow."

Here was a brief silence. Then Fletcher sat forward on his chair, regarding his young guest with great kindliness and some keenness.

"You are quite sure, I suppose, of your feelings for this young lady? In youth one makes many mistakes which are difficult to undo."

Tom appeared surprised and a little indignant at the suggestion.

"Of course I am sure. If I were not sure, I wouldn't be here speaking to you about her like this."

"And she?"

"She doesn't say much. She is a model of reticence and modesty, all that a woman should be, and if my mother were only moderately reasonable—"

"Remember what trouble she is in," interpolated Fletcher gently, "and don't add to it."

"That's the only reason why I don't carry things more high-handedly. I put it to you, Sir Rafe. Suppose for a moment that the woman you cared about was in dire poverty, dependent for her daily bread on her daily toil, and that for some paltry reason that was suddenly taken from her, wouldn't you be inclined to behave rashly?"

"The blood flows more sluggishly at forty, dear boy," replied Fletcher with his rare, slow smile.

"But you are not that!" cried Tom incredulously.

"Very near it. I am thirty-eight."

"You don't look it. Oh, I don't think my blood will ever cool. I don't want it to. I should hate to be slow and calculating and not keen where wrong and injustice are concerned. I have lost a good deal over this one way and another—among other things, the two friends whom I liked best in the world, and on whom I thought I could absolutely count."

"Who are they?"

"Miss Lundie and David Alister—the surgeon who lives in the Overgate."

Fletcher nodded, deeply interested.

"But you think she is worth it, and that she will make up to you for all that you have lost?"

"Why, of course, there isn't any doubt about it."

"I shall be more than interested to see Miss Durie, I assure you."

"You won't be disappointed. You have met Miss Lundie? Of course, you dined at their house, I remember now. We were more intimate then, though it is not so long since those days. But when a great many experiences are crowded into a short space, time seems to be obliterated."

"Miss Lundie and her father dined here last night."

"A nice old man, isn't he? What did you think of her?"

"I admired her exceedingly."

"She's the woman whom my people are crazy to have me marry."

"I can understand that. What I don't understand is why you should not be willing to fall in with so excellent an arrangement."

"Does anybody ever want to fall in, as you term it, with excellent arrangements made for them by other people?" asked Tom rather scornfully. "In this case everything was against it. We have known each other too long, and been too intimate as friends. Marriage is an inspiration, not an ordained path which we can tread by command."

Fletcher sat back, laughing silently, and much entertained by Tom's philosophy of life, delivered with all the assurance befitting a man of double his age.

"If they had wanted me to marry Katherine Lundie they should have left us alone. And my grandfather, whom I thought was my best friend, ruined everything by an absurd and wicked codicil to his will, which leaves me the place at Newport on condition that Miss Lundie and I marry within eighteen months."

"And if you fail to fulfil the condition you lose the place?"

"Exactly. And my people, but especially my mother, are, of course, furious and cannot understand why the condition is impossible to fulfil."

"Your life seems to be a bit complicated at present, my boy," said Fletcher kindly: "I hope the tangles will smooth themselves out soon. Then you are actually engaged to Miss Durie. She has promised to marry you?"

"She knows I will not marry any one else, and she's letting me do all sorts of things for her. Yes, of course she has promised. But, as I have said, she is very reserved—in fact she's the very opposite of everything that my mother thinks she is, and if she would be only reasonable and meet her, I am sure all her objections would melt away."

Fletcher felt doubtful, but he did not say so.

"Well, I must go, I've bored you inexcusably," said Tom as he rose to his feet.

"Not at all—you have interested me very much. I shall see something of you, I hope, later on when your feet will naturally turn up the Caddam road."

Tom laughed a little shamefacedly.

"Of course I'll be at the lodge a good deal, if you are so kind as to let them have it. Did you say you would see them to-morrow?"

"I shall make a point of it—"

"You will see only Mrs. Durie of course in the day-time, Mary being at her place of business all day. She does not get home till seven o'clock. But I forgot that to-morrow is the half-holiday. So you will see her any time after three. I had promised to take her out, but I shall have to explain that while my father is away I must stick in at the mill."

The shadow again fell across his face as all the shame and sorrow of that day's happening swept over him.

Fletcher felt sorry for him as he let him out.

"A fine spirit, but one that will suffer much. Poor boy!" he said to himself musingly as he went back to his solitary pipe. The story had interested him not a little, and he was able to fill in the gaps.

He had no doubt whatever that Katherine was not so indifferent as Tom had made out. He remembered the expression in her face.

CAHPTER XXX

BRIGHTENING HOPES

ABOUT three o'clock next afternoon Mary Durie arrived at the two small rooms above a baker's shop in Lochee, where she and her mother had found a temporary home.

The rooms had been recommended to her by the outfitter in Burgess Street, who had given her much-needed employment. They belonged to a cousin of her own, who was glad to let them to respectable people. The locality and the neighbours were many degrees superior to those of Wilson's Court, and some peace was restored to the lives of these beaten women who had been tried so hard in the furnace of affliction. But times were still very hard with them, and the future sometimes appeared desperate to Mary.

Her mother suffered fewer qualms. She was not yet aware of Tom Speed's identity. Mary, with a scheming which surprised herself, had begged him not to reveal himself to her mother in the meantime. She did not know what she feared, but placing so little reliance on her mother's prudence, she preferred that she should not know the name of their benefactor. He had been extraordinarily kind to them, but Mary was not aware that he had actually given money to her mother. He had not, of course, dared to offer it to her.

But there was no brightness in her face nor buoyancy in her step as she approached the new home that wintry afternoon. She felt, indeed, somewhat desperate about the future. Her own heart and conscience were never for a moment at rest, because she had given a false pledge to a man for whom she cared nothing.

The worst part of herself had asserted itself in her dealings with Tom Speed. To her he was little more than the medium through which her own wrongs and those of her mother should be avenged.

The intimacy, daily increasing—for Tom came every day to Lochee—was beginning to tell on her, causing her to realise what she had done. Though she was grateful for his kindness, for his chivalrous championship, her heart was as cold to him as the nether millstone. Yet she had promised to marry him some day. That "some day" was her sheet-anchor of hope, so many things might happen before "some day" came.

It had been a relief to her when she had received a note written from the mills, explaining that he could not see her until late in the evening as till then he would not be completely free from the duties of the day.

As she approached her new home her face wore an expression of gloom that somewhat detracted from its charm. These days of anxiety and of brooding on bitter thoughts had told upon Mary Durie, and had made her look years older. But that was a matter of small account to one who had little interest in her looks.

She passed up the little, narrow passage by the side of the shop to a stair in the yard behind, by which she had to ascend to the rooms.

There was nothing beautiful or attractive in that dismal back-yard, shut in by a red brick wall. A few articles of clothing hung on the lines, scarcely flapping in the still November air. A hen in the little wire hen-run was clucking noisily and thereby proclaiming to the world that she had fulfilled her function in life.

Mary paused for a moment on the stairhead, and looked up and down over all the back-yards, which were exactly alike as peas in a pod. There were no green things to be seen just then, and from that particular point of vantage, while above, the giant chimney-stalks of innumerable works pointed to the dull sky and belched forth clouds of black smoke to add to the general gloom.

Could this be life ? she asked herself as she placed her fingers on the handle of the door. Setting it a little ajar she heard voices within, indicating that some one was visiting her mother. Hearing a man's voice she supposed it would be the clergyman of the district come, as in duty bound, to look them up.

Being in no mood to make herself agreeable to strangers she felt annoyed, and was for the moment tempted to turn back, and in order to escape, go for a walk along some country road.

A second thought decided her to remain, and she walked through the little passage to the place which was at once kitchen and living room.

Her mother, who had certainly showed some signs of improvement since they had left Wilson's Court, was up and dressed, sitting in her basket-chair and talking with apparent ease and freedom to a tall stranger wearing a tweed shooting suit, who leaned against the little table set across the window, and who appeared to be listening with the greatest possible interest. On Mary's entrance hs stood up, and she was at once conscious of the keenness of his scrutiny.

" Mary," cried her mother fussily, " this is Sir Rafe Fletcher, and what do you think he has come to offer us ! The place of lodge-keeper at Caddam ! Very kind of him, isn't it ? His offer comes, it seems, through the Speeds—a thing which I don't quite understand."

Mary looked desperately uncomfortable, and she returned Sir Rafe's pleasant salutation with the curtest nod.

" It is very kind indeed," she said lamely. " But, I am afraid, we have no qualifications for such a post."

" Why not ? " he asked with a frank smile. " There are no special qualifications required. If your mother is well enough to attend to the opening of the gate when necessary, that is really all that is needed. I understand that you would continue your occupation in Dundee."

" Yes, I suppose I should," she said, vaguely wondering how he knew so much about them. Tom in his note had not mentioned anything about Sir Rafe Fletcher or his promise to call that day. But that omission did not mean much, for Tom was very casual in many of his proceedings, and he left a good deal to chance. His mind, moreover, had been fully occupied with other interests all that day, and he had decided to leave further discussion of the future of the Duries until he should see them in the evening. A telegram, received from his father, which intimated that they had a clue to Netta's whereabouts, had served to keep his wandering thoughts nearer home than usual all day.

" My mother is not very strong, as you see, Sir Rafe," Mary said, and he was quick to note the ease of her manner and the educated tone of her voice. " I should not like to undertake anything that we could not accomplish well, though I understand what a boon it would be to us, and especially to my mother, to live in the country. She has not been much used to town life, and it tries her too much."

" I think you are the very people I am looking for. Could you walk out to Caddam this afternoon and see the cottage ? It is not more than half an hour's walk, and, if you will, I can meet you there in an hour's time."

" Thank you," said Mary, grasping the respite from the necessity for immediate decision, and also the relief from the undoubted strain of the moment. " Yes. I can be there in an hour's time."

Sir Rafe immediately took his leave.

The mother had left no impression on his mind. She was weak, vacillating, even underbred, but the daughter filled him with astonishment. He no longer wondered at Tom Speed's infatuation—she was the sort of woman to inspire it.

Yet the casual observer would have found it difficult to specify Mary Durie's charm, which proceeded entirely from her strong and interesting personality.

" We're going to have a spell of good luck now, Mary," said her mother delightedly. " But why were you so standoffish with Sir Rafe ? Such a pleasant-spoken gentleman and so willing to be friendly ! I assure you that he came into this little kitchen as respectfully as if it had been a drawing-room."

" And why shouldn't he ? " inquired Mary with that defiant note in her voice which her mother had learned to dread. " Did he say anything about payment for the work, or are you supposed to open the gate as a return for the privilege of living at the lodge ? "

" No, he offered five shillings a week."

"And I can make ten, and we should sit rent free. Yes, we must take it, mother."

"We can't afford to refuse it, my dear," replied Mrs. Durie. "Already we have been too much indebted to Mr. Halliwell, but we can't go on taking from him."

"Taking from him, mother? What do you mean?" asked Mary, flushing angrily.

Mrs. Durie immediately began to whimper, as she invariably did, when blamed in the slightest degree.

"Don't glare and shout at me. He has given me a little money, and if you are going to marry him, as he seems to think, I don't see that it can matter at all. You are so queer, Mary, and uncomfortable. Nobody knows just now how you are going to behave."

Mary turned away, sick at heart.

"We'll accept Sir Rafe Fletcher's offer. Only you must promise to take no more money from Mr. Halliwell. It humiliates me too much. I must make you jot down what you have had, and I'll pay him back. With fifteen shillings a week and no rent to pay we can save a little. At least I shall try."

"You are getting very hard and unsympathetic, Mary, and more difficult to live with every day," said Mrs. Durie through her tears.

Mary sighed as she turned away to set out their simple meal.

Perhaps it was true. Certainly she felt as hard as the nether millstone, and the bitterness of her heart was like to overwhelm her.

Her mother, who still clung to the habits of the helpless invalid, and who did very little to add to the comfort of their bare and hard life, leaned back in her chair with the languid air of one who is resigned to inevitable fate. Mary laid the cloth, got out the cups and saucers, and put two chops on the fire to cook for the meal, which must be both dinner and tea for them. They ate it in uncomfortable silence.

"If I'm to be in time for my appointment with your new master I'll have to leave you to clear the table. If you don't feel equal to it you can let it stand till I come back."

Mary did not speak graciously, and once more her mother wept. Certainly she did not feel gracious—things were utterly out of joint.

She got beyond the narrow limits of the poor home with relief, and once more out upon the open road she felt the load slightly lift.

She made some inquiries, and she was directed up the winding road to the gates of Caddam, which she reached about five minutes before the appointed time. She was not sorry for that, because it gave her an opportunity of taking her bearings and obtaining a good look at the exterior of the little house.

It delighted her; the latticed casements, the thatched roof, the low doorway, and, above all, the situation on the edge of the great park and of the winter woods of Caddam promised complete seclusion from the sordid life to which she had never grown accustomed. Humble it might be, but it could be made a real home. She was wandering in the thicket behind the house, scaring the rabbits who scuttered by in terror, while a small, bright-eyed squirrel watched her from the topmost boughs, when the sudden, sharp bark of a dog warned her of Sir Rafe's approach.

He came forward, lifted his cap, and took a key from his pocket.

"You are punctual. Some one had called for me when I got back, and I was detained. I hope I have the right key. I think you will like the little house. It is very small, of course, but I think it could be made comfortable."

"I like it very much," she answered simply, not being at any time possessed of superfluous words. She felt more silent than usual indeed in the presence of this man, whose face was stern, but whose heart was kind.

He fitted the key, threw open the door, and stood aside for her to pass in first. This small attention, which in the circumstances might easily, and, perhaps naturally, have been omitted, caused the colour to rise quickly to her pale cheek. She thanked him, and passed into the queer, little, octagon room with the quaint fireplace and the latticed windows.

Some few articles of old furniture stood about, a gate-legged table and an old settee by the fireplace, which were wholly in keeping with the character of the house.

"I'm afraid it's a little damp," said Sir Rafe critically. "But I can order some fires to be put on immediately if you agree to come. Are you bound for any time to the place where you are now living?"

"No; we are only weekly tenants."

" Then how soon could you come ? "

" Our week is ended on Saturday. But perhaps that would be too early for you."

" Not at all. It makes no difference to me, and indeed the sooner the house is occupied the better I shall be pleased. If you let me know when you will be ready I can send a cart for your things on Saturday."

" Thank you very much."

" You are willing to come, then, on the terms which I mentioned to your mother—five shillings a week and the house ? You may also have as much wood as you care to burn. They're thinning out the plantations now, and there's enough to spare. You may have a load at any time."

Mary lifted her eyes to his face and tried to speak her thanks for the vista of comfort and independence which thus seemed to be opened out before her. Only those who have suffered privations such as hers will be able to appreciate what the prospect meant for her.

She essayed to speak her thanks, but words would not come.

Her beautiful eyes, from which all the hardness had fled, filled with tears.

CHAPTER XXXI

THE OLD CAMPAIGNER

IN those days none suffered more than Katherine Lundie, who was the prey of an unavailing regret. She might, had she only spoken out in time, have prevented the catastrophe which had plunged the Speeds into such sorrow. Her fine reticence regarding Netta had become a crime. She bore in her face evidences of her unhappiness, and nothing that her father could say dispelled the gloom.

Each morning she telephoned to The Rowans asking when Mr. and Mrs. Speed were expected home, and at last she heard that they had unexpectedly arrived by the night train from London. They had been absent from Dundee for thirteen days, in the course of which they had followed the pair as far as Milan, never having overtaken them *en route*—so expert was Marchesi in travelling expedients—nor did they come up with them until he was safely in his own land, where he was able to meet them with greater assurance. He had no actual realisation of what such an elopement meant to people like the Speeds; that what he considered a glowing romance was to them merely sordid disgrace.

Learning that Mrs. Speed had not gone to bed after her journey, but was busy about the house as usual, Katherine dressed and proceeded to West Ferry by train. She felt very humble—even resigned to be rebuked by Mrs. Speed.

She was admitted without the smallest demur, and Mrs. Speed at once came to her in the morning-room. Beyond looking a little paler than usual, Mrs. Speed did not bear any traces of her grief or of her long, fatiguing journey.

"How are you, my dear?" she said almost affectionately, and at the same time kissing Katherine on both cheeks. "How good of you to come over so soon. Beith has told me how kind you have been, asking every day. But, my dear, I simply couldn't write. There wasn't time, and, besides, it was all too ghastly."

"I have come to confess, Mrs. Speed," said Katherine faintly. "I knew something about what was going on, and I did not tell you."

Mrs. Speed looked at her keenly, but in no way angrily.

"How much did you actually know? Netta told me that you knew something."

Katherine related all that had passed between them on the subject.

"It was probably by that time too late to have averted the elopment, my dear," she said with a magnanimity that Katherine had hardly expected. "Indeed, Netta told me that everything except the merest details was already settled. Could you have imagined our little Netta capable of so much duplicity? But she is clever, Katherine. Unfortunately, all my children are."

"Tell me about her if you can," said Katherine, almost falteringly, a great deal more upset than the mother herself seemed to be.

"Oh, she is married right enough, and the man has no other wife, the dread of which was the spectre haunting her father night and day. I assure you that he never closed an eye until we reached Milan and had met them."

"You've been at Milan?" exclaimed Katherine in amazement.

"Yes, and discovered that it might be worse. Marchesi, though very nervous, was quite courageous, and answered all our questions with great frankness. He is very poor, but his people are respectable, even noble. So many of the Italian aristocracy are poor, and have to work in a way that our nobility know nothing about. When an elderly cousin dies Marchesi will have a title. So, you see, it might be worse."

Katherine thankfully accepted these crumbs of comfort, unaware that they were to a large extent manufactured by Mrs. Speed, who had on the homeward journey arranged a complete plan of campaign, determined with a courage that did her credit to make the best of everything.

" But will she be happy, do you think, away in Milan among strangers with a husband that she knows so little about ? "

" In the meantime she is infatuated with Marchesi, who, I must say, is a very charming fellow. We have arranged everything on the best possible basis, and her father will give her an income on which it will be possible for her to live independently of Marchesi. I am telling you all this, Katherine, relying on your help to remove false public impressions, and to let people understand that, though we, of course, disapproved of the elopement, things have turned out better than we expected."

Katherine regarded her with growing astonishment and even with a kind of unwilling respect. Certainly she was wonderful, and reminded one of an old campaigner who is never at a loss in any circumstances.

" After I have seen to things here I shall go over to St. Andrews and have one straight talk with Lady Barter. She is responsible for introducing Marchesi to an unsuspecting public, and I shall see that she helps me to put the best complexion on the affair for my daughter's sake. Don't you think I am right ? "

" It will be a difficult and most unpleasant task," said Katherine, without committing herself.

" It is my duty, and it shall be done. In the course of the year we shall have Netta home on a visit, and the affair will die down gradually. Of course it is horrible for us, and happening, as it has done, on the top of the disappointment about grandpa Speed's property, it has worried me very much. George really looks quite ill, and I have not yet been able to get him to take the sensible view of things. He harps on Netta's unhappiness all the time. He's certain she's going to be unhappy later on, and I assure you that if it hadn't been for me he and Marchesi would have come to blows. In dealing with such difficult elements as I find in my family, Katherine, one would need to unite the wisdom of the serpent and the softness of the dove."

In spite of herself Katherine smiled, but George Speed's careworn face rose up before her and caused the smile to die away. Her sympathy was naturally with him.

" He expected Marchesi to grovel, but a triumphant lover does not grovel, Katherine, and in the South they look at things differently, of course. An elopement more or less in Milan does not even ruffle the surface of family life. One's point of view is, I think, a mere matter of temperament."

" It is good for you that you can take such a view," Katherine could not help saying.

" Nothing is easier if one will keep common sense to the fore. What is the use of shrieking after the steed is stolen ? Surely it is best to look at the bright side. I was angry with Netta, of course. She ought to have trusted me, but I forgave her. Why ? Because there was no use in doing anything else. The deed was done."

Katherine admitted the advantages of common sense, but she was not enthusiastic. Suddenly Mrs. Speed regarded her with a more intimate and friendly glance.

" Yes, I do think it was sweet of you to come over like this, so informally and so sympathetically. I hope it means that you are really interested in us, dear."

" I felt so horribly anxious about Netta, and I so much blamed myself," said Katherine a little hurriedly as she rose to her feet.

" Oh, don't go yet. There's only Tom left, and if he disappoints us I don't know what will happen. Has he returned to his allegiance to you ? Like Netta, he will come to himself one of these days, and I hope you will be kind to him then."

" Mrs. Speed, I don't think you have the right to speak to me like that," said Katherine hotly. " There is not, and there never has been, anything between Tom and me."

" My dear, you can't expect me to believe that. Why, Tom has cared about you ever since you were children, and you used to spend the day at each other's houses. You can't so easily get away from old associations. For a time he has been carried away by some idiotic infatuation, but I am in hope that all that will soon be nipped in the bud, and that we shall be made truly happy by hearing of your engagement to him. That would compensate us—but especially my husband—for all we have suffered."

Katherine, feeling the futility of speech, remained silent, and began to move towards the door.

"If I weren't so driven, I should ask you to remain to lunch. But I've got to go over all Netta's things and get them despatched to her. Would you believe it? She made all that long journey with only a dressing-bag."

"She is going to remain in Milan, then?"

"For the meantime, yes. Marchesi is a Professor of the College there, and is well known. Mr. Speed made every inquiry, and the British Consul helped him. Oh, I assure you that we did the thing thoroughly, and will continue to do the right thing."

Katherine retired, considerably comforted in respect of Netta's welfare. Her heart in these days was rather empty and sad. Several weeks had now elapsed since she had had speech with Tom Speed, and it was impossible for her not to feel the blank. He had so long occupied so large a portion of her horizon that life without him seemed purposeless and vain. She was no longer the confidante and partner of his ideals and plans for the future; he had put her outside his life. In this somewhat pensive mood she met Sir Rafe Fletcher, who manifested much pleasure at the meeting, and his friendliness created a little brightness.

"You look very sad, Miss Lundie. I have been watching you for a few moments from the other side of the street. Does life seem to you flat, stale, and unprofitable?"

"Very much so," she answered emphatically. "I've been at West Ferry seeing Mrs. Speed. I suppose you know what had happened in the family?"

"Yes. I had the whole story from young Speed, and I felt very sorry for them. I hope that they have been able to make some arrangement."

"Netta is now Madame—or, rather, Signora—Marchesi," replied Katherine, "and they have left her at Milan. I can't realise it."

"You were intimate friends, I suppose?"

"Oh, no, not intimate, but we have always known one another. Life is rather a tangle just at present, Sir Rafe. I am inclined to quarrel with it."

"I have been in thrall to that mood. I suffered from it badly when first I came home from Rhodesia. A sort of hunger for freedom; that's what you are suffering from."

She smiled a little under his keen, kind gaze.

"Yes. What a thing it is to have lived and to be able always to understand! But you are happy now at Caddam? I should be happy with such big interests and so much responsibility as you have. My life is too narrow."

"You make your father very happy, and that is a great thing," he said quietly.

"Yes, I don't make little of that, but there—I must not be discontented."

"I have wanted to see you lately. I have got the people at the North Lodge."

"Mrs. Durie and her daughter, do you mean?"

He nodded. "They interest me very much. There's a big story behind these two lives, Miss Lundie, and I am busy unravelling it. I'm not sure whether what is coming is not more interesting than what is past."

"How do you mean?" she asked with an eagerness that she could scarcely hide.

"Your friend young Speed is a frequent—almost a daily—visitor at Caddam. It's a very pretty love story."

"It will cause more trouble," said Katherine a little hardly. "If you had heard Mrs. Speed talking about her family to-day you would understand."

"But the girl is not impossible," he suggested.

"From Mrs. Speed's point of view she is utterly impossible."

"Well, her mind may be relieved, for I don't believe that there will ever be a marriage between these two."

"What do you mean by that?" she asked with the same eagerness—an eagerness of which she was secretly ashamed.

" I have not very much ground to go upon, but my private opinion is that the affair is wholly one-sided, and that if it is left alone it will fizzle out. If you get an opportunity of talking to Mrs. Speed about it you might give her that bit of timely warning from a staid old bachelor, who, never having had any affairs himself, has acquired all the guile of a practised looker-on."

Katherine smiled.

" You are very amusing," she said. " It will interest me very much to learn in due time whether you are a true prophet."

CHAPTER XXXII

IN CADDAM WOODS

Tom Speed and Mary Durie walked together in the Caddam woods.

It was a Saturday afternoon in February—one of those soft, exquisite days when we are tempted to believe that winter is really over and gone. A soft haze was over the sky, and through it the sun shone tenderly, a west wind scarcely stirred the leafless trees, and there was that indescribable hush of expectancy in the air which is one of the sure harbingers of spring. The catkins, downy on the willows, were as yet the only courageous exponents of the coming bounty of the year. There were no wild flowers yet, though the spikes of the snowdrops showed here and there a willing bud waiting for the sun.

The Caddam woods from time immemorial had been a spot beloved of lovers. None of the woodland ways were forbidden, and in the green glades and bosky recesses amid the great encircling trees there were many mossy trunks which might have had their tales to tell.

But one pair walked soberly, decorously apart, and there were no tokens to proclaim them lovers. Gloom sat on the young man's brow, and the girl's face wore an expression of a woman whose mind and heart were ill at ease.

"I don't see how we can go on like this," she said in a low voice. "It is horrible."

"But I explained to you at the beginning that it would be a slow process—that there would be mountains of prejudice to remove, and you understood that because of the trouble with my sister we should have to wait even longer."

"I understand all that quite, but—but I was not prepared for this."

She stood still on a mossy bridge that spanned the Caddam burn, and she drew a letter from her pocket. Tom noted its black border, and something told him that the handwriting was his mother's even before he saw it.

She passed it over and, turning away from him while he read it, leaned her arms on the mossy parapet, and looked down into the clear depths of the water playing beneath. It was a beautiful burn, dancing and gurgling over a pebbly bed with many alluring pools in which trout were hidden, and with mossy banks where in their season all sorts of wild flowers found a home.

The letter was dated from Ravenscraig, and it ran as follows :—

"Dear Miss Durie,—You will doubtless be surprised to hear from me—or perhaps you will not. I make my anxiety concerning my son's future my excuse. I am writing without my husband's knowledge, though it is for his sake that I write. His family troubles are bearing heavily upon him, and I fear that if he is grievously disappointed in his only son the consequences are likely to be serious. I do not wish to say one disparaging word of yourself. I have seen you, and I have also heard what an exemplary daughter you are, and how admirable in many other ways. But as a wife for my son—ah, that is a different matter ! Had we been rich people we might have afforded to allow him to have his way ; but, though we have to keep up large appearances, we really are in financial straits. The future, which my son can make or mar for himself, will determine whether our anxieties are to be lessened or increased. I don't know whether he has told you about the terms of his grandfather's will, by which he is left handsomely provided for if he fulfils the conditions attached. One of these is that he marries the young lady to whom he was engaged before he met and became infatuated with you. If he persists in marrying you, and if you hold him to his promise, it simply means ruin to him and the certain loss of all his grandfather's property. I know that young people in love do not top to think of these things, but, in the event of your marriage, the day will surely come when he would look back and know all that he had forfeited. I appeal to you as one woman to another to be generous and let him go. I hardly know how to express myself, but I should like to say that my husband would only too willingly pay any compensation you thought adequate. He is brooding over this, and it is making him an old man. I have humbled myself to you when I might easily have taken a different line. If you would see me I should come—only too gladly—out to Caddam on any day you may appoint. In fact there is nothing I would not do to get this matter amicably arranged and to free my boy so that he may be at liberty to fulfil his honourable engagements and enjoy the great benefits of his grandfather's will.

" I have given you a very full confidence, and I have tried to write kindly and to put myself in your place. And I beg for the like consideration at your hands, or at least for a courteous acknowledgment of this letter.—Yours faithfully,

" Marian Halliwell Speed."

Tom crushed the letter into his pocket and his eyes blazed.

" I will answer this letter," he said a trifle hoarsely. " Look round, Mary."

She was a moment in complying. Then he laid his hand on her shoulder and gently turned her round. The discontented, fretful expression had left her face, her contemplation of the dreaming water having for the moment made her calm.

" It is a hard thing to say of my mother, but there is hardly a word of truth in her letter. I could take it sentence by sentence and tear it to shreds."

" It reads very convincingly," she said quietly.

" She appeals to you at the beginning about my father. He is certainly dull and looks rather ill, but that is solely on account of my sister. I don't believe that he cares a fig about my future ; at least not in the way my mother says. He is a man himself—he knows that outsiders can't tinker with a man's life, that he has got to live it himself."

Mary answered nothing, but, leaning against the mossy parapet, she stared into space.

" What she says about my grandfather's will is true enough in essence, but it is not true that my refusal to fulfil the arbitrary condition will make my parents poor. As a matter of fact, they are the better now by five thousand pounds coming to them through my grandfather's death."

" But your promise to the young lady of whom your mother speaks ? I understand that she means Miss Lundie."

Tom's face flushed, and his hand involuntarily clenched.

" There is no promise, and never was a promise," he cried excitedly. " I will swear it to you on oath, if you like."

" Oh, I don't want any oath," she said slowly. " And besides, it is possible to make promises otherwise than in actual words. There are deeds as binding, though I know that men cannot be held to such."

" But I never was guilty of anything of that kind. I admired and liked Miss Lundie exceedingly, just as I do still, though I haven't seen much of her in the last two months. We have always known each other and been the best of friends. She was my chum, you understand, and we were a lot together, I admit, but never has one word of love passed between us. I have never cared for anybody but you, Mary. You are absolutely the first."

The assurance which, to a woman who truly loved, would have bridged the widening gulf, left her wholly unmoved.

" It is an impossible position. I think we had better part. I could never enter a family who regarded me as your mother does, and so far as you are concerned I should always be thinking of the other woman to whom you were pledged before you met me."

" Then you don't take my word for it, Mary ? You think I'm in the great deception too ? " he asked bitterly.

" I don't know what to think, but that letter is enough. I repeat, I think we'd better part."

Tom stood still, tugging at his moustache, and regarding her in a sort of passionate silence. She had held him at arm's length during the brief and stormy period of their engagement, and her very coolness had acted as a spur to his ardour. He had been accustomed to obtain most things on which he had set his heart, and this woman's reticence, the difficulty in winning anything more than the promise she had given him at the beginning baffled him. He attributed it to every cause under heaven except the true one—that she did not care and had never cared for him as a woman cares who will give up all without a question or a doubt.

" Give me back the letter," she said, holding out her hand.

But he merely shook his head.

" No. I will take it to my mother and ask her to explain, and she will take back every word of it."

" Give it to me. It is mine, and I have to answer it," she repeated quietly.

" No, I will not, and you will not answer it, promise me, Mary, until I give you leave."

She smiled a little inscrutably and turned away. He was very masterful, and she was too weary to insist. After all, what could affect the main issue, already a foregone conclusion ?

He moved to her side, and he tried to draw her to him again and to read her unwilling face.

" I believe myself it's the bit about Miss Lundie that rankles most," he said man-like. " So certain am I of my position with her that I have only to ask her, and she will come or write to you and corroborate what I have said. She's my chum, and she would do that for me with the utmost pleasure."

" I should think it would be a very difficult thing to say to Miss Lundie or to any woman," was all she answered.

" Difficult ! Why should it be difficult ? She's my comrade, I tell you, and she knows what good comradeship means. There would be a lot more of it in the world if men and women would give it a chance to flourish."

" It seems to me," said Mary, after a moment's silence, " that such comradeship as you describe would be a very much better foundation for marriage than the unsatisfactory relations between us. I am unsuited to you in every way. I am not in your station, I should be full of imaginations, and live in an atmosphere of resentment over slights real or imaginary. Whereas if you married Miss Lundie, all your people would be pleased, and you would enter on your grandfather's property. It is certainly the right thing to do."

" But I don't want to do it," said Tom sharply. " It is you I want and will have, and all these obstacles that they're trying to pile up only serve to make me more determined. I'll have it out with my mother this very day, I assure you, and if you don't have an apology I'll know the reason why."

Mary did not look elated at the prospect.

" And I'll get Miss Lundie to come and see you. She'll be only too glad to do that for an old pal. Then you'll understand all that I've been trying to tell you. If I can compass these ends, Mary, will you be more contented in the prospect of the future ? If I did not know how true you were, and how incapable of deceit you were I might on my side begin to fear that there was some one else."

Her face was still turned away, and her hands were pressed against her cheeks so that he did not see the flame which sprang to them.

" Nothing will alter the fact that I'm an unsuitable wife for you—a poor seamstress in a shop."

" Is it Alister ? " he cried jealously. " He comes a jolly sight too much here. I'll tell him to mind his own business."

She smiled at that, meeting his gaze frankly.

" Dr. Alister is the best friend I have in the world. I don't know what we should do without him. He is my comrade, if you like—he has been like a brother during the last nine months, and he has helped us more than we can ever acknowledge or repay."

" Brothers have a way of developing into lovers," he said moodily. " Don't try me too far, Mary. I could be horribly jealous and disagreeable."

" I know that," she answered. " That is why I don't think we are suited to each other. We shall certainly quarrel. We don't think in the same way about anything. Be warned in time."

" I like you because you have the courage of your opinions and because you are not built after the pattern of other women. You can't play bogey to me, Mary. You are the only woman I want for a wife, and the one I mean to have, and I won't wait very long until I have you, either. All these obstacles exist only to be demolished. Just you wait till to-morrow—I'll come back to-morrow triumphant."

Mary showed no elation, but she said no more. Something told her that the march of destiny would neither be hindered nor advanced by any intervention of hers, and that for the nonce they were mere puppets in the game of fate. It was a somewhat dangerous belief for a woman in her position to hold.

She let him babble on, in his usual hot-headed fashion, her own thoughts being far enough away. In the Lovers' Walk in Caddam Woods that spring afternoon, there was only one lover. The heart of the girl was as cold as ice.

CHAPTER XXXIII

AT THE KELPIE'S BRIDGE

MARY parted from her lover on the path near the highway, and he went out by the wicket-gate. She had persistently refused to be seen with him on the roads or in any public place, and she had absolutely forbidden him to come to her place of business.

She was very happy there with an old-fashioned woman of business who had been only too glad to obtain an assistant so much superior to the raw girls that had so long been her despair. An excellent needlewoman, Mary had applied herself to learn the few things in business-life of which she was ignorant, and she had thus become the old lady's veritable prop. She was often behind the counter, too, and she had rapidly made herself mistress of the whole routine of the little shop, which was known to many substantial people in Dundee, who were not to be lured from it by the newer and more showy emporiums springing up everywhere to keep advance with the growing prosperity of the city.

Relieved of sordid anxiety, Mary Durie had yet a good deal on her mind, and it was her private affairs which kept the worried look on her face. In a moment of mental excitement and in pursuit of a most unworthy aim she had engaged herself to Tom Speed—an engagement which she now regretted with all her might. She had told him so quite frankly, but so far he had absolutely refused to take his dismissal. He did not for a moment believe her indifferent, and he attributed all her aloofness to the superiority of her nature. Although the letter of Mrs. Speed had filled her with a natural indignation, she had welcomed it as affording an excellent pretext for bringing the engagement to an end.

She had come out with that determination, but had failed to achieve her purpose. As Tom himself expressed it, he encountered obstacles only to remove them. Instead of proceeding back to the house where her mother was doubtless waiting tea for her, she returned by the way they had come, and she once more found herself on the old bridge across the burn where she spent in reverie so many leisure hours.

She could not help contrasting the circumstances of her present lot with the hardship of the year that was past, and a consuming gratitude to the man who had so kindly and willingly given them such a shelter was for ever uppermost in her mind. Fletcher would have been surprised could he have known how he was enshrined in her heart. They had met not above half a dozen times, and on these occasions only in a most casual manner, though he often dropped into the lodge during the day and had a talk with the mother.

It is possible that had he not been aware of the love-affair between her and Tom Speed he might have timed his visits differently, for the girl certainly interested him. But he had met them more than once in the woods and had done his best to avoid them, though never in any case had he surprised them in any lover-like attitude. Of late he had avoided on Sundays certain parts of his domain lest he should come across them.

Mary sat down on the low parapet and, pulling a strip of moss from the grey stone, began to pick it in pieces. Her brows were knit, her mouth set in quite a harsh line, her whole attitude one of perplexity and discontent.

Fletcher, descending the sides of the ravine with his gun over his shoulder, saw her a good way off, and was quick to note the extreme dejection of her look. He jumped to the conclusion, which in the circumstances was natural, that there had been a lover's quarrel. The temptation to speak to her, however, overcame his natural reluctance to intrude upon her at an awkward moment. She presently heard his foot in the dry bracken and stood up, expecting to behold one of the keepers whom she knew quite well by sight and speech. Fletcher raised his hat and came forward, smiling pleasantly.

"I hardly expected to find you alone on a Saturday afternoon, Miss Durie," he said significantly. "I hope you are quite well? It must be several weeks since I saw you last."

"It is a long time," she answered impulsively.

"Has Speed not been out this afternoon?"

"Yes—he has been here," she replied, and turned her head aside.

Sir Rafe rested his gun on the ground, and, leaning on it, looked at her intently.

"You don't look very happy," he said quietly.

"I don't feel so," she answered, apparently in no way surprised at the remark, and responding to it with transparent frankness.

"It will blow over," he said cheerily. "Such breezes always do. Tom's a bit hot-tempered, isn't he?—a small volcano liable to burst forth in unexpected places, but a first-rate chap."

"Oh, yes, I suppose he is that," she said dully, and then smiled very faintly and made as if to leave the place.

"It is very kind of you, Sir Rafe, to take such an interest is us. My mother is always telling me of your kind visits, and you can see for yourself how much better she is since we came here; she has never been so well since my father left us. The change has saved us from despair. If only I had waited a little!"

"Waited! For what?" he asked gently.

She hesitated a moment, realising how passing strange it was that she should feel tempted to lay bare the misery of her soul to this man, who was a stranger to her, and who stood in the capacity of a master. At any rate her mother was his servant, though his delicate consideration had somtimes led them almost to forget it.

"You look as if you were troubled about something," he said in his kind, frank manner. "If I can help you, I shall be glad,"

She remained silent until he spoke again.

"I think I understand. This—this love-affair of yours is not going smoothly. Pray, don't think I wish to intrude, but Speed, of course, has trusted me so far that I know practically how you stand."

"You could not understand, I am sure," she said, somewhat embarrassed.

"It is his people, of course. They are difficult—they were bound to be, but a little patience and things will come right. They always do if people have only courage to wait long enough."

"It is not their opposition that troubles me, Sir Rafe, though all the objections that you mention certainly exist. I had a letter from Mrs. Halliwell Speed this morning which was very bitter reading for me. But I can sympathise with her. I have tried to explain to—to Tom that it will be much better for us to part."

"Tom did not listen, of course? He never will consent to that, and I question if, feeling as you both do, it would be right to let others spoil your lives."

"That is not the real trouble, Sir Rafe. I want to be free."

He regarded her in the silence of a great astonishment.

"You want to be free! What do you mean? Don't you care for him?"

She shook her head.

"I don't know why I speak to you like this, Sir Rafe," she said, struggling with a most unwonted emotion. "The reason, I suppose, must be that you have been so truly kind and that in all the world I have not one friend."

"Your mother," he said quickly.

She shook her head.

"Mother and I are beginning to understand each other. Since she has grown so much better in health she sees things differently. But if one could only cut out certain portions of life, how much simpler it would be altogether."

"How long is it since your father died?" he asked.

She waited a moment before answering, as if debating with herself what that answer should be. Long battle with fate had robbed this woman in her bloom of her youth, of that sublime unconsciousness and of that careless outlook upon life and its consequences which is the birthright of youth in happier circumstances, and the chief weapon with which it conquers fate.

Fletcher, watching the play of her features, understood more than she imagined.

"My father is not dead," she said in a low voice. "My mother and he were unhappy, and separated."

"Not so uncommon a story, and, as you could not be held to blame for that, you need not look so ashamed."

"It has always been a grief to me, for I love my father dearly. He was a silent, reserved man who could not find that ease in speech which makes life simpler for those differently constituted. He was one of the unfortunates. Nothing that he touched succeeded, and he lost heart—chiefly because my mother, having lost faith in him, took no pains to hide the fact. He left us without even saying good-bye."

"You have heard nothing of him since?"

She shook her head.

"Nothing—and my mother thinks he is dead. It is a reasonable view; for, if he has succeeded, he would surely have written to one of us. It was a terrible tragedy all through, and the beginning of it was that my mother married him while caring for another man."

"And your father knew it?"

"Oh yes. It was common talk in the place where they lived, but my father thought, I suppose, that time would be on his side. But she never changed—nor attempted to change," she said bitterly. Then, after a moment's hesitation, she added—"The other man was George Speed."

Fletcher uttered an exclamation of surprise.

"The father of the man to whom you are engaged?"

She nodded.

"My nature seems to have been warped somehow by all that we have gone through," she said, marvelling more and more at the ease with which she could unburden her soul to this man with the grave face and the kindly eyes.

"I seemed suddenly to become possessed of one idea—namely, to take revenge for the suffering of three people. George Speed was the author of it all. My mother was engaged to him for seven years. She gave him the best days of her youth, and then he left her that he might marry one who would further his worldly interests. It really broke my mother's heart."

"You came here with the intention of "getting even," as men say, with George Speed?"

She bent her head in assent.

"My mother was easy to persuade. I did not know how it was going to be done, but I felt certain that I should succeed. I did not tell her when I went to work in the Eliot Mills that it was with George Speed that I had found employment. I could not trust to her discretion, and to this day she thinks that Tom Speed's name is Halliwell. So you see what a web of deceit I have woven and what a poor, wicked creature I am."

"You would have sacrificed yourself to this very mistaken idea. But since you have been able to speak of it to me, I take it that you have repented, and that you would draw back?"

"Yes," she said with a sigh, "but it is not so easy to do so. I will yet find a way out, however. I must be free."

After a moment she somewhat timidly raised her eyes to his face.

"I hope you do not think too hardly of me, and that you will not, now you know the kind of woman I am, send us away, for in that case my mother would again suffer as she has done in the past. It is your kindness that has tempted me to be honest with you. Now you know the worst."

"It is not very bad," he said with a reassuring smile, "and this desperate tangle will in the end be unravelled. But I feel strangely interested in the story you have told me—in the part particularly which concerns your father. You say that you do not know where he went?"

" He went to America, I think, but we've had no means of knowing what ultimately became of him."

" What was his Christian name ? "

" Charlie."

Fletcher laid his gun across the broad, low parapet of the bridge and took from his pocket a well-filled letter-case out of which he drew an envelope.

" Would you know his handwriting again ? " he asked as he held it towards her.

CHAPTER XXXIV

THE UNEXPECTED

MARY DURIE grasped the proffered envelope with a somewhat unsteady hand. The small, neat characters, a little cramped but very plain and legible, gave her a strange thrill, and her face grew a shade paler.

"It certainly looks like my father's handwriting," she said faintly. "But it would be impossible."

He took it from her hand again, opened out the thin sheet, and showed her the signature—"From your old pal, Charlie Durie."

"Where did this come from?" she asked, beginning to tremble very much.

"From my old quarters, Umtali in Rhodesia, where your father had had considerable success. Do you know what is the substance—the very *raison d'etre* of this letter?"

She shook her head.

"A request that I should go to Edinburgh and seek you out. It is a long letter. See, it contains practically the story you have just told me. We were very intimate in Umtali, and I knew, of course—as we all did—that there was a story behind Charlie's sad face. How strange that I should find the whole mystery solved here at my own door!"

"It is almost unbelievable," she said, and her eyes, with a strange wistfulness in their depths, seemed to cleave to his face.

"I must have known that there was something—some link between us—or how should I have dared to talk to you as I have done? But if my father was your intimate friend, as you say, how was such a thing possible? He was a poor man, though he was not an uneducated one."

"A true gentleman and one of the best chaps that ever lived. He is adored in Rhodesia, and is beginning to be known."

"He ought to have written to us, then," she said hardly—"to me at least, for I loved him dearly, and I tried as well as a wretched girl could to make up to him for the unhappiness of our home."

"He has never forgotten you. He says in this letter that the one hope of his life if to find you, and get you to come out to him. You must not run away with the idea that he has been living on the fat of the land out there, while you have been paying the price here. Success in the Colonies comes very slowly—often not at all—to those who most deserve it. He worked and struggled a long time without recompense, making little more than enough to keep body and soul together. When I left he had not been long in Umtali, to which he had come as a trader to the stores. He has lately had several strokes of luck, and is now in a fair way to make—if not a fortune—at least a competency."

"It seems incredible that you should know my father. It eclipses everything else."

"It may very easily alter everything at least," he assented. "What shall we do about this letter? I got it only to-day, and though I felt nearly certain that the wife and daughter of my old chum were so near, I had to make sure."

"I don't know what to do about it. I don't even know how my mother may take it. And don't you see that however much I might wish to go out to my father, and that though I should welcome it just now—you don't know how eagerly—as a means of escape from circumstances that have become intolerable, I could not leave her."

"We can think it over and afterwards talk it over together. Meantime may I counsel you not to persist in this engagement which can only end disastrously? Be warned by the tragedy of your mother's life."

Her face slowly flushed as she turned to go.

"I don't know how to thank you for your kind interest in us," she said brokenly.

"It is easy to be interested in such a case," he assured her frankly. "I have knocked about the world a good bit, and I have learned to look things straight in the face. I wish to help you. I must help you. The question is how. Would it not be the fairest way to tell Tom Speed the story that you have just told me?"

"It would hardly be fair seeing that it involves other lives, and that it might alter his feelings towards his father. That would be cruel. No, I can't. I must get out of it some other way."

"Meantime, may I answer your father's letter and tell him that I have you at my very gates?"

A smile of surpassing sweetness suddenly illumined her face, and made a marvellous change there.

"If you will."

"And when I have written the letter may I bring it to you, so that you may send him a little message by your own hand?"

The tears started in her eyes.

"How thoughtful you are! But it might be easier if you gave me the address. Then I could write him a separate letter."

"But we must talk about it again," he said eagerly. "Are you to see Speed to-morrow?"

"I don't know. There was nothing said about meeting again when we parted. He was very angry with his mother. I believe he has gone to her now. Very likely he will come."

"Then you could not meet me here to-morrow afternoon?"

She looked undecided, though she was greatly tempted to make tryst there and then, for her heart was beating with a new hope and joy which she did not attempt to analyse. She only knew that in some strange manner the whole aspect of the world had changed.

Seeing her embarrassment, he blamed himself for having inconsiderately caused it.

"I shall call at the lodge some time to-morrow. We can leave it at that."

"Thank you, Sir Rafe," she replied, and her eyes were full of the gratitude that her lips did not utter.

As she walked slowly towards the house she pondered in bewilderment over all that had passed, and yet it all seemed to her to have happened naturally and without any effort to bring it about. The greatest miracle of all was the frankness with which she had been able to speak to this man whom she had known for such a short time, and who was so far above her in social position. Many a one in her circumstances would have trembled in his presence. Woman-like she could not help comparing him with the other man who had swept so stormily into her life, and who now sought to dominate it completely. And though in point of looks and other qualities by which youth is attracted, Tom Speed ought to have stood higher than Sir Rafe, he suffered by that comparison.

Wide experience had taught Fletcher a certain indescribable lore—had given him almost a sixth sense which enabled him to go at once to the heart of things. It was due solely to his ease of manner that in this unusual interview there had been no sense of embarrassment. He had with one word demolished the barriers which a man of lesser mind would have obtrusively maintained between them.

He was more interested in this obscure woman than any of the more highly-born dames who vied with each other for his smiles, and the fact that he had discovered that which would be a genuine bond between them, filled him with a satisfaction which he on his part was by no means anxious to analyse.

Meanwhile Tom Speed had repaired in hot haste across the water to Newport.

The family were now settled there, and the terms upon which they occupied Ravenscraig were known to very few. Mrs. Speed lived on from day to day in the hope that something would happen which would turn the tide in favour of her cherished ambitions. She had schemed in every possible direction—had even planned out how Tom would fulfil the condition by marrying Katherine and by them refusing to live at Ravenscraig—a contingency which had not been foreseen by old George Speed. Some arrangement could doubtless be arrived at whereby his father and mother could continue in residence, while they made a home elsewhere. A little later on she might entertain the Marquise Marchesi; already to one or two of her intimates Mrs. Speed, when speaking of her daughter, had made use of an imaginary title.

Into this atmosphere of personal and unquenchable ambition Tom burst that Saturday afternoon. His father had gone for his usual Saturday game of golf on Monifieth Links, and he was informed that his mother was having tea in the boudoir—as she had christened a small sitting-room in the tower that she had annexed for her own use.

She had been writing to Netta, asking for a great many details of her life in Milan which had not been furnished. The tea-table stood close to her desk, and when Tom entered she was filling out a second cup.

She looked round, surprised to see him, but she spoke in an amiable tone to him, although something warned her that there was trouble in the air. She hardly expected, however, that she would be brought to book so quickly for a letter that she had written only the previous day.

"An unexpected treat," she said almost gaily. "When did we have tea together on a Saturday afternoon? Not since you ceased to play tennis at home. Ring the bell, dear. There, it is just behind you at the door. It was very awkward getting a bell fitted here. Grandpa had evidently not intended the turret to be used except as a lumber-room, or a place from which to view the landscape. Haven't I made it very cosy?"

"I don't want any tea," he said gloomily, as he closed the door with no gentle hand, and then leaned his back against it. His mother stirred her tea and raised the cup to her lips.

"I've been writing to Netta. The letter isn't closed. Would you like to put in a message? She complained last time she wrote that she hadn't had a line from you since Christmas."

For a moment Tom did not answer. His usual hot-headed rashness of speech seemed to desert him for the nonce in face of his mother's admirable ease of manner. It would obviously be impossible to convict her of any mistake in judgment.

She looked across at him, her placid face unruffled, her eyes straight and smiling, completely mistress of herself, albeit she knew now perfectly well that she was about to be called to account for the letter which she had written at that very desk, and after much consideration, had dispatched to Mary Durie at Caddam Lodge.

"You look about as lively as a funeral," she said, with a shrug of her shoulders. "It is to be hoped that my cheerfulness under the most depressing circumstances will be counted to me for righteousness somewhere. I'm astonished at it myself."

"Mother," he said quietly, "why did you write that beastly letter? It was uncalled-for, it was cruel—and a lot of it was untrue."

CHAPTER XXXV

THE DEEPENING SHADOW

MRS. SPEED put down her cup and calmly met her son's irate gaze. It was the first time that the subject which was the bone of contention between them had been mentioned since the old man's death, and she welcomed the opportunity it gave her of clearing the air. Experience had taught her that a scheme is sometimes best furthered, and that the end is most surely gained, by silence and waiting.

These having failed, as she imagined, she was glad to try other methods.

" I wrote the letter—I omit the unpleasant adjective that you have applied to it—because it was my duty."

" It can never be a duty to make two people so bitterly unhappy. If you had known her you never would have written it. She is incapable of all that you would attribute to her, and it is a letter that she will never forgive."

" The forgiveness ought to be exercised on my side," she answered coldly. " How do you think that I or your father can forgive her for what she has done ? "

" She has done nothing. If there is any blame, I am ready to take it. She is a woman in a thousand, and she is too good for me."

" That may be a matter of opinion."

" I understand, of course, that Ravenscraig is the insurmountable barrier, but even if you succeed in parting us the condition will remain unfulfilled all the same. And, mother, it was not playing the game to tell her that I was engaged to Katherine Lundie. That's the bit where I find it hardest of all to forgive. It was a lie."

" You were as good as engaged," she maintained stoutly, " and I happen to know that Katherine thought so too."

She watched him narrowly while she drew this bow at a venture. The statement happened to be nearer the truth than most of her assertions.

" I don't believe it—nothing will ever make me believe that," he cried hotly. " And, after all, I had the best means of judging. Why can't you leave me alone, mother ? "

" I have tried to, and I have been wrong. A nice example we have of the no action policy in the case of Netta. Can't you see how these troubles are aging your father, Tom ? His children, who ought to be a comfort to him now at an age when he should be getting a little rest, are his chief care. He does not sleep at nights for worrying over you and Netta. I think I have got him persuaded to make the best of Netta's marriage, but with you proceeding on the same lines I don't know what the end will be. He'll have a shock of some kind. Then no doubt you will be satisfied."

Tom winced, and, seeing it, she hastened to follow up her advantage.

" Your father isn't a fighter. If he had been you would have been taken in hand long ago, and it would have been ever so much the better for you and for us all. Where we have erred has been in giving you so much of your own way. But I warn you that if you persist in this disastrous affair, you will have to cut yourself off from us. We shall never consent to your marriage or in any way recognise the girl, and we shall be so ashamed of the escapades of our family that we shall have to leave Dundee. I could never face the humiliation of seeing this place given up to a charity, and of all the talk that it would entail. You ought to give these things some thought, Tom. You who are so great on duty to your fellow-men should remember where charity begins."

There was sufficient truth in her words to give them a sting.

" You don't give us a fair chance, mother. If only you would go and see Mary and have a good long talk with her, you would change your mind, I feel sure. And, anyhow, I think it is due to me that you should tell her there was no truth in that part of your letter about Katherine."

"I might go and see her—that would be easy enough—but I shall take back nothing, Tom. I wrote moderately and kindly, and I read the letter many times before I posted it. I have nothing to add to it or to take away. It embodied my views—the views which your father shares and which any sane person would endorse. You have the ultimatum. If you marry this girl, the best thing that could happen to us would be for you to go out permanently to the East and let Edward Mouat come home here to take your place."

This suggestion, which seemed to bear the mpress of careful consideration and arrangement, was merely struck out on the spur of the moment, and she was surprised to see that it went home.

"I must talk to Dad," he said gloomily. "I'm very unhappy, mother. I suppose that doesn't count, however. I really care for this girl, and I shall never care for any one else. And if it's going to make the complete breach you speak of, I think it's very hard. Many a man has married out of his station—as you put it—and found his happiness in that marriage. But you have implanted in her mind the suspicion that I've disappointed another woman. That has changed everything. As I have said, it isn't playing the game. If there's going to be war, let it at least be fair, and do remember that I'm a man and claim my right to live my life as I may think best."

"That idea doesn't blend very well with the first principles of Socialism. I thought its motto was "Each for all." Apply that grand-sounding principle to the acts of your daily life, Tom, and we'll begin to believe in you."

"Mother, will you let me bring her here to see you?" he asked, making a last appeal.

"No. It would be perfectly futile and most uncomfortable. I have already seen her. I know more about her than you think, and my opinion is not likely to change. She has looks of a kind, I admit, but she is sly, Tom. A woman with eyes like hers is capable of any plotting, and I am nearly certain that it is your position that she's after—not you. When she finds that it will be shorn of a good deal of its glory, if you marry her, she may repent in time. If I were you, I should lay the state of affairs very clearly before her. Indeed, you owe it to her. To have misled one woman is surely enough to have on your conscience."

It was a stinging blow, and Tom's hot temper was roused by it. Afraid that he should no longer be able to govern his tongue, he flung himself out of the room, leaving his mother not so much agitated as disappointed at the complete failure of her last move. She did not now believe that any power on earth would prevent Tom from marrying Mary Durie. Her next task therefore must be to make the best of her second defeat.

That she found the disappointment bitter was evidenced by the singularly careworn look which overspread her face. In this brooding temper her husband found her when he returned from his golf at half-past five. By this time Tom had left the house, and nobody knew where he had gone, but his movements were so seldom registered at home, and he gave so little time to his own people, that any fresh vagary scarcely called for remark.

Learning that his wife was in the boudoir, Speed proceeded upstairs to talk to her, declining the offer of tea, which he had already had at the club-house.

She looked round when the door opened, and with a sudden little rush of wifely affection she extended her hand to him.

"So you have come back, dear? Did you have a nice game, and would you like some tea?"

George Speed, touched by the expression on her face, bent down and kissed her. She had been a good wife to him, and throughout Netta's affair she had behaved admirably, showing a courage and resource which he could not emulate.

It is not too much to say that George Speed would never fully recover from the shock of his daughter's clandestine marriage. The youngest of the flock, she was also his dearest. His love was now mingled with an indescribable longing, and with many sharp pangs of apprehension such as visit the heart of a loving father when he knows his ewe-lamb to be out unprotected in a wintry world.

Speed placed no reliance on Marchesi's protestations and promises, and he had done his best to safeguard her so far as money was concerned, but the wound to his affection remained both raw and deep.

" I've just had an earthquake—in fact, the deluge in the shape of a visit from Tom, dear," she said as she drew a chair up. " Sit down and let us talk about it. He's quite determined to marry that impossible girl. And all that we can do now is to resign ourselves, but I do find it hard. What have we done to deserve such treatment at our children's hands ? We have tried to be good to them, but Florrie is the only one in whom we have any comfort. If I had not married her young, she would probably have gone the way of the rest."

" What brought matters to a crisis to-day ? "

She hesitated a moment.

" Well, as a matter of fact, it was a letter that I wrote to the girl."

" Where is she to be found ? " he asked interestedly. " I understood that she had left her old lodgings in Wilson's Court."

" Fancy having a son making love in Wilson's Court ! " she said with curling lip. " Oh, they left Wilson's Court long ago. They're living at the North Lodge at Caddam, on the bounty of Sir Rafe Fletcher, I presume. Don't ask me how they got there. I don't know. I discovered it by the merest accident only yesterday from a letter addressed to her that Tom had inadvertently left on the hall-table. Beith lifted it with mine and came to ask me whether she should post it."

" And she did it ? "

" Yes, of course. Don't look at me as if I had confiscated it, dear, though I may tell you frankly that I was tempted to do it. I followed that letter with one of my own, however, pointing out a few things which might not have occurred to her."

" Useless, Marian," said Speed, shaking his head. " I could have told you that."

" Well, but, dear, every course must be tried while there is a chance to avert catastrophe. But after what he said this afternoon all that is left for us to do is to resign ourselves to the inevitable, wait till Tom consummates his folly by marrying this impossible creature, hand over Ravenscraig to the old men and women, and ourselves retire to hide our diminished heads in the obscurity which we have doubtless deserved, but which I at least will find it very hard to bear."

Tears of genuine mortification rose in her eyes and stood there, wounding George Speed more than he cared to own.

He could not for a few moments command any words. He was casting his memory back across all the years of his family life, trying to solve the problem of how they had completely missed the way in dealing with their children.

" We don't seem to have gained their confidence, Marian." he said with difficulty. " I have been too busy trying to make money, and you have been engrossed with your other ambitions. It's only the people who put their children first that have any real pleasure in them."

" Nay, I don't agree with you," she snapped back rather sharply. " The people who make themselves slaves to their children get all their thanks in one day. But there's a cross strain in ours, George—there's no doubt about that."

He smiled a little dully.

" Write up to Florrie, will you ? and ask her to come down with the bairns for a month or so. We should all be the better for it, and I'll have a word with Tom myself—perhaps to-night. It's well anyhow that we should know exactly where we are standing, and if he's determined to marry her, then we had better try to make the best of it. I don't want to lose the boy altogether, Marian, and we will unless we show him a little sympathy now."

" I can't pretend sympathy, George. I'll never recover from this double disappointment."

" It will be easier when we have accepted the inevitable, wife."

" I told him this afternoon that if he persisted, the best thing that could happen would be that he should go out to Calcutta with her and that we should have Edward Mouat home here. His conduct in this matter is like a thorn in our flesh, but it wouldn't be so aggravating if the pair of them were removed beyond the sea."

George Speed rose somewhat heavily to his feet.

" We can talk things over. Yes. I'll have it out with him to-night, and then we shall see whether we can't establish our family relations on a better basis. All this worry is killing me, Marian. I suppose I haven't the buoyance of spirit that I used to have, and things just at present look very gloomy to me."

"I don't wonder at that! You don't look well. I rubbed all that into Tom, I do assure you, but he's so infatuated about that creature that he can't see an inch beyond her. All his duty and responsibility elsewhere are lost sight of. As I told him, he ought to start fair with the first principle of the Socialism that he's so keen about, and remember that charity begins at home."

George Speed smiled a curious little detached smile as he left the room.

His wife was very clever—she would never miss the point of an argument, but she was undoubtedly hard. It is not cleverness which makes the home and binds its inmates in indissoluble bonds. It is love that rules the world.

CHAPTER XXXVI

THE GHOSTS

In the little smoking-room downstairs George Speed kept some private papers in a lock-up cabinet that had been brought over from The Rowans. He lit a pipe when he entered the room, and taking his keys from his pocket opened the door. In one of the drawers at the back was a packet of old letters which prudence had often prompted him to destroy, but somehow he had never found courage sufficient for the task.

They were held together by a band of broad elastic. That they had not often been taken out and had not been tampered with was evidenced by the snap which the brittle band gave when it was touched. The letters, loosely held, fell at his feet in a shower. He stooped and picked them up, and he opened one or two at random.

All were in the same writing—a small, rather precise woman's hand, not educated, but rather laboured, as if she had made great efforts to make the performance worthy of the person for whose eyes it was destined. The terms in which they were couched brought a dull red flush to his cheek, and something told him that he ought not to have kept them—that even now their proper and final resting-place was the fire. He looked at it smouldering within the bars, and once more at the letters which he had gathered up.

Only a mere sentiment now bound him to the past. The flame of that old passion had been long since quenched in the prose of workaday life. But most men and women have some inner shrine from which even those who walk and sit with them are shut out. The sentiment which had never had fitting scope in George Speed's life was epitomised in that bundle of old love-letters, and he was loth to destroy them. There was no disloyalty to his wife in his regard for them, and he put them back—a little tenderly, perhaps—in their place, telling himself that he would choose some more convenient season for their destruction—that very night, perhaps, after the rest of the household had gone to bed.

As he turned the key in the cabinet a sudden impulse came to him, and at that moment the clock struck six. Two persons were to dine with them an hour later than usual that night to suit the convenience of a guest who was coming from a considerable distance and would stay the night. He had time, if he was expeditious to go to Lochee and be back to dress for dinner at half-past eight.

Unaccustomed as he was to act on impulse, he did not hesitate on this occasion, but left the house as he was, only putting a covert-coat over his golfing suit and a tweed cap on his head. He was fortunate in not being delayed on the cross journey, and a good cab-horse took him up the Caddam Road at a quick pace. He got down about a hundred yards from the gate at the end of the road and told the cabman to wait for him. Then he strode up to the little lodge, from whose front window a bright light shed its radiance across the road.

For once he had acted simply on an impulse similar to those which Tom had permitted to govern so many of the actions of his life.

The big gates were closed, but the wicket yielded to his touch, and he passed within hesitating for a moment in the little porch.

What should he say to the mother and to the daughter, and how would Helen Drever receive him after all these years? That she was Helen Drever—the woman whose letters he had kept and whose image had never been wholly effaced from his heart he felt absolutely certain. His hand went forth with a certain unwillingness and lifted the knocker, letting it fall again with a short, sharp tap. He heard a chair being pushed back, a somewhat slow step crossing the little room within, and then the door was opened.

"Who is there?" asked Mrs. Durie in a sharp, rather nervous voice, and though she stood with her back to the light he could discern her features well.

"If you will let me come in, Helen, you won't need to ask the question twice."

He half expected her to scream, but she remained quite silent and stood aside, motioning him to enter. Then with a hand that was wonderfully steady she closed the door, and they faced one another in the cheerful atmosphere of the little living-room which was really a home.

Helen Drever had often pictured some possible meeting with her old lover, and she had even worked herself up into excitement over it. The actual happening found her perfectly calm.

He put his cap on the table, and he looked at her with an indescribable sadness. Her face—her aged, somewhat broken looks, told their tale. As usual, the woman had paid the heavier price.

"You are greatly changed, Helen," he said quietly. "And we're both growing old."

"Won't you sit down?" she said with difficulty. "I don't know why you are here. My daughter has gone to Dundee, and I am alone. Why have you come?"

He shook his head.

"I don't know. I learned that you were here, and some impulse brought me. Won't you sit down? You are tired, perhaps—indeed, you look it."

The tenderness of his tone was almost more than she could bear.

She trembled a little as she walked to a chair and sat down. She had no questions to ask, she could not analyse the strange, dull feeling at her heart. There was no rush of fond elation at the sight of the man whom she had never forgotten. She realised in a moment that everything had changed, that above all Time had had his revenge, and that the car of Destiny had not stayed for an old love story from which all the romance had fled.

The lover of her youth was gone for ever. She remembered him as a slim, handsome youth—all that a girl's heart could most readily idealise. He came to her now with hair grey at the temples and the cares of the world writ large on his somewhat haggard face.

"I want to know how long you have been in Dundee?" he asked.

"Not long—only a few months."

"I heard that you had made a home in Edinburgh."

"I went there when I married Charlie Durie. I never had a home there," she answered, telling him the whole truth without a moment's hesitation.

"How long have you been a widow?"

"I'm not a widow. Charlie left because he was unfortunate and because we didn't get on. He went to South America, but I have never heard of him since."

"And you have had a hard struggle?"

"Oh yes, and bad health. I have never had any health since I left Rattray, and I have been dependent on my daughter. It is she who has had the struggle."

"It was the very irony of fate that she should come to work in my mills, Helen. You should not have allowed that—you might for old times' sake have appealed to me in a different way."

"I never thought of appealing to you," she said truly enough. "And Mary never asked my leave to go to your mills. In fact, I never knew that it was in your mills that she worked until she had left them."

"I suppose these things are taken out of our control, but it seems strange that she should have been there only two short weeks and yet long enough to alter the whole outlook on life for so many. I suppose you have encouraged this affair with my son. There is a kind of rough justice about it which prevents my being astonished that it has all come about in such a strange way."

She stared at him uncomprehendingly.

"Your son? I have never seen him!" she exclaimed. "What can you be talking about?"

"He comes here often, and I understand from my wife that he is engaged to your daughter. So history repeats itself, Helen, and we're after all little more than the puppets of fate."

"The young man who comes here, who has been so good a friend to us, who calls himself Mr. Halliwell, is your son, George Speed!" she said slowly.

"It is my son who comes here, though why he should have introduced himself to you in his mother's name I am at a loss to understand."

"It was Mary who told me at the beginning—the first time I saw him—that his name was Halliwell."

"I am glad that he did not tell you so himself," he said grimly. "There could be nothing very honourable in presenting himself to you under a false name."

"Oh, there isn't anything false about him! He is a splendid fellow! Your son, George, and my daughter! Could the irony of fate go further than that or could anything in this world more unlikely ever have happened?"

He regarded her very gravely.

"As I have said, we are the puppets of fate. This will make trouble, Helen, at my home, but I own it is not undeserved. I treated you badly, and I am here very late to make what reparation is possible. I shall not oppose Tom's marriage with your daughter. I have come here to tell her so. Where is she?"

"Gone into the town," repeated Helen Drever faintly, almost as if overcome by the magnitude of her astonishment. "Your son and my girl, George! I can't take it in!"

"It has not been in our hands, Helen," he said in a low voice as he passed his hand across his forehead like a man who is perplexed. "There will be trouble before this affair can be amicably settled. My wife had other views for her boy, but he will be stronger than I was. He will take his own way, and it will be better for himself in the end."

When she did not reply he regarded her steadily for a moment, wondering at the expression of her face. Much of the beauty that in her early youth had been so rare was gone, and discontent had left its dull, peevish lines on her face. The pathos of a life that had failed of realising all its ideals was there, and the sharpness of a great remorse was his.

For he was guilty. His treachery had robbed this woman of hope and love in the spring-time of her days, the result being that all the seasons following were barren and empty.

"Tell me," he said suddenly, "does your daughter know of the old acquaintance between us?"

"Yes, she knows the whole story."

"Ah, then, I can comprehend her motive in introducing Tom to you under a false name. His is not so easy to understand. I hope she has not told him the story. I have had very little joy in my children, Helen. Somehow things have missed the mark with me nearly all my life."

"You don't look very happy," she said gently, and all the bitterness that had so long corroded her heart died out of it for ever. And with it, too, there fled the last shred of the romance which she had hugged to her breast, whose memory she had suffered to poison existence not only for herself but for those of her own household, and whose indulgence had driven her husband forth into the wilderness. In that strange, searching moment clearness of vision returned to Helen Drever, and she became once more a woman strong and purposeful and not afraid to speak her mind.

She leaned her elbows on the table and looked across at her old lover without so much as a shadow in her eyes.

"You have blamed yourself and made yourself miserable, I can see, through these years, thinking about me while I never dreamed that you even remembered what had been between us. It was cruel at the time, George. I will not seek to say otherwise, because it would be a lie. But I too have been wrong and wicked all through, grieving and grumbling when I might have made the best of what I had. I drove a good man away from my side, robbed my girl of her father, and cut both her and myself adrift from all that counts in the lives of women. For, whatever they may say, it is only matters of the heart that count with them—these are their whole life."

"With some only, Helen," he corrected. "But notwithstanding all you say, I have been to blame too. I have come here to tell you that my father was always sorry on your account, and that one of his last thoughts was for you. He laid upon me a charge to seek you out, and see that you wanted for nothing. I have been a long time about it, Helen, but I was afraid of what the search might reveal."

She smiled sadly.

"And now time has stepped in and joined our lives once more. For all that i past, George, I do forgive you, if you are seeking my forgiveness. It may be that it was best after all that we should part, for we might not have been happy together. But my girl must not suffer in the same way. That is the only reparation I seek."

"She shall not. That is what I am here for—to tell her so. As I have said, there will be trouble at home, but to-night I shall tell my wife the whole story. There comes a time when all the barriers have to be swept aside and when everything has to be staked on one chance. Perhaps my chance is frail. My wife has had many disappointments. She takes different views of life from me, but she has been a good wife to me, and I would not hurt a hair of her head if I could avoid it."

"Perhaps it would be better not to go back on the past, George," said Helen Drever with the new clearness of vision that had come to her, showing the contingencies that might arise in the case. "Could you not just tell her that you will permit the marriage, and that if she would please you she will try to make the best of it? I am no fool now, George, though I have very often behaved like one. And I understand that it must be a disappointment to a lady like your wife to accept my daughter as a wife for her son."

He rose somewhat heavily to his feet.

"No, I'll tell her the whole truth. I will trust her generosity and hope for a happy ending to our anxieties. Then you will be cared for and provided for. My father left a thousand pounds for the purpose."

"I couldn't touch it. If it should come that I see my Mary happily married to your son, I shall go out into the world and search for my husband, and if he is willing to renew our union, I shall try to make up to him for all the suffering I caused him."

"Through me," groaned George Speed, still stung by the scorpions of remorse.

"No, no! I took exaggerated views," she cried, as eager now to excuse as she had formerly been to blame him. "Don t look so wretched. Let us bury the past and try to make the best of what is left."

CHAPTER XXXVII

THE PRICE OF FRIENDSHIP

SHE held out her hand to him, and after a moment he took it and pressed it; but the gloom did not leave his face.

Her kindness was harder to bear than reproaches would have been, and once more memory was busy among the old days on the pleasant Rattray braes in the summer of his life.

He had thrown away the sweet kernel of happiness and had been starving on the husks all these years. The bitterness of unavailing regret was his.

"You will leave this to me, Helen," he said quietly. "This is my affair, understand, and I shall arrange it in my own time and way. But of this you may be assured. Your daughter shall not suffer. That will be my one care."

"Mary is strong-minded," said Helen with a sigh. "She has always treated me like a child. Of—of course, I have behaved like one, but she is also proud, and she will not enter into any family where she is not welcome. Your wife will have to come here, I know. Mary will not go to her."

"That shall be my affair," he repeated in the quiet, determined voice of a man who sees the straight path and will pursue it at whatever cost.

"Take my advice, and say nothing to your wife about the past," she persisted. "It is dead, and it is always a mistake to go back on what can't be undone. She might take it ill, George, and give you—give you no peace."

"I have had very little of that," he said rather sadly. "And to tell the simple truth will, I think, be but justice to her and the best way of clearing the ground."

She shook her head in dissent.

"I am a woman and I know how a woman feels about these things. Say nothing."

At that moment the handle of the door was turned, and Mary entered with her little market-basket on her arm.

The sight of her former employer standing at the table and of the expression on her mother's face so astonished her that she nearly dropped her basket.

"Mary, this is Mr. Speed, whom you know already. He has been so kind as to come out and see me for old times' sake."

Mary did not know what to say. She perceived from the manner of both that the veil had been lifted and that they had arrived at an understanding that had made her mother look a different woman. Speed took up his cap, and as he turned to go took Mary's hand and raised it to his lips. Then he passed out, her mother following him to the outer door of the little porch, where she heard her say "Good-bye. God bless you!" in a tone which indicated that some deep well of tenderness and compassion had been opened.

The door was shut, and after a moment Helen Drever returned to the little living-room and sat down.

"A strange thing has happened, Mary," she said quietly. "I have looked into my own heart."

"Have you, mother; and what did you find there? Mostly we women are afraid to do that."

It was a curious answer, but Helen Drever, full of her own concerns, did not notice it.

"I found there the ashes of an old passion which I have been trying all these years to keep alive. I suppose I cared for him once; but that was long ago, and now I have merely pity for him as a man who has had little happiness in his life—less even than I have had in mine, though the fault was my own."

The spirit of this deliverance, so opposed to the usual selfish view taken by her mother of her own acts and of all the troubles that had darkened her life awoke in Mary a fresh surprise.

"What did he come for, and how did he find you out?" she asked bluntly.

"I did not ask him how he found us, but I suppose that his son has told him. I suppose you had your own reasons for withholding your sweetheart's name from me, Mary, but it would have been better perhaps had I known all along."

"I did not think so. I was afraid. Did Mr. Speed come here, to-night, then, after a talk with Tom?"

"He did not say anything about that, nor did I ask him. But he will make no objection to your marriage. It is very strange how time equalises things. You will be Mrs. Speed to make up for what I missed. Well, I think I am pleased since you are to be happy with him. He is a well-disposed young man, and has been most kind and respectful to me, never hinting at the difference in our stations. I hope, my dear, that you will have the happiness in life that I have missed. I think he is one to make a woman happy. There is no hardness in his nature, and he has sympathy—which few men have—with a woman's point of view."

Mary was silent for a moment. She had been fighting her own battle during her solitary walk to the shopping centres, and she had almost come to a decision. But in the interval matters seemed to have been lifted out of her hands, and she did not know whether she should give her mother her full confidence or withhold it till a more convenient season.

"I suppose that Mr. Speed knew of the letter I received this morning from his wife," she said in order to gain a little time for reflection.

"He did not mention it. What did she write about, and how?"

"It was not a kind letter, mother. I gave it to Tom, and he took it away with him. She mentioned all the objections, and carefully explained that she at least would have nothing to do with me. In the face of such opposition from his family I would not marry him, though he was the best man in the world, mother. I have too much pride."

"But Mr. Speed will put everything right. He said that he would, and he meant it."

Mary looked dubious.

"He may think that he will, but it is not so easy to do so. No, no; it will be better for us all—as I said to Tom this afternoon—that everything should come to an end. I was wrong from the beginning in encouraging him. I ought to have known that nothing but trouble would come of it."

"But if you cared for him, Mary," said her mother in a low voice, for these are subjects that Scotswomen do not easily discuss, and, when necessity arises, it is done shamefacedly, and as if they were doing something wrong.

"But that's the crux of the whole matter, mother," replied Mary unexpectedly. "I don't care for him. I never have cared, and I never will care."

"Then what did you mean by leading him on? He is very fond of you. You can see it in his eye and hear it in the very tones of his voice. It was wicked and cruel, Mary, and I don't understand it!"

"The temptation came to me in a desperate moment, when I had been unjustly treated at the mills by—as I thought—his father's orders. My sole desire was for revenge, but I did not know what a difficult path I was preparing for myself. I thought that I could be doubly revenged on them—for what George Speed had done to you, and for what I had suffered through them. But—as I have said—I didn't understand how hard it would be or what horrible complications would arise."

Helen Drever stood staring fixedly at her daughter's bowed head, overwhelmed by the discovery of the wheels within wheels in this life-story of which she was the central figure.

"Mary, this is terrible, and you must now at any price be honest with the young man. I know what it is to marry without love—what a hell upon earth for both. This dissimulation must be ended here and now."

"Yes. The engagement must come to an end, as I told him this afternoon at Kelpie's Bridge. I told him that now I would never marry him after his mother's letter."

"And what did he say to that?"

"What did he say! Nothing at all—he wouldn't even listen. And he left me in a towering rage with his mother, saying that he would make her take back her words. I am so tired of it all. I should like to run away somewhere and be at rest."

"There won't be any rest, Mary, for either of us until this thing is settled on the right lines."

"In her letter Mrs. Speed said another thing which rankles in my soul—that Tom was engaged to another girl. I think she meant Miss Lundie, though she did not say so, and that he has broken faith with her for my sake. How am I to extricate myself from the difficulties in which I have involved myself? You must help me."

The tables were now strangely turned. She who had hitherto led and governed was now a suppliant for help and guidance. She had tried the crooked path and found it stony ground.

"The same story over again," Helen Drever said in a breathless whisper. "Life is a queer thing—almost it makes me afraid," she added, more to herself than to her daughter. "Listen, Mary. When your sweetheart comes here again you must leave him to me. I will help you out of this tangle, but it must be once for all. You have had a terrible example before you, and you must profit by it. If only your father were here to help me! He had a wonderfully clear judgment, and a reasonable way of looking at things that few men or women have, which amounted almost to second sight."

Mary flung up her head, not certain that she heard aright.

Again she hesitated. Was this the right moment for divulging the other harmless secret that she shared with Sir Rafe Fletcher? Her mother's tone seemed to indicate that she would welcome news of her husband's whereabouts. Yet Mary hesitated, greatly fearing to make some fresh mistake.

"Something will perhaps happen to make a change in our lives, mother, so that we can get away from all these worries. We were far happier in our little flat in the Causewayside of Edinburgh, though times were hard. We had at least no troubles of this kind."

She rose, unbuttoned her jacket, and passed into the inner room to put it away, and to remove her boots. She felt really unhappy, and her mind was strangely full of Katherine Lundie. She remembered the expression of her face on that day when she had leaned from the carriage to speak so kindly to her. She could have wished that she herself had been less aggressive—not so swift to throw back the proffered kindness in her teeth.

It may well have been that the second sight spoken of by her mother was hers at that moment, for Katherine was simultaneously going through another sharp trial.

When Tom left the house after his interview with his mother he returned to Dundee and made his way to Albion Terrace. He had not seen or spoken with Katherine for a long time, and he suddenly realised that he missed her out of his life. He needed a friend. If the old bond of friendship counted for anything surely Katherine would not fail him now. He was admitted at once, though the servant, who had been long in the house, looked surprised to see him. His long absence had naturally occasioned remark among those who were interested, and who had always expected a happy marriage to be the fitting crown to such close intimacy. Katherine, however, had comported herself so well that none of them could say that she was fretting over it.

He was shown at once to the drawing-room, where Katherine was at work precisely as she had been on the last occasion on which they had talked intimately together. Tom greatly admired her at that moment. How could he help it? She was the very embodiment of gracious womanhood. Such was her repose of manner, her harmony of colour, her perfection of detail.

Disappointment of heart would never tempt Katherine to forget her duty to others or her duty to herself. She continued to give of her best to the conduct of her daily life, and to those whom she loved and who loved her.

She was taken by surprise when he entered, having made use of his old privilege to come unannounced into her drawing-room, but she rose to receive him with a quiet smile of welcome.

"This is like old times, Tom," she said pleasantly. "I hope you are very well."

"Yes, thank you. It's good of you to be pleased to see me. I have been very remiss lately, but I hope you have understood."

"At least I haven't misunderstood," she replied, "and that is something. Papa is dining at Caddam to-night. Sir Rafe has a bachelor dinner. Will you stay and keep me company ?"

"I can't. We have guests at home. I'm here, Katherine, only because I'm in trouble. I want your help. Was I right to come to my old chum ?"

He sat down near her and he leaned forward in his chair in order that he might see her face under the lamp-shade.

"Yes, of course. Why not ?" she asked cheerfully. "I am just the same as I always was."

"Then, I must tell you everything. I'm engaged, Katherine, to that girl whom we spoke of long ago, and whom you have seen. She used to work in the mills."

"Yes, I know, and she is now living with her mother at Caddam Lodge."

"Well, my mother, of course, is furious. You can understand that, so I needn't expatiate upon it. She wrote a letter only last night to Mary, telling her a parcel of lies. It's a hard thing for a chap to say about his mother, but I must tell you the whole truth. You can imagine the kind of things that my mother would say in a letter of that sort. But she didn't keep your name out of it, Katherine—she told Mary that you and I had been engaged and that I had deserted you. You can understand, of course, what effect such a statement would have on a woman like my sweetheart. I have denied it, of course, but she isn't convinced. May I ask you to help me, Katherine ? Reduced to cold words it seems beastly, but you know what I mean."

"Yes. I know quite well that you want me to write to Miss Durie and also to deny the charge."

CHAPTER XXXVIII

CRUEL AS THE GRAVE

AFTER her husband had left the room Mrs. Speed sat still, thinking over the events of the afternoon. She feared that there was now little chance of any of her cherished hopes being realised. Tom had completely broken away from the trammels of her authority. Her face grew sharp in outline and her mouth exceeding bitter as she pondered on the significance of this. She had been in too much haste to remove her household goods to Ravenscraig ; great would be her humiliation when she should have to leave it. She felt that she had been hardly dealt with—that she had not deserved so many crushing defeats.

Her musings were disturbed by the entrance of Beith with a telegram.

" Wait a moment. There may be an answer required."

She tore open the envelope, looked surprised, then distinctly relieved.

" It is from the gentlemen who were to dine and sleep here to-night. They can't come owing to the sudden illness of Captain Dunn. Tell cook that she needn't make the entrée, and that we shall dine at the usual hour if she can be ready."

" Yes, ma'am. Can I take the tray now ? "

" Yes ; and tell Jessie not to light the bedroom fire. I am just as well pleased, Beith, that the gentlemen are not coming. I don't feel in the humour for guests to-night."

" No, ma'am," murmured Beith respectfully, and deftly gathering the things on to the tray she carried it out. Her mistress left the room almost immediately after to seek for her husband. But she did not find him in any of his usual haunts. She came at last to the little sanctum where he often spent the interval between dinner and tea when he happened to be in the house.

The odour of his cigar was there still, but he was gone. She turned to leave the room when her eye was arrested by an envelope lying on the floor—a small, narrow envelope of a shape that she had never seen. She stooped to pick it up, and she observed that it was directed to her husband at an address which she remembered to have been that of his father's first house in Dundee. Curious, but in no way jealous or apprehensive, she opened it and withdrew the letter. It contained only a few lines written on a half-sheet of paper, and at first sight these seemed to her incoherent, but she quickly realised that she was reading an old love-letter. She read it through twice, and then she studied the envelope with a strange expression on her face. It bore the postmark of Rattray, and a date in September twenty-seven years before.

Twenty-seven years before ! And where had it come from that on this day of all days it was lying in her husband's room ? She smiled a little hardly and read it again. Then she stood still and looked about her vaguely, pondering the thing in her mind, and trying to arrive at some explanation of it. That the letter had been treasured was evident from its being so clean and well-pressed ; but how had it come there ? Her restless eye presently fell upon the cabinet, the keys of which her husband always carried about with him, and into which she had never troubled to look. Nor had she ever cared to inquire what it contained. She had never doubted him or suffered one jealous pang. In his haste and preoccupation, George Speed had left his keys in the door of the cabinet, though he had turned the lock. His wife stepped across and threw it open. A number of documents, docketed and numbered, were in the pigeon-holes. The deep, narrow drawer under these had another key in it which she turned without a moment's hesitation, and there lay the bundle of letters, loose as Speed had deposited them after they had escaped from their elastic band. She lifted the packet in her hand and carried it to the window, where, though the evening was now closing in, the light was still good.

There were a great many letters—certainly not fewer than fifty or sixty, all written apparently by the same hand. She deliberately sat down with them in her lap and began to read. And for the first time in her life she learned that her husband had had a love affair before he met her, and that he had been absolutely pledged to another woman.

The letters were such as Marian Halliwell even in her girlhood could never have penned. They showed an unselfish devotion—an utter surrender which is only possible to the most womanly type of woman. No calculation of marriage had in these days entered into Helen Drever's thoughts. She would cheerfully have followed her lover to earth's utmost end without a question or a doubt.

Contempt and anger were strangely tempered by a feeling of envy as she read, and very soon growing weary, she put them down. They were monotonous—yes, as the outpourings of an affectionate heart must ever be to a critical and casual onlooker. It grew quite dark in the room, but when the maid came to the door to draw the blinds and see to the fire her mistress dismissed her.

" I'm resting a bit in the dark, Jessie," she said in a quite natural voice. " I'll ring when I want you to come up."

Only one fact concerning these letters was of immediate interest to George Speed's wife—the fact that he should have kept them all these years, and that he had evidently been reading them lately.

It was strange, unheard of, inexplicable—the very last thing that she would have expected of him who showed so little sentiment in his ordinary life. She forgot that the atmosphere which she had created had never been favourable to sentiment and that she herself had often laughed at it. But she was conscious now of a very real and deep pang.

Not wishing to be found there when her husband should return, she returned the letters to their place in the cabinet and went upstairs.

The evening gown that she had intended to wear was lying across the chair in her dressing-room, where the fire burned cheerily. She shivered a little as with sudden cold, and drawing in a chair, sat very close to the fire, astonished at the dull misery and resentment in her heart.

Her nature was cold, but it was also proud, and the idea that she had had a rival all these years was intolerable. Her imagination, actively at work for the first time over a purely personal experience, was quick to fill up gaps and to rear mountains of impossibility out of the slender evidence in her hands. Probably he had been writing to the woman—perhaps seeing her through all these years ; and it was certain he must still regret her, else why keep the old letters which had long since fulfilled their purpose ?

All the anguish of the jealous woman was hers, and it came to her swiftly, falling upon her like the stroke of a two-edged sword and causing her suffering such as she had not dreamed of as possible to be meted out to her.

By the time Speed returned to his home his wife had wrought herself up to a pitch of nervous wrath and excitement which boded ill for his domestic peace.

She heard his foot on the stairs, and he came into the room without a moment's hesitation.

" So they're not coming, Marian. Poor old Dunn ! It's hard on him to be taken ill in a hotel like that. Did you wire back ? "

" No, I didn't," she answered, and pushing back her chair she turned to look at him. Then he saw something in her face which staggered him.

" You're ill yourself, Marian," he said anxiously.

" Not in body, but in mind, George," she replied. " You can ask yourself, if you like, what's the cause."

He did not ask himself. An unerring intuition told him exactly what had occurred—even before he had fumbled in his pocket for the keys that were not there.

" You have been looking over these old letters, Marian," he said in a low voice. " And sorry reading they make after all these years. A man is a fool to keep such truck about him, and no man ever can give a satisfactory reason why he does keep them."

" The reason is quite obvious—he hasn't forgotten the person who wrote them," she answered hardly. " Coming on the top of all the rest of my troubles, the knowledge that you have never cared for me all these years, George, and that our marriage has been a mere mockery is far from pleasant."

" Don't be unjust, Marian," he said quietly. " I grant that it was disloyal to you to keep these letters and that I was a fool over them ; but I give you my word of honour that I have never written to the woman who wrote them since I married you."

" It's hard to believe it. So many of us are deceived," she said quietly.

" But you have not been, my dear," he answered with a great gentleness. " It is strange that this should have happened to-night, because I was coming to you with a story, praying and hoping that you would take a kindly view of it, and that after you had heard it we might be better friends than we have ever been."

She made no answer, but drew in her chair again and fixed her dull eyes on the dancing flames. Speed had never seen her in such a mood, and it baffled him. They had had many family jars throughout which she had usually carried herself high-handedly. He felt disconcerted now.

" Listen, dear," he said gently.

" Don't call me dear," she interrupted, with an impatient toss of her head.

" I must go back a long time," he continued patiently.

" Yes ! Right to the time these letters were written. You were making love to two of us at the same time."

" I was not. The moment you promised to marry me I gave up writing to Helen Drever. If you had taken the trouble to read the letters carefully and had compared the dates you would have discovered that for yourself."

" It hasn't got much to do with it, anyhow."

" It has everything to do with it—it shows that I tried to do my duty by you."

" Tried—but did not succeed."

" You remember the terms of our engagement and to what a limited extent sentiment entered into it. You told me then that you believed the happiest marriages were those based on mutual interest and that sentiment spoiled everything. There never was any love-making between us before we were married, and very little after it. You adhered to your part of the contract, and so have I to mine. I have been absolutely true to you through all these years, Marian, whether you believe it or not."

" But you can't say you have never thought of the other woman. The very fact that you have kept her letters proves that you have, and how am I to be certain that you have never seen her ? "

" I can only give you my word, Marian. She married soon after I did ; since then I have never heard from her or seen her till to-night, but I have come from her now."

CHAPTER XXXIX

THE WHIRLWIND

SHE threw up her head and looked at him almost haughtily.

"You dare to stand there and tell me that you have come from her now! Has she been in Dundee all these years, then, and have you been visiting her regularly?"

"You have the right, I suppose, to say such things, Marian, but do give me a chance to explain. The woman who wrote these letters and to whom, I frankly confess, I was engaged before I met you is the mother of the girl that Tom is running after and that he is determined to marry."

"And has she always lived in Dundee, and have you known this all along?"

"No. I only suspected it shortly after the girl came to our employment, because her appearance reminded me of her mother. I have been certain of it only for a few weeks."

"It is horrible!" she cried indignantly. "And I don't know what to believe."

"We were brought up in the same village of Rattray, and after I left it and we were married, she married a chap of the name of Durie and removed with him to Edinburgh. I heard that only through a traveller who came from Rattray and who knew most of the gossip about the folk. Her husband isn't dead, but for some reason or another they are living apart."

"Probably he discovered that he had been deceived—as I have done—and couldn't endure it."

"It wasn't that. He knew perfectly well that we had been sweethearts, for he too belonged to Rattray. But they didn't get on, and he went abroad. About six months ago, as I understand, the mother and her daughter came to Dundee."

"Doubtless with the idea of seeing you again," she snapped hotly. "And probably she wrote, appealing to you for old times' sake."

George Speed looked at her gravely. The task which he had set himself was more difficult than he had anticipated. His attempt to clear the whole ground under his feet in order that his home might be built on the sure foundation of peace was now complicated by a woman's jealous fears. And the set, hard expression on her face indicated that she would not be easy to convince.

"Marian, I entreat you to believe that I am telling you the absolute truth. I have never until to-day seen Helen Drever, and I should not have seen her now had it not been that I wanted to get at the bottom of this affair of Tom's."

The mention of her son's name gave Mrs. Speed another opening.

"I can't think why things are like this—why I have to be so punished. Tom must be told of this entanglement, and he will surely now see how impossible it is that this preposterous engagement can continue. Will you tell him or shall I?"

"I shall tell him myself," replied George Speed heavily. "He shall know the whole truth, though I question very much whether it will make any difference to him. It might even make him keener on fulfilling his promise. You know what his ideas of justice are."

"And you would encourage him in it. You would make him help to pay off old scores," she said sourly.

Speed answered nothing. Some such thought had undoubtedly more than once occurred to him, but, presented to him in his wife's cold, hard tone of voice, it assumed the character of a fresh offence.

He leaned against the mantelpiece and bent his head on his arm.

His attitude indicated hopelessness—despair of ever arriving at any satisfactory understanding. It did not, however, move his wife to compassion—her own wound was yet too new and hard to bear. Yet in spite of her hard looks and words Marian Speed was nearer being a real womanly woman at that moment than she had ever been in her life. The innermost recesses of her heart were stirred, and she realised the depth of her love for her husband in a manner which astonished herself—as it would have astonished him had he understood. He believed at that moment that her good will was alienated from him for ever. He had blundered, and Helen had been right after all.

"What are you going to do, then, Marian?" he presently asked in the voice of a man who would give up unequal strife. "I have told you the whole—the absolute truth. You don't believe me, so there is no use in saying any more. But I don't for a moment suppose that you'll let it end here."

"If Tom persists in marrying that girl, and if her mother remains in Dundee, I shall leave it," she said calmly.

"Where would you go?" he asked helplessly.

"To Colchester to Florrie, or out to Milan to Netta. Oh, I shall find a place, and I believe that you would be glad to see me go, George. You have never cared for me; now I know it. I attributed your coldness to your Scottish ways, but these letters have proved to me that even the Scots know how to love and to express themselves too. The tone of your letters would be similar. I suppose that she has kept them too?"

"I did not ask her, but she will will tell you, I don't doubt, if you go to her," he said, stung to self-defence by the goading accents of her tongue.

There was a moment's silence.

Suddenly he flung up his head and looked her straight in the face.

"I want to be done with this thing here and now, Marian. You have had the whole truth—nothing more and nothing less. I did care for her. She was my first sweetheart, and I ought to have married her. But it began and ended there. From the moment I was engaged to you and during all the years in which we have lived together I have never seen or heard of her. And so loth was I to stir up an old affair that I have been five months in making the inquiry which my father asked me to make before he died—to see that Helen Drever wanted for nothing."

"He said that to you before he died! Then he knew, of course, and he was sorry all his life through that you had not married her. Now I begin to see light—to understand Grandpa Speed's dislike to me."

"I don't think that had anything to do with it, Marian, believe me, and the matter was never once mentioned between us."

"Ah, but it rankled, and no doubt others among your friends knew the story and regarded me as an interloper. Yes, I begin to understand a lot of things which were dark before."

George Speed turned wearily away. His wife's active brain, busied on a new track, would find a thousand devious ways to cross it; and the chance of arriving at any better understanding with her seemed to become every moment more remote.

"I'll go down, I think, Marian. Further talking about this matter seems futile at present. We are both feeling it too acutely. But I hope for all our sakes that you will give me the benefit of the doubt," he added with a fleeting smile. "Most men have had an early love affair. I have been so unfortunate as to keep a record of mine—that's all the difference. But in doing so there was not a single disloyal thought towards you, and that's my last word on it."

He walked out of the room, but he came back in a moment to ask whether she would go down to dinner.

"No. Tell them to bring me something here. I'll go soon to bed. My head is splitting, and don't, whatever you do, let Tom come up, supposing that he should do us the honour to come back for dinner as he promised."

George Speed closed the door and stole rather miserably downstairs.

In his own sanctum he found the keys in the cabinet door as he had left them, but he did not touch them. The letters could remain. Sorry reading they might make, but the dates would verify his own assurance that the last had been received before his marriage. Some dim idea that his wife might push the matter to its utmost conclusion moved him thus to safeguard himself.

He drew in his chair and took down his pipe. He was in need of some comfort, though at the moment he did not know where to turn for it. Before he had time to light up—while he was still preparing the fill with that abstraction of manner, which betokens thought fully engrossed—Tom came in.

"I hear they're not coming after all, dad," he said cheerily. "I wish I had had any means of knowing. I was at Albion Terrace, and I could have stopped to dinner with Katherine. Mr. Lundie is dining at Caddam."

"Yes. Dunn has taken ill in Edinburgh. So you have been at Albion Terrace, have you? Your feet, I take it, have almost forgotten the way there."

"Not quite so bad as that, though, of course, I've been taken up elsewhere," he answered ingenuously. "Where's mother?"

"In her room? She isn't very well, Tom, and won't be down. Don't go up to her. She has—she has had an upset."

"I couldn't help it, dad," cried Tom. "She shouldn't have written that beastly letter to my girl. There was hardly a word of truth in it from beginning to end. There it is. I have it with me."

He drew it out and passed it over. Speed opened it and read it in silence.

"Your mother says what she means—and a bit over, Tom; but don't let us be too hard on her. This is an awful disappointment to her—and indeed she has had a good many of them lately."

"Yes. But, hang it all, it isn't playing the game. That bit about Katherine, you know, it's—it's a lie. I've been up to see Katherine to ask her to help me."

"You asked Katherine to deny it to Miss Durie, you mean? You—you are colossal, Tom! There isn't one man in a thousand who would have your courage in his relations with women."

"It was the only way out, and it will prove what my relations—as you call them—with Katherine really were. I have always said that we were only chums."

"And is she going to do what you ask?"

"Of course, she is."

George Speed put the match to his pipe.

"It's a queer world."

"There's nothing wrong with the world. It's the people that put things wrong, dad. Don't you see that Mary is going to throw me over for this? That's the kind of girl she is."

"Then you are determined to carry this thing through? I was in hopes that it was only a passing fancy."

"I don t have passing fancies, dad. I fall in love once only, and if I can't marry Mary, I won't marry anybody. If people would only let us alone and give us a fair chance!"

Speed sat silent for a moment, drawing heavily at his pipe.

Should he or should he not tell Tom the story of the past? He had nothing to guide him to a decision—no guarantee of how Tom would take it. It might cause him to fly off at another tangent, and things might thus become further complicated.

"If only you would go and see her and her mother," said Tom presently. "They're gentle folk, dad."

"I have been to see them to-night," was the unexpected answer.

"You have! What for? Did my mother send you?"

"No. I went on my own account, and my visit had nothing to do with your affairs."

"Did you see Mary? Did you speak to her?"

"No—I didn't speak to her."

"But her mother. I am sure she is quite presentable—a very sweet woman, and I don't wonder that Mary is devoted to her."

"Yes, that is all true."

"Then you are going to be on my side!" cried Tom eagerly. "And you'll speak to my mother and try to persuade her to be reasonable. Mary told me this afternoon that she would not have anything to do with me on any other condition. She must be recognised by my family. Of course, it's her right, and she's perfectly justified in insisting upon it. But, you see what it means to me—she'll give me up if my mother and you don't yield."

"Your mother is not in a good mood just now, Tom. We shall have to leave it over for a little time."

"But I can't wait. Mary won't see me until things are cleared up. It isn't fair.

You can't understand what this actually means to me, father, or you would be more reasonable."

The door opened at that moment, and Beith announced that dinner was served.

The two men ate it together in a sort of strained silence, broken only by a very occasional remark. A tray was taken up to Mrs. Speed's room, but it was sent down again almost untouched.

Later in the evening George Speed went upstairs, his heart yearning over his wife, his very soul sick of strife. He opened the door softly. The lights were low, and she was in bed, apparently asleep.

He stole across the floor and bent over her. Her eyes were closed, but two tears lay undried upon her cheek.

He stooped down and kissed them away.

CHAPTER XL

TWO WOMEN

KATHERINE seldom left the house on a Sunday afternoon, being in the habit of keeping open house for her working friends on that day.

No matter how stormy the day, some guests always turned up—one of the Club girls, perhaps, to get help in some difficulty, or, perhaps, some tired mother, to whom an hour spent in that beautiful drawing-room was well-spent time, sending her back with better heart to the daily round of care and toil.

Katherine possessed the rare gift of being able to make them all feel perfectly at home. She had won their confidence and affection, and the rest was easy. Her father would sometimes come in at tea-time and help her, but it was now his habit to rest for the greater part of the Sunday afternoon, and so they seldom met between dinner and tea.

After the early dinner on the Sunday following Tom Speed's last visit to Albion Terrace Katherine called Susan Beveridge, the middle-aged factotum, who was her right hand, and who had been of immense help to her in dealing with the girls and in training the young ones who had entered her service.

Susan belonged to the old order of things. "Discreet" was the word which summed up her many good qualities. With her rosy and unwrinkled face she looked very young, an easy conscience and a contented mind assisting nature to do her part.

"I have to go to Lochee this afternoon, Susan," Katherine explained.

"To Lochee, Miss Katie! But look at the rain!"

"Oh, it won't hurt me, and, as it is so wet, perhaps we shall not have many visitors to-day. But I know of two who will certainly come—Minnie Cochrane and that big girl from Dawes Street. Don't let her away, whatever you do. I want to get hold of her. But I shall certainly be back by four o'clock."

"It's just two now, Miss Katie; but will ye no get a cab or let Meldrum bring up the carriage?"

"No, no, that wouldn't suit me at all. I can easily be back. You must do the best you can, and begin with tea whenever they come, if I shouldn't happen to be at home."

Susan buttoned up her mistress's waterproof with some misgiving, and watched her descend the long flight of steps to the outer gate, wondering what special business took her forth at such an unusual time.

Katherine was fortunate in finding in the street a stray cab, which she hired to drive her to Caddam, but which she left at some distance from the gate, bidding the cabman wait for her there.

When she left the cab she was pleased to discover that the rain had ceased, and that the sky was breaking overhead. The air was very soft and delicious and pure, as if it had been cleansed by the benediction of the rain. Everywhere the smell of the awakening earth was good, and the bare boughs were beginning to show a green tinge, which to-morrow's sun would open into buds.

There was only one prayer in Katherine's heart, and that was that she should not find Tom Speed at the North Lodge. His presence would make the task impossible. She stood a moment inside the little porch, and listened for the sound of a man's voice from within, but there was neither sound nor movement to be heard. Thereupon she tapped lightly at the door.

She had to wait for a few seconds, which seemed longer than they actually were. Then some one crossed the floor, and the door was opened—not by Mary Durie, as Katherine had hoped, but by her mother.

"I wish to see Miss Durie for a moment, if you please. Is she at home?"

"She is not in the house. She went out a few minutes ago when the rain stopped."

"Oh," said Katherine disappointedly. "I wanted very much to see her."

"She can't be far away," said Mrs. Durie quickly. "She had been in the house all day, and she said that she must have a mouthful of fresh air. She did not even wait to put her hat on. If you'll come in and wait a little I'll go out and try to find her."

"Oh no, thank you. If you can give me some idea of what direction she took I shall go and find her myself."

"She will be at the bridge over the burn—what they call the Kelpie's Bridge. But, perhaps, you don't know the Caddam Woods?"

"No. I have never been through them, but if you show me the path I shall quickly find the bridge."

Mrs. Durie stepped out and directed her. Katherine waited only to ask another question.

"Is she alone? What I mean is that if any one has gone with her it would be useless for me to seek her. I wish to talk to her alone."

"There is nobody with her, though we are expecting a gentleman to tea."

Katherine thanked her with a bright, fleeting smile, and plunged into the beaten path which led down to the glen and to the bridge over the burn.

She felt glad to think that there was a chance of the meeting taking place in the open, for doubtless it would be an ordeal for them both. Katherine was surprised at herself for having come, but she had given her promise, and she had felt that it was best to fulfil it at the earliest possible moment. She may be forgiven, however, for thinking with a touch of bitterness that it was a promise which should not have been exacted from her, and that the asking showed a selfishness and an obtuseness on Tom's part which had disappointed her.

In these trying days the halo that had illumed her idol had vanished, leaving an image composed of very human clay. Tom had shown himself to be gifted with a wonderful power of insistence on purely selfish interests and aims. He would have been indeed surprised had he been vouchsafed a glimpse of Katherine's singular clearness of vision, and had he known how capable she was of weighing him up, and how bereft of ideal adornment he stood before her.

Yet such partial disillusionment on Katherine's part had in no way altered or diminished her love. She was one of those women who are faithful even unto death.

The Caddam Woods were indescribably lovely that spring afternoon, albeit the paths were sodden and the rain-drops glittered on every bough in tremulous beauty, so that the faintest motion sent them showering down.

Usually quick to be touched by every phase of nature's moods, Katherine for the first time felt irresponsive, and her heart began to beat when she saw a black figure standing idly against the parapet of the bridge and staring into space.

Mary was feeling the impossibility of meeting Tom Speed that day, and the absolute necessity of a brief respite—of some little time in which to possess her soul and decide upon what she must do in the future. She did not see Katherine until she was quite close to her. Then with a start and a blush she at once recognised her, feeling assured that no common errand had brought her at such a time to such a place.

"Good afternoon," said Katherine in her clear voice, but, remembering perhaps her past experience with Mary, she did not offer her hand. "I am very glad to find you here. I have only a very few words to say, but they will be more easily said in the open than in a house."

"Yes," murmured Mary in confusion.

A sudden sense of her own unworthiness, of the transparent nobility of Katherine Lundie's soul oppressed, almost overwhelmed her, and she did homage without making any outward sign.

"You remember me, of course. I am Katherine Lundie."

"Yes, I remember you very well."

"You will not know why I am here to-day?"

Mary shook her head. She may have had a faint idea, but it was impossible to put it into words.

"I came to remove some misunderstanding in your mind about Tom Speed and myself. He called upon me last night to ask me to help him to remove it."

Mary's face flushed yet more deeply, and she half turned away.

Could she have been capable of such a gracious act? Did she know another woman who would? She thought not.

"He has told me of the trouble, and if that is all that separates you," continued Katherine, speaking a little quickly, but clearly and quietly, "you may put it away from you for ever. We have never been engaged. He did not break any pledge to me when he asked you to be his wife. We have been very good friends all our ives, and that is all."

Mary turned away, her breath coming a little quickly, her shoulders heaving.

Katherine waited a moment. Her task being done, the natural impulse was to flee the place, yet something held her—some sisterly impulse towards this sister-woman, who certainly did not carry on her face the happiness that she might be supposed to enjoy.

"Don't be distressed," she said kindly. "I know how badly you must have felt about it. No right-thinking woman could bear to be happy at another's expense. But you may put it away from you now for ever; indeed, you may."

Mary suddenly turned with an extraordinary flash of passion in her eyes, its heat ringing in her voice.

"I don't want to put it away. It doesn't make much difference to me anyway. I don't care for him, and I shall never be his wife."

"You are speaking in anger and haste, my dear," said Katherine in precisely the same, even, gentle tone that she used to the many girls whom she had wisely advised when they came to her with their troubles. "You must try and take things quietly, and reason them out, and remember that the happiness of two lives can't be lightly played with."

"Oh, how kind and good you are, and what a fool I was to be so rude to you that day when you stopped your carriage in the street. If only I had made friends with you then how differently things might have turned out! I never could have dreamed of such a thing as your coming like this to try to help me. Not one woman in a thousand would have done it."

"My dear, that isn't much to do for another woman and for one's friend," said Katherine in a low voice. "And I do hope that you will be happy, and that you will always understand one another. He is one of the best of men; but a good wife will be very good for him, and he is very fond of you."

Mary Durie never forgot the tones of the voice which uttered these words. It had some rare quality which set it apart from all the voices that she had ever heard, or ever would hear.

She dashed aside the half-angry moisture from her eyes, stood up, and looked Katherine straight in the face.

"I have been a wicked woman, but I'll be true now you have shown me the way. I have never cared for Tom Speed. I never shall care for him, though he should come after me for a hundred years. At the beginning of it all I encouraged him out of a feeling of revenge, because I had been unjustly treated at the mills, and because my mother was at one time engaged to his father, who deserted her to marry a rich wife. All these things and the misery of our lives distorted my views of things, and I thought only of revenge. I resolved that I would make the Speeds suffer through their son, and even that I would marry him to—to spite them, and to become the wife of a rich man and be able to help my mother. But I didn't reckon with other things, nor did I realise how hard it is for a woman to play a part which she hates. So, now you know the truth, you will hate and despise me, and never speak to me again."

Katherine's heart was filled with dismay unspeakable, but she did not suffer it to display itself.

"My dear, this is terrible, but what a blessed thing that you have come to yourself before it is too late?"

"Oh, I never could have married him! I knew that quite at the beginning. But he is so difficult—he will not take a last word. Last night I told him as plainly as I am telling you now that I would not marry him, and that everything must come to an end, but he would not listen. You know that, for he must have gone straight to you. Oh, that was a cruel thing to do, and no really kind man would have asked any woman to do such a thing as he asked you to do."

Katherine scarcely winced.

"We must forgive him everything, for he is very fond of you. I am sorry for him."

Mary Durie was silent for a moment. Then she raised her eyes with a sweet humility to the beautiful face looking down upon her.

"Miss Lundie, may I say something? Your heavenly kindness has made a great difference—it has lifted something that lay on my heart like lead. But I do assure you that it is only the opposition which he has had to encounter that has made him determined to marry me. I have not had much experience, but something in my heart tells me that I am right. He does not really care for me, and if his people had been wise and left him alone his infatuation would have died out long ago. You have known him a long time, and you know how little his nature can brook opposition. Well, that's how it is between him and me. If all his relatives had approved his choice, then he would have discovered that he did not want to marry me at all."

"If you are right, then he must be a very weak character surely," said Katherine impulsively, "unstable as water, and no woman could ever be happy with him, whether you or another."

"Oh, he is not weak, only very young—much younger than his years. He will be a splendid man by and by when he has had more experience and when he has proved all his mistakes; and then, if he can marry the right woman, he will live a noble life, and will be a power for good in the world,"

"Where did you get all this wonderful wisdom from?" asked Katherine, touched and arrested by the quiet, convincing passion with which she spoke.

"I don't know. It's just here, but I feel that I am right this time, and I shall never be able to thank you for what you have done."

"I don't want any thanks, my dear, and I shall always be glad that I came; and we must meet sometimes in the future, mustn't we?"

"If you wish, though I think we shall be leaving Dundee. Will you forget that day on the causeway and offer me your hand again?"

Katherine's eyes filled, and, bending forwards, she put her hand on Mary Durie's shoulder and kissed her.

It was more than a kiss of peace. The heart of each was laid bare to the other's eyes, and both understood.

CHAPTER XLI

THE TWICE TOLD TALE

KATHERINE went quickly away, feeling that it was better to say no more. Mary did not offer to follow her, and in a few minutes' time she was on the open road, and had beckoned to her cabman, who thereupon drove swiftly up to meet her.

Tom Speed, walking at a long, swinging pace, saw the whole little scene and understood. He would have stopped the cab to speak some words of grateful thanks, but Katherine, waving her hand, called to the man to drive on. She did not feel that she could at that moment stop to speak to Tom Speed. Tom, albeit a little disappointed at Katherine's rebuff, hastened on to the North Lodge, and, being directed, took the path which she had so lately trod. He found Mary at the bridge, and he would have taken her in his arms had she not drawn away from him and shaken her head.

" No, no," she said quickly. " Things are the same as they were yesterday. I told you that everything between us had come to an end."

" But Miss Lundie has been here," he said blankly. " I passed her cab. I did not speak to her, but it's impossible that she can have said anything to—to make things worse."

" Don't speak about her—you and I are not fit to speak about her. She's an angel ! I shall never forget her as long as I live."

" She told you the truth about our friendship, didn't she ? "

" Yes ; but it won't make any difference."

" But why ? I made sure yesterday that that was the chief difficulty, and I took the best way to get it removed. I haven't been able to bring my mother to reason, but she'll come round by and by, I don't doubt, when she sees that we don't fear obstacles."

She listened to him in silence ; and in silence they stood for a few moments, she looking away from him down into the brown depths of the water that the rain had troubled.

" Do you hear, Mary ? If we are going to be happy we must take our own way—we must marry and allow them to reconcile themselves to it afterwards. Would you be afraid ? "

He spoke with the eagerness of a man who has counted the cost, and who is prepared to take the final plunge.

She turned somewhat slowly to him, and he beheld a new look on her face, but he did not know what it might portend.

" Listen," she said quietly. " I should not be afraid if I cared as people ought to care who contemplate marriage. I do not love you—that is what is wrong. I tried to tell you yesterday, only you would not listen, and I did not speak plainly enough. I allowed you to go away thinking that it was your mother's letter which had made the great difference. Now I am ashamed, and I will speak the truth."

" I shall never believe that you don't care for me, Mary," he said stubbornly. " And I should not be surprised if this is the outcome of Katherine's talk with you."

" You have no right to say that."

" What did she say to you ? Did she tell you what I said she would tell you ? "

" Yes. She assured me that there had never been anything between you."

" And you believed her, Mary ? Surely she was convincing. Everybody believes what Katherine says. She is always as true as steel."

" Oh, I know she is that! Don't let us talk about her! She is too far above both you and me."

Tom stared at her somewhat stupidly. He was not in haste to concede Katherine's nobility, but was, on the contrary, rather inclined to blame her for this sudden change of front on Mary's part.

" Something else has come between us," he said gloomily. " I wish I could get to the bottom of these machinations. It is impossible for a man to steer a straight course, and I don't think you have treated me fairly, Mary."

" I haven't, and I ask your pardon for it. I never cared for you. I only let you come, and promised to marry you because—because of other reasons which I don't want to enter into here."

" You mean because you thought it would be a pleasant thing perhaps to be the wife of a man in better circumstances than yourself."

" You may think that if you like. It can't matter much," she said in a low voice. " I am sorry—I ask your pardon for it, and please go away now and try to forget all about me."

He continued to look steadily at her, quite unconvinced. His own self-esteem repudiated the idea that he had failed to make the smallest impression on her mind and heart, and he was still inclined to the belief that the interference of others was at the bottom of all the trouble. He even blamed Katherine for words that she had never spoken.

" I won t take my dismissal like this, Mary. You're my promised wife, and I mean to have you."

She shook her head a trifle drearily.

" If you will only look back you will be forced to admit that I have never promised very much—that I have never even made much pretence."

" I attributed that to the fact that you are different from all the girls whom I had ever met before, and far superior," he promptly replied.

She almost laughed aloud.

" You have set me on an impossible pedestal, and I'm nothing—nothing at all. I am sorry, I repeat, that I ever crossed your path. I ask you to forgive me for having deceived you, and I hope you will forget me as quickly as you can."

His face flushed hotly then as he understood that this was in reality a final dismissal.

" I could have staked my life on your constancy, Mary. I thought you were the sort of woman to stick to a man through thick and thin; and yet the moment I am down on my luck you go back on me. I suppose that's the way of women. I wish that I had never seen you—I wish to God I never had!"

" So do I," she said miserably. " But you must remember that it was you who did all the seeking, and that I tried to keep you at arm's length at the beginning."

" I'm not satisfied about it all yet, and I'll sift it to the foundation. I still believe that my people are at the bottom of this, and that I haven't got the truth from you. And I promise you that I shan't rest until I get to the very root of it. I can't believe that you have refused me because you are afraid that it will make a difference in my position if my parents don't consent to our marriage."

" You may believe just what you like," she said with a sudden hardening of her voice. " I have tried to tell you the truth."

She thereupon walked away from him, and he did not seek to follow her. He left the woods by another path, and he plunged back into the town in a white heat of anger and disappointment, not knowing where or how to vent it.

Mary walked back to the house, remembering that Sir Rafe Fletcher had promised to call at the lodge some time that day, and wondering whether he might be even then with her mother. She felt weak, miserable, and ashamed of the part which she had played in these last months. And now that she had finally dismissed the lover for whom she had never cared, she was disposed to exaggerate every detail of her conduct. She could not help contrasting the spirit which had animated her with Katherine Lundie's clear, beautiful conception of duty. She was one who at whatever cost to herself would keep in the straight path.

It was a relief to her to find her mother alone, but one glance at her face showed that she was in a state of the highest mental excitement.

" Where have you been so long, Mary? What an afternoon I have had! First of all there was a lady asking for you, to whom I showed the way to the Kelpie's

Bridge. But I suppose that you have missed her after all——"

"No, I saw her," interrupted Mary.

"Then there was Tom. What have you done with him?"

"He has gone away home, I think."

"Home! What for? Isn't he coming back to tea? Have you quarrelled or what? But I can't stop to talk about that now," she cried breathlessly. "Who, do you think, has been here besides? Sir Rafe; and he brought me a letter from your father! It seems that he knows where he is, that he met him in South Africa, though I can't give you the outlandish name of the place. And—oh! oh! I can believe that he is alive!"

She sank crying into a chair, and Mary, lifted for a moment out of herself and her own troubles, did her best to soothe her. A long time had now passed since she had had a hysterical attack; but on this occasion there was some excuse for it, and Mary treated her with great tenderness.

"I am sorry that I was out when Sir Rafe came. He told me about my father yesterday, and I have been trying to summon up my courage to pass on the news to you."

"Summon up your courage! What on earth do you mean? Did you ever hear of good news hurting anybody?"

"I wasn't sure whether you would think it good news."

"The idea!" cried Mrs. Durie with the air of one mortally offended. "When you are married yourself, Mary, if that ever happens—which is doubtful if you go on as you are doing now—you will understand something of how a wife feels. Why, Sir Rafe understood everything far better than you do, and he spoke to me as if he had been my son or my brother. Everybody is kinder to me than you."

"Dear mother," said Mary, undecided whether to laugh or to cry, "I am sure they are! Then it's good news, and you will write to father, won't you?"

"Write to him! Why, of course I will, and ask him to come home!"

Then suddenly she dropped her hands on her lap, and something seemed to come over her.

"Oh, Mary, it will be a letter that will take a lot of writing, lassie, and maybe I'll need your help. Sir Rafe, he says that all I require to say is just 'Come'; and he has filled me with joy and pride by telling me what a favourite your father is out there and how much respected he is. I never did him justice. Eh, me, what a long road the man has had to travel to get justice!"

Mary smiled in spite of herself. There was something delicious in her mother's inconsequence.

"Mother," she said suddenly, "what I should like better than anything else in the world would be that you and I should rise up to-morrow morning and set out for South Africa to join father and never return to Scotland."

"That's what I may do," replied Mrs. Durie with great dignity. "You, being engaged to be married, are tied to Scotland. Sir Rafe has even said that he will advance me the money, being sure that your father will pay it back again! Isn't it a wonderful Providence that has guided us to this, Mary?"

"I don't know about Providence," said Mary with a faint sigh. "I have made a nice muddle of my life, and I don't know how I am to get out of it."

"A nice muddle! You are engaged to a good man and a well-to-do one! It will make a difference to Madam Speed, maybe, when she learns that we are somebody after all—that your father's a man of substance out in South Africa, and that he has been, and still is, an intimate friend of Sir Rafe Fletcher. Don't you see what a difference it will make to us all?"

Mary made no answer. She was weary of speech, weary of explanations, weary of trying to find reasons and excuses for her conduct. Her one desire was to fly away and be at rest.

"He's coming back—Sir Rafe, I mean—in the evening, maybe—to see what you think. The morn's the mail-day, and he has written, and he wants me to have my letter ready. Get me the paper and the pens and I'll try."

For the time being everything had faded from Helen Durie's ken except that her husband was still alive and that her written word could reach him. Her mind was a fevered tangle of words that she would write, of apologies that she would make for her share in the stormy past that had culminated in his being driven out into the wilderness.

But after all the few words that she actually achieved seemed poor and inadequate, though they sufficed to fill with joy the heart of the lonely man who read them on the South African veldt.

This is how the letter ran :—

" Dear Charlie,—Sir Rafe Fletcher has told us that you are alive, and has shown me your handwriting and has bidden me write a letter.

" My mind is full of confused thoughts, and no skill of mine could ever set them down. I am sorry for all I have been and done, and I have suffered for it, Charlie—that you may believe. If you have it in your heart to write to me, or to send for me, do it by the quickest way you know, and I shall rise up and come to you—on my knees, if need be—and try to make up for the past.—Helen."

CHAPTER XLII

THE OBSTINATE

MEANWHILE " the poor people's doctor " was pursuing his solitary way.

He occasionally called at Caddam North Lodge, where he had to listen to praises of his successful rival—a searching experience even for the man of forbearance and peace. He timed his visits so that he should not see Mary, and they had not met for many weeks. Neither had he seen Tom Speed save casually on the streets.

The man in love has no scruples about casting off his old friends, whom nevertheless he expects to pick up again when it suits his convenience. All the world loves a lover ; and so this course of unblushing selfishness causes fewer wrecks of friendship than might be imagined.

There were times, however, when Alister, the friend whom Tom had alienated by his plain speech, missed the solace of friendship—days on which he was sick of his own existence, when he experienced wild desires for change. The sea with its suggestions of voyaging beckoned him as he passed to and from the harbour and round about it, and as he witnessed the preparations for the whale-fishing he had wild dreams of throwing everything to the winds and faring forth in search of freedom and adventure.

But the poor people restrained him, the exigencies of a growing business whispered prudence. The bounds of Alister's practice were gradually extending—the West-End was beginning to talk about the clever young surgeon whose work, done in lowly places, but always conscientiously and efficiently, was beginning to tell. The success which had once seemed so far off was now within sight. Old George Speed's legacy had brought him luck, though it lay untouched, uninvested in the bank, the purpose for which it had been whimsically given farther off than ever. Alister had rashly concluded that now he would never marry, and thus it came about that " the poor people's doctor " pursued his solitary way.

To beguile the tedium of many dull hours he began to write a book. A thing of shadowy proportions at the beginning, it quickly took shape and began to engross such portion of his life as was not devoted to his profession. It took the place of lover and of friend, and, being thus regarded, it bade fair to become a thing of beauty and of value. He now looked forward to the coming of Sunday, because of the extra hours which he could devote to the idol, and time became more precious, more crowded than ever.

Into this atmosphere of quiet and delightful absorption Tom Speed burst like a whirlwind in the cool of the spring Sunday evening, shouting his quarrel with fate. Alister heard the ring at the door-bell with dismay—to such a pass had his literary labours brought him, and he waited anxiously for his housekeeper's message, apprehensive lest it should summon him afar. Instead of her decorous knock the door seemed to burst open, and Tom tumbled in—not exactly dishevelled, but looking pale and upset.

" How are you Alister ? I thought I'd find you in at this time," he said in an off-hand way, as if he had called the previous evening and left his card and had now returned to pay the call in person.

Alister accepted the situation, and simply replied—" Hulloa, Tom."

Then he shut up his big blotting-book with a snap and began to put his sheets of foolscap together with hasty hand. He was shy yet about the new love of his life ; but he need not have been afraid of any display of inquisitive interest on Tom's part. Tom was wholly absorbed in his own woes.

" It's all up, Alister," he said with a groan as he dropped into a chair. " Among them they've managed to make a mess of my life."

" What has happened ? "

Alister s voice was not very sympathetic. Perhaps that would have been too much to expect, but it was at least kind, for he could not bear to see a fellow-creature in distress. Tom, however, had always made mountains out of molehills, all his troubles being incurable as his joys were transcendent and his hopes soared to the clouds.

" Everything has happened ! She has—she has given me up."

" Has she ? What for ? "

" Oh, well, you can understand. You used to understand, anyway, without much jaw, but you have gone back on me like the rest of them. You have not been the same for a long time."

Alister heard this indictment unmoved. It did not surprise him—few things did—and Tom of the impulsive tongue said many things which his better judgment condemned—when he gave it a chance. But at that moment Alister forgave him everything. Having been dismissed finally by Mary Durie, a man must be excused no matter what he said or did.

" I'm sorry, old chap," was all he said, and then he waited. It was no part of his duty to question here. If Tom chose to tell, good and well. If not—no matter.

" They've been meddling. Of course, you knew they would—or you would have known if you hadn't ceased to take the smallest interest in me and my affairs. I don't know why I came here to-day. A chap must tell somebody, I suppose ; but I've a good mind to end it all in the dock-basin."

" I'd choose a cleaner place," observed Alister drily. " Have your people managed to bring it all to an end ? "

" Yes. My mother wrote her a letter—on Friday, was it ? I've endured so much that the time seems much longer. She told her among other things that I had been engaged to Katherine Lundie and had deserted her. No woman of spirit could stand that, of course, and she doesn't believe my denial. Oh, if I only could have choked that lie at the beginning ! What Katherine and I have suffered by it nobody will ever know."

" Didn't you try to explain ? "

" Yes, and Katherine went to see her too. I tell you we've done everything, and it's all of no use. She has sent me away, and I don't care if I go to the devil now. The sooner the better."

Alister suffered the threat to pass—he had heard it before.

He was puzzled by the denouement, and did not quite know what to make of it.

" Isn't there any chance of bringing your people to reason ? If you really care for each other, your lives ought not to be spoiled like this. You have counted the cost. Why not act on your own responsibility now ? "

" How do you mean ? "

" Marry her in spite of them, man. Run away with her—that's what I would do."

" You can't run away with a woman who won't run," answered Tom, gloomily resentful over a suggestion which coincided very well with his inclinations, but which bristled with impossibility. " I tell you you don't understand what kind of a woman she is. My mother speaks about her as if she was the dust under her feet. Why, man, there isn't any pride among the Speeds or Lundies or any of the crowd to come up to hers ! I tell you she'll have her pound of flesh."

" You mean that, until she has the fullest recognition and welcome from your family, she won't have anything more to do with you."

" That's it," answered Tom, and he spoke as he believed.

To him it seemed inconceivable that she could not care for him who cared so greatly for her.

Alister, still puzzled, stared into the fire and suggested a pipe. The suggestion was scorned ; but he quietly filled a pipe and passed it over.

" A chap in the Foregate whose leg I saved brought me that baccy from Rotterdam, Tom. Try it—it's uncommon good, and I don't offer it to every one."

After a brief hesitation Tom gave in, lit the pipe, and sat back in the depths of the big chair.

" The first comfortable moment that I have had in many weeks. It was too bad of you also to go back on me, Alister. Katherine's the only brick. What a woman that is—better than ten men pals ! "

Alister smiled wearily and made haste to get his own pipe in working order lest he should be tempted to jeering or imprudent remarks. He forgave Tom for his untimely interruption because of the freshness of sensation that he brought with him.

" I accused her of having other strings to her bow—of encouraging you, Alister. A man has to say something, you know, and I had to fish for a valid reason."

" I've only spoken to her once since she went to the North Lodge, so your use of my name was superfluous."

" I dare say ; but one had to say something. Do you think that she'll ever turn round ? What I mean is that she's really giving up a lot, you know. That's where she's so splendid. The considerations that influence other women simply don't count with her. Even though she didn't know where her next meal was to come from she'd act just the same."

" She has certainly both courage and resource," admitted Alister readily enough.

" Yes. Well, why won't she apply them to our own case ? If only she'd agree to marry me now without further trouble, what a thing it would be for me ! Why, I'd be strong enough to conquer fate."

" It would imperil your position at the mills ? " suggested Alister.

" They'd send me to India. I should like that if she were with me. I think I must have one more try at the governor. My mother is quite hopeless. I had it out with her yesterday—was it yesterday ? Yes, and she told me that I had to choose between Mary and them. So I will."

" But she has dismissed you," Alister remarked. " For good, I think, you said."

" If you'd ever been in love," replied Tom in his loftiest manner, " you'd know that a man doesn't ever take a woman's ' No ' as final."

His manner differed from that with which he had left Mary's presence when finally dismissed.

The optimistic temperament asserted itself, and for the next hour Alister had to listen to a rhapsody of glowing visions of a future in which he could take only a languid interest. He allowed himself to be bored with exemplary patience ; but when he was left alone he found his thread of thought hopelessly lost, and he could not go on with the work which Tom had interrupted.

Tom proceeded home to Newport with some idea of arranging his future on a different basis. He would tell his father that he was quite willing to go to India and would ask what provision would be made for him there. Then with an assured position in his hand, a double passage perhaps taken out, he would go to Mary and present his ultimatum. Ultimatums were in the air. Had Tom been less absorbed by his own affairs he could not have failed to notice the atmosphere of strain at Ravenscraig. His mother had not been down at breakfast, and at luncheon a man had returned with his father from church, so that the conversation had been more general than usual. He had observed that his mother had less to say than she ordinarily had, but that otherwise things seemed right enough. She was polite and affable to him.

He found his father in his own sanctum sitting gloomily before the fire, not even smoking, but merely staring in front of him with an expression of dejection on his face. Tom, of course, was not aware that there was a breach between his father and his mother and that they had not exchanged a word since the previous afternoon. This involved a strain which a man of George Speed's temperament could not stand for any length of time.

" Hulloa, father, all alone ? Where's the mater ? "

" In the boudoir, I think. I haven't seen her since Mr. Courtenay left."

" Isn't she well, or what ? "

" Not very. Sit down, won't you ? Where have you been all the afternoon ? "

" At Lochee," replied Tom, and leaning his arm on the mantel, he added suddenly—" Father, I think I'll go to India, if you don't mind."

Speed looked up in surprise.

" You are too late, Tom. Have you forgotten that Soutar sailed yesterday ? "

" Soutar sailed yesterday ! In heaven's name what for ? "

" To look after our interests in the Azra case. We think that your uncle, James Mouat, has been a little slack. That's a job that you ought to have been able to do,

Tom, and I'm disappointed in you, though Soutar, of course, will manage perfectly. He will, however, have to be handsomely paid for it—probably with a partnership."

"Why didn't you tell me this before?" said Tom blankly. "I would have gone."

A slight expression of irritation crossed his father's face.

"You are aggravating at every turn, and if you didn't know that the Indian matter had become acute, then you ought to have known. It's impossible that busy men can take time to instruct you in the A B C of the business, and I may point out to you that if you think you have been unfairly treated, you have only got the treatment you have deserved—neither more nor less—and that's the lot of most men. Things get equalised sooner or later."

These straight remarks were by no means to Tom's liking; but he took them rather more meekly than his father expected.

"I shall never do any good here, dad," he said unexpectedly. "Let me go to Calcutta, as you suggested a short time ago, and remain there for five years or so; and Edward Mouat can take my place. I am sure it would be good for everybody."

"I have no doubt of it," was the answer, "and I shall try whether it can be arranged. It's a pity you didn't speak two days ago. Then I could have given Soutar instructions to arrange the exchange as soon as he landed."

"I prefer not to be arranged by Soutar—I hate the bounder," said Tom under his breath.

"He's a good servant, and I don't know where we should have been without him at this crisis," was the dry response.

CHAPTER XLIII

THE CLIMAX

THE deep, sonorous chime of the great clock in the hall at Ravenscraig rang seven. Sitting over the evening paper in the library, Mrs. Speed was startled by it. She sat up, listened for a moment, and then touched the bell.

Beith, laying the table for dinner in the next room, answered it immediately.

"Has the master come home yet, Beith?"

"No, ma'am, not yet."

"You are sure?"

"I think so, ma'am. At least I've never heard him."

"Go to the smoking-room and see."

The girl departed, but returned in about two minutes to say that there was no one there.

"Hasn't Mr. Tom come home either?"

"No, ma'am."

"Extraordinary!—especially for your master. I never remember his having been so late. This is mail day, of course, and he has more to do since Mr. Soutar went away. I wonder if it would be of any use to telephone to the office."

"Can I do it for you, ma'am?"

"Well, you may ring them up. There will be somebody there to answer, I dare say."

Beith went out into the hall and rang up the Exchange. After a delay of some minutes she was put on to the Eliot Mills, but she waited there for an answer in vain.

"There doesn't seem to be anybody there, ma'am," she came back to say. "Shall I ring off?"

"Of course, if you can't get an answer. Doubtless they will be home soon."

She sank back in her chair again, and listlessly took up the paper which she had thrown down. She looked tired and pale, the air of assurance and self-satisfaction which had so long characterised her having disappeared. The change in their mistress had not failed to be observed by the servants, and Beith, who waited on the family at the evening meal, admitted that something had gone amiss. The long silences between her master and mistress and the feeling of strain in the air were most marked. And this state of things had lasted for five days. For the first time in her life Marian Speed was actively unhappy on her own account. She had not recovered from the shock of finding the old love letters, and in addition to the bitterness of disillusionment she had experienced a very new and strange sensation—she had learned that she loved her husband dearly, and that she grudged with her whole heart and soul the passing thought which he had given to another woman.

Too proud to stoop or to crave for the love for which she longed and which was hers for the asking, she suffered the breach to widen, giving him cold looks and colder words, which drove him farther from her side. Matters were very bad indeed at Ravenscraig, seeing that all were living at cross purposes, and that there was apparently little prospect of any change for the better.

In these few days of acute mental distress Marian Speed had lost weight and colour and spirit. Yet her altered looks gave to her a sort of pathetic charm. Her husband had looked at her that morning across the breakfast table with a sudden, startled air, and had left the house with an acute pang.

He did not know how to approach or how to conciliate her. He had made use of all his arguments, but to no purpose, and hopelessness rather than pride kept him silent now. He only could wait, though he did not know for what he was waiting. He was an unhappy as any man could possibly, and he had now nearly reached the limit of his endurance.

Not yet seriously alarmed, for she had heard her husband and son say that they had had a great influx of business which had indeed already detained them later than usual for several nights, she waited expectantly till a quarter to eight. Then she went out to the telephone herself and rang up the Lundies at Albion Terrace.

Katherine answered, and in response to Mrs. Speed's question said that her father had come home as usual, shortly after six o'clock.

"Just ask him to speak to me, will you?" she asked, and the next moment Henry Lundie himself took Katherine's place at the telephone.

"George hasn't come home yet," she said, "nor Tom. Is there any reason why they should be so late at the mills?"

"None, so far as I am aware. I myself left at ten minutes to six, and George had by that time got through most of the letters. I left him writing to Soutar."

"Did he seem all right?"

"Quite. He bade me good-night as usual. Was there no other business to keep him in Dundee?"

"Nothing that I know of. What do you think I should do? It's of no use to ring up the mills—there seems to be nobody there to answer."

Henry Lundie hesitated for a moment.

"Tom hasn't come home yet either, you say? If you like I shall send somebody in to the mills. It is easier to do so from here."

"Oh, don't do that. I'm sure it's unnecessary. If they don't come soon I'll send a messenger myself," she said, and rang off.

But Henry Lundie felt oddly anxious, and said so to Katherine when he returned to the library, where the coffee had been served. They had finished dinner, and they had been preparing to spend their quiet evening in the usual way.

"I don't feel easy in my mind, Katherine. I think I shall go to the mills."

"To the mills, papa! Why? You can't suppose that Mr. Speed has stopped there all this time."

"I'm not comfortable in my mind, Kate, I tell you. He wasn't like himself to-day. I couldn't help remarking it, though I didn't mention it to Mrs. Speed. I did not wish to cause her perhaps needless alarm. Yes—I think I'll go."

"Will there be any one there except the night-watchman?" asked Katherine.

"Oh yes—the men at the furnaces, and, at any rate, it will satisfy me."

"I shall come with you. Yes, I will—don't say I must not. I am coming," said Katherine jumping up decidedly. "I won't keep you a moment. I'll just put on a short skirt and a long coat, and then I shall be ready. Shall we take a cab?"

"Off the rank. Yes, if we can get one. All right, dear, if you think the infant capable of making such a short journey unattended."

Katherine laughed as she flew upstairs to get ready, and in a few minutes they were out of doors.

Nine o'clock pealed from all the church bells as they turned away from the gate in search of a cab. They had to walk some distance, but were fortunate at last, though a tired horse took them very slowly up the hill to the gates of the mills.

"Don't ask the man to wait, father," urged Katherine. "The horse is dead tired, and ought to be in his stable. We can easily walk home."

"He can wait a few minutes, dear," said Henry Lundie prudently. "He may as well take us to the bottom of the hill again."

He did not voice his real reason for detaining the man, which was an intuition that they might want him for another purpose.

The gates were locked, and when he rang the bell its sonorous echoes, never heard amid the many noises of the day, struck a sudden note of alarm.

"It sounds ghastly, father—like a prelude to a tragedy," said Katherine with a little shudder.

"I hope it won't be that, dear," replied Henry Lundie gravely.

The porter in mingled astonishment and alarm hurried out of his house, such a summons never having occurred during his whole period of office at the Eliot Mills.

"Don't look so scared, Thomson, it's only me," said the master. "Just open the wicket, and I'll explain."

"Did ye forget something, sir," he asked as he made haste to undo the bolts.

"No. But Mr. Speed has not gone home to Newport, and nobody seems to know where he is. Mrs. Speed has telephoned to inquire. I suppose he isn't by any chance here?"

"Oh no, sir. That's impossible," said Thomson a little blankly yet with an air of conviction.

"I left about six o'clock when he was writing a letter for Mr. Soutar. Was that sent out?"

"I couldna say, sir. The bag gaed doon as usual, of course."

"Did you see him leave—that's what I want to be at?"

"No, sir, I didna; but then I hardly ever do. Mr. Tom left aboot seevin, or just efter it. I thocht at the time hoo late he was."

"He left alone?"

Thomson nodded.

"Well, my man, we'll just go up to the office and see. Don't look so scared," he repeated a trifle irritably. "I don't suspect anything wrong, but it's just possible that Mr. Speed may have taken ill in his room and been unable to call for assistance. Such things have happened."

"Oh yes, sir," assented Thomson as he closed the wicket.

"You have the key, I suppose?"

"I havena. Galbraith usually tak's that hame wi' him."

"Well, if Galbraith has taken the key home with him, there's an end of it. We can go up and see." Katherine was conscious of a growing excitement and apprehension. They turned silently and walked up the farther slope to the open space where the offices stood.

"It's a' dark," observed Thomson cautiously. "I dinna think he can be there."

Henry Lundie pressed forward. Anxiety and apprehension had become certainty, and something told him that he should find his friend and partner there. They tried all the doors, but none yielded to their touch.

"I must get in somehow, Thomson," said Henry Lundie quietly. "Now I have come I must make sure. Try the windows."

"There's ane aff the snib. I can see it, sir," he answered quickly. "If I can climb up I'll easily get in."

He wringgled up the smooth surface of the stones with the agility of a cat, which, his years and weight considered, was something of a feat. Once he was on the ledge the rest was easy, though the sash was stiff with much rain and yielded very slowly. At last, however, he got it sufficiently open to obtain a good grip, and he pushed it high enough to admit him.

"I'll turn up the licht," he said, not in the least afraid, and the next moment the electric light had flooded the passage and brought with it a sudden sense of relief. The dark and all the possibilities it may hide is seldom cheering or inspiring, and most men have quicker kinship with the light. He came towards the door, and he then observed to his surprise that it was merely bolted from within and that the key was gone. For the first time a curious thrill of apprehension chilled him, and he looked over his shoulder fearfully as if in dread of what might lie beyond.

The next moment he had drawn back the bolt and thrown open the door.

"Is the key in the door?" Henry Lundie inquired.

"No, sir; the big bolt was slippit in. There must be somebody aboot the place, the door bein' bolted frae the inside. Burglars, eh?"

Katherine paled, and her hand instinctively went forth to clutch her father's arm.

"Will you stay here, dear, while Thomson and I go to Mr. Speed's room?"

She nodded, but when they stepped forward some instinct made her follow.

There were panels of obscure glass in the door of the private room, but there was no light behind them. They tried the handle, but the door was locked. They stared at one another blankly, in no doubt that something had happened within.

"We'd better gang for Jamieson an' the rest an' force the door," suggested Thomson. "I've nae tools at my place, but there's plenty in the engine-house."

" Try the other door through to the counting-house, or perhaps we may get in by my room."

Thomson obeyed, and they went in single file through the passage and arrived at the other door, which opened to their touch. Thomson turned on the swtich. The communicating door between the rooms of the two partners was just opposite. Henry Lundie stepped forward and threw it open. The borrowed light from where they stood struck in a straight shaft across the floor, and revealed what Henry Lundie at least had fully expected to find—the prostrate body of George Speed on the floor.

CHAPTER XLIV

THE TRAGEDY

KATHERINE did not scream. A curious stillness seemed to descend upon her as she stood waiting, she scarcely knew for what. Henry Lundie stepped into the room and turned up the light.

"Ah!" he exclaimed. "See, there is the explanation!"

A revolver lay upon the floor near the body, as if it had fallen from the hand that used it. Katherine, with the womanly instinct to help and save, sprang forward and knelt down by the side of the prostrate man.

"Papa, he isn't dead!" she cried. "Do let us get him to the cab and to a doctor as soon as possible. Dr. Alister's house is quite near. We can take him there."

"Go down, Thomson, and open the gates and bring up our cab to the door," said Henry Lundie. "But help me first to lift him to the sofa."

"Don't father," said Katherine quickly. "I don't know much, but I am sure the best thing is not to move him too much. Oh, poor Mr. Speed! What a dreadful thing!"

The blood was oozing from a wound in the neck. Katherine, now the first shock was over, thought only of how she could help. She took her own handkerchief and the wounded man's from his pocket, and made a tourniquet, as she had been taught at the ambulance class which she had attended after she had left school. In a few seconds Thomson was back with the cab, and with great care and tenderness they lifted the prostrate man, who groaned deeply as they carried him to the cab.

It was a ghastly experience, and they greatly feared that his life might ebb out before they could come within reach of the doctor's aid. They drove very slowly—the time seemed an eternity to Katherine—until they arrived at the familiar door of the house in the Foregate, which was known to so many in trouble.

Fortunately Alister was in, bending low at the table over his beloved book. When he heard the cab stop at the door he made haste to put his work into the big drawer of the old-fashioned dining-table, and stepped out into the hall.

To his surprise he was met there by Henry Lundie.

"Thank God that you are in the house, Doctor!" he said quickly. "Something terrible has happened. We have found Mr. Speed shot at the office, and we have brought him here."

Alister did not speak a word. In an instant of time the professional instinct, the keen, surgical interest thrust everything else into the background, and he was the right man in the right place. In an astonishingly short time they had George Speed lying in Alister's own bed, and everything that was possible was being done.

"He has lost a good deal of blood, and is frightfully weak," he said. "We had better telephone for his wife and son."

The wisdom of this was obvious, and Henry Lundie moved out to the hall to ring up Ravenscraig.

The message given, he put on his coat for the purpose of going to meet Mrs. Speed at the Ferry.

"Would you like to go home, dear? It is very little we can do now."

"No," Katherine answered; "I'll wait till Mrs. Speed comes—it would only be kind. Perhaps we can both leave then. But, papa, it seems hardly necessary for you to go to the Ferry. Tom will be with her."

"No; Tom has not been home," replied Lundie shortly as he went out.

The tone of his voice rather than the words suggested impossible things to Katherine's quick imagination. Tom had not gone home! Nobody seemed to know where he was. He had left the mills, alone just after seven o'clock. If he were not at Caddam North Lodge, then what was the explanation? Katherine's heart seemed to turn to stone in her breast. What if the father and the son had quarrelled, and in a moment of passion Tom's hand had dealt the blow—the cowardly blow that had perhaps set a limit to George Speed's life?

The relations at Ravenscraig had long been strained. The explanation seemed not only feasible but probable. Swift anguish did its work in a loving woman's heart. Sitting there in the silence, Katherine seemed to live years of crowded life. When Alister presently came down he noticed the signs of suffering, and he partly understood what had brought them there.

"How is he now?"

"About the same. I have telephoned for Professor Gilruth to come. The bullet will have to be extracted, but I must have another opinion before I do much else."

"Do you think he will die?"

Alister shook his head.

"It is impossible to say."

She was silent for a moment, and then she lifted her heavy eyes to his face. Alister never forgot that look. It moved him to the heart.

"Can you tell me, Doctor, whether in a case of this kind the wound has been self-inflicted?"

"In this case it is impossible to tell."

"The revolver was lying close to his hand," she said eagerly.

"That in itself proves nothing."

She bowed her head on her hands.

"You are thinking of Tom," he said gently; "but put that out of your mind at once and for ever, Miss Katherine. I know him well, and though we haven't always sailed in the same boat, he is incapable, believe me, of such a dastardly outrage. Nothing would make me credit it."

"Thank you. Oh, thank you. I was afraid that he might be blamed—that's all. But where can he be?"

"Probably at Caddam North Lodge," he answered drily.

"But they might have quarrelled desperately?" she persisted. "I suppose that you know something about the family troubles at Ravenscraig—between Tom and his people, I mean?"

"Oh yes, I know. Tom was here last Sunday night and spoke out very frankly about it all; but I do assure you he is incapable of what you think. Even if he had run away, I should never believe that was the reason."

Katherine said "Thank you" again, and did not seem to think that Alister might wonder what he had done to deserve thanks. As a matter of fact, he did not wonder at all—he fully understood. What he did wonder—and that with all his might—was how Tom Speed could have been so utterly blind to the direction in which his best happiness lay. For undoubtedly she was a peerless creature on whose love a man might build his happiness, sure of its standing the test of time and circumstance to the very end of life.

Time passes slowly to all who wait, weighed down by apprenhensive fears. Marian Speed, crossing in the boat from Newport, could scarcely bear herself. Beith was with her, and Beith had never seen her mistress in so sore a strait. She could not be still; her extreme nervousness made itself manifest in her every movement, though she did not speak at all during the passage.

At Craig Pier Henry Lundie awaited her, and she clutched his arm, her eyes fixing themselves wildly on his face.

"You have come to tell me that he is dead," she said, and Beith never forgot the expression on her face. Any hard thoughts which he may from time to time have cherished against her mistress were wiped away by that look of dire distress.

"No, no. He is still alive, and while there is life there is hope," said Henry Lundie, as he guided her steps to the waiting cab. "I was hoping that Tom would be with you."

"I don't know where he is. I haven't seen him since last night. He always leaves the house in the morning before I come down, and he has not been home all day. Has anybody sent to Caddam for him?"

"There has not been time, but we can send now," said Henry Lundie, as he helped her into the cab, Beith standing sympathetically by.

She climbed to the box beside the driver. Then Mrs. Speed turned swiftly to the man at her side.

" He has taken his own life—or tried to take it—and I am to blame," she said, with unnatural calmness. " And I know he will die, and I shall not have an opportunity of telling him how sorry I am."

He saw—and felt glad if it—that she attached no blame to Tom, that apparently it had not occured to her that he could possibly have had any hand in the affair, but he did not understand her allusion to herself.

" He is in the best of hands," he whispered reassuringly. " Alister is one of the cleverest young surgeons that we have. We were fortunate in finding him at home, and there was no time lost."

" Tell me exactly how you found him, and how you thought of seeking him at the mills. Keep on talking. I can't be silent or still. I feel as if I was being consumed with fire."

Fortunately the drive was not a long one. In a very few minutes they drew up at Alister's door. She was out of the cab almost before it stopped, and Katherine, listening for the sound if approaching wheels, opened the door.

" Dear Mrs. Speed, I am sorry—so very sorry for you."

Katherine put her arm around Mrs. Speed's waist and led her up the steps into the drawing-room, where she had been waiting alone.

" I want to go upstairs or wherever he is. Is he dead, Katherine ? "

" No, no—still alive, and they are quite hopeful. Professor Gilruth has arrived, and I think that they are doing something now. Will you wait, or shall I tell them that you are here ? "

" Take me to him."

While Katherine still hesitated, Alister himself, having heard the arrival of the cab, appeared on the stairs.

" Mrs. Speed—yes, come up, if you please. Mr. Speed is still unconscious,but his pulse is strong, and we have every hope."

He ran down the bottom steps, and took her by the arm and guided her feet up the narrow stairs. All were kind to the striken woman, including even those whom her tongue had not spared. She had not spoken to Alister since old George Speed's funeral day. Her manner then had been cutting, her words few and ungracious. But Alister remembered these things not at all.

" There is nothing to shock or frighten you," he assured her. " He is, of course, deadly pale through shock and loss of blood, and he will not know you ; but I assure you that there is hope."

They went in, and the door was shut. Henry Lundie and his daughter remained in silence in the little hall. Then he turned to the door again.

" I'll take the cab out to Caddam and fetch Tom if he is there. What he should be doing there, though, at this time of night I can't think. Has he been dining with Fletcher ? "

" No. You needn't seek him at the Castle," said Katherine, remembering that her father knew nothing about Tom Speed's love affair. " He will be at the North Lodge ; he's engaged to the girl who lives there."

Henry Lundie stared incredulously.

" Engaged to a girl at the North Lodge ! To the lodge-keeper's daughter, do you mean ? "

" Yes. Go quickly and fetch him, father. I shall stay with Mrs. Speed until you come back."

Henry Lundie, much mystified, departed on a perfectly futile errand. He arrived at the North Lodge, only to be told by a girl with wonderful eyes that he had not been there at all that day.

Where, then, was Tom ?

Henry Lundie had now no doubt in his mind that there had been a quarrel between father and son, and that Tom had fled to escape the dreadful consequences of his crime.

CHAPTER XLV

THE DREADFUL DAY

ILL news travels fast, and before the whistles blew for breakfast next morning it was known at the mills that there had been a tragedy in the night. The wildest rumours were afloat, and when Henry Lundie arrived shortly after eight o'clock—an unprecedented occurrence—the excitement increased. He had learned by telephoning to Ravenscraig that Tom Speed had not slept at home, and nothing being known of him at Caddam North Lodge or at Dr. Alister's, the affair began to assume a very grave complexion indeed. Henry Lundie had called at Alister's where he had learned that the condition of George Speed, though he was still alive, was not much improved, and that his wife had not left his bedside all night.

He had not asked to see him, but had proceeded to the mills to take up the business of the day, an unwonted sense of responsibility resting upon him now that he was the sole representative of the firm able to take a personal interest in its affairs.

A few moments after the whistle had blown, and while the tramp of many feet was still filling the air, a clerk knocked at Mr. Lundie's door and said that one of the women-workers wished to speak to him.

Surprised at this interruption, he directed her to be at once shown in ; and Betsy Baxter entered with her shawl pinned across her breast, and as it was a rainy morning, also a small one on her head.

Henry Lundie did not, of course, recognise her. He took the most shadowy interest in the hands, for though he would willingly legislate for them in the mass, he was content to leave personal dealing with them to his daughter. Nevertheless, he turned to her and bade her a kindly good-morning, casually thinking what a plain, unlovely object she was.

" Guid-mornin', sir ! I've something to tell ye, sir, if ye please——"

" Well, tell on."

" Maister Tom, sir—he's no here this mornin', they're saying. It's true, isn't it ? "

" Quite true, my good woman ; there is no use of hiding it. Mr. Tom is missing. He did not go home last night. Have you any light to throw on the unhappy business ? "

" Yes, sir. Maybe ye ken, or maybe ye dinna ken, that last nicht twa o' the boats left for the whalin'."

" I saw it mentioned in the evening paper, I believe."

" Weel, my guid-brither, Andrew Fernie, is skipper o' the *Bonnie Jean*, an' me an' my man an' the bairns were doon at the quay seein' him aff."

Henry Lundie nodded understandingly.

" There was a michty crood, as usual, an' jist as they were shovin' aff, wha should come tearin' through it but the young maister; an' he lap the distance between the boat an' the quay-side—it maun hae been six or seevin feet—an' got safe aboard. The crood cheered, an' naebody thocht onything aboot it, for Maister Tom has often been doon when they gaed aff ; in fact, he's nearly aye there. We thocht he wad only drap doon the Firth a mile or twa, maybe, an' come back in a sma' boat. Ye never ken what the young maister wull dae next. He's aye at something different frae ither folk."

" True, my good woman ; and you think perhaps that he did not come back in the small boat, but that he may have gone on to Greenland ? "

" It micht be, sir. He seemed flurried, an' noo as things ha'e turned oot it micht explain something. At least, I thocht I wad better come an' tell ye."

" Quite right ! Thank you very much," said Henry Lundie, absently, now in no doubt that Tom had gone off to Greenland in the whaling ship, and that only one complexion could be put on his action—that he had fled to escape the consequences of his crime.

Mrs. Baxter saw that he had forgotten her, but before she left the room she ventured on a question concerning the welfare of Mr. Speed.

"He's still alive, Mrs. Baxter, thank you. You need not talk any more about this than you can help," he added, suddenly bending his deep, penetrating eyes full on her face. "Least said is soonest mended."

"Deed is't sir; an' I'll haud my tongue," she answered as she took herself off.

Henry Lundie, having obtained fresh food for thought, found it difficult to concentrate his attention on the immediate business of the day, which fortunately did not happen to be of a pressing nature.

He was presently relieved to hear that he was wanted at the telephone. He found that it was Katherine who was speaking from Alister's house in the Foregate.

"They think him much better, papa," she cried, and the glad note in her voice was distinctly discernible. "They are quite hopeful."

"I am indeed thankful to hear that; and how is Mrs. Speed?"

"It has made her a different woman. I am so sorry for her. We have been misjudging her all along."

"Ah, perhaps so. I don't suppose that George has spoken, has he?"

"Oh, no. He is not even conscious—he is only stronger in every way. They really are quite hopeful."

"Ah! I was hoping that he might have spoken and been able to throw some light on Tom's disappearance."

Henry Lundie deliberately opened up this painful part of the affair because it was easier to speak to Katherine when he was not face to face with her.

There was a moment's silence. Then Katherine's voice, a little altered, put the question, "What do you mean, papa? Has Tom really disappeared?"

"He was not at home at Ravenscraig last night, my dear, and he is not here this morning. I have just heard from a *protégée* of yours—Mrs. Baxter—that he leapt on board one of the whalers last night at the very moment of sailing. Those who saw him thought his doing so was a mere escapade, and that he would leave the vessel—probably in a small boat—a little lower down the Firth. But as things have turned out, it looks as if he had deliberately gone off to Greenland, or at least to some place where he will be out of the way if wanted."

"Tell me what exactly you mean, papa," came Katherine's voice, sharp and shrill.

"I mean, of course, that on the face of it it looks as if his father and he had quarrelled. You know what an impetuous disposition Tom has, and though he would not mean to kill his father, I am sure, still passion is responsible for many tragedies."

"I shall never believe it of Tom Speed—never as long as I live. Whatever the evidence against him, I shall not believe that dreadful thing until his father himself accuses him. I pray God that he may recover so that the mystery may be cleared up."

She thereupon dropped the receiver, and Henry Lundie, with a sigh, returned to his desk.

He had guessed Katherine's secret, and he may be forgiven for the bitterness which he could not help cherishing against the man who had so lightly esteemed the priceless treasure of Katherine's love. Having scorned that, surely he deserved little favour at the hands of fate?

The day wore on, each hour heightening the chances of life for George Speed, lying unconscious in David Alister's bedroom in the Foregate, ministered to by such skill and love as might well have drawn him back to conscious life.

Nothing could exceed Alister's attention and tenderness, and his whole estimate of Mrs. Speed was raised. Not knowing the inner kernel of the story, he was amazed and greatly touched by her wifely devotion, and he showed it in his manner to the stricken woman, who was now so humble and so grateful for all his care and kindness. She accepted unquestioningly the whole circumstances of the situation. As long as they were fighting for a precious life all else must remain in the background. What most puzzled Alister was that she seemed to have dismissed from her mind every other consideration, including even any thought concerning her children; and though she had been informed that Tom was missing, she did not seem to trouble about his absence or to associate him in any way with the tragedy.

When Katherine retired from the telephone Alister came out of the surgery.

"Doctor," she said hurriedly, "that was my father to whom I was speaking, and he said that he had heard about Tom. Mrs. Baxter, one of the workers, whose brother-in-law is skipper of one of the whaling ships, has told him that Tom jumped on board one of them yesterday evening at the last moment."

Alister thrust his hands into his pockets and gave vent to a low whistle.

"Greenland looks bad, doesn't it, Miss Katherine?"

"So papa seems to think; but surely we know better," she said desperately. "What is to be done about Mrs. Speed? Shall we tell her?"

"She is not troubling her head about Tom, I assure you. She has eyes and thoughts only for her husband. I admit frankly that I have not been just to Mrs. Speed, Miss Lundie. I have never seen such devotion as hers."

"Do you think it will be long before Mr. Speed becomes conscious—before he can tell us what happened, and put an end to suspicion and suspense?"

"Some time to-day, I should think; but the greatest care will have to be exercised. You can understand that every exciting topic will have to be avoided if we are to get him pulled through."

Katherine quite understood.

"I can't be of much use here, and yet it seems kinder to stop," she said vaguely.

"Do stop, if you can. I am sure that Mrs. Speed likes to have you here," said Alister quickly. After a moment he remarked, as if casually, "I shall be driving in Lochee direction this morning, and I think I shall call at the lodge at Caddam and see if they can throw any light on the affair."

"You will not see Miss Durie. She will be at her place of business in Burgess Street. I thought of going there myself presently."

"Well, that would be excellent," said Alister, though inwardly surprised.

"I think I shall go now," she added. "Mrs. Speed won't be coming down just yet, I suppose."

"No; she will not leave the room if she can avoid it, and she has not slept all night. She can't spend another such night. I'm sending in a couple of nurses to-day."

"Perhaps it won't be necessary to keep them long," said Katherine, as she walked into the dining-room to get her gloves. She smiled a little as she looked at Alister's face when she was ready to go out.

"It is astonishing how much at home one feels with you, and what use we make of you, Dr. Alister. I begin to understand why you are called the poor people's doctor."

Alister shook his head and hastened away.

Katherine took the car to Burgess Street, and when she entered the little shop she found Mary behind the counter. She closed the little glass door and stepped forward, wondering whether Mary had heard what had happened. Her face certainly showed that she knew something of the matter. It was wan and drawn, and under her eyes were great dark shadows.

Katherine at once offered her hand, and spoke frankly.

"I thought that I would come and see you this morning in case you might be worrying yourself too much. Mr. Speed is still alive. He is at Dr. Alister's house, and his wife is with him."

Mary stood quite still for a moment, saying nothing—too deeply moved, indeed, by this act of true kindness to speak.

Katherine did not misunderstand that silence, and after a brief interval she continued, "You understand all that may lie behind this dreadful thing, don't you? Tom has disappeared. May I ask you whether you saw him yesterday?"

"Yes; he was waiting for me when I left my work yesterday afternoon at three o'clock, and he walked home with me."

"It was the half-holiday, of course. I had forgotten that."

"We had a very stormy interview. He would not leave me, nor would he believe what I told him, and when at last he did go it was, he said, to try to get his father to intervene."

"Ah, that explains many things. But do you—could you—believe him capable of lifting his hand to his father?"

"No," said Mary sharply and clearly. "If people are saying that they are telling lies."

Katherine drew a quick breath of relief.

"Yet it looks as if he had gone away in the whaler to Greenland. What do you say to that?"

"Still I say that he had no hand in this deed, Miss Lundie, except that the interview between them may have helped to work his father up to the rash act. I am as certain of this as that I am standing here."

"Thank you, so am I. You have comforted me very much."

Katherine spoke the words quite simply, and as at this moment a customer came into the shop, she walked out, bidding Mary a brief good-morning, accompanied by a glance which said much more.

She found the doctor's brougham at the door of the house in the Foregate, signifying that he had not yet started on his round. She softly rang the muffled bell, and he opened the door himself.

"He is conscious," he said, with a look of quiet exultation. "His heart is fairly strong, and his pulse regular. Beyond a doubt we shall save him."

"Has he said anything?" asked Katherine in a voice of breathless gladness.

"Not very much. He must not be encouraged to talk. Will you impress that upon Mrs. Speed? But I think she understands, and the nurse has my full instructions."

"Could I see him, do you think?"

"I should not advise you to go up just yet," replied Alister. "I left her by his bedside on her knees."

CHAPTER XLVI

INTO THE HAVEN

On a glorious afternoon in October Katherine walked on Lunan sands with a lithe, quick step, and her eyes, turned seaward, were full of a happy light. The tide was full, the long waves rolled in upon that incomparable golden stretch, and then they broke softly almost at her feet.

The few summer visitors who had discovered the joys of that enchanted spot had already gone home, and only those who for some private reason cared to linger now remained. The dwellers in the house of the cliff were the last to leave, as they had been the first to come.

It had been continuously occupied that year since the first of May, when George Speed and his wife, after his recovery from his long and tedious illness, had come thither to spend their first honeymoon. They had come alone, and there, within sight of the spacious sea and sky, far from all the distracting interests of their city life, they had found a key to happiness which they would never again lose.

Now, at Katherine's earnest invitation, they had returned to spend a few more days before the house should be closed for the winter. She had left them in the garden, and she had climbed down by the cliff path to take her walk alone on the sandy shore, pursued by a strange restlessness which was half-joy, half-pain.

Turning westward she walked on rapidly to a little cove in the rocks, which completely screened her from the view of any straggler on the beach.

There she sat down on a piece of shelving sandstone. The swift walk had brought a rich glow to her cheeks, and never had she looked lovelier or happier, though, had she been asked why she was happy, she could not perhaps have given an answer in specific words.

The summer had been uneventful, but the tangles seemed somehow to have smoothed themselves out of her life and the lives of those in whom she was interested, and everywhere there was the feeling and the benediction of peace. It was in sea and sky to-day—on the wide expanse of calm waters, in the rhythmic beat of the waves on the shore. And she told herself that peace was better than happiness because the heart can be stayed upon it, secure from wintry terrors which work only devastation. She who had so often prayed to live in the full and vivid sense now craved peace only.

She was idly drawing some figures on the sand when a shadow suddenly crossed the shaft of sunshine at her feet, and, lifting her eyes, she saw her old friend, the companion of her youth, before her.

She was not surprised, because he was expected that afternoon, along with David Alister, to spend the last Sunday at Lunan with them.

She smiled and held out her hand, rising to meet him without visible sign of embarrassment.

"I thought you would be here, Katherine," he said. "I haven't been here myself for over a year."

"I thought it was longer," she answered simply.

"Were you thinking about it just now?" he asked, with his grave eyes on her face.

Tom was nearly always grave now. The careless, irresponsible way, the mercurial touch had left him, apparently for ever. The events of the past year had sobered him and made an indelible impression upon him.

But Katherine loved that gravity, which undoubtedly betokened the awakening of a nobler manhood, purged of all the errors of youth.

Never had she been prouder of her friend, never had their friendship been so perfect, so satisfying a thing. The comradeship had been very slowly restored to her—it had taken Tom Speed a long time to recover from the shock of what had happened in the spring, and there had been a time when it seemed as if he would sink altogether. But courage and strength and hope had returned to him, and he knew the blessedness of being forgiven by those whose hearts he had wrung.

" This is where we used to talk," he said, as he begged her to sit down again. " Here I used to blow my own horn loudly enough to rend the skies. Heavens, Katherine, how did you have patience with me ? I am filled with wonder when I look back."

" You were always interesting," she answered with a little tremulous smile.

" I couldn't have been. The man who talks incessantly about himself is an insufferable bore. You would have been kinder to me, dear, if you had nipped my little enthusiasms in the bud."

" Oh, no," she rejoined. " But if you will remember, I was always something of a restraint. Sometimes you thought me uncomprehending and dull—a sort of clod."

Tom dug his stick into the soft sand in a savage acquiescence.

" How you must have despised me, Katherine ! How you must despise me now ! "

" Oh no. I could discern the real thing beneath, and you are not going to bury all these fine enthusiasms for ever. They are going to bear their genuine fruit now. Did David come with you ? "

" Oh yes ; and David is at the present moment receiving the usual adoration from my mother. If I were inclined to jealousy, as I used to be in the degenerate days, Katherine, I should now desire to punch David. He has undoubtedly ousted me at home."

" Nonsense ! It is only because your mother is grateful for what he did at the time of the trouble."

Tom's face shadowed. He dropped his stick and turned to her a very sad but resolute face.

" Katherine, you have never let me talk about that awful time. I'm going to talk to-day. I came for the purpose."

" It is past," she said in a low voice, " and none of us want to remember it, now that everything has been put right, and that we are all so happy."

" You must bear with me, Katherine. You have already borne many things with and from me. This one more I must lay upon your patient heart. I heard from Alister only last night how you championed me all through that dreadful time."

" I was not the only one who did so," she answered. " David believed in you also, and so did Mary Durie. Don't forget that. Those who knew you best knew, too, that you were incapable of such a cruel thing."

" I might easily have been guilty of it. I was very angry, Katherine, and my father's indifference stung me. When I flung out of his presence that night after he had told me that he was weary of me and of everything belonging to me, I did not care what became of me. I had thoughts of suicide, if you like, but of murder—no ! Yet the thing was black against me. I don't know how you preserved your faith in me."

" The trial lasted only for a few days—only, indeed, till your father was able to speak and set everything right."

" I did not understand. The selfish man never does, because he can't see an inch beyond his own petty troubles. Do you know, Katherine, I have had a long talk with the Dad since I came home, and that not so long either ? He told me everything, laying bare his very heart. What a life he has had—not an atom of happiness in it—and he blamed himself for it all ! Yet we might have helped him more. If I had been less of a trial he never would have got strung up to the pitch of misery which makes a man try to take his own life."

" Don't let us talk about it. He is happy now—don't you think he is ? " said Katherine in a low voice full of pain.

" Oh yes, thank God ! It is the biggest joy of my life to see my mother and him together ; and now that they are relieved about Netta and her future, there doesn't seem to be a cloud in their sky."

" So Netta is coming to Dundee next month—a real Marquise after all ! " said Katherine with a little smile.

" A real Marquise ! And the mater's delight over it is comical. Poor mater, it's unnatural to see her as she now is. She simply never seems to want to think about herself at all."

"Oh, don't say that it is unnatural, Tom. She is as sweet as she can be, and it is the loveliest thing in the world to see her and your father together. Why, they are nothing but lovers open and unashamed."

"It's good, I admit, but it has cost something, Katherine."

"Everything that is worth having costs," said Katherine, with her sweet eyes turned dreamily out to sea.

Tom leaned his elbow on his knee, and he fixed his glowing eyes on her face, so that presently she was embarrassed by it, and would have risen, but he drew her back.

"I was just thinking that you are the only one who has never changed, who has been perfect and unselfish all through. A long way behind you comes Alister, and neither of you has gone back on me, poor fool though I am! That's the most wonderful thing of all!"

"Don't abase yourself, Tom," she said hotly. "I hate to hear it. I won't listen. The man who constantly abases himself ends by being abased. I am sure of that."

She spoke with a touch of the old queenly spirit, and her glorious eyes flashed.

"A man must always be right to abase himself before nobility like yours, Katherine. He were ignoble else."

"Let us go home. You are morbid, Tom. Come at once!"

"Not yet. There is just one more thing to say. Dare I say it, Katherine?"

She did not answer, and he drew a paper from his pocket, smoothed it on his knee, and handed it to her.

"This evening's *Telegraph*, you observe," he said. "Read that. I drew my pencil across it. How does it strike you?"

The pencilled lines were under the marriage announcements, and when she caught the names she gave a little cry.

"At Umtali, Rhodesia, on the 15th September, Sir Rafe Fletcher, Bart. of Caddam and Reres, Forfarshire, to Mary Helen, only daughter of Charles and Helen Durie, late of Edinburgh."

"So that is the explanation of Sir Rafe's sudden and mysterious journey to the Cape, while I was attributing it to the hunger of the lawless spirit fretting at the bondage of convention," she said with a low laugh.

She did not ask how the announcement had affected Tom, and, handing him back the paper, she suggested once more that they should go home.

"In a moment. Dare I speak, Katherine? My eyes are opened, and I see what I have missed, what I scarcely dare to aspire to now. But I am afraid with all this marrying in the air that some worse loss may befall me. Will you give me the chance to win you, Katherine—to prove the love which I cannot utter?"

Her eyes swam, her face softly flushed, an exquisite sweetness seemed to pervade and envelop her as she gave him her hand. He grasped it close, and raised it to his lips, his eager eyes fixed upon her changeful face, while he waited for the spoken word.

It was long of coming; and then it was not a word, but it was a gesture, which told him all.

Katherine belonged to the order of womanhood which gives royally—or not at all. And though Tom Speed accepted very humbly the happiness of which he was now worthier than he had been, even he did not fully realise the greatness of the gift.

It was a long, long time before they presented themselves with a certain shamefacedness in the garden on the cliff, where George Speed and his wife waited for them, hoping all things, yet a little afraid.

They did not say much about their love for Katherine Lundie. It had become part of their lives, and when they spoke—as they often did—of the goodness of God, who had led them, after all their own imperfect steering, into quiet waters, they scarcely restrained the expression of their longing for one crowning mercy still to be vouchsafed.

"Here they come, Marian!" said George Speed a little nervously. "Can you see Katherine's face? Do you think they have made it up?"

She did not answer, but she laid her hand on his, while the two came up the path together.

" Is this our new daughter ? Please God, it is," said George Speed as he laid out both his hands.

Katherine lifted her face for his kiss ; then she bent down and laid her glowing cheek for a moment against the mother's.

And that was all.

" What's that ? " said Tom after a moment when the sudden crackling of a bush broke the full silence.

They peered over the projecting cliff, and presently they saw a tall figure emerge upon the steep incline to the shore.

It was only Alister pursuing his solitary way—the way which would be always solitary now—towards the sounding sea.

. . . .

All the conditions attached to old George Speed's bequest to his grandson were amply fulfilled before the time-limit expired.

The spirit as well as the letter of that bequest has been adhered to, and none will suffer, seeing that Ravenscraig has at last accomplished its primary purpose and become a happy home, enlivened by the music of children's voices, and the cradle of a thousand lovely hopes for the future. The husband and wife who dwell there regard their position and their means as a great trust ; and the needy, the sorrowful, and the old will have occasion to bless the name of George Speed and his heirs for ever.

THE END

Waterlow & Sons Limited, Printers, London, Dunstable and Watford.